D0552610

A SCARPETTA OMNIBUS

Volume 3

CAUSE OF DEATH
UNNATURAL EXPOSURE
POINT OF ORIGIN

ALSO BY PATRICIA CORNWELL

THE SCARPETTA NOVELS
Postmortem
Body of Evidence
All That Remains
Cruel and Unusual
The Body Farm
From Potter's Field
Black Notice
The Last Precinct
Blow Fly
Trace
Predator

ANDY BRAZIL SERIES
Hornet's Nest
Southern Cross
Isle of Dogs

NON-FICTION
Portrait of a Killer: Jack the Ripper – Case Closed

BIOGRAPHY
Ruth, A Portrait: The Story of Ruth Bell Graham

OTHER WORKS
Food to Die For: Secrets from Scarpetta's Kitchen
Life's Little Fable
Scarpetta's Winter Table

PATRICIA CORNWELL

A Scarpetta Omnibus

Volume 3

CAUSE OF DEATH
UNNATURAL EXPOSURE
POINT OF ORIGIN

Three Novels in One Volume

LITTLE, BROWN

LITTLE, BROWN

First published in this omnibus edition in 2002 by Little, Brown
Reprinted 2006

A Scarpetta Omnibus: Volume 3 copyright © 2001 by Cornwell Enterprises, Inc.
Cause of Death copyright © 1996 by Patricia Daniels Cornwell
Unnatural Exposure copyright © 1997 by Patricia Daniels Cornwell
Point of Origin copyright © 1998 by Cornwell Enterprises, Inc.

The moral right of the author has been asserted.

All rights reserved.
No part of this publication may be reproduced,
stored in a retrieval system, or transmitted, in any form
or by any means, without the prior permission in writing
of the publisher, nor be otherwise circulated in any form
of binding or cover other than that in which it is published
and without a similar condition including this condition
being imposed on the subequent purchaser.

*All characters in this publication are fictitious
and any resemblance to real persons, living or dead,
is purely coincidental.*

A CIP catalogue record for this book
is available from the British Library.

ISBN-13: 978-0-3167-2472-2
ISBN-10: 0-3167-2472-6

Typeset in Palatino by Palimpsest Book Production Limited,
Polmont, Stirlingshire
Printed and bound in Great Britain by
Clays Ltd, St Ives plc

Little, Brown
An imprint of
Time Warner Book Group UK
Brettenham House
Lancaster Place
London WC2E 7EN

www.twbg.co.uk

CAUSE OF DEATH

And he said unto them the third time, Why, what evil hath he done? I have found no cause of death in him.

Luke 23:22

1
___

On the last morning of Virginia's bloodiest year since the Civil War, I built a fire and sat facing a window of darkness where at sunrise I knew I would find the sea. I was in my robe in lamplight, reviewing my office's annual statistics for car crashes, hangings, beatings, shootings, stabbings, when the telephone rudely rang at five-fifteen.

'Damn,' I muttered, for I was beginning to feel less charitable about answering Dr Philip Mant's phone. 'All right, all right.'

His weathered cottage was tucked behind a dune in a stark coastal Virginia subdivision called Sandbridge, between the U.S. Naval Amphibious Base and Back Bay National Wildlife Refuge. Mant was my deputy chief medical examiner for the Tidewater District, and, sadly, his mother had died last week on Christmas Eve. Under ordinary circumstances, his returning to London to get family affairs in order would not have constituted an emergency for the Virginia medical examiner system. But his assistant forensic pathologist was already out on maternity leave, and, recently, the morgue supervisor had quit.

'Mant residence,' I answered as wind tore the dark shapes of pines beyond windowpanes.

'This is Officer Young with the Chesapeake Police,' said someone who sounded like a white male born and bred in the South. 'I'm trying to reach Dr Mant.'

'He is out of the country,' I answered. 'How may I help you?'

'Are you Mrs Mant?'

'I'm Dr Kay Scarpetta, the chief medical examiner. I'm covering for Dr Mant.'

The voice hesitated, then went on, 'We got a tip about a death. An anonymous call.'

'Do you know where this death supposedly took place?' I was making notes.

'Supposedly the Inactive Naval Ship Yard.'

'Excuse me?' I looked up.

He repeated what he had said.

'What are we talking about, a Navy SEAL?' I was baffled, for it was my understanding that SEALs on maneuvers were the only divers permitted around old ships moored at the Inactive Yard.

'We don't know who it is but he might have been looking for Civil War relics.'

'After dark?'

'Ma'am, the area's off-limits unless you have clearance. But that hasn't stopped people from being curious before. They sneak their boats in and always it's after dark.'

'This scenario is what the anonymous caller suggested?'

'Pretty much.'

'That's rather interesting.'

'I thought so.'

'And the body hasn't been located yet,' I said as I continued to wonder why this officer had taken it upon himself to call a medical examiner at such an early hour when it was not known for a fact that there was a body or even someone missing.

'We're out looking now, and the Navy's sending in a few divers, so we'll get the situation handled if it pans out. But I just wanted you to have a heads up. And be sure you give Dr Mant my condolences.'

'Your condolences?' I puzzled, for if he had known about Mant's circumstances, why did he call here asking for him?

'I heard his mother passed on.'

I rested the tip of the pen on the sheet of paper. 'Would you tell me your full name and how you can be reached, please?'

'S. T. Young.' He gave me a telephone number and we hung up.

I stared into the low fire, feeling uneasy and lonely as I got up to add more wood. I wished I were in Richmond in my own home with its candles in the windows and Fraser fir decorated with Christmases from my past. I wanted Mozart and Handel instead of wind shrilly rushing around the roof, and I wished I had not taken Mant up on his kind offer that I could stay in his home instead of a hotel. I resumed proofreading the statistical report, but my mind would not stop drifting. I imagined the sluggish water of the Elizabeth River, which this time of year would be less than sixty degrees, visibility, at best, maybe eighteen inches.

In the winter, it was one thing to dive for oysters in the Chesapeake Bay or go thirty miles offshore in the Atlantic Ocean to explore a sunken aircraft carrier or German submarine and other wonders worth a wet suit. But in the Elizabeth River, where the Navy parked its decommissioned ships, I could think of nothing enticing, no matter the weather. I could not imagine who would dive there alone in winter after dark to look for artifacts or anything, and believed the tip would prove to be a crank.

Leaving the recliner chair, I walked into the master bedroom where my belongings had metastasized throughout most of the small, chilly space. I undressed quickly and took a hurried shower, having discovered my first day here that the hot-water heater had its limitations. In fact, I did not like Dr Mant's drafty house with its knotty pine paneling the color of amber and dark brown painted floors that showed every particle of dust. My British deputy chief seemed to live in the dark clutches of gusting wind, and every moment in his minimally furnished home was cold and unsettled by shifting sounds that sometimes caused me to sit up in my sleep and reach for my gun.

Swathed in a robe with a towel wrapped around my hair, I checked the guest bedroom and bath to make certain all was in order for the midday arrival of Lucy, my niece. Then I surveyed the kitchen, which was pitiful compared to the one I had at home. I did not seem to have forgotten anything yesterday when I had driven to Virginia Beach to shop, although I would have to do without garlic press, pasta maker, food processor and microwave oven. I was seriously beginning to wonder if Mant ever ate in or even stayed here. At least I had thought to bring my own cutlery and cookware, and as long as I had good knives and pots there wasn't much I couldn't manage.

I read some more and fell asleep in the glow of a gooseneck lamp. The telephone startled me again and I grabbed the receiver as my eyes adjusted to sunlight in my face.

'This is Detective C. T. Roche with Chesapeake,' said another male voice I did not know. 'I understand you're covering for Dr Mant, and we need an answer from you real quick. Looks like we got a diving fatality in the Inactive Naval Ship Yard, and we need to go ahead and recover the body.'

'I'm assuming this is the case one of your officers called me about earlier?'

His long pause was followed by the rather defensive remark, 'As far as I know, I'm the first one notifying you.'

'An officer named Young called me at quarter past five this morning. Let me see.' I checked the call sheet. 'Initials S as in Sam, T as in Tom.'

Another pause, then he said in the same tone, 'Well, I got no idea who you're talking about since we don't have anybody by that name.'

Adrenaline was pumping as I took notes. The time was thirteen minutes past nine o'clock. I was baffled by what he had just said. If the first caller really wasn't police, then who was he, why had he called, and how did he know Mant?

'When was the body found?' I asked Roche.

'Around six a security guard for the shipyard noticed a johnboat anchored behind one of the ships. There was a long hose in the water, like maybe there was someone diving at the other end. And when it hadn't budged an hour later, we were called. One diver was sent down and like I said, there is a body.'

'Do we have an identification?'

'We recovered a wallet from the boat. The driver's license is that of a white male named Theodore Andrew Eddings.'

'The reporter?' I said in disbelief. 'That Ted Eddings?'

'Thirty-two years old, brown hair, blue eyes, based on his picture. He has a Richmond address of West Grace Street.'

The Ted Eddings I knew was an award-winning investigative reporter for the Associated Press. Scarcely a week went by when he didn't call me about something. For a moment, I almost couldn't think.

'We also recovered a nine-millimeter pistol from the boat,' he said.

When I spoke again, it was very firmly. 'His identification absolutely is not to be released to the press or anyone else until it has been confirmed.'

'I already told everybody that. Not to worry.'

'Good. And no one has any idea why this individual might have been diving in the Inactive Ship Yard?' I asked.

'He might have been looking for Civil War stuff.'

'You speculate that based on what?'

'A lot of people like to look in the rivers around here for cannonballs and things,' he said. 'Okay. So we'll go on and pull him in so he's not down there any longer than necessary.'

'I do not want him touched, and leaving him in the water a little longer isn't going to change anything.'

'What is it you're gonna do?' He sounded defensive again.

'I won't know until I get there.'

'Well, I don't think it's necessary for you to come here . . .'

'Detective Roche,' I interrupted him. 'The necessity of my coming to the scene and what I do when I'm there is not for you to decide.'

'Well, there's all these people I've got on hold, and this afternoon it's supposed to snow. Nobody wants to be standing around out there on the piers.'

'According to the Code of Virginia, the body is my jurisdiction, not yours or any other police, fire, rescue or funeral person's. Nobody touches the body until I say so.' I spoke with just enough edge to let him know I could be sharp.

'Like I said, I'm going to have to tell all the rescue and shipyard people to just hang out, and they aren't going to be happy. The Navy's already leaning on me pretty hard to clear the area before the media shows up.'

'This is not a Navy case.'

'You tell them that. It's their ships.'

'I'll be happy to tell them that. In the meantime, you just tell everyone that I'm on my way,' I said to him before I hung up.

Realizing it could be many hours before I returned to the cottage, I left a note taped to the front door that cryptically instructed Lucy how to let herself in should I not be here. I hid a key only she could find, then loaded medical bag and dive equipment into the trunk of my black Mercedes. At quarter of ten the temperature had risen to thirty-eight degrees, and my attempts to reach Captain Pete Marino in Richmond were frustrating.

'Thank God,' I muttered when my car phone finally rang.

I snatched it up. 'Scarpetta.'

'Yo.'

'You've got your pager on. I'm shocked,' I said to him.

'If you're so shocked, then why the hell'd you call it?' He sounded pleased to hear from me. 'What's up?'

'You know that reporter you dislike so much?' I was careful not to divulge details because we were on the air and could be monitored by scanners.

'As in which one?'

'As in the one who works for AP and is always dropping by my office.'

He thought a moment, then said, 'So what's the deal? You have a run-in with him?'

'Unfortunately, I may be about to. I'm on my way to the Elizabeth River. Chesapeake just called.'

'Wait a minute. Not that kind of run-in.' His tone was ominous.

'I'm afraid so.'

'Holy shit.'

'We've got only a driver's license. So we can't be certain, yet. I'm going to go in and take a look before we move him.'

'Now wait a damn minute,' he said. 'Why the hell do you need to do something like that? Can't other people take care of it?'

'I need to see him before he's moved,' I repeated.

Marino was very displeased because he was overly protective. He didn't have to say another word for me to know that.

'I just thought you might want to check out his residence in Richmond,' I told him.

'Yeah. I sure as hell will.'

'I don't know what we're going to find.'

'Well, I just wish you'd let them find it first.'

In Chesapeake, I took the Elizabeth River exit, then turned left on High Street, passing brick churches, used-car lots and mobile homes. Beyond the city jail and police headquarters, naval barracks dissolved into the expansive, depressing landscape of a salvage yard surrounded by a rusty fence topped with barbed wire. In the midst of acres littered with metal and overrun by weeds was a power plant that appeared to burn trash and coal to supply the shipyard with energy to run its dismal, inert business. Smoke-stacks and train tracks were quiet today, all dry-dock cranes out of work. It was, after all, New Year's Eve.

I drove on toward a headquarters built of boring tan cinder-block, beyond which were long paved piers. At the guard gate, a young man in civilian clothes and hard hat stepped out of his booth. I rolled my window down as clouds churned in the wind-swept sky.

'This is a restricted area.' His face was completely devoid of expression.

'I'm Dr Kay Scarpetta, the chief medical examiner,' I said as I displayed the brass shield that symbolized my jurisdiction over every sudden, unattended, unexplained or violent death in the Commonwealth of Virginia.

Leaning closer, he studied my credentials. Several times he glanced up at my face and stared at my car.

'You're the chief medical examiner?' he asked. 'So how come you're not driving a hearse?'

I had heard this before and was patient when I replied, 'People who work in funeral homes drive hearses. I don't work in a funeral home. I am a medical examiner.'

'I'm going to need some other form of identification.'

I gave him my driver's license, and had no doubt that this sort of interference wasn't going to improve once he allowed me to drive through. He stepped back from my car, lifting a portable radio to his lips.

'Unit eleven to unit two.' He turned away from me as if about to tell secrets.

'Two,' floated back the reply.

'I got a Dr Scaylatta here.' He mispronounced my name worse than most people did.

'Ten-four. We're standing by.'

'Ma'am,' the security guard said to me, 'just drive through and you'll find a parking lot on your right.' He pointed. 'You need to leave your car there and walk to Pier Two, where you'll find Captain Green. That's who you need to see.'

'And where will I find Detective Roche?' I asked.

'Captain Green's who you need to see,' he repeated.

I rolled my window up as he opened a gate posted with signs warning that I was about to enter an industrial area where spray painting was an imminent hazard, safety equipment was required and parking was at my own risk. In the distance, dull gray cargo and tank landing ships, and mine sweepers, frigates and hydrofoils intimidated the cold horizon. On the second pier, emergency vehicles, police cars and a small group of men had gathered.

Leaving my car as instructed, I briskly walked toward them as they stared. I had left my medical bag and dive gear in the car, so I was an empty-handed, middle-aged woman in hiking boots, wool slacks and pale army-green Schoffel coat. The instant I set foot on the pier, a distinguished, graying man in uniform intercepted me as if I were trespassing. Unsmiling, he stepped in my path.

'May I help you?' he asked in a tone that said halt as the wind lifted his hair and colored his cheeks.

I again explained who I was.

'Oh, good.' He certainly did not sound as if he meant it. 'I'm

Captain Green with Navy Investigative Service. We really do need to get on with this. Listen,' he turned away from me and spoke to someone else. 'We gotta get those CPs off . . .'

'Excuse me. You're with NIS?' I cut in, for I was going to get this cleared up now. 'It was my belief that this shipyard is not Navy property. If it is Navy property, I shouldn't be here. The case should be the Navy's and autopsied by Navy pathologists.'

'Ma'am,' he said as if I tried his patience, 'this shipyard is a civilian contractor-operated facility, and therefore not Naval property. But we have an obvious interest because it appears someone was diving unauthorized around our vessels.'

'Do you have a theory as to why someone might have done that?' I looked around.

'Some treasure hunters think they're going to find cannonballs, old ship bells and whatnot in waters around here.'

We were standing between the cargo ship *El Paso* and the submarine *Exploiter*, both of them lusterless and rigid in the river. The water looked like cappuccino, and I realized that visibility was going to be even worse than I had feared. Near the submarine, there was a dive platform. But I saw no sign of the victim or the rescuers and police supposedly working his death. I asked Green about this as wind blowing off the water numbed my face, and his reply was to give me his back again.

'Look, I can't be here all day waiting for Stu,' he said to a man in coveralls and a filthy ski jacket.

'We could haul Bo's butt in here, Cap'n,' was the reply.

'No way José,' Green said, and he seemed quite familiar with these shipyard men. 'No point in calling that boy.'

'Hell,' said another man with a long tangled beard. 'We all know he ain't gonna be sober this late in the morning.'

'Well, now if that isn't the pot calling the kettle black,' Green said, and all of them laughed.

The bearded man had a complexion like raw hamburger. He slyly eyed me as he lit a cigarette, shielding it from the wind in rough bare hands.

'I hadn't had a drink since yesterday. Not even water,' he swore as his mates laughed some more. 'Damn, it's cold as a witch's titty.' He hugged himself. 'I should'a wore a better coat.'

'I tell you what's cold is that one over yonder.' Another worker spoke, dentures clicking as he talked about what I realized was the dead diver. 'Now that boy's cold.'

'He don't feel it now.'

I controlled my mounting irritation as I said to Green, 'I know you're eager to get started, and so am I. But I don't see any rescuers or police. I haven't seen the johnboat or the area of the river where the body is located.'

I felt half a dozen pairs of eyes on me, and I scanned the eroded faces of what easily could have been a small band of pirates dressed for modern times. I was not invited into their secret club and was reminded of those early years when rudeness and isolation could still make me cry.

Green finally answered, 'The police are inside using the phones. In the main building there, the one with the big anchor in front. The divers are probably in there too staying warm. The rescue squad is at a landing on the other side of the river where they've been waiting for you to get here. And you might be interested in knowing that this same landing is where the police just found a truck and trailer they believe belonged to the deceased. If you follow me.' He began walking. 'I'll show you the location you're interested in. I understand you plan on going in with the other divers.'

'That's right.' I walked with him along the pier.

'I sure as hell don't know what you expect to see.'

'I learned long ago to have no expectations, Captain Green.'

As we passed old, tired ships, I noticed many fine metal lines leading from them into the water. 'What are those?' I asked.

'CPs – cathodic protectors,' he answered. 'They're electrically charged to reduce corrosion.'

'I certainly hope someone has turned them off.'

'An electrician's on the way. He'll turn off the whole pier.'

'So the diver could have run into CPs. I doubt it would have been easy to see them.'

'It wouldn't matter. The charge is very mild,' he said as if anyone should know that. 'It's like getting zapped with a nine-volt battery. CPs didn't kill him. You can already mark that one off your list.'

We had stopped at the end of the pier where the rear of the partially submerged submarine was in plain view. Anchored no more than twenty feet from it was the dark green aluminum johnboat with its long black hose leading from the compressor, which was nestled in an inner tube on the passenger's side. The floor of the boat was scattered with tools, scuba equipment and other objects that I suspected had been rather carelessly gone through by someone. My chest tightened, for I was angrier than I would show.

'He probably just drowned,' Green was saying. 'Almost every diving death I've seen was a drowning. You die in water as shallow as this, that's what it's going to be.'

'I certainly find his equipment unusual.' I ignored his medical pontifications.

He stared at the johnboat barely stirred by the current. 'A hookah. Yeah, it's unusual for around here.'

'Was it running when the boat was found?'

'Out of gas.'

'What can you tell me about it? Homemade?'

'Commercial,' he said. 'A five-horsepower gasoline-driven compressor that draws in surface air through a low-pressure hose connected to a second-stage regulator. He could have stayed down four, five hours. As long as his fuel lasted.' He continued to stare off.

'Four or five hours? For what?' I looked at him. 'I can understand that if you're collecting lobsters or abalone.'

He was silent.

'What is down there?' I said. 'And don't tell me Civil War artifacts because we both know you're not going to find those here.'

'In truth, not a damn thing's down there.'

'Well,' I said, 'he thought something was.'

'Unfortunately for him, he thought wrong. Look at those clouds moving in. We're definitely going to get it.' He flipped his coat collar up around his ears. 'I assume you're a certified diver.'

'For many years.'

'I'm going to need to see your dive card.'

I looked out at the johnboat and the submarine nearby as I wondered just how uncooperative these people intended to be.

'You've got to have that with you if you're going in,' he said. 'I thought you would have known that.'

'And I thought the military did not run this shipyard.'

'I know the rules here. It doesn't matter who runs it.' He stared at me.

'I see.' I stared back. 'And I suppose I'm going to need a permit if I want to park my car on this pier so I don't have to carry my gear half a mile.'

'You do need a permit to park on the pier.'

'Well, I don't have one of those. I don't have my PADI advanced and rescue dive cards or my dive log. I don't have my licenses to practice medicine in Virginia, Maryland or Florida.'

I spoke very smoothly and quietly, and because he could not rattle me, he became more determined. He blinked several times, and I could feel his hate.

'This is the last time I'm going to ask you to allow me to do my job,' I went on. 'We have an unnatural death here that is in my jurisdiction. If you would rather not cooperate, I will be happy to call the state police, the U.S. Marshal, FBI. Your choice. I can probably get somebody here in twenty minutes. I've got my portable phone right here in my pocket.' I patted it.

'You want to dive' – he shrugged – 'then go right ahead. But you'll have to sign a waiver relieving the shipyard of any responsibility, should something unfortunate happen. And I seriously doubt there are any forms like that here.'

'I see. Now I need to sign something you don't have.'

'That's correct.'

'Fine,' I said. 'Then I'll just draft a waiver for you.'

'A lawyer would have to do that, and it's a holiday.'

'I am a lawyer and I work on holidays.'

His jaw muscles knotted, and I knew he wasn't going to bother with any forms now that it was possible to have one. We started walking back, and my stomach tightened with dread. I did not want to make this dive and I did not like the people I had encountered this day. Certainly, I had gotten entangled in bureaucratic barbed wire before when cases involved government or big business. But this was different.

'Tell me something,' Green spoke again in his scornful tone, 'do chief medical examiners always personally go in after bodies?'

'Rarely.'

'Explain why you think it is necessary this time.'

'The scene of death will be gone the moment the body is moved. I think the circumstances are unusual enough to merit my taking a look while I can. And I'm temporarily covering my Tidewater District, so I happened to be here when the call came in.'

He paused, then unnerved me by saying, 'I certainly was sorry to hear about Dr Mant's mother. When will he be back to work?'

I tried to remember this morning's phone call and the man called Young with his exaggerated southern accent. Green did not sound native to the South, but then neither did I, and that didn't mean either of us couldn't imitate a drawl.

'I'm not certain when he'll return,' I warily replied. 'But I'm wondering how you know him.'

'Sometimes cases overlap, whether they should or not.'

I was not sure what he was implying.

'Dr Mant understands the importance of not interfering,' Green went on. 'People like that are good to work with.'

'The importance of not interfering with what, Captain Green?'

'If a case is the Navy's, for example, or this jurisdiction or that. There are many different ways that people can interfere. All are a problem and can be harmful. That diver, for example. He went where he didn't belong and look what happened.'

I had stopped walking and was staring at him in disbelief. 'It must be my imagination,' I said, 'but I think you're threatening me.'

'Go get your gear. You can park closer in, by the fence over there,' he said, walking off.

2

Long after he had disappeared inside the building with the anchor in front, I was sitting on the pier, struggling to pull a thick wet suit over my dive skin. Not far from me, several rescuers prepared a flat-bottomed boat they had moored to a piling. Shipyard workers wandered about curiously, and on the dive platform, two men in royal blue neoprene tested buddy phones and seemed very thorough in their inspection of scuba gear, which included mine.

I watched the divers talk to each other, but I could not make out a word they said as they unscrewed hoses and fitted belts with weights. Occasionally, they glanced my way, and I was surprised when one of them decided to climb the ladder that led up to my pier. He walked over to where I was and sat beside me on my little patch of cold pavement.

'This seat taken?' He was a handsome young man, black and built like an Olympic athlete.

'There are a lot of people who want it, but I don't know where they are.' I fought with the wet suit some more. 'Damn. I hate these things.'

'Just think of it as putting on an inner tube.'

'Yes, that's an enormous help.'

'I need to talk to you about underwater comm equipment. You ever used it before?' he said.

I glanced up at his serious face and asked, 'Are you with a squad?'

'Nope. I'm just plain ole Navy. And I don't know about you, but this sure isn't the way I planned to spend my New Year's Eve. Don't know why anybody'd want to dive in this river unless they got some sort of fantasy about being a blind tadpole in a mud puddle. Or maybe if you got iron-poor blood and think all the rust in there will help.'

'All the rust in there will do is give you tetanus.' I looked around. 'Who else here is Navy versus squad?'

'The two with the rescue boat are squad. Ki Soo down there on the dive platform is the only other Navy except our intrepid investigator with NIS. Ki's good. He's my buddy.'

He gave an okay sign to Ki Soo, who gave it back, and I found all of this rather interesting and very different from what I had experienced so far.

'Now listen up.' My new acquaintance spoke as if he had worked with me for years. 'Comm equipment's tricky if you've never used it. It can be real dangerous.' His face was earnest.

'I'm familiar with it,' I assured him with more ease than I felt.

'Well, you gotta be more than familiar. You gotta be buddies with it, because like your dive buddy, it can save your life.' He paused. 'It can also kill you.'

I had used underwater communication equipment on only one other dive, and was still nervous about having my regulator replaced by a tightly sealed mask fitted with a mouthpiece and no purge valve. I worried about the mask flooding, about having to tear it off as I frantically groped for my alternate air source, or octopus. But I was not going to mention this, not here.

'I'll be fine,' I assured him again.

'Great. I heard you were a pro,' he said. 'By the way, my name's Jerod, and I already know who you are.' Sitting Indian-style, he was tossing gravel into the water and seemed fascinated by the slowly spreading ripples. 'I've heard a lot of nice things about you. In fact, when my wife finds out I met you, she's going to be jealous.'

I was not certain why a diver in the Navy would have heard anything about me beyond what was in the news, which wasn't always nice. But his words were a welcome salve to my raw mood, and I was about to let him know this when he glanced at his watch, then stared down at the platform and met Ki Soo's eyes.

'Dr Scarpetta,' Jerod said as he got up. 'I think we're ready to rock and roll. How about you?'

'I'm as ready as I'm going to be.' I got up, too. 'What's going to be the best approach?'

'The best way – in fact, the only way – is to follow his hose down.'

We stepped closer to the edge of the pier and he pointed to the johnboat.

'I've already been down once, and if you don't follow the hose you'll never find him. You ever had to wade through a sewer with no lights on?'

'That one hasn't happened to me yet.'

'Well, you can't see shit. And that's the same thing here.'

'To your knowledge, no one has disturbed the body,' I said.

'No one's been near it but me.'

He watched as I picked up my buoyancy control vest, or BC, and tucked a flashlight in a pocket.

'I wouldn't even bother. In these conditions, all a flashlight's going to do is get in your way.'

But I was going to bring it because I wanted any advantage I could possibly have. Jerod and I climbed down the ladder to the dive platform so we could finish preparations, and I ignored overt stares from shipyard men as I massaged cream rinse into my hair and pulled on the neoprene hood. I strapped a knife to my inner right calf, and then grabbed each end of a fifteen-pound weight belt and quickly hoisted it around my waist. I checked safety releases, and pulled on gloves.

'I'm ready,' I said to Ki Soo.

He carried over communication equipment and my regulator.

'I will attach your air hose to the face mask.' He spoke with no accent. 'I understand you've used comm equipment like this before.'

'That's correct,' I said.

He squatted beside me and lowered his voice as if we were about to conspire. 'You, Jerod and I will be in constant contact with each other over the buddy phones.'

They looked like bright red gas masks with a five-strap harness in back. Jerod moved behind me and helped me into my BC and air tank while his buddy talked on.

'As you know,' Ki Soo was saying, 'you breathe normally and use the push-to-talk button on the mouthpiece when you want to communicate.' He demonstrated. 'Now we need to get this nice and secure over your hood and tuck it in. There, you get the rest of your hair tucked in and let me make sure this is nice and tight in back.'

I hated buddy phones the most when I wasn't in the water because it was difficult to breathe. I sucked in air as best I could as I peered out through plastic at these two divers I had just entrusted with my life.

'There will be two rescuers in a boat and they will be monitoring us with a transducer that will be lowered into the water. Whatever we say will be heard by whoever is listening on the surface. Do you understand?' Ki Soo looked at me and I knew I had just been given a warning.

I nodded, my breathing loud and labored in my ears.

'You want your fins on now?'

I shook my head and pointed at the water.

'Then you go first and I will toss them to you.'

Weighing at least eighty pounds more than when I had arrived, I cautiously made my way to the edge of the dive platform and checked again to make certain my mask was tucked into my hood. Cathodic protectors were like catfish whiskers trailing from the huge dormant ships, the water ruffled by wind. I steeled myself for the most unnerving giant stride I had ever made.

The cold at first was a shock, and my body took its time warming the water leaking into my rubber sheath as I pulled on my fins. Worse, I could not see my computer console or its compass. I could not see my hand in front of my face, and I now understood why it was useless to bring a flashlight. The suspended sediment absorbed light like a blotter, forcing me to surface at frequent intervals to get my bearings as I swam toward the spot where the hose led from the johnboat and disappeared beneath the surface of the river.

'Everybody ten-four?' Ki Soo's voice sounded in the receiver pressed against the bone of my skull.

'Ten-four,' I spoke into the mouthpiece and tried to relax as I slowly kicked barely below the surface.

'You're on the hose?' It was Jerod who spoke this time.

'I've got my hands on it now.' It seemed oddly taut, and I was careful to disturb it as little as possible.

'Keep following it down. Maybe thirty feet. He should be floating right above the bottom.'

I began my descent, pausing at intervals to equalize the pressure in my ears as I tried not to panic. I could not see. My heart was pounding as I tried to will myself to relax and take deep breaths. For a moment I stopped and floated as I shut my eyes and slowly breathed. I resumed following the hose down and panic seized me again when a thick rusting cable suddenly materialized in front of me.

I tried to get under it, but I could not see where it was coming from or going to, and I was really more buoyant than I wanted to be and could have used more weight in my belt or the pockets of my BC. The cable got me from the rear, clipping my K-valve hard. I felt my regulator tug as if someone were grabbing it from behind, and the loosened tank began to slide down my back, pulling me with it. Ripping open the Velcro straps of my BC, I quickly worked my way out of it as I tried to block out everything except the procedure I had been trained to do.

'Everything ten-four?' Ki Soo's voice sounded in my mask.

'Technical problem,' I said.

I maneuvered the tank between my legs so I could float on it as if I were riding a rocket in cold, murky space. I readjusted straps and fought off fear.

'Need help?'

'Negative. Watch for cables,' I said.

'You gotta watch for anything,' his voice came back.

It entered my mind that there were many ways to die down here as I slipped my arms inside the BC. Rolling over on my back, I snugly strapped myself in.

'Everything ten-four?' Ki Soo's voice sounded again.

'Ten-four. You're breaking up.'

'Too much interference. All these big tubs. We're coming down behind you. Do you want us closer?'

'Not yet,' I said.

They were maintaining a prudent distance because they knew I wanted to see the body without distraction or interference. We did not need to get in each other's way. Slowly, I dropped deeper, and closer to the bottom, I realized the hose must be snagged, explaining why it was so taut. I was not sure which way to move, and tried going several feet to my left, where something brushed against me. I turned and met the dead man face to face, his body bumping and nudging as I involuntarily jerked away. Languidly, he twisted and drifted on the end of his tether, rubber-sheathed arms out like a sleepwalker's as my motion pulled him after me.

I let him drift close, and he nudged and bumped some more, but now I was not afraid because I was no longer surprised. It was as if he were trying to get my attention or wanted to dance with me through the hellish darkness of the river that had claimed him. I maintained neutral buoyancy, barely moving my fins for I did not want to stir up the bottom or cut myself on rusting shipyard debris.

'I've got him. Or maybe I should say he got me.' I depressed the push-to-talk button. 'Can you copy?'

'Barely. We're maybe ten feet above you. Holding.'

'Hold a few minutes more. Then we'll get him out.'

I tried my flashlight one last time, just in case, but it still proved useless, and I realized I would have to see this scene with my hands. Tucking the light back in my BC, I held my computer console almost against my mask. I could barely make out that my depth was almost thirty feet and I had more than half a tank of air. I began to hover in the dead man's face, and through the murkiness could make out only the vague shape of features and hair that had floated free of his hood.

Gripping his shoulders, I carefully felt around his chest, tracing the hose. It was threaded through his weight belt and I began following it toward whatever it was caught on. In less than ten feet, a huge rusty screw blossomed before my eyes. I touched the barnacle-covered metal of a ship's side, steadying myself so I did not float any closer. I did not want to drift under a vessel the size of a playing field and have to blindly feel my way out before I ran out of air.

The hose was tangled and I felt along it to see if it might be folded or compressed in a way that might have cut off the flow of air, but I could find no evidence of that. In fact, when I tried to free it from the screw, I found this was not hard to do. I saw no reason why the diver could not have freed himself, and I was suspicious his hose had gotten snagged after death.

'His air hose was caught.' I got on the radio again. 'On one of the ships. I don't know which.'

'Need some help?' It was Jerod who spoke.

'No. I've got him. You can start pulling.'

I felt the hose move.

'Okay. I'm going to guide him up,' I said. 'You keep pulling. Very slowly.'

I locked my arms under the body's from behind and began kicking with my ankles and knees instead of my hips because movement was restricted.

'Easy,' I warned into the microphone, for my ascent could be no more than one foot a second. 'Slowly. Slowly.'

Periodically, I looked up but could not see where I was until we broke the surface. Then suddenly the sky was painted with slate-gray clouds, and the rescue boat was rocking nearby. Inflating the dead man's BC and mine, I turned him on his belly and released his weight belt, almost dropping it because it seemed so heavy. But I managed to hand it up to rescuers who were wearing wet suits and seemed to know what they were doing in their old flat-bottomed boat.

Jerod, Ki Soo and I had to leave our masks on because we still had to swim back to the platform. So we were talking by buddy phone and breathing from our tanks as we maneuvered the body inside a chicken-wire basket. We swam it flush against the boat, then helped the rescuers lift it in as water poured everywhere.

'We need to take his mask off,' I said, and I motioned to the rescuers.

They seemed confused, and wherever the transducer was, it clearly wasn't with them. They couldn't hear a word we said.

'You need some help getting your mask off?' one of them asked as he reached toward me.

I waved him off and shook my head. Grabbing the side of the boat, I hoisted myself up enough to reach the basket. I pulled off the dead man's mask, emptied it of water, and laid it next to his hooded head with its straying long wet hair. It was then I knew him, despite the deep oval impression etched around his eyes. I knew the straight nose and dark mustache framing his full mouth. I recognized the reporter who had always been so fair with me.

'Okay?' One of the rescuers shrugged.

I gave them an okay, although I could tell they did not understand the importance of what I had just done. My reason was cosmetic, for the longer the mask caused pressure against skin fast losing elasticity, the slighter the chance that the indentation would fade. This was an unimportant concern to investigators and paramedics, but not to loved ones who would want to see Ted Eddings's face.

'Am I transmitting?' I then asked Ki Soo and Jerod as we bobbed in the water.

'You're fine. What do you want done with all this hose?' Jerod asked.

'Cut it about eight feet from the body and clamp off the end,' I said. 'Seal that and his regulator in a plastic bag.'

'I got a salvage bag in my BC,' Ki Soo volunteered.

'Sure. That will work.'

After we had done what we could, we rested for a moment, floating and looking across muddy water to the johnboat and the hookah. As I surveyed where we had been, I realized that the screw Eddings's hose had snagged on belonged to the *Exploiter*. The submarine looked post-World War II, maybe around the time of the Korean War, and I wondered if it had been stripped of its finer parts and was on its way to being sold for scrap. I wondered if Eddings had been diving around it for a reason, or if, after death, he had drifted there.

The rescue boat was halfway to the landing on the other side of the river where an ambulance waited to take the body to the morgue. Jerod gave me the okay sign and I returned it, although everything did not feel okay at all. Air rushed as we deflated our BCs, and we dipped back under water the color of old pennies.

There was a ladder leading from the river to the dive platform, and then another to the pier. My legs trembled as I climbed, for I was not as strong as Jerod and Ki Soo, who moved in all their gear as if it weighed the same as skin. But I got out of my BC and tank myself and did not ask for help. A police cruiser rumbled near my car, and someone was towing Eddings's johnboat across the river to the landing. Identity would have to be verified, but I had no doubt.

'So what do you think?' a voice overhead suddenly asked.

I looked up to find Captain Green standing next to a tall, slender man on the pier. Green was apparently now feeling charitable, and reached down to help. 'Here,' he said. 'Hand me your tank.'

'I won't know a thing until I examine him,' I said as I lifted it up, then the other gear. 'Thanks. The johnboat with the hose and every-thing else should go straight to the morgue,' I added.

'Really? What are you going to do with it?' he asked.

'The hookah gets an autopsy, too.'

'You're going to want to rinse your stuff really good,' the slender man said to me as if he knew more than Jacques Cousteau, and his voice was familiar. 'There's a lot of oil and rust in there.'

'There certainly is,' I agreed, climbing up to the pier.

'I'm Detective Roche,' he then said, and he was oddly dressed in jeans and an old letter jacket. 'I heard you say his hose was caught on something?'

'I did, and I'm wondering when you heard me say that.' I was on the pier now and not at all looking forward to carrying my dirty, wet gear back to my car.

'Of course, we monitored the recovery of the body.' It was Green who spoke. 'Detective Roche and I were listening inside the building.'

I remembered Ki Soo's warning to me and I glanced at the plat-form below where he and Jerod were working on their own gear.

'The hose was snagged,' I answered. 'But I can't tell you when that happened. Maybe before his death, maybe after.'

Roche didn't seem all that interested as he continued to stare at me in a manner that made me self-aware. He was very young and almost pretty, with delicate features, generous lips and short curly dark hair. But I did not like his eyes, and thought they were invasive and smug. I pulled off my hood and ran my fingers through my slippery hair, and he watched as I unzipped my wet suit and pulled the top of it down to my hips. The last layer was my dive skin, and water trapped between it and my flesh was chilling quickly. Soon I would be unbearably cold. Already, my fingernails were blue.

'One of the rescuers tells me his face looks really red,' the captain said as I tied the wet suit's sleeves around my waist. 'I'm wondering if that means anything.'

'Cold livor,' I replied.

He looked expectantly at me.

'Bodies exposed to the cold get bright pink,' I said as I began to shiver.

'I see. So it doesn't—'

'No,' I cut him off, because I was too uncomfortable to listen to them. 'It doesn't necessarily mean anything. Look, is there a ladies' room so I can get out of these wet things?' I cast about and saw nothing promising.

'Over there.' Green pointed at a small trailer near the administration building. 'Would you like Detective Roche to accompany you and show you where everything is?'

'That's not necessary.'

'Hopefully, it's not locked,' Green added.

That would be my luck, I thought. But it wasn't, and it was awful, with only toilet and sink, and nothing seemed to have been cleaned in recent history. A door leading to the men's room on the other side was secured by a two-by-four with padlock and chain, as if one gender or the other were very worried about privacy.

There was no heat. I stripped, only to find there was no hot water. Cleaning up as best I could, I hurried into a sweat suit, after-ski boots and cap. By now it was one-thirty and Lucy was probably at Mant's house. I hadn't even started the tomato sauce yet. Exhausted, I was desperate for a long hot shower or bath.

Because I could not get rid of him, Green walked me to my car and helped place my dive gear into the trunk. By now the johnboat had been loaded on a trailer and should have been en route to my office in Norfolk. I did not see Jerod or Ki Soo and was sorry I could not say good-bye to them.

'When will you do the autopsy?' Green asked me.

I looked at him, and he was so typical of weak people with power or rank. He had done his best to scare me off, and when that had accomplished nothing he had decided we would be friends.

'I will do it now.' I started the car and turned the heat up high.

He looked surprised. 'Your office is open today?'

'I just opened it,' I said.

I had not shut the door, and he propped his arms on top of the frame and stared down at me. He was so close, I could see broken blood vessels along his cheekbones and the wings of his nose, and changes in pigmentation from the sun.

'You will call me with your report?'

'When I determine cause and manner of death, certainly I will discuss them with you,' I said.

'Manner?' He frowned. 'You mean there's some question that he's an accidental death?'

'There can and will always be questions, Captain Green. It is my job to question.'

'Well, if you find a knife or bullet in his back, I hope you'll call me first,' he said with quiet irony as he gave me one of his cards.

I drove away looking up the number for Mant's morgue assistant and hoping I would find him home. I did.

'Danny, it's Dr Scarpetta,' I said.

'Oh, yes, ma'am,' he said, surprised.

Christmas music sounded in the background and I heard the voices of people arguing. Danny Webster was in his early twenties and still lived with his family.

'I'm so sorry to bother you on New Year's Eve,' I said, 'but we've got a case I need to autopsy without delay. I'm on my way to the office now.'

'You need me?' He sounded quite open to the idea.

'If you could help me, I can't tell you how much I would appreciate it. There's a johnboat and a body headed to the office as we speak.'

'No problem, Dr Scarpetta,' he cheerfully said. 'I'll be right there.'

I tried Mant's house, but Lucy did not pick up, so I entered a code to check the answering machine's messages. There were two, both left by friends of Mant, expressing their sympathy. Snow had begun drifting down from a leaden sky, the interstate busy with people driving faster than was safe. I wondered if my niece had gotten delayed and why she hadn't called. Lucy was twenty-three and barely graduated from the FBI Academy. I still worried about her as if she needed my protection.

My Tidewater District Office was located in a small, crowded annex on the grounds of Sentara Norfolk General Hospital. We shared the building with the Department of Health, which unfortunately included the office of Shell Fish Sanitation. So between the stench of decomposing bodies and decaying fish, the parking lot was not a good place to be, no matter the time of year or day. Danny's ancient Toyota was already there, and when I unlocked the bay I was pleased to find the johnboat waiting.

I lowered the door behind me and walked around, looking. The long low-pressure hose had been neatly coiled, and as I had requested one severed end and the regulator it was attached to were sealed inside plastic. The other end was still connected to the small compressor strapped to the inner tube. Nearby were a gallon of gasoline and the expected miscellaneous assortment of dive and boat equipment, including extra weights, a tank containing three thousand pounds per square inch of air, a paddle, life preserver, flashlight, blanket and flare gun.

Eddings also had attached an extra five-horsepower trolling engine that he clearly had used to enter the restricted area where he had died. The main thirty-five-horsepower engine was pulled back and locked, so its propeller would have been out of the water, and I remembered this was the position it was in when I saw the johnboat at the scene. But what interested me more than any of this was a hard plastic carrying case open on the floor. Nestled in its foam lining were various camera attachments and boxes of Kodak 100 ASA film. But I saw no camera or strobe, and I imagined they were forever lost on the bottom of the Elizabeth River.

I walked up a ramp and unlocked another door, and inside the white-tiled corridor, Ted Eddings was zipped inside a pouch on top of a gurney parked near the X-ray room. His stiff arms pushed against black vinyl as if he were trying to fight his way free, and water slowly dripped on the floor. I was about to look for Danny when he limped around a corner, carrying a stack of towels, his right knee in a bright red sports brace from a soccer injury that had necessitated a reconstruction of his anterior cruciate ligament.

'We really should get him in the autopsy suite,' I said. 'You know how I feel about leaving bodies unattended in the hall.'

'I was afraid someone would slip,' he said, mopping up water with the towels.

'Well, the only someones here today are you and me.' I smiled at him. 'But thank you for the thought, and I certainly don't want you to slip. How's the knee?'

'I don't think it's ever going to get better. It's already been almost three months and I still can barely go downstairs.'

'Patience, keep up your physio, and yes, it will get better,' I repeated what I had said before. 'Have you rayed him yet?'

Danny had worked diving deaths before. He knew it was highly improbable that we were looking for projectiles or broken bones, but what an X-ray might reveal was pneumothorax or a mediastinal shift caused by air leaking from lungs due to barotrauma.

'Yes, ma'am. The film's in the developer.' He paused, his expression turning unpleasant. 'And Detective Roche with Chesapeake's on his way. He wants to be present for the post.'

Although I encouraged detectives to watch their cases autopsied, Roche was not someone I particularly wanted in my morgue.

'Do you know him?' I asked.

'He's been down here before. I'll let you judge him for yourself.'

He straightened up and gathered his dark hair into a ponytail again, because strands had escaped and were getting in his eyes. Lithe and graceful, he looked like a young Cherokee with a brilliant grin. I often wondered why he wanted to work here. I helped him roll the body into the autopsy suite, and while he weighed and measured it, I disappeared inside the locker room and took a shower. As I was dressing in scrubs, Marino called my pager.

'What's up?' I asked when I got him on the phone.

'It's who we thought, right?' he asked.

'Tentatively, yes.'

'You posting him now?'

'I'm about to start,' I said.

'Give me fifteen minutes. I'm almost there.'

'You're coming here?' I said, perplexed.

'I'm on my car phone. We'll talk later. I'll be there soon.'

As I wondered what this was about, I also knew that Marino must have found something in Richmond. Otherwise, his coming to Norfolk made no sense. Ted Eddings's death was not Marino's jurisdiction unless the FBI had already gotten involved, and that would not make sense, either.

Both Marino and I were consultants for the Bureau's Criminal Investigative Analysis program, more commonly known as the profiling unit which specialized in assisting police with unusually heinous and difficult deaths. We routinely got involved in cases outside of our domains, but by invitation only, and it was a little early for Chesapeake to be calling the FBI about anything.

Detective Roche arrived before Marino did, and he was carrying a paper bag and insisting that I give him gown, gloves, face shield, cap and shoe covers. While he was in the locker room fussing with his biological armor, Danny and I began taking photographs and looking at Eddings exactly as he had come to us, which was still in a full wet suit that continued to slowly drip on the floor.

'He's been dead a while,' I said. 'I have a feeling that whatever happened to him occurred shortly after he went into the river.'

'Do we know when that was?' Danny asked as he fit scalpel handles with new blades.

'We're assuming it was sometime after dark.'

'He doesn't look very old.'

'Thirty-two.'

He stared at Eddings's face and his own got sad. 'It's like when kids end up in here or that basketball player who dropped dead in the gym the other week.' He looked at me. 'Does it ever get to you?'

'I can't let it get to me because they need me to do a good job for them,' I said as I made notes.

'What about when you're done?' He glanced up.

'We're never done, Danny,' I said. 'Our hearts will stay broken for the rest of our lives, and we will never be done with the people who pass through here.'

'Because we can't forget them.' He lined a bucket with a viscera bag and put it near me on the floor. 'At least I can't.'

'If we forget them, then something is wrong with us,' I said.

Roche emerged from the locker room looking like a disposable astronaut in his face shield and paper suit. He kept his distance from the gurney but got as close as he could to me.

I said to him, 'I've looked inside the boat. What items have you removed?'

'His gun and wallet. I got both of them here with me,' he replied. 'Over there in the bag. How many pairs of gloves you got on?'

'What about a camera, film, anything like that?'

'What's in the boat is all there is. Looks like you got on more than one pair of gloves.' He leaned close, his shoulder pressing against mine.

'I've double-gloved.' I moved away from him.

'I guess I need another pair.'

I unzipped Eddings's soggy dive boots and said, 'They're in the cabinet over there.'

With a scalpel I opened the wet suit and dive skin at the seams because they would be too difficult to pull off a fully rigorous body. As I freed him from neoprene, I could see that he was uniformly pink due to the cold. I removed his blue bikini bathing suit, and Danny and I lifted him onto the autopsy table, where we broke the rigidity of the arms and began taking more photographs.

Eddings had no injuries except several old scars, mostly on his knees. But biology had dealt him an earlier blow called hypospadias, which meant his urethra opened onto the underside of his penis instead of in the center. This moderate defect would have caused him a great deal of anxiety, especially as a boy. As a man he may have suffered sufficient shame that he was reluctant to have sex.

Certainly, he had never been shy or passive during professional encounters. In fact, I had always found him quite confident and charming, when someone like me was rarely charmed by anyone, least of all a journalist. But I also knew appearances meant nothing in terms of how people behaved when two of them were alone, and then I tried to stop right there.

I did not want to remember him alive as I made annotations and measurements on diagrams fastened to my clipboard. But a part of my mind tackled my will, and I returned to the last occasion I had seen him. It was the week before Christmas and I was in my Richmond office with my back to the door, sorting through slides in a carousel. I did not hear him behind me until he spoke, and when I turned around, I found him in my doorway, holding a potted Christmas pepper thick with bright red fruit.

'You mind if I come in?' he asked. 'Or do you want me to walk all the way back to my car with this.'

I said good afternoon to him while I thought with frustration of the front office staff. They knew not to let reporters beyond the locked bulletproof partition in the lobby unless I was asked, but the female clerks, in particular, liked Eddings a little too much. He walked in and set the plant on the carpet by my desk, and when he smiled, his entire face did.

'I just thought there ought to be something alive and happy in this place.' His blue eyes fixed on mine.

'I hope that isn't a comment about me.' I could not help but laugh.

'Are you ready to turn him?'

The body diagram on my clipboard came into focus, and I realized Danny was speaking to me.

'I'm sorry,' I muttered.

He was eyeing me with concern while Roche wandered around as if he had never been inside a morgue, peering through glass cabinets and glancing back in my direction.

'Everything all right?' Danny asked me in his sensitive way.

'We can turn him now,' I said.

My spirit shook inside like a small hot flame. Eddings had worn khaki range pants and a black commando sweater that day, and I tried to remember the look in his eyes. I wondered if there had been anything behind them that might have presaged this.

Refrigerated by the river, his body was cold to my touch, and I began discovering other aspects of him that distorted the familiar, making me feel even more disturbed. The absence of first molars signaled orthodonture. He had extensive, very expensive porcelain crowns, and contact lenses tinted to enhance eyes already vivid. Remarkably, the right lens had not been washed away when his mask had flooded, and his dull gaze was weirdly asymmetrical, as if two dead people were staring out from sleepy lids.

I was almost finished with the external examination, but what was left was the most invasive, for in any unnatural death, it was necessary to investigate a patient's sexual practices. Rarely was I given a sign as obvious as a tattoo depicting one orientation or another, and as a rule, no one the individual was intimate with was going to step forth to volunteer information, either. But it really would not have mattered what I was told or by whom. I would still check for evidence of anal intercourse.

'What are you looking for?' Roche returned to the table and stood close behind me.

'Proctitis, anal tunneling, small fissures, thickening of the epithelium from trauma,' I replied as I worked.

'Then you're assuming he's queer.' He peered over my shoulder.

The color mounted to Danny's cheeks, and anger sparked in his eyes.

'Anal ring, epithelium are unremarkable,' I said, scribbling notes. 'In other words, he has no injury that would be consistent with an active homosexual lifestyle. And, Detective Roche, you're going to have to give me a little more room.'

I could feel his breath on my neck.

'You know, he's been in this area a lot doing interviews.'

'What sort of interviews?' I asked, and he was seriously getting on my nerves.

'That I don't know.'

'Who was he interviewing?'

'Last fall he did a piece on the Inactive Ship Yard. Captain Green could probably tell you more.'

'I was just with Captain Green, and he didn't tell me about that.'

'The story ran in *The Virginian Pilot*, back in October, I think. It wasn't a big deal. Just your typical feature,' he said. 'My personal opinion is he decided to come back to snoop around for something bigger.'

'Such as?'

'Don't ask me. I'm not a reporter.' He glanced across the table at Danny. 'I personally hate the media. They're always coming up with these wild theories and will do anything to prove them. Now this guy's kinda famous around here, being a big-shot reporter for the AP and all. Rumor has it when he gets with girls it's window dressing. You get beyond it and nothing's there, if you know what I mean.' He had a cruel smile on his face, and I could not believe how much I did not like him when we had only met today.

'Where are you getting your information?' I asked.

'I hear things.'

'Danny, let's get hair and fingernail samples,' I said.

'You know, I take the time to talk to people on the street,' Roche added as he brushed against my hip.

'You want his mustache plucked, too?' Danny fetched forceps and envelopes from a surgical cart.

'May as well.'

'I guess you're going to test him for HIV.' Roche brushed against me again.

'Yes,' I replied.

'Then you're thinking he might be queer.'

I stopped what I was doing because I'd had enough. 'Detective Roche' – I turned around to face him, and my voice was hard – 'if you are going to be in my morgue, then you will give me room to work. You will stop rubbing against me, and you will treat my patients with respect. This man did not ask to be here dead and naked on this table. And I don't like the word queer.'

'Well, regardless of what you call it, his orientation might somehow be important.' He was nonplussed, if not pleased by my irritation.

'I don't know for a fact that this man was or was not gay,' I said. 'But I do know for a fact that he did not die of AIDS.'

I grabbed a scalpel off a surgical cart and his demeanor abruptly changed. He backed off, suddenly unnerved because I was about to start cutting, so now I had that problem to cope with, too.

'Have you ever seen an autopsy?' I said to him.

'A few.' He looked like he might throw up.

'Why don't you go sit down over there,' I suggested none too kindly as I wondered why Chesapeake had assigned him to this case or any case. 'Or go out in the bay.'

'It's just hot in here.'

'If you get sick, go for the nearest trash can.' It was all Danny could do not to laugh.

'I'll just sit over here for a minute.' Roche went to the desk near the door.

I swiftly made the Y incision, the blade running from shoulders to sternum to pelvis. As blood was exposed to air, I thought I detected an odor that made me stop what I was doing.

'You know, Lipshaw's got a really good sharpener out I wish we could get,' Danny was saying. 'It hone-grinds with water so you can just stick the knives in there and leave them.'

What I was smelling was unmistakable, but I could not believe it.

'I was just looking at their new catalog,' he went on. 'Makes me crazy all the cool things we can't afford.'

This could not be right.

'Danny, open the doors,' I said with a quiet urgency that startled him.

'What is it?' he asked in alarm.

'Let's get plenty of air in here. Now,' I said.

He moved fast with his bad knee and opened double doors that led into the hall.

'What's wrong?' Roche sat up straighter.

'This man has a peculiar odor.' I was unwilling to voice my suspicions right then, especially to him.

'I don't smell anything.' He got up and looked around, as if this mysterious odor might be something he could see.

Eddings's blood reeked of a bitter almond smell, and it did not surprise me that neither Roche nor Danny could detect it. The ability to smell cyanide is a sex-linked recessive trait that is inherited by less than thirty percent of the population. I was among the fortunate few.

'Trust me.' I was reflecting back skin from ribs, careful not to puncture the intercostal muscles. 'He smells very strange.'

'And what does that mean?' Roche wanted to know.

'I won't be able to answer that until tests are conducted,' I said. 'In the meantime, we'll thoroughly check out all of his equipment to make sure everything was functioning and that he didn't, for example, get exhaust fumes down his hose.'

'You know much about hookahs?' Danny asked me, and he had returned to the table to help.

'I've never used one.'

I undermined the midline chest incision laterally. Reflecting back tissue, I formed a pocket in a side of skin, which Danny filled with water. Then I immersed my hand and inserted the scalpel blade between two ribs. I checked for a release of bubbles that might indicate a diving injury had caused air to leak into the chest cavity. But there were none.

'Let's get the hookah and the hose out of the boat and bring them in,' I decided. 'It would be good if we could get hold of a dive consultant for a second opinion. Do you know anyone around here we might be able to reach on a holiday?'

'There's a dive shop in Hampton Roads that Dr Mant sometimes uses.'

He got the numbers and called, but the shop was closed this snowy New Year's Eve, and the owner did not seem to be at home. Then Danny went out to the bay, and when he returned a brief time later, I could hear a familiar voice talking loudly with him as heavy footsteps sounded along the hallway.

'They wouldn't let you if you were a cop,' Pete Marino's voice projected into the autopsy suite.

'I know, but I don't understand it,' Danny said.

'Well, I'll give you one damn good reason. Hair as long as yours gives the assholes out there one more thing to grab. Me? I'd cut it off. Besides, the girls would like you better.'

He had arrived in time to help carry in the hookah and coils of hose, and was giving Danny a fatherly lecture. It had never been hard for me to understand why Marino had terrible problems with his own grown son.

'You know anything about hookahs?' I asked Marino as he walked in. He looked blankly at the body. 'What? He's got some weirdo disease?'

'The thing you're carrying is called a hookah,' I explained.

He and Danny set the equipment on top of an empty steel table next to mine.

'Looks like dive shops are closed for the next few days,' I added. 'But the compressor seems pretty simple – a pump driven by a five-horsepower engine which pulls air through a filtered intake valve, then through the low-pressure hose connected to the diver's second-stage regulator. Filter looks all right. Fuel line is intact. That's all I can tell you.'

'The tank's empty,' Marino observed.

'I think he ran out of gas after death.'

'Why?' Roche had walked over to where we were, and he stared intensely at me and the front of my scrubs as if he and I were the only two people in the room. 'How do you know he didn't lose track of time down there and run out of gas?'

'Because even if his air supply quit, he still had plenty of time to get to the surface. He was only thirty feet down,' I said.

'That's a long way if maybe your hose has gotten hung up on something.'

'It would be. But in that scenario, he could have dropped his weight belt.'

'Has the smell gone away?' he asked.

'No, but it's not as overpowering.'

'What smell?' Marino wanted to know.

'His blood has a weird odor.'

'You mean like booze?'

'No, not like that.'

He sniffed several times and shrugged as Roche moved past me, averting his gaze from what was on the table. I could not believe it when he brushed against me again though he had plenty of room and I had given him a warning. Marino was big and balding in a fleece-lined coat, and his eyes followed him.

'So, who's this?' he asked me.

'Yes, I guess the two of you haven't met,' I said. 'Detective Roche of Chesapeake, this is Captain Marino with Richmond.'

Roche was looking closely at the hookah, and the sound of Danny cutting through ribs with shears on the next table was getting to him. His complexion was the shade of milk glass again, his mouth bowed down.

Marino lit a cigarette and I could tell by the expression on his face that he had made his decision about Roche, and Roche was about to know it.

'I don't know about you,' he said to the detective, 'but one thing I discovered early on, is once you come to this joint, you never feel the same about liver. You watch.' He tucked the lighter back inside his shirt pocket. 'Me, I used to love it smothered in onions.' He blew out smoke. 'Now, on the pain of death you couldn't make me touch it.'

Roche leaned closer to the hookah, almost burying his face in it, as if the smell of rubber and gasoline was the antidote he needed. I resumed work.

'Hey, Danny,' Marino went on, 'you ever eat shit like kidneys and gizzards since you started working here?'

'I've never ate any of that my entire life,' he said as we removed the breastplate. 'But I know what you mean. When I see people order big slabs of liver in restaurants, I almost have to dive for the door. Especially if it's even the slightest bit pink.'

The odor intensified as organs were exposed, and I leaned back.

'You smelling it?' Danny asked.

'Oh, yeah,' I said.

Roche retreated to his distant corner, and now that Marino had had his fun, he walked over and stood next to me.

'So you think he drowned?' Marino quickly asked.

'At the moment I'm not thinking that. But certainly, I'm going to look for it,' I said.

'What can you do to figure out he didn't drown?'

Marino was not very familiar with drownings, since people rarely committed murder that way, so he was intensely curious. He wanted to understand everything I was doing.

'Actually, there are a lot of things I'm doing,' I said as I worked. 'I've already made a skin pocket on the side of the chest, filled it with water and inserted a blade in the thorax to check for bubbles. I'm going to fill the pericardial sac with water and insert a needle into the heart, again to see if any bubbles form. And I'll check the brain for petechial hemorrhages, and look at the soft tissue of the mediastinum for extraalveolar air.'

'What will all that show?' he asked.

'Possibly pneumothorax or air embolism, which can occur in less than fifteen feet of water if the diver is breathing inadequately. The problem is that excessive pressure in the lungs can result in small tears of the alveolar walls, causing hemorrhages and air leaks into one or both pleural cavities.'

'And I'm assuming that could kill you,' he said.

'Yes,' I said. 'That most certainly could.'

'What about when you come up and go down too fast?' He had moved to the other side of the table so he could watch.

'Pressure changes, or barotrauma, associated with descent or ascent aren't very likely in the depth he was diving. And as you can see, his tissues aren't spongy as I would expect them to be were he a death by barotrauma. Would you like some protective clothing?'

'So I can look like I work for Terminex?' Marino looked in Roche's direction.

'Just hope you don't get AIDS,' Roche wanly said from far away.

Marino put on apron and gloves as I began explaining the pertinent negatives I needed to look for in order to also rule out a death by decompression or the bends, or drowning. It was when I inserted an eighteen-gauge needle into the trachea to obtain a sample of air for cyanide testing that Roche decided to leave. He rapidly walked across the room, paper rattling as he collected his evidence bag from a counter.

'So we won't know anything until you do tests,' he said from the doorway.

'That's correct. For now his cause and manner of death are pending.' I paused and looked up at him. 'You'll get a copy of my report when it's complete. And I'd like to see his personal effects before you leave.'

He would come no closer, and my hands were bloody.

I looked at Marino. 'Would you mind?'

'It would be my pleasure.'

He went to him, took the bag and gruffly said, 'Come on. We'll go through it in the hall so you can get some air.'

They walked just beyond the doorway, and as I continued to work, paper rattled some more. I heard Marino drop the magazine from a pistol, open the slide and loudly complain that the gun had not been made safe.

'I can't believe you're carrying this thing around loaded,' Marino's voice boomed. 'Jesus Christ! You know, it's not like this is your friggin' lunch in a bag.'

'It's not been processed for prints yet.'

'Well, then you put on gloves and dump the ammo like I just did. And then you clear the chamber, the way I just did. Where'd you go? The Keystone Police Academy where they also must have taught you your gentlemanly manners?'

Marino went on, and it was now clear to me why he had taken Roche into the hall, and it wasn't for fresh air. Danny glanced across the table at me and grinned.

Moments later Marino returned to us shaking his head, and Roche was gone. I was relieved, and it showed.

'Good God,' I said. 'What is his story?'

'He thinks with the head God gave him,' Marino said. 'The one between his legs.'

'Like I said,' Danny replied, 'he's been down here a couple of times before bothering Dr Mant about things. But what I didn't tell you is he always talked to him upstairs. He never would come down to the morgue.'

'I'm shocked,' Marino drolly said.

'I heard that when he was in the police academy he called in sick the day they were supposed to come down here for the demo autopsy,' Danny went on. 'Plus, he just got transferred over from juvenile. So he's been a homicide detective for only about two months.'

'Oh, now that's good,' Marino said. 'Just the kind of person we want working something like this.'

I asked him, 'Can you smell the cyanide?'

'Nope. Right now all I smell is my cigarette, which is exactly how I want it.'

'Danny?'

'No, ma'am.' He sounded disappointed.

'So far I'm seeing no evidence that this is a diving death. No bubbles in the heart or thorax. No subcutaneous emphysema. No water in the stomach or lungs. I can't tell if he's congested.' I cut another section of heart. 'Well, he does have congestion of the heart, but is it due to the left heart failing the right – just due to dying, in other words? And he does have some reddening of the stomach wall, which is consistent with cyanide.'

'Doc,' Marino said, 'how well did you know him?'

'Personally, really not at all.'

'Well, I'm going to tell you what was in the bag because Roche didn't know what he was looking at and I didn't want to tell him.'

He at last slipped out of his coat and looked for a safe place to hang it, deciding on the back of a chair. He lit another cigarette.

'Damn, these floors kill my feet,' he said as he went to the table where hookah and hose were piled, and leaned against the edge. 'It must kill your knee,' he said to Danny.

'Totally kills it.'

'Eddings's got a Browning nine-millimeter pistol with a Birdsong desert brown finish,' Marino said.

'What's Birdsong?' Danny placed the spleen in a hanging scale.

'The Rembrandt of pistol finishes. Mr Birdsong's the guy you send your weapon to if you want it waterproofed and painted to blend with the environment,' Marino answered. 'What he does, basically, is strip it, sandblast it and then spray it with Teflon, which is baked on. All of HRT's pistols have a Birdsong finish.'

HRT was the FBI's Hostage Rescue Team. I felt sure that given the number of stories Eddings had done on law enforcement, he would have been exposed to the FBI Academy at Quantico and its finest trained agents.

'Sounds like something Navy SEALs would have, too,' Danny suggested.

'Them, SWAT teams, counterterrorists, guys like me.' Marino was looking again at the hookah's fuel line and intake valves. 'And most of us have Novak sights like he's got, too. But what we don't have is KTW metal-piercing ammo, also known as cop killers.'

'He's got Teflon-coated ammo?' I glanced up.

'Seventeen rounds, one in the chamber. All with red lacquer around the primer for waterproofing.'

'Well, he didn't get armor-piercing ammo here. At least not legally, because it's been outlawed in Virginia for years. And as for the finish on his pistol, are you certain it's Birdsong, the same company the Bureau uses?'

'Looks like Birdsong's magic touch to me,' Marino replied. ''Course, there are other outfits that do similar work.'

I opened the stomach as mine continued to close like a fist. Eddings had seemed such a fan of law enforcement. I had heard he used to ride along with the police, and go to their picnics and their balls. He had never struck me as gung-ho about weapons, and I was stunned that he would have loaded a pistol with illegal ammunition notorious for being used to murder and maim the very people who were his sources and perhaps his friends.

'Gastric contents are just a small amount of brownish fluid,' I continued. 'He didn't eat near the time of death, not that I would have expected him to if he planned to dive.'

'Any chance fuel exhaust could have gotten to him, say if the wind blew just right?' Marino continued studying the hookah. 'Couldn't that also make him pink?'

'Certainly, we'll test for carbon monoxide. But that doesn't explain what I'm smelling.'

'And you're sure?'

'I know what I'm smelling,' I said.

'You think he's a homicide, don't you,' Danny said to me.

'No one should be talking about this.' I pulled a cord down from an overhead reel and plugged in the Stryker saw. 'Not to the Chesapeake police. Not to anyone. Not until all tests are concluded and I make an official release. I don't know what's going on here. I don't know what was going on at the scene. So we must exercise even more caution than usual.'

Marino was looking at Danny. 'How long you been working in this joint?' he asked.

'Eight months.'

'You heard what the doc just said, right?'

Danny looked up, surprised by Marino's change in tone.

'You know how to keep your mouth shut, right?' Marino went on. 'That means no bragging to the boys, no trying to impress your family or your girlfriend. You got that?'

Danny held in his anger as he made an incision low around the back of the head, ear to ear.

'See, if anything leaks, me and the doc here are going to know where it came from,' Marino continued an attack that seemed completely unprovoked.

Danny reflected back the scalp. He pulled it forward over the eyes to expose the skull, and Eddings's face collapsed, sad and slack, as if he knew what was happening and was grieving. I turned on the saw, and the room was filled with the high whine of blade cutting bone.

3

At three-thirty the sun had dipped low behind a veil of gray, and snow was several inches deep and hung like smoke in the air. Marino and I followed Danny's footsteps across the parking lot, for the young man had already gone, and I felt bad for him.

'Marino,' I said, 'you just can't talk to people like that. My staff knows about discretion. Danny did nothing to merit your treating him so rudely, and I don't appreciate it.'

'He's a kid,' he said. 'You raise him right and he'll take good care of you. Thing is, you got to believe in discipline.'

'It is not your job to discipline my staff. And I have never had a problem with him.'

'Yeah? And maybe this is one time when you don't need a problem with him,' he replied.

'I really would appreciate it if you wouldn't try to run my office.'

I was tired and out of sorts, and Lucy still was not answering the phone at Mant's house. Marino had parked next to me, and I unlocked my driver's door.

'So, what's Lucy doing for the New Year?' he asked as if he knew my concerns.

'Hopefully, spending it with me. But I haven't heard from her.' I got into the car.

'The snow started up north, so Quantico got hit first,' he said. 'Maybe she got caught. You know how 95 can be.'

'She's got a car phone. Besides, she's driving from Charlottesville,' I said.

'How come?'

'The Academy's decided to send her back to UVA for another graduate course.'

'In what? Advanced Rocket Science?'

'Apparently, she's doing a special study in virtual reality.'

'So maybe she got stuck somewhere between here and Charlottesville.' He did not want me to leave.

'She could have left a message.'

He stared around the parking lot. It was empty save for the dark blue morgue wagon, which was covered with snow. Flakes clung to his wispy hair and must have been cold on his balding head, but he did not seem to mind.

'Do you have New Year plans?' I started the engine, then the wipers to plow snow off the windshield.

'A couple of us guys are supposed to play poker and eat chili.'

'That sounds like fun.' I looked up at his big, flushed face as he continued staring off.

'Doc. I went through Eddings's apartment back in Richmond and didn't want to get into it in front of Danny. I think you're going to want to go through it, too.'

Marino wanted to talk. He did not want to be with the guys or alone. He wanted to be with me, but he would never admit that. In all the years I had known him, his feelings for me were a confession he could not make, no matter how obvious they might be.

'I can't compete with a poker game,' I said to him as I fastened my shoulder harness, 'but I was going to make lasagne tonight. And it doesn't look like Lucy's going to get in. So if—'

'It don't look like driving back after midnight would be a smart thing,' he cut me off as snow swirled across the tarmac in small white storms.

'I've got a guest room,' I went on.

He looked at his watch, and decided it was a good time to smoke.

'In fact, driving back now isn't even a good idea,' I stated. 'And it looks like we need to talk.'

'Yeah, well, you're probably right,' he said.

What neither of us counted on as he slowly followed me to Sandbridge was that when we arrived, smoke would be drifting up from the chimney. Lucy's vintage green Suburban was parked in the drive and blanketed with snow, so I knew she had been here for a while.

'I don't understand,' I said to Marino as we slammed car doors shut. 'I called three times.'

'Maybe I'd better leave.' He stood by his Ford, not sure what to do.

'That's ridiculous. Come on. We'll figure out something. There is a couch. Besides, Lucy will be thrilled to see you.'

'You got your diving shit?' he said.

'In the trunk.'

We got it out together and carried it up to Dr Mant's house, which looked even smaller and more forlorn in the weather. At the back was a screened-in porch, and we went in that way and deposited my gear on the wooden floor. Lucy opened the door leading into the kitchen, and we were enveloped by the aroma of tomatoes and garlic. She looked baffled as she stared at Marino and the dive equipment.

'What the hell's going on?' she said.

I could tell she was upset. This had been our night to be alone, and we did not have special nights like this often in our complicated lives.

'It's a long story.' I met her eyes.

We followed her inside, where a large pot was simmering on the stove. Nearby on the counter was a cutting board, and Lucy apparently had been slicing peppers and onions when we arrived. She was dressed in FBI sweats and ski socks and looked flawlessly healthy, but I could tell she had not been getting much sleep.

'There's a hose in the pantry, and just off the porch near a spigot is an empty plastic trash can,' I said to Marino. 'If you'd fill that, we can soak my gear.'

'I'll help,' Lucy said.

'You most certainly won't.' I gave her a hug. 'Not until we've visited for a minute.'

We waited until Marino was outside, then I pulled her over to the stove and lifted the lid from the pot. A delicious steam rose and I felt happy.

'I can't believe you,' I said. 'God bless you.'

'When you weren't back by four I figured I'd better make the sauce or we weren't going to be eating lasagne tonight.'

'It might need a little more red wine. And maybe more basil and a pinch of salt. I was going to use artichokes instead of meat, although Marino won't be happy about that, but he can just eat prosciutto. How does that sound?' I returned the lid to the pot.

'Aunt Kay, why is he here?' she asked.

'Did you get my note?'

'Sure. That's how I got in. But all it said was you had gone to a scene.'

'I'm sorry. But I called several times.'

'I wasn't going to answer a phone in somebody else's house,' she said. 'And you didn't leave a message.'

'My point is that I didn't think you were here, so I invited Marino. I didn't want him to drive back to Richmond in the snow.'

Disappointment glinted in her intense green eyes. 'It's not a problem. As long as he and I don't have to sleep in the same room,' she dryly remarked. 'But I don't understand what he was even doing in Tidewater.'

'Like I said, it's a long story,' I answered. 'The case in question has a Richmond connection.'

We went out to the frigid porch and quickly swished fins, dive skin, wet suit and other gear in icy water. Then we carried all of it up to the attic, where nothing would freeze, and placed it on multiple layers of towels. I took as long a shower as the water heater would allow, and thought it unreal that Lucy, Marino and I were together in this tiny coastal cottage on a snowy New Year's Eve.

When I emerged from my bedroom, I found them in the kitchen drinking Italian beer and reading about making bread.

'All right,' I said to them. 'That's it. Now I take over.'

'Watch out,' Lucy said.

I shooed them out of the way and began measuring high gluten flour, yeast, a little sugar and olive oil into a large bowl. I turned the oven on low and opened a bottle of Côte Rôtie, which was for the cook to sip as she began her serious work. I would serve a Chianti with the meal.

'Did you go through Eddings's wallet?' I asked Marino as I chopped porcini mushrooms.

'Who's Eddings?' Lucy asked.

She was sitting on a countertop, sipping Peroni. Through the windows behind her snow streaked the gathering dark. I explained more about what had happened today, and she asked no further questions, but was silent as Marino talked.

'Nothing jumped out,' he said. 'One MasterCard, one Visa, AmEx, insurance info. Crap like that and a couple receipts. They look like restaurants, but we'll check. You mind if I get another one of these?' He dropped an empty bottle into the trash and opened the refrigerator door. 'Let's see what else.' Glass clattered. 'He wasn't carrying much cash. Twenty-seven bucks.'

'What about photographs?' I asked, kneading dough on a board dusted with flour.

'Nothing.' He shut the refrigerator. 'And as you know, he wasn't married.'

'We don't know that he didn't have a significant relationship with someone,' I said.

'That could be true because there sure isn't a hell of a lot we know.' He looked at Lucy. 'You know what Birdsong is?'

'My Sig's got a Birdsong finish.' She looked over at me. 'So does Aunt Kay's Browning.'

'Well, this guy Eddings had a Browning nine-mil just like what your aunt's got and it has a desert brown Birdsong finish. Plus, his ammo's Teflon-coated and has red lacquer on the primer. I mean you could shoot the shit through twelve phone books in the friggin' pouring rain.'

She was surprised. 'What's a journalist doing with something like that?'

'Some people are just very enthusiastic about guns and ammo,' I said. 'Although I never knew Eddings was. He never mentioned it to me – not that he necessarily would have.'

'I've never seen KTW in Richmond at all,' Marino said, referring to the brand name of the Teflon-coated cartridges. 'Legal or other-wise.'

'Could he have gotten it at a gun show?' I asked.

'Maybe. One thing's for sure. This guy probably went to a lot of them. I ain't told you about his apartment yet.'

I covered the dough with a damp towel and put the bowl in the oven on the lowest setting.

'I won't give you the whole tour,' he went on. 'Just the important parts, starting with the room where he's apparently been reloading his own ammo. Now where he's been shooting all these rounds, who knows. But he's got plenty of guns to choose from, including several other handguns, an AK-47, an MP5 and an M16. Not exactly what you use for varmint hunting. Plus, he subscribed to a number of survivalist magazines, including *Soldier of Fortune, U.S. Cavalry Magazine,* and *Brigade Quartermaster*. Finally' – Marino took another swallow of beer – 'we found some videotapes on how to be a sniper. You know, special forces training and shit like that.'

I folded eggs and Parmesan reggiano with ricotta. 'Any hint as to what he may have been involved in?' I asked as the mystery of the dead man deepened and unsettled me more.

'No, but he sure as hell seemed to be after something.'

'Or something was after him,' I said.

'He was scared,' Lucy spoke as if she knew. 'You don't go diving after dark and carry along a waterproof nine-mil loaded with armor-piercing ammo unless you're scared. That's the behavior of someone who thinks there's a contract out on him.'

It was then I told them about my strange early-morning phone call from an Officer Young who did not seem to exist. I mentioned Captain Green and described his behavior.

'Why would he call, if he's the one who did?' Marino frowned.

'Clearly, he didn't want me at the scene,' I said. 'And maybe if I were given ample information by the police, I would just wait for the body to come in, as I usually do.'

'Well, it sounds to me like you were being bullied,' Lucy said.

'I believe that was the overall plan,' I agreed.

'Have you tried the phone number this nonexistent Officer Young gave you?' she asked.

'No,' I said.

'Where is it?'

I got it for her and she dialed it.

'It's the number for the local weather report,' she said, hanging up.

Marino pulled out a chair from the checker cloth-covered breakfast table and straddled it, his arms folded on top of the back. Nobody spoke for a while as we sifted through data that were getting only stranger by the minute.

'Listen, Doc.' Marino cracked his knuckles. 'I really gotta smoke. You going to let me or do I have to go outside?'

'Outside,' Lucy said, jabbing her thumb toward the door and looking meaner than I knew she felt.

'And what if I fall into a snowdrift, you little runt?' he said.

'It's four inches deep out there. The only drift you're going to fall into is the one in your mind.'

'Tomorrow we'll go out on the beach and shoot cans,' he said. 'Now and then you need someone to give you a little humility, Special Agent Lucy.'

'You most certainly will not be shooting anything on this beach,' I said to both of them.

'I guess we could let Pete open the window and blow smoke out,'

Lucy said. 'But it just shows you how addicted you are.'

'As long as you smoke fast,' I said to him. 'This house is cold enough as it is.'

The window was stubborn, but no more so than Marino, who managed to get it open after a violent struggle. Moving his chair nearby, he lit up and blew smoke out the screen. Lucy and I placed silverware and napkins in the living room, deciding it would be cozier to eat in front of the fire than in Dr Mant's kitchen or cramped, drafty dining room.

'You haven't even told me how you're doing,' I said to my niece as she started working on the fire.

'I'm doing great.'

Sparks swarmed up the chimney's sooty throat as she shoved more wood inside, and veins stood out in her hands, muscles flexing in her back. Her gifts were in computer science and, most recently, robotics, which she had studied at MIT. They were areas of expertise that had made her very attractive to the FBI's Hostage Rescue Team, but the expectation of her was cerebral, not physical. No woman had ever passed HRT's punishing requirements, and I worried that she was not going to accept her limits.

'How much are you working out?' I asked her.

She closed the screen and sat on the hearth, looking at me. 'A lot.'

'If your body fat gets much lower, you won't be healthy.'

'I'm very healthy and actually have too much body fat.'

'If you're getting anorexic, I'm not going to have my head in the sand about it, Lucy. I know that eating disorders kill. I've seen their victims.'

'I don't have an eating disorder.'

I came over and sat next to her, the fire warming our backs.

'I guess I'll have to take your word on that.'

'Good.'

'Listen' – I patted her leg – 'you've been assigned to HRT as their technical consultant. It has never been anyone's assumption that you will fast-rope out of helicopters and run four-minute miles with the men.'

She looked over at me with flashing eyes. 'You're one to talk about limitations. I don't see that you've ever let your gender hold you back.'

'I absolutely know my limitations,' I disagreed. 'And I work around them with my mind. That is how I have survived.'

'Look,' she said with feeling, 'I'm tired of programming computers and robots, and then every time something big goes down – like the bombing in Oklahoma City – the guys head off to Andrews Air Force Base and I get left. Or even if I go with them, they lock me in some little room somewhere like I'm nothing but a nerd. I'm not a goddamn nerd. I don't want to be a latchkey agent.'

Her eyes were suddenly bright with tears and she averted them from me. 'I can run any obstacle course they put me on. I can rappel, sniper-shoot and scuba-dive. More important, I can take it when they act like assholes. You know, not all of them are exactly happy to have me around.'

I had no doubt of that. Lucy had always been an extremely polarizing human being, because she was brilliant and could be so difficult. She was also beautiful in a sharp-featured, strong way, and I frankly wondered how she survived at all on a special forces team of fifty men, not one of whom she would ever date.

'How is Janet?' I asked.

'They transferred her out to the Washington Field Office to do white-collar crime. So at least she's not far away.'

'This must have been recent.' I was puzzled.

'Real recent.' Lucy rested her forearms on her knees.

'And where is she tonight?'

'Her family's got a condo in Aspen.'

My silence asked the question, and her voice was irritated as she answered it. 'No, I wasn't invited. And not just because Janet and I aren't getting along. It just wasn't a good idea.'

'I see.' I hesitated before adding, 'Then her parents still don't know.'

'Hell, who does know? You think we don't hide it at work? So we go to things together and each of us gets to watch the other being hit on by men. That's a special pleasure,' she bitterly said.

'I know what it's like at work,' I said. 'It's no different than I told you it would be. What I'm more interested in is Janet's family.'

Lucy stared at her hands. 'It's mostly her mom. To tell you the truth, I don't think her dad would care. He's not going to assume it's because of something he did wrong, like my mother assumes. Only she assumes it's because of something you did wrong since you pretty much raised me and are my mother, according to her.'

There was little point in my defending myself against the ignorant notions of my only sister, Dorothy, who unfortunately happened to be Lucy's parent.

'And Mother has another theory now, too. She says you're the first woman I fell in love with, and somehow that explains everything,'

Lucy went on in an ironic tone. 'Never mind that this would be called incest or that you're straight. Remember, she writes these insightful children's books, so she's an expert in psychology and apparently is a sex therapist, too.'

'I'm sorry you have to go through all this on top of everything else,' I said with feeling. I never knew quite what to do when we had these conversations. They were still new to me, and in some ways scary.

'Look' – she got up as Marino walked into the living room – 'some things you just live with.'

'Well, I got news for you,' Marino announced, 'the weather forecast is that this crap is going to melt. So come tomorrow morning, all of us should be able to get out of here.'

'Tomorrow's New Year's Day,' Lucy said. 'For the sake of argument, why should we get out of here?'

'Because I need to take your aunt to Eddings's crib.' He paused before adding, 'And Benton needs to get his ass there, too.'

I did not visibly react. Benton Wesley was the unit chief of the Bureau's Criminal Investigative Analysis program, and I had hoped I would not have to see him during the holidays.

'What are you telling me?' I quietly said.

He sat down on the sofa and regarded me thoughtfully for a pause. Then he answered my question with one of his own. 'I'm curious about something, Doc. How would you poison someone underwater?'

'Maybe it didn't happen underwater,' Lucy suggested. 'Maybe he swallowed cyanide before he went diving.'

'No. That's not what happened,' I said. 'Cyanide is very corrosive, and had he taken it orally, I would have seen extensive damage to his stomach. Probably to his esophagus and mouth, as well.'

'So what could have happened?' Marino asked.

'I think he inhaled cyanide gas.'

He looked baffled. 'How? Through the compressor?'

'It draws air through an intake valve that's covered with a filter,' I reminded him. 'What someone could have done was simply mix a little hydrochloric acid with a cyanide tablet and hold the vial close enough to the intake valve for the gas to be drawn in.'

'If Eddings inhaled cyanide gas while he was down there,' Lucy said, 'what would have happened?'

'A seizure, then death. In seconds.'

I thought of the snagged air hose and wondered if Eddings had been close to the *Exploiter*'s screw when he suddenly inhaled cyanide gas through his regulator. That might explain the position he was in when I found him.

'Can you test the hookah for cyanide?' Lucy asked.

'Well, we can try,' I said, 'but I don't expect to find anything unless the cyanide tablet was placed directly on the valve's filter. Even so, things may have been tampered with by the time I got there. We might have better luck with the section of hose that was closest to the body. I'll start tox testing tomorrow, if I can get anybody to come into the lab on a holiday.'

My niece walked over to a window to look out. 'It's still coming down hard. It's amazing how it lights up the night. I can see the ocean. It's this black wall,' she said in a pensive tone.

'What you're seeing is a wall,' Marino said. 'The brick wall at the back of the yard.'

She did not speak for a while, and I thought of how much I missed her. Although I had seen little of her during her undergraduate years at UVA, now we saw each other less, for even when a case brought me to Quantico there was never a guarantee we would find time to visit. It saddened me that her childhood was gone, and a part of me wished she had chosen a life and a career less harsh than what hers must be.

Then she mused as she still gazed out the glass, 'So we've got a reporter who's into survivalist weaponry. Somehow he's poisoned with cyanide gas while diving around decommissioned ships in a restricted area at night.'

'That's just a possibility,' I reminded her. 'His case is pending. We should be careful not to forget that.'

She turned around. 'Where would you get cyanide if you wanted to poison someone? Would that be hard?'

'You could get it from a variety of industrial settings,' I said.

'Such as?'

'Well, for example, it's used to extract gold from ore. It's also used in metal plating, and as a fumigant, and to manufacture phosphoric acid from bones,' I said. 'In other words, anyone from a jeweler to a worker in an industrial plant to an exterminator could have access to cyanide. Plus, you're going to find it and hydrochloric acid in any chemical lab.'

'Well,' it was Marino who spoke, 'if someone poisoned Eddings, then they had to know he was going to be out in his boat. They had to know where and when.'

'Someone had to know many things,' I agreed. 'For example, one would have had to know what type of breathing apparatus Eddings planned to use because had he gone down with scuba gear instead of a hookah, the MO would have had to be entirely different.'

'I just wish we knew what the hell he was doing down there.' Marino opened the screen to tend to the fire.

'Whatever it was,' I said, 'it seems to have involved photography. And based on the camera equipment it appears he had with him, he was serious.'

'But no underwater camera was found,' Lucy said.

'No,' I said. 'The current could have carried it anywhere, or it might be buried in silt. Unfortunately, the kind of equipment he apparently had doesn't float.'

'I sure would like to get hold of the film.' She was still looking out at the snowy night, and I wondered if she was thinking of Aspen.

'One thing's for damn sure, he wasn't taking pictures of fish.' Marino jabbed a fat log that was a little too green. 'So that pretty much leaves ships. And I think he was doing a story somebody didn't want him to do.'

'He may have been doing a story,' I agreed, 'but that doesn't mean it's related to his death. Someone could have used his being out diving as an opportunity to kill him for another reason.'

'Where do you keep the kindling?' He gave up on the fire.

'Outside under a tarp,' I answered. 'Dr Mant won't allow it in the house. He's afraid of termites.'

'Well, he ought to be more afraid of the fires and wind shear in this dump.'

'In back, just off the porch,' I said. 'Thanks, Marino.'

He put on gloves but no coat and went outside as the fire smoked stubbornly and the wind made eerie moaning sounds in the leaning brick chimney. I watched my niece, who was still at the window.

'We should work on dinner, don't you think?' I said to her.

'What's he doing?' she said with her back to me.

'Marino?'

'Yes. The big idiot's gotten lost. Look, he's all the way up by the wall. Wait a minute. I can't see him now. He turned his flashlight off. That's kind of weird.'

Her words lifted the hair on my neck and instantly I was on my feet. I dashed into the bedroom and grabbed my pistol off the night-stand. Lucy was on my heels.

'What is it?' she exclaimed.

'He doesn't have a flashlight,' I said as I ran.

4

In the kitchen, I flung open the door leading to the porch and ran into Marino. We almost knocked each other down.

'What the shit . . . ?' he yelled behind a load of wood.

'There's a prowler,' I spoke with quiet urgency.

Kindling thudded loudly to the floor and he ran back out into the yard, his pistol drawn. By now, Lucy had fetched her gun and was outside, too, and we were ready to handle a riot.

'Check the perimeter of the house,' Marino ordered. 'I'm going over here.'

I went back in for flashlights, and for a while Lucy and I circled the cottage, straining eyes and ears, but the only sight and sound was our shoes crunching as we left impressions in the snow. I heard Marino decock his pistol as we reconvened in deep shadows near the porch.

'There are footprints by the wall,' he said, and his breath was white. 'It's real strange. They lead down to the beach and then just disappear near the water.' He looked around. 'You got any neighbors who might have been out for a stroll?'

'I don't know Dr Mant's neighbors,' I replied. 'But they should not have been in his yard. And who in his right mind would walk on the beach in weather like this?'

'Where on this property do the footprints go?' Lucy asked.

'Looks like he came over the wall and went about six feet inside the yard before backtracking,' Marino answered.

I thought of Lucy standing before the window, backlit by the fire and lamps. Maybe the prowler had spotted her and had been scared off.

Then I thought of something else. 'How do we know this person was a he?'

'If it ain't, I feel sorry for a woman with boats that big,' Marino said. 'The shoes are about the same size as mine.'

'Shoes or boots?' I asked, heading toward the wall.

'I don't know. They got some sort of cross-hatch tread pattern.' He followed me.

The footprints I saw gave me cause for more alarm. They were not from typical boots or athletic shoes.

'My God,' I said. 'I think this person was wearing dive boots or something with a moccasin shape like dive boots. Look.'

I pointed out the pattern to Lucy and Marino. They had gotten down next to me, footprints obliquely illuminated by my flashlight.

'No arch,' Lucy noted. 'They sure look like dive boots or aqua shoes to me. Now that's bizarre.'

I got up and stared out over the wall at dark, heaving water. It seemed inconceivable that someone could have come up from the sea.

'Can you get photos of these?' I asked Marino.

'Sure. But I got nothing to make casts.'

Then we returned to the house. He gathered the wood and carried it into the living room while Lucy and I returned our attention to dinner, which I was no longer certain I could eat because I was so tense. I poured another glass of wine and tried to dismiss the prowler as a coincidence, a harmless peregrination on the part of someone who enjoyed the snow or perhaps diving at night.

But I knew better, and kept my gun nearby and frequently glanced out the window. My spirit was heavy as I slid the lasagne into the oven. I found the Parmesan reggiano in the refrigerator and began grating it, then I arranged figs and melon on plates, adding plenty of prosciutto for Marino's share. Lucy made salad, and for a while we worked in silence.

When she finally spoke, she was not happy. 'You've really gotten into something, Aunt Kay. Why does this always happen to you?'

'Let's not allow our imaginations to run wild,' I said.

'You're out here alone in the middle of nowhere with no burglar alarm and locks as flimsy as flip-top aluminum cans—'

'Have you chilled the champagne yet?' I interrupted. 'It will be midnight soon. The lasagne will only take about ten minutes, maybe fifteen, unless Dr Mant's oven works like everything else does around here. Then it could take until this time next year. I've never understood why people cook lasagne for hours. And then they wonder why everything is leathery.'

Lucy was staring at me, resting a paring knife on a side of the salad bowl. She had cut enough celery and carrots for a marching band.

'One day I will really make lasagne coi carciofi for you. It has artichokes, only you use béchamel sauce instead of marinara—'

'Aunt Kay,' she impatiently cut me off. 'I hate it when you do this. And I'm not going to let you do this. I don't give a shit about lasagne right now. What matters is that this morning you got a weird phone call. Then there was a bizarre death and people treated you suspiciously at the scene. Now tonight you had a prowler who might have been in a damn wet suit.'

'It's not likely the person will be back. Whoever it was. Not unless he wants to take on the three of us.'

'Aunt Kay, you can't stay here,' she said.

'I have to cover Dr Mant's district, and I can't do that from Richmond,' I told her as I again looked out the window over the sink. 'Where's Marino? Is he still out taking pictures?'

'He came in a while ago.' Her frustration was as palpable as a storm about to start.

I walked into the living room and found him asleep on the couch, the fire blazing. My eyes wandered to the window where Lucy had looked out, and I went to it. Beyond cold glass the snowy yard glowed faintly like a pale moon, and was pockmarked by elliptical shadows left by our feet. The brick wall was dark, and I could not see beyond it, where coarse sand tumbled into the sea.

'Lucy's right,' Marino's sleepy voice said to my back.

I turned around. 'I thought you were down for the count.'

'I hear and see everything, even when I'm down for the count,' he said. I could not help but smile.

'Get the hell out of here. That's my vote.' He worked his way up to a sitting position. 'No way I'd stay in this crate out in the middle of nowhere. Something happens, ain't no one going to hear you scream.' His eyes fixed on me. 'By the time anyone finds you, you'll be freeze-dried. If a hurricane don't blow you out to sea, first.'

'Enough,' I said.

He retrieved his gun from the coffee table, got up and tucked it in the back of his pants. 'You could get one of your other doctors to come out here and cover Tidewater.'

'I'm the only one without family. It's easier for me to move, especially this time of year.'

'What a lot of bullshit. You don't have to apologize for being divorced and not having kids.'

'I am not apologizing.'

'And it's not like you're asking someone to relocate for six months. Besides, you're the friggin' chief. You should make other people relocate, family or not. You should be in your own house.'

'I actually hadn't thought coming here would be all that unpleasant,' I said. 'Some people pay a lot of money to stay in cottages on the ocean.'

He stretched. 'You got anything American to drink around here?'

'Milk.'

'I was thinking more along the lines of Miller.'

'I want to know why you're calling Benton. I personally think it's too soon for the Bureau to be involved.'

'And I personally don't think you're in a position to be objective about him.'

'Don't goad me,' I warned. 'It's too late and I'm too tired.'

'I'm just being straight with you.' He knocked a Marlboro out of the pack and tucked it between his lips. 'And he will come to Richmond. I got no doubt about that. He and the wife didn't go nowhere for the holidays, so my guess is he's ready for a little field trip right about now. And this is going to be a good one.'

I could not hold his gaze, and I resented that he knew why.

'Besides,' he went on, 'at the moment it ain't Chesapeake who's asking the FBI anything. It's me, and I have a right. In case you've forgot, I'm the commander of the precinct where Eddings's apartment is. As far as I'm concerned right now, this is a multi-jurisdictional investigation.'

'The case is Chesapeake's, not Richmond's,' I stated. 'Chesapeake is where the body was found. You can't bulldoze your way into their jurisdiction, and you know it. You can't invite the FBI on their behalf.'

'Look,' he went on, 'after going through Eddings's apartment and finding what I did—'

I interrupted him, 'Finding what you did? You keep referring to whatever it is you found. You mean, his arsenal?'

'I mean more than that. I mean worse than that. We haven't gotten to that part yet.' He looked at me and took the cigarette out of his mouth. 'The bottom line is Richmond's got a reason to be interested in this case. So consider yourself invited.'

'I'm afraid I was invited when Eddings died in Virginia.'

'Don't sound to me like you felt all that invited this morning when you were at the shipyard.'

I didn't say anything, because he was right.

'Maybe you had a guest on your property tonight so you would realize just how uninvited you are,' he went on. 'I want the FBI in this thing now because there's more to it than some guy in a john-boat you had to fish out of the river.'

'What else did you find in Eddings's apartment?' I asked him.

I could see his reluctance as he stared off, and I did not understand it.

'I'll serve dinner first and then we'll sit down and talk,' I said.

'If it could wait until tomorrow, it would be better.' He glanced toward the kitchen as if worried that Lucy might overhear.

'Marino, since when have you ever worried about telling me something?'

'This is different.' He rubbed his face in his hands. 'I think Eddings got himself tangled up with the New Zionists,' he finally said.

The lasagne was superb because I had drained fresh mozzarella in dishcloths so it did not weep too much during baking, and, of course, the pasta was fresh. I had served the dish tender instead of cooking it bubbly and brown, and a light sprinkling of Parmesan reggiano at the table had made it perfect.

Marino ate virtually all of the bread, which he slathered with butter, layered with prosciutto and sopped with tomato sauce, while Lucy mostly picked at the small portion on her plate. The snow had gotten heavier, and Marino told us about the New Zionist bible he had found as fireworks sounded in Sandbridge.

I pushed back my chair. 'It's midnight. We should open the champagne.'

I was more disturbed than I had supposed, for what Marino had to say was worse than I feared. Over the years, I had heard quite a lot about Joel Hand and his fascist followers who called themselves the New Zionists. They were going to cause a new order, create an ideal land. I had always feared they were quiet behind their Virginia compound walls because they were plotting a disaster.

'What we need to do is raid the asshole's farm,' Marino said as he got up from the table. 'That should have been done a long time ago.'

'What probable cause would anybody have?' Lucy said.

'You ask me, with squirrels like him, you shouldn't need probable cause.'

'Oh, good idea. You should suggest that one to Gradecki,' she drolly said, referring to the U.S. attorney general.

'Look, I know some guys in Suffolk where Hand lives, and the neighbors say some really weird shit goes on there.'

'Neighbors always think weird shit goes on with their neighbors,' she said.

Marino got the champagne out of the refrigerator while I fetched glasses.

'What sort of weird shit?' I asked him.

'Barges pull up to the Nansemond River and unload crates so big they got to use cranes. Nobody knows what goes on there, except pilots have spotted bonfires at night, like maybe there's occult rituals. Local people swear they hear gunshots all the time and that there have been murders on his farm.'

I walked into the living room because we would clean up later.

I said, 'I know about the homicides in this state, and I've never heard the New Zionists mentioned in connection with any of them, or with any crime at all, for that matter. I've never heard they are involved in the occult, either. Only on-the-fringe politics and oddball extremism. They seem to hate America and would probably be happy if they could have their own little country somewhere where Hand could be king. Or God. Or whatever he is to them.'

'You want me to pop this thing?' Marino held up the champagne.

'The new year's not getting any younger,' I said. 'Now let me get this straight.' I settled on the couch. 'Eddings had some link with the New Zionists?'

'Only because he had one of their bibles, like I already told you,' Marino said. 'I found it when we was going through his house.'

'That's what you were worried about me seeing?' I looked quizzically at him.

'Tonight, yes,' he said. 'Because I'm more worried about her seeing it, if you want to know.' He looked at Lucy.

'Pete,' my niece spoke very reasonably, 'you don't need to protect me anymore, even though I appreciate it.'

He was silent.

'What sort of bible?' I asked him.

'Not any sort you've ever carried to Mass.'

'Satanic?'

'No, I can't say it's like that. At least not like the ones I've seen, because it's not about worshiping Satan and doesn't have any of the sort of symbolism that you associate with that. But it sure as hell isn't something you'd want to read before going to bed.' He glanced at Lucy again.

'Where is it?' I wanted to know.

He peeled foil off the top of the bottle and unwound wire. The cork popped loudly, and he poured champagne the way he poured beer, tilting the glasses sharply to prevent a head.

'Lucy, how about bringing my briefcase here. It's in the kitchen,' he said, and he looked at me as she left the room and lowered his voice. 'I wouldn't have brought it with me if I thought I was going to be seeing her.'

'She's a grown woman. She's an FBI agent, for God's sake,' I said.

'Yeah, and she gets whacked out sometimes, and you know that, too. She don't need to be looking at spooky stuff like this. I'm telling you, I read it because I had to, and I felt really creepy. I felt like I needed to go to Mass, and when have you ever heard me say that?' His face was intense.

I had never heard him say that, and I was uneasy. Lucy had been through hard times that had seriously frightened me. She had been self-destructive and unstable before.

'It is not my right to protect her,' I said as she returned to the living room.

'I hope you're not talking about me,' she said as she handed Marino his briefcase.

'Yeah, we were talking about you,' he said, 'because I don't think you should be looking at this.'

Clasps sprang open.

'It's your case.' Her eyes were calm as they turned to me. 'I am interested in it and would like to help in even the smallest way, if I can. But I'll leave the room, if you want me to.'

Oddly, the decision was one of the hardest ones I'd had to make, because my allowing her to look at evidence I wanted to protect her from was my concession to her professional accomplishment. As wind shook windows and rushed around the roof, sounding like spirits in distress, I moved over on the couch.

'You can sit next to me, Lucy,' I said. 'We'll look at it together.'

The New Zionist bible was actually titled the *Book of Hand*, for its author had been inspired by God and had modestly named the manuscript after himself. Written in Renaissance script on India paper, it was bound in tooled black leather that was scuffed and stained and lettered with the name of someone I did not know. For more than an hour, Lucy leaned against me and we read while Marino prowled about, carrying in more wood and smoking, his restlessness as palpable as the fire's wavering light.

Like the Christian Bible, much of what the manuscript had to say was conveyed in parables, and prophesies and proverbs, thus making the text illustrative and human. This was one of many reasons why reading it was so hard. Pages were populated with people and images that penetrated to deeper layers of the brain. The Book, as we came to call it during the beginning of this new year, showed in exquisite detail how to kill and maim, frighten, brainwash and torture. The explicit section on the necessity of pogroms, including illustrations, made me quake.

I found the violence reminiscent of the Inquisition, and it was, in fact, explained that the New Zionists were here on earth to effect a new Inquisition, of sorts.

'We are in an age when the wrongful ones must be purged from our midst,' Hand had written, 'and in doing so we must be loud and obvious like cymbals. We must feel their weak blood cool on our bare skin as we wallow in their annihilation. We must follow the One into glory, and even unto death.'

I read other ruinations and runes, and perused strange preoccupations with fusion and fuels that could be used to change the balance of the land. By the Book's end, a terrible darkness seemed to have enveloped me and the entire cottage. I felt sullied and sickened by the reminder that there were people in our midst who might think like this.

It was Lucy who finally spoke, for our silence had been unbroken for more than an hour. 'It speaks of the One and their loyalty to him,' she said. 'Is this a person or a deity of some sort?'

'It's Hand, who probably thinks he's Jesus friggin' Christ,' Marino said, pouring more champagne. 'Remember that time we saw him in court?' He glanced up at me.

'That I'm not likely to forget any time soon,' I said.

'He came in with this entourage, including a Washington attorney who has this big gold pocket watch and a silver-topped cane,' he said to Lucy. 'Hand is wearing some fancy designer suit, and he's got long blond hair in a ponytail, and women are waiting outside the courthouse to get a peek at him like he's Michael Bolton or something, if you can believe that.'

'What was he in court for?' Lucy looked at me.

'He'd filed a petition for disclosure, which the attorney general had denied, so it went before a judge.'

'What did he want?' she asked.

'Basically, he was trying to force me to turn over copies of Senator Len Cooper's death records.'

'Why?'

'He was alleging that the late senator was poisoned by political enemies. In fact, Cooper died of an acute hemorrhage into a brain tumor. The judge granted Hand nothing.'

'I guess Joel Hand doesn't like you too much,' she said to me.

'I expect he doesn't.' I looked at the Book on the coffee table, and asked Marino, 'This name on the cover. Do you know who Dwain Shapiro is?'

'I was about to get to that,' he said. 'This is as much as we could pull up on the computer. He lived on the New Zionists' compound in Suffolk until last fall when he defected. About a month later he got killed in a carjacking in Maryland.'

We were quiet for a moment, and I felt the cottage's dark windows as if they were big, square eyes.

Then I asked, 'Any suspects or witnesses?'

'None anybody knows of.'

'How did Eddings get hold of Shapiro's bible?' said Lucy.

'Obviously, that's the twenty-thousand-dollar question,' Marino replied. 'Maybe Eddings talked to him at some point, or maybe to his relatives. This thing ain't a photocopy, and it also says right in the beginning of it that you're not supposed to let your Book ever leave your hands. And if you're ever caught with someone else's Book, you can kiss your ass good-bye.'

'That's pretty much what happened to Eddings,' Lucy said.

I did not want the Book anywhere near us and wished I could throw it into the fire. 'I don't like this,' I said. 'I don't like it at all.'

Lucy looked curiously at me. 'You're not getting superstitious on us, are you?'

'These people are consorting with evil,' I said. 'And I respect that there is evil in the world and it is not to be taken lightly. Where exactly in Eddings's house did you find this God-awful book?' I asked Marino.

'Under his bed,' he said.

'Seriously.'

'I'm very serious.'

'And we're certain Eddings lived alone?' I asked.

'Appears that way.'

'What about family?'

'Father's deceased, a brother's in Maine and the mother lives in Richmond. Real close to where you live, as a matter of fact.'

'You've talked to her?' I asked.

'I stopped by and told her the bad news and asked if we could conduct a more thorough search of her son's house, which we'll do tomorrow.' He glanced at his watch. 'Or I guess I should say today.'

Lucy got up and moved to the hearth. She propped an elbow on a knee and cupped her chin in her hand. Behind her, coals glowed in a deep bed of ashes.

'How do you know this bible originally came from the New Zionists?' she said. 'Seems to me all you know is it came from Shapiro, and how can we be sure where he got it?'

Marino said, 'Shapiro was a New Zionist until just three months ago. I've heard that Hand isn't real understanding when people want to leave him. Let me ask you something. How many ex-New Zionists do you know?'

Lucy could not say. Certainly, I couldn't either.

'He's had followers for at least ten years. And we never hear anything about anyone leaving?' he went on. 'How the hell do we know who he's got buried on his farm?'

'How come I've never heard of him?' she wanted to know.

Marino got up to top off our champagne.

He said, 'Because they don't teach subjects like him at MIT and UVA.'

5

At dawn, I lay in bed and looked out at Mant's backyard. The snow was very deep and piled high on the wall, and beyond the dune the sun was polishing the sea. For a while I shut my eyes and thought of Benton Wesley. I wondered what he would say about where I was living now, and what we would say to each other when we met later this day. We had not spoken since the second week of December, when we had agreed that our relationship must end.

I turned to one side and pulled the covers up to my ears as I heard quiet footsteps. Next I felt Lucy perch on the edge of my bed.

'Good morning, favorite niece in the world,' I mumbled.

'I'm your only niece in the world.' She said what she always did. 'And how did you know it was me?'

'It had better be you. Someone else might get hurt.'

'I brought you coffee,' she said.

'You're an angel.'

'"Yo," to quote Marino. That's what everybody says about me.'

'I was just trying to be nice.' I yawned.

She bent over to hug me, and I smelled the English soap I had placed in her bathroom. I felt her strength and firmness, and I felt old.

'You make me feel like hell.' I rolled on my back, placing my hands behind my head.

'Why do you say that?' She wore a pair of my loose cotton flannel pajamas and looked puzzled.

'Because I don't think I could even do the Yellow Brick Road anymore,' I said, referring to the Academy's obstacle course.

'I've never heard anyone call it easy.'

'It is for you.'

She hesitated. 'Well, it is now. But it's not like you have to hang out with HRT.'

'For that I am thankful.'

She paused, then added with a sigh, 'You know, at first I was pissed when the Academy decided to send me back to UVA for a month. But it may end up being a relief. I can work in the lab, ride my bike and jog around the campus like a normal person.'

Lucy was not a normal person, nor would she ever be. I had decided that in many sad ways, individuals with IQs as high as hers are as different from others as are the mentally impaired. She was gazing out the window and the snow was becoming bright. Her hair was rosegold in shy morning light, and I was amazed I could be related to anyone so beautiful.

'It may be a relief not being around Quantico right now, too.' She paused, her face very serious when she turned back to me. 'Aunt Kay, there's something I need to tell you. I'm not sure you're really going to want to hear this. Or maybe it would be easier if you didn't hear it. I would have told you yesterday if Marino hadn't been here.'

'I'm listening.' I was immediately tense.

She paused again. 'Especially since you may be seeing Wesley today, I think you ought to know. There's a rumor in the Bureau that he and Connie have split.'

I did not know what to say.

'Obviously, I can't verify that this is true,' she went on. 'But I've heard some of what's being said. And some of it concerns you.'

'Why would any of it concern me?' I said too quickly.

'Come on.' She met my eyes. 'There have been suspicions ever since you started working so many cases with him. Some of the agents think that's the only reason you agreed to be a consultant. So you could be with him, travel with him, you know.'

'That's patently untrue,' I angrily said as I sat up. 'I agreed to be the consulting forensic pathologist because the director asked Benton, who asked me, not the other way around. I assist in cases as a service to the FBI and—'

'Aunt Kay,' she interrupted me. 'You don't have to defend yourself.'

But I would not be soothed. 'That is an absolutely outrageous thing for anyone to say. I have never allowed a friendship with anyone to interfere with my professional integrity.'

Lucy got quiet, then spoke again. 'We're not talking about a mere friendship.'

'Benton and I are very good friends.'

'You are more than friends.'

'At this moment, no, we are not. And it is none of your business.' She impatiently got up from my bed. 'It's not right for you to get mad at me.'

She stared at me but I could not speak, for I was very close to tears.

'All I'm doing is reporting to you what I've heard so you don't end up hearing it from someone else,' she said.

Still, I said nothing, and she started to leave.

I reached for her hand. 'I'm not angry with you. Please try to understand. It's inevitable I'm going to react when I hear something like this. I feel certain you would, too.'

She pulled away from me. 'What makes you think I didn't react when I heard it?'

I watched in frustration as she stalked out of my room, and I thought she was the most difficult person I knew. All our lives together we had fought. She never relented until I had suffered as long as she thought I should, when she knew how much I cared. It was so unfair, I told myself as I planted my feet on the floor.

I ran my fingers through my hair as I contemplated getting up and coping with the day. My spirit felt heavy, shadowed by dreams that were now unclear but I sensed had been strange. It seemed there had been water and people who were cruel, and I had been ineffective and afraid. In the bathroom I showered, then got a robe off a hook on the back of the door and found my slippers. Marino and my niece were dressed and in the kitchen when I finally appeared.

'Good morning,' I announced as if Lucy and I had not seen each other this day.

'Yo. It's good all right.' Marino looked as if he had been awake all night and was feeling hateful.

I pulled out a chair and joined them at the small breakfast table. By now the sun was up, the snow on fire.

'What's wrong?' I asked as my nerves tightened more.

'You remember those footprints out by the wall last night?' His face was boiled red.

'Of course.'

'Well, now we've got more of them.' He set down his coffee mug.

'Only this time they're out by our cars and were left by regular boots with a Vibram tread. And guess what, Doc?' he asked as I already feared what he was about to say. 'The three of us ain't going anywhere today until a tow truck gets here first.'

I remained silent.

'Someone punctured our tires.' Lucy's face was stone. 'Every goddamn one of them. With some kind of wide blade, it looks to me. Maybe a big knife or machete.'

'The moral of the story is that it sure as hell wasn't some misguided neighbor or night diver on your property,' he went on. 'I think we're talking about someone who had a mission. And when he got scared off, he came back or somebody else did.'

I got up for coffee. 'How long will it take to get our cars fixed?'

'Today?' he said. 'I don't think it's possible for you or Lucy to get your rides fixed today.'

'It's got to be possible,' I matter-of-factly stated. 'We have to get out of here, Marino. We need to see Eddings's house. And right now it doesn't seem all too safe in this one.'

'I'd say that's a fair assessment,' Lucy said.

I moved close to the window over the sink and could plainly see our vehicles with tires that looked like black rubber puddles in the snow.

'They're punctured on the sides versus the tread, and can't be plugged,' Marino said.

'Then what are we going to do?' I asked.

'Richmond's got reciprocal agreements with other police departments, and I've already talked to Virginia Beach. They're on their way.'

His car needed police tires and rims, while Lucy's and mine needed Goodyears and Michelins because, unlike Marino, we were here in our personal vehicles. I pointed all this out to him.

'We got a flatbed truck on the way for you,' he said as I sat back down. 'Sometime during the next few hours they'll load up your Benz and Lucy's piece of shit and haul them into Bell Tire Service on Virginia Beach Boulevard.'

'It's not a piece of shit,' Lucy said.

'Why the hell did you buy anything the color of parrot shit? That your Miami roots coming out, or what?'

'No, it's my budget coming out. I got it for nine hundred dollars.'

'What about in the meantime?' I asked. 'You know they won't take care of this speedily. It's New Year's Day.'

'You got that right,' he said. 'And it's pretty simple, Doc. If you're going to Richmond, you're riding with me.'

'Fine.' I wasn't going to argue. 'Then let's get as much done now as we can so we can leave.'

'Starting with your getting packed,' he said to me. 'In my opinion, you should boogie right on out of here for good.'

'I have no choice but to stay here until Dr Mant returns from London.'

Yet I packed as if I might not be coming back to his cottage during this life. Then we conducted the best forensic investigation we could on our own, for slashing tires was a misdemeanor, and we knew the local police would not be especially enthused about our case. Ill-equipped to make tread-pattern casts, we simply took photographs to scale of the footprints around our cars, although I suspected the most we would ever be able to tell from them was that the suspect was large and wore a generic-type boot or shoe with a Vibram seal on the arch of the rugged tread.

When a youthful policeman named Sanders and a red tow truck arrived late morning, I took two ruined radials and locked them inside the trunk of Marino's car. For a while I watched men in jumpsuits and insulated jackets twirl handjacks with amazing speed as a winch held the Ford's front end rampant in the air, as if Marino's car were about to fly. Virginia Beach officer Sanders asked if my being the chief medical examiner might possibly be related to what had been done to our vehicles. I told him I did not think so.

'It's my deputy chief who lives at this address,' I went on to explain. 'Dr Philip Mant. He's in London for a month or so. I'm simply covering for him.'

'And no one knows you're staying here?' asked Sanders, who was no fool.

'Certainly, some people know. I've been taking his calls.'

'So you don't see that this might be related to who you are and what you do, ma'am.' He was taking notes.

'At this time I have no evidence that there is a relationship,' I replied. 'In fact, we really can't say that the culprit wasn't some kid blowing off steam on New Year's Eve.'

Sanders kept looking at Lucy, who was talking to Marino by our cars. 'Who is that?' he asked.

'My niece. She's with the FBI,' I answered, and I spelled her name.

While he went to speak to her, I made one last trip inside the cottage, entering through the plain front door. The air was warmed by sunlight that blazed through glass, bleaching furniture of color, and I could still smell garlic from last night's meal. In my bedroom I looked around once more, opening drawers and riffling through clothes hanging in the closet while I was saddened by my disenchantment. In the beginning, I had thought I would like it here.

Down the hall I checked where Lucy had slept, then moved into the living room where we had sat until early morning reading the *Book of Hand*. The memory of that unsettled me like my dream, and my arms turned to gooseflesh. My blood was thrilled by fear, and suddenly I could not stay inside my colleague's simple home a moment longer. I dashed to the screened-in porch, and out the door into the backyard. In sunlight I felt reassured, and as I gazed out at the ocean, I got interested in the wall again.

Snow was to the top of my boots as I drew close to it, footprints from the night before gone. The intruder, whose flashlight Lucy had seen, had climbed over the wall and then quickly left. But he must have showed up later, or someone else must have, because the footprints around our cars clearly had been made after snow had quit falling, and they hadn't been made by dive boots or surf shoes. I looked over the wall and beyond the dune to the wide beach below. Snow was spun-sugar heaped in drifts with sea oats protruding like ragged feathers. The water was a ruffled dark blue and I saw no sign of anyone as my eyes followed the shore as far as they could.

I looked out for a long time, completely absorbed in speculations and worries. When I turned around to walk back, I was shocked to find Detective Roche standing so close he could have grabbed me.

'My God,' I gasped. 'Don't ever sneak up on me like that.'

'I walked in your tracks. That's why you didn't hear me.' He was chewing gum and had his hands in the pockets of a leather coat. 'Being quiet's one thing I'm good at when I want to be.'

I stared at him, my dislike of him finding new depths. He wore dark trousers and boots, and I could not see his eyes behind their aviator's glasses. But it did not matter. I knew what Detective Roche was about. I knew his type well.

'I heard about your vandalism and came to see if I could be of assistance,' he said.

'I wasn't aware we called the Chesapeake police,' I replied.

'Virginia Beach and Chesapeake have a mutual aid channel, so I heard about your problem on that,' he said. 'I have to confess that the first thing to go through my mind was there might be a connection.'

'A connection to what?'

'To our case.' He stepped closer. 'Looks like someone really did a number on your cars. Sounds like a warning. You know, like just maybe you're poking your nose where someone doesn't think it belongs.'

My eyes wandered to his feet, to his lace-up Gore-Tex boots made of leather the color of liver, and I saw the tread pattern they had left in the snow. Roche had big feet and hands, and was wearing Vibram soles. I looked back at a face that would have been handsome were the spirit behind it not so petty and mean. I did not say a word for a while, but when I did I was very direct.

'You sound a lot like Captain Green. So tell me. Are you threatening me, too?'

'I'm just passing along an observation.'

He stepped even closer, and now I was backed against the wall. Melting snow heaped on top of it dripped down the collar of my coat while my blood ran hotter.

'By the way,' he went on, edging ever nearer, 'what's new with this case of ours?'

'Please step back,' I said to him.

'I'm just not sure at all that you're telling me everything. I think you have a real good idea about what happened to Ted Eddings, and you're withholding information.'

'We're not going to discuss that case or any other right now,' I said.

'See? That puts me in a bad spot because I have people I answer to.' I couldn't believe it when he placed his hand on my shoulder as he added, 'I know you wouldn't want to cause me trouble.'

'Don't touch me,' I warned. 'Don't push this any further.'

'I think you and me need to get together so we can overcome our communication problem.' He left his hand where it was. 'Maybe we can catch dinner in some quiet little laid-back place. You like seafood? I know a real private place on the Sound.'

I was silent as I wondered whether to jam my finger in his windpipe.

'Don't be shy. Trust me. It's all right. This isn't the Capital of the Confederacy with all these snobby old has-beens you got in Richmond. We believe in live and let live around here. You know what I mean?'

I tried to move past him and he grabbed my arm.

'I'm talking to you.' He was beginning to sound angry. 'You don't go walking off when I'm talking to you.'

'Let go of me,' I demanded.

I tried to wrench my arm away. But he was surprisingly strong.

'No matter how many fancy degrees you got, you're no match for me,' he said under breath that smelled like spearmint.

I stared straight into his Ray-Bans.

'Get your hands off me now,' I said in a loud, hard voice. 'Now!' I exclaimed as if I would kill him instantly.

Roche suddenly let go, and I trudged with purpose through the snow as my heart flew off on its own. When I reached the front of the house, I stopped, out of breath and dazed.

'There are footprints in the backyard that should be photographed,' I addressed everyone. 'Detective Roche's footprints. He was just back there. And I want all of my belongings out of the house.'

'What the hell do you mean he was just back there?' Marino said.

'We had a conversation.'

'How the hell did he get back there without us seeing him?'

I scanned the street and did not see a car that might have been Roche's. 'I don't know how he got back there,' I said. 'I guess he cut through someone else's backyard. Or maybe he came up from the beach.'

Lucy did not know what to think as she looked at me. 'You won't be coming back here?' she asked me. 'Not at all?'

'No,' I said. 'I will not be coming back here ever again, if I have my way about it.'

She helped me pack the remainder of my belongings, and I did not relay what had happened in the backyard until we were in Marino's car driving fast on 64 West toward Richmond.

'Shit,' he exclaimed. 'The friggin' bastard hit on you. Goddamn it. Why didn't you yell?'

'I think his mission was to harass me on the behalf of someone else,' I said.

'I don't care what his mission was. He still hit on you. You got to take out a warrant.'

'Hitting on someone is not against the law,' I said.

'He grabbed you.'

'So I'm going to have him arrested for grabbing my arm?'

'He shouldn't have grabbed nothing.' He was furious as he drove. 'You told him to let go and he didn't. That's abduction. At the very least, it's simple assault. Damn, this thing's out of alignment.'

'You've got to report him to Internal Affairs,' Lucy said from the front seat, where she was fooling with the scanner because it was hard for her hands to be still. 'Hey, Pete, the squelch isn't right,' she added to him. 'And you can't hear a thing on channel three. That's Third Precinct, right?'

'What do you expect when I'm way the hell near Williamsburg? You think I'm a state trooper?'

'No, but if you want to talk to one, I can probably figure that out.'

'I'm sure you could tune in to the damn space shuttle,' he irritably remarked.

'If you can,' I said to her, 'how about getting me on it.'

6

We arrived in Richmond at half past two, and a guard raised a gate and allowed us into the secluded neighborhood where I very recently had moved. Typical for this area of Virginia, there had been no snow, and water dripped profusely from trees because rain had turned to ice during the night. Then the temperature had risen.

My stone house was set back from the street on a bluff that over-looked a rocky bend in the James River, the wooded lot surrounded by a wrought-iron fence neighboring children could not squeeze through. I knew no one on any side of me, and had no intention of changing that.

I had not anticipated problems when I had decided for the first time in my life that I would build, but whether it had been the slate roof, the brick pavers or the color of my front door, it seemed everyone had a criticism. When it had gotten to the point where my contractor's frustrated telephone calls were interrupting me in the morgue, I had threatened the neighborhood association that I would sue. Needless to say, invitations to parties in this subdivision, thus far, had been few.

'I'm sure your neighbors will be delighted to see you're home,' my niece dryly said as we got out of the car.

'I don't think they pay that much attention to me anymore.' I dug for my keys.

'Bullshit,' Marino said. 'You're the only one they got who spends her days at murder scenes and cutting up dead bodies. They probably look out their windows the entire time you're home. Hell, the guards probably call every one of them to let 'em know when you roll in.'

'Thank you so much,' I said, unlocking the front door. 'And just when I was beginning to feel a little better about living here.'

The burglar alarm loudly buzzed its warning that I had better quickly press the appropriate keys, and I looked around as I always did, because my home was still a stranger to me. I feared the roof would leak, plaster would fall or something else would fail, and when everything was fine, I took intense pleasure in my accomplishment. My house was two levels and very open, with windows placed to catch every photon of light. The living room was a wall of glass that captured miles of the James, and late in the day I could watch the sun set over trees on the river's banks.

Adjoining my bedroom was an office that finally was big enough for me to work in, and I checked it first for faxes and found I had four.

'Anything important?' asked Lucy, who had followed me while Marino was getting boxes and bags.

'As a matter of fact, they're all for you from your mother.' I handed them to her.

She frowned. 'Why would she fax me here?'

'I never told her I was temporarily relocating to Sandbridge. Did you?'

'No. But Grans would know where you are, right?' Lucy said.

'Of course. But my mother and yours don't always get things straight.' I glanced at what she was reading. 'Everything okay?'

'She's so weird. You know, I installed a modem and CD ROM in her computer and showed her how to use them. My mistake. Now she's always got questions. Each of these faxes is a computer question.' She irritably shuffled through the pages.

I was put out with her mother, Dorothy, too. She was my sister, my only sibling, and she could not be bothered to so much as wish her only child a happy New Year.

'She sent these today,' my niece went on. 'It's a holiday and she's writing away on another one of her goofy children's books.'

'To be fair,' I said, 'her books aren't goofy.'

'Yeah, go figure. I don't know where she did her research, but it wasn't where I grew up.'

'I wish you two weren't at odds.' I made the same comment I had made throughout Lucy's life. 'Someday you will have to come to terms with her. Especially when she dies.'

'You always think about death.'

'I do because I know about it, and it is the other side of life. You can't ignore it any more than you can ignore night. You will have to deal with Dorothy.'

'No, I won't.' She swiveled my leather desk chair around and sat in it, facing me. 'There's no point. She doesn't understand the first thing about me and never has.'

That was probably true.

'You're welcome to use my computer,' I said.

'It will just take me a minute.'

'Marino will pick us up about four,' I said.

'I didn't know he left.'

'Briefly.'

Keys tapped as I went into my bedroom and began to unpack and plot. I needed a car and wondered if I should rent one, and I needed to change my clothes but did not know what to wear. It bothered me that the thought of Wesley would still make me conscious of what I put on, and as minutes crept forward I became truly afraid to see him.

Marino picked us up when he said he would, and somewhere he had found a carwash open and had filled the tank with gas. We drove east along Monument Avenue into the district known as the Fan, where gracious mansions lined historic avenues and college students crowded old homes. At the statue of Robert E. Lee, he cut over to Grace Street, where Ted Eddings had lived in a white Spanish duplex with a red Santa flag hanging over a wooden front porch with a swing. Bright yellow crime scene tape stretched from post to post in a morbid parody of Christmas wrapping, its bold black letters warning the curious not to come.

'Under the circumstances, I didn't want nobody inside, and I didn't know who else might have a key,' Marino explained as he unlocked the front door. 'What I don't need is some nosy landlord deciding he's going to check his friggin' inventory.'

I did not see any sign of Wesley, and was deciding he wasn't going to show up when I heard the throaty roar of his gray BMW. It parked on the side of the street, and I watched the radio antenna retract as he cut the engine.

'Doc, I'll wait for him if you want to go on in,' Marino said to me.

'I need to talk to him.' Lucy headed back down the steps as I put on cotton gloves.

'I'll be inside,' I said as if Wesley were not someone I knew.

I entered Eddings's foyer and his presence instantly overwhelmed me everywhere I looked. I felt his meticulous personality in minimalist furniture, Indian rugs and polished floors, and his warmth in sunny yellow walls hung with bold monotype prints. Dust had formed a fine layer that was disturbed anywhere police might recently have been to open cabinets or drawers. Begonias, ficus, creeping fig and cyclamen seemed to be mourning the loss of their master, and I looked around for a watering can. Finding one in the laundry room, I filled it and began tending plants because I saw no point in allowing them to die. I did not hear Benton Wesley walk in.

'Kay?' His voice was quiet behind me.

I turned and he caught sorrow not meant for him.

'What are you doing?' He stared as I poured water into a pot.

'Exactly what it looks like.'

He got quiet, his eyes on mine.

'I knew him, knew Ted,' I said. 'Not terribly well. But he was popular with my staff. He interviewed me many times and I respected . . . Well . . .' My mind left the path.

Wesley was thin, which made his features seem even sharper, his hair by now completely white, although he wasn't much older than I. He did look tired, but everyone I knew looked tired, and what he did not look was separated. He did not look miserable to be away from his wife or from me.

'Pete told me about your cars,' he said.

'Pretty unbelievable,' I said as I poured.

'And the detective. What's his name? Roche? I've got to talk to his chief anyway. We're playing telephone tag, but when we hook up, I'll say something.'

'I don't need you to do that.'

'I certainly don't mind,' he said.

'I'd rather you didn't.'

'Fine.' He raised his hands in a small surrender, and looked around the room. 'He had money and was gone a lot,' he said.

'Someone took care of his plants,' I replied.

'How often?' He looked at them.

'Non-blooming plants, at least once a week, the rest, every other day, depending on how warm it gets in here.'

'So these haven't been watered for a week?'

'Or longer,' I said.

By now, Lucy and Marino had entered the duplex and gone down the hall.

'I want to check the kitchen,' I added as I set down the can.

'Good idea.'

It was small and looked like it had not been renovated since the sixties. Inside cupboards I found old cookware and dozens of canned goods like tuna fish and soup, and snack foods like pretzels. As for what Eddings had kept in his refrigerator, that was mostly beer. But I was interested in a single bottle of Louis Roederer Cristal Champagne tied in a big red bow.

'Find something?' Wesley was looking under the sink.

'Maybe.' I was still peering inside the refrigerator. 'This will set you back as much as a hundred and fifty dollars in a restaurant, maybe a hundred and twenty if you buy it off the shelf.'

'Do we know how much this guy got paid?'

'I don't know. But I suspect it wasn't a whole lot.'

'He's got a lot of shoe polish and cleansers down here, and that's about it,' Wesley said as he stood.

I turned the bottle around and read a sticker on the label. 'A hundred and thirty dollars, and it wasn't purchased locally. As far as I know, Richmond doesn't have a wine shop called The Wine Merchant.'

'Maybe a gift. Explaining the bow.'

'What about D.C.?'

'I don't know. I don't buy much wine in D.C. these days,' he said.

I shut the refrigerator door, secretly pleased, for he and I had enjoyed wine. We once had liked to pick and choose and drink as we sat close to each other on the couch or in bed.

'He didn't shop much,' I said. 'I see no evidence that he ever ate in.'

'It doesn't look to me like he was ever even here,' he said.

I felt his closeness as he moved near me, and I almost could not bear it. His cologne was always subtle and evocative of cinnamon and wood, and whenever I smelled it anywhere, for an instant I was caught as I was now.

'Are you all right?' he asked in a voice meant for no one but me as he paused in the doorway.

'No,' I said. 'This is pretty awful.' I shut a cabinet door a little too hard.

He stepped into the hallway. 'Well, we need to take a hard look at his financial status, to see where he was getting money for eating out and expensive champagne.'

Those papers were in the office, and the police had not gone through them yet because officially there had been no crime. Despite my suspicions about Eddings's cause of death and the strange events surrounding it, at this moment we legally had no homicide.

'Has anyone gone into this computer?' asked Lucy, who was looking at the 486 machine on the desk.

'Nope,' said Marino as he sorted through files in a green metal cabinet. 'One of the guys said we're locked out.'

She touched the mouse and a password window appeared on the screen.

'Okay,' she said. 'He's got a password, which isn't unusual. But what is a little strange is he's got no disk in his backup drive. Hey, Pete? You guys find any disks in here?'

'Yeah, there's a whole box of them up there.' He pointed at a bookcase, which was crowded with histories of the Civil War and an elaborate leather-bound set of encyclopedias.

Lucy took the box down and opened it.

'No. These are programming disks for WordPerfect.' She looked at us. 'All I'm saying is most people would have a backup of their work, assuming he was working on something here in his house.'

No one knew if he had been. We knew only that Eddings was employed by the AP office downtown on Fourth Street. We had no reason to know what he did at home, until Lucy rebooted his computer, did her magic and somehow got into programming files. She disabled the screen saver, then started sorting through WordPerfect directories, all of which were empty. Eddings did not have a single file.

'Shit,' she said. 'Now that really is bizarre unless he never used his computer.'

'I can't imagine that,' I said. 'Even if he did work downtown, he must have had an office at home for a reason.'

She typed some more, while Marino and Wesley sifted through various financial records that Eddings had neatly stored in a basket inside a filing cabinet drawer.

'I just hope he didn't blow away his entire subdirectory,' said Lucy, who was in the operating system now. 'I can't store that without a backup, and he doesn't seem to have a backup.'

I watched her type *undelete*.* and hit the enter key. Miraculously, a file named *killdrug.old* appeared, and after she was prompted to keep it, another name followed. By the time she was finished, she had recovered twenty-six files as we watched in amazement.

'That's what's cool about DOS 6,' she simply said as she began printing.

'Can you tell when they were deleted?' Wesley asked.

'The time and date on the files is all the same,' she replied. 'Damn. December thirty-first, between one-oh-one and one-thirty-five A.M. You would have thought he'd already be dead by then.'

'It depends on what time he went to Chesapeake,' I said. 'His boat wasn't spotted until six A.M.'

'By the way, the clock's set right on the computer. So these times ought to be good,' she added.

'Would it take more than half an hour to delete that many files?' I asked.

'No. You could do it in minutes.'

'Then someone might have been reading them as he was deleting them,' I said.

'That's what a lot of people do. We need more paper for the printer. Wait, I'll steal some from the fax machine.'

'Speaking of that,' I said, 'can we get a journal report?'

'Sure.'

She produced a list of meaningless fax diagnostics and telephone numbers that I had an idea about checking later. But at least we knew with certainty that around the time Eddings had died, someone had gone into his computer and had deleted every one of his files. Whoever was responsible wasn't terribly sophisticated, Lucy went on to explain, because a computer expert would have removed the files' subdirectory, too, rendering the undelete command useless.

'This isn't making sense,' I said. 'A writer is going to back up his work, and it is evident that he was anything but careless. What about his gun safe?' I asked Marino. 'Did you find any disks in there?'

'Nope.'

'That doesn't mean someone didn't get into it, and the house, for that matter,' I said.

'If they did, they knew the combination of the safe and the code for the burglar alarm system.'

'Are they the same?' I asked.

'Yeah. He uses his D.O.B. for everything.'

'And how did you find that out?'

'His mother,' he said.

'What about keys?' I said. 'None came in with the body. He must have had some to drive his truck.'

'Roche said there aren't any,' Marino said, and I thought that odd, too.

Wesley was watching pages of undeleted files come off the printer. 'These all look like newspaper stories,' he said.

'Published?' I asked.

'Some may have been because they look pretty old. The plane that crashed into the White House, for example. And Vince Foster's suicide.'

'Maybe Eddings was just cleaning house,' Lucy proposed.

'Oh, now here we go.' Marino was reviewing a bank statement. 'On December tenth, three thousand dollars was wired to his account.' He opened another envelope and looked some more. 'Same thing for November.'

It was also true for October and the rest of the year, and based on other information, Eddings definitely needed to supplement his income. His mortgage payment was a thousand dollars a month, his monthly charge card bills sometimes as much, yet his annual salary was barely forty-five thousand dollars.

'Shit. With all this extra cash coming in, he was sucking in almost eighty grand a year,' Marino said. 'Not bad.'

Wesley left the printer and walked over to where I stood. He quietly placed a page in my hand.

'The obituary for Dwain Shapiro,' he said. '*Washington Post*, October sixteenth of last year.'

The article was brief and simply stated that Shapiro had been a mechanic at a Ford dealership in D.C., and was shot to death in a carjacking while on his way home from a bar late at night. He was survived by people who lived nowhere near Virginia, and the New Zionists were not mentioned.

'Eddings didn't write this,' I said. 'A reporter for the *Post* did.'

'Then how did he get the Book?' Marino said. 'And why the hell was it under his bed?'

'He might have been reading it,' I answered simply. 'And maybe he didn't want anyone else – a housekeeper, for example – to see it.'

'These are notes now.' Lucy was engrossed in the screen, opening one file after another and hitting the print command. 'Okay, now we're getting to the good stuff. Damn.' She was getting excited as text scrolled by and the LaserJet hummed and clicked. 'How wild.' She stopped what she was doing and turned around to Wesley. 'He's got all this stuff about North Korea mixed in with info about Joel Hand and the New Zionists.'

'What about North Korea?' He was reading pages while Marino went through another drawer.

'The problem our government had with theirs several years ago when they were trying to make weapons-grade plutonium at one of their nuclear power plants.'

'Supposedly, Hand is very interested in fusion, energy, that sort of thing,' I said. 'There's an allusion to that in the Book.'

'Okay,' said Wesley, 'then maybe this is just a big profile on him. Or better stated, the raw makings of a big piece on him.'

'Why would Eddings delete the file of a big article he had not yet finished?' I wanted to know. 'And is it a coincidence that he did this the night he died?'

'That could be consistent with someone planning to commit suicide,' Wesley said. 'And we really can't be certain he didn't do that.'

'Right,' Lucy said. 'He wipes out all his work so that after he's gone, no one's going to see anything he doesn't want them to see. Then he stages his death to look like an accident. Maybe it mattered a lot to him that people not think he killed himself.'

'A strong possibility,' Wesley agreed. 'He may have been involved in something he couldn't get out of, thus explaining the money wired to his bank account every month. Or he could have suffered from depression or from an intense personal loss that we know nothing of.'

'Someone else could have deleted the files and taken any backup disks or printouts,' I said. 'Someone may have done this after he was already dead.'

'Then this person had a key, knew codes and combinations,' he said. 'He knew Eddings wasn't home and wasn't going to be.' He glanced up at me.

'Yes,' I said.

'That's pretty complicated.'

'This case is very complicated,' I said, 'but I can tell you with certainty that if Eddings were poisoned underwater with cyanide gas, he could not have done this to himself. And I want to know why he had so many guns. I want to know why the one he was carrying in his johnboat has a Birdsong coating and was loaded with KTWs.'

Wesley glanced again at me, and his unflappability was hitting me hard. 'Certainly, one could view his survivalist tendencies as an indicator of instability,' he said.

'Or fear of being murdered,' I said.

Then we went into that room. Submachine guns were on a rack on the wall, and pistols, revolvers and ammunition were inside the Browning safe that police had opened this morning. Ted Eddings had equipped a small bedroom with an arbor press, digital scale, case trimmer, reloading dies and everything else needed to keep him in cartridges. Copper tubing and primers were stored in a drawer. Gunpowder was in an old military case, and it seemed he had been fond of laser sights and spotting scopes.

'I think this shows a tilted mind-set.' It was Lucy who spoke as she squatted before the safe, opening hard plastic gun cases. 'I'd call all of this more than a little paranoid. It's like he thought an army was coming.'

'Paranoia is healthy if there really is someone after you,' I said.

'Me, I'm beginning to think the guy was wacky,' Marino replied.

I did not care about their theories. 'I smelled cyanide in the morgue,' I reminded them as my patience wore thinner. 'He didn't gas himself before going into the river, or he would have been dead when he hit the water.'

'You smelled cyanide,' Wesley said, pointedly. 'No one else did, and we don't have tox results yet.'

'What are you implying, that he drowned himself?' I stared at him. 'I don't know.'

'I saw nothing to indicate drowning,' I said.

'Do you always see indications in drownings?' he reasonably asked. 'I thought drownings were notoriously difficult, explaining why expert witnesses from South Florida are often flown in to help with such cases.'

'I began my career in South Florida and am considered an expert witness in drownings,' I sharply said.

We continued arguing outside on the sidewalk by his car because I wanted him to take me home so we could finish our fight. The moon was vague, the nearest streetlight a block away, and we could not see each other well.

'For God's sake, Kay, I was not implying that you don't know what you're doing,' he was saying.

'You most certainly were.' I was standing by the driver's door as if the car were mine and I was about to leave in it. 'You're picking on me. You're acting like an ass.'

'We're investigating a death,' he said in that steady tone of his. 'This is not the time or place for anything to be taken personally.'

'Well, let me tell you something, Benton, people aren't machines. They do take things personally.'

'And that's really what this is all about.' He moved beside me and unlocked the door. 'You're reacting personally because of me. I'm not sure this was a good idea.' Locks rushed up. 'Maybe I shouldn't have come here today.' He slid into the driver's seat. 'But I felt it was important. I was trying to do the right thing and thought you would do the same.'

I walked around to the other side and got in, and wondered why he had not opened my door when he usually did. Suddenly, I was very weary and afraid I might cry.

'It is important, and you did do the right thing,' I said. 'A man is dead. I not only believe he was murdered, but I think he might have been caught up in something bigger that I fear may be very ugly. I don't think he deleted his own computer files and disposed of all backups because that would imply he knew he was going to die.'

'Yes. It would imply suicide.'

'Which this case is not.'

We looked at each other in the dark.

'I think someone entered his house late the night of his death.'

'Someone he knew.'

'Or someone who knew someone else who had access. Like a colleague or close friend, or a significant other. As for keys to get in, his are missing.'

'You think this has to do with the New Zionists.' He was beginning to mellow.

'I'm afraid of that. And someone is warning me to back off.'

'That would implicate the Chesapeake police.'

'Maybe not the entire department,' I said. 'Maybe just Roche.'

'If what you're saying is true, he's superficial in this, an outer layer far removed from the core. His interest in you is a separate issue, I suspect.'

'His only interest is to intimidate, to bully,' I said. 'And, therefore, I suspect it is related.'

Wesley got quiet, looking out the windshield, and for a moment I indulged myself and stared at him.

Then he turned to me. 'Kay, has Dr Mant ever said anything about being threatened?'

'Not to me. But I don't know if he would say anything. Especially if he were frightened.'

'Of what? That's what I'm having a very hard time imagining,' he said as he started the car and pulled out onto the street. 'If Eddings were linked to the New Zionists, then how could that possibly connect to Dr Mant?'

I did not know, and was quiet as he drove.

He spoke again. 'Any possibility your British colleague simply skipped town? Do you know for a fact that his mother died?'

I thought of my Tidewater morgue supervisor, who had quit before Christmas without giving notice or a reason. Then Mant suddenly had left, too.

'I know only what he told me,' I said. 'But I have no reason to think he is lying.'

'When does your other deputy chief come back, the one out on maternity leave?'

'She just had her baby.'

'Well, that's a little hard to fake,' he said.

We were turning on Malvern, and the rain was tiny pinpricks against the glass. Welling up inside me were words I could not say, and when we turned on Cary Street I began to feel desperate. I wanted to tell Wesley that we had made the right decision, but ending a relationship doesn't end feelings. I wanted to inquire after Connie, his wife. I wanted to invite him into my home as I had done in the past, and ask him why he never called me anymore. Old Locke Lane was without light as we followed it toward the river, and he drove slowly in low gear.

'Are you going back to Fredericksburg tonight?' I asked.

He was silent, then said, 'Connie and I are getting a divorce.'

I made no reply.

'It's a long story and will probably be a rather long drawn-out messy thing. Thank God, at least, the kids are pretty much grown.' He rolled down his window and the guard waved us through.

'Benton, I'm very sorry,' I said, and his BMW was loud on my empty, wet street.

'Well, you probably could say I got what I deserved. She's been seeing another man for the better part of a year, and I was clueless. Some profiler I am, right?'

'Who is it?'

'He's a contractor in Fredericksburg and was doing some work on the house.'

'Does she know about us?' I almost could not ask, for I had always liked Connie and was certain the truth would make her hate me.

We turned into my driveway and he did not answer until we had parked near my front door.

'I don't know.' He took a deep breath and looked down at his hands on the wheel. 'She's probably heard rumors, but she really doesn't listen to rumors, much less believe them.' He paused. 'She knows we've spent a lot of time together, taken trips, that sort of thing. But I really suspect she thinks that's solely because of work.'

'I feel awful about all of this.'

He said nothing.

'Are you still at home?' I asked.

'She wanted to move out,' he replied. 'She moved into an apartment where I guess she and Doug can regularly meet.'

'That's the contractor's name.'

His face was hard as he stared out the windshield. I reached over and gently took one of his hands.

'Look,' I said quietly. 'I want to help in any way I can. But you'll have to tell me what I can do.'

He glanced at me, and for an instant his eyes shone with tears that I believed were for her. He still loved his wife, and though I understood, I did not want to see it.

'I can't let you do much for me.' He cleared his throat. 'Right now especially. For pretty much the next year. This guy she's with likes money and knows I have some, you know, from my family. I don't want to lose everything.'

'I don't see how you can, in light of what she's done.'

'It's complicated. I have to be careful. I want my children to still care about me, to respect me.' He looked at me and withdrew his hand. 'You know how I feel. Please try to just leave it at that.'

'Did you know about her in December, when we decided to stop—'

He interrupted me, 'Yes. I knew.'

'I see.' My voice was tight. 'I wish you could have told me. It might have made it easier.'

'I don't think anything could have made it easier.'

'Good night, Benton,' I said as I got out of his car, and I did not turn around to watch him drive away.

Inside, Lucy was playing Melissa Etheridge, and I was glad my niece was here and that there was music in the house. I forced myself to not think about him, as if I could walk into a different room in my mind and lock him out. Lucy was inside the kitchen, and I took my coat off and set my pocketbook on the counter.

'Everything okay?' She shut the refrigerator door with a shoulder and carried eggs to the sink.

'Actually, everything's pretty rotten,' I said.

'What you need is something to eat, and as luck would have it, I'm cooking.'

'Lucy' – I leaned against the counter – 'if someone is trying to disguise Eddings's death as an accident or suicide, then I can see how subsequent threats or intrigue concerning my Norfolk office might make sense. But why would threats have been made to any member of my staff in the past? Your deductive skills are good. You tell me.'

She was beating egg whites into a bowl and thawing a bagel in the microwave. Her nonfat routines were depressing, and I did not know how she kept them up.

'You don't know that anyone was threatened in the past,' she matter-of-factly said.

'I realize I don't know, at least not yet.' I had begun making Viennese coffee. 'But I'm simply trying to reason this out. I'm looking for a motive and coming up empty-handed. Why don't you add a little onion, parsley and ground pepper to that? A pinch of salt can't hurt you, either.'

'You want me to fix you one?' she asked as she whisked.

'I'm not very hungry. Maybe I'll eat soup later.'

She glanced up at me. 'Sorry everything's rotten.'

I knew she referred to Wesley, and she knew I wasn't going to discuss him.

'Eddings's mother lives near here,' I said. 'I think I should talk to her.'

'Tonight? At the last minute?' The whisk lightly clicked against the sides of the bowl.

'She very well may want to talk tonight, at the last minute,' I said. 'She's been told her son is dead and not much more.'

'Yeah,' Lucy muttered. 'Happy New Year.'

7

I did not have to ask anyone for a residential listing or telephone number because the dead reporter's mother was the only Eddings with a Windsor Farms address. According to the city directory, she lived on the lovely tree-lined street of Sulgrave, which was well known for wealthy estates and the sixteenth-century Tudor manors called Virginia House and Agecroft that in the 1920s had been shipped from England in crates. The night was still young when I called, but she sounded as if she had been asleep.

'Mrs Eddings?' I said, and I told her who I was.

'I'm afraid I drifted off.' She sounded frightened. 'I'm sitting in my living room watching TV. Goodness, I don't even know what's on now. It was *My Brilliant Career* on PBS. Have you seen that?'

'Mrs Eddings,' I said again, 'I have questions about your son, Ted. I'm the medical examiner for his case. And I was hopeful we might talk. I live but a few blocks from you.'

'Someone told me you did.' Her thick southern voice got thicker with tears. 'That you lived close by.'

'Would now be a convenient time?' I asked after a pause.

'Well, I would appreciate it very much. And my name is Elizabeth Glenn,' she said as she began to cry.

I reached Marino at his home, where his television was turned up so high I did not know how he could hear anything else. He was on the other line and clearly did not want to keep whoever it was on hold.

'Sure, see what you can find out,' he said when I told him what I was about to do. 'Me, I'm up to my ass right now. Got a situation down in Mosby Court that could turn into a riot.'

'That's all we need,' I said.

'I'm on my way over there. Otherwise I'd go with you.'

We hung up and I dressed for the weather because I did not have a car. Lucy was on the phone in my office, talking to Janet, I suspected, based on her intense demeanor and quiet tone. I waved from the hallway and indicated by pointing at my watch I'd be back in about an hour. As I left my house and started walking in the cold, wet dark, my spirit began to crawl inside me like a creature trying to hide. Coping with the loved ones tragedy leaves behind remained one of the cruelest features of my career.

Over the years, I had experienced a multitude of reactions ranging from my being turned into a scapegoat to families begging me to somehow make the death untrue. I had seen people weep, wail, rant, rage and not react in the least, and throughout I was always the physician, always appropriately dispassionate yet kind, for that was what I was trained to be.

My own responses had to be mine. Those moments no one saw, not even when I was married, when I became expert at covering moods or crying in the shower. I remembered breaking out in hives one year and telling Tony I was allergic to plants, shellfish, the sulfite in red wine. My former husband was so easy because he did not want to hear.

Windsor Farms was eerily still as I entered it from the back, near the river. Fog clung to Victorian iron lamps reminiscent of England, and although windows were lighted in most of the stately homes, it did not seem anyone was up or out. Leaves were like soggy paper on pavement, rain lightly smacking and beginning to freeze. It occurred to me that I had foolishly walked out of my house with no umbrella.

When I reached the Sulgrave address, it was familiar, for I knew the judge who lived next door and had been to many of his parties. Three-story brick, the Eddings home was Federal-style with paired end chimneys, arched dormer windows and an elliptical fanlight over the paneled front door. To the left of the entry porch was the same stone lion that had been standing guard for years. I climbed slick steps, and had to ring the bell twice before a voice sounded faintly on the other side of thick wood.

'It's Dr Scarpetta,' I answered, and the door slowly opened.

'I thought it would be you.' An anxious face peered out as the space got wider. 'Please come in and get warm. It is a terrible night.'

'It's getting very icy,' I said as I stepped inside.

Mrs Eddings was attractive in a well-bred, vain way, with refined features, and spun-white hair swept back from a high, smooth brow. She had dressed in a Black Watch suit and cashmere turtleneck sweater, as if she had been bravely receiving company all day. But her eyes could not hide her irrecoverable loss, and as she led me into the foyer, her gait was unsteady and I suspected she had been drinking.

'This is gorgeous,' I said as she took my coat. 'I've walked and driven past your house I don't know how many times and had no idea who lives here.'

'And you live where?'

'Over there. Just west of Windsor Farms.' I pointed. 'My house is new. In fact, I just moved in last fall.'

'Oh yes, I know where you are.' She closed the closet door and led me down a hall. 'I know quite a number of people over there.'

The gathering room she showed me was a museum of antique Persian rugs, Tiffany lamps, and yew wood furniture in the style of Biedermeier. I sat on a black-upholstered couch that was lovely but stiff, and was already beginning to wonder how well mother had gotten along with son. The decors of both their dwellings painted portraits of people who could be stubborn and disconnected.

'Your son interviewed me a number of times,' I began our conversation as we got seated.

'Oh, did he?' She tried to smile but her expression collapsed.

'I'm sorry. I know this is hard,' I gently said as she tried to compose herself in her red leather chair. 'Ted was someone I happened to like quite a lot. My staff liked him, too.'

'Everyone likes Ted,' she said. 'From day one, he could charm. I remember the first big interview he got in Richmond.' She stared into the fire, hands tightly clasped. 'It was with Governor Meadows, and I'm sure you remember him. Ted got him to talk when no one else could. That was when everyone was saying the governor was using drugs and associating with immoral women.'

'Oh, yes,' I replied as if the same had never been said of other governors.

She stared off, her face distressed, and her hand trembled as she reached up to smooth her hair. 'How could this happen? Oh Lord, how could he drown?'

'Mrs Eddings, I don't think he did.'

Startled, she stared at me with wide eyes. 'Then what happened?'

'I'm not sure yet. There are tests to be done.'

'What else could it be?' She began dabbing tears with a tissue. 'The policeman who came to see me said it happened underwater. Ted was diving in the river with that contraption of his.'

'There could be a number of possible causes,' I answered. 'A malfunction of the breathing apparatus he was using, for example. He could have been overcome by fumes. I don't know right this minute.'

'I told him not to use that thing. I can't tell you how many times I begged him not to go off and dive with that thing.'

'Then he had used it before.'

'He loved to look for Civil War relics. He'd go diving almost anywhere with one of those metal detectors. I believe he found a few cannonballs in the James last year. I'm surprised you didn't know. He's written several stories about his adventures.'

'Generally, divers have a partner with them, a buddy,' I said. 'Do you know who he usually went with?'

'Well, he may have taken someone with him now and then. I really don't know because he didn't discuss his friends with me very much.'

'Did he ever say anything to you about going diving in the Elizabeth River to look for Civil War relics?' I asked.

'I don't know anything about him going there. He never mentioned it to me. I thought he was coming here today.' She shut her eyes, brow furrowed, and her bosom deeply rose and fell as if there were not enough air in the room.

'What about these Civil War relics he collected?' I went on. 'Do you know where he kept them?'

She did not respond.

'Mrs Eddings,' I went on, 'we found nothing like that in his house. Not a single button, belt buckle or minié ball. Nor did we find a metal detector.'

She was silent, hands shaking as she clutched the tissue hard.

'It is very important that we establish what your son might have been doing at the Inactive Ship Yard in Chesapeake,' I spoke to her again. 'He was diving in a classified area around Navy decommissioned ships and no one seems to know why. It's hard to imagine he was looking for Civil War relics there.'

She stared at the fire and in a distant voice said, 'Ted goes through phases. Once he collected butterflies. When he was ten. Then he gave them all away and started collecting gems. I remember he would pan for gold in the oddest places and pluck up garnets from the roadside with a pair of tweezers. He went from that to coins, and those he mostly spent because the Coke machine doesn't care if the quarter's pure silver or not. Baseball cards, stamps, girls. He never kept anything long. He told me he likes journalism because it's never the same.'

I listened as she tragically went on.

'Why, I think he would have traded in his mother for a different one if that could have been arranged.' A tear slid down her cheek. 'I know he must have gotten so bored with me.'

'Too bored to accept your financial help, Mrs Eddings?' I delicately said.

She lifted her chin. 'Now I believe you're getting a bit too personal.'

'Yes, I am, and I regret that you have to be subjected to it. But I am a doctor, and right now, your son is my patient. It is my mission to do everything I can to determine what might have happened to him.'

She took a deep, tremulous breath and fingered the top button of her jacket. I waited as she fought back tears.

'I sent him money every month. You know how inheritance taxes are, and Ted was accustomed to living beyond his means. I suppose his father and I are to blame.' She could barely continue. 'Life was not hard enough for my sons. I don't suppose life was very hard for me until Arthur passed on.'

'What did your husband do?'

'He worked in tobacco. We met during the war when most of the world's cigarettes were made around here and you could find hardly a one, or stockings either.'

Her reminiscing soothed her, and I did not interrupt.

'One night I went to a party at the Officers' Service Club at the Jefferson Hotel. Arthur was a captain in a unit of the Army called the Richmond Grays, and he could dance.' She smiled. 'Oh, he could dance like he breathed music and had it in his veins, and I spotted him right away. Our eyes needed to meet but once, and then we were never without each other.'

She stared off, and the fire snapped and waved as if it had something important to say.

'Of course, that was part of the problem,' she went on. 'Arthur and I never stopped being absorbed with each other and I think the boys sometimes felt they were in the way.' She was looking directly at me now. 'I didn't even ask if you'd like tea or perhaps a touch of something stronger.'

'Thank you. I'm fine. Was Ted close to his brother?'

'I already gave the policeman Jeff's number. What was his name? Martino or something. I actually found him rather rude. You know, a little Goldschlager is good on a night like this.'

'No, thank you.'

'I discovered it through Ted,' she oddly went on as tears suddenly spilled down. 'He found it when he was skiing out west and brought a bottle home. It tastes like liquid fire with a little cinnamon. That's what he said when he gave it to me. He was always bringing me little things.'

'Did he ever bring you champagne?'

She delicately blew her nose.

'You said he was to have visited you today,' I reminded her.

'He was supposed to come for lunch,' she said.

'There is a very nice bottle of champagne in his refrigerator. It has a bow tied around it, and I'm wondering if this might have been something he had intended to bring when he came by for lunch today.'

'Oh my.' Her voice shook. 'That must have been for some other celebration he planned. I don't drink champagne. It gives me a headache.'

'We're looking for his computer disks,' I said. 'We're looking for any notes pertaining to what he might have been recently writing. Did he ever ask you to store anything for him here?'

'Some of his athletic equipment is in the attic but it's old as Methuselah.' Her voice caught and she cleared it. 'And papers from school.'

'Are you aware of his having a safe deposit box, perhaps?'

'No.' She shook her head.

'What about a friend he might have entrusted these things to?'

'I don't know about his friends,' she said again as freezing rain clicked against glass.

'And he didn't mention any romantic interests? You're saying he had none?'

She pressed her lips tight.

'Please tell me if I am misunderstanding something.'

'There was a girl he brought by some months back. I guess it was in the summer and apparently she's some sort of scientist.' She paused. 'Seems he was doing a story or something, they met that way. We had a bit of a disagreement over her.'

'Why?'

'She was attractive and one of these academic types. Maybe she's a professor. I can't recall but she's from overseas somewhere.'

I waited, but she had nothing more to say.

'What was your disagreement?' I asked.

'I knew the minute I met her that she was not of good character, and she was not permitted in my home,' Mrs Eddings replied.

'Does she live in this area?' I asked.

'One would expect so, but I wouldn't know where she is.'

'But he might have still been seeing her.'

'I have no idea who Ted was seeing,' she said, and I believed she was lying.

'Mrs Eddings,' I said, 'by all appearances, your son was not home much.'

She just looked at me.

'Did he have a housekeeper? For example, someone who took care of his plants?'

'I sent my housekeeper by when needed,' she said. 'Corian. Sometimes she brings him food. Ted can never bother with cooking.'

'When was the last time she went by?'

'I don't know,' she said, and I could tell she was getting weary of questions. 'Some time before Christmas, I suspect, because she's had the flu.'

'Did Corian ever mention to you what is in his house?'

'I guess you mean his guns,' she said. 'Just another something he started to collect a year or so back. That's all he wanted for his birthday – a gift certificate for one of those gun stores around here. As if a woman would dare walk into such a place.'

It was pointless to probe further, for she had the single desire for her son to be alive. Beyond that, any activity or inquiry was simply an invasion she was determined to sidestep. At close to ten, I headed home, and almost slipped twice on vacant streets where it was too dark to see. The night was bitterly cold and filled with sharp wet sounds as ice coated trees and glazed the ground.

I felt discouraged because it did not seem anyone knew Eddings beyond what he had been like on the surface or in the past. I had learned he had collected coins and butterflies and had always been charming. He was an ambitious reporter with a limited attention span, and I thought how odd it was that I should be walking through his old neighborhood in such weather to talk about this man. I wondered what he would think could I tell him, and I felt very sad.

I did not want to chat with anyone when I walked into my house, but went straight to my room. I was warming my hands with hot water and washing my face when Lucy appeared in the doorway. I knew instantly that she was in one of her moods.

'Did you get enough to eat?' I looked at her in the mirror over the sink.

'I never get enough to eat,' she irritably replied. 'Someone named Danny from your Norfolk office called. He said the answering service was contacted about our cars.'

For a moment my mind went blank. Then I remembered. 'I gave the towing service the office number.' I dried my face with a towel. 'So I guess the answering service reached Danny at home.'

'Whatever. He wants you to call.' She stared at me in the mirror as if I had done something wrong.

'What is it?' I stared back.

'I've just got to get out of here.'

'I'll try to get the cars here tomorrow,' I said, stung.

I walked out of the bathroom, and she followed.

'I need to get back to UVA.'

'Of course you do, Lucy,' I said.

'You don't understand. I've got so much to do.'

'I didn't realize your independent study or whatever it is had already started.' I walked into the gathering room and headed for the bar.

'It doesn't matter if it's started. I've got a lot to set up. And I don't understand how you're going to get the cars here. Maybe Marino can take me to get mine.'

'Marino is very busy and my plan is simple,' I said. 'Danny will drive my car to Richmond and he has a reliable friend who will drive your Suburban. Then Danny and his friend will take the bus back to Norfolk.'

'What time?'

'That's the only snag. I can't permit Danny to do any of this until after hours, because he can't deliver my personal car on state time.' I was opening a bottle of Chardonnay.

'Shit,' Lucy impatiently said. 'So I won't have transportation tomorrow, either?'

'I'm afraid neither of us will,' I said.

'And what are you going to do, then?'

I handed her a glass of wine. 'I'll be going into my office and probably spending a lot of time on the phone. Anything you might be able to do at the field office here?'

She shrugged. 'I know a couple people who went through the Academy with me.'

At the very least she could find another agent to take her to the gym so she could work off her ugly mood, I started to say, but held my tongue.

'I don't want wine.' She set the glass down on the bar. 'I think I'll just drink beer for a while.'

'Why are you so angry?'

'I'm not angry.' She got a Beck's Light out of the small refrigerator and popped off the cap.

'Do you want to sit down?'

'No,' she said. 'By the way, I've got the Book, so don't get alarmed when you don't find it in your briefcase.'

'What do you mean, you have it?' I looked uneasily at her.

'I was reading it while you were out talking to Mrs Eddings.' She took a swallow of beer. 'I thought it would be a good idea to go over it again in case there's something we didn't notice.'

'I think you've looked at it quite enough,' I flatly said. 'In fact, I think all of us have.'

'There's a lot of Old Testament-type stuff in there. I mean, it's not like it's satanic, really.'

I watched her in silence as I wondered what was really going on in that incredibly complicated brain.

'I actually find it rather interesting, and believe it has power only if you allow it to have power. I don't allow it, so it doesn't bother me,' she was saying.

I set down my glass. 'Well, something certainly is.'

'Only thing bothering me is I'm stranded and tired. So I guess I'll just go to bed,' she said. 'I hope you sleep well.'

But I did not. Instead, I sat before the fire worrying about her, for I probably knew my niece better than anyone did. Perhaps she and Janet had simply had a fight and repairs would be made in the morning, or maybe she really did have too much to do, and not being able to return to Charlottesville was more of a problem than I knew.

I turned the fire off and checked the burglar alarm one more time to make certain it was armed, then I walked back to my bedroom and shut the door. Still, I could not sleep, so I sat up in lamplight listening to the weather as I studied the journal that had been printed by Eddings's fax machine. There were eighteen numbers dialed over the past two weeks, and all of them were curious and suggestive that he certainly had been home at least some of the time and doing something in his office.

What also struck me right away was that if he had worked at home, I would have expected numerous transmissions to the AP office downtown. But this was not the case. Since mid-December, he had faxed his office only twice, at least from the machine we had found at his house. This was simple enough to determine because he had entered a speed dial label for the wire service's fax number, so 'AP DESK' appeared in the journal's identification column, along with less obvious labels like 'NVSE,' 'DRMS,' 'CPT,' and 'LM.' Three of those numbers had Tidewater, Central and Northern Virginia area codes and exchanges, while the area code for DRMS was Memphis, Tennessee.

I tried to sleep but information drifted past my eyes and questions spoke because I could not shut them off. I wondered who Eddings had been contacting in these different places, or if it mattered. But what I could not get away from was where he had died. I could still see his body suspended in that murky river, tethered by a useless hose caught on a rusting screw. I could feel his stiffness as I held him in my arms and swam him up with me. I had known before I had ever reached the surface that he had been dead many hours.

At three A.M. I sat up in bed and stared at the darkness. The house was quiet except for its usual shifting sounds, and I simply could not turn off my conscious mind. Reluctantly, I put my feet on the floor, my heart beating hard, as if it were startled that I should stir at such an hour. In my office I shut the door and wrote the following brief letter:

TO WHOM IT MAY CONCERN:
I realize this is a fax number, otherwise I would call in person. I need to know your identification, if possible, as your number has shown up on the printout of a recently deceased individual's fax machine. Please contact me at your earliest convenience. If you need verification of the authenticity of this communication, contact Captain Pete Marino of the Richmond Police Department.

I gave telephone numbers and signed my title and my name, and I faxed the letter to every speed dial listing in Eddings's journal, except, of course, the Associated Press. For a while I sat at my desk, staring rather glazed, as if my fax machine were going to solve this case immediately. But it remained silent as I read and waited. At the reasonable hour of six A.M., I called Marino.

'I take it there was no riot,' I said after the phone banged and dropped and his voice mumbled over the line. 'Good, you're awake,' I added.

'What time is it?' He sounded as if he were in a stupor.

'It's time for you to rise and shine.'

'We locked up maybe five people. The rest got quiet after that and went back inside. What are you doing awake?'

'I'm always awake. And by the way, I could use a ride to work today and I need groceries.'

'Well, put on some coffee,' he said. 'I guess I'm coming over.'

8

When he arrived, Lucy was still in bed and I was making fresh fruit salad and coffee. I let him in, dismayed again when I looked out at my street. Overnight, Richmond had turned to glass, and I had heard on the news that falling branches and trees had knocked down power lines in several sections of the city.

'Did you have any trouble?' I asked, shutting the front door.

'Depends on what kind you mean.' Marino set down groceries, took off his coat and handed it to me.

'Driving.'

'I got chains. But I was out till after midnight and I'm tired as hell.'

'Come on. Let's get you some coffee.'

'None of that unleaded shit.'

'Guatemalan, and I promise it's leaded.'

'Where's the kid?'

'Asleep.'

'Yo. Must be nice.' He yawned again.

We walked into the kitchen with its many windows. Through them the river was pewter and slow. Rocks were glazed, the woods a fantasy just beginning to sparkle in the wan morning light. Marino poured his own coffee, adding plenty of sugar and cream.

'You want some?' he asked.

'Black, please.'

'I think by now you don't have to tell me.'

'I never make assumptions,' I said, getting plates out of a cabinet. 'Especially about men, who seem to have a Mendelian trait which precludes them from remembering details important to women.'

'Yeah, well, I could give you a list of things Doris never remembered, starting with using my tools and not putting them back,' he said of his ex-wife.

I worked at the counter while he looked around as if he wanted to smoke. I wasn't going to let him.

'I guess Tony never fixed coffee for you,' he said.

'Tony never did much of anything for me except try to get me pregnant.'

'He didn't do a very good job unless you didn't want kids.'

'Not with him I didn't.'

'What about now?'

'I still don't want them with him. Here.' I handed Marino a plate. 'Let's sit.'

'Wait a minute. This is it?'

'What else do you want?'

'Shit, Doc. This ain't food. And what the hell are these little green slices with black things.'

'The kiwi fruit I told you to get. I'm sure you must have had it before,' I patiently said. 'I've got bagels in the freezer.'

'Yeah, that'd be good. With cream cheese. You got any poppyseed?'

'If you have a drug test today you'll come up positive for morphine.'

'And don't give me any of the nonfat stuff. It's like eating paste.'

'No, it's not,' I said. 'Paste is better.'

I left off the butter, determined to make him live for a while. By now Marino and I were more than partners or even friends. We were dependent on each other in a way neither could explain.

'So tell me what all you did,' he said as we sat at my breakfast table by a wide pane of glass. 'I know you been up all night doing something.' He took a large bite of bagel and reached for his juice.

I told him about my visit with Mrs Eddings, and about the note I had written and sent to numbers belonging to places I did not know.

'It's weird he was faxing things everywhere but his office.'

'He sent two faxes to his office,' I reminded him.

'I need to talk to those people.'

'Good luck. Remember, they're reporters.'

'That's what I'm afraid of. To those drones, Eddings is just another story. Only thing they care about is what they're going to do with the info. The worse his death is, the better they like it.'

'Well, I don't know. But I suspect whoever he associated with in that office is going to be extremely careful about what is said. I'm not sure I blame them. A death investigation is frightening to people who did not ask to be invited.'

'What's the status of his tox?' Marino asked.

'Hopefully today,' I said.

'Good. You get your verification it's cyanide, then maybe we can work this thing the way it ought to be worked. As it is, I'm trying to explain superstitions to the commander of A Squad and wondering what the hell I'm going to do about the Keystone Kops in Chesapeake. And I'm telling Wesley it's a homicide and he's asking for proof because he's on the spot, too.'

The mention of his name was disturbing, and I looked out the window at unnavigable water moving thickly between big, dark rocks. The sun was lighting up gray clouds in the eastern part of the sky, and I heard the shower running in the back part of the house where Lucy was staying.

'Sounds like Sleeping Beauty's awake,' Marino said. 'She need a ride?'

'I think she's involved with the field office today. We should get going,' I added, for staff meeting at my office was always at eight-thirty.

He helped gather dishes and we put them in the sink. Minutes later, I had on my coat, my medical bag and briefcase in hand, when my niece appeared in the foyer, hair wet, her robe pulled tight.

'I had a dream,' she said in a depressed voice. 'Someone shot us in our sleep. Nine-millimeter to the back of the head. They made it look like a robbery.'

'Oh really?' Marino asked, pulling on rabbit-fur-lined gloves. 'And where was yours truly? 'Cause that ain't going to happen if I'm in the house.'

'You weren't here.'

He gave her an odd look as he realized she was serious. 'What the hell'd you eat last night?'

'It was like a movie. It must have gone on for hours.' She looked at me, and her eyes were puffy and exhausted.

'Would you like to come to the office with me?' I asked.

'No, no. I'll be fine. The last thing I feel like being around right now is a bunch of dead bodies.'

'You're going to get together with some of the agents you know in town?' I uneasily said.

'I don't know. We were going to work with closed-cycle oxygen respiration, but I just don't think I feel up to putting on a wet suit and getting in some indoor pool that stinks like chlorine. I think I'll just wait around for my car, then leave.'

Marino and I didn't talk much as we drove downtown, his mighty tires gouging glazed streets with clanking teeth. I knew he was worried about Lucy. As much as he abused her, if anyone else tried to do the same Marino would destroy that person with his big bare hands. He had known her since she was ten. It was Marino who had taught her to drive a five-speed pickup truck and shoot a gun.

'Doc, I got to ask you something,' he finally spoke as the rhythm of chains slowed at the toll booth. 'Do you think Lucy's doing okay?'

'Everyone has nightmares,' I said.

'Hey, Bonita,' he called to the toll taker as he handed his pass card out the window, 'when you going to do something about this weather?'

'Don't you be blaming this on me, Cap'n.' She returned his card, and the gate lifted. 'You told me you're in charge.'

Her mirthful voice followed us as we drove on, and I thought how sad it was that we lived in a day when even toll booth attendants had to wear plastic gloves for fear their flesh may come in contact with someone else's flesh. I wondered if we would reach a point when all of us lived in bubbles so we did not die of diseases like the Ebola virus and AIDS.

'I just think she's acting a little weird,' Marino went on as his window rolled up. After a pause, he asked, 'Where's Janet?'

'With her family in Aspen, I think.'

He stared straight ahead and drove.

'After what happened at Dr Mant's house, I don't blame Lucy for being a little rattled,' I added.

'Hell, she's usually the one who looks for trouble,' he said. 'She doesn't get rattled. That's why the Bureau lets her hang out with HRT. You ain't allowed to get rattled when you're dealing with white supremacists and terrorists. You don't call in sick because you've had a friggin' bad dream.'

Off the expressway, he took the Seventh Street exit into the old cobblestone lanes of Shockoe Slip, then turned north onto Fourteenth, where I went to work every day when I was in town. Virginia's Office of the Chief Medical Examiner, or OCME, was a squat stucco building with tiny dark windows that reminded me of unattractive, suspicious eyes. They overlooked slums to the east and the banking district to the west, and suspended overhead were highways and railroad tracks cutting through the sky.

Marino pulled into the back parking lot, where there was an impressive number of cars considering the condition of the roads. I got out in front of the shut bay door and used a key to enter another door to one side. Following the ramp intended for stretchers, I entered the morgue, and could hear the noise of people working down the hall. The autopsy suite was past the walk-in refrigerator, and doors were open wide. I walked in while Fielding, my deputy chief, removed various tubes and a catheter from the body of a young woman on the second table.

'You ice-skate in?' he asked and he did not seem surprised to see me.

'Close to it. I may have to borrow the wagon today. At the moment I'm without a car.'

He leaned closer to his patient, frowning a bit as he studied the tattoo of a rattlesnake coiled around the dead woman's sagging left breast, its gaping mouth disturbingly aimed at her nipple.

'You tell me why the hell somebody gets something like this,' Fielding said.

'I'd say the tattoo artist got the best end of that deal,' I said. 'Check the inside of her lower lip. She's probably got a tattoo there.'

He pulled down her lower lip, and inside it in big crooked letters was *Fuck You*.

Fielding looked at me in astonishment. 'How'd you know that?'

'The tattoos are homemade, she looks like a biker-type and my guess is she's no stranger to jail.'

'Right on all counts.' He grabbed a clean towel and wiped his face.

My body-building associate always looked as if he were about to split his scrubs, and he perspired while the rest of us were never quite warm. But he was a competent forensic pathologist. He was pleasant and caring, and I believed he was loyal.

'Possible overdose,' he explained as he sketched the tattoo on a chart. 'I guess her New Year was a little too happy.'

'Jack,' I said to him, 'how many dealings have you had with the Chesapeake police?'

He continued to draw. 'Very little.'

'None recently?' I asked.

'I really don't think so. Why?' He glanced up at me.

'I had a rather odd encounter with one of their detectives.'

'In connection with Eddings?' He began to rinse the body, and long dark hair flowed over bright steel.

'Right.'

'You know, it's weird but Eddings had just called me. It couldn't have been more than a day before he died,' Fielding said as he moved the hose.

'What did he want?' I asked.

'I was down here doing a case, so I never talked to him. Now I wish I had.' He climbed up a stepladder and began taking photographs with a Polaroid camera. 'You in town long?'

'I don't know,' I said.

'Well, if you need me to help out in Tidewater some, I will.' The flash went off and he waited for the print. 'I don't know if I told you, but Ginny's pregnant again and would probably love to get out of the house. And she likes the ocean. Tell me the name of the detective you're worried about, and I'll take care of him.'

'I wish somebody would,' I said.

The camera flashed again, and I thought about Mant's cottage and could not imagine putting Fielding and his wife in there or even nearby.

'It makes sense for you to stay here anyway,' he added. 'And hopefully Dr Mant isn't going to stay in England forever.'

'Thank you,' I said to him with feeling. 'Maybe if you could just commute several times a week.'

'No problem. Could you hand me the Nikon?'

'Which one?'

'Uh, the N-50 with the single-reflex lens. I think it's in the cabinet over there.' He pointed.

'We'll work out a schedule,' I said as I got the camera for him. 'But you and Ginny don't need to be in Dr Mant's house, and you're going to have to trust me on that.'

'You have a problem?' He ripped out another print and handed it down.

'Marino, Lucy and I started our New Year with slashed tires.'

He lowered the camera and looked at me, shocked. 'Shit. You think it was random?'

'No, I do not,' I said.

I took the elevator up to the next floor and unlocked my office and the sight of Eddings's Christmas pepper surprised me like a blow. I could not leave it on the credenza, so I picked it up and then did not know where to move it. For a moment, I walked around, confused and upset, until I finally put it back where it had been, because I could not throw it out or subject some other member of my staff to its memories.

Looking through Rose's adjoining doorway, I was not surprised that she wasn't here yet. My secretary was advancing in years and did not like to drive downtown even on the nicest days. Hanging up my coat, I carefully looked around, satisfied that all seemed in order except for the cleaning job done by the custodial crew that came in after hours. But then, none of the sanitation engineers, as they were called by the state, wanted to work in this building. Few lasted long and none would go downstairs.

I had inherited my quarters from the previous chief, but beyond the paneling, nothing was as it had been back in those cigar-smoky days when forensic pathologists like Cagney nipped bourbon with cops and funeral home directors, and touched bodies with bare hands. My predecessor had not worried much about alternate light sources and DNA.

I remembered the first time I had been shown his space after he had died and I was being interviewed for his position. I had surveyed macho mementos he had proudly displayed, and when one of them turned out to be a silicone breast implant from a woman who had been raped and murdered, I had been tempted to stay in Miami.

I did not think the former chief would like his office now, for it was nonsmoking, and disrespect and sophomoric behavior were left outside the door. The oak furniture was not the state's but my own, and I had hidden the tile floor with a Sarouk prayer rug that was machine-made but bright. There were corn plants and a ficus tree, but I did not bother with art, because, like a psychiatrist, I wanted nothing provocative on my walls, and, frankly, I needed all the space I could find for filing cabinets and books. As for trophies, Cagney would not have been impressed with the toy cars, trucks and trains I used to help investigators reconstruct accidents.

I took several minutes to look through my in-basket, which was full of red-bordered death certificates for medical examiner cases and green-bordered ones for those that were not. Other reports also awaited my initialing, and a message on my computer screen told me I needed to check my electronic mail. All that could wait, I thought, and I walked back out into the hall to see who else was here. Only Cleta was, I discovered, when I reached the front office, but she was just who I needed to see.

'Dr Scarpetta,' she said, startled. 'I didn't know you were here.'

'I thought it was a good idea for me to return to Richmond right now,' I said, pulling a chair close to her desk. 'Dr Fielding and I are going to try to cover Tidewater from here.'

Cleta was from Florence, South Carolina, and wore a lot of makeup and her skirts too short because she believed that happiness was being pretty, which was something she would never be. In the midst of sorting grim photographs by case number, she sat straight in her chair, a magnifying glass in hand, bifocals on. Nearby was a sausage biscuit on a napkin that she probably had gotten from the cafeteria next door, and she was drinking Tab.

'Well, I think the roads are starting to melt,' she let me know.

'Good.' I smiled. 'I'm glad you're here.'

She seemed very pleased as she plucked more photographs out of the shallow box.

'Cleta,' I said, 'you remember Ted Eddings, don't you?'

'Oh yes, ma'am.' She suddenly looked as if she might cry. 'He was always so nice when he would come in here. I still can't believe it.' She bit her lower lip.

'Dr Fielding says Eddings called down here the end of last week,' I said. 'I'm wondering if you might remember that.'

She nodded. 'Yes, ma'am, I sure do. In fact, I can't stop thinking about it.'

'Did he talk to you?'

'Yes.'

'Can you remember what he said?'

'Well, he wanted to speak to Dr Fielding, but his line was busy. So I asked if I could take a message, and we kidded around some. You know how he was.' Her eyes got bright and her voice wavered. 'He asked me if I was still eating so much maple syrup because I had to be eating plenty of it to talk like this. And he asked me out.'

I listened as her cheeks turned red.

'Of course, he didn't mean it. He was always saying, you know, "When are we going out on that date?" He didn't mean it,' she said again.

'It's all right if he did,' I kindly told her.

'Well, he already had a girlfriend.'

'How do you know that?' I asked.

'He said he was going to bring her by sometime, and I got the impression he was pretty serious about her. I believe her name is Loren, but I don't know anything else about her.'

I thought of Eddings engaging in personal conversations like this with my staff, and was even less surprised that he had seemed to gain access to me more easily than most reporters who called. I could not help but wonder if this same talent had led to his death, and I suspected it had.

'Did he ever mention to you what he wanted to talk to Dr Fielding about?' I said as I got up.

She thought hard for a moment, absently rummaging through pictures the world should never see. 'Wait a minute. Oh, I know. It was something about radiation. About what the findings would be if someone died from that.'

'What kind of radiation?' I said.

'Well, I was thinking he was doing some sort of story on X-ray machines. You know, there's been a lot in the news lately because of all the people afraid of things like letter bombs.'

I did not recall seeing anything in Eddings's house that might indicate he was researching such a story. I returned to my office, and started on paperwork and began returning telephone calls. Hours later, I was eating a late lunch at my desk when Marino walked in.

'What's it doing out there?' I said, surprised to see him. 'Would you like half a tuna-fish sandwich?'

Shutting both doors, he sat with his coat still on, and the look on his face frightened me. 'Have you talked to Lucy?' he said.

'Not since I left the house.' I put the sandwich down. 'Why?'

'She called me' – he glanced at his watch – 'roughly an hour ago. Wanted to know how to get in touch with Danny so she could call him about her car. And she sounded drunk.'

I was silent for a moment, my eyes on his. Then I looked away. I did not ask him if he were certain because Marino knew about such matters, and Lucy's past was quite familiar to him.

'Should I go home?' I quietly asked.

'Naw. I think she's in some kind of mood and is blowing things off. At least she's got no car to drive.'

I took a deep breath.

'Point is, I think she's safe at the moment. But I thought you should know, Doc.'

'Thank you,' I grimly said.

I had hoped my niece's proclivity to abuse alcohol was a problem she had left behind, for I had seen no worrisome signs since those early self-destructive days when she had driven drunk and almost died. If nothing else, her odd behavior at the house this morning in addition to what Marino had just revealed made me know that something was very wrong. I wasn't certain what to do.

'One other thing,' he added as he got up. 'You don't want her going back to the Academy like this.'

'No,' I said. 'Of course not.'

He left, and for a while I stayed behind shut doors, depressed, my thoughts like the sluggish river behind my home. I did not know if I was angry or frightened, but as I thought of the times I had offered wine to Lucy or gotten her a beer, I felt betrayed. Then I was almost desperate as I considered the magnitude of what she had accomplished, and what she had to lose, and suddenly other images came to me, too. I envisioned terrible scenes penned by a man who wanted to be a deity, and I knew that my niece with all her brilliance did not understand the darkness of that power. She did not understand malignancy the way I did.

I put my coat and gloves on, because I knew just where I should go. I was about to let the front office know I was leaving, when my phone rang, and I picked it up in the event it might be Lucy. But it was the Chesapeake police chief, who told me his name was Steels and that he had just moved here from Chicago.

'I'm sorry this is the way we have to meet,' he said, and he sounded sincere. 'But I need to talk to you about a detective of mine named Roche.'

'I need to talk to you about him, too,' I said. 'Maybe you can explain to me exactly what his problem is.'

'According to him, the problem's you,' he said.

'That's ridiculous,' I said, unable to restrain my anger. 'To cut to the chase, Chief Steels, your detective is inappropriate, unprofessional and an obstruction in this investigation. He is banned from my morgue.'

'You realize Internal Affairs is going to have to thoroughly investigate this,' he said, 'and I'm probably going to need you to come in at some point so we can talk to you.'

'Exactly what is the accusation?'

'Sexual harassment.'

'That's certainly popular these days,' I ironically said. 'However, I wasn't aware I had power over him, since he works for you, not me, and by definition, sexual harassment is about the abuse of power. But it's all moot since the roles are reversed in this case. Your detective is the one who made sexual advances toward me, and when they were not reciprocated, he's the one who became abusive.'

Steels said after a pause, 'Then it sounds to me like it's your word against his.'

'No, what it sounds like is a lot of bullshit. And if he touches me one more time, I will get a warrant and have him arrested.'

He was silent.

'Chief Steels,' I went on, 'I think what should be of glaring importance right now is a very frightening situation that is going on in your jurisdiction. Might we talk about Ted Eddings for a moment?'

He cleared his throat. 'Certainly.'

'You're familiar with the case?'

'Absolutely. I've been thoroughly briefed and am very familiar with it.'

'Good. Then I'm sure you'll agree that we should investigate it to our fullest capacity.'

'Well, I think we should look hard at everybody who dies, but in the Eddings case the answer's pretty plain to me.'

I listened as I got only more furious.

'You may or may not know that he was into Civil War stuff – had a collection, and all. Apparently, there were some battles not so far from where he went diving, and it may be he was looking for artifacts like cannonballs.'

I realized that Roche must have talked to Mrs Eddings, or perhaps the chief had seen some of the newspaper articles Eddings supposedly had written about his underwater treasure hunts. I was no historian, but I knew enough to see the obvious problem with what was becoming a ridiculous theory.

I said to Steels, 'The biggest battle on or near water in your area was between the *Merrimac* and the *Monitor*. And that was miles away in Hampton Roads. I have never heard of any battles in or near the part of the Elizabeth River where the shipyard is located.'

'But Dr Scarpetta, we really just don't know, do we?' he thoughtfully said. 'Could be anything that was fired, any garbage dumped, and anybody killed at any place back then. It's not like there were television cameras or millions of reporters all over. Just Mathew Brady, and by the way, I'm a big fan of history and have read a lot about the Civil War. I'm personally of the belief that this guy, Eddings, went down in that shipyard so he could comb the river bottom for relics. He inhaled noxious gases from his machine and died, and whatever he had in his hands – like a metal detector – got lost in the silt.'

'I am working this case as a possible homicide,' I firmly said.

'And I don't agree with you, based on what I've been told.'

'I expect the prosecutor will agree with me when I speak to her.'
The chief said nothing to that.

'I should assume you don't intend to invite the Bureau's Criminal Investigative Analysis people into this,' I added. 'Since you have decided we're dealing with an accident.'

'At this point, I see no reason in the world to bother the FBI. And I've told them that.'

'Well, I see every reason,' I answered, and it was all I could do not to hang up on him.

'Damn, damn, damn!' I muttered as I angrily grabbed my belongings and marched out the door.

Downstairs in the morgue office, I removed a set of keys from the wall, and I went outside to the parking lot and unlocked the driver's door of the dark blue station wagon we sometimes used to transport bodies. It was not as obvious as a hearse, but it wasn't what one might expect to see in a neighbor's driveway, either. Oversized, it had tinted windows obscured with blinds similar to those used by funeral homes, and in lieu of seats in back, the floor was covered with plywood fitted with fasteners to keep stretchers from sliding during transport. My morgue supervisor had hung several air fresheners from the rearview mirror, and the scent of cedar was cloying.

I opened my window part of the way and drove onto Main Street, grateful that by now roads were only wet, and rush-hour traffic not too bad. Damp, cold air felt good on my face, and I knew what I must do. It had been a while since I had stopped at church on my way home, for I thought to do this only when I was in crisis, when life had pushed me as far as I could go. At Three Chopt Road and Grove Avenue, I turned into the parking lot of Saint Bridget's, which was built of brick and slate and no longer kept its doors unlocked at night, because of what the world had become. But Alcoholics Anonymous met at this hour, and I always knew when I could get in and that I would not be bothered.

Entering through a side door, I blessed myself with holy water as I walked into the sanctuary with its statues of saints guarding the cross, and crucifixion scenes in brilliant stained glass. I chose the last row of pews, and I wished for candles to light, but that ritual had stopped here with Vatican II. Kneeling on the bench, I prayed for Ted Eddings and his mother. I prayed for Marino and Wesley. In my private, dark space, I prayed for my niece. Then I sat in silence with my eyes shut, and I felt my tension begin to ease.

At almost six P.M., I was about to leave when I paused in the narthex and saw the lighted doorway of the library down a hall. I wasn't certain why I was guided in that direction, but it did occur to me that an evil book might be countered by one that was holy, and a few moments with the catechism might be what the priest would prescribe. When I walked in, I found an older woman inside, returning books to shelves.

'Dr Scarpetta?' she asked, and she seemed both surprised and pleased.

'Good evening.' I was ashamed I did not remember her name.

'I'm Mrs Edwards.'

I remembered she was in charge of social services at the church, and trained converts in Catholicism, which some days I thought should include me since it was so rare I went to Mass. Small and slightly plump, she had never seen a convent but still inspired the same guilt in me that the good nuns had when I was young.

'I don't often see you here at this hour,' she said.

'I just stopped by,' I answered. 'After work. I'm afraid I missed evening prayer.'

'That was on Sunday.'

'Of course.'

'Well, I'm so glad I happened to see you on my way out.' Her eyes lingered on my face and I knew she sensed my need.

I scanned bookcases.

'Might I help you find something?' she asked.

'A copy of the catechism,' I said.

She crossed the room and pulled one off a shelf, and handed it to me. It was a large volume and I wondered if I had made a good decision, for I was very tired right now and I doubted Lucy was in a condition to read.

'Perhaps there is something I might help you with?' Her voice was kind.

'Maybe if I could speak to the priest for a few moments, that would be good,' I said.

'Father O'Connor is making hospital visits.' Her eyes continued searching. 'Might I help you in some way?'

'Maybe you can.'

'We can sit right here,' she suggested.

We pulled chairs out from a plain wooden table reminiscent of ones I had sat at in parochial school when I was a girl in Miami. I suddenly remembered the wonder of what had awaited me on the pages of those books, for learning was what I loved, and any mental escape from home had been a blessing. Mrs Edwards and I faced each other like friends, but the words were hard to say because it was rare I talked this frankly.

'I can't go into much detail because my difficulty relates to a case I am working,' I began.

'I understand.' She nodded.

'But suffice it to say that I have become exposed to a satanic-type bible. Not devil worship, per se, but something evil.'

She did not react but continued to look me in the eye.

'And Lucy was, as well. Lucy is my twenty-three-year-old niece. She also read this manuscript.'

'And you're having problems as a result?' Mrs Edwards asked.

I took a deep breath and felt foolish. 'I know this sounds rather weird.'

'Of course it doesn't,' she said. 'We must never underestimate the power of evil, and we should avoid brushing up against it whenever we can.'

'I can't always avoid that,' I said. 'It is evil that usually brings my patients to my door. But rarely do I have to look at documents like the one I'm talking about now. I've been having disturbing dreams, and my niece is acting erratically and has spent a lot of time with the Book. Mostly, I'm worried about her. That's why I'm here.'

'"But continue thou in the things which thou hast learned and hast been assured of,"' she quoted to me. 'It's really that simple.' She smiled.

'I'm not certain I understand,' I replied.

'Dr Scarpetta, there is no cure for what you've just shared with me. I can't lay hands on you and push the darkness and bad dreams away. Father O'Connor can't, either. We have no ritual or ceremony that works. We can pray for you and, of course, we will. But what you and Lucy must do right now is return to your own faith. You need to do whatever it is that has given you strength in the past.'

'That's why I came here today,' I said again.

'Good. Tell Lucy to return to the religious community and pray. She should come to church.'

That would be the day, I thought as I drove toward home, and my fears only intensified when I walked through my front door. It was not quite seven P.M. and Lucy was in bed.

'Are you asleep?' I sat next to her in the dark and placed my hand on her back. 'Lucy?'

She did not answer and I was grateful that our cars had not arrived.

I was afraid she might have tried to drive back to Charlottesville. I was so afraid she was about to repeat every terrible mistake she had ever made.

'Lucy?' I said again.

She slowly rolled over. 'What?' she said.

'I'm just checking on you,' I said in a hushed tone.

I saw her wipe her eyes and realized she was not asleep but crying.

'What is it?' I said.

'Nothing.'

'I know it's something. And it's time we talk. You've not been your-self and I want to help.'

She would not answer.

'Lucy, I will sit right here until you talk to me.'

She was quiet some more, and I could see her eyelids move as she stared up at the ceiling. 'Janet told them,' she said. 'She told her mom and dad. They argued with her, as if they know more about her feel-ings than she does. As if somehow she is wrong about herself.'

Her voice was getting angrier and she worked her way up to a half-sitting position, stuffing pillows behind her back.

'They want her to go to counseling,' she added.

'I'm sorry,' I said. 'I'm not sure I know what to say except that the problem lies with them and not with the two of you.'

'I don't know what she's going to do. It's bad enough that we have to worry about the Bureau finding out.'

'You have to be strong and true to who you are.'

'Whoever that is. Some days I don't know.' She got more upset. 'I hate this. It's so hard. It's so unfair.' She leaned her head against my shoulder. 'Why couldn't I have been like you? Why couldn't it have been easy?'

'I'm not sure you want to be like me,' I said. 'And my life certainly isn't easy, and almost nothing that matters is easy. You and Janet can work things out if you are committed to do so. And if you truly love each other.'

She took a deep breath and slowly blew out air.

'No more destructive behavior.' I got up from her bed in the shadows of her room. 'Where's the Book?'

'On the desk,' she said.

'In my office?'

'Yes. I put it there.'

We looked at each other, and her eyes shone. She sniffed loudly and blew her nose.

'Do you understand why it's not good to dwell on something like that?' I asked.

'Look what you have to dwell on all the time. It goes with the turf.'

'No,' I said, 'what goes with the turf is knowing where to step and where not to stand. You must respect an enemy's power as much as you despise it. Otherwise, you will lose, Lucy. You had better learn this now.'

'I understand,' she quietly said as she reached for the catechism I had set on the foot of the bed. 'What is this, and do I have to read it all tonight?'

'Something I picked up for you at church. I thought you might like to look at it.'

'Forget church,' she said.

'Why?'

'Because it's forgotten me. It thinks people like me are aberrant, as if I should go to hell or jail for the way I am. That's what I'm talking about. You don't know what it's like to be isolated.'

'Lucy, I've been isolated most of my life. You don't even know what discrimination is until you're one of only three women in your medical school class. Or in law school, the men won't share their notes if you're sick and miss class. That's why I don't get sick. That's why I don't get drunk and hide in bed.' I sounded hard because I knew I needed to be.

'This is different,' she said.

'I think you want to believe it's different so you can make excuses and feel sorry for yourself,' I said. 'It seems to me that the person doing all of the forgetting and rejecting here is you. It's not the church. It's not society. It's not even Janet's parents, who simply may not understand. I thought you were stronger than this.'

'I am strong.'

'Well, I've had enough,' I said. 'Don't you come to my house and get drunk and pull the covers over your head so that I worry about you all day. And then when I try to help, you push me and everyone else away.'

She was silent as she stared at me. Finally she said, 'Did you really go to church because of me?'

'I went because of me,' I said. 'But you were the main topic of conversation.'

She threw the covers off. '"A person's chief end is to glorify God and enjoy God forever,"' she said as she got up.

I paused in her doorway.

'Catechism. Using inclusive language, of course. I had a religion course at UVA. Do you want dinner?'

'What would you like?' I said.

'Whatever's easy.' She came over and hugged me. 'Aunt Kay, I'm sorry,' she said.

In the kitchen I opened the freezer first and was not inspired by anything I saw. Next I looked inside the refrigerator, but my appetite had gone into hiding along with my peace of mind. I ate a banana and made a pot of coffee. At half past eight, the base station on the counter startled me.

'Unit six hundred to base station one,' Marino's voice came over the air.

I picked up the microphone and answered him, 'Base station one.'

'Can you call me at a number?'

'Give it to me,' I said, and I had a bad feeling.

It was possible the radio frequency used by my office could be monitored, and whenever a case was especially sensitive, the detectives tried to keep all of us off the air. The number Marino gave me was for a pay phone.

When he answered, he said, 'Sorry, I didn't have any change.'

'What's going on?' I didn't waste time.

'I'm skipping the M.E. on call because I knew you'd want us to get hold of you first.'

'What is it?'

'Shit, Doc, I'm really sorry. But we've got Danny.'

'Danny?' I said in confusion.

'Danny Webster. From your Norfolk office.'

'What do you mean you've got him?' I was gripped by fear. 'What did he do?' I imagined he had gotten arrested driving my car. Or maybe he had wrecked it.

Marino said, 'Doc, he's dead.'

Then there was silence on his end and mine.

'Oh God.' I leaned against the counter and shut my eyes. 'Oh my God,' I said. 'What happened?'

'Look, I think the best thing is for you to get down here.'

'Where are you?'

'Sugar Bottom, where the old train tunnel is. Your car's about a block uphill at Libby Hill Park.'

I asked nothing further but told Lucy I was leaving and probably would not be home until late. I grabbed my medical bag and my pistol, for I was familiar with the skid row part of town where the tunnel was, and I could not imagine what might have lured Danny there. He and his friend were to have driven my car and Lucy's Suburban to my office, where my administrator was to meet them in back and give them a ride to the bus station. Certainly, Church Hill was not far from the OCME, but I could not imagine why Danny would have driven anywhere in my Mercedes other than where he knew he was to be. He did not seem the type to abuse my trust.

I drove swiftly along West Cary Street, passing huge brick homes with roofs of copper and slate, and entrances barricaded by tall black wrought-iron gates. It seemed surreal to be speeding in the morgue wagon through this elegant part of the city while one of my employees lay dead, and I fretted over leaving Lucy alone again. I could not remember if I had armed the alarm system and turned the motion sensors off on my way out. My hands were shaking and I wished I could smoke.

Libby Hill Park was on one of Richmond's seven hills in an area where real estate was now considered prime. Century-old row houses and Greek Revival homes had been brilliantly restored by people bold enough to reclaim a historic section of the city from the clutches of decay and crime. For most residents, the chance they took had turned out fine, but I knew I could not live near housing projects and depressed areas where the major industry was drugs. I did not want to work cases in my neighborhood.

Police cruisers with lights throbbing red and blue lined both sides of Franklin Street. The night was very dark, and I could barely make out the octagonal bandstand or the bronze soldier on his tall granite pedestal facing the James. My Mercedes was surrounded by officers and a television crew, and people had emerged on wide porches to watch. As I slowly drove past, I could not tell if my car had been damaged, but the driver's door was open, the interior light on.

East past 29th Street, the road sloped down to a low-lying section known as Sugar Bottom, named for prostitutes once kept in business by Virginia gentlemen, or maybe it was for moonshine. I wasn't sure of the lore. Restored homes abruptly turned into slumlord apartments and leaning tarpaper shacks, and off the pavement, midway down the steep hill, were woods thick and dense where the C&O tunnel had collapsed in the twenties.

I remembered flying over this area in a state police helicopter once, and the tunnel's black opening had peeked out of trees at me, its railroad bed a muddy scar leading to the river. I thought of the train cars and laborers supposedly still sealed inside, and, again, I could not imagine why Danny would have come here willingly. If nothing else, he would have worried about his injured knee. Pulling over, I parked as close to Marino's Ford as I could, and instantly was spotted by reporters.

'Dr Scarpetta, is it true that's your car up the hill?' asked a woman journalist as she hurried to my side. 'I understand the Mercedes is registered to you. What color is it? Is it black?' she persisted when I did not reply.

'Can you explain how it got there?' A man pushed a microphone close to my face.

'Did you drive it there?' asked someone else.

'Was it stolen from you? Did the victim steal it from you? Do you think this is about drugs?'

Voices folded into each other because no one would wait his turn and I would not speak. When several uniformed officers realized I had arrived, they loudly intervened.

'Hey, get back.'

'Now. You heard me.'

'Let the lady through.'

'Come on. We got a crime scene to work here. I hope that's all right with you.'

Marino was suddenly holding on to my arm. 'Bunch of squirrels,' he said as he glared at them. 'Be real careful where you step. We got to go through the woods almost all the way to where the tunnel is. What kind of shoes you got on?'

'I'll be all right.'

There was a path, and it was long and led steeply down from the street. Lights had been set up to illuminate the way, and they cut a swath like the moon on a dangerous bay. On the margins, woods dissolved into blackness stirred by a subtle wind.

'Be real careful,' he said again. 'It's muddy and there's shit all over the place.'

'What shit?' I asked.

I turned on my flashlight and directed it straight down at the narrow muddy path of broken glass, rotting paper, and discarded shoes that glinted and glowed a washed-out white amid brambles and winter trees.

'The neighbors have been trying to turn this into a landfill,' he said.

'He could not have gotten down here with his bad knee,' I said. 'What's the best way to approach this?'

'On my arm.'

'No. I need to look at this alone.'

'Well, you're not going down there alone. We don't know if someone else might still be down there somewhere.'

'There's blood there.' I pointed the flashlight, and several large drops glistened on dead leaves about six feet down from where I was.

'There's a lot of it up here.'

'Any up by the street?'

'No. It looks like it pretty much starts right here. But we've found some on the path going all the way down to where he is.'

'All right. Let's do it.' I looked around and began careful steps, Marino's heavier ones behind me.

Police had run bright yellow tape from tree to tree, securing as much of the area as possible, for right now we did not know how big this scene might be. I could not see the body until I emerged from the woods into a clearing where the old railroad bed led to the river south of me and disappeared into the tunnel's yawning mouth to the west. Danny Webster lay half on his back, half on his side in an awkward tangle of arms and legs. A large puddle of blood was beneath his head. I slowly explored him with the flashlight and saw an abundance of dirt and grass on his sweater and jeans, and bits of leaves and other debris clung to his blood-matted hair.

'He rolled down the hill,' I said as I noted that several straps had come loose in his bright red brace, and debris was caught in the Velcro. 'He was already dead or almost dead when he came to rest in this position.'

'Yeah, I think it's pretty clear he was shot up there,' Marino said. 'My first question was whether he bled while he maybe tried to get away. And he makes it about this far, then collapses and rolls the rest of the way.'

'Or maybe he was made to think he was being given a chance to get away.' Emotion crept into my voice. 'You see this knee brace he has on? Do you have any idea how slowly he would have moved were he trying to get down this path? Do you know what it's like to inch your way along on a bad leg?'

'So some asshole was shooting fish in a barrel,' Marino said.

I did not answer him as I directed the light at grass and trash leading up to the street. Drops of blood glistened dark red on a flattened milk carton whitened by weather and time.

'What about his wallet?' I asked.

'It was in his back pocket. Eleven bucks and charge cards still in it,' Marino said, his eyes constantly moving.

I took photographs, then knelt by the body and turned it so I could get a better look at the back of Danny's ruined head. I felt his neck, and he was still warm, the blood beneath him coagulating. I opened my medical bag.

'Here.' I unfolded a plastic sheet and gave it to Marino. 'Hold this up while I take his temperature.'

He shielded the body from any eyes but ours as I pulled down jeans and undershorts, finding that both were soiled. Although it was not uncommon for people to urinate and defecate at the instant of death, sometimes this was the body's response to terror.

'You got any idea if he fooled around with drugs?' Marino asked.

'I have no reason to think so,' I said. 'But I have no idea.'

'For example, he ever look like he lived beyond his means? I mean, how much did he earn?'

'He earned about twenty-one thousand dollars a year. I don't know if he lived beyond his means. He still lived at home.'

The body temperature was 94.5, and I set the thermometer on top of my bag to get a reading of the ambient air. I moved arms and legs, and rigor mortis had started only in small muscles like his fingers and eyes. For the most part, Danny was still warm and limber as in life, and as I bent close to him I could smell his cologne and knew I would recognize it forever. Making sure the sheet was completely under him, I turned him on his back, and more blood spilled as I began looking for other wounds.

'What time did you get the call?' I asked Marino, who was moving slowly near the tunnel, probing its tangled growths of vines and brush with his light.

'One of the neighbors heard a gunshot coming from this area and dialed 911 at seven-oh-five P.M. We found your car and him maybe fifteen minutes after that. So we're talking about two hours ago. Does that work with what you're finding?'

'It's almost freezing out. He's heavily clothed and he's lost about four degrees. Yes, that works. How about handing me those bags over there. Do we know what happened to the friend who was supposed to be driving Lucy's Suburban?'

I slipped the brown paper bags over the hands and secured them at the wrist with rubber bands to preserve fragile evidence like gunshot residue, or fibers or flesh beneath fingernails, supposing he had struggled with his assailant. But I did not think he had. Whatever had happened, I suspected Danny had done exactly as he had been told.

'At the present time we don't know anything about whoever his friend is,' Marino said. 'I can send a unit down to your office to check.'

'I think that's a good idea. We don't know that the friend isn't somehow connected to this.'

'One hundred,' Marino said into his portable radio as I began taking photographs again.

'One hundred,' the dispatcher came back.

'Ten-five any unit that might be in the area of the medical examiner's office at Fourteenth and Franklin.'

Danny had been shot from behind, the wound close range, if not contact. I started to ask Marino about cartridge cases when I heard a noise I knew all too well.

'Oh no,' I said as the beating sound got louder. 'Marino, don't let them get near.'

But it was too late, and we looked up as a news helicopter appeared and began circling low. Its searchlight swept the tunnel and the cold, hard ground where I was on my knees, brains and blood all over my hands. I shielded my eyes from the blinding glare as leaves and dirt stormed and bare trees rocked. I could not hear what Marino yelled as he furiously waved his flashlight at the sky while I shielded the body with my own as best I could.

I enclosed Danny's head in a plastic bag and covered him with a sheet while the crew for Channel 7 destroyed the scene because they were ignorant or did not care, or maybe both. The helicopter's passenger door had been removed, and the cameraman hung out in the night as the light nailed me for the eleven o'clock news. Then the blades began their thunderous retreat.

'Goddamnsonofabitch!' Marino was screaming as he shook his fist after them. 'I ought to shoot your ass out of the air!'

9

While a car was dispatched there, I zipped the body inside a pouch, and when I stood I felt faint. For an instant I had to steady myself as my face got cold and I could not see.

'The squad can move him,' I told Marino. 'Can't someone get those goddamn television cameras out of here?'

Their bright lights floated like satellites up on the dark street as they waited for us to emerge. He gave me a look because we both knew nobody could do a thing about reporters or what they used to record us. As long as they did not interfere with the scene, they could do as they pleased, especially if they were in helicopters we could not stop or catch.

'You going to transport him yourself?' he asked me.

'No. A squad's already there,' I said. 'And we need some help getting him back up there. Tell them to come on now.'

He got on the radio as our flashlights continued to lick over trash and leaves and potholes filled with muddy water.

Then Marino said to me, 'I'm going to keep a few guys out here poking around for a while. Unless the perp collected his cartridge case, it's got to be out here somewhere.' He looked up the hill. 'Problem is, some of those mothers can eject a long way and that goddamn chopper blew stuff all the hell over the place.'

Within minutes, paramedics were coming down with a stretcher, feet crunching broken glass, metal clanging. We waited until they had lifted the body, and I probed the ground where it had been. I stared into the black opening of a tunnel that long ago had been dug into a mountainside too soft to support it, and I moved closer until I was just inside its mouth. A wall sealed it deep inside, and whitewash on bricks glinted in my light. Rusting railroad spikes protruded from rotting ties covered with mud, and scattered about were old tires and bottles.

'Doc, there's nothing in there.' Marino was picking his way right behind me. 'Shit.' He almost slipped. 'We've already looked.'

'Well, obviously, he couldn't have escaped through here,' I said as my light discovered cobblestones and dead weeds. 'And no one could hide in here. And your average person shouldn't have known about this place, either.'

'Come on.' Marino's voice was gentle but firm as he touched my arm.

'This wasn't picked randomly. Not many people around here even know where this is.' My light moved more. 'This was someone who knew exactly what he was doing.'

'Doc,' he said as water dripped, 'this ain't safe.'

'I doubt Danny knew about this place. This was premeditated and cold-blooded.' My voice echoed off old, dark walls.

Marino held my arm this time, and I did not resist him. 'You've done all you can do here. Let's go.'

Mud sucked at my boots and oozed over his black military shoes as we followed the rotting railroad bed back out into the night. Together, we climbed up the littered hillside, carefully stepping around blood spilled when Danny's body had been rolled down the steep slope like garbage. Much of it had been displaced by the helicopter's violent wind, and that would one day matter if a defense attorney thought it did. I averted my face from the glare of cameras and flashing strobes. Marino and I got out of the way, and we did not talk to anyone.

'I want to see my car,' I said to him as his unit number blared.

'One hundred,' he answered, holding the radio close to his mouth.

'Go ahead, one-seventeen,' the dispatcher said to somebody else.

'I checked the lot front and back, Captain,' Unit 117 said to Marino. 'No sign of the vehicle you described.'

'Ten-four.' Marino lowered the radio and looked very annoyed. 'Lucy's Suburban ain't at your office. I don't get it,' he said to me. 'None of this is making sense.'

We began walking back to Libby Hill Park because it really wasn't far, and we wanted to talk.

'What it's looking like to me is Danny might have picked some-body up,' Marino said as he lit a cigarette. 'Sure sounds like it could be drugs.'

'He wouldn't do that when he was delivering my car,' I said, and I knew I sounded naive. 'He wouldn't pick anybody up.'

Marino turned to me. 'Come on,' he said. 'You don't know that.'

'I've never had any reason to think he was irresponsible or into drugs or anything else.'

'Well, I think it's obvious he was into an alternative life, as they say.'

'I don't know that at all.' I was tired of that talk.

'You better find out because you got a lot of blood on you.'

'These days I worry about that no matter who it is.'

'Look, what I'm saying is people you know do disappointing things,' he went on as the lights of the city spread below us. 'And sometimes people you don't know very well are worse than ones you don't know at all. You trusted Danny because you liked him and thought he did a good job. But he could have been into anything behind the scenes, and you weren't going to know.'

I did not reply. What he said was true.

'He's a nice-looking kid, a pretty boy. And now he's driving this unbelievable ride. The best could have been tempted to maybe do a little trolling before turning in the boss's ride. Or maybe he just wanted to score a little dope.'

I was more concerned that Danny had fallen prey to an attempted carjacking, and I pointed out that there had been a rash of them down-town and in this area.

'Maybe,' Marino said as my car came into view. 'But your ride's still here. Why do you walk someone down the street and shoot them, and leave the car right where it is? Why not steal it? Maybe we should be worried about a gay bashing. You thought about that?'

We had arrived at my Mercedes, and reporters took more photo-graphs and asked more questions as if this were the crime of all time. We ignored them as we moved around to the open driver's door and looked inside my S–320. I scanned armrests, ashtrays, dashboard and saddle leather upholstery, and saw nothing out of place. I saw no sign of a struggle, but the floor mat on the passenger's side was dirty. I noted the faint impressions left by shoes.

'This was the way it was found?' I asked. 'What about the door being opened?'

'We opened the door. It was unlocked,' Marino said.

'Nobody got inside?'

'No.'

'This wasn't there before.' I pointed to the floor mat.

'What?' Marino asked.

'See those shoe impressions and the dirt?' I spoke quietly so reporters could not hear. 'There shouldn't have been anybody in the passenger's seat. Not while Danny was driving, and not earlier when it was being repaired at Virginia Beach.'

'What about Lucy?'

'No. She hasn't ridden with me recently. I can't think of anybody who has since it was cleaned last.'

'Don't worry, we're going to vacuum everything.' He looked away from me and reluctantly added, 'You know we're going to have to impound it, Doc.'

'I understand,' I said, and we started walking back to the street near the tunnel, where we had parked.

'I'm wondering if Danny was familiar with Richmond,' Marino said.

'He's been to my office before,' I replied, and my soul felt heavy. 'In fact, when he was first hired, he did a week's internship with us. I don't remember where he stayed, but I think it was the Comfort Inn on Broad Street.'

We walked in silence for a moment, and I added, 'Obviously, he knew the area around my office.'

'Yeah, and that includes here since your office is only about fifteen blocks from here.'

Something occurred to me. 'We don't know that he didn't just come up here tonight to get something to eat before the bus ride home. How do we know he wasn't just doing something mundane like that?'

Our cars were near several cruisers and a crime scene van, and the reporters had gone. I unlocked the station wagon door and got in. Marino stood with his hands in his pockets, a suspicious expression on his face because he knew me so well.

'You aren't posting him tonight, are you?' he said.

'No.' It wasn't necessary and I wouldn't put myself through it.

'And you don't want to go home. I can tell.'

'There are things to do,' I said. 'The longer we wait, the more we might lose.'

'Which places do you want to try?' he asked, because he knew what it was like to have someone you worked with killed.

'Well, there's a number of places to eat right around here. Millie's, for example.'

'Nope. Too high-dollar. Same with Patrick Henry's and most of the joints in the Slip and Shockoe Bottom. Remember, Danny's not going to have a lot of money unless he's getting it from places we don't know about.'

'Let's assume he's getting nothing from anywhere,' I said. 'Let's assume he wanted something that was a straight shot from my office, so he stayed on Broad Street.'

'Poe's, which isn't on Broad, but is very close to Libby Hill Park. And of course there's the Cafe,' he said.

'That's what I would say, too,' I agreed.

When we walked into Poe's, the manager was ringing up the check of the last customer for the night. We waited what seemed a long time, only to be told that dinner had been slow and no one resembling Danny had come in. Returning to our cars, we continued east on Broad to the Hill Cafe at 28th Street, and my pulse picked up when I realized the restaurant was but one street down from where my Mercedes had been found.

Known for its Bloody Marys and chili, the cafe was on the corner, and over the years had been a favorite hangout for cops. So I had been here many times, usually with Marino. It was a true neighborhood bar, and at this hour, tables were still full, smoke thick in the air, the television loudly playing old Howie Long clips on ESPN. Daigo was drying glasses behind the bar when she saw Marino and gave him a toothy grin.

'Now what you doing in here so late?' she said as if it had never happened before. 'Where were you earlier when things were popping?'

'So tell me,' Marino said to her, 'in the joint that makes the best steak sandwich in town, how's business been tonight?' He moved closer so others could not hear what he had to say.

Daigo was a wiry black woman, and she was eyeing me as if she had seen me somewhere before. 'They were crawling in from everywhere earlier,' she said. 'I thought I was going to drop. Can I get something for you and your friend, Captain?'

'Maybe,' he said. 'You know the doc here, don't ya?'

She frowned and then recognition gleamed in her eyes. 'I knew I seen you in here before. With him. You two married yet?' She laughed as if this were the funniest thing she had ever said.

'Listen, Daigo,' Marino went on, 'we're wondering if a kid might have come in here today. White male, slender, long dark hair, real nice-looking. Would have been wearing a leather jacket, jeans, a sweater, tennis shoes, and a bright red knee brace. About twenty-five years old and driving a new black Mercedes-Benz with a lot of antennas on it.'

Her eyes narrowed and her face got grim as Marino continued to talk, the dish towel limp in her hand. I suspected the police had asked her questions in the past about other unpleasant matters, and I could tell by the set of her mouth that she had no use for lazy, bad people who felt nothing when they ruined decent lives.

'Oh, I know exactly who you mean,' she said.

Her words had the effect of a fired gun. She had our complete attention, both of us startled.

'He came in, I guess it was around five, 'cause it was still early,' she said. 'You know, there were some in here drinking beer just like always. But not too many in for dinner yet. He sat right over there.'

She pointed at an empty table beneath a hanging spider plant all the way in back, where there was a painting of a rooster on the white brick wall. As I stared at the table where Danny had eaten last while in this city because of me, I saw him in my mind. He was alive and helpful with his clean features and shiny long hair, and then he was bloody and muddy on a dark hillside strewn with garbage. My chest hurt and, for a moment, I had to look away. I had to do something else with my eyes.

When I was more composed, I turned to Daigo and said, 'He worked for me at the medical examiner's office. His name was Danny Webster.'

She looked at me a long time, my meaning very clear. 'Uh-oh,' she said in a low voice. 'That's him. Oh sweet Jesus, I can't believe it. It's been all over the news, people in here talking about it all night 'cause it's just down the street.'

'Yes,' I said.

She looked at Marino as if pleading with him. 'He was just a boy. Come in here not minding no one, and all he did was eat his sailor sandwich and then someone kills him! I tell you' – she angrily wiped down the counter – 'there's too much meanness. Too damn much! I'm sick of it. You understand me? People just kill like it's nothing.'

Several diners nearby overheard our conversation, but they continued their own without stares or asides. Marino was in uniform. He clearly was the brass, and that tended to inspire people to mind their own affairs. We waited until Daigo had sufficiently vented her spleen, and we found a table in the quietest corner of the bar. Then she nodded for a waitress to stop by.

'What you want, sugar?' Daigo asked me.

I did not think I could ever eat again, and ordered herbal tea, but she would not hear of that.

'I tell you what, you bring the chief here a bowl of my bread pudding with Jack Daniel's sauce; don't worry, the whiskey's cooked off,' she said, and she was the doctor now. 'And a cup of strong coffee. Captain?' She looked at Marino. 'You want your usual, honey? Uh-huh,' she said before he could respond. 'That will be one steak sandwich medium rare, grilled onions, extra fries. And he likes A.1., ketchup, mustard, mayo. No dessert. We want to keep this man alive.'

'You mind?' Marino got out his cigarettes, as if he needed one more thing that might kill him this day.

Daigo lit up a cigarette, too, and told us more about what she remembered, which was everything because the Hill Cafe was the sort of bar where people noticed strangers. Danny, she said, had stayed less than an hour. He had come and gone alone, and it had not appeared that he was expecting anyone to join him. He had seemed mindful of the time because he frequently checked his watch, and he had ordered a sailor sandwich with fries and a Pepsi. Danny Webster's last meal had cost him six dollars and twenty-seven cents. His waitress was named Cissy, and he had tipped her a dollar.

'And you didn't see anybody in the area that made your antenna go up? Not at any point today?' Marino asked.

Daigo shook her head. 'No, sir. Now that doesn't mean there wasn't some son of a bitch hanging out somewhere on the street. 'Cause they're out there. You don't have to go far to find 'em. But if there was somebody, I didn't see him. Nobody who came in here complained about anybody out there like that, either.'

'Well, we need to check with your customers, as many as we can,' Marino said. 'Maybe a car was noticed around the time Danny went out.'

'We got charge receipts.' She plucked at her hair and by now it was looking wild. 'Most people who been in here we know anyhow.'

We were about to leave but there was one more detail I needed to know. 'Daigo,' I asked, 'did he take anything with him to go?'

She looked perplexed and got up from the table. 'Let me ask.'

Marino crushed out another cigarette, and his face was deep red.

'Are you all right?' I said.

He mopped his face with a napkin. 'It's hot as shit in here.'

'He took his fries,' Daigo announced when she got back. 'Cissy says he ate his sandwich and slaw but she wrapped almost all of his fries. Plus when he got to the register, he bought a jumbo pack of gum.'

'What kind?' I asked.

'She's pretty sure it was Dentyne.'

As Marino and I stepped outside, he loosened the neck of his white uniform shirt and yanked off his tie. 'Damn, some days I wish I'd never left A-Squad,' he said, for when he had commanded detectives it had been in street clothes. 'I don't care who's watching,' he muttered. 'I'm about to die.'

'Please tell me if you're serious,' I said.

'Don't worry, I'm not ready for one of your tables yet. I just ate too much.'

'Yes, you did,' I said. 'And you smoked too much, too. And that's what prepares people for my tables, goddamn it. Don't you even think about dying. I'm tired of people dying.'

We had reached my station wagon and he was staring at me, searching for anything I might not want him to see. 'Are you okay?'

'What do you think? Danny worked for me.' My hand shook as I fumbled with the key. 'He seemed nice and decent. It seemed he always tried to do what was right. He was driving my car here from Virginia Beach because I asked him to and now he's missing the back of his head. How the hell do you think I feel?'

'I think you feel like this is somehow your fault.'

'And maybe it is.'

We stood in the dark, looking at each other.

'No, it's not,' he said. 'It's the fault of the asshole who pulled the trigger. You had nothing in the world to do with that. But if it was me, I'd feel the same way.'

'My God,' I suddenly said.

'What?' He was alarmed, and he looked around as if I had spotted something.

'His doggie bag. What happened to it? It wasn't inside my Mercedes. There was nothing in there that I could see. Not even a gum wrapper,' I said.

'Damn, you're right. And I didn't see nothing on the street where your ride was parked. Nothing with the body or anywhere at the scene, either.'

There was one place no one had looked, and it was right where we were, on this street by the restaurant. So Marino and I got out flashlights again and prowled. We looked along Broad Street, but it was on 28th near the curb where we found the small white bag as a large dog began barking from a yard. The bag's location suggested that Danny had parked my car as close to the cafe as possible in an area where buildings and trees cast dense shadows and lights were few.

'You got a couple pencils or pens inside your purse?' Marino squatted by what we suspected might be the remains of Danny's dinner.

I found one pen and a long-handled comb, which I gave to him. Using these simple instruments, he opened the bag without touching it as he probed. Inside were cold French fries wrapped in foil and a jumbo pack of Dentyne gum. The sight of them was jolting and told a terrible story. Danny had been confronted as he had walked out of the cafe to my car. Perhaps someone emerged from shadows and pulled a gun as Danny was unlocking the door. We did not know, but it seemed likely he was forced to drive a street away, where he was walked to a remote wooded hillside to die.

'I wish that damn dog would shut up,' Marino said as he stood. 'Don't go anywhere. I'll be right back.'

He crossed the street to his car and opened the trunk. When he returned, he was carrying the usual large brown paper bag police used for evidence. While I held it open, he maneuvered the comb and pen to drop Danny's leftovers inside.

'I know I should take this into the property room, but they don't like food in there. Besides, there's no fridge.' Paper crackled as he folded shut the top of the evidence bag.

Our feet made scuffing noises on pavement as we walked.

'Hell, it's colder than any refrigerator out here,' he went on. 'If we get any prints they'll probably be his. But I'll get the labs to check anyway.'

He locked the bag inside his trunk, where I knew he had stored evidence many times before. Marino's reluctance to follow departmental rules went beyond his dress.

I looked around the dark street lined with cars. 'Whatever happened started right here,' I said.

Marino was silent as he looked around, too. Then he asked, 'You think it was your Benz? You think that was the motive?'

'I don't know,' I replied.

'Well, it could be robbery. The car made him look rich even if he wasn't.'

I was overwhelmed by guilt again.

'But I still think he might have met someone he wanted to pick up.'

'Maybe it would be easier if he had been up to no good,' I said. 'Maybe it would be easier for all of us because then we could blame him for being killed.'

Marino was silent as he looked at me. 'Go home and get some sleep. You want me to follow you?'

'Thank you. I'll be fine.'

But I wasn't, really. The drive was longer and darker than I remembered, and I felt unusually unskilled at everything I tried to do. Even rolling down the window at the toll booth and finding the right change was hard. Then the token I tossed missed the bin, and when someone behind me honked, I jumped. I was so out of sorts I could think of nothing that might calm me down, not even whiskey. I returned to my neighborhood at nearly one A.M., and the guard who let me through was grim, and I expected he had heard the news, too, and knew where I had been. When I pulled up to my house, I was stunned to see Lucy's Suburban parked in the drive.

She was up and seemed recovered, sitting in the gathering room. The fire was on, and she had a blanket over her legs, and on TV, Robin Williams was hilarious at the Met.

'What happened?' I sat in a chair nearby. 'How did your car get here?'

She had glasses on and was reading some sort of manual that had been published by the FBI. 'Your answering service called,' she said. 'This guy who was driving my car arrived at your office downtown and your assistant never showed up. What's his name, Danny? So the guy in my car calls, and next thing the phone's ringing here. I had him drive to the guard booth, and that's where I met him.'

'But what happened?' I asked again. 'I don't even know the name of this person. He was supposed to be an acquaintance of Danny's. Danny was driving my car. They were supposed to park both vehicles behind my office.' I stopped and simply stared. 'Lucy, do you have any idea what's going on? Do you know why I'm home so late?'

She picked up the remote control and turned the television off. 'All I know is you got called out on a case. That's what you said to me right before you left.'

So I told her. I told her who Danny was and that he was dead, and I explained about my car. I gave her every detail.

'Lucy, do you have any idea who this person was who dropped off your car?' I then said.

'I don't know.' She was sitting up now. 'Some Hispanic guy named Rick. He had an earring, short hair and looked maybe twenty-two, twenty-three. He was very polite, nice.'

'Where is he now?' I said. 'You didn't just take your car from him.'

'Oh no. I drove him to the bus station, which George gave me directions to.'

'George?'

'The guard on duty at the time. At the guard gate. I guess this would have been close to nine.'

'Then Rick's gone back to Norfolk.'

'I don't know what he's done,' she said. 'He told me as we were driving that he was certain Danny would show up. He probably has no idea.'

'God. Let's hope he doesn't unless he heard it on the news. Let's hope he wasn't there,' I said.

The thought of Lucy alone with this stranger in her car filled me with terror, and in my mind I saw Danny's head. I felt shattered bone beneath gloves slippery with his blood.

'Rick's considered a suspect?' She was surprised.

'At the moment, just about anybody is.'

I picked up the phone at the bar. Marino had just gotten home, too, and before I could say anything, he butted in.

'We found the cartridge case.'

'Great,' I said, relieved. 'Where?'

'If you're on the road looking down toward the tunnel, it was in a bunch of undergrowth about ten feet to the right of the path where the blood starts.'

'A right port ejector,' I said.

'Had to be, unless both Danny and his killer were going downhill backwards. And this asshole meant business. He was shooting a forty-five. The ammo's Winchester.'

'Overkill,' I said.

'You got that right. Someone wanted to make sure he was dead.'

'Marino,' I said, 'Lucy met Danny's friend tonight.'

'You mean the guy driving her car?'

'Yes,' and I explained what I knew.

'Maybe this thing's making a little more sense,' he said. 'The two of them got separated on the road, but in Danny's mind it didn't matter because he'd given his pal directions and a phone number.'

'Can someone try to find out who Rick is before he disappears? Maybe intercept him when he gets off the bus?' I asked.

'I'll call Norfolk P.D. I got to anyway because somebody's got to go over to Danny's house and notify his family before they hear about this from the media.'

'His family lives in Chesapeake,' I told him the bad news, and I knew I would need to talk to them, too.

'Shit,' Marino said.

'Don't talk to Detective Roche about any of this, and I don't want him anywhere near Danny's family.'

'Don't worry. And you'd better get hold of Dr Mant.'

I tried the number for his mother's flat in London, but there was no answer, and I left an urgent message. There were so many calls to make, and I was drained. I sat next to Lucy on the couch.

'How are you doing?'

'Well, I looked at the catechism but I don't think I'm ready to be confirmed.'

'I hope someday you will be.'

'I have a headache that won't go away.'

'You deserve one.'

'You're absolutely right.' She rubbed her temples.

'Why do you do it after all you've been through?' I could not help but ask.

'I don't always know why. Maybe because I have to be such a tight-ass all the time. Same thing with a lot of the agents. We run and lift and do everything right. Then we blow it off on Friday night.'

'Well, at least you were in a safe place to do that this time.'

'Don't you ever lose control?' She met my eyes. 'Because I've never seen it.'

'I've never wanted you to see it,' I said. 'That's all you ever saw with your mother, and you've needed someone to feel safe with.'

'But you didn't answer my question.' She held my gaze.

'What? Have I ever been drunk?'

She nodded.

'It isn't something to be proud of, and I'm going to bed.' I got up.

'More than once?' Her voice followed me as I walked off.

I stopped in the doorway and faced her. 'Lucy, throughout my long, hard life there isn't much I haven't done. And I have never judged you for anything you've done. I've only worried when I thought your behavior placed you in harm's way.' I spoke in understatements yet again.

'Are you worried about me now?'

I smiled a little. 'I will worry about you for the rest of my life.'

I went to my room and shut the door. I placed my Browning by my bed, and took a Benadryl because otherwise I would not sleep the few hours that were left. When I awakened at dawn, I was sitting up with the lamp on, the latest *Journal of the American Bar Association* still in my lap. I got up and walked out into the hall, where I was surprised to find Lucy's door open, her bed unmade. She was not in the gathering room on the couch, and I hurried into the dining room at the front of the house. I stared out windows at an empty expanse of frosted brick pavers and grass, and it was obvious the Suburban had been gone for some time.

'Lucy,' I muttered as if she could hear me. 'Damn you, Lucy,' I said.

10

I was ten minutes late for the staff meeting, which was unusual, but no one commented or seemed to care. The murder of Danny Webster was heavy in the air, as if tragedy might suddenly rain down on us all. My staff was slow-moving and stunned, no one thinking very clearly. After all these years, Rose had brought me coffee and had forgotten I drink it black.

The conference room, which had been recently refurbished, seemed very cozy with its deep blue carpet, long new table and dark paneling. But anatomical models on tables and the human skeleton beneath his plastic shroud were reminders of the hard realities discussed in here. Of course, there were no windows, and art consisted of portraits of previous chiefs, all of them men who stared sternly down at us from the walls.

Seated on either side of me this morning were my chief and assistant chief administrators, and the chief toxicologist from the Division of Forensic Science upstairs. Fielding, to my left, was eating plain yogurt with a plastic spoon, while next to him sat the assistant chief and the new fellow, who was a woman.

'I know you've heard the terrible news about Danny Webster,' I somberly proceeded from the head of the table, where I always sat. 'Needless to say, it is impossible to describe how a senseless death like this affects each one of us.'

'Dr Scarpetta,' said the assistant chief, 'is there anything new?'

'At the moment we know the following,' I said, and I repeated all that I knew. 'It appeared at the scene last night that he had at least one gunshot wound to the back of the head,' I concluded.

'What about cartridge cases?' Fielding asked.

'Police recovered one in woods not too far from the street.'

'So he was shot there at Sugar Bottom versus in or near the car.'

'It does not appear he was shot inside or near the car,' I said.

'Inside whose car?' asked the fellow, who had gone to medical school late in life and was far too serious.

'Inside my car. The Mercedes.'

The fellow seemed very confused until I explained the scenario again. Then she made a rather salient comment. 'Is there any possibility you were the intended victim?'

'Jesus,' Fielding irritably said as he set down the yogurt cup. 'You shouldn't even say something like that.'

'Reality isn't always pleasant,' said the fellow, who was very smart and just as tedious. 'I'm simply suggesting that if Dr Scarpetta's car was parked outside a restaurant she has gone to numerous times before, maybe someone was waiting for her and got surprised. Or maybe someone was following and didn't know it wasn't her inside, since it was dark by the time Danny was on the road heading here.'

'Let's move on to this morning's other cases,' I said, as I took a sip of Rose's saccharine coffee whitened with nondairy creamer.

Fielding moved the call sheet in front of him and in his usual impatient Northern tone went down the list. In addition to Danny, there were three autopsies. One was a fire death, another a prisoner with a history of heart disease, and a seventy-year-old woman with a defibrillator and pacemaker.

'She has a history of depression, mostly over her heart problems,' Fielding was saying, 'and this morning at about three o'clock her husband heard her get out of bed. Apparently she went into the den and shot herself in the chest.'

Possible views were of other poor souls who during the night had died from myocardial infarcts and wrecks in cars. I turned down an elderly woman who clearly was a victim of cancer, and an indigent man who had succumbed to his coronary disease. Finally, we pushed back chairs and I went downstairs. My staff was respectful of my space and did not question what I was going through. No one spoke in the elevator as I stared straight ahead at shut doors, and in the locker room we put on gowns and washed our hands in silence. I was pulling on shoe covers and gloves when Fielding got close to me and spoke in my ear.

'Why don't you let me take care of him.' His eyes were earnest on mine.

'I'll handle it,' I said. 'But thank you.'

'Dr Scarpetta, don't put yourself through it, you know? I wasn't here the week he came in. I never met him.'

'It's okay, Jack.' I walked away.

This was not the first time I had autopsied a person I knew, and most police and even the other doctors did not always understand. They argued that the findings were more objective if someone else did the case, and this simply wasn't true as long as there were witnesses. Certainly, I had not known Danny intimately or for long, but he had worked for me, and in a way had died for me. I would give him the best that I had.

He was on a gurney parked next to table one, where I usually did my cases, and the sight of him this morning was worse and hit me with staggering force. He was cold and in full rigor, as if what had been human in him had given up during the night, after I had left him. Dried blood smeared his face, and his lips were parted as if he had tried to speak when life had fled from him. His eyes stared the slitted dull stare of the dead, and I saw his red brace and remembered him mopping the floor. I remembered his cheerfulness, and the sad look on his face when he talked about Ted Eddings and other young people suddenly gone.

'Jack.' I motioned for Fielding.

He almost trotted to my side. 'Yes, ma'am,' he said.

'I'm going to take you up on your offer.' I began labeling test tubes on a surgical cart. 'I could use your help if you're sure you're up to it.'

'What do you want me to do?'

'We'll do him together.'

'Not a problem. You want me to scribe?'

'Let's photograph him as he is but let's cover the table with a sheet first,' I said.

Danny's case number was ME–3096, which meant he was the thirtieth case of the new year in the central district of Virginia. After hours of refrigeration he was not cooperative, and when we lifted him onto the table, arms and legs loudly banged against stainless steel as if protesting what we were about to do. We removed dirty, bloody clothing. Arms resisted coming out of sleeves, and tight-fitting jeans were stubborn. I dipped my hands in pockets, and came up with twenty-seven cents in change, a Chap Stick and a ring of keys.

'That's weird,' I said as we folded garments and placed them on top of the gurney covered by a disposable sheet. 'What happened to my car key?'

'Was it one of those remote-control ones?'

'Right.' Velcro ripped as I removed the knee brace.

'And obviously, it wasn't anywhere at the scene.'

'We didn't find it. And since it wasn't in the ignition, I assumed Danny would have had it.' I was pulling off thick athletic socks.

'Well, I guess the killer could have taken it, or it could have gotten lost.'

I thought of the helicopter making a bigger mess, and I had heard that Marino had been on the news. He was shaking his fist and yelling for all the world to see, and I was there, too.

'Okay, he's got tattoos.' Fielding picked up the clipboard.

Danny had a pair of dice inked into the top of his feet.

'Snake eyes,' Fielding said. 'Ouch, that must have hurt.'

I found a faint scar from an appendectomy, and another old one on Danny's left knee that may have come from an accident when he was a child. On his right knee, scars from recent arthroscopic surgery were purple, the muscles in that leg showing minimal atrophy. I collected samples of his fingernails and hair, and at a glance saw nothing indicative of a struggle. I saw no reason to assume he had resisted whomever he had encountered outside the Hill Cafe when he had dropped his bag of leftovers.

'Let's turn him,' I said.

Fielding held the legs while I gripped my hands under the arms. We got him on his belly and I used a lens and a strong light to examine the back of his head. Long dark hair was tangled with clotted blood and debris, and I palpated the scalp some more.

'I need to shave this here so I can be sure. But it looks like we've got a contact gunshot wound behind his right ear. Where are his films?'

'They should be ready.' Fielding looked around.

'We need to reconstruct this.'

'Shit.' He helped me hold together what was a profound stellate wound that looked more like an exit, because it was so huge.

'It's definitely an entrance,' I said as I used a scalpel blade to carefully shave that part of the scalp. 'See, we've got a faint muzzle mark up here. Very faint. Right there.' I traced it with a gloved bloody finger. 'This is very destructive. Almost like a rifle.'

'Forty-five?'

'A half-inch hole,' I said almost to myself as I used a ruler. 'Yes, that's definitely consistent with a forty-five.'

I was removing the skull cap in pieces to look at the brain when the autopsy technician appeared and slapped films on a nearby light box. The bright white shape of the bullet was lodged in the frontal sinus, three inches from the top of the head.

'My God,' I muttered as I stared at it.

'What the hell is that?' Fielding asked as both of us left the table to get closer.

The deformed bullet was big with sharp petals folded back like a claw.

'Hydra-Shok doesn't do that,' my deputy chief said.

'No, it does not. This is some kind of special high-performance ammo.'

'Maybe Starfire or Golden Sabre?'

'Like that, yes,' I answered, and I had never seen this ammunition in the morgue. 'But I'm thinking Black Talon because the cartridge case recovered isn't PMC or Remington. It's Winchester. And Winchester made Black Talon until it was taken off the market.'

'Winchester makes Silvertip.'

'This is definitely not Silvertip,' I replied. 'You ever seen a Black Talon?'

'Only in magazines.'

'Black-coated, brass-jacketed with a notched hollow point that blossoms like this. See the points.' I showed him on the film. 'Unbelievably destructive. It goes through you like a buzz saw. Great for law enforcement but a nightmare if in the wrong hands.'

'Jesus,' Fielding said, amazed. 'It looks like a damn octopus.'

I pulled off latex gloves and replaced them with ones made of a tightly woven cloth, for ammunition like Black Talon was dangerous in the ER and the morgue. It was a bigger threat than a needle stick, and I did not know if Danny had hepatitis or AIDS. I did not want to cut myself on the jagged metal that had killed him so his assailant could end up taking two lives instead of one.

Fielding put on a pair of blue Nitrile gloves, which were sturdier than latex, but not good enough.

'You can wear those for scribing,' I said. 'But that's it.'

'That bad?'

'Yes,' I said, plugging in the autopsy saw. 'You wear those and handle this and you're going to get cut.'

'This doesn't seem like a carjacking. This seems like someone who was very serious.'

'Believe me,' I raised my voice above the loud whine of the saw, 'it doesn't get any more serious than this.'

The story told by what lay beneath the scalp only got worse. The bullet had shattered the temporal, occipital, parietal and frontal bones of the skull. In fact, had it not lost its energy fragmenting the thick petrous ridge, the twisted claw would have exited, and we would have lost what was a very important piece of evidence. As for the brain, what the Black Talon had done to it was awful. The explosion of gas and shredding caused by copper and lead had plowed a terrible path through the miraculous matter that had made Danny who he was. I rinsed the bullet, then cleaned it thoroughly in a weak solution of Clorox, because body fluids can be infectious and are notorious for oxidizing metal evidence.

At almost noon, I double-bagged it in plastic envelopes and carried it upstairs to the firearms lab, where weapons of every sort were tagged and deposited on countertops, or wrapped in brown paper bags. There were knives to be examined for tool marks, submachine guns and even a sword. Henry Frost, who was new to Richmond but well known in his field, was staring into a computer screen.

'Has Marino been up here?' I asked him as I walked in.

Frost looked up, hazel eyes focusing, as if he had just arrived from some distant place where I had never been. 'About two hours ago.' He tapped several keys.

'Then he gave you the cartridge case.' I moved beside his chair.

'I'm working on it now,' he said. 'The word is, this case is a number-one priority.'

Frost, I guessed, was about my age and had been divorced at least twice. He was attractive and athletic, with well-proportioned features and short black hair. According to the typical legends people always claimed about their peers, he ran marathons, was an expert in white-water rafting, and could shoot a fly off an elephant at a hundred paces. What I did know from personal observation was that he loved his trade better than any woman, and there was nothing he would rather talk about than guns.

'You've entered the forty-five?' I asked him.

'We don't know for a fact it's connected to the crime, do we?' He glanced at me.

'No,' I said. 'We don't know for a fact.' I spotted a chair with wheels close by and pulled it over. 'The cartridge case was found about ten feet from where we believe he was shot. In the woods. It's clean. It looks new. And I've got this.' I dipped into a pocket of my lab coat and withdrew the envelope containing the Black Talon bullet.

'Wow,' he said.

'Consistent with a Winchester forty-five?'

'Man alive. There is always a first time.' He opened the envelope and was suddenly excited. 'I'll measure lands and grooves and tell you in a minute whether it's a forty-five.'

He moved before the comparison microscope and used the Air Gap method to fix the bullet to the stage, which meant he used wax so he didn't leave any marks on metal that weren't already there.

'Okay,' he talked without looking up, 'the rifling is to the left, and we've got six lands and grooves.' He began measuring with micrometer jaws. 'Land impressions are point oh-seven-four. Groove impressions are point one-five-three. I'm going to enter that into the GRC,' he said, referring to the FBI's computerized General Rifling Characteristics. 'Now let's determine the caliber,' he spoke abstractedly as he typed.

While the computer raced through its databases, Frost checked the bullet with a vernier measuring device. Unsurprisingly, what he found was that the caliber of the Black Talon was .45, and then the GRC came back with a list of twelve brands of firearms that could have fired it. All, except Sig Sauer and several Colts, were military pistols.

'What about the cartridge case?' I said. 'Do we know anything about it?'

'I've got it on live video but I haven't run it yet.'

He returned to the chair where I had found him when I had first come in and began typing on a workstation connected by modem to an FBI firearms evidence imaging system called DRUGFIRE. The application was part of the massive Crime Analysis Information Network known as CAIN, which Lucy had developed, and the point was to link firearms-related crimes. Succinctly put, I wanted to know if the gun that had killed Danny might have killed or maimed before, especially since the type of ammunition hinted that the assailant was no novice.

The workstation was simple, with its 486 turbo PC connected to a video camera and comparison microscope that made it possible to capture images in real time and in color on a twenty-inch screen. Frost went into another menu and the video display was suddenly filled with a checkerboard of silvery disks representing other .45 cartridge cases, each with unique impressions. The breech face of the

Winchester .45 connected to my case was on the top left-hand side, and I could see every mark made by breech block, firing pin, ejector or any other metal part of the gun that had fired the round into Danny's head.

'Yours had a big drag to the left.' Frost showed me what looked like a tail coming out of the circular dent left by the firing pin. 'And there's this other mark here, also to the left.' He touched the screen with his finger.

'Ejector?' I said.

'Nope, I'd say that's from the firing pin bouncing back.'

'Unusual?'

'Well, I'd just say it's unique to this weapon,' he replied as he stared. 'So we can run this if you want.'

'Let's.'

He pulled up another screen and entered the information he had, such as the hemispherical shape the firing pin had impressed in the soft metal of the primer, and the direction of twist and parallel striation of the microscopic characteristics of the breech face. We did not enter anything about the bullet I had recovered from Danny's brain, for we could not prove that the Black Talon and the cartridge case were related, no matter how much we might suspect it. The examination of those two items of evidence was really unrelated, for lands and grooves and firing pin impressions are as different as fingerprints and footwear. All one can hope is that the stories the witnesses tell are the same.

Amazingly, in this case they were. When Frost executed his search, we had to wait only a minute or two before DRUGFIRE let us know that it had several candidates that might match the small, nickel-plated cylinder found ten feet from Danny's blood.

'Let's see what we've got here.' Frost talked to himself as he positioned the top of the list on his screen. 'This is your front runner.' He dragged his finger across the glass. 'No contest. This one's way ahead of the pack.'

'A Sig forty-five P220,' I said, looking at him in astonishment. 'The cartridge case is matching with a weapon versus another cartridge case?'

'Yes. Damn if it isn't. Je-sus Christ.'

'Let me make sure I understand this.' I could not believe what I was seeing. 'You wouldn't have the characteristics of a firearm entered into DRUGFIRE unless that firearm had been turned into a lab. By the police, for some reason.'

'That's how it's done,' Frost agreed as he began to print screens. 'This Sig forty-five that's in the computer is coming up as the same one that fired the cartridge found near Danny Webster's body. That much we know right this second. What I've got to do is pull the actual cartridge case from the test fire done when we originally got the gun.' He stood.

I did not move as I continued staring at the list in DRUGFIRE with its symbols and abbreviations that told us about this pistol. It left recoil and drag marks, or its fingerprints, on the cartridge cases of every round it spent. I thought of Ted Eddings's stiff body in the cold waters of the Elizabeth River. I thought of Danny dead near a tunnel that no longer led anywhere.

'Then this gun somehow got back out on the street,' I said.

Frost pursed his lips as he opened file drawers. 'It would appear that way. But I really don't know the details of why it was entered into the system to begin with.' Still rooting around, he added, 'I believe the police department that originally turned the weapon in to us was Henrico County. Let's see, where's CVA5471? We are seriously running out of room in this place.'

'This was submitted last fall.' I noted the date on the computer screen. 'September twenty-ninth.'

'Right. That should be the date the form was completed.'

'Do you know why the police turned the gun in?'

'You'd have to call them,' Frost said.

'Let's get Marino on it now.'

'Good idea.'

I called Marino's pager as Frost pulled a file folder. Inside was the usual clear plastic envelope that we used to store the thousands of cartridge cases and shotgun shells that came through Virginia's labs every year.

'Here we go,' he said.

'You have any Sig P220s in here?' I got up, too.

'One. It should be on the rack with the other forty-five auto loads.'

While he mounted his test-fire cartridge case on the microscope's stage, I walked into a room that was either a nightmare or a toy store, depending on your point of view. Walls were pegboards crowded with pistols, revolvers, and Tec-11s and Tec-9s. It was depressing to think how many deaths were represented by the weapons in this one cramped room, and how many of the cases had been mine. The Sig Sauer P220 was black, and looked so much like the nine-millimeter carried by Richmond police that at a glance I could not have told them apart. Of course, on close inspection, the .45 was somewhat bigger, and I suspected its muzzle mark might be different, too.

'Where's the ink pad?' I asked Frost as he leaned over the microscope, lining up both cartridge cases so he could physically compare them side by side.

'In my top desk drawer,' he said as the telephone rang. 'Towards the back.'

I got out the small tin of fingerprint ink and unfolded a snowy clean cotton twill cloth, which I placed on a thin, soft plastic pad. Frost picked up the phone.

'Hey, Bud. We got a hit on DRUGFIRE,' he said, and I knew he was talking to Marino. 'Can you run something down?'

He proceeded to tell Marino what he knew. Then Frost said to me as he hung up, 'He's going to check with Henrico even as we speak.'

'Good,' I abstractedly said as I pressed the pistol's barrel into the ink, and then onto the cloth.

'These are definitely distinctive,' I said right off as I studied several blackened muzzle marks that clearly showed the combat pistol's front sight blade, recoil guide and shape of the slide.

'You think we could identify that specific type of pistol?' he asked, and he was peering into the microscope again.

'On a contact wound, theoretically, we could,' I said. 'The obvious problem is that a forty-five loaded with high-performance ammunition is so incredibly destructive, you aren't likely to find a good pattern, not on the head.'

This had been true in Danny's case, even after I had conjured up my plastic surgery skills to reconstruct the entrance wound as best I could. But as I compared the cloth to diagrams and photographs I had made downstairs in the morgue, I found nothing inconsistent with a Sig P220 being the murder weapon. In fact, I thought I might have matched a sight mark protruding from the margin of the entrance.

'This is our confirmation,' Frost said, adjusting the focus as he continued staring into the comparison microscope.

We both turned at the sound of someone running down the hall.

'You want to see?' he asked.

'Yes, I do,' I said as yet another person ran past, keys jingling madly from a belt.

'What the hell?' Frost got up, frowning toward the door.

Voices had gotten louder outside in the hall, and now people were hurrying by, but going the other way. Frost and I stepped outside the lab at the same moment several security guards rushed past, heading for their station. Scientists in lab coats stood in doorways casting about. Everyone was asking everyone else what was going on, when suddenly the fire alarm hammered overhead and red lights in the ceiling flashed.

'What the hell is this, a fire drill?' Frost yelled.

'There isn't one scheduled.' I held my hands over my ears as people ran.

'Does that mean there's a fire?' He looked stunned.

I glanced up at sprinkler heads in the ceilings, and said, 'We've got to get out of here.'

I ran downstairs and had just pushed through doors into the hall on my floor when a violent white storm of cool halon gas blasted from the ceiling. It sounded as if I were surrounded by huge cymbals being beaten madly with a million sticks as I dashed in and out of rooms. Fielding was gone, and every other office I checked had been evacuated so fast that drawers were left open, and slide displays and microscopes were on. Cool clouds rolled over me, and I had the surreal sensation I was flying through a hurricane in the middle of an air raid. I dashed into the library, the restrooms, and when I was satisfied that everyone was safely out, I ran down the hall and pushed my way out of the front doors. For a moment, I stood to catch my breath and let my heart slow down.

The procedure for alarms and drills was as rigidly structured as most routines in the state. I knew I would find my staff gathered on the second floor of the Monroe Tower parking deck across Franklin Street. By now, all Consolidated Lab employees should be in their designated spots, except for section chiefs and agency heads, and of those, it seemed, I was the last to leave, except for the director of general services, who was in charge of my building. He was briskly crossing the street in front of me, a hard hat tucked under his arm. When I called out to him, he turned around and squinted as if he did not know me at all.

'What in God's name is going on?' I asked as I caught up with him and we crossed to the sidewalk.

'What's going on is you better not have requested anything extra in your budget this year.' He was an old man who was always well dressed and unpleasant. Today he was in a rage.

I stared at the building and saw no smoke as fire trucks screamed and blared several streets away.

'Some jackass tripped the damn deluge system, which doesn't stop until all the chemicals are dumped.' He glared at me as if I were to blame. 'I had the damn thing set on a delay to prevent this very thing.'

'Which wasn't going to help if there was a chemical fire or explosion in a lab,' I couldn't resist pointing out, because most of his decisions were about this bad. 'You don't want a thirty-second delay when something like that happens.'

'Well, something like that didn't happen. Do you have any idea how much this is going to cost?'

I thought of the paperwork on my desk and other important items flung far and wide and possibly damaged. 'Why would anyone trip the system?' I asked.

'Look, at the moment I'm about as informed as you are.'

'But thousands of gallons of chemicals have been dumped over all of my offices, and the morgue and the anatomical division.' We climbed stairs, my frustration becoming harder to contain.

'You won't know it was even there.' He rudely waved off the remark. 'It disappears like a vapor.'

'It's sprayed all over bodies we are autopsying, including several homicides. Let's hope a defense attorney never brings that up in court.'

'What you'd better hope is that somehow we can pay for this. To refill those halon tanks, we're talking several hundred thousand dollars. That's what ought to make you stay awake at night.'

The second level of the parking deck was crowded with hundreds of state employees on an unexpected break. Ordinarily, drills and false alarms were an invitation to play, and people were in good moods as long as the weather was nice. But no one was relaxed this day. It was cold and gray, and people were talking in excited voices. The director abruptly walked off to speak to one of his henchmen, and I began to look around. I had just spotted my staff when I felt a hand on my arm.

'Geez, what's the matter?' Marino asked when I jumped. 'You got post-traumatic stress syndrome?'

'I'm sure I do,' I said. 'Were you in the building?'

'Nope, but not far away. I heard about your full fire alarm on the radio and thought I'd check it out.'

He hitched up his police belt with all its heavy gear, his eyes roaming the crowd. 'You mind telling me what the hell's going on? You finally have a case of spontaneous combustion?'

'I don't know exactly what's going on. But what I've been told is that someone apparently tripped a false alarm that set off the deluge system throughout the entire building. Why are you here?'

'I see Fielding way over there.' Marino nodded. 'And Rose. They're all together. You look cold as shit.'

'You were just in the area?' I asked, because when he was evasive, I knew something was up.

'I could hear the damn alarm all the way on Broad Street,' he said.

As if on cue, the awful clanging across the street suddenly stopped. I stepped closer to the parking deck wall and looked over the top of it as I worried more about what I would find when all of us were allowed to return to the building. Fire trucks rumbled loudly in parking lots, and firefighters in protective gear were entering through several different doors.

'When I saw what was going on,' he added, 'I figured you'd be up here. So I thought I'd check on you.'

'You figured right,' I said, and my fingernails had turned blue. 'You know anything about this Henrico case, the forty-five cartridge case that seems to have been fired by the same Sig P220 that killed Danny?' I asked as I continued to lean against the cold concrete wall and stare out at the city.

'What makes you think I'd find anything out that fast?'

'Because everybody's scared of you.'

'Yeah, well they sure as hell should be.'

Marino moved closer to me. He leaned against the wall, only facing the other way, for he did not like having his back to people, and this had nothing to do with manners. He adjusted his belt again and crossed his arms at his chest. He avoided my eyes, and I could tell he was angry.

'On December eleventh,' he said, 'Henrico had a traffic stop at 64 and Mechanicsville Turnpike. As the Henrico officer approached the car, the subject got out and ran, and the officer pursued on foot. This was at night.' He got out his cigarettes. 'The foot pursuit crossed the county line into the city, eventually ending in Whitcomb Court.' He fired his lighter. 'No one's real sure what happened, but at some point during all this, the officer lost his gun.'

It took a moment for me to remember that several years ago the Henrico County Police Department had switched from nine-millimeters to Sig Sauer P220 .45 caliber pistols.

'And that's the pistol in question?' I uneasily asked.

'Yup.' He inhaled smoke. 'You see, Henrico's got this policy. Every Sig gets entered into DRUGFIRE in the event this very thing happens.'

'I didn't know that.'

'Right. Cops lose their guns and have them stolen like anybody else. So it's not a bad thing to track them after they're gone, in case they're used in the commission of crimes.'

'Then the gun that killed Danny is the one this Henrico officer lost,' I wanted to make sure.

'It would appear that way.'

'It was lost in the projects about a month ago,' I went on. 'And now it's been used for murder. It was used on Danny.'

Marino turned toward me, flicking an ash. 'At least it wasn't you in the car outside the Hill Cafe.'

There was nothing I could say.

'That area of town ain't exactly far from Whitcomb Court and other bad neighborhoods,' he said. 'So we could be talking about a carjacking, after all.'

'No.' I still would not accept that. 'My car wasn't taken.'

'Something could have happened to make the squirrel change his mind,' he said.

I did not respond.

'It could have been anything. A neighbor turns a light on. A siren sounds somewhere. Someone's burglar alarm accidentally goes off. Maybe he got spooked after shooting Danny and didn't finish what he started.'

'He didn't have to shoot him.' I watched traffic slowly rolling past on the street below. 'He could have just stolen my Mercedes outside the cafe. Why drive him off and walk him down the hill into the woods?' My voice got harder. 'Why do all of that for a car you don't end up taking?'

'Things happen,' he said again. 'I don't know.'

'What about the tow lot in Virginia Beach,' I said. 'Has anybody checked with them?'

'Danny picked up your ride around three-thirty, which is the time they told you it would be ready.'

'What do you mean, the time they told me?'

'The time they told you when you called.'

I looked at him and said, 'I never called.'

He flicked an ash. 'They said you did.'

'No.' I shook my head. 'Danny called. That was his job. He dealt with them and my office's answering service.'

'Well, someone who claimed to be Dr Scarpetta called. Maybe Lucy?'

'I seriously doubt she would say she was me. Was this person who called a woman?'

He hesitated. 'Good question. But you probably should ask Lucy, just to make sure she didn't call.'

Firefighters were emerging from the building, and I knew that soon we would be allowed to return to our offices. We would spend the rest of the day checking everything, speculating and complaining as we hoped that no more cases came in.

'The ammo's the thing that's really eating at me,' Marino then said.

'Frost should be back in his lab within the hour,' I said, but Marino did not seem to care.

'I'll call him. I'm not going up there in all this mess.'

I could tell he did not want to leave me and his mind was on more than this case.

'Something's troubling you,' I said.

'Yeah, Doc. Something always is.'

'What this time?'

He got out his pack of Marlboros again, and I thought of my mother, whose constant companion now was an oxygen tank, because she once had been as bad as him.

'Don't look at me like that,' he warned as he fished for his lighter again.

'I don't want you to kill yourself. And today you seem to be really trying.'

'We're all going to die.'

'Attention,' blared a fire truck's P.A. system. 'This is the Richmond Fire Department. The emergency has ended. You may reenter the building,' sounded the mechanical broadcast with its jarring repetitive beeps and monotonous tones. 'Attention. The emergency has ended. You may reenter the building . . .'

'Me,' Marino went on, unmindful of the commotion, 'I want to croak while I'm drinking beer, eating nachos with chili and sour cream, smoking, downing shots of Jack Black and watching the game.'

'You may as well have sex while you're at it.' I did not smile, for I found nothing amusing about his health risks.

'Doris cured me of sex.' Marino was serious, too, as he referred to the woman he had been married to most of his life.

'When did you hear from her last?' I asked, as I realized she was probably the explanation for his mood.

He moved away from the wall and smoothed back his thinning

hair. He tugged at his belt again, as if he hated the accoutrements of his profession and the layers of fat that had rudely inserted themselves into his life. I had seen photographs of him when he was a New York cop astride a motorcycle or horse, when he had been powerful and lean, with thick dark hair and tall leather boots. There had been a day when Doris must have found Pete Marino handsome.

'Last night. You know, she calls now and then. Mostly to talk about Rocky,' he said of their son.

Marino was scanning state employees as they began to make their way toward the stairs. He stretched his fingers and arms, then took in a large volume of air. He rubbed the back of his neck as people exited the parking deck, most of them cold and cranky and trying to salvage what a false alarm had done to their day.

'What does she want from you?' I felt compelled to ask.

He looked around some more. 'Well, it seems she's gotten married,' he said. 'That's the headline of the day.'

I was quite taken aback. 'Marino,' I quietly said. 'I'm so sorry.'

'Her and the drone with the big car with leather seats. Don't you love it? One minute she leaves. Then she wants me back. Then Molly quits dating me. Then Doris gets married, just like that.'

'I'm sorry,' I said again.

'You better get back inside before you catch pneumonia,' he said. 'I got to get back to the precinct and call Wesley about what's going on. He's going to want to know about the gun, and to be honest with you' – he glanced over at me as we walked – 'I know what the Bureau's going to say.'

'They're going to say that Danny's death is random,' I said.

'And I'm not so sure that ain't exactly right. It's looking more like Danny might have been trying to score a little crack or something and ran into the wrong guy who happened to have found a policeman's gun.'

'I still don't believe that,' I said.

We crossed Franklin Street, and I looked down it to the north, where the imposing old Gothic red brick train station with its clock tower blocked my view of Church Hill. Danny had strayed very little from the area where he was supposed to have been last night when he was to deliver my car. I had found nothing that might hint he intended to do drugs. I had found no physical indication that he used drugs, for that matter. Of course, his toxicology reports were not in, yet, although I did know he had not been drinking.

'By the way,' Marino said as he unlocked his Ford. 'I stopped by the substation at Seventh and Duval, and you should get your Mercedes back this afternoon.'

'They've already processed it?'

'Oh yeah. We did that last night and had everything in by the time the labs opened this morning 'cause I've made it clear we ain't shitting around with this case. Everything else moves to the back of the line.'

'What did you find?' I asked, and the thought of my car and what had happened inside it was almost more than I could stand.

'Prints, we don't know whose. We got vacuumings. That's really it.' He climbed in and left the door open. 'Anyway, I'll make sure it's here so you have a way home.'

I thanked him, but as I walked inside my building, I knew I could not drive that car. I knew I could not drive it ever. I did not believe I could even unlock its doors or sit inside it again.

Cleta was mopping the lobby while the receptionist wiped down furniture with towels, and I tried explaining to them that this wasn't necessary. The point of an inert gas like halon, I patiently said, was that it did not damage paper or sensitive instruments.

'It evaporates and doesn't leave a residue,' I promised. 'You don't have to clean up. But paintings on the walls will need to be straightened, and it looks like Megan's desk is a terrible mess.'

In the receptionist's area, requests for anatomical donations and a variety of other forms were scattered all over the floor.

'I still think some of it smells funny,' Megan said.

'Yeah, magazines, that's what you smell, you goofball,' said Cleta. 'They always have a funny smell.' She asked me, 'What about the computers?'

'They shouldn't be affected in the least,' I said. 'What worries me more are the floors that you're getting wet. Let's go ahead and dry them off so nobody slips.'

With a growing sense of hopelessness, I carefully walked over slippery tile while they mopped and wiped. As my office came in sight, I braced myself, then stopped inside my doorway. My secretary was already at work inside.

'Okay,' I said to Rose. 'How bad is it?'

'Not a problem except some of your paperwork's blown to Oz. I've already straightened out your plants.' She was an imperious woman old enough to retire, and she peered at me over reading glasses. 'You've always wanted to keep your in and out baskets empty, well, now they are.'

Wherever I looked, death certificates, call sheets and autopsy reports had blown about like autumn leaves. They were on the floor, in bookshelves and caught in the branches of my ficus tree.

'I also believe you shouldn't assume that just because you can't see something doesn't mean it's not a problem. So I think you ought to let this paperwork air out. I'm going to rig up a clothesline here with paper clips.' She talked as she worked, and gray hair strayed from her French twist.

'I don't think we're going to need anything like that,' I started the same old speech again. 'Halon disappears when it dries.'

'I noticed you never got your hard hat off the shelf.'

'I didn't have time,' I said.

'Too bad we don't have windows.' Rose said this at least once a week.

'Really, all we need to do is pick things up,' I said. 'You're paranoid, every last one of you.'

'You ever been gassed by this stuff before?'

'No,' I said.

'Uh-huh,' she said as she set a stack of towels nearby. 'Then we can't be too careful.'

I sat at my desk and opened the top drawer, where I pulled out several boxes of paper clips. Despair fluttered in my breast and I feared I would dissolve right there. My secretary knew me better than my mother, and she caught my every expression, but she did not stop working.

After a long silence, she said, 'Dr Scarpetta, why don't you go home? I'll take care of this.'

'Rose, we will take care of this together,' I stubbornly replied.

'I can't believe that stupid security guard.'

'What security guard?' I stopped what I was doing and looked at her.

'The one who set off the system because he thought we were going to have some sort of radioactive meltdown upstairs.'

I stared at her as she lifted a death certificate from the carpet. With paper clips, she hung it from the twine while I continued to rearrange the top of my desk.

'What in the world are you talking about?' I asked.

'That's all I know. They were discussing it on the parking deck.' She pressed the small of her back and looked around. 'I can't get over how fast this stuff dries. It's like something out of a science fiction movie.' She hung another death certificate. 'I think this is going to work out just fine.'

I did not comment as I thought again of my car. I was honestly terrified of seeing it, and I covered my face with my hands. Rose did not quite know what to do because she had never seen me cry.

'Can I get you some coffee?' she asked.

I shook my head.

'This is like a big windstorm blew through. Tomorrow it will be like it never happened.' She tried to make me feel better.

I was grateful when I heard her leave. She quietly shut both of my doors, and I leaned back in my chair and was spent. I picked up the phone and tried Marino's number, but he was not in, so I looked up McGeorge Mercedes and hoped that Walter wasn't off somewhere.

He wasn't.

'Walter? It's Dr Scarpetta,' I said with no preamble. 'Can you please come get my car?' I faltered, 'I guess I need to explain.'

'No explanation necessary. How much was it damaged?' he asked, and he clearly had been following the news.

'For me it's totaled,' I said. 'For someone else, it's as good as new.'

'I understand and I don't blame you,' he said. 'What do you want to do?'

'Can you trade it for something right now?'

'I got almost the identical car. But it's used.'

'How used?'

'Barely. It belonged to my wife. An S-500, black with saddle interior.'

'Can you have someone drive it to my parking space in back and we'll swap?'

'My dear, I'm on the way.'

He arrived at half past five, when it was already dark out, which was a good time for a salesman to show a used car to someone as desperate as me. But, in truth, I had dealt with Walter for years and really would have bought the car sight unseen because I trusted him that much. He was a very distinguished-looking man with an immaculate mustache and close-cropped hair. He dressed better than most lawyers I knew, and wore a gold Medic Alert bracelet because he was allergic to bees.

'I'm really sorry about all this,' he said as I cleaned out my trunk.

'I'm sorry about it, too.' I made no attempt at being friendly or hiding my mood. 'Here is one key. Consider the other one lost. And what I'd like to do, if you don't mind, is to drive off this minute. I don't want to see you get into my car. I just want to leave. We'll worry about the radio equipment later.'

'I understand. We'll get into the details another time.'

I did not care about them at all. At the moment I was not interested in the cost-effectiveness of what I had just done, or if it was true that the condition of this car was as good as the one I had traded away. I could have been driving a cement truck and that would have been fine. Pushing a button on the console, I locked the doors and tucked my pistol between the seats.

I drove south on Fourteenth Street and turned off on Canal toward the interstate I usually took home, and several exits later I got off and turned around. I wanted to follow the route I suspected Danny had taken last night, and if he were coming from Norfolk he would have taken 64 West. The easiest exit for him would have been the one for the Medical College of Virginia, for this would have brought him almost to the OCME. But I did not think this was what he had done.

By the time he reached Richmond, he would have been thinking about food, and there was nothing much to interest him close to my office. Danny obviously would have known that since he had spent time with us before. I suspected he had exited at Fifth Street, as I was doing now, and had followed it to Broad. It was very dark as I passed construction and empty lots that would soon be Virginia's Biomedical Research Park, where my division would be moved one day.

Several police cruisers quietly floated past, and I stopped behind one of them at a traffic light next to the Marriott. I watched the officer ahead as he turned on an interior light and wrote something on a metal clipboard. He was very young with light blond hair, and he unhooked the microphone of his radio and began to speak. I could see his lips move as he gazed out at the dark shape of the mini-precinct on the corner. He got off the air and sipped from a 7-Eleven cup, and I knew he had not been a cop long, because he had not read his surroundings. He did not seem aware that he was being watched.

I moved on and turned left on Broad, past a Rite Aid and the old Miller & Rhoads department store that had permanently closed its doors as fewer people shopped downtown. The old city hall was a granite Gothic fortress on one side of the street, and then on the other was the campus of MCV, which may have been familiar to me, but not to Danny. I doubted he would have known about The Skull & Bones, where medical staff and students ate. I doubted he would have known where to park my car around here.

I believed he had done what anyone would do if he were relatively unfamiliar with a city and driving his boss's expensive car. He would have driven straight and stopped at the first decent place he found. That, quite literally, was the Hill Cafe. I circled the block, as he had to have done to park southbound, where we had found his bag of leftovers. Pulling over beneath that magnificent magnolia tree, I got out as I slid the pistol into a pocket of my coat. Instantly, the barking behind the chain-link fence began again. The dog sounded big and as if we had a history that had filled him with hate. Lights went on in the upstairs of his owner's small home.

Crossing the street, I entered the cafe, which was typically busy and loud. Daigo was mixing whiskey sours and did not notice me until I was pulling out a chair at the bar.

'You look like you need something strong tonight, honey,' she said, dropping an orange slice and a cherry into each glass.

'I do but I'm working,' I said, and the dog's barking had stopped.

'That's the problem with you and the Captain, both. You're always working.' She caught a waiter's eye.

He came over and got the drinks, and Daigo started on the next order.

'Are you aware of the dog directly across the street from you? Across Twenty-eighth Street?' I asked in a quiet voice.

'You must mean Outlaw. Least that's what I call that son of a bitch dog. You have any idea how many customers that mangy thing's scared off from here?' She glanced at me as she angrily sliced a lime. 'You know he's half shepherd and half wolf,' she went on before I could reply. 'He bother you or something?'

'It's just that his barking is very fierce and loud, and I'm wondering if he might have barked after Danny Webster left here last night. Especially since we are suspicious he was parked under the magnolia tree, which is in the dog's yard.'

'Well, that damn dog barks all the time.'

'Then you don't remember, not that I would expect you—'

She cut me off as she read an order and popped open a beer, 'Course I remember. Like I said, he barks all the time. Wasn't no different with that poor boy. Outlaw barked up a storm when he went out. That damn dog barks at the wind.'

'What about before Danny went out?' I asked.

She paused to think, then her eyes lit up. 'Well, now that you mention it, it seems like the barking was pretty constant early in the evening. In fact, I made a comment about it, said it was driving me crazy and I had half a mind to call the damn thing's owner.'

'What about other customers?' I asked. 'Did many other people come in while Danny was in here?'

'No.' Of that she was sure. 'First of all, he came in early. Other than the usual barflies, there was no one here when he arrived. Fact is, I don't remember anybody coming in to eat until at least seven. And by then he'd already left.'

'And how long did the dog bark after he left?'

'On and off the rest of the night, like he always does.'

'On and off but not solidly.'

'No one would take that all night. Not solidly.' She eyed me shrewdly. 'Now if you're wondering if that dog was barking because somebody was out there waiting for that boy' – she pointed her knife at me – 'I don't think so. The kind of riffraff that would show up here is going to run like hell when that dog starts in. That's why they have him. Those people over there.' She pointed with her knife again.

I thought again of the stolen Sig used to shoot Danny, and of where the officer had lost it, and I knew exactly what Daigo meant. The average street criminal would be afraid of a big, loud dog and the attention its barking might bring. I thanked her and walked back outside. For a moment I stood on the sidewalk and surveyed smudges of gas lamps set far apart along narrow, dark streets. Spaces between buildings and homes were thick with shadows, and anyone could wait in them and not be seen.

I looked across at my new car, and the small yard beyond it where the dog lay in wait. He was silent just now, and I walked north on the sidewalk for several yards to see what he might do. But he did not seem interested until I neared his yard. Then I heard the low, evil growling that raised the hair on the back of my neck. By the time I was unlocking my car door, he was on his hind legs, barking and shaking the fence.

'You're just guarding your turf, aren't you, boy?' I said. 'I wish you could tell me what you saw last night.'

I looked at the small house as an upstairs window suddenly slid up.

'Bozo, shut up!' yelled a fat man with tousled hair. 'Shut up, you stupid mutt!' The window slammed shut.

'All right, Bozo,' I said to the dog who was not really called Outlaw, unfortunately for him. 'I'm leaving you alone now.' I looked around one last time and got into my car.

The drive from Daigo's restaurant to the restored area on Franklin where police had found my former car took less than three minutes if one were driving the posted speed. I turned around at the hill leading to Sugar Bottom, for to drive down there, especially in a Mercedes, was out of the question. That thought led to another.

I wondered why the assailant would have chosen to remain on foot in a restored area with a Neighborhood Watch program as widely publicized as the one here. Church Hill published its own newsletter, and residents looked out their windows and did not hesitate to call the cops, especially after shots had been fired. It seemed it might have been safer to have casually returned to my car and driven a safe distance away.

Yet the killer did not do this, and I wondered if he knew this area's landmarks but not the culture because he really was not from here. I wondered if he had not taken my car because his own was parked nearby and mine was of no interest. He didn't need it for money or to get away. That theory made sense if Danny had been followed instead of happened upon. While he was eating dinner, his assailant could have parked, then returned to the cafe on foot and waited in the dark near the Mercedes while the dog barked.

I was passing my building on Franklin when my pager vibrated against my side. I slipped it off and turned on its light so I could see. I had neither radio nor phone yet, and made a quick decision to turn into the OCME back parking lot. Letting myself in through a side door, I entered our security code, walked into the morgue and took the elevator upstairs. Traces of the day's false alarm had vanished, but Rose's death certificates suspended in air were an eerie display. Sitting behind my desk, I returned Marino's page.

'Where the hell are you?' he said right off.

'The office,' I said, staring up at the clock.

'Well, I think that's the last place you ought to be right now. And I bet you're alone. You eaten yet?'

'What do you mean, this is the last place I should be right now?'

'Let's meet and I'll explain.'

We agreed to go to the Linden Row Inn, which was downtown and private. I took my time because Marino lived on the other side of the river, but he was quick. When I arrived, he was sitting at a table before the fire in the parlor. Off duty, he was drinking a beer. The bartender was a quaint older man in a black bow tie, and he was carrying in a big bucket of ice while Pachelbel played.

'What is it?' I said to Marino as I sat. 'What's happened now?'

He was dressed in a black golf shirt, and his belly strained against the knitted fabric and flowed roundly over the waistband of his jeans.

The ashtray was already littered with cigarette butts, and I suspected the beer he was drinking wasn't his first or last.

'Would you like to hear the story of your false alarm this afternoon, or has someone gotten to you first?' He lifted the mug to his lips.

'No one has gotten to me about much of anything. Although I've heard a rumor about some radioactivity scare,' I said as the bartender appeared with fruit and cheese. 'Pellegrino with lemon, please,' I ordered.

'Apparently, it's more than a rumor,' Marino said.

'What?' I gave him a frown. 'And why would you know more about what's going on inside my building than I do?'

'Because this radioactive situation has to do with evidence in a city homicide case.' He took another swallow of beer. 'Danny Webster's homicide, to be exact.'

He allowed me a moment to grasp what he had just said, but my limits were unwilling to stretch.

'Are you implying that Danny's body was radioactive?' I asked as if he were crazy.

'No. But the debris we vacuumed from the inside of your car apparently is. And I'm telling you, the guys that did the processing are scared shitless, and I'm not happy about it either because I poked around inside your ride, too. That's one thing I got a big damn problem with like some people do with spiders and snakes. It's like these guys who got exposed to Agent Orange in Nam, and now they're dying of cancer.'

The expression on my face now was incredulous. 'You're talking about the front seat passenger's side of my black Mercedes?'

'Yeah, and if I were you, I wouldn't drive it anymore. How do you know that shit won't get to you over a long time?'

'I won't be driving that car anymore,' I said. 'Don't worry. But who told you the vacuumings were radioactive?'

'The lady who runs that SEM thing.'

'The scanning electron microscope.'

'Yeah. It picked up uranium, which set the Geiger counter off. Which I'm told has never happened before.'

'I'm sure it hasn't.'

'So next we have a panic on the part of security, which are right down the hall, as you know,' he went on. 'And this one guard makes the executive decision to evacuate the building. Only problem is, he forgets that when he breaks the glass on the little red box and yanks the handle, he's also going to set off the deluge system.'

'To my knowledge,' I said, 'it's never been used. I could see how someone might forget. In fact, he might not even have known about it.' I thought of the director of general services, and I knew what his attitude would be. 'Good God. All this happened because of my car. In a sense, because of me.'

'No, Doc.' Marino met my eyes and his face was hard. 'It all happened because some asshole killed Danny. How many times I got to tell you that?'

'I think I'd like a glass of wine.'

'Quit blaming yourself. I know what you're doing. I know how you get.'

I searched for the bartender, and the fire was beginning to feel too hot. Four people had sat nearby and they were talking loudly about the 'enchanted garden' in the Inn's courtyard where Edgar Allan Poe used to play when he was a boy in Richmond.

'He wrote about it in one of his poems,' a woman was saying.

'They say the crab cakes are good here.'

'I don't like it when you get like this,' Marino went on, leaning closer to me and pointing a finger. 'Next thing I know you're doing things on your own, and me? I don't sleep.'

The bartender saw me and made a quick detour in our direction. I changed my mind about Chardonnay and ordered Scotch as I took off my jacket and draped it over a chair. I was perspiring and uncomfortable in my skin.

'Give me one of your Marlboros,' I said to Marino.

His lips parted as he stared at me, shocked.

'Please.' I held out my hand.

'Oh no you don't.' He was adamant.

'I'll make a deal with you. I'll smoke one and you'll smoke one and then both of us will quit.'

He hesitated. 'You ain't serious.'

'The hell I'm not.'

'I don't see anything in it for me.'

'Except being alive. If it's not too late.'

'Thank you. But no deal.' Picking up his pack, he knocked out a cigarette for each of us, his lighter in hand.

'How long has it been?'

'I don't know. Maybe three years.' The cigarette tasted bland, but holding it with my lips felt wonderful, as if lips had been created for such a fit.

The first hit cut my lungs like a blade, and I was instantly light-headed. I felt as I had when I smoked my first Camel at the age of sixteen. Then nicotine enveloped my brain, just as it had back then, and the world spun more slowly and my thoughts coalesced.

'God, I have missed this,' I mourned as I tapped an ash.

'So don't nag me anymore.'

'Someone needs to.'

'Hey, it's not like it's marijuana or something.'

'I haven't smoked that. But if it wasn't illegal, maybe today I would.'

'Shit. Now you're beginning to scare me.'

I inhaled one last time and put the cigarette out while Marino watched me with a weird expression on his face. He always slightly panicked if I acted in a way he did not know.

'Listen.' I got down to business. 'I think Danny was followed last night, that his death isn't a random crime motivated by robbery, gay bashing or drugs. I think his killer waited for him, maybe as long as an hour, then confronted him as he returned to my car in the dark shadows near the magnolia tree on Twenty-eight Street. You know that dog, the one who lives right there? He barked the entire time Danny was inside the Hill Cafe, according to Daigo.'

Marino regarded me in silence for a moment. 'See, that's what I was just saying. You went there tonight.'

'Yes, I did.'

His jaw muscles bunched as he looked away. 'That's exactly what I mean.'

'Daigo remembers the dog barking nonstop.'

He said nothing.

'I was there earlier and the dog doesn't bark unless you get close to his property. Then he goes berserk. Do you understand what I'm saying?'

His eyes came back to me. 'Who's going to hang out there for an hour when a dog's acting like that? Come on, Doc.'

'Not your average killer,' I answered as my drink appeared. 'That's my point.'

I waited until the bartender served us, and after he was gone from our table I said, 'I think Danny may have been a professional hit.'

'Okay.' He drained his beer. 'Why? What the hell did that kid know? Unless he was into drugs or some type of organized crime.'

'What he was into was Tidewater,' I said. 'He lived there. He worked in my office there. He was at least peripherally involved in the Eddings case, and we know whoever killed Eddings was very sophisticated. That, too, was premeditated and carefully planned.'

Marino was thoughtfully rubbing his face. 'So you're convinced there's a connection.'

'I think nobody wanted us to know there was. I think whoever is behind this assumed he would look like a carjacking gone bad or some other street crime.'

'Yeah, and that's what everybody still thinks.'

'Not everybody.' I held his eyes. 'Absolutely, not everybody.'

'And you're convinced Danny was the intended victim, saying this was a professional hit.'

'It could have been me. It could have been him to scare me,' I said. 'We may never know.'

'You got tox yet on Eddings?' He motioned for another round.

'You know what today was like. Hopefully, I'll know something tomorrow. Tell me what's going on with Chesapeake.'

He shrugged. 'Don't got a clue.'

'How can you not have a clue?' I impatiently said. 'They must have three hundred officers. Isn't anybody working on Ted Eddings's death?'

'Doesn't matter if they have three thousand officers. All you need is one division screwed up, and in this instance it's homicide. So that's a barricade we can't get around because Detective Roche is still on the case.'

'I don't understand it,' I said.

'Yeah, well, he's still on your case, too.'

I didn't listen for he wasn't worth my time.

'I'd watch my back, if I were you.' He met my eyes. 'I wouldn't take it lightly.' He paused. 'You know how cops talk, so I hear things. And there's a rumor being spread out there that you hit on Roche, and his chief's going to try to get the governor to fire you.'

'People can gossip about whatever they like,' I impatiently said.

'Well, part of the problem is they look at him and how young he is, and some people don't have a hard time imagining that you might be attracted.' He hesitated, and I could tell he despised Roche and wanted to maim him at the very least. 'I hate to tell you,' Marino added, 'but you'd be a whole lot better off if he wasn't good-looking.'

'Harassment is not about how people look, Marino. But he has no case, and I'm not worried about it.'

'Point is, he wants to hurt you, Doc, and he's already trying hard. One way or another he's going to screw you, if he can.'

'He can wait in line with all the other people who want to.'

'The person who called the tow lot in Virginia Beach and said they was you was a man.' He stared at me. 'Just so you know.'

'Danny wouldn't have done that,' was all I could say.

'I wouldn't think so. But maybe Roche would,' Marino replied.

'What are you doing tomorrow?'

He sighed. 'I don't have time to tell you.'

'We may need to make a trip to Charlottesville.'

'What for?' He frowned. 'Don't tell me Lucy's still acting screwy.'

'That's not why we need to go. But maybe we'll see her, too,' I said.

11

The next morning, I made evidence rounds, and my first stop was the Scanning Electron Microscopy lab where I found forensic scientist Betsy Eckles sputter-coating a square of tire rubber. She was sitting with her back to me, and I watched her mount the sample on a platform, which would next go into a vacuum chamber of glass so it could be coated by atomic particles of gold. I noted the cut in the center of the rubber, and thought it looked familiar, but couldn't be sure.

'Good morning,' I said.

She turned around from her intimidating console of pressure gauges, dials, and digital microscopes that built images in pixels instead of lines on video screens. Graying and trim in a long lab coat, she seemed more harried than usual this Thursday.

'Oh, good morning, Dr Scarpetta,' she said as she placed the sample of punctured rubber into the chamber.

'Slashed tires?' I asked.

'Firearms asked me to coat the sample. They said it had to be done right now. Don't ask me why.'

She was not happy about it in the least, for this was an unusual response to what was generally not considered a serious crime. I did not understand why it would be a priority today when labs were backed up to the moon, but this was not why I was here.

'I came to talk to you about the uranium,' I said.

'That's the first time I've ever found anything like that.' She was opening a plastic envelope. 'We're talking twenty-two years.'

'We need to know which isotope of uranium we're dealing with,' I said.

'I agree, and since this has never come up before, I'm not sure where to do that. But I can't do it here.'

Using double sticky tape, she began mounting what looked like particles of dirt on a stub that would go into a storage vial. She got vacuumings every day and was never caught up.

'Where is the radioactive sample now?' I asked.

'Right where I left it. I haven't opened that chamber back up and don't think I want to.'

'May I see what we've got?'

'Absolutely.'

She moved to another digitalized scope, turned on the monitor, and it filled with a black universe scattered with stars of different sizes and shapes. Some were a very bright white while others were dim, and all were invisible to the unaided eye.

'I'm zooming it up to three thousand,' she said as she turned dials. 'You want it higher?'

'I think this will do the trick,' I replied.

We stared at what could have been a scene from inside an observatory. Metal spheres looked like three-dimensional planets surrounded by smaller moons and stars.

'That's what came out of your car,' she let me know. 'The bright particles are uranium. Duller ones are iron oxide, like you find in soil. Plus there's aluminum, which is used in just about everything these days. And silicon, or sand.'

'Very typical for what someone might have on the bottom of his shoes,' I said. 'Except for the uranium.'

'And there's something else I'll point out,' she went on. 'The uranium has two shapes. The lobed or spherical, which resulted from some process in which the uranium was molten. But here.' She pointed. 'We have irregular shapes with sharp edges, meaning these came from a process involving a machine.'

'CP&L would use uranium for their nuclear power plants.' I referred to Commonwealth Power & Light, which supplied electricity for all of Virginia and some areas of North Carolina.

'Yes, they would.'

'Any other business around here that might?' I asked.

She thought for a minute. 'There are no mines around here or processing plants. Well, there's the reactor at UVA, but I think that's mainly for teaching.'

I continued to stare at the small storm of radioactive material that had been tracked into my car by whoever had killed Danny. I thought of the Black Talon bullet with its savage claws, and the weird phone call I had gotten in Sandbridge which was followed by someone climbing over my wall. I believed Eddings was somehow the common link, and that was because of his interest in the New Zionists.

'Look,' I said to Eckles, 'just because a Geiger counter's gone off doesn't mean the radioactivity is harmful. And, in fact, uranium isn't harmful.'

'The problem is we don't have a precedent for something like this,' she said.

I patiently explained, 'It's very simple. This material is evidence in a homicide investigation. I am the medical examiner in that case, and it is Captain Marino's jurisdiction. What you need to do is receipt this vacuuming to Marino and me. We will drive it to UVA and have the nuclear physicist there determine which isotope it is.'

Of course, this could not be accomplished without a telephone conference that included the director of the Bureau of Forensic Science, along with the health commissioner, who was my direct boss. They worried about a possible conflict of interest because the uranium had been found in my car, and, of course, Danny had worked for me. When I pointed out that I was not a suspect in the case, they were appeased, and in the end, relieved to have this radioactive sample taken off their hands.

I returned to the SEM lab and Eckles opened that frightful chamber while I slipped on cotton gloves. Carefully, I removed the sticky tape from its stub and tucked it inside a plastic bag, which I sealed and labeled. Before I left her floor, I stopped by Firearms, where Frost was seated before a comparison microscope, examining an old military bayonet on top of a stage. I asked him about the punctured rubber he was having sputter-coated with gold, because I had a feeling.

'We've got a possible suspect in your tire-slashing case,' he said, adjusting the focus as he moved the blade.

'This bayonet?' I knew the answer before I asked.

'That's right. It was just turned in this morning.'

'By whom?' I said as my suspicions grew.

He looked at a folded paper bag on a nearby table. I saw the case number and date, and the last name 'Roche.'

'Chesapeake,' Frost replied.

'Do you know anything about where it came from?' I felt enraged.

'The trunk of a car. That's all I was told. Apparently, there's a hell-fire rush on it for some reason.'

I went upstairs to Toxicology because it was a last round I certainly needed to make. But my mood was bad, and I was not cheered when I finally found someone home who could confirm what my nose had told me in the Norfolk morgue. Dr Rathbone was a big, older man whose hair was still very black. I found him at his desk signing lab reports.

'I just called you.' He looked up at me. 'How was your New Year?'

'It was new and different. How about you?'

'I got a son in Utah, so we were there. I swear I'd move if I could find a job, but I reckon Mormons don't have much use for my trade.'

'I think your trade is good anywhere,' I said. 'And I assume you've got results on the Eddings case,' I added as I thought of the bayonet.

'The concentration of cyanide in his blood sample is point five milligrams per liter, which is lethal, as you know.' He continued signing his name.

'What about the hookah's intake valve and tubes and so on?'

'Inconclusive.'

I was not surprised, nor did it really matter since there was now no doubt that Eddings had been poisoned with cyanide gas, his manner of death unequivocally a homicide. I knew the prosecutor in Chesapeake and stopped by my office long enough to give her a call so she could encourage the police to do the right thing.

'You shouldn't have to ring me up for that,' she said.

'You're right, I shouldn't.'

'Don't give it another thought.' She sounded angry. 'What a bunch of idiots. Has the FBI gotten into this one at all?'

'Chesapeake doesn't need their help.'

'Oh good. I guess they work homicidal cyanide gas poisonings in diving deaths all the time. I'll get back to you.'

Hanging up, I collected coat and bag, and walked out into what was becoming a beautiful day. Marino's car was parked on the side of Franklin Street, and he was sitting inside with the engine running and his window down. As I headed toward him he opened his door and released the trunk.

'Where is it?' he said.

I held up a manila envelope, and he looked shocked.

'That's all you've got it in?' he exclaimed, eyes wide. 'I thought you'd at least put it in one of those metal paint cans.'

'Don't be ridiculous,' I said. 'You could hold uranium in your bare hand and it wouldn't hurt you.'

I shut the envelope inside the trunk.

'Then how come the Geiger counter went off?' he continued arguing as I climbed in. 'It went off because the friggin' shit is radioactive, right?'

'Without a doubt, uranium is radioactive, but, by itself, not very, because it is decaying at such a slow rate. Plus, the sample in your trunk is extremely small.'

'Look, a little radioactive is like a little pregnant or a little dead, in my opinion. And if you ain't worried about it how come you sold your Benz?'

'That's not why I sold it.'

'I don't want to be rayed, if it's all the same to you,' he irritably said.

'You're not going to be rayed.'

But he railed on, 'I can't believe you'd expose me and my car to uranium.'

'Marino,' I tried again, 'a lot of my patients come into the morgue with very grim diseases like tuberculosis, hepatitis, meningitis, AIDS. And you've been present for their autopsies, and you've always been safe with me.'

He drove fast along the interstate, cutting in and out of traffic.

'I should think that you would know by now that I would never deliberately place you in harm's way,' I added.

'Deliberately is right. Maybe you're into something you don't know about,' he said. 'When was the last time you had a radioactive case?'

'In the first place,' I explained, 'the case itself is not radioactive, only some microscopic debris associated with it is. And secondly, I do know about radioactivity. I know about X-rays, MRIs and isotopes like cobalt, iodine and technetium that are used to treat cancer. Physicians learn about a lot of things, including radiation sickness. Would you please slow down and choose a lane?'

I stared at him with growing alarm as he eased up on the accelerator. Sweat was beaded on top of his head and rolling down his temples, his face dark red. With jaw muscles clenched, he gripped the steering wheel hard, his breathing labored.

'Pull over,' I demanded.

He did not respond.

'Marino, pull over. Now,' I repeated in a tone he knew not to resist.

The shoulder was wide and paved on this stretch of 64, and without a word I got out and walked around to his side of the car. I motioned with my thumb for him to get out, and he did. The back of his uniform was soaking wet and I could see the outline of his undershirt through it.

'I think I must be getting the flu,' he said.

I adjusted the seat and mirrors.

'I don't know what's wrong with me.' He mopped his face with a handkerchief.

'You're having a panic attack,' I said. 'Take deep breaths and try to calm down. Bend over and touch your toes. Go limp, relax.'

'Anybody sees you driving a city car, my ass is on report,' he said, pulling the shoulder harness across his chest.

'Right now the city should be grateful that you're not driving anything,' I said. 'You shouldn't be operating any machinery at this moment. In fact, you should probably be sitting in a psychiatrist's office.' I looked over at him and sensed his shame.

'I don't know what's wrong,' he mumbled, staring out his window.

'Are you still upset about Doris?'

'I don't know if I ever told you about one of the last big fights she and I had before she left.' He mopped his face again. 'It was about these damn dishes she got at a yard sale. I mean, she'd been thinking about getting new dishes for a long time, right? And I come home from work one night and here's this big set of blaze orange dishes spread out on the dining-room table.' He looked at me. 'You ever heard of Fiesta Ware?'

'Vaguely.'

'Well, there was something in the glaze of this particular line that I come to find out will set a Geiger counter off.'

'It doesn't take much radioactivity to set a Geiger counter off.' I made that point again.

'Well, there'd been stories written about the stuff, which had been taken off the market,' he went on. 'Doris wouldn't listen. She thought I was overreacting.'

'And you probably were.'

'Look, some people are phobic of all kinds of things. Me, it's radiation. You know how much I hate even being in the X-ray room with you, and when I turn on the microwave, I leave the kitchen. So I packed up all the dishes and dumped them without telling her where.'

He got quiet and wiped his face again. He cleared his throat several times.

Then he said, 'A month later she left.'

'Listen,' I softened my voice, 'I wouldn't want to eat off those dishes, either. Even though I know better. I understand fear, and fear isn't always rational.'

'Yeah, Doc, well maybe in my case it is.' He opened his window a crack. 'I'm afraid of dying. Every morning I get up and think about it, if you want to know. Every day I think I'm going to stroke out or be told I got cancer. I dread going to bed because I'm afraid I'll die in my sleep.' He paused, and it was with great difficulty that he added, 'That's the real reason Molly stopped seeing me, if you want to know.'

'That wasn't a very kind reason.' What he just said hurt me.

'Well' – he got more uncomfortable – 'she's a lot younger than me. And part of the way I feel these days is I don't want to do anything that might exert myself.'

'Then you're afraid of having sex.'

'Shit,' he said, 'why don't you just wave it like a flag.'

'Marino, I'm a doctor. All I want to do is help, if I can.'

'Molly said I made her feel rejected,' he went on.

'And you probably did. How long have you had this problem?'

'I don't know, Thanksgiving.'

'Did something happen?'

He hesitated again. 'Well, you know I've been off my medicine.'

'Which medication? Your adrenergic blocker or the finasteride? And no, I didn't know.'

'Both.'

'Now why would you do anything that foolish?'

'Because when I'm on it nothing works right,' he blurted out. 'I quit taking it when I started dating Molly. Then I started again around Thanksgiving after I had a checkup and my blood pressure was really up there and my prostate was getting bad again. It scared me.'

'No woman is worth dying for,' I said. 'And what this is all about is depression, which you're a perfect candidate for, by the way.'

'Yeah, it's depressing when you can't do it. You don't understand.'

'Of course, I understand. It's depressing when your body fails you, when you get older and have other stressors in your life like change. And you've had a lot of change in the past few years.'

'No, what's depressing,' he said, and his voice was getting louder, 'is when you can't get it up. And then sometimes you get it up and it won't go down. And you can't pee when you feel like you got to go, and other times you go when you don't feel like it. And then there's the whole problem of not being in the mood when you got a girlfriend almost young enough to be your daughter.' He was glaring at me, veins standing out in his neck. 'Yeah, I'm depressed. You're fucking right I am!'

'Please don't be angry with me.'

He looked away, breathing hard.

'I want you to make appointments with your cardiologist and your urologist,' I said.

'Uh-uh. No way.' He shook his head. 'This damn new healthcare plan I'm on has me assigned to a woman urologist. I can't go in there and tell a woman all this shit.'

'Why not? You just told me.'

He fell silent, staring out the window. He looked in the side mirror and said, 'By the way, some drone in a gold Lexus has been behind us since Richmond.'

I looked in the rearview mirror. The car was a newer model and the person driving was talking on the phone.

'Do you think we're being followed?' I asked.

'Hell if I know, but I wouldn't want to pay his damn phone bill.'

We were close to Charlottesville, and the gentle landscape we had left had rounded into western hills that were winter-gray between evergreens. The air was colder and there was more snow, although the interstate was dry. I asked Marino if we could turn the scanner off because I was tired of hearing police chatter, and I took 29 North toward the University of Virginia.

For a while, the scenery was sheer rocky faces interspersed with trees spreading from woods to roadsides. Then we reached the outer limits of the campus, and blocks were crowded with places for pizzas and subs, convenience stores and filling stations. The university was still on Christmas break, but my niece was not the only person in the world to ignore that fact. At Scott Stadium, I turned on Maury Avenue, where students perched on benches and rode by on bikes, wearing backpacks or holding satchels that seemed full of work. There were plenty of cars.

'You ever been to a game here?' Marino had perked up.

'I can't say that I have.'

'Now that ought to be against the law. You have a niece going here and you never once saw the Hoos? What'd you do when you came to town? I mean, what did you and Lucy do?'

In fact, we had done very little. Our time together generally was spent taking long walks on the campus or talking inside her room on the Lawn. Of course we had many dinners at restaurants like The

Ivy and Boar's Head, and I had met her professors and even gone to class. But I did not see friends, what few of them she had. They, like the places where she met them, were not something shared with me.

I realized Marino was still talking.

'I'll never forget when I saw him play,' he was saying.

'I'm sorry,' I said.

'Can you imagine being seven feet tall? You know he lives in Richmond now.'

'Let's see.' I studied buildings we were passing. 'We want the School of Engineering, which starts right here. But we need Mechanical, Aerospace and Nuclear Engineering.'

I slowed down as a brick building with white trim came in sight, and then I saw the sign. Parking was not hard to find, but Dr Alfred Matthews was. He had promised to meet me in his office at eleven-thirty, but apparently had forgotten.

'Then where the hell is he?' asked Marino, who was still worried about what was in his trunk.

'The reactor facility.' I got back in the car.

'Oh great.'

It was really called the High Energy Physics Lab, and was on top of a mountain that was also shared by an observatory. The university's nuclear reactor was a large silo made of brick. It was surrounded by woods that were fenced in, and Marino was acting phobic again.

'Come on. You'll find this interesting.' I opened my door.

'I got no interest in this at all.'

'Okay. Then you stay here and I'll go in.'

'You won't get an argument out of me,' he replied.

I retrieved the sample from the trunk, and at the facility's main entrance, I rang a bell and someone released a lock. Inside was a small lobby where I told a young man behind glass that I was looking for Dr Matthews. A list was checked and I was informed that the head of the physics department, whom I knew only in a limited way, was this moment by the reactor's pool. The young man then picked up an in-house phone while sliding out a visitor's pass and a detector for radiation. I clipped them to my jacket, and he left his station to escort me through a heavy steel door beneath a red light sign that indicated the reactor was on.

The room was windowless with high tile walls, and every object I saw was marked with a bright yellow radioactive tag. At one end of the lighted pool, Cerenkov radiation caused the water to glow a fantastic blue as unstable atoms spontaneously disintegrated in the fuel assembly twenty feet down. Dr Matthews was conferring with a student who, I gathered as I heard them talk, was using cobalt instead of an autoclave to sterilize micropipettes used for in vitro fertilization.

'I thought you were coming tomorrow,' the nuclear physicist said to me, a distressed expression on his face.

'No, it was today. But thank you for seeing me at all. I have the sample with me.' I held up the envelope.

'Okay, George,' he said to the young man. 'Will you be all right?'

'Yes, sir. Thanks.'

'Come on,' Matthews said to me. 'We'll take it down there now and get started. Do you know how much you've got here?'

'I don't know exactly.'

'If we've got enough, we can do it while you wait.'

Beyond a heavy door, we turned left and paused at a tall box that monitored the radiation of our hands and feet. We passed with bright green colors and went on to stairs that led to the neutron radiography lab, which was in a basement of machine shops and forklifts, and big black barrels containing low-level nuclear waste waiting to be shipped. There was emergency equipment at almost every turn, and a control room locked inside a cage. Most remote to all of this was the low background counting room. Built of thick windowless concrete, it was stocked with fifty-gallon canisters of liquid nitrogen, and germanium detectors and amplifiers, and bricks made of lead.

The process for identifying my sample was surprisingly simple. Matthews, wearing no special protection other than lab coat and gloves, placed the piece of sticky tape into a tube, which he then set inside a two-foot-long aluminum container housing the germanium crystal. Finally, he stacked lead bricks on every side to shield the sample from background radiation.

Activating the process required a simple computer command, and a counter on the canister began measuring radioactivity so it could tell us which isotope we had. This was all rather strange to see, for I was accustomed to arcane instruments like scanning electron microscopes and gas chromatographs. This detector, on the other hand, was a rather formless house of lead cooled by liquid nitrogen, and did not seem capable of intelligent thought.

'Now, if you'll just sign this evidence receipt,' I said, 'I'll be on my way.'

'It could take an hour or two. It's hard to say,' he answered.

He signed the form and I gave him a copy.

'I'll stop by after I check on Lucy.'

'Come on, I'll escort you up to make sure you don't set anything off. How is she?' he asked as we passed detectors without a complaint. 'Did she ever go on to MIT?'

'She did do an internship there last fall,' I said. 'In robotics. You know, she's back here. For at least a month.'

'I didn't know. That's wonderful. Studying what?'

'Virtual reality, I think she said.'

Matthews looked perplexed for a moment. 'Didn't she take that when she was here?'

'I expect this is more advanced.'

'I expect it would have to be.' He smiled. 'I wish I had at least one of her in every class.'

Lucy had probably been the only non-physics major at UVA to take a course in nuclear design for fun. I walked outside, and Marino was leaning against the car, smoking.

'So what now?' he said, and he still looked glum.

'I thought I'd surprise my niece and take her to lunch. You're more than welcome to join us.'

'I'm going to drop by the Exxon station down the street and use the pay phone,' he said. 'I got some calls to make.'

12

He drove me to the rotunda, brilliant white in sunlight and my favorite building Thomas Jefferson had designed. I followed old brick colonnaded walkways beneath ancient trees, where Federal pavilions formed two rows of privileged housing known as the Lawn.

Living here was an award for academic achievement, yet it might have been considered a dubious honor by some. Showers and toilets were located in another building in back, the sparsely furnished rooms not necessarily intended for comfort. Yet I had never heard Lucy complain, for she had truly loved her life at UVA.

She was staying on the West Lawn in Pavilion III, with its Corinthian capitals of Carrara marble that had been carved in Italy. Wooden shutters outside room 11 were drawn, the morning paper still on the mat, and I wondered, perplexed, if she had not gotten up yet. I rapped on the door several times and heard someone stirring.

'Who is it?' my niece's voice called out.

'It's me,' I said.

There was a pause, then a surprised, 'Aunt Kay?'

'Are you going to open the door?' My good mood was fading fast for she did not sound pleased.

'Uh, hold on a minute. I'm coming.'

The door unlocked and opened.

'Hi,' she said as she let me in.

'I hope I didn't wake you up.' I handed her the newspaper.

'Oh, T.C. gets that,' she said, referring to the friend who really belonged to this room. 'She forgot to cancel it before she left for Germany. I never get around to reading it.'

I entered an apartment not so different from where I had visited my niece last year. The space was small with bed and sink, and crowded bookcases. Heart of pine floors were bare, with no art on whitewashed walls except a single poster of Anthony Hopkins in *Shadowlands*. Lucy's technical preoccupations had taken over tables, desk and even several chairs. Other equipment, like the fax machine and what looked like a small robot, was out cold on the floor.

Additional telephone lines had been installed, and these were connected to modems winking with green lights. But I did not get the impression that my niece was living here alone, for on the sink were two toothbrushes, and solution for contact lenses that she did not wear. Both sides of the twin bed were unmade, and on top of it was a briefcase I did not recognize, either.

'Here.' She lifted a printer off a chair and put me close to the fire. 'Sorry everything's such a mess.' She wore a bright orange UVA sweat-shirt and jeans, and her hair was wet. 'I can heat up some water,' she said, and she was very distracted.

'If you're offering tea, I accept,' I said.

I watched her closely as she filled a pot with water and plugged it in. Nearby, on a dresser top, were FBI credentials, a pistol, and car keys. I spotted file folders and pieces of paper scribbled with notes, and I spotted unfamiliar clothing hanging inside the closet.

'Tell me about T. C.,' I said.

Lucy opened a tea bag. 'A German major. She's spending the next six weeks in Munich. So she said I could stay here.'

'That was very nice of her. Would you like me to help you pack up her things or at least make room for yours?'

'You don't need to do any work at all right now.'

I glanced toward the window, hearing someone.

'You still take your tea black?' Lucy said.

The fire crackled, smoking wood shifted, and I wasn't surprised when the door opened and another woman walked in. But I was not expecting Janet, and she was not expecting me.

'Dr Scarpetta,' she said in surprise as she glanced at Lucy. 'How great of you to drop by.'

She was carrying shower items, a baseball cap pulled over wet hair that was almost to her shoulders. Dressed in sweats and tennis shoes, she was lovely and healthy, and like Lucy, seemed even younger because she was on a university campus again.

'Please join us,' Lucy said to her as she handed me a mug of tea.

'We were out running.' Janet smiled. 'Sorry about the hair. So what brings you here?' she asked as she sat on the floor.

'I need some help with a case,' was all I said. 'Are you taking this virtual reality course too?' I studied both of their faces.

'Right,' Janet said. 'Lucy and I are here together. As you may or may not know, I was transferred to the Washington Field Office late last year.'

'Lucy mentioned it.'

'I've been assigned to white-collar crime,' she went on. 'Especially anything that might be related to a violation of the IOC.'

'Which is?' I asked.

It was Lucy who replied as she sat next to me, 'Interception of Communication statute. We've got the only group in the country with experts who can handle these cases.'

'Then the Bureau has sent both of you here for training because of this group.' I tried to understand. 'But I guess I don't see what virtual reality might have to do with hackers breaking into major databases,' I added.

Janet was silent as she took off her cap and combed her hair, staring into the fire. I could tell she was very uncomfortable, and I wondered how much of it had to do with what had happened in Aspen over the holidays. My niece moved to the hearth and sat facing me.

'We're not here for a class, Aunt Kay,' she said with quiet seriousness. 'That's how it's supposed to look to everybody else. Now, I'm going to tell you this when I shouldn't, but it's too late for any more lies.'

'You don't have to tell me,' I said. 'I understand.'

'No.' Her eyes were intense. 'I want you to understand what's going on. And to give you a quick, dirty summary, last fall Commonwealth Power & Light began experiencing problems when what appeared to be a hacker started getting inside their computer system. The attempts were frequent – sometimes four or five times a day. But there was no success in identifying this individual until he left tracks in an audit log after accessing and printing customer billing information. We were called, and remotely we managed to trace the perpetrator to UVA.'

'Then you haven't caught whoever it is,' I said.

'No.' It was Janet who spoke. 'We interviewed the graduate student whose I.D. it was, but he definitely isn't the hacker. We have reasons to be very sure of that.'

'Point is,' said Lucy, 'several other I.D.s have been stolen from students here since, and the perpetrator was also trying to access CP&L along with the university computer and one in Pittsburgh.'

'Was?' I asked.

'Actually, he's been pretty quiet lately, which makes it harder for us,' Janet said. 'Mostly, we've been chasing him through the university computer.'

'Right,' Lucy said. 'We haven't tracked him in CP&L's computer for almost a week. I figure because of the holidays.'

'Why might someone be doing this?' I asked. 'Do you have a theory?'

'A power trip, no pun intended,' Janet simply said. 'Maybe so he can turn lights on and off throughout Virginia and the Carolinas. Who knows?'

'But what we believe is that whoever's doing it is on campus, and is getting in via the Internet and another link called Telnet,' Lucy said, adding confidently, 'We'll get him.'

'You mind if I ask why all the secrecy?' I said to my niece. 'Could you not just tell me you were on a case you couldn't discuss?'

She hesitated before responding. 'You're on the faculty here, Aunt Kay.'

This was true, and I had not even thought of that. Though I was only a visiting professor in pathology and legal medicine, I decided Lucy's point was well taken, and I supposed I did not blame her for keeping this from me for yet another reason. She wanted her independence, especially in this place where for the duration of her undergraduate studies it had been well known that she was related to me.

I looked at her. 'Is this why you left Richmond so abruptly the other night?'

'I got paged.'

'By me,' Janet said. 'I was flying in from Aspen, got delayed, et cetera. Lucy picked me up at the airport and we came back here.'

'And were there any other attempted break-ins over the holidays?'

'Some. The system is constantly being monitored,' Lucy said. 'We're not alone in this by any means. We've just been assigned an undercover post here so we can do some hands-on detective work.'

'Why don't you walk me to the Rotunda.' I got up, and so did they. 'Marino should be back with the car.' I hugged Janet and her hair smelled like lemon. 'You take care and come see me more often,' I said to her. 'I consider you family. Lord knows it's about time I had some help in taking care of this one.' I smiled as I put my arm around Lucy.

Outside in the sun, the afternoon was warm enough for only sweaters, and I wished I could stay longer. Lucy did not linger during our brief walk, and I could tell she was anxious about anyone seeing us together.

'It's just like the old days,' I said lightly to hide my hurt.

'How's that?' she asked.

'Your ambivalence about being seen with me.'

'That's not true. I used to be proud of it.'

'And now you're not,' I said with irony.

'Maybe I'd like you to feel proud to be seen with me,' she said. 'Instead of it always the other way. That's what I meant.'

'I am proud of you and always have been, even when you were such a mess that sometimes I wanted to lock you in the basement.'

'I believe that's called child abuse.'

'No, the jury would vote for aunt abuse in your case. Trust me,' I said. 'And I'm glad you and Janet seem to be getting along. I'm glad she's back from Aspen and the two of you are together.'

My niece stopped and looked at me, squinting in the sun. 'Thanks for what you said to her. Right now, especially, that meant a lot.'

'I spoke the truth, that's all,' I said. 'Maybe someday her family will speak it, too.'

We were in sight of Marino's car, and he was sitting in it, as usual, and puffing away.

Lucy walked up to his door. 'Hey, Pete,' she said, 'you need to wash your ride.'

'No, I don't,' he grumbled as he immediately tossed the cigarette and got out.

He looked around, and the sight of him hitching up his pants and inspecting his car because he could not help himself was too much. Lucy and I both laughed, and then he tried not to smile. In truth, he secretly enjoyed it when we teased. We bantered a little bit more, and then Lucy left as a late-model gold Lexus with tinted glass drove past. It was the same one we had seen earlier on the road, but the driver was obliterated by glare.

'This is beginning to get on my nerves.' Marino's eyes followed the car.

'Maybe you should run the plate number,' I stated the obvious.

'Oh, I already done that.' He started the car and began backing. 'DMV's down.'

DMV was the Department of Motor Vehicles computer, and it was down a lot, it seemed. We headed back up to the reactor facility, and when we got there, Marino again refused to go inside. So I left him in the parking lot, and this time the young man in the control room behind glass told me I could enter unescorted.

'He's down in the basement,' he said with eyes on his computer screen.

I found Matthews in the low background counting room again, sitting before a computer screen displaying a spectrum in black and white.

'Oh, hello,' he said, when he realized I was beside him.

'Looks like you've had some luck,' I said. 'Although I'm not sure what I'm seeing. And I might be too early.'

'No, no, you're not too early. These vertical lines here indicate the energies of the significant gamma rays detected. One line equals one energy. But most of the lines we're seeing here are for background radiation.' He showed me on the screen. 'You know, even the lead bricks don't get rid of all of that.'

I sat next to him.

'I guess what I'm trying to show you, Dr Scarpetta, is that the sample you brought in isn't giving off high-energy gamma rays when it decays. If you look here on this energy spectrum' – he was staring at the screen – 'it looks like this characteristic gamma ray on the spectrum is for uranium two-thirty-five.' He tapped a spike on the glass.

'Okay,' I said. 'And what does that mean?'

'That's the good stuff.' He looked over at me.

'Such as is used in nuclear reactors,' I said.

'Exactly. That's what we use to make fuel pellets or rods. But as you probably know, only point three percent of uranium is two-thirty-five. The rest is depleted.'

'Right. The rest is uranium two-thirty-eight,' I said.

'And that's what we've got here.'

'If it isn't giving off high-energy gamma rays,' I said. 'How can you tell that from this energy spectrum?'

'Because what the germanium crystal is detecting is uranium two-thirty-five. And since the percentage of it is so low, this indicates that the sample we're dealing with must be depleted uranium.'

'It couldn't be spent fuel from a reactor,' I thought out loud.

'No, it couldn't,' he said. 'There's no fission material mixed in with your sample. No strontium, cesium, iodine, barium. You would have already seen those with SEM.'

'No isotopes like that came up,' I agreed. 'Only uranium and other nonessential elements that you might expect with soil tracked in on the bottom of someone's shoes.'

I looked at peaks and valleys of what could have been a scary cardiogram while Matthews made notes.

'Would you like printouts of all of this?' he asked.

'Please. What is depleted uranium used for?'

'Generally, it's worthless.' He hit several keys.

'If it didn't come from a nuclear power plant, then from where?'

'Most likely a facility that does isotopic separation.'

'Such as Oak Ridge, Tennessee,' I suggested.

'Well, they don't do that anymore. But they certainly did for decades, and they must have warehouses of uranium metal. Now there also are plants in Portsmouth, Ohio, and Paducah, Kentucky.'

'Dr Matthews,' I said. 'It appears someone had depleted uranium metal on the bottom of his shoes and tracked it into a car. Can you give me any logical explanation as to how or why?'

'No.' His expression was blank. 'I don't think I can.'

I thought of the jagged and spherical shapes the scanning electron microscope had revealed to me, and tried again. 'Why would someone melt uranium two-thirty-eight? Why would they shape it with a machine?'

Still, he did not seem to have a clue.

'Is depleted uranium used for anything at all?' I then asked.

'In general, big industry doesn't use uranium metal,' he answered. 'Not even in nuclear power plants, because in those the fuel rods or pellets are uranium oxide, a ceramic.'

'Then maybe I should ask what depleted uranium metal could, in theory, be used for,' I restated.

'At one time there was some talk by the Defense Department about using it for armor plating on tanks. And it's been suggested that it could be used to make bullets or other types of projectiles. Let's see. I guess the only other thing we know that it's good for is shielding radioactive material.'

'What sort of radioactive material?' I said as my adrenal glands woke up. 'Spent fuel assemblies, for example?'

'That would be the idea if we knew how to get rid of nuclear waste in this country,' he wryly said. 'You see, if we could remove it to be buried a thousand feet beneath Yucca Mountain, Nevada, for example, then U-238 could be used to line the casks needed for transport.'

'In other words,' I said, 'if the spent assemblies are to be removed from a nuclear power plant, they will have to be put in something, and depleted uranium is a better shield than lead.'

He said this was precisely what he meant, and receipted my sample back to me, because it was evidence and one day could end up in court. So I could not leave it here, even though I knew how Marino would feel when I returned it to his trunk. I found him walking around, his sunglasses on.

'What now?' he said.

'Please pop the trunk.'

He reached inside the car and pulled a release as he said, 'I'm telling you right now, that it ain't going in no evidence locker in my precinct or at HQ. No one's going to cooperate, even if I wanted them to.'

'It has to be stored,' I simply said. 'There's a twelve-pack of beer in here.'

'So I didn't want to have to bother stopping for it later.'

'One of these days you're going to get in trouble.' I shut the trunk of his city-owned police car.

'Well, how about you store the uranium at your office,' he said.

'Fine.' I got in. 'I can do that.'

'So, how was it?' he asked, starting the engine.

I gave him a summary, leaving out as much scientific detail as I could.

'You're telling me that someone tracked nuclear waste into your Benz?' he asked, baffled.

'That's the way it appears. I need to stop by and talk to Lucy again.'

'Why? What's she got to do with it?'

'I don't know that she does,' I said as he drove down the mountain. 'I have a rather wild idea.'

'I hate it when you get those.'

Janet looked worried when I was back at their door, this time with Marino.

'Is everything all right?' she asked, letting us in.

'I think I need your help,' I said. 'Strike that. What I mean is that both of us do.'

Lucy was sitting on the bed, a notebook open in her lap. She looked at Marino. 'Fire away. But we charge for consultations.'

He sat by the fire, while I took a chair close to him.

'This person who has been getting into CP&L's computer,' I said. 'Do we know what else he has gotten into besides customer billing?'

'I can't say we know everything,' Lucy replied. 'But the billing is a certainty, and customer info is in general.'

'Meaning what?' Marino asked.

'Meaning that the information about customers includes billing addresses, phone numbers, special services, energy-use averaging, and some customers are part of a stock-sharing program—'

'Let's talk about stock sharing,' I stopped her. 'I'm involved in that program. Part of my check every month buys stock in CP&L, and therefore the company has some financial information on me, including my bank account and social security numbers.' I paused, thinking. 'Could that sort of thing be important to this hacker?'

'Theoretically, it could,' Lucy said. 'Because you've got to remember that a huge database like CP&L's isn't going to reside in any one place. They've got other systems with gateways leading to them, which might explain the hacker's interest in the mainframe in Pittsburgh.'

'Maybe it explains something to you,' said Marino, who always got impatient with Lucy's computer talk. 'But it don't explain shit to me.'

'If you think of the gateways as major corridors on a map – like I-95, for example,' she patiently said, 'then if you go from one to the other, theoretically you could start cruising the global web. You could pretty much get into anything you want.'

'Like what?' he asked. 'Give me an example that I can relate to.'

She rested the notebook in her lap and shrugged. 'If I broke into the Pittsburgh computer, my next stop would be at AT&T.'

'That computer's a gateway into the telephone system?' I asked.

'It's one of them. And that's one of the suspicions Jan and I have been working on – that this hacker's trying to figure out ways to steal electricity and phone time.'

'Of course, at the moment this is just a theory,' Janet said. 'So far, nothing has come up that might tell us what the hacker's motive is. But from the FBI's perspective, the break-ins are against the law. That's what counts.'

'Do you know which CP&L customer records were accessed?' I asked.

'We know that this person has access to all customers,' Lucy replied. 'And we're talking millions. But as for individual records that we know were looked at in more detail, those were few. And we have them.'

'I'm wondering if I could see them,' I said.

Lucy and Janet paused.

'What for?' Marino asked as he continued to stare at me. 'What are you getting at, Doc?'

'I'm getting at that uranium fuels nuclear power plants, and CP&L has two nuclear power plants in Virginia and one in Delaware. Their mainframe is being broken into. Ted Eddings called my office with radioactivity questions. In his home PC he had all sorts of files on North Korea and suspicions that they were attempting to manufacture weapons-grade plutonium in a nuclear reactor.'

'And the minute we start looking into anything in Sandbridge we get a prowler,' Lucy added. 'Then someone slashes our tires and Detective Roche threatens you. Now Danny Webster comes to Richmond and ends up dead and it appears that whoever killed him tracked uranium into your car.' She looked at me. 'Tell me what you need to see.'

I did not require a complete customer list, for that would be virtually all of Virginia, including my office and me. But I was interested in any detailed billing records that were accessed, and what I was shown was curious but short. Out of five names, I recognized all but one.

'Does anybody know who Joshua Hayes is? He has a post office box in Suffolk,' I said.

'All we know so far,' said Janet, 'is that he's a farmer.'

'All right,' I moved on. 'We've got Brett West, who is an executive at CP&L. I can't remember his title.' I looked at the printout.

'Executive Vice President in charge of Operations,' Janet said.

'He lives in one of those brick mansions near you, Doc,' Marino said. 'In Windsor Farms.'

'He used to. If you study his billing address,' Janet pointed out, 'you'll see it changed as of last October. It appears he moved to Williamsburg.'

There were two other CP&L executives whose records had been perused by whoever was illegally prowling the Internet. One was the CEO, the other the president. But it was the identity of the fifth electronic victim that truly frightened me.

'Captain Green.' I stared at Marino, stunned.

His face was vague. 'I got no idea who you're talking about.'

'He was present at the Inactive Ship Yard when I got Eddings's body out of the water,' I said. 'He's with Navy Investigative Services.'

'I hear you.' Marino's face darkened, and Lucy and Janet's IOC case dramatically shifted before their eyes.

'Maybe it's not surprising this person breaking in would be curious about the highest-ranking officials of the corporation he's violating, but I don't see how NIS fits in,' Janet said.

'I'm not sure I want to know how it might,' I said. 'But if what Lucy has to say about gateways is relevant, then maybe the final stop for this hacker is certain people's telephone records.'

'Why?' Marino asked.

'To see who they were calling.' I paused. 'The sort of information a reporter might be interested in, for example.'

Getting up from the chair, I began to pace about as fear tingled along my nerves. I thought of Eddings poisoned in his boat, of Black Talons and uranium, and I remembered that Joel Hand's farm was in Tidewater somewhere.

'This person named Dwain Shapiro who owned the bible you found in Eddings's house,' I said to Marino. 'He allegedly died in a carjacking. Do we have any further information on that?'

'Right now we don't.'

'Danny's death could have been signed out as the same sort of thing,' I said.

'Or yours could have. Especially because of the type of car. If this were a hit, maybe the assailant didn't know that Dr Scarpetta isn't a man,' Janet said. 'Maybe the gunman was cocky and only knew what you would be driving.'

I stopped by the hearth as she went on.

'Or maybe the killer didn't figure out Danny wasn't you until it was too late. Then Danny had to be dealt with.'

'Why me?' I said. 'What would be the motive?'

It was Lucy who replied. 'Obviously, they think you know something.'

'They?'

'Maybe the New Zionists. The same reason they killed Ted Eddings,' she said. 'They thought he knew something or was going to expose something.'

I looked at my niece and Janet as my anxieties got more inflamed.

'For God's sake,' I said to them with feeling, 'don't do anything more on this until you talk to Benton or someone. Damn! I don't want them thinking you know something, too.'

But I knew Lucy, at least, would not listen. She would be on her keyboard with renewed vigor the moment I shut the door.

'Janet?' I held the gaze of my only hope for their playing it safe. 'Your hacker is very possibly connected to people being murdered.'

'Dr Scarpetta,' she said. 'I understand.'

Marino and I left UVA, and the gold Lexus we had already seen twice this day was behind us all the way back to Richmond. Marino drove with his eyes constantly on his mirrors. He was sweating and mad because the DMV computer wasn't up yet, and the plate number he had called in was taking forever to come back. The person behind us in the car was young and white. He wore dark glasses and a cap.

'He doesn't care if you know who he is,' I said. 'If he cared, he wouldn't be so obvious, Marino. This is just one more intimidation attempt.'

'Yeah, well, let's see who intimidates who,' he said, slowing down.

He stared in the rearview mirror again, slowing more, and the car got closer. Suddenly, he hit his brakes hard. I didn't know who was more shocked, our tailgater or me, as the Lexus's brakes screeched, horns blaring all around, and the car clipped the rear end of Marino's Ford.

'Uh-oh,' he said. 'Looks like someone's just rear-ended a policeman.'

He got out and subtly unsnapped his holster while I looked on in disbelief. I slipped out my pistol and dropped it in a pocket of my coat as I decided I should get out, too, since I had no idea what was about to happen. Marino was by the Lexus's driver's door, watching the traffic at his back as he talked into his portable radio.

'Keep your hands where I can see them at all times,' he ordered the driver again in a loud, authoritative voice. 'Now I want you to give me your driver's license. Slow.'

I was on the other side of the car, near the passenger's door, and I knew who the offender was before Marino saw the license, and the photograph on it.

'Well, well, Detective Roche,' Marino raised his voice above the rush of traffic. 'Fancy we should run into you. Or vice versa.' His tone turned hard. 'Get out of the car. Now. You got any firearms on you?'

'It's between the seats. In plain view,' he said, coldly.

Then Roche slowly got out of the car. He was tall and slender in fatigue pants, a denim jacket, boots and a large black dive watch. Marino turned him around and ordered him again to keep his hands in plain view. I stood where I was while Roche's sunglasses fixed on me, his mouth smug.

'So tell me, Detective Cock-Roche,' Marino said, 'who you snitching for today? Might it be Captain Green you've been talking to on your portable phone? You been telling him everywhere we've been going today and what we're doing, and how much you've been scaring our asses as we spot you in our mirrors? Or are you obvious just because you're a dumb shit?'

Roche said nothing, his face hard.

'Is that what you did to Danny, too? You called the tow lot and said you were the doc and wanted to know about your car. Then you passed the info down the line, only it just so happened it wasn't the doc driving that night. And now a kid's missing half his head because some soldier of fortune didn't know the doc ain't a man or maybe mistook Danny for a medical examiner.'

'You can't prove anything,' Roche said with the same mocking smile.

'We'll see how much I can prove when I get hold of your cellular phone bills.' Marino moved closer so Roche could feel his big presence, his belly almost touching him. 'And when I find something, you're going to have a lot more to worry about than a driving penalty. At the very least I'm going to nail your pretty ass for being an accomplice to murder prior to the fact. That ought to get you about fifty years.

'In the meantime' – Marino jabbed a thick finger at his face – 'I'd better never see you even within a mile of me again. And I wouldn't recommend you getting anywhere close to the doc, either. You've never seen her when she gets irritated.'

Marino lifted his radio and got back on the air to check the status of getting an officer to the scene, and even as his request was broadcast again, a cruiser appeared on 64. It pulled in behind us on the shoulder, and a uniformed female sergeant from Richmond P.D. got out. She walked our way with purpose, her hand discreetly near her gun.

'Captain, good afternoon.' She adjusted the volume on the radio on her belt. 'What seems to be the problem?'

'Well, Sergeant Schroeder, it seems this person's been tailgating me for the better part of the day,' Marino said. 'And unfortunately, when I was forced to apply my brakes due to a white dog running in front of my vehicle, he struck me from the rear.'

'Was this the same white dog?' the sergeant asked without a trace of a smile.

'Looked like the same one we've had problems with.'

They went on with what must have been the oldest police joke, for when it came to single-car accidents, it seemed a ubiquitous white canine was always to blame. It darted in front of vehicles and then was gone until it darted in front of the next bad driver and again got blamed.

'He has at least one firearm inside his vehicle,' Marino added in his most serious police tone. 'I want him thoroughly searched before we get him inside.'

'All right, sir, you need to spread your arms and legs.'

'I'm a cop,' Roche snapped.

'Yes, sir, so you should know exactly what I'm doing,' Sergeant Schroeder matter-of-factly stated.

She patted him down, and discovered an ankle holster on his inner left leg.

'Now ain't that sweet,' Marino said.

'Sir,' the sergeant said a little more loudly as another unmarked unit pulled up, 'I'm going to have to ask you to remove the pistol from your ankle holster and place it inside your vehicle.'

A deputy chief got out, resplendent in patent leather, navy and brass, and not exactly thrilled to be on the scene. But it was procedure to call him whenever a captain was involved in any police matter, no matter how small. He silently looked on as Roche removed a Colt .380 from the black nylon holster. He locked it inside the Lexus and was red with rage as he was placed in the back of the patrol car. The sergeant and deputy chief interviewed him and Marino while I waited inside the damaged Ford.

'Now what happens?' I asked Marino when he returned.

'He'll be charged with following too close and be released on a Virginia Uniform Summons.' He buckled up and seemed pleased.

'That's it?'

'Yup. Except court. The good news is, I ruined his day. The better news is now we got something to investigate that may eventually send his ass to Mecklenburg where, as sweet-looking as he is, he'll have lots of friends.'

'Did you know it was him before he hit us?' I asked.

'Nope. I had no idea.' We pulled back out into traffic.

'And what did he say when he was questioned?'

'What you'd expect. I stopped suddenly.'

'Well, you did.'

'And by law it's all right to do that.'

'What about following us? Did he have an explanation?'

'He's been out all day running errands and sightseeing. He doesn't know what we're talking about.'

'I see. If you're going to run errands, you need to bring along at least two guns.'

'You want to tell me how the hell he can afford a car like that?' Marino glanced over at me. 'He probably doesn't make half what I do, and that Lexus he's got probably cost close to fifty grand.'

'The Colt he was carrying isn't cheap, either,' I said. 'He's getting money from somewhere.'

'Snitches always do.'

'That's all you think he is?'

'Yeah, for the most part. I think he's been doing shit work, probably for Green.'

The radio suddenly interrupted us with the loud blare of an alert tone, and then we were given answers that were even worse than any we might have feared.

'All units be advised that we have just received a teletype from state police that gives the following information,' a dispatcher repeated. 'The nuclear power plant at Old Point has been taken over by terrorists. Shots have been fired and there are fatalities.'

I was shocked speechless as the message went on and on.

'The chief of police has ordered that the department move to emergency plan A. Until further notice all day-shift units will remain on their posts. Updates will follow. All division commanders will report to the command post at the police academy immediately.'

'Hell no,' Marino said as he slammed the accelerator to the floor. 'We're going to your office.'

13

The invasion of the Old Point nuclear power plant had happened swiftly and horrifically, and in disbelief we listened to the news while Marino sped through town. We did not utter a sound as an almost hysterical reporter at the scene rambled in a voice several octaves above what it usually was.

'Old Point nuclear power plant has been seized by terrorists,' he repeated. 'This happened about forty-five minutes ago when a bus carrying at least twenty men posing as CP&L employees stormed the main administration building. It is believed that at least three civilians are dead.' His voice was shaking and we could hear helicopters overhead. 'I can see police vehicles and fire trucks everywhere, but they can't get close. Oh my God, this is awful . . .'

Marino parked on the side of the street by my building. For a while we could not move as we listened to the same information again and again. It did not seem real, for less than a hundred miles from Old Point, here in Richmond, the afternoon was bright. Traffic was normal and people walked along sidewalks as if nothing had happened. My eyes stared without focusing, my thoughts flying through lists of what I must do.

'Come on, Doc.' Marino cut the engine off. 'Let's go inside. I got to use the phone and get hold of one of my lieutenants. I've got to get things mobilized in case the lights go out in Richmond, or worse.'

I had my own mobilizing to do, and started with assembling everyone in the conference room, where I declared a statewide emergency.

'Each district must be on standby and ready to implement their part of the disaster plan,' I announced to everyone in the room. 'A nuclear disaster could affect all districts. Obviously, Tidewater is the most imperiled and the least covered. Dr Fielding,' I said to my deputy chief, 'I'd like to put you in charge of Tidewater and make you acting chief when I can't be there.'

'I'll do the best I can,' he said bravely, although no one of sound mind would want the assignment I just gave him.

'Now, I won't always know where I'm going to be throughout this,' I said to other anxious faces. 'Business goes on as usual here, but I want any bodies brought here. Any bodies from Old Point, I'm saying, starting with the shooting fatalities.'

'What about other Tidewater cases?' Fielding wanted to know.

'Routine cases are done as usual. I understand we do have another autopsy technician to fill in until we can find a permanent replacement.'

'Any chance these bodies you want here might be contaminated?' my administrator asked, and he had always been a worrier.

'So far we're talking about shooting victims,' I said.

'And they couldn't be.'

'No.'

'But what about later?' he went on.

'Mild contamination isn't a problem,' I said. 'We just scrub the bodies and get rid of the soapy water and clothes. Acute exposure to radiation is another matter, especially if the bodies are badly burned, if debris is burned into them, as it was in Chernobyl. Those bodies will need to be shielded in a special refrigerated truck, and all exposed personnel will wear lead-lined suits.'

'Those bodies we'll cremate?'

'I would recommend that. Which is another reason why they need to come here to Richmond. We can use the crematorium in the anatomical division.'

Marino stuck his head inside the conference room. 'Doc?' He motioned me out.

I got up and we spoke in the hall.

'Benton wants us at Quantico now,' he said.

'Well, it won't be now,' I said.

I glanced back at the conference room. Through the doorway I could see Fielding making some point, while one of the other doctors looked tense and unhappy.

'You got an overnight bag with you?' Marino went on, and he knew I always kept one here.

'Is this really necessary?' I complained.

'I'd tell you if it wasn't.'

'Give me just fifteen minutes to finish up this meeting.'

I brought confusion and fear to closure as best I could, and told the other doctors I could be gone for days because I'd just been summoned to Quantico. But I would wear my pager. Then Marino and I took my car instead of his, since he had already made arrangements for repairs to the bumper Roche had hit. We sped north on 95 with the radio on, and by now we had heard the story so many times we knew it as well as the reporters.

In the past two hours, no one else had died at Old Point, at least not that anybody knew of, and the terrorists had let dozens of people go. These fortunate ones had been allowed to leave in twos and threes, according to the news. Emergency medical personnel, state police and the FBI intercepted them for examinations and interviews.

We arrived at Quantico at almost five, and Marines in camouflage were vigorously blasting the rapid approach of night. They were crowded in trucks and behind sandbags on the range, and when we passed close to a knot of them gathered by the road, I was pained by their young faces. I rounded a bend, where tall tan brick buildings suddenly rose above trees. The complex did not look military, and, in fact, could have been a university were it not for the rooftops of antennae. A road leading to it stopped midway at an entrance gate where tire shredders bared teeth to people going the wrong way.

An armed guard emerged from his booth and smiled because we were no strangers, and he let us through. We parked in the big lot across from the tallest building, called Jefferson, which was basically the Academy's self-contained downtown. Inside were the post office, the indoor range, dining hall, and PX, with upper floors for dormitory rooms, including security suites for protected witnesses and spies.

New agents in khaki and dark blue were honing weapons in the gun-cleaning room. It seemed I had smelled the solvents all of my life, and could hear in my mind compressed air blasting through barrels and other parts whenever I wanted to. My history had become entwined with this place. There was scarcely a corner that did not evoke emotion, for I had been in love here, and had brought into this building my most terrible cases. I had taught and consulted in their classrooms, and inadvertently given them my niece.

'God knows what we're about to walk into,' Marino said as we got on the elevator.

'We'll just take it one inch at a time,' I said as the new agents in their FBI caps vanished behind shutting steel doors.

He pressed the button for the lower level, which had been intended as Hoover's bomb shelter in a different age. The profiling unit, as the world still called it, was sixty feet below ground, with no windows or any other relief from the horrors it found. I frankly had never understood how Wesley could endure it year after year, for whenever I sat in consultations that lasted more than a day, I was crazed. I had to walk or drive my car. I had to get away.

'An inch at a time?' Marino repeated as the elevator stopped. 'There ain't no inch or mile that's going to help this scenario. We're a day late and a dollar short. We started putting the pieces together after the game was goddamn over.'

'It isn't over,' I said.

We walked past the receptionist and around a corner, where a hallway led to the unit chief's office.

'Yeah, well, let's hope it don't end with a bang. Shit. If only we had figured it out sooner.' His stride was long and angry.

'Marino, we couldn't have known. There isn't a way.'

'Well, I think we should have figured out something sooner. Like in Sandbridge, when you got the weird phone call and then everything else.'

'Oh for God's sake,' I said. 'What? A phone call should have tipped us off that terrorists were about to seize a nuclear power plant?'

Wesley's secretary was new and I could not remember her name.

'Good afternoon,' I said to her. 'Is he in?'

'May I tell him who you are?' she asked with a smile.

We told her, and were patient as she rang him. They did not speak long.

When she looked back at us she said, 'You may go in.'

Wesley was behind his desk, and when we walked in he stood. He was typically preoccupied and somber in a gray herringbone suit and black and gray tie.

'We can go in the conference room,' he said.

'Why?' Marino took a chair. 'You got some other people coming?'

'Actually, I do,' he replied.

I stood where I was and would not give him my eyes any longer than was polite.

'I'll tell you what,' he reconsidered. 'We can stay in here. Hold on.' He walked to the door. 'Emily, can you find another chair?'

We got settled while she brought one in, and Wesley was having a hard time keeping his thoughts in one place and making decisions. I knew what he was like when he was overwhelmed. I knew when he was unnerved.

'You know what's going on,' he said as if we did.

'We know what everybody else does,' I replied. 'We've heard the same news on the radio probably a hundred times.'

'So how about starting from the beginning,' Marino said.

'CP&L has a district office in Suffolk,' Wesley began. 'At least twenty people left there this afternoon in a bus for an alleged in-service in the mock control room of the Old Point plant. They were men, white, thirties to early forties, posing as employees, which they obviously are not. And they managed to get into the main building where the control room is located.'

'They were armed,' I said.

'Yes. When it was time for them to go through the X-ray machines and other detectors at the main building, they pulled out semiautomatic weapons. As you know, people have been killed – we think at least three CP&L employees, including a nuclear physicist who just happened to be paying a site visit today and was going through security at the wrong time.'

'What are their demands?' I asked, and I wondered how much Wesley had known and for how long. 'Have they said what they want?'

He met my eyes. 'That's what worries us the most. We don't know what they want.'

'But they're letting people go,' Marino said.

'I know. And that worries me, too,' Wesley stated. 'Terrorists generally don't do that.' His telephone rang. 'This is different.' He picked up the receiver. 'Yes,' he said. 'Good. Send him in.'

Major General Lynwood Sessions was in the uniform of the Navy he served when he entered the office and shook hands with each of us. He was black, maybe forty-five and handsome in a way that was not to be dismissed. He did not take off his jacket or even loosen a button as he formally took a chair and set a fat briefcase beside him.

'General, thank you for coming,' Wesley began.

'I wish it were for a happier reason,' he said as he bent over to get out a file folder and legal pad.

'Don't we all,' Wesley said. 'This is Captain Pete Marino with

Richmond, and Dr Kay Scarpetta, the chief medical examiner of Virginia.' He looked at me and held my gaze. 'They work with us. Dr Scarpetta, as a matter of fact, is the medical examiner in the cases that we believe are related to what is happening today.'

General Sessions nodded and made no comment.

Wesley said to Marino and me, 'Let me try to tell you what we know beyond the immediate crisis. We have reason to believe that vessels in the Inactive Ship Yard are being sold to countries that should not have them. This includes Iran, Iraq, Libya, North Korea, Algeria.'

'What sort of vessels?' Marino asked.

'Mainly submarines. We also suspect that this shipyard is buying vessels from places like Russia and then reselling them.'

'And why have we not been told this before?' I asked.

Wesley hesitated. 'No one had proof.'

'Ted Eddings was diving in the Inactive Yard when he died,' I said. 'He was near a submarine.'

No one replied.

Then the general said, 'He was a reporter. It's been suggested that he might have been looking for Civil War relics.'

'And what was Danny doing?' I measured my words because I was getting tired of this. 'Exploring a historic train tunnel in Richmond?'

'It's hard to know what Danny Webster was into,' he said. 'But I understand the Chesapeake police found a bayonet in the trunk of his car, and it is consistent with the tool marks left on your slashed tires.'

I looked a long time at him. 'I don't know where you got your information, but if what you've said is true, then I suspect Detective Roche turned that evidence in.'

'I believe he turned in the bayonet, yes.'

'I believe all of us in this room can be trusted.' I kept my eyes on his. 'If there is a nuclear disaster, I am mandated by law to take care of the dead. There are already too many dead at Old Point.' I paused. 'General Sessions, now would be a very good time to tell the truth.'

The men were silent for a moment.

Then the general said, 'NAVSEA has been concerned about that shipyard for a while.'

'NAVSEA? What the hell is that?' Marino asked.

'Naval Sea Systems Command,' he said. 'They're the people responsible for making certain that shipyards like the one in question abide by the appropriate standards.'

'Eddings had the label N-V-S-E programmed into his fax machine,' I said. 'Was he in communication with them?'

'He had asked questions,' General Sessions said. 'We were aware of Mr Eddings. But we could not give him the answers he wanted. Just as we could not answer you, Dr Scarpetta, when you sent us a fax asking who we were.' His face was inscrutable. 'I'm certain you can understand that.'

'What is D-R-M-S out of Memphis?' I then asked.

'Another fax number that Eddings called, as did you,' he said. 'Defense Reutilization Marketing Service. They handle all surplus sales, which must be approved by NAVSEA.'

'This is making sense,' I said. 'I can see why Eddings would have been in touch with these people. He was on to what was happening at the Inactive Yard, that the Navy's standards were being violated in a rather shocking way. And he was probing for his story.'

'Tell me more about these standards,' Marino said. 'Exactly what is the shipyard supposed to abide by?'

'I'll give you an example. If Jacksonville wants the *Saratoga* or some other aircraft carrier, then NAVSEA makes certain that any work done to it meets the Navy's standards.'

'Like in what way?'

'For example, the city has to have the five million it will take to fix it up, and the two million for maintenance each year. And the water in the harbor must be at least thirty feet deep. On the other hand, where the ship is moored, someone from NAVSEA, probably a civilian, is going to appear about once a month and inspect the work being done to the vessel.'

'And this has been happening at the Inactive Ship Yard?' I asked.

'Well, right now, we're not sure of the civilian doing it.' The general looked straight at me.

Then it was Wesley who spoke, 'That's the problem. There are civilians everywhere, some of them mercenaries who would buy or sell anything with absolute reckless disregard for national security. As you know, a civilian company runs the Inactive Yard. It inspects the ships being sold to cities or for salvage.'

'What about the submarine in there now, the *Exploiter*?' I asked. 'The one I saw when I recovered Eddings's body?'

'A Zulu V class ballistic missile sub. Ten torpedo tubes plus two missile tubes. It was made from 1955 to 1957,' General Sessions said. 'Since the sixties, all subs built in the U.S. are nuclear-powered.'

'So the sub we're talking about is old,' Marino said. 'It's not nuclear.'

The general replied, 'It couldn't be nuclear-powered. But you can put any type of warhead on a missile or torpedo you want.'

'Are you saying that the sub I dove near might be retrofitted to fire nuclear weapons?' I asked as this frightening specter just loomed bigger.

'Dr Scarpetta,' the general said as he leaned closer to me. 'We're not assuming that sub has been retrofitted here in the United States. All that was needed was for it to be brought back up to speed and sent out to sea where it might be intercepted by a principality that should not have it. Work could be done there. But what Iraq or Algeria cannot do for themselves on their own soil is produce weapons-grade plutonium.'

'And where is that going to come from?' Marino asked. 'It's not like you can get that from a power plant. And if the terrorists think otherwise, then I guess we're dealing with a bunch of redneck dumb shits.'

'It would be extremely hard, if not close to impossible, to get plutonium from Old Point,' I agreed.

'An anarchist like Joel Hand doesn't think about how hard it might be,' Wesley said.

'And it is possible,' Sessions added. 'For about two months after new fuel rods have been placed in a reactor, there is a window in which you can get plutonium.'

'How often are the rods replaced?' Marino asked.

'Old Point replaces one-third of them every fifteen months. That's eighty assemblies, or about three atom bombs if you shut down the reactors and get the assemblies out during that two-month window.'

'Then Hand had to know the schedule,' I said.

'Oh, yes.'

I thought of the telephone records of CP&L executives that someone like Eddings might have illegally accessed.

'So someone was on the take,' I said.

'We think we know who. One high-ranking officer, really,' Sessions said. 'Someone who had a lot of say in the decision to locate the CP&L field office on property adjacent to Hand's farm.'

'A farm belonging to Joshua Hayes?'

'Yes.'

'Shit,' Marino said. 'Hand had to be planning this for years, and he sure as hell was getting a lot of bucks from somewhere.'

'No question about either,' the general agreed. 'Something like this would have to be planned for years, and someone was paying for it.'

'You need to remember that for a fanatic like Hand,' Wesley said, 'what he is engaged in is a religious war of eternal significance. He can afford to be patient.'

'General Sessions,' I went on, 'if the submarine we're speaking of is destined for a distant port, might NAVSEA know that?'

'Absolutely.'

'How?' Marino wanted to know.

'A number of things,' he said. 'For example, when ships are stored at the Inactive Yard, their missile and torpedo tubes are covered with steel plates outside the hull. And a plate is welded over the shaft inside the ship so the screw is fixed. Obviously, all guns and communications are removed.'

'Meaning that a violation of at least some of these regulations could be inspected from the outside,' I said. 'You could tell by looking at the vessel if you were near it in the water.'

He looked at me and caught my meaning precisely. 'Yes, you could tell.'

'You could dive around this sub and find that the torpedo tubes, for example, are not sealed. You might even be able to tell that the screw was not welded.'

'Yes,' he said again. 'All of that you could tell.'

'That's what Ted Eddings was doing.'

'I'm afraid so.' It was Wesley who spoke. 'Divers recovered his camera and we've looked at the film, which had only three exposures. All blurred images of the *Exploiter*'s screw. So it doesn't appear he was in the water long before he died.'

'And where is that submarine now?' I asked.

The general paused. 'You might say that we're in subtle pursuit of it.'

'Then it's gone.'

'I'm afraid it left port about the same time the nuclear power plant was stormed.'

I looked at the three men. 'Well, I certainly think we know why Eddings had gotten increasingly paranoid about self-protection.'

'Someone must have set him up,' Marino said. 'You can't just decide at the last minute to poison someone with cyanide gas.'

'His was a premeditated murder committed by someone he must have trusted,' Wesley said. 'He wouldn't have told just anybody what he was doing that night.'

I thought of another label in Eddings's fax machine. CPT could stand for captain, and I mentioned Captain Green's name to them.

'Well, Eddings must have had at least one inside source for his story,' was Wesley's comment. 'Someone was leaking information to him and I suspect this same someone set him up or at least assisted in it.' He looked at me. 'And we know from his phone bills that over the past few months, he had quite a lot of communication with Green, by phone and fax, that seems to have begun last fall when Eddings did a rather harmless profile on the shipyard.'

'Then he started digging too deep,' I said.

'His curiosity was actually helpful to us,' General Sessions said. 'We started digging deeper, too. We've been investigating this situation longer than you might imagine.' He paused, and smiled a little. 'In fact, Dr Scarpetta, you have not been as alone at some points as you might have thought.'

'I sincerely hope you'll thank Jerod and Ki Soo,' I said, assuming they were SEALs.

But it was Wesley who replied, 'I will, or perhaps you can yourself next time you visit HRT.'

'General Sessions,' I moved on to what seemed a rather more mundane topic. 'Would you happen to know if rats are a concern in decommissioned ships?'

'Rats are always a worry in any ship,' he said.

'One of the uses of cyanide is to exterminate rodents in the hulls of ships,' I said. 'The Inactive Yard may keep a supply of it.'

'As I've indicated, Captain Green is of great concern to us.' He knew just what I meant.

'Vis-à-vis the New Zionists?' I asked.

'No,' Wesley answered for him. 'Not as opposed to but as with. My speculation is that Green is the New Zionists' direct link to anything military, such as the shipyard, while Roche is simply his toady. Roche is the one who harasses, snoops and snitches.'

'He didn't kill Danny,' I said.

'Danny was killed by a psychopathic individual who blends well enough with normal society that he did not draw any attention to himself as he waited outside the Hill Cafe. I'd profile this individual as a white male, early thirties to early forties, experienced in hunting and in guns, in general.'

'Sounds like the spitting image of the drones who took over Old Point,' Marino remarked.

'Yes,' Wesley said. 'Killing Danny, whether he was the intended victim or not, was a hunting assignment, like shooting a groundhog. The individual who did this probably bought the Sig forty-five at the same gun show where he got the Black Talons.'

'I thought you said the Sig once belonged to a cop,' the general reminded him.

'Right. It ends up on the street and eventually gets sold second-hand,' Wesley said.

'To one of Hand's followers,' Marino said. 'The same kind of guy that took out Shapiro in Maryland.'

'The exact same kind of guy.'

'My big question is what they think you know,' the general asked me.

'I've thought about that a lot and can't come up with anything,' I replied.

'You have to think like they do,' Wesley said to me. 'What is it they think you might know that others don't?'

'They might think I have the Book,' I said for lack of anything else that came to mind. 'And apparently that is as sacred as an Indian burial ground to them.'

'What's in it that they wouldn't want anyone else to know?' Sessions asked.

'It would seem that the revelation most dangerous to them would be the plan they've already carried out,' I replied.

'Of course. They couldn't carry it out if someone tipped their hand.' Wesley looked at me, a thousand thoughts in his eyes. 'What does Dr Mant know?'

'I haven't had the chance to ask him. He doesn't answer my calls, and I've left messages numerous times.'

'You don't think that's rather strange?'

'I absolutely think it's strange,' I said to him. 'But I don't think anything extreme has happened, or we would have heard. I think he's afraid.'

Wesley explained to the general, 'He's the medical examiner in charge of the Tidewater District.'

'Well, then, perhaps you should go see him,' the general suggested to me.

'In light of circumstances, this doesn't seem the ideal time,' I said.

'On the contrary,' the general said. 'I think this is precisely the ideal time.'

'You might be right,' Wesley agreed. 'Our only hope, really, is to get inside these people's heads. Maybe Mant has information that could help. Maybe that's why he's hiding.'

General Sessions shifted in his chair. 'Well, I vote for it,' he said. 'For one thing, we've got to worry about this same kind of thing happening over there, as you and I have already discussed, Benton. So that business already awaits anyway, doesn't it? It won't be any big deal for another person to go along, providing British Airways doesn't mind, short notice and all.' He seemed amused in a wry way. 'If they do, I expect I'll just have to call the Pentagon.'

'Kay,' Wesley explained this to me while Marino looked on with angry eyes, 'we don't know that an Old Point isn't already happening in Europe because what's going on in Virginia didn't happen overnight. We're worried about major cities elsewhere.'

'So, are you telling me these New Zionist fruit loops are in England, too?' It was Marino who asked, and he was about to boil over.

'Not that we are aware of, but unfortunately, there are plenty of others to take their place,' Wesley said.

'Well, I got an opinion.' Marino looked accusingly at me. 'We got a possible nuclear disaster on our hands. Don't you think you ought to stick around?'

'That would be my preference.'

The general made the salient remark, 'If you help, hopefully it won't be necessary for you to stick around because there won't be anything for you to do.'

'I understand that, too,' I said. 'No one believes in prevention more than I do.'

'Can you manage it?' Wesley asked.

'My offices are already mobilizing to handle whatever happens,' I said. 'The other doctors know what to do. You know I'll help in any way I possibly can.'

But Marino was not to be soothed. 'It ain't safe.' He stared at Wesley now. 'You can't just go sending the doc through airports and all the hell over the place when we don't know who's out there or what they want.'

'You're right, Pete,' Wesley thoughtfully said. 'And we're not going to do that.'

14

That night I went home because I needed clothes, and my passport was in the safe. I packed with nervous hands as I waited for my pager to beep. Fielding had been calling me on the hour to hear updates and air his concerns. The bodies at Old Point remained where the gunmen had left them, as best we knew, and we did not know how many of the plant's workers remained imprisoned inside.

I slept restlessly under the watch of a police car parked on my street, and I sat up when the alarm clock startled me awake at five A.M. An hour and a half later, a Learjet awaited me at the Millionaire Terminal in Henrico Country, where the area's wealthiest businessmen parked their helicopters and corporate planes. Wesley and I were polite but guarded as we greeted each other, and I was having trouble believing we were about to fly overseas together. But it had been planned that he would visit the embassy before it was suggested that I should go to London, too, and General Sessions did not know about our history. Or at least this was how I chose to view a situation that was out of my hands.

'I'm not sure I trust your motives,' I said to Wesley as the jet took off like a race car with wings. 'And what about this?' I looked around. 'Since when does the Bureau use Learjets, or did the Pentagon arrange this, too?'

'We use whatever we need,' he said. 'CP&L has made available any resource it has to help us resolve this crisis, and this Learjet belongs to them.'

The white jet was sleek, with burlwood and teal green leather seats, but it was loud, so we could not speak softly.

'You don't have to worry about using something of theirs?' I said.

'They're just as unhappy about all this as we are. As far as we know, with the exception of one or two bad apples, CP&L is blameless. In fact, it and its employees are clearly the most profoundly victimized.'

He stared ahead at the cockpit and its two well-built pilots dressed in suits. 'Besides, the pilots are HRT,' he added. 'And we checked every nut and bolt of this thing before we took off. Don't worry. As for my going with you' – he looked at me – 'I'll say it again. What happens now is operational. The ball has been passed to HRT. I will be needed when terrorists begin to communicate with us, when we can at least identify them. But I don't think that will be for several days.'

'How can you possibly know that?' I poured coffee.

He took the cup from my hand and our fingers brushed. 'I know because they're busy. They want those assemblies, and there are only so many they can get per day.'

'Have the reactors been shut down?'

'According to the power company, the terrorists shut down the reactors immediately after storming the plant. So they know what they want, and they are down to business.'

'And there are twenty of them.'

'That's approximately how many went in for their alleged seminar in the mock control room. But we really can't be sure how many are there now.'

'This tour,' I said, 'when was it scheduled?'

'The power company said it was originally scheduled in early December for the end of February.'

'Then they moved it up.' I wasn't surprised in light of what had happened lately.

'Yes,' he said. 'It was suddenly rescheduled a couple of days before Eddings was killed.'

'It sounds like they're desperate, Benton.'

'And probably more reckless and not as prepared,' he said. 'And that's better and worse for us.'

'And what about hostages? Is it likely they will let all of them go, based on your experience?'

'I don't know about all of them,' he said, staring out the window, his face grim in soft side lights.

'Lord,' I said, 'if they try to get the fuel out, we could have a national disaster on our hands. And I don't see how they think they can pull this off. Those assemblies probably weigh several tons each and are so radioactive they could cause instant death if you got close. And how will they get them away from Old Point?'

'The plant's surrounded by water for purposes of cooling the reactors. And nearby, on the James, we're watching a barge we believe belongs to them.'

I remembered Marino telling me of barges delivering large crates to the New Zionist compound, and I said, 'Can we take it?'

'No. We can't take barges, submarines, nothing right now. Not until we can get those hostages out.' He sipped coffee, and the horizon was turning a pale gold.

'Then the best-case scenario is they will take what they want and leave without killing anybody else,' I supposed, although I did not think this could happen.

'No. The best-case scenario is we stop them there.' He looked at me. 'We don't want a barge full of highly radioactive material on Virginia's rivers or out at sea. What are we going to do, threaten to sink it? Besides, my guess is they'll take hostages with them.' He paused. 'Eventually, they'll shoot them all.'

I could not help but imagine those poor people now as fright shocked every nerve cell every moment they breathed. I knew about the physical and mental manifestations of fear, and the images were searing and I seethed inside. I felt a wave of hatred for these men who called themselves the New Zionists, and I clenched my fists.

Wesley looked down at my white knuckles on the armrests, and thought I was afraid of flying. 'It's only a few more minutes,' he said. 'We're starting our descent.'

We landed at Kennedy, and a shuttle waited for us on the tarmac. It was driven by two more fit men in suits, and I did not ask Wesley about them because I already knew. One of them walked us inside the terminal to British Airways, which had been kind enough to cooperate with the Bureau, or maybe it was the Pentagon, by making two seats available on their next Concorde flight to London. At the counter, we discreetly showed our credentials and said we had not packed guns. The agent assigned to keep us safe walked with us to the lounge, and when I looked for him next, he was perusing stacks of foreign newspapers.

Wesley and I found seats before expansive windows looking out over the tarmac where the supersonic plane waited like a giant white heron being fed fuel through a thick hose attached to its side. The Concorde looked more like a rocket than any commercial craft I had seen, and it appeared that most of its passengers were no longer capable of being impressed by it or much of anything. They served themselves pastries and fruit, and some were already mixing Bloody Marys and mimosas.

Wesley and I talked little and constantly scanned the crowd as we held up newspapers like every other proverbial spy or fugitive on the run. I could tell that Middle Easterners, in particular, caught his eye, while I was more wary of people who looked like us, for I remembered Joel Hand that day I had faced him in court and had found him attractive and genteel. If he sat next to me right now and I did not know him, I would have thought he belonged in this lounge more than we.

'How are you doing?' Wesley lowered his paper.

'I don't know.' I was agitated. 'So tell me. Are we alone or is your friend still here?'

His eyes smiled.

'I don't see what's amusing about this.'

'So you thought the Secret Service might be nearby. Or undercover agents.'

'I see. I guess that man in the suit who walked us here is special services for British Airways.'

'Let me answer your question this way. If we're not alone, Kay, I'm not going to tell you.'

We looked at each other a moment longer – we had never traveled abroad together, and now did not seem like a good time to start. He was wearing a blue suit so dark it was almost black, and his usual white shirt and conservative tie. I had dressed with similar somber deliberation, and both of us had our glasses on. I thought we looked like partners in a law firm, and as I noticed other women in the room I was reminded that what I did not look like was anybody's wife.

Paper rustled as he folded the London *Times* and glanced at his watch. 'I think that's us,' he said, getting up as Flight 2 was called again.

The Concorde held a hundred people in two cabins with two seats on either side of the aisle. The decor was muted gray carpet and leather, with spaceship windows too small to gaze out. Flight attendants were British and typically polite, and if they knew we were the two passengers from the FBI, Navy, or God knows, the CIA, they did not indicate so in any way. Their only concern seemed to be what we wanted to drink, and I ordered whiskey.

'It's a little early, isn't it?' Wesley said.

'Not in London it's not,' I told him. 'It's five hours later there.'

'Thank you. I'll set my watch,' he dryly said as if he'd never been anywhere in his life. 'I guess I'll have a beer,' he told the attendant.

'There, now that we're on the proper time zone, it's easier to drink,' I said, and I could not keep the bite out of my voice.

He turned to me and met my eyes. 'You sound angry.'

'That's why you're a profiler, because you can figure out things like that.'

He subtly looked around us, but we were behind the bulkhead with no one across the aisle, and I almost did not care who was at our rear.

'Can we talk reasonably?' he quietly asked.

'It's hard to be reasonable, Benton, when you always want to talk after the fact.'

'I'm not sure I understand what you mean. I think there's a transition missing somewhere.'

I was about to give him one. 'Everyone knew about your separation except me,' I said. 'Lucy told me because she heard about it from other agents. I would just like to be included in our relationship for once.'

'Christ, I wish you wouldn't get so upset.'

'Not half as much as I do.'

'I didn't tell you because I didn't want to be influenced by you,' he said.

We were talking in low voices, leaning forward and together so that our shoulders were touching. Despite the grim circumstances, I was aware of his every move and how it felt against me. I smelled his wool jacket and the cologne he liked to wear.

'Any decision about my marriage can't include you,' he went on as our drinks arrived. 'I know you must understand that.'

My body wasn't used to whiskey at this hour, and the effect of it was quick and strong. I instantly began to relax, and shut my eyes during the roar of takeoff as the jet leaned back and throbbed, thundering up through the air. From then on, the world below became nothing but a vague horizon, if I could see anything out the window at all. The noise of engines remained loud, making it necessary for us to continue sitting very close to each other as we intensely talked on.

'I know how I feel about you,' Wesley was saying. 'I have known that for a long time.'

'You have no right,' I said. 'You have never had a right.'

'And what about you? Did you have a right to do what you did, Kay? Or was I the only one in the room.'

'At least I'm not married or even with anyone,' I said. 'But no, I shouldn't have.'

He was still drinking beer and neither of us was interested in the canapes and caviar that I suspected would prove the first inning of a long gourmet game. For a while we fell silent, flipping through magazines and professional journals while almost everyone else inside our cabin did the same. I noticed that people on the Concorde did not talk to each other much, and I decided that being rich and famous or royal must be rather boring.

'So I guess we've resolved that issue then,' Wesley started again, leaning closer as I picked at asparagus.

'What issue?' I set down my fork, because I was left-handed and he was in the way.

'You know. About what we should and shouldn't do.' He brushed against my breast and then his arm stayed there as if all we had said earlier was voided at Mach two.

'Yes,' I said.

'Yes?' His voice was curious. 'What do you mean, yes?'

'Yes about what you just said.' With each breath I took, my body moved against him. 'About resolving things.'

'Then that's what we'll do,' he agreed.

'Of course we will,' I said, not entirely certain what we had just agreed to. 'One other thing,' I added. 'If you ever get divorced and we want to see each other, we start over.'

'Absolutely. That makes perfect sense.'

'In the meantime, we're colleagues and friends.'

'That's exactly what I want, too,' he said.

At half past six, we sped along Park Lane, both of us silent in the backseat of a Rover driven by an officer of the Metropolitan Police. In darkness, I watched the lights of London go by, and I was disoriented and vividly alive. Hyde Park was a sea of spreading darkness, lamps smudges of light along winding paths.

The flat where we were staying was very close to the Dorchester Hotel, and Pakistanis pooled around that grand old hotel this night, protesting their visiting prime minister with fervor. Riot police and dogs were out in numbers, but our driver seemed unconcerned.

'There is a doorman,' he said as he pulled in front of a tall building that looked relatively new. 'Just go in and give him your identification. He will get you into your accommodations. Do you need help with your bags?'

Wesley opened his door. 'Thanks. We can manage.'

We got out and went inside a small reception area, where an alert older man smiled warmly at us from behind a polished desk.

'Oh right. I've been expecting you,' he said.

He got up and took our bags. 'If you'll just follow me to the lift here.'

We got on and rose to the fifth floor, where he showed us a three-bedroom flat with wide windows, bright fabrics and African art. My room was comfortably appointed, with the typical English tub large enough to drown in and toilet that flushed with a chain. Furniture was Victorian with hardwood floors covered in worn Turkish rugs, and I went over to the window and turned the radiator up high. I switched off lamps and gazed out at cars rushing past and dark trees in the park moving in the wind.

Wesley's room was down the hall at the far end, and I did not hear him walk in until he spoke.

'Kay?' He waited near my doorway, and I heard ice softly rattle. 'Whoever lives here keeps very fine Scotch. I've been told we are to help ourselves.'

He walked in and set tumblers on the sill.

'Are you trying to get me drunk?' I asked.

'It's never been necessary in the past.'

He stood next to me, and we drank and leaned against each other as we looked out together. For a long time we spoke in small, quiet sentences, and then he touched my hair, and kissed my ear and jaw. I touched him, too, and our love for each other got deeper as our kisses and caresses did.

'I've missed you so much,' he whispered as clothing became loosened and undone.

We made love because we could not help ourselves. That was our only excuse and would hold up in no court I knew. Separation had been very hard, so we were hungry with each other all night. Then at dawn I drifted off to sleep long enough to awaken and find him gone, as if it all had been a dream. I lay beneath a down-filled duvet, and images were slow and lyrical in my mind. Lights danced beneath my lids and I felt as if I were being rocked, as if I were a little girl again and my father were not dying of a disease I did not understand back then.

I had never gotten over him. I supposed my attachments to all men had sadly relived my being left by him. It was a dance I moved to without trying, and then found myself in silence in the empty room of my most private life. I realized how much Lucy and I were alike. We both loved in secret and would not speak of pain.

Getting dressed, I went out into the hall and found Wesley in the living room drinking coffee as he looked out at a cloudy day. He was dressed in suit and tie, and did not seem tired.

'There's coffee on,' he said. 'Can I get you some?'

'Thanks, I'll get it.' I stepped into the kitchen. 'Have you been up long?'

'For a while.'

He made coffee very strong, and it struck me that there were so many domestic details about him I did not know. We did not cook together or go on vacations or do sports when I knew we both enjoyed so many of the same things. I walked into the living room and set my cup and saucer on a windowsill because I wanted to look out at the park.

'How are you?' His eyes lingered on mine.

'I'm fine. What about you?'

'You don't look fine.'

'You always know just the thing to say.'

'You look like you didn't get much sleep. That's what I meant.'

'I got virtually no sleep, and you're to blame.'

He smiled. 'That and jet lag.'

'The lag you cause is worse, Special Agent Wesley.'

Already traffic was loud rushing past, and punctuated periodically by the odd cacophony of British sirens. In the cold, early light, people were walking briskly along sidewalks, and some were jogging. Wesley got up from his chair.

'We should be going soon.' He rubbed the back of my neck and kissed it. 'We should get a little something to eat. It's going to be a long day.'

'Benton, I don't like living this way,' I said as he shut the door.

We followed Park Lane past the Dorchester Hotel, where some Pakistanis were still taking their stand. Then we took Mount Street to South Audley where we found a small restaurant open called Richoux. Inside were exotic French pastries and boxes of chocolates beautiful enough to display as art. People were dressed for business and reading newspapers at small tables. I drank fresh orange juice and got hungry. Our Filipino waitress was puzzled because Wesley had only toast while I ordered bacon and eggs with mushrooms and tomatoes.

'You wish to share?' she asked.

'No, thank you.' I smiled.

At not quite ten A.M., we continued on South Audley to Grosvenor Square, where the American Embassy was an unfortunate granite block of 1950s architecture guarded by a bronze eagle rampant on the roof. Security was extremely tight, with somber guards everywhere. We produced passports and credentials, and our photographs were taken. Finally, we were escorted to the second floor where we were to meet with the FBI's senior legal attaché, or legate, for Great Britain. Chuck Olson's corner office afforded a perfect view of people waiting in long lines for visas and green cards. He was a stocky man in a dark suit, his neatly trimmed hair almost as silver as Wesley's.

'A pleasure,' he said as he shook our hands. 'Please have a seat. Would anybody like coffee?'

Wesley and I chose a couch across from a desk that was clear except for a notepad and file folders. On a cork board behind Olson's head were drawings that I assumed were done by his children, and above these hung a large Department of Justice seal. Other than shelves of books and various commendations, the office was the simple space of a busy person unimpressed with his job or self.

'Chuck,' Wesley began, 'I'm sure you already know that Dr Scarpetta is our consulting forensic pathologist, and though she does have her own situation in Virginia to handle, she could be called back here later.'

'God forbid,' Olson said, for if there was a nuclear disaster in England or anywhere in Europe, chances were I would be brought in to help handle the dead.

'So I wonder if you could give her a clearer picture of our concerns,' Wesley said.

'Well, there's the obvious,' Olson said to me. 'About a third of England's electricity is generated by nuclear power. We're worried about a similar terrorist strike, and don't know, in fact, if one hasn't already been planned by these same people.'

'But the New Zionists are rooted in Virginia,' I said. 'Are you saying they have international connections?'

'They aren't the driving force in this,' he said. 'They aren't the ones who want plutonium.'

'Who specifically, then?' I said.

'Libya.'

'I think the world has known that for a while,' I replied.

'Well, now it's happening,' Wesley said. 'It's happening at Old Point.'

'As you no doubt know,' Olson went on, 'Qaddafi has wanted nuclear weapons for a very long time and has been thwarted in his every attempt. It appears he finally found a way. He found the New Zionists in Virginia, and certainly, there are extremist groups he could use over here. We also have many Arabs.'

'How do you know it's Libya?' I asked.

It was Wesley who replied, 'For one thing, we've been going through Joel Hand's telephone records and they include numerous calls – mainly to Tripoli and Benghāzī – made over the past two years.'

'But you don't know that Qaddafi is trying anything here in London,' I said.

'What we fear is how vulnerable we would be. London is the stepping-off point to Europe, the U.S. and the Middle East. It is a tremendous financial center. Just because Libya steals fire from the U.S. doesn't mean the U.S. is the ultimate target.'

'Fire?' I asked.

'As in the myth about Prometheus. Fire is our code for plutonium.'

'I understand,' I said. 'What you're saying makes chilling sense. Tell me what I can do.'

'Well, we need to explore the mind-set of this thing, both for purposes of what's happening now and what might happen later,' Olson said. 'We need to get a better handle on how these terrorists think, and that, obviously, is Wesley's department. Yours is to get information. I understand you have a colleague here who might prove useful.'

'We can only hope,' I said. 'But I intend to speak to him.'

'What about security?' Wesley asked him. 'Do we need to put someone with her?'

Olson looked at me oddly as if assessing my strength, as if I were not myself but an object or fighter about to step into the ring.

'No,' he said. 'I think she's absolutely safe here, unless you know otherwise.'

'I'm not sure,' Wesley said as he looked at me, too. 'Maybe we should send someone with her.'

'Absolutely not. No one knows I'm in London,' I said. 'And Dr

Mant already is reluctant, if not scared to death, so he's certainly not going to open up to me if someone else is along. Then the point of this trip is defeated.'

'All right,' Wesley reluctantly said. 'Just so long as we know where you are, and we need to meet back here no later than four if we're going to catch that plane.'

'I'll call you if I get hung up,' I said. 'You'll be here?'

'If we're not, my secretary will know where to find us,' Olson said.

I went down to the lobby where water splashed loudly in a fountain and a bronze Lincoln was enthroned within walls lined with portraits of former U.S. representatives. Guards were severe as they studied passports and visitors. They let me pass with cool stares, and I felt their eyes follow me out the door. On the street in the cold, damp morning, I hailed a cab and gave the driver an address not very far away in Belgravia off Eaton Square.

The elderly Mrs Mant had lived in Ebury Mews in a three-story town house that had been divided into flats. Her building was stucco with red chimney pots piled high on a variegated shingle roof, and window boxes were filled with daffodils, crocuses and ivy. I climbed stairs to the second floor and knocked on her door, but when it was answered, it was not by my deputy chief. The matronly woman peering out at me looked as confused as I did.

'Excuse me,' I said to her. 'I guess this has already been sold.'

'No, I'm sorry. It's not for sale a'tall,' she firmly said.

'I'm looking for Philip Mant,' I went on. 'Clearly I must have the wrong . . .'

'Oh,' she said. 'Philip's my brother.' She smiled pleasantly. 'He just left for work. You just missed him.'

'Work?' I said.

'Oh yes, he always leaves right about this time. To avoid traffic, you know. Although I don't think that's really possible.' She hesitated, suddenly aware of the stranger before her. 'Might I tell him who dropped by?'

'Dr Kay Scarpetta,' I said. 'And I really must find him.'

'Why of course.' She seemed as pleased as she was surprised. 'I've heard him speak of you. He's enormously fond of you and will be absolutely delighted to hear you came by. What brings you to London?'

'I never miss an opportunity to visit here. Might you tell me where I could find him?' I asked again.

'Of course. The Westminster Public Mortuary on Horseferry Road.'

She hesitated, uncertain. 'I should have thought he would have told you.'

'Yes.' I smiled. 'And I'm very pleased for him.'

I wasn't certain what I was talking about, but she seemed very pleased, too.

'Don't tell him I'm coming,' I went on. 'I intend to surprise him.'

'Oh, that's brilliant. He will be absolutely thrilled.'

I caught another taxi as I thought about what I believed she had just said. No matter Mant's reason for what he had done, I could not help but feel slightly furious.

'You going to the Coroner's Court, ma'am?' the driver asked me. 'It's right there.' He pointed out the open window at a handsome brick building.

'No, I'm going to the actual mortuary,' I said.

'All right. Well that's right here. Better that you walk in,' he said with a hoarse laugh.

I got out money as he parked in front of a building small by London standards. Brick with granite trim and a strange parapet along the roof, it was surrounded by an ornate wrought-iron fence painted the color of rust. According to the date on a plaque at the entrance, the mortuary was more than a hundred years old, and I thought about how grim it would have been to practice forensic medicine in those days. There would have been few witnesses to tell the story except for the human kind, and I wondered if people had lied less in earlier times.

The mortuary's reception area was small but pleasantly furnished like a typical lobby for a normal business. Through an open door was a corridor, and since I did not see anyone, I headed that way just as a woman emerged from a room, her arms loaded with oversized books.

'Sorry,' she said, startled. 'But you can't come back here.'

'I'm looking for Dr Mant,' I said.

She wore a loose-fitting long dress and sweater, and spoke with a Scottish accent. 'And who may I tell him is here to see him?' she politely said.

I showed her my credentials.

'Oh very good. I see. And he must be expecting you.'

'I shouldn't think so,' I said.

'I see.' She shifted the books to another arm, and she was very confused.

'He used to work with me in the States,' I said. 'I'd like to surprise him, so I prefer to find him if you'll just tell me where.'

'Dear me, that would be the Foul Room just now. If you go through this door here.' She nodded at it. 'And you'll see locker rooms to the left of the main mortuary. Everything you need is there, then turn left again through another set of doors, and right beyond that. Is that clear?' She smiled.

'Thank you,' I said.

In the locker room I put on booties, gloves and mask, and loosely tied a gown around me to keep the odor out of my clothes. I passed through a tiled room where six stainless-steel tables and a wall of white refrigerators gleamed. The doctors wore blue, and Westminster was keeping them busy this morning. They scarcely glanced at me as I walked past. Down the hall I found my deputy chief in tall rubber boots, standing on a footstool as he worked on a badly decomposing body that I suspected had been in water for a while. The stench was terrible, and I shut the door behind me.

'Dr Mant,' I said.

He turned around and for an instant did not seem to know who I was or where he was. Then he simply looked shocked.

'Dr Scarpetta? My God, why I'll be bloody damned.' He heavily stepped off the stool, for he was not a small man. 'I'm so surprised. I'm rather speechless!' He was sputtering, and his eyes wavered with fear.

'I'm surprised, too,' I somberly said.

'I quite imagine that you are. Come on. No need to talk in here with this rather ghastly floater. Found him in the Thames yesterday afternoon. Looks like a stabbing to me but we have no identity. We should go to the lounge,' he nervously talked on.

Philip Mant was a charming old gentleman impossible not to like, with thick white hair and heavy brows over keen pale eyes. He showed me around the corner to showers, where we disinfected our feet, stripped off gloves and masks and stuffed scrubs into a bin. Then we went to the lounge, which opened onto the parking lot in back. Like everything else in London, the stale smoke in this room had a long history, too.

'May I offer you some refreshment?' he asked as he got out a pack of Players. 'I know you don't smoke anymore, so I won't offer.'

'I don't need a thing except some answers from you,' I said.

His hands trembled slightly as he struck a match.

'Dr Mant, what in God's name are you doing here?' I started in. 'You're supposed to be in London because you had a death in the family.'

'I did. Coincidentally.'

'Coincidentally?' I said. 'And what does that mean?'

'Dr Scarpetta, I fully intended to leave anyway and then my mother suddenly died and that made it easy to choose a time.'

'Then you've had no intention of coming back,' I said, stung.

'I'm quite sorry. But no, I have not.' He delicately tapped an ash.

'You could at least have told me so I could have begun looking for your replacement. I've tried to call you several times.'

'I didn't tell you and I didn't call because I didn't want them to know.'

'Them?' The word seemed to hang in the air. 'Exactly who do you mean, Dr Mant?'

He was very matter-of-fact as he smoked, legs crossed and belly roundly swelling over his belt. 'I have no idea who they are, but they certainly know who we are. That's what alarms me. I can tell you exactly when it all began. October thirteenth, and you may or may not remember the case.'

I had no idea what he was talking about.

'Well, the Navy did the autopsy because the death was at their shipyard in Norfolk.'

'The man who was accidentally crushed in a dry dock?' I vaguely recalled it.

'The very one.'

'You're right. That was a Navy case, not ours,' I said as I began to anticipate what he had to say. 'Tell me what that has to do with us.'

'You see, the rescue squad made a mistake,' he continued. 'Instead of transporting the body to Portsmouth Naval Hospital, where it belonged, they brought it to my office, and young Danny didn't know. He began drawing blood, doing paperwork, that sort of thing, and in the process found something very unusual amongst the decedent's personal effects.'

I realized Mant did not know about Danny.

'The victim had a canvas satchel with him,' he went on. 'And the squad had simply placed it on top of the body and covered everything with a sheet. Poor form as it may be, I suppose had that not occurred we wouldn't have had a clue.'

'A clue about what?'

'What this fellow had, apparently, was a copy of a rather sinister bible that I came to find out later is connected to a cult. The New Zionists. An absolutely terrible thing, that book was, describing in detail torture, murder, things like that. It was terribly unsettling, in my view.'

'Was it called the *Book of Hand*?' I asked.

'Why yes.' His eyes lit up. 'It was, indeed.'

'Was it in a black leather binder?'

'I believe it was. With a name stamped on it that oddly enough was not the name of the decedent. Shapiro, or something.'

'Dwain Shapiro.'

'Of course,' he said. 'Then you already know about this.'

'I know about the Book but not why this individual had it in his possession, because certainly his name was not Dwain Shapiro.'

He paused to rub his face. 'I think his name was Catlett.'

'But he could have been Dwain Shapiro's killer,' I said. 'That could be why he had the bible.'

Mant did not know. 'When I realized we had a naval case in our morgue,' he said, 'I had Danny transport the body to Portsmouth. Clearly, the poor man's effects should have gone with him.'

'But Danny kept the book,' I said.

'I'm afraid so.' He leaned forward and crushed out the cigarette in an ashtray on the coffee table.

'Why would he do that?'

'I happened to walk into his office and spotted it, and I asked him why in the world he had it. His explanation was that since the book had another individual's name on it, he wondered if it hadn't been accidentally picked up at the scene. That perhaps the satchel belonged to someone else, as well.' He paused. 'You see, he was still rather new and I think he'd simply made an honest mistake.'

'Tell me something,' I said, 'were any reporters calling the office or coming around at this time? For example, might anyone have inquired about the man crushed to death in the shipyard?'

'Oh yes, Mr Eddings showed up. I remember that because he was rather keen on finding out every detail, which puzzled me a bit. To my knowledge, he never wrote anything about it.'

'Might Danny have talked to Eddings?'

Mant stared off in thought. 'It seems I did see the two of them talking some. But young Danny certainly knew better than to give him a quote.'

'Might he have given Eddings the Book, assuming that Eddings was doing a story on the New Zionists?'

'Actually, I wouldn't know. I never saw the Book again and assumed Danny had returned it to the Navy. I miss the lad. How is he, by the way? How is his knee? I called him Hop-Along, you know.' He laughed.

But I did not answer his question or even smile. 'Tell me what happened after that. What made you afraid?'

'Strange things. Hang-ups. I felt I was being followed. My morgue supervisor, as you recall, abruptly quit with no good explanation. And one day when I went out to the parking lot, there was blood all over the windshield of my car. I actually had it tested in the lab, and it was type butcher shop. From a cow, in other words.'

'I presume you have met Detective Roche,' I said.

'Unfortunately. I don't fancy him a'tall.'

'Did he ever try to get information from you?'

'He would drop by. Not for postmortems, of course. He doesn't have the stomach for them.'

'What did he want to know?'

'Well, the Navy death we talked about. He had questions about that.'

'Did he ask about his personal effects? The satchel that inadvertently came into the morgue along with the body?'

Mant was trying to remember. 'Well, now that you're prodding this rather pathetic memory of mine, it seems I do recall him asking about the satchel. And I referred him to Danny, I believe.'

'Well, Danny obviously never gave it to him,' I said. 'Or at least not the Book, because that has turned up since.'

I did not tell him how because I did not want to upset him.

'That bloody Book must be terribly important to someone,' he mused.

I paused as he smoked again. Then I said, 'Why didn't you tell me? Why did you just run and never say a word?'

'Frankly, I didn't want you dragged into it, as well. And it all sounded rather fantastic.' He paused, and I could tell by his face he sensed other bad events had occurred since he had left Virginia. 'Dr Scarpetta, I'm not a young man. I only want to peacefully do my job a little while longer before I retire.'

I did not want to criticize him further because I understood what he had done. I frankly could not blame him and was glad he had fled, for he probably had saved his own life. Ironically, there had been nothing important he knew, and had he been murdered, it would have been for no cause, as Danny's murder was for no cause.

Then I told the truth as I pushed back images of a knee brace as bright red as blood spilled, and leaves and trash clinging to gory hair. I remembered Danny's brilliant smile and would never forget the small white bag he had carried out of the cafe on a hill, where a dog had barked half the night. In my mind, I would always see the sadness and fear in his eyes when he helped me with the murdered Ted Eddings, who I now realized he had known. Together, the two young men had inadvertently led each other a step closer to their eventual violent deaths.

'Dear Lord. The poor boy,' was all Mant could say.

He covered his eyes with a handkerchief, and when I left him, he was still crying.

15

Wesley and I flew back to New York that night, and arrived early because tail winds were more than a hundred knots. We went through customs and got our bags, then the same shuttle met us at the curb and returned us to the private airport where the Learjet was still waiting.

The weather had suddenly warmed and was threatening rain, and we flew between colossal black thunderheads lighting up with violent thoughts. The storm loudly cracked and flashed as we sped through what seemed the middle of a feud. I had been briefed a little as to the current state of affairs, and it had come as no surprise that the Bureau had established an outpost along with others set up by police and rescue crews.

Lucy, I was relieved to hear, had been brought in from the field, and was working again in the Engineering Research Facility, or ERF, where she was safe. What Wesley did not tell me until we reached the Academy was that she had been deployed along with the rest of HRT and would not be at Quantico long.

'Out of the question,' I said to him as if I were a mother refusing permission.

'I'm afraid you don't have a say in this,' he replied.

He was helping me carry my bags through the Jefferson lobby, which was deserted this Saturday night. We waved to the young women at the registration desk as we continued arguing.

'For God's sake,' I went on, 'she's brand new. You can't just throw her into the middle of a nuclear crisis.'

'We're not throwing her into anything.' He pushed open glass doors. 'All we need are her technical skills. She's not going to be doing any sniper-shooting or jumping out of planes.'

'Where is she now?' I asked as we got on an elevator.

'Hopefully in bed.'

'Oh.' I looked at my watch. 'I guess it is midnight. I thought it was tomorrow and I should be getting up.'

'I know. I'm screwed up, too.'

Our eyes met and I looked away. 'I guess we're supposed to pretend nothing happened,' I said with an edge to my voice, for there had been no discussion of what had happened between us.

We walked out into the hall and he pressed a code into a digitalized keypad. A lock released and he opened another glass door.

'What good would it do to pretend?' he said, entering another code and opening another door.

'Just tell me what you want to do,' I said.

We were inside the security suite where I usually stayed when work or danger kept me here overnight. He carried my bags into the bedroom as I drew draperies across the large window in the living room. The decor was comfortable but plain, and when Wesley did not respond, I remembered it probably was not safe to talk intimately in this place where I knew at the very least phones were monitored. I followed him back out into the hall and repeated my question.

'Be patient,' he said, and he looked sad, or maybe he was just weary. 'Look, Kay, I've got to go home. First thing in the morning we've got to do a surveillance by air with Marcia Gradecki and Senator Lord.'

Gradecki was the United States attorney general, and Frank Lord was the chairman of the Judiciary Committee and an old friend.

'I'd like you along since overall you seem to know more of what's been going on than anyone else. Maybe you can explain to them the importance of the bible these wackos believe. That they'll kill for it. They'll die for it.'

He sighed and rubbed his eyes. 'And we need to talk about how we're going to – God forbid – handle the contaminated dead should these goddamn assholes decide to blow up the reactors.' He looked at me again. 'All we can do is try,' he said, and I knew he referred to more than the present crisis.

'That's what I'm doing, Benton,' I said, and I walked back inside my suite.

I called the switchboard and asked them to ring Lucy's room, and when there was no answer, I knew what that meant. She was at ERF, and I could not call there because I did not know where in that building the size of a football field she might be. So I put on my coat and walked out of Jefferson because I could not sleep until I saw my niece.

ERF had its own guard gate not far from the one at the entrance of the Academy, and most of the FBI police, by now, knew me pretty well. The guard on duty looked surprised when I appeared, and he walked outside to see what I wanted.

'I think my niece is working late,' I began to explain.

'Yes, ma'am. I did see her go in earlier.'

'Is there any way you can contact her?'

'Hmmm.' He frowned. 'Might you have any idea what area she'd likely be in?'

'Maybe the computer room.'

He tried that to no avail, then looked at me. 'This is important.'

'Yes, it is,' I said with gratitude.

He raised his radio to his mouth.

'Unit forty-two to base,' he said.

'Forty-two, come in.'

'You ten-twenty-five me at ERF gate?'

'Ten-four.'

We waited for the guard to arrive, and he occupied the booth while his partner let me inside the building. For a while we roamed long empty hallways, trying locked doors that led into machine shops and laboratories where my niece might be. After about fifteen minutes of this, we got lucky. He tried a door and it opened onto an expansive room that was a Santa's workshop of scientific activity.

Central to this was Lucy, who was wearing a data glove and head-mounted display connected to long thick black cables snaking over the floor.

'Will you be okay?' the guard asked me.

'Yes,' I said. 'Thank you so much.'

Co-workers in lab coats and coveralls were busy with computers, interface devices and large video screens, and they all saw me walk in. But Lucy was blind. She really was not in this room but the one in the small CRTs covering her eyes as she conducted a virtual-reality walk-through along a catwalk in what I suspected was the Old Point nuclear power plant.

'I'm going to zoom in now,' she was saying as she pressed a button on top of the glove.

The area on the video screen suddenly got bigger as the figure that was Lucy stopped at steep grated stairs.

'Shit, I'm zooming out,' she said impatiently. 'No way this is going to work.'

'I promise it can,' said a young man monitoring a big black box. 'But it's tricky.'

She paused and made some other adjustment. 'I don't know, Jim, is this really high-res data or is the problem me?'

'I think the problem's you.'

'Maybe I'm getting cyber sick,' my niece then said as she moved around inside what looked like conveyor belts and huge turbines that I could see on the video screen.

'I'll take a look at the algorithm.'

'You know,' she said, making her way down the virtual stairs, 'maybe we should just put it in C code and go from a delay of three-four to three hundred and four microseconds, et cetera, instead of whatever's in the software we got.'

'Yeah. The transfer sequences are off,' said someone else. 'We got to adjust the timing loops.'

'What we don't have is the luxury of massaging this too much,' another opinion sounded. 'And, Lucy, your aunt's here.'

She briefly paused, then went on as if she had not heard what the person just said. 'Look, I'll do the C code before morning. We gotta be sharp or Toto's going to end up stuck or falling down stairs. And then we're totally screwed.'

Toto, I could only conclude, was the odd bubble head with one video eye that was mounted on a boxy steel body no more than three feet high. Legs were cleated tracks, arms had grippers, and in general he reminded me of a small animated tank. Toto was parked to one side, not far from his master, who was taking off her helmet.

'We got to change the bio-controllers on this glove,' she said as she began carefully pulling it off. 'I'm used to one finger meaning forward and two meaning back. Not the other way around. I can't afford a mix-up like that when we're in the field.'

'That's an easy one,' said Jim, and he went to her and took the glove.

Lucy looked keyed up to the point of being crazed when she met me near the door.

'How'd you get in?' She wasn't the least bit friendly.

'One of the guards.'

'Good thing they know you.'

'Benton told me they'd brought you back, that HRT needs you,' I said.

She watched her colleagues continue to work. 'Most of the guys are already there.'

'At Old Point,' I said.

'We've got divers around the area, snipers set up nearby, choppers waiting. But nothing's going to do any good unless we can get at least one person in.'

'And obviously, that's not you,' I said, knowing that if she claimed otherwise I would kill the FBI, the entire Bureau, all of them at once.

'In a way it's me going in,' my niece said. 'I'll be the one working Toto. Hey, Jim,' she called out. 'While you're at it, let's add a fly command to the pad.'

'So Toto's gonna have wings,' someone cracked. 'Good thing. We're gonna need a smart guardian angel.'

'Lucy, do you have any idea how dangerous these people are?' I could not help but say.

She looked at me and sighed. 'I mean, what do you think, Aunt Kay? Do you think I'm just a kid playing with Tinkertoys?'

'I think that I can't help but feel very worried.'

'We should all be worried right now,' she said, drained. 'Look, I got to get back to work.' She glanced at her watch and blew out a big breath. 'You want a quick overview of my plan so you at least know what's going on?'

'Please.'

'It starts with this.' She sat on the floor and I got down beside her, our backs against the wall. 'Normally, a robot like Toto would be controlled by radio, which would never work inside a facility with so much concrete and steel. So I've come up with what I think is a better way. Basically, he'll carry a spool of fiber optic cable that he'll leave behind like a snail's trail as he moves around.'

'And where is he going to move around?' I asked. 'Inside the power plant?'

'We're trying to determine that now,' she said. 'But a lot will depend on what happens. We could be covert, such as in information gathering. Or we could end up with an overt deployment on our hands, such as if the terrorists want a hostage phone, which we're banking on. Toto has to be ready to go anywhere instantly.'

'Except stairs.'

'He can do stairs. Some better than others.'

'The fiber optics cable will be your eyes?' I said.

'It will hook right into my data gloves.' She held up both hands. 'And I will move as if it's me going in instead of Toto. Virtual reality will allow me to have a remote presence so I can react instantly to whatever his sensors pick up. And by the way, most of them are in that lovely shade of gray we made him.' She pointed to her friend across the room. 'His smart paint helps him not to bump into things,' she added as if she might have feelings for him.

'Did Janet come back with you?' I then asked.

'She's finishing up in Charlottesville.'

'Finishing up?'

'We know who's been breaking into CP&L's computer,' she said. 'A woman graduate assistant in nuclear physics. Surprise, surprise.'

'What's her name?'

'Loren something.' She rubbed her face with her hands. 'God, I should never have sat down. You know cyberspace really can make you dizzy if you stay in it too long. Lately, it's almost been making me sick. Uh.' She snapped her fingers several times. 'McComb. Loren McComb.'

'And she's how old?' I asked as I remembered Cleta saying that the name of Eddings's girlfriend was Loren.

'Late twenties.'

'Where is she from?'

'England. But she's actually South African. She's black.'

'Thus explaining her poor character, according to Mrs Eddings.'

'Huh?' Lucy looked bizarrely at me.

'What about a connection with the New Zionists?' I asked.

'Apparently she got associated with them over the net. She's very militant and antigovernment. My theory is she got brainwashed by them the longer they communicated.'

'Lucy,' I said, 'I think she was Eddings's girlfriend and source, and in the end, she may have helped the New Zionists kill him, probably by way of Captain Green.'

'Why would she help him and then do that?'

'She may have believed she had no choice. If she had assisted him with information that could have hurt Hand's cause, she may have been convinced to help them or they may have threatened her.'

I thought of the Cristal Champagne in Eddings's refrigerator, and wondered if he had planned to spend New Year's Eve with his girlfriend.

'How would they have wanted her to help them?' Lucy was asking.

'She probably knew his burglar alarm code, maybe even the combination to his safe.' My final thought was the worst. 'She may have been with him in the boat the night he died. For that matter, we don't know that she wasn't the one who poisoned him. After all, she's a scientist.'

'Damn.'

'I'm assuming you've interviewed her,' I said.

'Janet has. McComb claims she was on the Internet about eighteen months ago when she came across a note posted on a bulletin board. Allegedly, some producer was working on a movie that had to do with terrorists taking over a nuclear power plant so they could re-create a North Korea situation and get weapons-grade plutonium, et cetera, et cetera. This alleged producer needed technical help, for which he was willing to pay.'

'Did she have a name for whoever this was?' I asked.

'He just always called himself "Alias," as if to imply he might be famous. She bit big time and the relationship began. She started sending him information from graduate papers she had access to because of her graduate assistantship. She gave this Alias asshole every recipe you might think of for essentially taking over Old Point and shipping fuel assemblies to the Arabs.'

'What about making casks?'

'Right. Steal tons of the depleted uranium from Oak Ridge. Have it sent to Iraq, Algeria, wherever, to be made into the hundred-twenty-five-ton casks. Then ship them back here where they're stored until the big day. And she went into the whole bit about when uranium turns into plutonium inside a reactor.' Lucy stopped and glanced over at me. 'She claims it never occurred to her that what she was doing might be real.'

'And was it real to her when she began breaking into CP&L's computer?'

'That's one she can't explain, nor will she supply a motive.'

'I expect motive is easy,' I said. 'Eddings was interested in any phone calls to Arab nations that certain people might have been making. And he got his list via the gateway in Pittsburgh.'

'You don't think she would have realized that the New Zionists wouldn't appreciate her helping her boyfriend, who happened to be a reporter?'

'I don't think she cared,' I angrily said. 'I suspect she enjoyed the drama of playing both sides. If nothing else, it had to make her feel very important when she probably had not felt that way before in her quiet academic world. I doubt reality hit until Eddings started poking around NAVSEA, Captain Green's office or who knows where, and then the New Zionists were tipped that their source, Ms McComb, was threatening the entire mission.'

'If Eddings had figured it out,' Lucy said, 'they never could have pulled it off.'

'Exactly,' I said. 'If any of us had figured it out in time, this wouldn't be happening.' I watched a woman in a lab coat maneuver Toto's arms to lift a box. 'Tell me,' I said, 'what was Loren McComb's demeanor when Janet interviewed her?'

'Detached. Absolutely no emotion.'

'Hand's people are very powerful.'

'I guess so if you can help your boyfriend one minute and they can get you to murder him the next.' Lucy was watching her robot, too, and didn't seem pleased by what she was seeing.

'Well, wherever the Bureau is detaining Ms McComb, I hope it's where the New Zionists can't find her.'

'She's secluded,' Lucy said as Toto suddenly stopped in his tracks and the box thudded heavily to the floor. 'What have you got the shoulder joint's rpm set at?' she called out.

'Eight.'

'Let's lower it to five. Damn.' She rubbed her face again. 'That's all we need.'

'Well, I'm going to leave you and go on back to Jefferson,' I said as I got up.

She got a strange look in her eyes. 'You staying on the security floor, as usual?' she asked.

'Yes.'

'I guess it doesn't matter, but that's where Loren McComb is,' she said.

In fact, my suite was next to hers, but, unlike me, she was confined. But as I sat up in bed for a while trying to read, I could hear her TV through the wall. I could hear channels switch, and then I recognized 'Star Trek' sounds as she watched an old episode rerun.

For hours we were only several feet apart and she did not know it. I imagined her calmly mixing hydrochloric acid and cyanide in a bottle, and directing gas into the compressor's intake valve. Instantly, the long black hose would have violently jerked in the water, and then only the river's sluggish current would have moved it anymore.

'See that in your sleep,' I said to her, though she could not hear me. 'In your sleep for the rest of your life. Every single goddamn night.' I angrily snapped off my lamp.

16

Early the next morning, fog was dense beyond my windows, and Quantico was quieter than usual. I did not hear a single gunshot on any range, and it seemed the Marines were sleeping in. As I walked out of double glass doors leading to the area where the elevators were, I heard a door shut and security locks click free next door to my room.

I punched the down button and glanced around as two female agents in conservative suits walked on either side of a light-skinned black woman who was staring straight at my face as if we had met before. Loren McComb had defiant dark eyes, and pride ran deep within her, as if it were the spring that fed her survival and made all that she did flourish.

'Good morning,' I said with no feeling.

'Dr Scarpetta,' one of the agents somberly greeted me as the four of us boarded the elevator together.

Then we were silent to the first floor, and I could smell the sour staleness of this woman who had taught Joel Hand how to build a bomb. She was wearing tight faded jeans, sneakers, and a long, full white blouse that could not hide an impressive build that must have contributed to Eddings's fatal error. I stood behind her and her wardens and watched the sliver of her face that I could see. She licked her lips often, staring straight ahead at doors which did not open soon enough for me.

Silence was thick like the fog outdoors, and then we were released on the first floor. I took my time getting off, and I watched the two agents lead McComb away without laying a finger on her. They did not have to, because they could, were it needed, just like that. They escorted Loren McComb down a corridor, then turned into one of the myriads of enclosed walkways called gerbil tubes, and I was surprised when she paused to look back at me again. She met my unfriendly stare and moved on, one step closer to what I hoped would be a long pilgrimage in the penitentiary.

Climbing stairs, I walked into the cafeteria where flags for every state in the union were hung on the walls. I met Wesley in a corner beneath Rhode Island.

'I just saw Loren McComb,' I said, setting down my tray.

He glanced at his watch. 'She'll be interviewed most of today.'

'Do you think she'll be able to tell us anything that might help?'

He slid salt and pepper closer. 'No. It's too late,' he simply said.

I ate scrambled egg whites and dry toast, and drank my coffee black as I watched new agents and cops in the National Academy fix omelets and waffles. Some made sandwiches with bacon and sausage, and I thought how boring it was to get old.

'We should go.' I picked up my tray, because sometimes eating wasn't worth it.

'I'm still eating, Chief.' He played with his spoon.

'You're eating granola and it's all gone.'

'I might get more.'

'No, you won't,' I said.

'I'm thinking.'

'Okay.' I looked at him, interested to hear what he had to say.

'Just how important is this *Book of Hand?*'

'Very. Part of the problem started when Danny basically took one and probably gave it to Eddings.'

'Why do you think it's so important?'

'You're a profiler. You should know. It tells us how they will behave. The Book makes them predictable.'

'A terrifying thought,' he said.

At nine A.M. we walked past firing ranges to a half acre of grass near the tire house HRT used in the very maneuvers they would need now. This morning, they were nowhere to be seen, all of them at Old Point except our pilot, Whit. He was typically silent and fit in a black flight suit, standing by a blue and white Bell 222, a corporate twin-engine helicopter also owned by CP&L.

'Whit.' Wesley nodded at him.

'Good morning,' I said as we boarded.

Inside were four seats in what looked like the cabin of a small plane and a co-pilot was busy studying a map. Senator Lord was completely engrossed in whatever he was reading, the attorney general across from him preoccupied with paperwork, too. They had been picked up first in Washington, and did not look like they had slept much, either, the last few nights.

'How are you, Kay?' The senator did not look up.

He was dressed in a dark suit and a white shirt with stiff collar. His tie was deep red, and he wore Senate cuff links. Marcia Gradecki, in contrast, wore a simple pale blue skirt and jacket, and pearls. She was a formidable woman with a face that was attractive in a strong, dynamic way. Although she had gotten her start in Virginia, before this moment we had never met.

Wesley made certain we knew each other as we lifted into a sky that was perfectly blue. We flew over bright yellow school buses that were empty this time of day, then buildings quickly gave way to swamps with duck blinds and vast acres of woods. Sunlight painted paths through the tops of trees, and as we began to follow the James, our reflection silently flew after us along the water.

'In a minute here, we're going to fly over Governor's Landing,' said Wesley, and we did not need headphones to speak to one another, only to the pilots. 'It's the real-estate arm of CP&L, and where Brett West lives. He's the vice president in charge of operations and lives in a nine-hundred-thousand-dollar house down there.' He paused as everybody looked down. 'You can just about see it. There. The big brick one with the pool and basketball court in back.'

The development had many huge brick homes that had pools and painfully young vegetation. There was also a golf course and a yacht club where we were told West kept a boat that right now was not there.

'And where is this Mr West?' the attorney general asked as our pilots turned north where the Chickahominy met the James.

'At the moment we don't know.' Wesley continued looking out the window.

'I'm assuming you believe he's involved,' the senator said.

'Without question. In fact, when CP&L decided to open a district office in Suffolk, they built it on land they bought from a farmer named Joshua Hayes.'

'His records were also accessed in their computer,' I interjected.

'By the hacker,' Gradecki said.

'Right.'

'And you have her in custody,' she said.

'We do. Apparently, she was dating Ted Eddings, and that's how he got into this and ended up murdered.' Wesley's face was hard. 'What I am convinced of is that West has been an accomplice to Joel Hand from the start. You can see the district office now.' He pointed. 'And what do you know,' he added ironically, 'it's right next to Hand's compound.'

The district office was basically a large parking lot of utility trucks and gas pumps, and modular buildings with CP&L painted in red on the roofs. As we flew around it and over a stand of trees, the terrain beneath us suddenly turned into the fifty-acre point on the Nansemond River where Joel Hand lived within a high metal fence that according to legend was electrified.

His compound was a cluster of multiple smaller homes and barracks, his own mansion weathered and with tall, white pillars. But it was not those buildings that worried us. It was others we saw, large wood structures that looked like warehouses built in a row along rail-road tracks leading to a massive private loading dock with huge cranes on the water.

'Those aren't normal barns,' the attorney general observed. 'What was being shipped off his farm?'

'Or on it,' the senator said.

I reminded them of what Danny's killer had tracked into the carpet of my former Mercedes. 'This might be where the casks were stored,' I added. 'The buildings are big enough, and you would need cranes and trains or trucks.'

'Then that would certainly link Danny Webster's homicide to the New Zionists,' the attorney general said to me as she nervously fingered her pearls.

'Or at least to someone who was going in and out of the ware-houses where the casks were kept,' I answered. 'Microscopic parti-cles of depleted uranium would be everywhere, saying that the casks are, in fact, lined with depleted uranium.'

'So this person could have had uranium on the bottom of his shoes and not known it,' Senator Lord said.

'Without a doubt.'

'Well, we need to raid this place and see what we find,' he then said.

'Yes, sir,' Wesley agreed. 'When we can.'

'Frank, so far they haven't done anything that we can prove,' Gradecki said to him. 'We don't have probable cause. The New Zionists haven't claimed responsibility.'

'Well, I know how it works, too, but it's ridiculous,' Lord said, looking out. 'There's no one down there but dogs, looks like to me. So you explain that, if the New Zionists are not involved. Where is everyone? Well, I think we damn well know.'

Doberman pinschers in a pen were barking and lunging at the air we circled.

'Christ,' Wesley said. 'I never thought all of them might be inside Old Point.'

Neither had I, and a very scary thought was forming.

'We've been assuming the New Zionists maintained their numbers over recent years,' Wesley went on. 'But maybe not. Maybe eventually the only people here were the ones in training for the attack.'

'And that would include Joel Hand.' I looked at Wesley.

'We know he's been living here,' he said. 'I think there's a very good chance he was on that bus. He's probably inside the power plant with the others. He's their leader.'

'No,' I said. 'He's their god.'

There was a long pause.

Then Gradecki said, 'The problem with that is he's insane.'

'No,' I said. 'The problem with that is he's not. Hand is evil, and that's infinitely worse.'

'And his fanaticism will affect everything he does in there,' Wesley added. 'If he is in there' – he measured his words – 'then the threat goes bizarrely beyond escaping with a barge of fuel assemblies. At any time, this could turn into a suicide mission.'

'I'm not sure why you're saying that,' said Gradecki, who did not want to hear it in the least. 'The motive is very clear.'

I thought of the *Book of Hand*, and of how hard it was for the un-initiated to understand just what a man like its author was capable of doing. I looked at the attorney general as we flew over rows of old gray tankers and transport ships, known as the Navy's Dead Fleet. They were parked in the James, and from a distance it looked like Virginia was under siege, which in a way, it was.

'I don't believe I've ever seen that,' she muttered in amazement as she looked down.

'Well, you should have,' Senator Lord retorted. 'You Democrats are responsible for the decommissioning of half the Navy's fleet. In fact we don't have room to park them. They're scattered here and there, ghosts of their former selves and not worth a tinker's damn if we need seaworthy vessels fast. By the time you'd get one of those old tubs going, the Persian Gulf would be as long past as that other war they fought around here.'

'Frank, you've made your point,' she crisply said. 'I believe we have other matters to attend to this morning.'

Wesley had put on a set of headphones so he could talk to the pilots. He asked for an update and then listened for a long time as he stared out at Jamestown and its ferry. When he got off the radio his face was anxious.

'We'll be at Old Point in several minutes. The terrorists still have refused contact and we don't know how many casualties might be inside.'

'I hear more helicopters,' I said.

We were silent, and then the sound of thudding blades was unmistakable. Wesley got back on the air.

'Listen, dammit, the FAA was supposed to restrict this airspace.' He paused as he listened. 'Absolutely not. No one else has clearance within a mile—' Interrupted, he listened again. 'Right, right.' He got angrier. 'Christ,' he exclaimed as the noise got louder.

Two Hueys and two Black Hawks loudly rumbled past, and Wesley unfastened his seat belt as if he were going somewhere. Furious, he rose and moved to the other side of the cabin, looking out windows.

He had his back to the senator when he said with controlled fury, 'Sir, you should not have called in the National Guard. We have a very delicate operation in place and cannot – let me repeat – cannot afford any sort of interference in either our planning or our airspace. And let me remind you the jurisdiction here is police, not military. This is the United States—'

Senator Lord cut in, 'I did not call them, and we're in complete agreement.'

'Then who did?' asked Gradecki, who was Wesley's ultimate boss.

'Probably your governor,' Senator Lord said, looking at me, and I knew by his manner that he was enraged, too. 'He would do something stupid like that because all he thinks about is the next election. Patch me into his office, and I mean now.'

The senator slipped the headset on and did not care who overheard when he launched in several minutes later.

'For God's sake, Dick, have you lost your mind?' he said to the man who held the Commonwealth's highest office. 'No, no, don't even bother telling me any of that,' he snapped. 'You are interfering with what we're doing out here, and if it costs lives you can be assured I'm going to announce who's to blame . . .'

He fell silent for a moment, and the expression on his face as he listened was scary. Then he made several other salient points as the governor ordered the National Guard back in. In fact, their huge helicopters never landed, but suddenly changed formation as they gained altitude. They flew right past Old Point, which just now we could see, its concrete containments rising in the clean blue air.

'I'm very sorry,' the senator apologized to us, because he was, above all, a gentleman.

We stared out at scores of police and law enforcement vehicles, ambulances and fire trucks, and flowering satellite dishes and news vans. Dozens of people were outside as if enjoying a lovely, brisk day, and Wesley informed us that where they were congregating was the visitors' center, which was the command post for the outer perimeter.

'As you can see,' he explained, 'it's no closer than half a mile away from the plant and the main building, which is there.' He pointed.

'The main building is where the control room is?' I asked.

'Right. That three-story beige brick building. That's where they are, at least most of them, we think, including the hostages.'

'Well, it's where they'd have to be if they planned on doing anything with the reactors, like shutting them down, which we know they've already done,' Senator Lord remarked.

'And then what?' the attorney general asked.

'There are backup generators, so no one's going to lose electricity. And the plant itself has an emergency power supply,' Lord said, and he was known for being an ardent advocate of nuclear energy.

Wide waterways ran on the plant's two sides, one leading from the nearby James, the other to a man-made lake nearby. Then there were acres of transformers and power lines, and parking lots with many cars, belonging to hostages and the people who had arrived to help. There did not seem an easy way to access the main building without being seen, for any nuclear power plant is designed with the most stringent security in mind. The point was to keep out everyone not authorized, and, unfortunately, that included us. A roof entry, for example, would require cutting holes in metal and concrete, and could not be done without risk of being seen.

I suspected Wesley was thinking about a possible amphibious plan, for HRT divers could enter undetected either the river or the lake, and follow a waterway very close to one side of the main building. It looked to me that they could swim within twenty yards of the very door the terrorists had stormed, but how the agents would escape detection once ashore, I could not imagine.

Wesley did not spell out any plan, for the senator and the attorney general were allies, even friends, but they were also politicians. Neither the FBI nor the police needed Washington inserting itself into this mission. What the governor had just done was bad enough.

'Now if you'll notice the large white RV that's close to the main building,' Wesley said, 'that's our inner perimeter command post.'

'I thought that belonged to a news crew,' the attorney general commented.

'That's where we try to establish a relationship with Mr Hand and his Merry Band.'

'How?'

'For starters, I want to talk with them,' Wesley said.

'No one's talked to them yet?' the senator asked.

'So far,' he said, 'they don't seem interested in talk.'

The Bell 222 slowly made its loud descent as news crews assembled near a helipad across the road from the visitors' center. We grabbed briefcases and bags, and disembarked in the strong wind of flying blades. Wesley and I walked swiftly and in silence. I glanced back only once and saw Senator Lord surrounded by microphones while our nation's most powerful lawyer delivered a string of emotional quotes.

We walked inside the visitors' center with its many displays intended for school children and the curious. But now the entire area was divided by local and state police. They were drinking sodas, eating fast food and snacks near plats and maps on easels, and I could not help but wonder how much of a difference any of us could make.

'Where's your outpost?' Wesley asked me.

'It should be out with the squads. I think I spotted our refrigerator truck from the air.'

His eyes were roaming around. They stopped on the men's room door opening and swinging shut. Marino walked out, hitching up his pants again. I had not expected to see him here. If for no other reason, I would have thought his fear of radiation would have kept him home.

'I'm getting coffee,' Wesley said. 'Anybody?'

'Yo. Make it a double.'

'Thanks,' I said, then to Marino I added, 'This is the last place I would have expected to see you.'

'See all these guys walking around in here?' he said. 'We're part of a task force so all the local jurisdictions got somebody here that can call home and say what the hell's going on. Bottom line is, the chief sent my ass out here, and no, I'm not thrilled about it. And by the way, I saw your buddy Chief Steels out here, and you'll be happy to know Roche has been suspended without pay.'

I did not reply, for Roche was not important right now.

'So that ought to make you feel a little better,' Marino went on.

I looked at him. His stiff white collar was rimmed in sweat, and his belt with all its gear creaked as he moved.

'While I'm here, I'll do my best to keep an eye on you. But I'd appreciate it if you didn't go wandering into the crosshairs of some drone's high-powered rifle,' he added, smoothing back strands of hair with a big, thick hand.

'I'd appreciate it if I didn't do that either. I need to check on my folks,' I said. 'Have you seen them?'

'Yeah, I saw Fielding in that big trailer the funeral home people bought for you. He was cooking eggs in the kitchen like he's camping out or something. There's a refrigerator truck, too.'

'Okay. I know exactly where it is.'

'I'll take you over there, if you want,' he nonchalantly said, as if he didn't care.

'I'm glad you're here,' I said, because I knew I was part of the reason, no matter what he claimed.

Wesley was back, and he had balanced a paper plate of doughnuts on top of cups of coffee. Marino helped himself while I looked out windows at the bright, cold day.

'Benton,' I said, 'where is Lucy?'

He did not reply, so I knew. My worst fears were confirmed right then.

'Kay, all of us have a job to do.' His eyes were kind, but he was unequivocal.

'Of course we do.' I set down my coffee because my nerves were bad enough. 'I'm going out to check on things.'

'Hold on,' Marino said as he started his second doughnut.

'I'll be fine.'

'Yeah, you will,' he said. 'I'm going to make sure of that.'

'You do need to be careful out there,' Wesley said to me. 'We know there's someone in every window, and they could start shooting whenever they want.'

I looked at the main building in the distance, and I pushed open the glass door that led outside. Marino was right behind me.

'Where's HRT?' I asked him.

'Where you can't see them.'

'Don't talk to me in riddles. I'm not in the mood.'

I walked with purpose, and because I could not see any sign of terrorism or its victims, this ordeal seemed a drill. Fire and refrigerator trucks and ambulances seemed part of a mock emergency, and even Fielding arranging disaster kits inside the large white trailer that was my outpost did not strike me as reality. He was opening one of the blue Army footlockers stamped with OCME, and inside was everything from eighteen-gauge needles to yellow pouches designed to hold the personal effects of the dead.

He looked up at me as if I had been here all along. 'You got any idea where the stakes are?' he asked.

'Those should be in separate boxes with hatchets, pliers, metal ties,' I replied.

'Well, I don't know where they are.'

'What about the yellow body pouches?' I scanned lockers and boxes stacked inside the trailer.

'I guess I'm just going to have to get all that from FEMA,' he said, referring to the Federal Emergency Management Agency.

'Where are they?' I asked, because hundreds of people from many agencies and departments were here.

'You go out and you'll see their trailer directly to the left, next to the guys from Fort Lee. Graves Registration. And FEMA's got the lead-lined suits.'

'And we'll pray we don't need them,' I said.

Fielding said to Marino, 'What's the latest on hostages? Do we know how many they've got in there?'

'We're not really sure because we don't know exactly how many employees were in the building,' he said. 'But the shift was small when they hit, which I'm sure was part of the plan. They've released thirty-two people. We're thinking there's maybe about a dozen left. We don't know how many of them are still alive.'

'Christ.' Fielding's eyes were angry as he shook his head. 'You ask me, every one of the assholes ought to be shot on the spot.'

'Yeah, well, you won't get an argument out of me,' Marino said.

'At this moment,' Fielding said to me, 'we can handle fifty. That's the max between the truck we got here and our morgue back in Richmond, which is already pretty crowded. Beyond that, MCV's mobilized if we need them for storage.'

'The dentists and radiologists are also mobilized,' I assumed.

'Right. Jenkins, Verner, Silverberg, Rollins. They're all on standby.'

I could smell eggs and bacon and didn't know if I felt hungry or sick. 'I'm on the radio, if you need me,' I said, opening the trailer's door.

'Don't walk so fast,' Marino complained when we were back outside.

'Have you checked out the mobile command post?' I asked. 'The big blue and white RV? I saw it when we were flying in.'

'I don't think we want to go over there.'

'Well, I do.'

'Doc, that's the inner perimeter.'

'That's where HRT is,' I said.

'Let's just check it out with Benton first. I know you're looking for Lucy, but for God's sake, use your head.'

'I am using my head and I am looking for Lucy.' I was getting angrier with Wesley by the moment.

Marino put his hand on my arm and stopped me, and we squinted at each other in the sun. 'Doc,' he said, 'listen to me. What's going down ain't personal. No one gives a shit that Lucy's your niece. She's a friggin' FBI agent, and it ain't Wesley's duty to give you a report on everything she's doing for them.'

I did not say anything, and he did not need to, either, for me to know the truth.

'So don't be pissed at him.' Marino was still gently holding my arm. 'You want to know? I don't like it, either. I couldn't stand it if something happened to her. I don't know what I'd do if anything happened to either of you. And right now I'm about as scared as I've ever been in my goddamn fucking life. But I got a job to do and so do you.'

'She's at the inner perimeter,' I said.

He paused. 'Come on, Doc. Let's go talk to Wesley.'

But we did not get a chance to do that, because when we walked into the visitors' center, we found him on the phone. His tone was iron-calm and he was standing tensely.

'Don't do anything until I get there, and it is very important that they know I'm on my way,' he was saying, slowly. 'No, no, no. Don't do that. Use a bullhorn so no one gets close.' He glanced at Marino and me. 'Just hold tight. Tell them you've got someone coming who will get a hostage phone to them immediately. Right.'

He hung up and headed straight for the door, and we were right behind him.

'What the hell's going on?' Marino asked.

'They want to communicate.'

'What'd they do? Send a letter?'

'One of them yelled out a window,' Wesley replied. 'They're very agitated.'

We walked fast past the helipad, and I noted it was empty, the senator and attorney general long gone.

'So they don't already have a phone?' I was very surprised.

'We shut down the phones in that building,' Wesley said. 'They have to get a phone from us, and before this minute they haven't wanted one. Now, suddenly they do.'

'So there's a problem,' I said.

'That's the way I'm reading it.' Marino was out of breath.

Wesley did not reply, but I could tell he was unnerved, and it was rare that anything made him this way. The narrow road led us through the sea of people and vehicles waiting to help, and the tan building loomed larger. The mobile command post gleamed in the sun and was parked on the grass, the conical containments and the waterway they needed for cooling so close I could have hit them with a stone.

I had no doubt that New Zionists had us in their rifle sights and could pull the trigger, if they chose, to pick us off one at a time. The windows where we believed they watched were open, but I could not see anything behind their screens.

We walked around to the front of the RV where half a dozen police and agents were in plain clothes surrounding Lucy, and the sight of her almost stopped my heart. She was in black fatigues and boots, and was attached to cables again, as she had been at ERF. Only this time she wore two gloves, and Toto was awake on the ground, his thick neck connected to a spool of fiber optics line that looked long enough to walk him to North Carolina.

'It's better if we tape down the receiver,' my niece was saying to men she could not see because of the CRTs over her eyes.

'Who's got tape?'

'Hold on.'

A man in a black jumpsuit reached inside a large toolbox and tossed a roll of tape to someone else. This person tore off several strips of it and secured the receiver to the cradle of a plain black phone in a box firmly held in the robot's grippers.

'Lucy,' Wesley spoke. 'This is Benton Wesley. I'm here.'

'Hi,' she said, and I could feel her nervousness.

'As soon as you get the phone to them, I'm going to start talking. I just want you to know what I'm doing.'

'Are we ready?' she asked, and she had no idea I was there.

'Let's do it,' Wesley tensely said.

She touched a button on her glove and Toto came to life in a quiet whir, and the one eye beneath his domed brain turned, as if focusing like a camera lens. His head swiveled as Lucy touched another button on a glove, and everyone watched in hushed anticipation as my niece's creation suddenly moved. It plowed forward on rubber tracks, telephone tight in its grippers, the fiber optics and telephone cable unrolling from spools.

Lucy silently conducted Toto's journey like an orchestra, her arms out and gently moving. Steadily, the robot rolled down the road, over gravel and through grass, until he was far enough away that one of the agents passed out field glasses. Following a sidewalk, Toto reached four cement steps leading up to the glass front entrance of the main building, and he stopped. Lucy took a deep breath as she continued to make her telepresence known to her metal and plastic friend. She touched another button, and the grippers extended with arms. They slowly lowered and set the telephone on the second step. Toto backed up and swiveled around, and Lucy began to bring him home.

The robot had not gotten far when all of us could see that glass door open, and a bearded man in khakis and a sweater swiftly emerged. He grabbed the telephone off the step and vanished inside.

'Good work, Lucy,' Wesley said, and he sounded very relieved. 'Okay, goddamn it, now call,' he added, and he was not talking to us, but them. 'Lucy,' he added, 'when you're ready, come on in.'

'Yes, sir,' she said as her arms coaxed Toto over every dip and bump.

Then Marino, Wesley and I climbed steps leading into the mobile command post, which was upholstered in gray and blue, with tables between seats. There was a small kitchen and bath, and windows were tinted so one could see out, but not in. Radio and computer equipment had been set up near the back, and overhead five televisions were turned to the major networks and CNN, the volume set low. A red phone on a table started ringing as we were walking down the aisle. It sounded urgent and demanding, and Wesley ran to pick it up.

'Wesley,' he said, staring out a window, and he pushed two buttons that both taped the caller and put him on speakerphone.

'We need a doctor.' The male voice sounded white and southern, and he was breathing hard.

'Okay, but you're going to need to tell me more.'

'Don't bullshit with me!' he screamed.

'Listen.' Wesley got very calm. 'We're not bullshitting, all right? We want to help, but I need more information.'

'He fell in the pool and went into like a coma.'

'Who did?'

'Why the fuck does it matter who?'

Wesley hesitated.

'He dies, we've got this place wired. You understand? We're going to blow you fucking up if you don't do something now!'

We knew who he meant, so Wesley did not ask again. Something had happened to Joel Hand, and I did not want to imagine what his followers might do if he died.

'Talk to me,' Wesley said.

'He can't swim.'

'Let me make certain I understand. Someone almost drowned?'

'Look. The water's radioactive. It had the fucking fuel assemblies in it, you understand?'

'He was inside one of the reactors.'

The man screamed again, 'Just shut the fuck up with your questions and get someone to help. He dies, everybody dies. You understand that?' he said as a gun loudly went off over the phone and cracked from the building at the same time.

Everyone froze, and then we could hear crying in the background. I thought my heart would beat out of my ribs.

'You make me wait another minute,' the man's excited voice was back on the line, 'and another one gets killed.'

I moved closer to the phone and before anyone could stop me, I said, 'I'm a doctor. I need to know exactly what happened when he fell into the reactor pool.'

Silence. Then the man said, 'He almost drowned, that's all I know. We tried to pump water out of him but he was already unconscious.'

'Did he swallow water?'

'I don't know. Maybe he did. Some was coming out of his mouth.' He was becoming more agitated. 'But if you don't do something, lady, I'm going to turn Virginia into a goddamn desert.'

'I'm going to help you,' I said. 'But I need to ask you several more questions. Tell me his condition now?'

'Like I said. He's out. It's like he's in a coma.'

'Where do you have him?'

'In the room here with us.' He sounded terrified. 'He don't react to anything, no matter what we try to do.'

'I'm going to have to bring in a lot of ice and medical supplies,' I said. 'It's going to take several trips unless I have some help.'

'You'd better not be FBI,' he raised his voice again.

'I'm a doctor out here with a lot of other medical personnel,' I said. 'Now, I'm going to come and help, but not if you're going to give me a hard time.'

He was silent. Then he said, 'Okay. But you come alone.'

'The robot will help me carry things. The same one that brought you your phone.'

He hung up, and when I did, Wesley and Marino were staring at me as if I had just committed murder.

'Absolutely not,' Wesley said. 'Jesus Christ, Kay. Have you lost your mind?'

'You ain't going if I have to put you in a goddamn police hold,' Marino chimed in.

'I have to,' I said simply. 'He's going to die,' I added.

'And that's the very reason why you can't go in there,' Wesley exclaimed.

'He has acute radiation sickness from swallowing water in the pool,' I said. 'He can't be saved. Soon he will die, and then I think we know what the consequences might be. His followers will probably set off the explosives.' I was looking at Wesley and Marino, and the commander of HRT. 'Don't you understand? I've read their Book. He is their messiah, and they won't just walk away when he dies. This whole thing will turn into a suicide mission, as you predicted.' I looked at Wesley again.

'We don't know that they'll do that,' he said to me.

'And you'll take the chance they won't?'

'And what if he comes to,' Marino said. 'Hand's going to recognize you and tell all his assholes who you are. Then what?'

'He's not going to come to.'

Wesley stared out a window, and it wasn't very hot in the RV, but he looked like it was summer. His shirt was limp from dampness, and he kept wiping his brow. He did not know what to do. I had one idea, and I did not think there could be another one.

'Listen to me,' I said. 'I can't save Joel Hand, but I can make them think he's not dead.'

Everyone just stared at me.

Then Marino said, 'What?'

I was getting frantic. 'He could die any minute,' I said. 'I've got to get in there now and buy you enough time to get in, too.'

'We can't get in,' Wesley said.

'Once I'm in there, maybe you can,' I said. 'We can use the robot to find a way. We'll get him in, and then he can stun and blind them long enough for your guys to get in. I know you have the equipment to do that.'

Wesley was grim and Marino looked miserable. I understood the way they felt, but I knew what must be done. I went out to the nearest ambulance and got what I needed from paramedics while other people found ice. Then Toto and I made our approach with Lucy at the controls. The robot carried fifty pounds of ice while I was in charge of a large medical chest. We walked toward the front door of Old Point's main building as if this were any other day and our visit was normal. I did not think of the men who had me in their scopes. I refused to imagine explosives or the barge loading up material that could help Libya build an atom bomb.

When we reached the door, it was immediately opened by what looked like the same bearded man who had appeared to get the hostage phone not long ago.

'Get in,' he gruffly said, and he was carrying an assault rifle on a strap.

'Help me with the ice,' I said.

He stared at the robot with its five bags held fast in grippers. He was reticent, as if Toto were a pit bull that might suddenly hurt him in some way. Then he reached for the ice and Lucy programmed her friend through fiber optics to release it. Next, this man and I were inside the building with the door shut, and I saw that the security area had been destroyed, X-ray and other scanning devices ripped out of place and riddled with bullets. There were blood drips and drag marks, and when I followed him around a corner, I smelled the bodies before I saw the slain guards who had been gathered into a ghastly, gory pile down the hall.

Fear rose in my throat like bile as we passed through a red door, and the rumble of combines shook my bones and made it impossible to hear anything said by this man who was a New Zionist. As I noticed the large black pistol on his belt, I thought about Danny and the .45 that had so coldly killed him. We climbed grated stairs painted red, and I did not look down because I would get dizzy. He led me along a catwalk to a door that was very heavy and painted with warnings, and he punched in a code as ice began to drip on the floor.

'Just do as you're told,' I vaguely heard him say as we walked into the control room. 'You understand me?' He nudged my back with his rifle.

'Yes,' I said.

There were maybe a dozen men inside, all dressed in slacks and sweaters or jackets, and carrying semiautomatic rifles and machine guns. They were very excited and angry, and seemed indifferent to the ten hostages sitting on the floor against a wall. Hands were tied in front of hostages, and pillow cases had been pulled over their heads. Through holes cut out for eyes, I could see their terror. The openings for their mouths were stained with saliva and they sucked in and out with rapid, shallow breaths. I noted bloody drag marks on the floor here, too, only these were fresh and led behind a console where the latest victim had been dumped. I wondered how many bodies I would later find should mine not be among them.

'Over there,' my escort ordered.

Joel Hand was on his back on the floor, covered by a curtain someone had ripped from a window. He was very pale and still wet from the pool where he had swallowed water that would kill him, no matter what I tried to do. I recognized his fair, full-lipped face from when I had seen him in court, only he looked puffier and older.

'How long has he been like this?' I spoke to the man who had brought me in.

'Maybe an hour and a half.'

He was smoking and pacing. He would not meet my eyes, one hand nervously resting on the barrel of his gun, which was aimed at my head as I set down the medical chest. I turned around and stared at him.

'Don't point that at me,' I said.

'You shut up.' He stopped pacing and looked as if he would crack my skull.

'I'm here because you invited me, and I'm trying to help.' I met his glassy gaze and my voice meant business, too. 'If you don't want me to help, then go ahead and shoot me or let me leave. Neither one is going to help him. I'm trying to save his life and don't need to be distracted by your goddamn gun.'

He did not know what to say as he leaned against a console with enough controls to fly a spaceship. Video displays on walls showed that both reactors were shut down, and areas in a grid lighted up red warned of problems I could not comprehend.

'Hey, Wooten, take it easy.' One of his peers lit a cigarette.

'Let's open the bags of ice now,' I said. 'I wish we had a tub, but we don't. I see some books on those countertops, and it looks like there's a lot of stacks of paper over there by that fax machine. Bring anything like that you can for a border.'

Men brought to me all sorts of thick manuals, reams of papers and briefcases that I assumed belonged to the employees they had captured. I formed a rectangular border around Hand as if I were in my backyard making a flower bed. Then I covered him with fifty pounds of ice, leaving only his face and an arm exposed.

'What will that do?' The man called Wooten had moved closer, and he sounded as if he were from out west somewhere.

'He's been acutely exposed to radiation,' I said. 'His system is being destroyed and the only way to put a stop to it is to slow everything down.'

I opened the medical chest and got out a needle, which I inserted into their dying leader's arm and secured with tape. I connected an IV line leading to a bag on a stand that contained nothing but saline, a harmless salty solution that would do nothing one way or another. It dripped as he got cooler beneath inches of ice.

Hand was barely alive, and my heart was thudding as I looked around at these sweating men who believed that this man I pretended to save was God. One had taken his sweater off, and his undershirt was almost gray, the sleeves drawn up from years of washing. Several of them had beards, while others had not shaved in days. I wondered where their women and children were, and I thought of the barge in the river and what must be going on in other parts of the plant.

'Excuse me,' a quavering voice barely said, identifying at least one of the hostages as a woman. 'I need to go to the bathroom.'

'Mullen, you take her. We don't want nobody shitting in here.'

'Excuse me, but I have to go, too,' said another hostage, who was a man.

'So do I.'

'All right, one at a time,' said Mullen, who was young and huge.

I knew at least one thing the FBI did not. The New Zionists had never intended to let anyone else go. Terrorists place hoods over their hostages because it is easier to kill people who have no faces. I got out a vial of saline and injected fifty milliliters into Hand's IV line, as if I were giving him some other magic dose.

'How's he doing?' one of the men loudly asked as another hostage was led off to the bathroom.

'I've got him stabilized at the moment,' I lied.

'When's he going to come around?' asked another.

I took their leader's pulse again, and it was so faint I almost could not find it. Suddenly, the man dropped down beside me and felt Hand's neck. Digging his fingers in the ice, he pressed them over the heart, and when he looked up on me, he was frightened and furious.

'I don't feel nothing!' he yelled, his face red.

'You're not supposed to feel anything. It's critical to keep him in a hypothermic state so we can arrest the rate of irradiation damage to blood vessels and organs,' I told him. 'He's on massive doses of diethylene triamine penta-acetic acid, and he is quite alive.'

He stood, his eyes wild as he stepped closer to me, finger on the trigger of his Tec-9. 'How do we know you aren't just bullshitting or making him worse.'

'You don't know.' I showed no emotion because I had accepted this was the day I would die, and I was not afraid of it. 'You have no choice but to trust that I know what I'm doing. I've profoundly slowed down his metabolism. And he's not going to come to any time soon. I'm simply trying to keep him alive.'

He averted his gaze.

'Hey, Bear, take it easy.'

'Leave the lady alone.'

I continued kneeling by Hand as his IV dripped and melting ice began to seep through the barricade, spreading over the floor. I took his vital signs many times and made notes, so it seemed that I was very busy in my attendance of him. I could not help but glance out windows whenever I could, and wonder about my comrades. At not quite three P.M., his organs failed him like followers that suddenly aren't interested anymore. Joel Hand died without a gesture or sound as cold water ran in small rivers across the floor.

'I need ice and I need more drugs,' I looked up and said.

'Then what?' Bear came closer.

'Then at some point you need to get him to a hospital.'

No one responded.

'If you don't give me these things I've requested, I can do nothing more for him,' I flatly said.

Bear went over to a desk and got on the hostage phone. He said we needed ice and more drugs. I knew Lucy and her team had better act now or I probably would be shot. I moved away from Hand's spreading puddle, and as I looked at his face it was hard for me to believe that he had so much power over others. But every man in this room and those in the reactor and on the barge would kill for him. In fact, they already had.

'The robot's bringing the shit. I'm going out to get it,' said Bear as he looked out the window. 'It's on its way now.'

'You go out there you're probably going to get your ass shot off.'

'Not with her in here.' Bear's eyes were hostile and crazed.

'The robot can bring it to you,' I surprised them by saying.

Bear laughed. 'You remember all those stairs? You think that tin-ass piece of shit's going to get up those?'

'It's perfectly capable,' I said, and I hoped this was true.

'Hey, make it bring the stuff in so no one has to go out,' another man said.

Bear got Wesley on the hostage phone again. 'Make the robot bring the supplies to the control room. We're not coming out.' He slammed the receiver down, not realizing what he had just done.

I thought of my niece and said a prayer for her because I knew this would be the hardest thing she had ever done, and I jumped as I suddenly felt the barrel of a gun against the back of my neck.

'You let him die, you're dead, too. You got that, bitch?'

I did not move.

'Pretty soon, we got to sail out of here, and he'd better be going with us.'

'As long as you keep me in supplies, I will keep him alive,' I quietly said.

He removed the gun from my neck and I injected the last vial of saline into their dead leader's IV line. Beads of sweat were rolling down my back, and the skirt of the gown I had put over my clothes was soaked. I imagined Lucy this minute outside the mobile outpost in her virtual reality gear. I imagined her moving her fingers and arms and stepping here and there as fiber optics made it possible for her to read every inch of the terrain on her CRTs. Her telepresence was the only hope that Toto would not get stuck in a corner or fall somewhere.

The men were looking out the window and commented when the robot's tracks carried him up the handicap ramp and he went inside.

'I wouldn't mind having one of those,' one of them said.

'You're too stupid to figure out how to use it.'

'No way. That baby ain't radio-controlled. Nothing radio-controlled would work in here. You got any idea how thick the walls are?'

'It'd be great for carrying in firewood when the weather sucks.'

'Excuse me, I need to use the bathroom,' one of the hostages timidly said.

'Shit. Not again.'

My tension got unbearable as I feared what would happen if they went out and were not back when Toto appeared.

'Hey, just make him wait. Damn, I wish we could close these windows. It's cold as shit in here.'

'Well, you won't get none of that clean, cold air in Tripoli. Better enjoy it while you can.'

Several of them laughed at the same time the door opened and another man walked in who I had not seen before. He was dark-skinned and bearded, wearing a heavy jacket and fatigues, and he was angry.

'We have only fifteen assemblies out and in casks on the barge,' he spoke with authority and a heavy accent. 'You must give us more time. Then we can get more.'

'Fifteen's a hell of a lot,' Bear said; and he did not seem to care for this man.

'We need twenty-five assemblies at the very least! That was the arrangement.'

'No one's told me that.'

'He knows that.' The man with the accent looked at Hand's body on the floor.

'Well, he ain't available to discuss it with you.' Bear crushed out a cigarette with the toe of his boot.

'Do you understand?' The foreign man was furious now. 'Each assembly weighs a ton, and the crane has to pull it from the flooded reactor to the pool, then get it into a cask. It is very slow and very difficult. It is very dangerous. You promised we would have at least twenty-five. Now you are rushing and sloppy because of him.' The man angrily pointed at Hand. 'We have an agreement!'

'My only agreement is to take care of him. We gotta get him on the barge and take the doctor with us. Then we get him to a hospital.'

'This is nonsense! He looks already dead to me! You are lunatics!'

'He's not dead.'

'Look at him. He is white as snow and does not breathe. He is dead!'

They were screaming at each other, and Bear's boots were loud as he strode over to me and demanded, 'He's not dead, is he?'

'No,' I said.

Sweat rolled down his face as he drew the pistol from his belt and pointed it first at me. Then he pointed it at the hostages, and all of them cowered and one began to cry.

'No, please. Oh please,' a man begged.

'Who is it who needs to use the john so bad?' Bear roared.

They were silent, shaking as hoods sucked in and out and wide eyes stared.

'Was it you?' The gun pointed at someone else.

The control-room door had been left open, and I could hear the whirring of Toto down the hall. He had made it up the stairs and along a catwalk, and he would be here in seconds. I retrieved a long metal flashlight that had been designed by ERF and tucked into the medical chest by my niece.

'Shit, I want to know if he's dead,' one of the men said, and I knew my charade was over.

'I'll show you,' I said as the whirring got louder.

I pointed the flashlight at Bear as I pushed a button, and he shrieked at the dazzling pop as he grabbed his eyes and I swung the heavy flashlight like a baseball bat. Bones shattered in his wrist, the pistol clattering to the floor, and the robot rolled in empty-handed. I flung myself down flat on my face, covering my eyes and ears as best I could, and the room exploded in blazing white light as a concussion bomb blew off the top of Toto's head. There was screaming and cursing as terrorists blindly fell against consoles and each other, and they could not hear or see when dozens of HRT agents stormed in.

'Freeze, motherfuckers!'

'Freeze or I'm gonna blow your motherfucking brains out!'

'Don't anybody move!'

I did not budge in Joel Hand's icy grave as helicopters shook windows and feet of fast-roping agents kicked in screens. Handcuffs snapped, and weapons clattered across the floor as they were kicked out of the way. I heard people crying and realized they were the hostages being taken away.

'It's all right. You're safe now.'

'Oh my God. Oh thank you, God.'

'Come on. We need to get you on out of here.'

When I finally felt a cool hand on the side of my neck, I realized the person was checking for vital signs because I looked dead.

'Aunt Kay?' It was Lucy's strained voice.

I turned over and slowly sat up. My hands and the side of my face that had been in water were numb, and I looked around, dazed. I was shaking so badly my teeth were chattering as she squatted beside me, gun in hand. Her eyes roamed the room as other agents in black fatigues were taking the last prisoners out.

'Come on, let me help you up,' she said.

She gave me her hand, and my muscles trembled as if I were about to have a seizure. I could not get warm, and my ears would not stop ringing. When I was standing, I could see Toto near the door. His eye had been scorched, his head blackened, the domed top of it gone. He stood silent in his cold trail of fiber optic cable, and no one paid him any mind as one by one all of the New Zionists were taken away.

Lucy looked down at the cold body on the floor, at the water and IV, the syringes and empty bags of saline.

'God,' she said.

'Is it safe to go out?' I had tears in my eyes.

'We've just now taken control of the containment area, and we took the barge the same time we took the control room. Several of them had to be shot because they wouldn't drop their weapons. Marino got one in the parking lot.'

'He shot one of them?'

'He had to,' she said. 'We think we got everyone – I guess about thirty – but we're still being careful. This place is wired with explosives, come on. Are you able to walk?'

'Of course I am.'

I untied my soaked gown and yanked it off because I could not stand it anymore. Tossing it on the floor, I pulled off my gloves and we walked quickly out of the control room. She snatched her radio off her belt and her boots were loud on the catwalk and the stairs Toto had maneuvered so well.

'Unit one-twenty to mobile unit one,' she said.

'One.'

'We're clearing out now. Everything secure?'

'You got the package?' I recognized Benton Wesley's voice.

'Ten-four. Package is a-okay.'

'Thank God,' came a reply unusually emotional for the radio. 'Tell the package we're waiting.'

'Ten-four, sir,' Lucy said. 'I believe the package knows.'

We walked fast beyond bodies and old blood, and turned in to a lobby that could not keep anyone in or out anymore. She pulled open a glass door, and the afternoon was so bright I had to shield my eyes. I did not know where to go and felt very unsteady on my feet.

'Watch the steps.' Lucy put an arm around my waist. 'Aunt Kay,' she said, 'just hold on to me.'

UNNATURAL EXPOSURE

And there came unto me one of the seven angels which had the seven vials full of the seven last plagues . . .

Revelation 21:9

1

—————

Night fell clean and cold in Dublin, and wind moaned beyond my room as if a million pipes played the air. Gusts shook old window-panes and sounded like spirits rushing past as I rearranged pillows one more time, finally resting on my back in a snarl of Irish linen. But sleep would not touch me, and images from the day returned. I saw bodies without limbs or heads, and sat up, sweating.

I switched on lamps, and the Shelbourne Hotel was suddenly around me in a warm glow of rich old woods and deep red plaids. I put on a robe, my eyes lingering on the phone by my fitfully-slept-in bed. It was almost two A.M. In Richmond, Virginia, it would be five hours earlier, and Pete Marino, commander of the city police department's homicide squad, should be up. He was probably watching TV, smoking, eating something bad for him unless he was on the street.

I dialed his number, and he grabbed the phone as if he were right next to it.

'Trick or treat.' He was loudly on his way to being drunk.

'You're a little early,' I said, already regretting the call. 'By a couple of weeks.'

'Doc?' He paused in confusion. 'That you? You back in Richmond?'

'Still in Dublin. What's all the commotion?'

'Just some of us guys with faces so ugly we don't need masks. So every day is Halloween. Hey! Bubba's bluffing,' he yelled out.

'You always think everybody's bluffing,' a voice fired back. 'It's from being a detective too long.'

'What you talking about? Marino can't even detect his own B.O.'

Laughter in the background was loud as the drunk, derisive comments continued.

'We're playing poker,' Marino said to me. 'What the hell time is it there?'

'You don't want to know,' I answered. 'I've got some unsettling news, but it doesn't sound like we should get into it now.'

'No. No, hold on. Let me just move the phone. Shit. I hate the way the cord gets twisted, you know what I mean? Goddamn it.' I could hear his heavy footsteps and a chair scraping. 'Okay, Doc. So what the hell's going on?'

'I spent most of today discussing the landfill cases with the state pathologist. Marino, I'm increasingly suspicious that Ireland's serial dismemberments are the work of the same individual we're dealing with in Virginia.'

He raised his voice. 'You guys hold it down in there!'

I could hear him moving farther away from his pals as I rearranged the duvet around me. I reached for the last few sips of Black Bush I had carried to bed.

'Dr Foley worked the five Dublin cases,' I went on. 'I've reviewed all of them. Torsos. Spines cut horizontally through the caudal aspect of the fifth cervical vertebral body. Arms and legs severed through the joints, which is unusual, as I've pointed out before. Victims are a racial mix, estimated ages between eighteen and thirty-five. All are unidentified and signed out as homicides by unspecified means. In each case, heads and limbs were never found, the remains discovered in privately owned landfills.'

'Damn, if that don't sound familiar.' he said.

'There are other details. But yes, the parallels are profound.'

'So maybe the squirrel's in the U.S. now,' he said. 'Guess it's a damn good thing you went over there, after all.'

He certainly hadn't thought so at first. No one really had. I was the chief medical examiner of Virginia, and when the Royal College of Surgeons had invited me to give a series of lectures at Trinity's medical school, I could not pass up an opportunity to investigate the Dublin crimes. Marino had thought it a waste of time, while the FBI had assumed the value of the research would prove to be little more than statistical.

Doubts were understandable. The homicides in Ireland were more than ten years old, and as was true in the Virginia cases, there was so little to go on. We did not have fingerprints, dentition, sinus configurations or witnesses for identification. We did not have biological samples from people missing to compare to the victims' DNA. We did not know the means of death. Therefore, it was very difficult to say much about the killer, except that I believed he was experienced with a meat saw and quite possibly used one in his profession, or had at one time.

'The last case in Ireland, that we know of, was a decade ago,' I was saying to Marino over the line. 'In the past two years we've had four in Virginia.'

'So you're thinking he stopped for eight years?' he said. 'Why? He was in prison, maybe, for some other crime?'

'I don't know. He may have been killing somewhere else and the cases haven't been connected,' I replied as wind made unearthly sounds.

'There's those serial cases in South Africa,' he thickly thought out loud. 'In Florence, Germany, Russia, Australia. Shit, now that you think of it, they're friggin' everywhere. Hey!' He put his hand over the phone. 'Smoke your own damn cigarettes! What do you think this is? Friggin' welfare!'

Male voices were rowdy in the background, and someone had put on Randy Travis.

'Sounds like you're having fun,' I dryly said. 'Please don't invite me next year, either.'

'Bunch of animals,' he mumbled. 'Don't ask me why I do this. Every time they drink me outa house, home. Cheat at cards.'

'The M.O. in these cases is very distinctive.' My tone was meant to sober.

'Okay,' he said. 'So if this guy started in Dublin, maybe we're looking for someone Irish. I think you should hurry back home.' He belched. 'Sounds like we need to go to Quantico and get on this. You told Benton yet?'

Benton Wesley headed the FBI's Child Abduction Serial Killer Unit, or CASKU, for which both Marino and I were consultants.

'I haven't had a chance to tell him yet,' I replied, hesitantly. 'Maybe you can give him a heads-up. I'll get home as soon as I can.'

'Tomorrow would be good.'

'I'm not finished with the lecture series here,' I said.

'Ain't a place in the world that don't want you to lecture. You could probably do that and nothing else,' he said, and I knew he was about to dig into me.

'We export our violence to other countries,' I said. 'The least we can do is teach them what we know, what we've learned from years of working these crimes . . .'

'Lectures ain't why you're staying in the land of leprechauns, Doc,' he interrupted as a flip-top popped. 'It ain't why, and you know it.'

'Marino,' I warned. 'Don't do this.'

But he kept on. 'Ever since Wesley's divorce, you've found one reason or another to skip along the Yellow Brick Road, right on out of town. And you don't want to come home now, I can tell from the way you sound, because you don't want to deal, take a look at your hand and take your chances. Let me tell you. Comes a time when you got to call or fold . . .'

'Point taken.' I was gentle as I cut off his besotted good intentions. 'Marino, don't stay up all night.'

The Coroner's Office was at No. 3 Store Street, across from the Custom House and central bus station, near docks and the river Liffey. The brick building was small and old, the alleyway leading to the back barred by a heavy black gate with MORGUE painted across it in bold white letters. Climbing steps to the Georgian entrance, I rang the bell and waited in mist.

It was cool this Tuesday morning, trees beginning to look like fall. I could feel my lack of sleep. My eyes burned, my head was dull, and I was unsettled by what Marino had said before I had almost hung up on him.

'Hello.' The administrator cheerfully let me in. 'How are we this morning, Dr Scarpetta?'

His name was Jimmy Shaw, and he was very young and Irish, with hair as fiery as copper ivy, and eyes as blue as sky.

'I've been better,' I confessed.

'Well, I was just boiling tea,' he said, shutting us inside a narrow, dimly lit hallway, which we followed to his office. 'Sounds like you could use a cup.'

'That would be lovely, Jimmy,' I said.

'As for the good doctor, she should be finishing up an inquest.' He glanced at his watch as we entered his cluttered small space. 'She should be out in no time.'

His desk was dominated by a large Coroner's Inquiries book, black and bound in heavy leather, and he had been reading a biography of Steve McQueen and eating toast before I arrived. Momentarily, he was setting a mug of tea within my reach, not asking how I took it, for by now he knew.

'A little toast with jam?' he asked as he did every morning.

'I ate at the hotel, thanks.' I gave the same reply as he sat behind his desk.

'Never stops me from eating again.' He smiled, slipping on glasses. 'I'll just go over your schedule, then. You lecture at eleven this morning, then again at one P.M. Both at the college, in the old pathology building. I should expect about seventy-five students for each, but there could be more. I don't know. You're awfully popular over here, Dr Kay Scarpetta,' he cheerfully said. 'Or maybe it's just that American violence is so exotic to us.'

'That's rather much like calling a plague *exotic*,' I said.

'Well, we can't help but be fascinated by what you see.'

'And I guess that bothers me,' I said in a friendly but ominous way. 'Don't be too fascinated.'

We were interrupted by the phone, which he snapped up with the impatience of one who answers it too often.

Listening for a moment, he brusquely said. 'Right, right. Well, we can't place an order like that just yet. I'll have to ring you back another time.'

'I've been wanting computers for years,' he complained to me as he hung up. 'No bloody money when you're the dog wagged by the Socialist tail.'

'There will never be enough money. Dead men don't vote.'

'The bloody truth. So what's the topic of the day?' he wanted to know.

'Sexual homicide,' I replied. 'Specifically the role DNA can play.'

'These dismemberments you're so interested in.' He sipped tea. 'Do you think they're sexual? I mean, would that be the motivation on the part of whoever would do this?' His eyes were keen with interest.

'It's certainly an element,' I replied.

'But how can you know that when none of the victims has ever been identified? Couldn't it just be someone who kills for sport? Like, say, your Son of Sam, for example?'

'What the Son of Sam did had a sexual element,' I said, looking around for my pathologist friend. 'Do you know how much longer she might be? I'm afraid I'm in a bit of a hurry.'

Shaw glanced at his watch again. 'You can check. Or I suppose she may have gone on to the morgue. We have a case coming in. A young male, suspected suicide.'

'I'll see if I can find her.' I got up.

Off the hallway near the entrance was the coroner's court, where inquests for unnatural deaths were held before a jury. This included industrial and traffic accidents, homicides and suicides, the proceedings *in camera*, for the press in Ireland was not allowed to print many details. I ducked inside a stark, chilly room of varnished benches and naked walls, and found several men inside, tucking paperwork into briefcases.

'I'm looking for the coroner,' I said.

'She slipped out about twenty minutes ago. Believe she had a viewing,' one of them said.

I left the building through the back door. Crossing a small parking lot, I headed to the morgue as an old man came out of it. He seemed disoriented, almost stumbling as he looked about, dazed. For an instant, he stared at me as if I held some answer, and my heart hurt for him. No business that had brought him here could possibly be kind. I watched him hurry toward the gate as Dr Margaret Foley suddenly emerged after him, harried, her graying hair disarrayed.

'My God!' She almost ran into me. 'I turn my back for a minute and he's gone.'

The man let himself out, the gate flung open wide as he fled. Foley trotted across the parking lot to shut and latch it again. When she got back to me, she was out of breath and almost tripped over a bump in the pavement.

'Kay, you're out and about early,' she said.

'A relative?' I asked.

'The father. Left without identifying him, before I could even pull back the sheet. That will foul me up the rest of the day.'

She led me inside the small brick morgue with its white porcelain autopsy tables that probably belonged in a medical museum and old iron stove that heated nothing anymore. The air was refrigerated-chilly, modern equipment nonexistent except for electric autopsy saws. Thin gray light seeped through opaque skylights, barely illuminating the white paper sheet covering a body that a father could not bear to see.

'It's always the hardest part,' she was saying. 'No one should ever have to look at anyone in here.'

I followed her into a small storeroom and helped carry out boxes of new syringes, masks and gloves.

'Strung himself up from the rafters in the barn,' she went on as we worked. 'Was being treated for a drink problem and depression.

More of the same. Unemployment, women, drugs. They hang themselves or jump off bridges.' She glanced at me as we restocked a surgical cart. 'Thank God we don't have guns. Especially since I don't have an X-ray machine.'

Foley was a slight woman with old-fashioned thick glasses and a penchant for tweed. We had met years ago at an international forensic science conference in Vienna, when female forensic pathologists were a rare breed, especially overseas. We quickly had become friends.

'Margaret, I'm going to have to head back to the States sooner than I thought,' I said, taking a deep breath, looking about, distracted. 'I didn't sleep worth a damn last night.'

She lit a cigarette, scrutinizing me. 'I can get you copies of whatever you want. How fast do you need them? Photographs may take a few days, but they can be sent.'

'I think there is always a sense of urgency when someone like this is on the loose,' I said.

'I'm not happy if he's now your problem. And I'd hoped after all these years he had bloody quit.' She irritably tapped an ash, exhaling the strong smoke of British tobacco. 'Let's take a load off for a minute. My shoes are already getting tight from the swelling. It's hell getting old on these bloody hard floors.'

The lounge was two squat wooden chairs in a corner, where Foley kept an ashtray on a gurney. She put her feet up on a box and indulged her vice.

'I can never forget those poor people.' She started talking about her serial cases again. 'When the first one came to me, I thought it was the IRA. Never seen people torn asunder like that except in bombings.'

I was reminded of Mark in a way I did not want to be, and my thoughts drifted to him when he was alive and we were in love. Suddenly he was in my mind, smiling with eyes full of a mischievous light that became electric when he laughed and teased. There had been a lot of that in law school at Georgetown, fun and fights and staying up all night, our hunger for each other impossible to appease. Over time we married other people, divorced and tried again. He was my leitmotif, here, gone, then back on the phone or at my door to break my heart and wreck my bed.

I could not banish him. It still did not seem possible that a bombing in a London train station would finally bring the tempest of our relationship to an end. I did not imagine him dead. I could not envision it, for there was no last image that might grant peace. I had never seen his body, had fled from any chance, just like the old Dubliner who could not view his son. I realized Foley was saying something to me.

'I'm sorry,' she repeated, her eyes sad, for she knew my history well. 'I didn't mean to bring up something painful. You seem blue enough this morning.'

'You made an interesting point.' I tried to be brave. 'I suspect the killer we're looking for is rather much like a bomber. He doesn't care who he kills. His victims are people with no faces or names. They are nothing but symbols of his private, evil credo.'

'Would it bother you terribly if I asked a question about Mark?' she said.

'Ask anything you want.' I smiled. 'You will anyway.'

'Have you ever gone to where it happened, visited that place where he died?'

'I don't know where it happened,' I quickly replied.

She looked at me as she smoked.

'What I mean is, I don't know where, exactly, in the train station.' I was evasive, almost stuttering.

Still she said nothing, crushing the cigarette beneath her foot.

'Actually,' I went on, 'I don't know that I've been in Victoria at all, not that particular station, since he died. I don't think I've had reason to take a train from there. Or arrive there. Waterloo was the last one I was in, I think.'

'The one crime scene the great Dr Kay Scarpetta will not visit.' She tapped another Consulate out of the pack. 'Would you like one?'

'God knows I would. But I can't.'

She sighed. 'I remember Vienna. All those men and the two of us smoking more than they did.'

'Probably the reason we smoked so much was all those men,' I said.

'That may be the cause, but for me, there seems to be no cure. It just goes to show that what we do is unrelated to what we know, and our feelings don't have a brain.' She shook out a match. 'I've seen smokers' lungs. And I've seen my share of fatty livers.'

'My lungs are better since I quit. I can't vouch for my liver,' I said. 'I haven't given up whiskey yet.'

'Don't, for God's sake. You'd be no fun.' She paused, adding pointedly, 'Course, feelings can be directed, educated, so they don't conspire against us.'

'I will probably leave tomorrow.' I got back to that.

'You have to go to London first to change planes.' She met my eyes. 'Linger there. A day.'

'Pardon?'

'It's unfinished business, Kay. I have felt this for a long time. You need to bury Mark James.'

'Margaret, what has suddenly prompted this?' I was tripping over words again.

'I know when someone is on the run. And you are, just as much as this killer is.'

'Now, that's a comforting thing to say,' I replied, and I did not want to have this conversation.

But she was not going to let me escape this time. 'For very different reasons and very similar reasons. He's evil, you're not. But neither of you wants to be caught.'

She had gotten to me and could tell.

'And just who or what is trying to catch me, in your opinion?' My tone was light but I felt the threat of tears.

'At this stage, I expect it's Benton Wesley.'

I stared off, past the gurney and its protruding pale foot tied with a tag. Light from above shifted by degrees as clouds moved over the sun, and the smell of death in tile and stone went back a hundred years.

'Kay, what do you want to do?' she asked kindly as I wiped my eyes.

'He wants to marry me,' I said.

I flew home to Richmond and days became weeks with the weather getting cold. Mornings were glazed with frost and evenings I spent in front of the fire, thinking and fretting. So much was unresolved and silent, and I coped the way I always did, working my way deeper into the labyrinth of my profession until I could not find a way out. It was making my secretary crazy.

'Dr Scarpetta?' She called out my name, her footsteps loud and brisk along the tile floor in the autopsy suite.

'In here,' I answered over running water.

It was October 30. I was in the morgue locker room, washing up with antibacterial soap.

'Where have you been?' Rose asked as she walked in.

'Working on a brain. The sudden death from the other day.'

She was holding my calendar and flipping pages. Her gray hair was neatly pinned back, and she was dressed in a dark red suit that

seemed appropriate for her mood. Rose was deeply angry with me
and had been since I'd left for Dublin without saying good-bye. Then
I forgot her birthday when I got back. I turned off the water and
dried my hands.

'Swelling, with widening of the gyri, narrowing of the sulci, all
good for ischemic encephalopathy brought on by his profound
systemic hypotension,' I cited.

'I've been trying to find you,' she said with strained patience.

'What did I do this time?' I threw up my hands.

'You were supposed to have lunch at the Skull and Bones with
Jon.'

'Oh, God,' I groaned as I thought of him and other medical school
advisees I had so little time to see.

'I reminded you this morning. You forgot him last week, too. He
really needs to talk to you about his residency, about the Cleveland
Clinic.'

'I know, I know.' I felt awful about it as I looked at my watch. 'It's
one-thirty. Maybe he can come by my office for coffee?'

'You have a deposition at two, a conference call at three about the
Norfolk-Southern case. A gunshot wound lecture to the Forensic
Science Academy at four, and a meeting at five with Investigator Ring
from the state police.' Rose went down the list.

I did not like Ring or his aggressive way of taking over cases. When
the second torso had been found, he had inserted himself into the
investigation and seemed to think he knew more than the FBI.

'Ring I can do without,' I said, shortly.

My secretary looked at me for a long moment, water and sponges
slapping in the autopsy suite next door.

'I'll cancel him and you can see Jon instead.' She eyed me over her
glasses like a stern headmistress. 'Then rest, and that's an order.
Tomorrow, Dr Scarpetta. Don't come in. Don't you dare let me see
you darken the door.'

I started to protest and she cut me off.

'Don't even think of arguing,' she firmly went on. 'You need a
mental health day, a long weekend. I wouldn't say that if I didn't
mean it.'

She was right, and as I thought about having a day to myself, my
spirits lifted.

'There's not a thing I can't reschedule,' she added. 'Besides.' She
smiled. 'We're having a touch of Indian summer and it's supposed
to be glorious, in the eighties with a big blue sky. Leaves are at their

peak, poplars an almost perfect yellow. Maples look like they're on fire. Not to mention, it's Halloween. You can carve a pumpkin.'

I got suit jacket and shoes out of my locker. 'You should have been a lawyer,' I said.

2

___

The next day, the weather was just what Rose predicted, and I woke up thrilled. As stores were opening, I set out to stock up for trick-or-treaters and dinner, and I drove far out on Hull Street to my favorite gardening center. Summer plantings had long since faded around my house, and I could not bear to see their dead stalks in pots. After lunch, I carried bags of black soil, boxes of plants and a watering can to my front porch.

I opened the door so I could hear Mozart playing inside as I gently tucked pansies into their rich, new bed. Bread was rising, homemade stew simmering on the stove, and I smelled garlic and wine and loamy soil as I worked. Marino was coming for dinner, and we were going to hand out chocolate bars to my small, scary neighbors. The world was a good place to live until three-thirty-five when my pager vibrated against my waist.

'Damn,' I exclaimed as it displayed the number for my answering service.

I hurried inside, washed my hands and reached for the phone. The service gave me a number for a Detective Grigg with the Sussex County Sheriff's Department, and I immediately called.

'Grigg,' a man answered in a deep voice.

'This is Dr Scarpetta,' I said as I stared dismally out windows at large terra cotta pots on the deck and the dead hibiscus in them.

'Oh good. Thank you for getting back to me so quick. I'm out here on a cellular phone, don't want to say much.' He spoke with the rhythm of the old South, and took his time.

'Where, exactly, is *here*?' I asked.

'Atlantic Waste Landfill on Reeves Road, off 460 East. They've turned something up I think you're going to want to take a look at.'

'Is this the same sort of thing that has turned up in similar places?' I cryptically asked as the day seemed to get darker.

'Afraid that's what it's looking like,' he said.

'Give me directions, and I'm on my way.'

I was in dirty khakis, and an FBI tee shirt that my niece, Lucy, had given to me, and did not have time to change. If I didn't recover the body before dark, it would have to stay where it was until morning, and that was unacceptable. Grabbing my medical bag, I hurried out the door, leaving soil, cabbage plants and geraniums scattered over the porch. Of course my black Mercedes was low on gas. I stopped at Amoco first and pumped my own, then was on my way.

The drive should have taken an hour, but I sped. Waning light flashed white on the underside of leaves, and rows of corn were brown in farms and gardens. Fields were ruffled green seas of soybeans, and goats grazed unrestrained in the yards of tired homes. Gaudy lightning rods with colored balls tilted from every peak and corner, and I always wondered what lying salesman had hit like a storm and played on fear by preaching more.

Soon grain elevators Grigg had told me to look for came into view. I turned on Reeves Road, passing tiny brick homes and trailer courts with pickup trucks and dogs with no collars. Billboards advertised Mountain Dew and the Virginia Diner, and I bumped over railroad tracks, red dust billowing up like smoke from my tires. Ahead, buzzards in the road picked at creatures that had been too slow, and it seemed a morbid harbinger.

At the entrance of the Atlantic Waste Landfill, I slowed my car to a stop and looked out at a moonscape of barren acres where the sun was setting like a planet on fire. Flatbed refuse trucks were sleek and white with polished chrome, crawling along the summit of a growing mountain of trash. Yellow Caterpillars were striking scorpions. I sat watching a moiling storm of dust heading away from the landfill, rocking over ruts at a high rate of speed. When it got to me it was a dirty red Ford Explorer driven by a young man who felt at home in this place.

'May I help you, ma'am?' he said in a Southern drawl, and he seemed anxious and excited.

'I'm Dr Kay Scarpetta,' I replied, displaying the brass shield in its small black wallet that I always pulled at scenes where I did not know anyone.

He studied my credentials, then his eyes were dark on mine. He was sweating through his denim shirt, hair wet at his neck and temples.

'They said the medical examiner would get here, and for me to watch for him,' he said to me.

'Well, that would be me,' I blandly replied.

'Oh yes, ma'am. I didn't mean anything . . .' His voice trailed off as his eyes wandered over my Mercedes, which was coated in dust so fine and persistent that nothing could keep it out. 'I suggest you leave your car here and ride with me,' he added.

I stared up at the landfill, at Caterpillars with rampant blades and buckets immobile on the summit. Two unmarked police cars and an ambulance awaited me up where the trouble was, and officers were small figures gathered near the tailgate of a truck smaller than the rest. Near it someone was poking the ground with a stick, and I got increasingly impatient to get to the body.

'Okay,' I said. 'Let's do it.'

Parking my car, I got my medical bag and scene clothes out of the trunk. The young man watched in curious silence as I sat in my driver's seat with the door open wide, and pulled on rubber boots, scarred and dull from years of wading in woods and rivers for people murdered and drowned. I covered myself with a big faded denim shirt that I had appropriated from my ex-husband, Tony, during a marriage that now did not seem real. Then I climbed inside the Explorer and sheathed my hands in two layers of gloves. I pulled a surgical mask over my head and left it loose around my neck.

'I can't say that I blame you,' my driver said. 'The smell's pretty rough. I can tell you that.'

'It's not the smell,' I said. 'Microorganisms are what make me worry.'

'Gee,' he said, anxiously. 'Maybe I should wear one of those things.'

'You shouldn't be getting close enough to have a problem.'

He made no reply, and I had no doubt that he already had gotten that close. Looking was too much of a temptation for most people to resist. The more gruesome the case, the more this was true.

'I sure am sorry about the dust,' he said as we drove through tangled goldenrod on the rim of a small fire pond populated with ducks. 'You can see we put a layer of tire chips everywhere to keep things settled, and a street cleaner sprays it down. But nothing seems to help all that much.' He nervously paused before going on. 'We do three thousand tons of trash a day out here.'

'From where?' I asked.

'Littleton, North Carolina, to Chicago.'

'What about Boston?' I asked, for the first four cases were believed to be from as far away as that.

'No, ma'am.' He shook his head. 'Maybe one of these days. We're so much less per ton down here. Twenty-five dollars compared to sixty-nine in New Jersey or eighty in New York. Plus, we recycle, test for hazardous waste, collect methane gas from decomposing trash.'

'What about your hours?'

'Open twenty-four hours a day, seven days a week,' he said with pride.

'And you have a way to track where the trucks come from?'

'A satellite system that uses a grid. We can at least tell you which trucks would have dumped trash during a certain time period in the area where the body was found.'

We splashed through a deep puddle near Porta-Johns, and rocked by a powerwash where trucks were being hosed off on their way back out to life's roads and highways.

'I can't say we've ever had anything like this,' he said. 'Now, they've had body parts at the Shoosmith dump. Or at least, that's the rumor.'

He glanced at me, assuming I would know if such a rumor were true. But I did not verify what he had just said as the Explorer sloshed through mud strewn with rubber chips, the sour stench of decomposing garbage drifting in. My attention was riveted to the small truck I had been watching since I had gotten here, thoughts racing along a thousand different tracks.

'By the way, my name's Keith Pleasants.' He wiped a hand on his pants and held it out to me. 'Pleased to meet you.'

My gloved hand shook his at an awkward angle as men holding handkerchiefs and rags over their noses watched us pull up. There were four of them, gathered around the back of what I now could see was a hydraulic packer, used for emptying Dumpsters and compressing the trash. *Cole's Trucking Co.* was painted on the doors.

'That guy poking garbage with a stick is the detective for Sussex,' Pleasants said to me.

He was older, in shirtsleeves, wearing a revolver on his hip. I felt I'd seen him somewhere before.

'Grigg?' I guessed, referring to the detective I had spoken to on the phone.

'That's right.' Sweat was rolling down Pleasants' face, and he was getting more keyed up. 'You know, I've never had any dealings with the sheriff's department, never even got a speeding ticket around here.'

We slowed down to a halt, and I could barely see through the boiling dust. Pleasants grabbed his door handle.

'Sit tight just a minute,' I told him.

I waited for dust to settle, looking out the windshield and surveying as I always did when approaching a crime scene. The loader's bucket was frozen midair, the packer beneath it almost full. All around, the landfill was busy and full of diesel sounds, work stopped only here. For a moment, I watched powerful white trucks roar uphill as Cats clawed and grabbed, and compactors crushed the ground with their chopper wheels.

The body would be transported by ambulance, and paramedics watched me through dusty windows as they sat in air conditioning, waiting to see what I was going to do. When they saw me fix the surgical mask over my nose and mouth and open my door, they climbed out, too. Doors slammed shut. The detective immediately walked to meet me.

'Detective Grigg, Sussex Sheriff's Department,' he said. 'I'm the one who called.'

'Have you been out here the entire time?' I asked him.

'Since we were notified at approximately thirteen hundred hours. Yes, ma'am. I've been right here to make sure nothing was disturbed.'

'Excuse me,' one of the paramedics said to me. 'You going to want us right now?'

'Maybe in fifteen. Someone will come get you,' I said as they wasted no time returning to their ambulance. 'I'm going to need some room here,' I said to everybody else.

Feet crunched as people stepped out of the way, revealing what they had been guarding and gawking at. Flesh was unnaturally pale in the dying light of the autumn afternoon, the torso a hideous stub that had tumbled from a scoop of trash and landed on its back. I thought it was Caucasian, but was not sure, and maggots teeming in the genital area made it difficult for me to determine gender at a glance. I could not even say with certainty whether the victim was pre- or postpubescent. Body fat was abnormally low, ribs protruding beneath flat breasts that may or may not have been female.

I squatted close and opened my medical bag. With forceps, I collected maggots into a jar for the entomologist to examine later, and decided upon closer inspection that the victim was, in fact, a woman. She had been decapitated low on the cervical spine, arms and legs severed. Stumps were dry and dark with age, and I knew right away that there was a difference between this case and the others.

This woman had been dismembered by cutting straight through the strong bones of the humerus and femur, versus the joints. Getting out a scalpel, I could feel the men staring as I made a half-inch incision on the torso's right side, and inserted a long chemical thermometer. I rested a second thermometer on top of my bag.

'What are you doing?' asked a man in a plaid shirt and baseball cap, who looked like he might get sick.

'I need the body's temperature to help determine time of death. A core liver temperature is the most accurate,' I patiently explained. 'And I also need to know the temperature out here.'

'Hot, that's what it is,' said another man. 'So, it's a woman, I guess.'

'It's too soon to say,' I replied. 'Is this your packer?'

'Yeah.'

He was young, with dark eyes and very white teeth, and tattoos on his fingers that I usually associated with people who have been in prison. A sweaty bandanna was tied around his head and knotted in back, and he could not look at the torso long without averting his gaze.

'In the wrong place at the wrong time,' he added, shaking his head with hostility.

'What do you mean?' Grigg had his eye on him.

'Wasn't from me. I know that,' the driver said as if it were the most important point he would ever make in his life. 'The Cat dug it up while it was spreading my load.'

'Then we don't know when it was dumped here?' I scanned faces around me.

It was Pleasants who replied, 'Twenty-three trucks unloaded in this spot since ten A.M., not counting this one.' He looked at the packer.

'Why ten A.M.?' I asked, for it seemed like a rather arbitrary time to start counting trucks.

'Because that's when we put down the last cover of tire chips. So there's no way it could have been dumped before then,' Pleasants explained, staring at the body. 'And in my opinion, it couldn't have been out long, anyway. It doesn't exactly look the way you'd expect if it's been run over by a fifty-ton compactor with chopper wheels, trucks or even this loader.'

He stared off at other sites where compacted trash was being gouged off trucks as huge tractors crushed and spread. The driver of the packer was getting increasingly agitated and angry.

'We got big machines all over the place up here,' Pleasants added. 'And they pretty much never stop.'

I looked at the packer, and the bright yellow loader with its empty cab. A tatter of black trash bag fluttered from the raised bucket.

'Where's the driver of the loader?' I asked.

Pleasants hesitated before answering, 'Well, I guess that would be me. We had somebody out sick. I was asked to work on the hill.'

Grigg moved closer to the loader, looking up at what was left of the trash bag as it moved in the hot, barren air.

'Tell me what you saw,' I said to Pleasants.

'Not much. I was unloading him.' He nodded at the driver. 'And my bucket caught the garbage bag, the one you see there. It tore and the body fell out to where it is now.' He paused, wiping his face on his sleeve and swatting at flies.

'But you don't know for sure where this came from,' I tried again, while Grigg listened, even though he probably had already taken their statements.

'I could've dug it up,' Pleasants conceded. 'I'm not saying it's impossible. I just don't think I did.'

'That's 'cause you don't want to think it.' The driver glared at him.

'I know what I think.' Pleasants didn't flinch. 'The bucket grabbed it off your packer when I was unloading it.'

'Man, you don't *know* it came from me,' the driver snapped at him.

'No, I don't know it for a fact. Makes sense, that's all.'

'Maybe to you.' The driver's face was menacing.

'Believe that will be about enough, boys,' Grigg warned, moving close again, his presence reminding them he was big and wore a gun.

'You got that right,' said the driver. 'I've had enough of this shit. When can I get out of here? I'm already late.'

'Something like this inconveniences everyone,' Grigg said to him with a steady look.

Rolling his eyes and muttering profanity, the driver stalked off and lit a cigarette.

I removed the thermometer from the body, and held it up. The core temperature was eighty-four degrees, the same as the ambient air. I turned the torso over to see what else was there and noted a curious crop of fluid-filled vesicles over the lower buttocks. As I checked more carefully, I found evidence of others in the area of the shoulders and thighs, at the edges of deep cuts.

'Double-pouch her,' I directed. 'I need the trash bag it came in, including what's caught on the bucket up there. And I want the trash immediately around and under her, send all of it in.'

Grigg unfolded a twenty-gallon trash bag and shook it open. He pulled gloves out of a pocket, squatted and started grabbing up garbage by the handful while paramedics opened the back of the ambulance. The driver of the packer was leaning against his cab, and I could feel his fury like heat.

'Where was your packer coming from?' I asked him.

'Look at the tags,' he replied in a surly tone.

'Where in Virginia?' I refused to be put off by him.

It was Pleasants who said, 'Tidewater area, ma'am. The packer belongs to us. We got a lot of them we lease.'

The landfill's administrative headquarters overlooked the fire pond and was quaintly out of sync with the loud, dusty surroundings. The building was pale peach stucco, with flowers in window boxes and sculpted shrubs bordering the walk. Shutters were painted cream, a brass pineapple knocker on the front door. Inside, I was greeted by clean, chilled air that was a wonderful relief and I knew why Investigator Percy Ring had chosen to conduct his interviews here. I bet he had not even been to the scene.

He was in the break room, sitting with an older man in shirtsleeves, drinking Diet Coke and looking at computer-printed diagrams.

'This is Dr Scarpetta. Sorry,' Pleasants said, adding to Ring, 'I don't know your first name.'

Ring gave me a big smile and a wink. 'The doc and I go way back.'

He was in a crisp blue suit, blond and exuding pure youthful innocence that was easy to believe. But he had never fooled me. He was a big-talking charmer who basically was lazy, and it had not escaped me that the moment he had become involved in these cases, we had been besieged by leaks to the press.

'And this is Mr Kitchen,' Pleasants was saying to me. 'The owner of the landfill.'

Kitchen was simple in jeans and Timberland boots, his eyes gray and sad as he offered a big rough hand.

'Please sit down,' he said, pulling out a chair. 'This is a bad, bad day. Especially for whoever that is out there.'

'That person's bad day happened earlier,' Ring said. 'Right now, she's feeling no pain.'

'Have you been up there?' I asked him.

'I just got here about an hour ago. And this isn't the crime scene, just where the body ended up,' he said. 'Number five.' He peeled open a stick of Juicy Fruit. 'He's not waiting as long, only two months in between 'em this time.'

I felt the usual rush of irritation. Ring loved to jump to conclusions and voice them with the certainty of one who doesn't know enough to realize he could be wrong. In part this was because he wanted results without work.

'I haven't examined the body yet or verified gender,' I said, hoping he would remember there were other people in the room. 'This is not a good time to be making assumptions.'

'Well, I'll leave ya,' Pleasants said nervously, on his way out the door.

'I need you back in an hour so I can get your statement,' Ring loudly reminded him.

Kitchen was quiet, looking at diagrams, and then Grigg walked in. He nodded at us and took a chair.

'I don't think it's an assumption to say that what we got here is a homicide,' Ring said to me.

'That you can safely say.' I held his gaze.

'And that it's just like the other ones.'

'That you can't safely say. I haven't examined the body yet,' I replied.

Kitchen shifted uncomfortably in his chair. 'Anybody want a soda. Maybe coffee?' he asked. 'We got rest rooms in the hall.'

'Same thing,' Ring said to me as if he knew. 'Another torso in a landfill.'

Grigg was watching with no expression, restlessly tapping his notebook. Clicking his pen twice, he said to Ring, 'I agree with Dr Scarpetta. Seems we shouldn't be connecting this case to anything yet. Especially not publicly.'

'Lord help me. I could do without that kind of publicity,' Kitchen said, blowing out a deep breath. 'You know, when you're in my business, you accept this can happen, especially when you're getting waste from places like New York, New Jersey, Chicago. But you never think it's going to land in your yard.' He looked at Grigg. 'I'd like to offer a reward to help catch whoever did this terrible thing. Ten thousand dollars for information leading to the arrest.'

'That's mighty generous,' Grigg said, impressed.

'That include investigators?' Ring grinned.

'I don't care who solves it.' Kitchen wasn't smiling as he turned to me. 'Now you tell me what I can do to help you, ma'am.'

'I understand you use a satellite tracking system,' I said. 'Is that what these diagrams are?'

'I was just explaining them,' Kitchen said.

He slid several of them to me. Their patterns of wavy lines looked like cross sections of geode, and they were marked with coordinates.

'This is a picture of the landfill face,' Kitchen explained. 'We can take it hourly, daily, weekly, whenever we want, to figure out where waste originated and where it was deposited. Locations on the map can be pinpointed by using these coordinates.' He tapped the paper. 'Sort of similar to how you plot a graph in geometry or algebra.' Looking up at me, he added, 'I reckon you suffered through some of that in school.'

'*Suffer* is the operative word.' I smiled at him. 'Then the point is you can compare these pictures to see how the landfill's face changes from load to load.'

He nodded. 'Yes, ma'am. That's it in a nutshell.'

'And what have you determined?'

He placed eight maps side by side. The wavy lines in each were different, like different wrinkles on the faces of the same person.

'Each line, basically, is a depth,' he said. 'So we can pretty much know which truck is responsible for which depth.'

Ring emptied his Coke can and tossed it in the trash. He flipped through his notepad as if looking for something.

'This body could not have been buried deep,' I said. 'It's very clean, considering the circumstances. There are no postmortem injuries, and based on what I observed out there, the Cats grab bales off the trucks, smash them open. They spread the trash on the ground so the compactor can doze it with the straight blade, chopping and compressing.'

'That's pretty much it.' Kitchen eyed me with interest. 'You want a job?'

I was preoccupied with images of earth-moving machines that looked like robotic dinosaurs, claws biting into plastic-shrouded bales on trucks. I was intimately acquainted with the injuries in the earlier cases, with human remains crushed and mauled. Except for what the killer had done, this victim was intact.

'Hard to find good women,' Kitchen was saying.

'You ain't kidding, brother,' Ring said as Grigg watched him with growing disgust.

'Seems like a good point,' Grigg said. 'If that body had been on the ground for any time at all, it would be pretty chewed up.'

'The first four were,' Ring said. 'Mangled like cube steak.' He eyed me. 'This one look compacted?'

'The body doesn't appear crushed,' I replied.

'Now that's interesting, too,' he mused. 'Why wouldn't it be?'

'It didn't start out at a transfer station where it was compacted and baled,' Kitchen said. 'It started in a Dumpster that was emptied by the packer.'

'And the packer doesn't pack?' Ring dramatically asked. 'Thought that's why they were called *packers*.' He shrugged and grinned at me.

'It depends on where the body was in relation to the other garbage when the compacting was done,' I said. 'It depends on a lot of things.'

'Or if it was compacted at all, depending on how full the truck was,' Kitchen said. 'I'm thinking it was the packer. Or at most, one of the two trucks before it, if we're talking about the exact coordinates where the body was found.'

'I guess I'm going to need the names of those trucks and where they're from,' Ring said. 'We gotta interview the drivers.'

'So you're looking at the drivers as suspects,' Grigg said, coolly, to him. 'Got to give you credit, that's original. The way I look at it, the trash didn't originate with them. It originated with the folks who pitched it. And I expect one of those folks is who we need to find.'

Ring stared at him, not the least bit perturbed. 'I'd just like to hear what the drivers have to say. You never know. It'd be a good way to stage something. You dump a body in a place that's on your route and make sure you deliver it yourself. Or, hell, you load it into your own truck. No one suspects you, right?'

Grigg pushed back his chair. He loosened his collar and worked his jaw as if it hurt. His neck popped, then his knuckles. Finally, he slapped his notebook down on the table and everybody looked at him as he glared at Ring.

'You mind if I work this thing?' he said to the young investigator. 'I'd sure hate not to do what the county hired me for. And I believe this is my case, not yours.'

'Just here to help,' Ring said easily as he shrugged again.

'I didn't know I needed help,' Grigg replied.

'The state police formed the multijurisdictional task force on homicides when the second torso showed up in a different county than the first one,' Ring said. 'You're a little late in the game, good buddy. Seems like you might want some background from somebody who's not.'

But Grigg had tuned him out, and he said to Kitchen, 'I'd like that vehicle information, too.'

'How about I get it for the last five trucks that were up there, to be safe,' Kitchen said to all of us.

'That will help a lot,' I said as I got up from the table. 'The sooner you could do that, the better.'

'What time you going to work on it tomorrow?' Ring asked me, remaining in his chair, as if there were little to do in life and so much time.

'Are you referring to the autopsy?' I asked.

'You bet.'

'I may not even open this one up for several days.'

'Why's that?'

'The most important part is the external examination. I will spend a very long time on that.' I could see his interest fade. 'I'll need to go through trash, search for trace, degrease and deflesh bones, get with an entomologist on the age of the maggots to see if I can get an idea of when the body was dumped, et cetera.'

'Maybe it's better if you just let me know what you find,' he decided.

Grigg followed me out the door and was shaking his head as he said in his slow, quiet way, 'When I got out of the army a long time ago, state police was what I wanted to be. I can't believe they got a bozo like that.'

'Fortunately, they're not all like him,' I said.

We walked out into the sun as the ambulance slowly made its way down the landfill in clouds of dust. Trucks were chugging in line and getting washed, as another layer of shredded modern America was added to the mountain. It was dark out when we reached our cars. Grigg paused by mine, looking it over.

'I wondered whose this was,' he said with admiration. 'One of these days I'm going to drive something like that. Just once.'

I smiled at him as I unlocked my door. 'Doesn't have the important things like a siren and lights.'

He laughed. 'Marino and me are in the same bowling league. His team's the Balls of Fire, mine's the Lucky Strikes. That ole boy's about the worst sport I ever seen. Drinks beer and eats. Then thinks everybody's cheating. He brought a girl the last time.' He shook his head. 'She bowled like the damn Flintstones, dressed like them, too. In this leopard-skin thing. All that was missing was a bone in her hair. Well, tell him we'll talk.'

He walked off, his keys jingling.

'Detective Grigg, thanks for your help,' I said.

He gave me a nod and climbed into his Caprice.

When I designed my house, I made sure the laundry room was directly off the garage because after working scenes like this one, I did not want to track death through the rooms of my private life. Within minutes of my getting out of my car, my clothes were in the washing machine, shoes and boots in an industrial sink, where I scrubbed them with detergent and a stiff brush.

Wrapping up in a robe I kept hanging on the back of the door, I headed to the master bedroom and took a long, hot shower. I was worn out and discouraged. Right now, I did not have the energy to imagine her, or her name, or who she had been, and I pushed images and odors from my mind. I fixed myself a drink and a salad, staring dismally at the big bowl of Halloween candy on the counter as I thought of plants waiting to be potted on the porch. Then I called Marino.

'Listen,' I said to him when he answered the phone. 'I think Benton should be here for this in the morning.'

There was a long pause. 'Okay,' he said. 'Meaning you want me to tell him to get his ass to Richmond. Versus your telling him.'

'If you wouldn't mind. I'm beat.'

'No problem. What time?'

'Whenever he wants. I'll be down there all day.'

I went back to the office in my house to check e-mail before I went to bed. Lucy rarely called when she could use the computer to tell me how and where she was. My niece was an FBI agent, the technical specialist for their Hostage Rescue Team, or HRT. She could be sent anywhere in the world at a moment's notice.

Like a fretful mother, I found myself frequently checking for messages from her, dreading the day her pager went off, sending her to Andrews Air Force Base with the boys, to board yet another C-141 cargo plane. Stepping around stacks of journals waiting to be read and thick medical tomes that I recently had bought but had not yet shelved, I sat at my desk. My office was the most lived-in room in my house, and I had designed it with a fireplace and large windows overlooking a rocky bend in the James River.

Logging on to America Online, or AOL, I was greeted by a mechanical male voice announcing that I had mail. I had e-mail about various cases, trials, professional meetings and journal articles, and one message from someone I did not recognize. His user name was *deadoc*. Immediately, I was uneasy. There was no description of what this person had sent, and when I opened what he had written to me, it simply said, *ten*.

A graphic file had been attached, and I downloaded and decompressed it. An image began to materialize on my screen, rolling down in color, one band of pixels at a time. I realized I was looking at a photograph of a wall the color of putty, and the edge of a table with some sort of pale blue cover on it that was smeared and pooled with something dark red. Then a ragged, gaping red wound was painted on the screen, followed by flesh tones that became bloody stumps and nipples.

I stared in disbelief as the horror was complete, and I grabbed the phone.

'Marino, I think you'd better get over here,' I said in a scared tone.

'What's wrong?' he said, alarmed.

'There's something here you need to see.'

'Are you okay?'

'I don't know.'

'Sit tight, Doc.' He took charge. 'I'm coming.'

I printed the file and saved it on my A drive, fearful it would somehow vanish before my eyes. While I waited for Marino, I dimmed the lights in my office to make details and colors brighter. My mind ran in a terrible loop as I stared at the butchery, the blood forming a vile portrait that for me, ordinarily, wasn't rare. Other physicians, scientists, lawyers and law enforcement officers frequently sent me photographs like this over the Internet. Routinely, I was asked, via e-mail, to examine crime scenes, organs, wounds, diagrams, even animated reconstructions of cases about to go to court.

This photograph could easily have been one sent by a detective, a colleague. It could have come from a Commonwealth's Attorney or CASKU. But there was one thing obviously wrong. So far we had no crime scene in this case, only a landfill where the victim had been dumped, and the trash and tattered bag that had been around her. Only the killer or someone else involved in the crime could have sent this file to me.

Fifteen minutes later, at almost midnight, my doorbell rang, and I jumped out of my chair. I ran down the hall to let Marino in.

'What the hell is it now?' he said right off.

He was sweating in a gray Richmond police tee shirt that was tight over his big body and gut, and baggy shorts and athletic shoes with

tube socks pulled up to his calves. I smelled stale sweat and cigarettes.

'Come on,' I said.

He followed me down the hall into my office, and when he saw
what was on the computer screen, he sat in my chair, scowling as he
stared.

'Is this what the shit I think it is?' he said.

'Appears the photograph was taken where the body was dismembered.' I was not used to having anyone in the private place where
I worked, and I could feel my anxiety level rise.

'This is what you found today.'

'What you're looking at was taken shortly after death,' I said. 'But
yes, this is the torso from the landfill.'

'How do you know?' Marino said.

His eyes were fastened to the screen, and he adjusted my chair.
Then his big feet shoved books on the floor as he made himself more
comfortable. When he picked up files and moved them to another
corner of my desk, I couldn't stand it any longer.

'I have things where I want them,' I pointedly said as I returned
the files to their original messy space.

'Hey, chill out, Doc,' he said as if it didn't matter. 'How do we
know that this thing ain't a hoax?'

Again, he moved the files out of his way, and now I was really
irritated.

'Marino, you're going to have to get up,' I said. 'I don't let anybody
sit at my desk. You're making me crazy.'

He shot me an angry look and got up out of my chair. 'Hey, do
me a favor. Next time call somebody else when you got a problem.'

'Try to be sensitive . . .'

He cut me off, losing his temper. 'No. *You* be sensitive and quit
being such a friggin' fussbudges. No wonder you and Wesley got
problems.'

'Marino,' I warned, 'you just crossed a line and better stop right
there.'

He was silent, looking around, sweating.

'Let's get back to this.' I sat in my chair, readjusting it. 'I don't
think this is a hoax, and I believe it's the torso from the landfill.'

'Why?' He would not look at me, hands in his pockets.

'Arms and legs are severed through the long bones, not the joints.'
I touched the screen. 'There are other similarities. It's her, unless another
victim with a similar body type has been killed and dismembered in

the same manner, and we've not found her yet. And I don't know how someone could have perpetrated a hoax like this without knowing how the victim was dismembered. Not to mention, this case hasn't hit the news yet.'

'Shit.' His face was deep red. 'So, is there something like a return address?'

'Yes. Someone on AOL with the name D-E-A-D-O-C.'

'As in *Dead-Doc*?' He was intrigued enough to forget his mood.

'I can only assume. The message was one word: *ten.*'

'That's it?'

'In lowercase letters.'

He looked at me, thinking. 'You count the ones in Ireland, this is number ten. You got a copy of this thing?'

'Yes. And the Dublin cases and their possible connection to the first four here have been in the news.' I handed him a printout. 'Anybody could know about it.'

'Don't matter. Assuming this is the same killer and he's just struck again, he knows damn well how many he's killed,' he said. 'But what I'm not getting is how he knew where to send this file to you?'

'My address in AOL wouldn't be hard to guess. It's my name.'

'Jesus, I can't believe you would do that,' he erupted again. 'That's like using your date of birth for your burglar alarm code.'

'I use e-mail almost exclusively to communicate with medical examiners, people in the Health Department, the police. They need something easy to remember. Besides,' I added as his stare continued to pass judgment on me, 'it's never been a problem.'

'Well, now it sure as hell is,' he said, looking at the printout. 'Good news is, maybe we'll find something in here that will help. Maybe he left a trail in the computer.'

'On the Web,' I said.

'Yeah, whatever,' he said. 'Maybe you should call Lucy.'

'Benton should do that,' I reminded him. 'I can't ask her help on a case just because I'm her aunt.'

'So I guess I got to call him about that, too.' He picked his way around my clutter, walking to the doorway. 'I hope you've got some beer in this joint.' He stopped and turned toward me. 'You know, Doc, it ain't none of my business, but you got to talk to him eventually.'

'You're right,' I said. 'It's none of your business.'

3

The next morning, I woke up to the muffled drumming of heavy rain on the roof and the persistent beeping of my alarm. The hour was early for a day that I was supposed to be taking off from work, and it struck me that during the night the month had turned into November. Winter was not far away, another year gone. Opening shades, I looked out at the day. Petals from my roses were beaten to the ground, the river swollen and flowing around rocks that looked black.

I felt bad about Marino. I had been impatient with him when I had sent him home without a beer last night. But I did not want to talk with him about matters he would not understand. For him, it was simple. I was divorced. Benton Wesley's wife had left him for another man. We'd been having an affair, so we might as well get married. For a while I had gone along with the plan. Last fall and winter, Wesley and I went skiing, diving, we shopped, cooked in and out and even worked in my yard. We did not get along worth a damn.

In fact, I didn't want him in my house any more than I wanted Marino sitting in my chair. When Wesley moved a piece of furniture or even returned dishes and silverware to the wrong cabinets and drawers, I felt a secret anger that surprised and dismayed me. I had never believed that our relationship was right when he was still married, but back then we had enjoyed each other more, especially in bed. I feared that my failure to feel what I thought I should revealed a trait that I could not bear to see.

I drove to my office with the windshield wipers working hard as the relentless downpour thrummed the roof. Traffic was thin because it was barely seven, and Richmond's downtown skyline came into view slowly and by degrees in the watery fog. I thought of the photograph again. I envisioned it slowly painting down my screen, and the hairs on my arms stood up as a chill crept over me. I was disturbed in a way I could not define as it occurred to me for the first time that the person who had sent it might be someone I knew.

Turning on the Seventh Street exit, I wound around Shockoe Slip, with its wet cobblestones and trendy restaurants that were dark at this hour. I passed parking lots barely beginning to fill, and turned into the one behind my four-story stucco building. I couldn't believe it when I found a television news van waiting in my parking place, which was clearly designated by a sign that read CHIEF MEDICAL EXAMINER. The crew knew that if they waited there long enough, they would be rewarded with me.

I pulled up close and motioned for them to move as the van's doors slid open. A cameraman in a rain suit jumped out, coming my way, a reporter in tow with a microphone. I rolled my window down several inches.

'Move,' I said, and I wasn't nice about it. 'You're in my parking place.'

They did not care as someone else got out with lights. For a moment I sat staring, anger turning me hard like amber. The reporter was blocking my door, her microphone shoved through the opening in the window.

'Dr Scarpetta, can you verify that the Butcher has struck again?' she asked, loudly, as the camera rolled and lights burned.

'Move your van,' I said with iron calm as I stared right at her and the camera.

'Is it in fact a torso that was found?' Rain was running off her hood as she pushed the microphone in farther.

'I'm going to ask you one last time to move your van out of my parking place,' I said like a judge about to cite contempt of court. 'You are trespassing.'

The cameraman found a new angle, zooming in, harsh lights in my eyes.

'Was it dismembered like the others . . . ?'

She jerked the microphone away just in time as my window went up. I shoved the car in gear and began backing, the crew scrambling out of the way as I made a three-hundred-and-sixty-degree turn. Tires spun and skidded as I parked right behind the van, pinning it between my Mercedes and the building.

'Wait a minute!'

'Hey! You can't do that!'

Their faces were disbelieving as I got out. Not bothering with an umbrella, I ran for the door and unlocked it.

'Hey!' the protests continued. 'We can't get out!'

Inside the bay, water was beaded on the oversized maroon station wagon and dripping to the concrete floor. I opened another door and walked into the corridor, looking around to see who else was here. White tile was spotless, the air heavy with industrial strength deodorizer, and as I walked to the morgue office, the massive stainless steel refrigerator door sucked open.

'Good morning!' Wingo said with a surprised grin. 'You're early.'

'Thanks for bringing the wagon in out of the rain,' I said.

'No more cases coming in that I know of, so I didn't think it would hurt to stick it in the bay.'

'Did you see anybody out there when you drove it?' I asked.

He looked puzzled. 'No. But that was about an hour ago.'

Wingo was the only member of my staff who routinely got to the office earlier than I did. He was lithe and attractive, with pretty features and shaggy dark hair. An obsessive-compulsive, he ironed his scrubs, washed the wagon and anatomical vans several times a week, and was forever polishing stainless steel until it shone like mirrors. His job was to run the morgue, and he did so with the precision and pride of a military leader. Carelessness and callousness were not allowed down here by either one of us, and no one dared dispose of hazardous waste or make sophomoric jokes about the dead.

'The landfill case is still in the fridge,' Wingo said to me. 'Do you want me to bring it out?'

'Let's wait until after staff meeting.' I said. 'The longer she's refrigerated, the better, and I don't want anybody wandering in here to look.'

'That won't happen,' he said as if I had just implied he might be delinquent in his duties.

'I don't even want anybody on the staff wandering in out of curiosity.'

'Oh.' Anger flashed in his eyes. 'I just don't understand people.'

He never would, because he was not like them.

'I'll let you alert security,' I said. 'The media's already in the parking lot.'

'You got to be kidding. This early?'

'Channel Eight was waiting for me when I pulled in.' I handed him the key to my car. 'Give them a few minutes, and then let them go.'

'What do you mean, let them go?' He frowned, staring at the remote control key in his hand.

'They're in my parking place.' I headed toward the elevator.

'They're what?'

'You'll see.' I boarded. 'If they so much as touch my car, I'll charge them with trespassing and malicious property damage. Then I'm going to have the A.G.'s office call their station's general manager. I might sue.' I smiled at him through shutting doors.

My office was on the second floor of the Consolidated Lab Building, which had been constructed in the seventies and was soon to be abandoned by us and the scientists upstairs. At last, we were to get spacious quarters in the city's new Biotech Park just off Broad Street, not far from the Marriott and the Coliseum.

Construction was already under way, and I spent far too much time arguing over details, blueprints and budgets. What had been home to me for years was now in disarray, stacks of boxes lining hallways, and clerks not wanting to file, since everything would have to be packed anyway. Averting my gaze from more boxes, I followed the hallway to my office, where my desk was in its usual state of avalanche.

I checked my e-mail again, almost expecting another anonymous file like the last, but only the same messages were there, and I scanned through them, sending brief replies. The address *deadoc* quietly waited in my mailbox, and I could not resist opening it and the file with the photograph. I was concentrating so hard, I did not hear Rose walk in.

'I think Noah had better build another ark,' she said.

Startled, I looked up to see her in the doorway adjoining my office and hers. She was taking off her raincoat, and looked worried.

'I didn't mean to scare you,' she said.

Hesitating, she stepped inside, scrutinizing me.

'I knew you'd be here, despite all advice,' she said. 'You look like you've seen a ghost.'

'What are you doing here so early?' I asked.

'I had a feeling you'd have your hands full.' She took off her coat. 'You saw the paper this morning?'

'Not yet.'

She opened her pocketbook and got out her glasses. 'All this *Butcher* business. You can imagine the uproar. While I was driving, I heard on the news that since these cases started, more handguns are being sold than you can shake a stick at. I sometimes wonder if the gun shops aren't behind things like this. Frighten us out of our wits so we all make a mad dash for the nearest .38 or semiautomatic pistol.'

Rose had hair the color of steel that she always wore up, her face patrician and keen. There was nothing she had not seen, and she was not afraid of anyone. I lived in the uneasy shadow of her retirement, for I knew her age. She did not have to work for me. She stayed only because she cared and had no one left at home.

'Take a look,' I said, pushing back my chair.

She came around to my side of the desk and stood so close I could smell White Musk, the fragrance of everything she had concocted at the Body Shop, where they were against testing with animals. Rose had recently adopted her fifth retired greyhound. She bred Siamese cats, kept several aquariums and was one step short of being dangerous to anyone who wore fur. She stared into my computer screen, and did not seem to know what she was looking at. Then her demeanor stiffened.

'My God,' she muttered, looking at me over the top of her bifocals. 'Is this what's downstairs?'

'I think an earlier version of it,' I said. 'Sent to me on AOL.'

She did not speak.

'Needless to say,' I went on, 'I will trust you to keep an eagle eye on this place while I'm downstairs. If anybody comes into the lobby we don't know or aren't expecting, I want security to intercept them. Don't you even think about going out to see what they want.' I looked pointedly at her, knowing what she was like.

'You think he would come here?' she matter-of-factly stated.

'I'm not sure what to think except that he clearly had some need to contact me.' I closed the file and got up. 'And he has.'

At not quite half past eight, Wingo rolled the body onto the floor scale, and we began what I knew would be a very long and painstaking examination. The torso weighed forty-six pounds and was twenty-one inches in length. Livormortis was faint posteriorly, meaning when her circulation had quit, blood had settled according to gravity, placing her on her back for hours or days after death. I could not look at her without seeing the savaged image on my computer screen, and believed it and the torso before me were the same.

'How big do you think she was?' Wingo glanced at me as he parallel parked the gurney next to the first autopsy table.

'We'll use heights of lumbar vertebrae to estimate height, since we obviously don't have tibias, femurs,' I said, tying a plastic apron over my gown. 'But she looks small. Frail, actually.'

Moments later, X-rays had finished processing and he was attaching them to light boxes. What I saw told a story that did not seem to make sense. The faces of the pubic symphysis, or the surfaces where one pubis joins the other, were no longer rugged and ridged, as in youth. Instead, bone was badly eroded with irregular, lipped margins. More X-rays revealed sternal rib ends with irregular bony growths, the bone very thin-walled with sharp edges, and there were degenerative changes to the lumbosacral vertebrae, as well.

Wingo was no anthropologist, but he saw the obvious, too.

'If I didn't know better, I'd think we got her films mixed up with somebody else's,' he said.

'This lady's old,' I said.

'How old, would you guess?'

'I don't like to guess.' I was studying her X-rays. 'But I'd say seventy, at least. Or to play it really safe, between sixty-five and eighty. Come on. Let's go through trash for a while.'

The next two hours were spent sifting through a large garbage bag of trash from the landfill that had been directly under and around the body. The garbage bag I believed she had been in was black, thirty-gallon size, and had been sealed with a yellow plastic-toothed tie. Wearing masks and gloves, Wingo and I picked through shredded tire and the fluff from upholstery stuffing that was used as a cover in the landfill. We examined countless tatters of slimy plastic and paper, picking out maggots and dead flies and dropping them into a carton.

Our treasures were few, a blue button that was probably unrelated, and, oddly, a child's tooth, which I imagined was tossed, a coin left under a pillow. We found a mangled comb, a flattened battery, several shards of broken china, a tangled wire coat hanger, and the cap of a Bic pen. Mostly, it was rubber, fluff, torn black plastic and soggy paper that we threw into a garbage can. Then we circled bright lights around the table and centered her on a clean white sheet.

Using a lens, I began going over her an inch at a time, her flesh a microscopic landfill of debris. With forceps, I collected pale fibers from the dark bloody stump that once had been her neck, and I found hairs, three of them, grayish-white, about fourteen inches long, adhering to dried blood, posteriorly.

'I need another envelope,' I said to Wingo as I came across something else I did not expect.

Embedded in the ends of each humerus, or the bone of the upper arm, and also in margins of muscle around it were more fibers and tiny fragments of fabric that looked pale blue, meaning the saw had to have gone through it.

'She was dismembered through her clothes or something else she was wrapped in,' I said, startled.

Wingo stopped what he was doing and looked at me. 'The others weren't.'

Those victims appeared to have been nude when they were sawn apart. He made more notes as I moved on, peering through the lens.

'Fibers and bits of fabric are also embedded in either femur.' I looked more closely.

'So she was covered from the waist down, too?' he said.

'That's the way it's looking.'

'So someone waited until after she was dismembered, and then took all her clothes off?' He looked at me, emotion in his eyes as he started to envision it.

'He wouldn't want us to get the clothes. There might be too much information there,' I said.

'Then why didn't he undress her, unwrap her or whatever to begin with?'

'Maybe he didn't want to look at her while he was dismembering her,' I said.

'Oh, so now he's getting sensitive on us,' Wingo said, as if he hated whoever it was.

'Make a note of the measurements,' I told him. 'Cervical spine is transected at the level of C-5. Residual femur on the right measures two inches below the lesser trochanter, and two and a half inches on the left, with saw marks visible. Right and left segments of humerus are one inch, saw marks visible. On the upper right hip is a three-quarters-of-an-inch old, healed vaccination scar.'

'What about that?' He referred to the numerous raised, fluid-filled vesicles scattered over buttocks, shoulders and upper thighs.

'I don't know,' I said, reaching for a syringe. 'I'm guessing herpes zoster virus.'

'Whoa!' Wingo jumped back from the table. 'I wish you'd told me that earlier.' He was scared.

'Shingles.' I began labeling a test tube. 'Maybe. I must confess, it's a little weird.'

'What do you mean?' He was getting more unnerved.

'With shingles,' I replied, 'the virus attacks sensory nerves. When the vesicles erupt, they do so in a swath along nerve distributions. Under a rib, for example. And the vesicles will be of varying ages. But this is a crop, and they all look the same age.'

'What else could it be?' he asked. 'Chicken pox?'

'Same virus. Children get chicken pox. Adults get shingles.'

'What if I get it?' Wingo said.

'Did you have chicken pox as a kid?'

'Got no idea.'

'What about the VZV vaccine?' I asked. 'Have you had that?'

'No.'

'Well, if you have no antibody to VZV, you should be vaccinated.' I glanced up at him. 'Are you immunosuppressed?'

He did not say anything as he went to a cart, snatching off his latex gloves and slamming them into the red can for biologically hazardous trash. Upset, he snatched a new pair made of heavier blue Nitrile. I stopped what I was doing, watching him until he returned to the table.

'I just think you could have warned me before now,' he said, and he sounded on the verge of tears. 'I mean, it's not like you can take any precautions in this place, like vaccinations, except for hepatitis B. So I depend on you to let me know what's coming in.'

'Calm down.'

I was gentle with him. Wingo was too sensitive for his own good, and that was really the only problem I ever had with him.

'You can't possibly get chicken pox or shingles from this lady unless you have an exchange of body fluids,' I said. 'So as long as you're wearing gloves and going about business in the usual way, and don't cut yourself or get a needle stick, you will not be exposed to the virus.'

For an instant, his eyes were bright, and he quickly looked away.

'I'll start taking pictures,' he said.

4

Marino and Benton Wesley appeared midafternoon, when the autopsy was well under way. There was nothing further I could do with the external examination, and Wingo had taken a late lunch, so I was alone. Wesley's eyes were on me as he walked through the door, and I could tell by his coat that it was still raining.

'Just so you know,' Marino said right off, 'there's a flood warning.'

Since there were no windows in the morgue, I never knew the weather.

'How serious a warning?' I asked, and Wesley had come close to the torso, and was looking at it.

'Serious enough that if this keeps up, somebody'd better start piling up sandbags,' Marino replied as he parked his umbrella in a corner.

My building was blocks from the James. Years ago, the lower level had flooded, bodies donated to science rising in overflowing vats, water poisoned pink with formalin seeping into the morgue and the parking lot in back.

'How worried should I be?' I asked with concern.

'It's going to stop,' Wesley said, as if he could profile the weather, too.

He took off his raincoat, and the suit beneath it was a dark blue that was almost black. He wore a starched white shirt and conservative silk tie, his silver hair a little longer than usual, but neat. His sharp features made him seem even keener and more intimidating than he was, but today his face was grim, and not just because of me. He and Marino went to a cart to put on gloves and masks.

'I'm sorry we're late,' Wesley said to me as I continued working. 'Every time I tried to get away from the house, the phone rang. This thing's a real problem.'

'Certainly for her it is,' I said.

'Shit.' Marino stared at what was left of a human being. 'How the hell does anybody do something like that?'

'I'll tell you how,' I said, cutting sections of spleen. 'First you pick an old woman and make sure she isn't properly watered or fed, and when she gets sick, forget medical care. Then you shoot or beat her in the head.' I glanced up at them. 'My bet is that she has a basilar skull fracture. Maybe some other type of trauma.'

Marino looked baffled. 'She doesn't have a head. How can you say that?'

'I can say it because there's blood in her airway.'

They got closer to see what I was talking about.

'One way that could have happened,' I went on, 'is if she had a basilar skull fracture and blood dripped down the back of her throat, and she aspirated it into her airway.'

Wesley looked carefully at the body with the demeanor of one who has seen mutilation and death a million times. He stared at the space where the head should be, as if he could imagine it.

'She has hemorrhage in muscle tissue.' I paused to let this sink in. 'She was still alive when the dismemberment began.'

'Jesus Christ,' Marino exclaimed in disgust as he lit a cigarette. 'Don't tell me that.'

'I'm not saying she was conscious,' I added. 'Most likely this was at or about the time of death. But she still had a blood pressure, feeble as it might have been. This was true around the neck, anyway. But not the arms and legs.'

'Then he severed her head first,' Wesley said to me.

'Yes.'

He was scanning X-rays on the walls.

'This doesn't fit with his victimology,' he said. 'Not at all.'

'Everything about this case doesn't fit,' I replied. 'Except that once again, a saw was used. I've also found some cuts on bone that are consistent with a knife.'

'What else can you tell us about her?' Wesley said, and I could feel his eyes on me as I dropped another section of organ into the stock jar of formalin.

'She has some sort of eruptions that might be shingles, and two scars of the right kidney that would indicate pyelonephritis, or kidney infection. Cervix is elongated and stellate, which could suggest she's had children. Her myocardium, or heart muscle, is soft.'

'Meaning?'

'Toxins do that. Toxins produced by microorganisms.' I looked up at him. 'As I've mentioned, she was sick.'

Marino was walking around, looking at the torso from different angles. 'Do you have any idea with what?'

'Based on secretions in her lungs, I know she had bronchitis. At the moment, I don't know what else, except her liver's in pretty grim shape.'

'From drinking,' Wesley said.

'Yellowish, nodular. Yes,' I said. 'And I would say that at one time she smoked.'

'She's skin and bones,' Marino said.

'She wasn't eating,' I said. 'Her stomach is tubular, empty and clean.' I showed them.

Wesley moved to a nearby desk and pulled out a chair. He stared off in thought as I yanked a cord down from an overhead reel and plugged in the Stryker saw. Marino, who liked this part of the procedure the least stepped back from the table. No one spoke as I sawed off the ends of arms and legs, a bony dust drifting on the air, the electric whir louder than a dentist's drill. I placed each section into a labeled carton, and said what I thought.

'I don't think we're dealing with the same killer this time.'

'I don't know what to think,' Marino said. 'But we got two big things in common. A torso, and it was dumped in central Virginia.'

'He's had a varied victimology all along,' said Wesley, wearing his surgical mask loose around his neck. 'One black, two whites, all female, and one black male. The five in Dublin were mixed, as well. But again, all were young.'

'So would you now expect him to choose an old woman?' I asked him.

'Frankly, I wouldn't. But these people aren't an exact science, Kay. This is somebody who does whatever the hell he feels like whenever he feels like it.'

'The dismemberment isn't the same, it's not through the joints,' I reminded them. 'And I think she was clothed or wrapped in something.'

'This one may have bothered him more,' Wesley said, taking the mask off altogether and dropping it on top of the desk. 'His urge to kill again may have been overwhelming, and she may have been easy.' He looked at the torso. 'So he strikes, but his M.O. shifts because the victimology has suddenly shifted, and he doesn't really like it. He leaves her at least partially dressed or covered because raping and killing an old woman aren't what turn him on. And he cuts off her head first so he doesn't have to look at her.'

'You see any sign of rape?' Marino asked me.

'You rarely do,' I said. 'I'm about to finish up here. She'll go in the freezer like the other ones in the hope we eventually get an identification. I've got muscle tissue and marrow for DNA, hoping that we'll eventually have a missing person to compare it with.'

I was discouraged, and it showed. Wesley collected his coat from the back of a door, leaving a small puddle on the floor.

'I'd like to see the photograph sent to you over AOL,' he said to me.

'That doesn't fit the M.O., either, by the way,' I said as I began suturing the Y-incision. 'I wasn't sent anything in the earlier cases.'

Marino was in a hurry, as if he had somewhere else to go. 'I'm heading out to Sussex,' he said, walking to the door. 'Gotta meet Lone Ranger Ring so he can give me lessons in how to investigate homicides.'

He abruptly left, and I knew the real reason why. Despite his preaching to me about marriage, my relationship with Wesley secretly bothered Marino. A part of him would always be jealous.

'Rose can show you the photograph,' I said to Wesley as I washed the body with hose and sponge. 'She knows how to get into my e-mail.'

Disappointment glinted in his eyes before he could mask it. I carried the cartons of bone ends to a distant counter where they would be boiled in a weak solution of bleach, to completely deflesh and degrease them. He stayed where he was, waiting and watching until I got back. I did not want him to go, but I did not know what to do with him anymore.

'Can't we talk, Kay?' he finally said. 'I've hardly seen you. Not in months. I know we're both busy, and this isn't a good time. But . . .'

'Benton,' I interrupted with feeling. 'Not here.'

'Of course not. I'm not suggesting we talk here.'

'It will just be more of the same.'

'I promise it won't.' He checked the clock on the wall. 'Look, it's already late. Why don't I just stay in town. We'll have dinner.'

I hesitated, ambivalence bouncing from one end of my brain to the other. I was afraid to see him and afraid not to see him.

'All right,' I said. 'My house at seven. I'll throw together something. Don't expect much.'

'I can take you out. I don't want you to go to any trouble.'

'The last place I want to be right now is out in public,' I said.

His eyes lingered on me a little longer as I labeled tags and tubes and various types of containers. The strike of his heels was sharp on tile as he left, and I heard him speak to someone as elevator doors opened in the hall. Seconds later, Wingo walked in.

'I would have got here sooner.' He went to a cart and began putting on new shoe covers, mask and gloves. 'But it's a zoo upstairs.'

'What's that supposed to mean?' I asked, untying my gown in back as he slipped into a fresh one.

'Reporters.' He put on a face shield and looked at me through clear plastic. 'In the lobby. Casing the building in their television vans.' He looked tensely at me. 'Hate to tell you, but now Channel Eight's got you blocked in. Their van's right behind your car so you can't get out, and nobody's in it.'

Anger rose like heat. 'Call the police and get them towed,' I said from the locker room. 'You finish up here. I'm going upstairs to take care of this.'

Slamming my balled-up gown into the laundry bin, I grabbed off gloves, shoe covers and cap. I vigorously scrubbed with antibacterial soap and yanked open my locker, my hands suddenly clumsy. I was very upset, this case, the press, Wesley, everything was getting to me.

'Dr Scarpetta?'

Wingo was suddenly in the doorway as I fumbled with buttons on my blouse, and his walking in on me while I was dressing was nothing new. It never bothered either of us, for I was as comfortable with him as I would be with a woman.

'I was wondering if you had time . . .' He hesitated. 'Well, I know you're busy today.'

I tossed bloody Reeboks into my locker and slipped on the shoes I had worn to work. Then I put on my lab coat.

'Actually, Wingo' – I checked my anger so I did not take it out on him – 'I'd like to talk to you, too. When you finish down here, come see me in my office.'

He did not have to tell me. I had a feeling I knew. I rode the elevator upstairs, my mood darkened like a storm about to strike. Wesley was still in my office, studying what was on my computer screen, and I walked past in the hallway without slowing my stride. It was Rose I wanted to find. When I got to the front office, clerks were frantically answering phones that would not stop, while my secretary and administrator were before a window overlooking the front parking lot.

The rain had not relented, and this had not seemed to deter a single journalist, cameraman or photographer in this town. They seemed crazed, as if the story must be huge for everyone else to be braving a downpour.

'Where are Fielding and Grant?' I asked about my deputy chief and this year's fellow.

My administrator was a retired sheriff who loved cologne and snappy suits. He stepped away from the window, while Rose continued to look out.

'Dr Fielding's in court,' he said. 'Dr Grant had to leave because his basement's flooding.'

Rose turned around with the demeanor of one ready to fight, as if her nest had been invaded. 'I put Jess in the filing room,' she said of the receptionist.

'So there's no one out front.' I looked toward the lobby.

'Oh, there are plenty of people, all right,' my secretary angrily said as phones rang and rang. 'I didn't want anybody sitting out there with all those vultures. I don't care if there is bulletproof glass.'

'How many reporters are in the lobby?'

'Fifteen, maybe twenty, last I checked,' my administrator answered. 'I went out there once and asked them to leave. They said they weren't going until they had a statement from you. So I thought we could write something up and . . .'

'I'll give them a statement, all right,' I snapped.

Rose put her hand on my arm. 'Dr Scarpetta, I'm not sure it's a good idea . . .'

I interrupted her, too. 'Leave this to me.'

The lobby was small, and the thick glass partition made it impossible for any unauthorized person to get in. When I rounded the corner, I could not believe how many people were crammed into the room, the floor filthy with footprints and dirty puddles. As soon as they saw me, camera lights blazed. Reporters began shouting, shoving microphones and tape recorders close as flash guns went off in my face.

I raised my voice above all of them. 'Please! Quiet!'

'Dr Scarpetta . . .'

'Quiet!' I said more loudly, as I blindly stared out at aggressive people I could not make out. 'Now, I am going to ask you politely to leave,' I said.

'Is it the Butcher again?' a woman raised her voice above the rest.

'Everything is pending further investigation,' I said.

'Dr Scarpetta.'

I could just barely make out the television reporter as Patty Denver, whose pretty face was on billboards all over the city.

'Sources say you're working this as another victim in these serial killings,' she said. 'Can you verify that?'

I did not respond.

'Is it true the victim is Asian, probably prepubescent, and came off a truck that is local?' she went on, to my dismay. 'And are we to assume that the killer may now be in Virginia?'

'Is the Butcher killing in Virginia now?'

'Possible he deliberately wanted the other bodies dumped here?'

I held up a hand to quiet them. 'This is not the time for assumptions,' I said. 'I can tell you only that we are treating this as a homicide. The victim is an unidentified white female. She is not prepubescent but an older adult, and we encourage people who might have information to call this office or the Sussex County Sheriff's Department.'

'What about the FBI?'

'The FBI is involved,' I said.

'Then you are treating this as the Butcher . . .'

Turning around, I entered a code on a keypad and the lock clicked free. I ignored the demanding voices, shutting the door behind me, my nerves humming with tension as I walked quickly down the hall. When I entered my office, Wesley was gone, and I sat behind my desk. I dialed Marino's pager number, and he called me right back.

'For God's sake, these leaks have got to stop!' I exclaimed over the line.

'We know damn well who it is,' Marino irritably said.

'Ring.' I had no doubt, but could not prove it.

'The drone was supposed to meet me at the landfill. That was almost an hour ago,' Marino went on.

'It doesn't appear the press had any trouble finding him.'

I told him what *sources* allegedly had divulged to a television crew.

'Goddamn idiot!' he said.

'Find him and tell him to keep his mouth shut,' I said. 'Reporters have practically put us out of business today, and now the city's going to believe there's a serial killer in their midst.'

'Yeah, well, unfortunately, that part could be true,' he said.

'I can't believe this.' I was only getting angrier. 'I have to release information to correct misinformation. I can't be put in this position, Marino.'

'Don't worry, I'm going to take care of this and a whole lot more,' he promised. 'I don't guess you know.'

'Know what?'

'Rumor has it that Ring's been seeing Patty Denver.'

'I thought she was married,' I said as I envisioned her from a few moments earlier.

'She is,' he said.

I began dictating case 1930–97, trying to focus my attention on what I was saying and reading from my notes.

'The body was received pouched and sealed,' I said into the tape recorder, rearranging paperwork smeared with blood from Wingo's gloves. 'The skin is doughy. The breasts are small, atrophic and wrinkled. There are skin folds over the abdomen suggestive of prior weight loss . . .'

'Dr Scarpetta?' Wingo was poking his head in the doorway. 'Oops. Sorry,' he said when he realized what I was doing. 'I guess now's not a good time.'

'Come in,' I said with a weary smile. 'Why don't you shut the door.'

He did and closed the one between my office and Rose's, too. Nervously, he pulled a chair close to my desk, and he was having a hard time meeting my eyes.

'Before you start, let me.' I was firm but kind. 'I've known you for many years, and your life is no secret to me. I don't make judgments. I don't label. In my mind, there are only two categories of people in this world. Those who are good. And those who aren't. But I worry about you because your orientation places you at risk.'

He nodded. 'I know,' he said, eyes bright with tears.

'If you're immunosuppressed,' I went on, 'you need to tell me. You probably shouldn't be in the morgue, at least not for some cases.'

'I'm HIV positive.' His voice trembled and he began to cry.

I let him go for a while, his arms over his face, as if he could not bear for anyone to see him. His shoulders shook, tears spotting his greens as his nose ran. Getting up with a box of tissues, I came over to him.

'Here.' I set the tissues nearby. 'It's all right.' I put my arm around him and let him weep. 'Wingo, I want you to try to get hold of yourself so we can talk about this, okay?'

He nodded, blowing his nose and wiping his eyes. For a moment he nuzzled his head against me, and I held him like a child. I gave him time before I faced him straight on, gripping his shoulders.

'Now is the time for courage, Wingo,' I said. 'Let's see what we can do to fight this thing.'

'I can't tell my family,' he choked. 'My father hates me anyway. And when my mother tries, he gets worse. To her. You know?'

I moved a chair close. 'What about your friend?'

'We broke up.'

'But he knows.'

'I just found out a couple weeks ago.'

'You've got to tell him and anybody else you've been intimate with,' I said. 'It's only fair. If someone had done that for you, maybe you wouldn't be sitting here now, crying.'

He was silent, staring down at his hands. Taking a deep breath, he said, 'I'm going to die, aren't I?'

'We're all going to die,' I gently told him.

'Not like this.'

'It could be like this,' I said. 'Every physical I get, I'm tested for HIV. You know what I'm exposed to. What you're going through could be me.'

He looked up at me, his eyes and cheeks burning. 'If I get AIDS, I'm going to kill myself.'

'No, you're not,' I said.

He began to cry again. 'Dr Scarpetta, I can't go through it! I don't want to end up in one of those places, a hospice, the Fan Free Clinic, in a bed next to other dying people I don't know!' Tears flowed, his face tragic and defiant. 'I'll be all alone just like I've always been.'

'Listen.' I waited until he calmed down. 'You will not go through this alone. You have me.'

He dissolved in tears again, covering his face and making sounds so loud I was certain they could be heard in the hall.

'I will take care of you,' I promised as I got up. 'Now I want you to go home. I want you to do what's right and tell your friends. Tomorrow, we'll talk more and figure out the best way to handle this. I need the name of your doctor and permission to talk to him or her.'

'Dr Alan Riley. At MCV.'

I nodded. 'I know him, and I want you to call him first thing in the morning. Let him know I'll be contacting him and that it's all right for him to talk to me.'

'Okay.' He looked furtively at me. 'But you'll be . . . You won't tell anyone.'

'Of course not,' I said with feeling.

'I don't want anyone here to know. Or Marino. I don't want him to.'

'No one will know,' I said. 'At least not from me.'

He slowly got up and stepped toward the door with the unsteadiness of someone drunk or dazed. 'You won't fire me, will you?' His hand was on the knob as he cast blood-shot eyes my way.

'Wingo, for God's sake,' I said with quiet emotion. 'I would hope you would think more of me than that.'

He opened the door. 'I think more of you than anyone.' Tears spilled again, and he wiped them on his scrubs, exposing his thin bare belly. 'I always have.'

His footsteps were rapid in the hall as he almost ran, and the elevator bell rang. I listened as he left my building for a world that did not give a damn. I rested my forehead on my fist and shut my eyes.

'Dear God,' I muttered. 'Please help.'

5

———

The rain was still heavy as I drove home, and traffic was terrible because an accident had closed lanes in both directions on I-64. There were fire trucks and ambulances, rescuers prying open doors and hurrying with stretchers and boards. Broken glass glistened on wet pavement, drivers slowing to stare at injured people. One car had flipped multiple times before catching fire. I saw blood on the shattered windshield of another and that the steering wheel was bent. I knew what that meant, and said a prayer for whoever the people were. I hoped I would not see them in my morgue.

In Carytown, I pulled off at P. T. Hasting's. Festooned with fish nets and floats, it sold the best seafood in the city. When I walked in, the air was spicy and pungent with fish and Old Bay, and filets looked thick and fresh on ice inside displays. Lobsters with bound claws crawled in their tank of water, and were in no danger from me. I was incapable of boiling anything alive and wouldn't touch meat if the cattle and pigs were first brought to my table. I couldn't even catch fish without throwing them back.

I was trying to decide what I wanted when Bev emerged from the back.

'What's good today?' I asked her.

'Well, look who's here,' she exclaimed warmly, wiping her hands on her apron. 'You're about the only person to brave the rain. So you sure got plenty to choose from.'

'I don't have much time, and need something easy and light,' I said.

A shadow passed over her face as she opened a jar of horseradish. 'I'm afraid I can imagine what you've been doing,' she said. 'Been hearing it on the news.' She shook her head. 'You must be plumb worn out. I don't know how you sleep. Let me tell you what to do for yourself tonight.'

She walked over to a case of chilled blue crabs. Without asking, she selected a pound of meat in a carton.

'Fresh from Tangier Island. Hand-picked it myself, and you tell me if you find even a trace of cartilage or shell. You're not eating alone, are you?' she said.

'No.'

'That's good to hear.'

She winked at me. I had brought Wesley in here before.

She picked out six jumbo shrimp, peeled and deveined, and wrapped them. Then she set a jar of her homemade cocktail sauce on the counter by the cash register.

'I got a little carried away with the horseradish,' she said, 'so it will make your eyes water, but it's good.' She began ringing up my purchases. 'You sauté the shrimp so quick their butts barely hit the pan, got it? Chill 'em, and have that as an appetizer. By the way, those and the sauce are on the house.'

'You don't need to . . .'

She waved me off. 'As for the crab, honey, listen up. One egg slightly beaten, one-half teaspoon dry mustard, a dash or two of Worcestershire sauce, four unsalted soda crackers, crushed. Chop up an onion, a Vidalia if you're still hoarding any from summer. One green pepper, chop that. A teaspoon or two of parsley, salt and pepper to taste.'

'Sounds fabulous,' I gratefully said. 'Bev, what would I do without you?'

'Now you gently mix all that together and shape it into patties.' She made the motion with her hands. 'Sauté in oil over medium heat until lightly browned. Maybe fix him a salad or get some of my slaw,' she said. 'And that's as much as I would fuss over any man.'

It was as much as I did. I got started as soon as I got home, and shrimp were chilling by the time I turned on music and climbed into a bath. I poured in aromatherapy salts that were supposed to reduce stress, and shut my eyes as steam carried soothing scents into my sinuses and pores. I thought about Wingo, and my heart ached and seemed to lose its rhythm like a bird in distress. For a while, I cried. He had started out with me in this city, then left to go back to school. Now he was back and dying. I could not bear it.

At seven P.M., I was in the kitchen again, and Wesley, always punctual, eased his silver BMW into my drive. He was still in the suit he had been wearing earlier, and he had a bottle of Cakebread chardonnay in one hand, and a fifth of Black Bush Irish whiskey in the other. The rain, at last, had stopped, clouds marching on to other fronts.

'Hi,' he said when I opened the door.

'You profiled the weather right.' I kissed him.

'They don't pay me this much money for nothing.'

'The money comes from your family.' I smiled as he followed me in. 'I know what the Bureau pays you.'

'If I was as smart with money as you are, I wouldn't need it from my family.'

In my great room was a bar, and I went behind it because I knew what he wanted.

'Black Bush?' I made sure.

'If you're serving it. Fine pusher that you are, you've managed to get me hooked.'

'As long as you bootleg it from D.C., I'll serve it any time you like,' I said.

I fixed our drinks on the rocks with a splash of seltzer water. Then we went into the kitchen and sat at a cozy table by an expansive window overlooking my wooded yard and the river. I wished I could tell him about Wingo and how it felt for me. But I could not break a confidence.

'Can I bring up a little business first?' Wesley took off his suit jacket and hung it on the back of a chair.

'I have some, too.'

'You first.' He sipped his drink, his eyes on mine.

I told him what had been leaked to the press, adding, 'Ring's a problem that's only getting worse.'

'If he's the one, and I'm not saying he is or isn't. The difficulty's getting proof.'

'There's no doubt in my mind.'

'Kay, that's not good enough. We can't just throw someone out of an investigation based on our intuition.'

'Marino's heard rumors that Ring's having an affair with a well-known local broadcaster,' I then said. 'She's with the same station that had the misinformation about the case, about the victim being Asian.'

He was silent. I knew he was thinking about proof again, and he was right. This all sounded circumstantial even as I said it.

Then he said, 'This guy's very smart. Are you aware of his background?'

'I know nothing about him,' I replied.

'Graduated with honors from William and Mary, double major in psychology and public administration. His uncle is the secretary of public safety.' He piled worse news upon bad. 'Harlow Dershin, who's an honorable guy, by the way. But it goes without saying this is not a good situation for making accusations unless you're one hundred percent damn sure of yourself.'

The secretary of public safety for Virginia was the immediate boss of the superintendent of the state police. Ring's uncle couldn't have been more powerful unless he had been the governor.

'So what you're saying is that Ring's untouchable,' I said.

'What I'm saying is, his educational background makes it clear he has high aspirations. Guys like him are looking to be a chief, a commissioner, a politician. They're not interested in being a cop.'

'Guys like him are interested only in themselves,' I impatiently said. 'Ring doesn't give a damn about the victims or the people left behind who have no idea what has happened to their loved one. He doesn't care if someone else gets killed.'

'Proof,' he reminded me. 'To be fair, there are a lot of people – including those working at the landfill – who could have leaked information to the press.'

I had no good argument, but nothing would shake me loose from my suspicions.

'What's important is breaking these cases,' he went on to say, 'and the best way to do that is for all of us to go about our business and ignore him, just like Marino and Grigg are doing. Follow every lead we can, steering around the impediments.' His eyes were almost amber in the overhead light, and soft when they met mine.

I pushed back my chair. 'We need to set the table.'

He got out dishes and opened wine as I arranged chilled shrimp on plates and spooned *Bev's Kicked By A Horse Cocktail Sauce* into a bowl. I halved lemons and wrapped them in gauze diapers, and fashioned crab cakes. Wesley and I ate shrimp cocktail as night drew closer and cast its shadow over the east.

'I've missed this,' he said. 'Maybe you don't want to hear it, but it's true.'

I did not say anything because I did not want to get into another big discussion that went on for hours, leaving both of us drained.

'Anyway.' He set his fork on his plate the way polite people do when they are finished. 'Thank you. I have missed you, Dr Scarpetta.' He smiled.

'I'm glad you're here, Special Agent Wesley.'

I smiled back at him as I got up. Turning on the stove, I heated oil in a pan while he cleared dishes.

'I want to tell you what I thought of the photograph that was sent to you,' he said. 'First, we need to establish that it is, in fact, of the victim you worked on today.'

'I'm going to establish that on Monday.'

'Assuming it is,' he went on, 'this is a very dramatic shift in the killer's M.O.'

'That and everything else.' Crab cakes went into the pan and began to sizzle.

'Right,' he said, serving coleslaw. 'It's very blatant this time, as if he's really trying to rub our noses in it. And, of course, the victim-ology's all wrong, too. That looks great,' he added, watching what I was cooking.

When we were seated again, I said with confidence, 'Benton, this is not the same guy.'

He hesitated before replying, 'I don't think it is, either, if you want to know the truth. But I'm not prepared to rule him out. We don't know what games he might be into now.'

I was feeling the frustration again. Nothing could be proven, but my intuition, my instincts, were screaming at me.

'Well, I don't think this murdered old woman has anything to do with the earlier cases from here or Ireland. Someone just wants us to assume she does. I think what we're dealing with is a copycat.'

'We'll get into it with everybody. Thursday. I think that's the date we set.' He tasted a crab cake. 'This is really incredibly good. Wow.' His eyes watered. 'Now that's cocktail sauce.'

'Staging. Disguising a crime that was committed for some other reason,' I said. 'And don't give me too much credit. This was Bev's recipe.'

'The photograph bothers me,' he said.

'You and me both.'

'I've talked to Lucy about it,' he said.

Now he really had my interest.

'You tell me when you want her here.' He reached for his wine.

'The sooner the better.' I paused, adding, 'How is she doing? I know what she tells me, but I'd like to hear it from you.'

I remembered we needed water, and got up for it. When I returned, he was quietly staring at me. Sometimes it was hard for me to look at his face, and my emotions began clashing like instruments out of tune. I loved his chiseled nose with its clean straight bridge, his eyes, which could draw me into depths I had never known and his mouth with its sensuous lower lip. I looked out the window, and could not see the river anymore.

'Lucy,' I reminded him. 'How about a performance evaluation for her aunt?'

'No one's sorry we hired her,' he dryly said of someone we all knew was a genius. 'Or maybe that's the understatement of the century. She's simply terrific. Most of the agents have come to respect her. They want her around. I'm not saying there aren't problems. Not everybody appreciates having a woman on HRT.'

'I continue to worry that she'll try to push it too far,' I said.

'Well, she's fit as hell. That's for sure. No way I'd take her on.'

'That's what I mean. She wants to keep up with them, when it really isn't possible. You know how she is.' I gave him my eyes again. 'She's always got to prove herself. If the guys are fast-roping and running through the mountains wearing sixty-pound packs, she thinks she's got to keep up, when she should just be content with her technical abilities, her robots and all the rest of it.'

'You're missing her biggest motivation, her biggest demon,' he said.

'What?'

'You. She feels she has to prove herself to you, Kay.'

'She has no reason to feel that way.' What he said was piercing. 'I don't want to feel I'm the reason she takes her life into her hands with all of these dangerous things she feels she must do.'

'This is not about blame,' he said, getting up from the table. 'This is about human nature. Lucy worships you. You're the only decent mother figure she's ever had. She wants to be like you, and she feels people compare her to you, and that's a pretty big act to follow. She wants you to admire her, too, Kay.'

'I do admire her, for God's sake.' I got up, too, and we began clearing dishes. 'Now you really have me worried.'

He began rinsing, and I loaded the dishwasher.

'You probably should worry.' He glanced at me. 'I will tell you this, she's one of these perfectionists who won't listen to anyone. Other than you, she's the most stubborn human being I've ever come across.'

'Thanks a lot.'

He smiled and put his arms around me, not caring that his hands were wet. 'Can we sit and talk for a while?' he said, his face, his body close to mine. 'Then I've got to hit the road.'

'And after that?'

'I'm going to talk to Marino in the morning, and in the afternoon I've got another case coming in. From Arizona. I know it's Sunday, but it can't wait.'

He continued talking as we carried our wine into the great room.

'A twelve-year-old girl abducted on her way home from school, body dumped in the Sonora desert,' he said. 'We think this guy's already killed three other kids.'

'It's hard to feel very optimistic, isn't it,' I said bitterly as we sat on the couch. 'It never stops.'

'No,' he replied. 'And I'm afraid it never will. As long as there are people on the planet. What are you going to do with what's left of the weekend?'

'Paperwork.'

One side of my great room was sliding glass doors, and beyond, my neighborhood was black with a full moon that looked like gold, clouds gauzy and drifting.

'Why are you so angry with me?' His voice was gentle, but he let me know his hurt.

'I don't know.' I would not look at him.

'You do know.' He took my hand and began to rub it with his thumb. 'I love your hands. They look like a pianist's, only stronger. As if what you do is an art.'

'It is,' I simply said, and he often talked about my hands. 'I think you have a fetish. As a profiler, that should concern you.'

He laughed, kissing knuckles, fingers, the way he often did. 'Believe me, I have a fetish for more than your hands.'

'Benton.' I looked at him. 'I am angry with you because you are ruining my life.'

He got very still, shocked.

I got up from the couch and began to pace. 'I had my life set up just the way I wanted it,' I said as emotions rose to a crescendo. 'I am building a new office. Yes, I've been smart with my money, made enough smart investments to afford this.' I swept my hand over my room. 'My own house that I designed. For me, everything was in its proper place until you . . .'

'Was it?' He was watching me intensely, wounded anger in his voice. 'You liked it better when I was married and we were always feeling rotten about it? When we were having an affair and lying to everyone?'

'Of course I didn't like that better!' I exclaimed. 'I just liked my life being mine.'

'Your problem is you're afraid of commitment. That's what this is about. How many times do I have to point that out? I think you should see someone. Really. Maybe Dr Zenner. You're friends. I know you trust her.'

'I'm not the one who needs a psychiatrist.' I regretted the words the instant I said them.

He angrily got up, as if ready to leave. It was not even nine o'clock.

'God. I'm too old and tired for this,' I muttered. 'Benton, I'm sorry. That wasn't fair. Please sit back down.'

He didn't at first, but stood in front of sliding glass doors, his back to me.

'I'm not trying to hurt you, Kay,' he said. 'I don't come around to see how badly I can fuck up your life, you know. I admire the hell out of everything you do. I just wish you'd let me in a little bit more.'

'I know. I'm sorry. Please don't leave.'

Blinking back tears, I sat down and stared up at the ceiling with its exposed beams and trowel marks visible on plaster. Wherever I looked there were details that had come from me. For a moment, I shut my eyes as tears rolled down my face. I did not wipe them away and Wesley knew when not to touch me. He knew when not to speak. He quietly sat beside me.

'I'm a middle-aged woman set in her ways,' I said as my voice shook. 'I can't help it. All I have is what I've built. No children. I can't stand my only sister and she can't stand me. My father was in bed dying my entire childhood, then gone when I was twelve. Mother's impossible, and now she's dying of emphysema. I can't be what you want, the good wife. I don't even know what the hell that is. I only know how to be Kay. And going to a psychiatrist isn't going to change a goddamn thing.'

He said to me, 'And I'm in love with you and want to marry you. And I can't seem to help that, either.'

I did not reply.

He added, 'And I thought you were in love with me.'

Still, I could not speak.

'At least you used to be,' he went on as pain overwhelmed his voice. 'I'm leaving.'

He started to get up again, and I put my hand on his arm.

'Not like this.' I looked at him. 'Don't do this to me.'

'To you?' He was incredulous.

I dimmed the lights until they were almost out, and the moon was a polished coin against a clear black sky scattered with stars. I got more wine and started the fire, while he watched everything I did.

'Sit closer to me,' I said.

He did, and I took his hands this time.

'Benton, patience. Don't rush me,' I said. 'Please. I'm not like Connie. Like other people.'

'I'm not asking you to be,' he said. 'I don't want you to be. I'm not like other people, either. We know what we see. Other people couldn't possibly understand. I could never talk to Connie about how I spend my days. But I can talk to you.'

He kissed me sweetly, and we went deeper, touching faces, tongues and nimbly undressing, doing what we once did best. He gathered me in his mouth and hands, and we stayed on the couch until early morning, as light from the moon turned chilled and thin. After he drove home, I carried wine throughout my house, pacing, wandering with music on and flowing out speakers in every room. I landed in my office, where I was a master at distraction.

I began going through journals, tearing out articles that needed to be filed. I began working on an article I was due to write. But I was not in the mood for any of it, and decided to check my e-mail to see if Lucy had left word about when she might make it to Richmond. AOL announced I had mail waiting, and when I checked my box I felt as if someone had struck me. The address *deadoc* awaited me like an evil stranger.

His message was in lowercase, with no punctuation except spaces. It said, *you think you re so smart*. I opened the attached file and once again watched color images paint down my screen, severed feet and hands lined up on a table covered with what appeared to be the same bluish cloth. For a while I stared, wondering why this person was doing this to me. I hoped he had just made a very big mistake as I grabbed the phone.

'Marino!' I exclaimed when I got him on the line.

'Huh? What happened?' he blurted as he came to.

I told him.

'Shit. It's three friggin' o'clock in the morning. Don't you ever sleep?'

He seemed pleased, and I suspected he figured I wouldn't have called him if Wesley had still been here.

'Are you okay?' he then asked.

'Listen. The hands are palm up,' I said. 'The photograph was taken at close range. I can see a lot of detail.'

'Like what kind of detail? Is there a tattoo or something?'

'Ridge detail,' I said.

Neils Vander was the section chief of fingerprint examination, an older man with wispy hair and voluminous lab coats perpetually stained purple and black with ninhydrin and dusting powder. Forever in a hurry and prepossessed, he was from genteel Virginia stock. Vander had never called me by my first name or referred to anything personal about me in all the years I had known him. But he had his way of showing he cared. Sometimes it was a doughnut on my desk in the morning or, in the summer, Hanover tomatoes from his garden.

Known for an eagle eye that could match loops and whorls at a glance, he was also the resident expert in image enhancement and, in fact, had been trained by NASA. Over the years, he and I had materialized a multitude of faces from photographic blurs. We had conjured up writing that wasn't there, read impressions and restored eradications, the concept really very simple even if the execution of it was not.

A high-resolution image processing system could see two hundred and fifty-six shades of gray, while the human eye could differentiate, at the most, thirty-two. Therefore, it was possible to scan something into the computer and let it see what we could not. Deadoc may have sent me more than he bargained for. The first task this morning was to compare a morgue photograph of the torso with the one sent to me through AOL.

'Let me get a little more gray over here,' Vander said as he worked computer keys. 'And I'm going to tilt this some.'

'That's better,' I agreed.

We were sitting side by side, both of us leaning into the nineteen-inch monitor. Nearby, both photographs were on the scanner, a video camera feeding their images to us live.

'A little more of that.' Another shade of gray washed over the screen. 'Let me bump this a tad more.'

He reached over to the scanner and repositioned one of the photographs. He put another filter over the camera lens.

'I don't know,' I said as I stared. 'I think it was easier to see before. Maybe you need to move it a little more to the right,' I added, as if we were hanging pictures.

'Better. But there's still a lot of background interference I'd like to get rid of.'

'I wish we had the original. What's the radiometric resolution of this thing?' I asked, referring to the system's capability of differentiating shades of gray.

'A whole lot better than it used to be. Since the early days, I guess we've doubled the number of pixels that can be digitalized.'

Pixels, like the dots in dot matrix, were the smallest elements of an image being viewed, the molecules, the impressionistic points of color forming a painting.

'We got some grants, you know. One of these days, I want to move us into ultraviolet imaging. I can't even tell you what I could do with cyanoacrylate,' he went on about Super Glue, which reacted to components in human perspiration and was excellent for developing fingerprints difficult to see with the unaided eye.

'Well, good luck,' I said, because money was always tight no matter who was in office.

Repositioning the photograph again, he placed a blue filter over the camera lens, and dilated the lighter pixel elements, brightening the image. He enhanced horizontal details, removing vertical ones. Two torsos were now side by side. Shadows appeared, gruesome details sharper and in contrast.

'You can see the bony ends.' I pointed. 'Left leg severed just proximal to the lesser trochanter. Right leg' – I moved my finger on the screen – 'about an inch lower, right through the shaft.'

'I wish I could correct the camera angle, the perspective distortion,' he muttered, talking to himself, which he often did. 'But I don't know the measurements of anything. Too bad whoever took this didn't include a nice little ruler as a scale.'

'Then I would really worry about who we were dealing with,' I commented.

'That's all we need. A killer who's like us.' He defined the edges, and readjusted the positions of the photographs one more time. 'Let's see what happens if I superimpose them.'

He did, and the overlay was amazing, bone ends and even the ragged flesh around the severed neck, identical.

'That does it for me,' I announced.

'No question about it in my mind,' he agreed. 'Let's print this out.'

He clicked the mouse and the laser printer hummed on. Removing the photographs from the scanner, he replaced them with the one of the feet and hands, moving it around until it was perfectly centered.

As he began to enlarge images, the sight became even more grotesque, blood staining the sheet bright red, as if it had just been spilled. The killer had neatly lined up feet like a pair of shoes, hands side by side like gloves.

'He should have turned them palm down,' Vander said. 'I wonder why he didn't?'

Using spatial filtering to retain important details, he began eliminating interference, such as the blood and the texture of the blue table cover.

'Can you get any ridge detail?' I asked leaning so close, I could smell his spicy aftershave.

'I think I can,' he said.

His voice was suddenly cheerful, for there was nothing he liked better than reading the hieroglyphics of fingers and feet. Beneath his gentle, distracted demeanor was a man who had sent thousands of people to the penitentiary, and dozens to the electric chair. He enlarged the photograph and assigned arbitrary colors to various intensities of gray, so we could see them better. Thumbs were small and pale like old parchment. There were ridges.

'The other fingers aren't going to work,' he said, staring, as if in a trance. 'They're too curled for me to see. But thumbs look pretty darn good. Let's capture this.' Clicking into a menu, he saved the image on the computer's hard disk. 'I'm going to want to work on this for a while.'

That was his cue for me to leave, and I pushed back my chair.

'If I get something, I'll run it through AFIS right away,' he said of the Automated Fingerprint Identification System, capable of comparing unknown latent prints against a databank of millions.

'That would be great,' I said. 'And I'll start with HALT.'

He gave me a curious look, because the Homicide Assessment and Lead Tracking System was a Virginia database maintained by the state police in conjunction with the FBI. It was the place to start if we suspected the case was local.

'Even though we have reason to suspect the other cases are not from here,' I explained to him, 'I think we should search everything we can. Including Virginia databases.'

Vander was still making adjustments, staring at the screen.

'As long as I don't have to fill out the forms,' he replied.

In the hallway were more boxes and white cartons marked *EVIDENCE* lining either side and stacked to the ceiling. Scientists walked past, preoccupied and in a hurry, paperwork and samples in hand that might send someone to court for murder. We greeted each other without slowing down as I headed to the fibers and trace evidence lab, which was big and quiet. More scientists in white coats were bent over microscopes and working at their desks, black counters haphazardly arranged with mysterious bundles wrapped in brown paper.

Aaron Koss was standing in front of an ultraviolet lamp that was glowing purple-red as he examined a slide through a magnifying lens to see what the reflective long wavelengths might tell him.

'Good morning,' I said.

'Same to you.' Koss grinned.

Dark and attractive, he seemed too young to be an expert in microscopic fibers, residues, paints and explosives. This morning, he was in faded jeans and running shoes.

'No court for you,' I said, for one could usually tell by the way people were dressed.

'Nope. Lucky me,' he said. 'Bet you're curious about your fibers.'

'I was in the neighborhood,' I said. 'Thought I'd drop by.'

I was notorious for making evidence rounds, and in the main, the scientists endured my intensity patiently, and in the end were grateful. I knew I pressured them when caseloads were already overwhelming. But when people were being murdered and dismembered, evidence needed to be examined now.

'Well, you've granted me a reprieve from working on our pipe-bomber,' he said with another smile.

'No luck with that,' I assumed.

'They had another one last night. I-195 North near Laburnum, right under the nose of Special Operations. You know, where Third Precinct used to be, if you can believe that?'

'Let's hope the person sticks with just blowing up traffic signs,' I said.

'Let's hope.' He stepped back from the UV lamp and got very serious. 'Here's what I've got so far from what you've turned in to me. Fibers from fabric remnants embedded in bone. Hair. And trace that was adhering to blood.'

'Her hair?' I asked, perplexed, for I had not receipted the long, grayish hairs to Koss. That was not his specialty.

'What I saw under the scope don't look human to me,' he replied. 'Maybe two different types of animal. I've sent them on to Roanoke.'

The state had only one hair expert, and he worked out of the western district forensic labs.

'What about the trace?' I asked.

'My guess is it's going to be debris from the landfill. But I want to look under the electron microscope. What I've got under UV now is fibers,' he went on. 'I should say they're fragments, really, that I gave an ultrasonic bath in distilled water to remove blood. You want to take a look?'

He gave me room to peer through the lens, and I smelled Obsession cologne. I could not help but smile, for I remembered being his age and still having the energy to preen. There were three mounted fragments fluorescing like neon lights. The fabric was white or off-white, one of them spangled with what looked like iridescent flecks of gold.

'What in the world is it?' I glanced up at him.

'Under the stereoscope, it looks synthetic,' he replied. 'The diameters regular, consistent like they would be if they were extruded through spinnerettes, versus being natural and irregular. Like cotton, let's say.'

'And the fluorescing flecks?' I was still looking.

'That's the interesting part,' he said. 'Though I've got to do further tests, at a glance it looks like paint.'

I paused for a moment to imagine this. 'What kind?' I asked.

'It's not flat and fine like automotive. This is gritty, more granular. Seems to be a pale, eggshell color. I'm thinking it's structural.'

'Are these the only fragments and fibers you've looked at?'

'I'm just getting started.' He moved to another countertop and pulled out a stool. 'I've looked at all of them under UV, and I'd say that about fifty percent of them have this paint-type substance soaked into the material. And although I can't definitively say what the fabric is, I do know that all of the samples you submitted are the same type, and probably from the same source.'

He placed a slide in the stage of a polarizing microscope, which, like Ray-Ban sunglasses, reduced glare, splitting light in different waves with different refractive index values to give us yet another clue as to the identity of the material.

'Now,' he said, adjusting the focus as he stared into the lens without blinking. 'This is the biggest fragment recovered, about the size of a dime. There are two sides to it.'

He moved out of the way and I looked at fibers reminiscent of blond hairs with speckles of pink and green along the shaft.

'Very consistent with polyester,' Koss explained. 'Speckles are delusterants used in manufacturing so the material isn't shiny. I also think there's some rayon mixed in, and based on all this would have decided what you've got here is a very common fabric that could be used in almost anything. Anything from blouses to bedspreads. But there's one big problem.'

He opened a bottle of liquid solvent used for temporary mountings, and with tweezers, removed the cover slide and carefully turned the fragment over. Dripping xylene, he covered the slide again and motioned for me to bend close.

'What do you see?' he asked, and he was proud of himself.

'Something grayish and solid. Not the same material as the other side.' I looked at him in surprise. 'This fabric has a backing on it?'

'Some kind of thermoplastic. Probably polyethylene terephthalate.'

'Which is used in what?' I wanted to know.

'Primarily soft drink bottles, film. Blister packs used in packing.'

I stared at him, baffled, for I did not see how those products could have anything to do with this case.

'What else?' I asked.

He thought. 'Strapping materials. And some of it, like bottles, can be recycled and used for carpet fibers, fiberfill, plastic lumber. Just about anything.'

'But not fabric for clothing.'

He shook his head, and said with certainty, 'No way. The fabric in question is a rather common, crude polyester blend lined with a plastic-type material. Definitely not like any clothing I've ever heard of. Plus, it appears to be saturated with paint.'

'Thank you, Aaron,' I said. 'This changes everything.'

When I got back to my office, I was surprised and annoyed to find Percy Ring sitting in a chair across from my desk, flipping through a notebook.

'I had to be in Richmond for an interview at Channel Twelve,' he innocently said, 'so I thought I might as well come by to see you. They want to talk to you, too.' He smiled.

I did not answer him, but my silence was loud as I sat in my chair.

'I didn't think you would do the interview. And that's what I told them,' he went on in his easy, affable way.

'And so tell me, what exactly did you say this time?' My tone was not nice.

'Excuse me?' His smile faded and his eyes got hard. 'What's that supposed to mean?'

'You're the investigator. Figure it out.' My eyes were just as hard as his.

He shrugged. 'I gave the usual. Just the basic information about the case and its similarities to the other ones.'

'Investigator Ring, let me make this very clear yet one more time,' I said with no attempt to hide my disdain for him. 'This case is not necessarily like the other ones, and we should not be discussing it with the media.'

'Well, now, it appears you and I have a different perspective, Dr Scarpetta.'

Handsome in a dark suit and paisley suspenders and tie, he looked remarkably credible. I could not help but recall what Wesley had said about Ring's ambitions and connections, and the idea that this egotistical idiot would one day run the state police or be elected to Congress was one I could not stand.

'I think the public has a right to know if there's a psycho in their midst,' he was saying.

'And that's what you said on TV.' My irritation flared hotter. 'That there's a psycho in our midst.'

'I don't remember my exact words. The real reason I stopped by is I'm wondering when I'm going to get a copy of the autopsy report.'

'Still pending.'

'I need it as soon as I can get it.' He looked me in the eye. 'The Commonwealth's Attorney wants to know what's going on.'

I couldn't believe what I'd just heard. He would not be talking to a C.A. unless there was a suspect.

'What are you saying?' I asked.

'I'm looking hard at Keith Pleasants.'

I was incredulous.

'There are a lot of circumstantial things,' he went on, 'not the least of which is how he just so happened to be the one operating the Cat when the torso was found. You know, he usually doesn't operate earth-moving equipment, and then just happens to be in the driver's seat at that exact moment?'

'I should think that makes him more a victim than a suspect. If he's the killer,' I continued, 'one might expect that he wouldn't have wanted to be within a hundred miles of the landfill when the body was found.'

'Psychopaths like to be right there,' he said as if he knew. 'They fantasize about what it would be like to be there when the victim is discovered. They get off on it, like that ambulance driver who murdered women, then dumped them in the area he covered. When it was time to go on duty, he'd call 911 so he was the one who ended up responding.'

In addition to his degree in psychology, he no doubt had attended a lecture on profiling, too. He knew it all.

'Keith lives with his mother, who I think he really resents,' he went on, smoothing his tie. 'She had him late in life, is in her sixties. He takes care of her.'

'Then his mother is still alive and accounted for,' I said.

'Right. But that doesn't mean he didn't take out his aggressions on some other poor old woman. Plus – and you won't believe this – in high school, he worked at the meat counter of a grocery store. He was a butcher's assistant.'

I did not tell him that I did not think a meat saw had been used in this case, but let him talk.

'He's never been very social, which again fits the profile.' He continued spinning his fantastic web. 'And it's rumored among the other guys who work at the landfill that he's homosexual.'

'Based on what?'

'On the fact he doesn't date women or even seem interested in them when the other guys make remarks, jokes. You know how it is with a bunch of rough guys.'

'Describe the house he lives in.' I thought of the photographs sent to me through e-mail.

'Two-story frame, three bedrooms, kitchen, living room. Middle class on its way to being poor. Like maybe in an earlier day when his old man was around, they had it pretty nice.'

'What happened to the father?'

'Ran off before Keith was born.'

'Brothers, sisters?' I asked.

'Grown, have been for a long time. I guess he was a surprise. I suspect Mr Pleasants isn't the father, explaining why he was already gone before Keith was even around.'

'And what is this suspicion based on?' I asked with an edge.

'My gut.'

'I see.'

'Where they live is remote, about ten miles from the landfill, in farmland,' he said. 'Got a pretty good-size yard, a garage that's detached from the house.' He crossed his legs, pausing, as if what he had to add next was important. 'There are a lot of tools, and a big workbench. Keith says he's a handyman and uses the garage when things need fixing around the house. I did see a hacksaw hanging up on a pegboard, and a machete he says he uses for cutting back kudzu and weeds.'

Slipping out of his jacket, he carefully draped it over his lap as he continued the tour of Keith Pleasants' life.

'You certainly had access to a lot of places without a warrant,' I cut him off.

'He was cooperative,' he replied, nonplussed. 'Let's talk about what's in this guy's head.' He tapped his own. 'First, he's smart, real smart, books, magazines, newspapers all over the place. Get this. He's been videotaping news accounts of this case, clipping articles.'

'Probably most of the people working at the landfill are,' I reminded him.

But Ring was not interested in one word I said.

'He reads all kinds of crime stuff. Thrillers. *Silence of the Lambs, Red Dragon*. Tom Clancy, Ann Rule . . .'

I interrupted again because I could not listen to him a moment longer. 'You've just described a typical American reading list. I can't tell you how to conduct your investigation, but let me try to persuade you to follow the evidence . . .'

'I am,' he interrupted right back. 'That's exactly what I'm doing.'

'That's exactly what you're not doing. You don't even know what the evidence is. You haven't received a single report from my office or the labs. You haven't received a profile from the FBI. Have you even talked to Marino or Grigg?'

'We keep missing each other.' He got up and put his jacket back on. 'I need those reports.' It sounded like an order. 'The C.A. will be calling you. By the way, how's Lucy?'

I did not want him to even know my niece's name, and it was evident by the surprised, angry look in my eyes.

'I wasn't aware the two of you were acquainted,' I coolly replied.

'I sat in on one of her classes, I don't know, a couple months back. She was talking about CAIN.'

I grabbed a stack of death certificates from the in-basket, and began initialing them.

'Afterwards she took us over to HRT for a robotics demo,' he said from the doorway. 'She seeing anyone?'

I had nothing to say.

'I mean, I know she lives with another agent. A woman. But they're just roommates, right?'

His meaning was plain, and I froze, looking up as he walked off, whistling. Furious, I collected an armload of paperwork and was getting up from my desk when Rose walked in.

'He can park his shoes under my bed anytime he wants,' she said in Ring's wake.

'Please!' I couldn't stand it. 'I thought you were an intelligent woman, Rose.'

'I think you need some hot tea,' she said.

'Maybe so.' I sighed.

'But we have another matter first,' she said in her businesslike way. 'Do you know someone named Keith Pleasants?'

'What about him?' For an instant, my mind locked.

'He's in the lobby,' she said. 'Very upset, refuses to leave until he sees you. I started to call security, but thought I should check . . .' The look on my face stopped her cold.

'Oh my God,' I exclaimed in dismay. 'Did he and Ring see each other?'

'I have no idea,' she said, and now she was very perplexed. 'Is something wrong?'

'Everything.' I sighed, dropping the paperwork back on my desk.

'Then you do or don't want me to call security?'

'Don't.' I walked briskly past her.

My heels were sharp and directed as I followed the hallway to the front, and around a corner into a lobby that had never been homey no matter how hard I had tried. No amount of tasteful furniture or prints on walls could disguise the terrible truths that brought people to these doors. Like Keith Pleasants, they sat woodenly on a blue upholstered couch that was supposed to be unprovocative and soothing. In shock, they stared at nothing or wept.

I pushed open the door as he sprung to his feet, eyes bloodshot. I could not quite tell if he were in a rage or a panic as he almost lunged at me. For an instant, I thought he was going to grab me or start swinging. But he awkwardly dropped his hands by his sides and glared at me, his face darkening as his outrage boiled over.

'You got no right to be saying things like that about me!' he exclaimed with clenched fists. 'You don't know me! Don't know anything about me!'

'Easy, Keith,' I said, calmly, but with authority.

Motioning for him to sit back down, I pulled up a chair so I could face him. He was breathing hard, trembling, eyes wounded and filled with furious tears.

'You met me one time.' He shot a finger at me. 'One lousy time and then say things.' His voice was quavering. 'I'm about to lose my job.' He covered his mouth with a fist, averting his eyes as he fought for control.

'In the first place,' I said, 'I have not said a word about you. Not to anyone.'

He glanced at me.

'I have no idea what you're talking about.' My eyes were steady on him, and I spoke with quiet confidence that made him waver. 'I wish you'd explain it to me.'

He was studying me with uncertainty, lies he had been led to believe about me wavering in his eyes.

'You didn't talk to Investigator Ring about me?' he said.

I checked my fury. 'No.'

'He came to my house this morning while my mama was still in bed.' His voice shook. 'Started interrogating me like I was a murderer or something. Said you had findings pointing right to me, so I better confess.'

'Findings? What findings?' I said as my disgust grew.

'Fibers that according to you looked like they came from what I had on the day we met. You said my size fit what you think the size is of the person who cut up that body. He said you could tell by the pressure applied with the saw that whoever did it was about my strength. He said you were demanding all kinds of things from me so you could do all these tests. DNA. That you thought I was weird when I drove you up to the site . . .'

I interrupted him, 'My God, Keith. I have never heard so much bullshit in my life. If I said even one of those things, I would be fired for incompetence.'

'That's the other thing,' Pleasants jumped in again, fire in his eyes. 'He's been talking with everyone I work with! They're all wondering if I'm some kind of axe murderer. I can tell by the way they look at me.'

He dissolved in tears as doors opened and several state troopers walked in. They paid us no mind as they were buzzed inside, on their way down to the morgue, where Fielding was working on a pedestrian death. Pleasants was too upset for me to discuss this with him any further, and I was so incensed with Ring that I did not know what else to say.

'Do you have a lawyer?' I asked him.

He shook his head.

'I think you'd better get one.'

'I don't know any.'

'I can give you some names,' I said as Wingo opened the door and was startled by the sight of Pleasants crying on the couch.

'Uh, Dr Scarpetta?' Wingo said. 'Dr Fielding wants to know if he can go ahead and receipt the personal effects to the funeral home.'

I stepped closer to Wingo, because I did not want Pleasants further upset by the business of this place.

'The troopers are on their way down,' I said in a low voice. 'If they don't want the personal effects, then yes. Receipt them to the funeral home.'

He was staring hard at Pleasants, as if he knew him from somewhere.

'Listen,' I said to Wingo. 'Get him the names and numbers of Jameson and Higgins.'

They were two very fine lawyers in town whom I considered friends.

'Then please see Mr Pleasants out.'

Wingo was still staring, as if transfixed by him.

'Wingo?' I gave him a questioning look, because he did not seem to have heard me.

'Yes, ma'am.' He glanced at me.

I went past him, heading downstairs. I needed to talk to Wesley, but maybe I should get hold of Marino first. As I rode the elevator down, I debated if I should call the C.A. in Sussex and warn her about Ring. At the same time all of this was going through my mind, I felt dreadfully sorry for Pleasants. I was scared for him. As far-fetched as it might seem, I knew he could end up charged with murder.

In the morgue, Fielding and the troopers were looking at the pedestrian on table one, and there wasn't the usual banter because the victim was the nine-year-old daughter of a city councilman. She had been walking to the bus stop early this morning when someone had swerved off the road at a high rate of speed. Based on the absence of skid marks, the driver had hit the girl from the rear and not even slowed.

'How are we doing?' I asked when I got to them.

'We got us a real tough one here,' said one of the troopers, his expression grave.

'The father's going ape shit,' Fielding told me as he went over the clothed body with a lens, collecting trace evidence.

'Any paint?' I asked, for a chip of it could identify the make and model of the car.

'Not so far.' My deputy chief was in a foul mood. He hated working on children.

I scanned torn, bloody jeans and a partial grille mark imprinted in fabric at the level of the buttocks. The front bumper had struck the back of the knees, and the head had hit the windshield. She had been wearing a small red knapsack. The bagged lunch, and books, papers and pens that had been taken out of it pricked my heart. I felt heavy inside.

'The grille mark seems pretty high,' I remarked.

'That's what I'm thinking, too,' another trooper spoke. 'Like you associate with pickup trucks and recreational vehicles. About the time it happened, a black Jeep Cherokee was observed in the area traveling at a high rate of speed.'

'Her father's been calling every half hour.' Fielding glanced up at me. 'Thinks this was more than an accident.'

'Implying what, exactly?' I asked.

'That it's political.' He resumed work, collecting fibers and bits of debris. 'A homicide.'

'Lord, let's hope not,' I said, walking away. 'What it is now is bad enough.'

On a steel counter in a remote corner of the morgue was a portable electric heater where we defleshed and degreased bones. The process was decidedly unpleasant, requiring the boiling of body parts in a ten-percent solution of bleach. The big, rattling steel pot, the smell, were dreadful, and I usually restricted this activity to nights and weekends when we were unlikely to have visitors.

Yesterday, I had left the bone ends from the torso to boil overnight. They had not required much time, and I turned off the heater. Pouring steaming, stinking water into a sink, I waited until the bones were cool enough to pick up. They were clean and white, about two inches long, cuts and saw marks clearly visible. As I examined each segment carefully, a sense of scary disbelief swept over me. I could not tell which saw marks had been made by the killer and which had been made by me.

'Jack,' I called out to Fielding. 'Could you come over here for a minute?'

He stopped what he was doing and walked to my corner of the room.

'What's up?' he asked.

I handed him one of the bones. 'Can you tell which end was cut with the Stryker saw?'

He turned it over and over, looking back and forth, at one end and then the other, frowning. 'Did you mark it?'

'For right and left I did,' I said. 'Beyond that, no. I should have. But usually it's so obvious which end is which, it's not necessary.'

'I'm not expert, but if I didn't know better, I'd say all these cuts were made with the same saw.' He handed the bone back to me and I began sealing it in an evidence bag. 'You got to take them to Canter anyway, right.'

'He's not going to be happy with me.' I said.

6

My house was built of stone on the edge of Windsor Farms, an old Richmond neighborhood with English street names, and stately Georgian and Tudor homes that some would call mansions. Lights were on in windows I passed, and beyond glass I could see fine furniture and chandeliers, and people moving or watching TV. No one seemed to close their curtains in this city, except me. Leaves had begun to fall. It was cool and overcast, and when I pulled into my driveway, smoke was drifting from the chimney, my niece's ancient green Suburban parked in front.

'Lucy?' I called out as I shut the door and turned off the alarm.

'I'm in here,' she replied from the end of the house where she always stayed.

As I headed for my office to deposit my briefcase and the pile I had brought home to work on tonight, she emerged from her bedroom, pulling a bright orange UVA sweatshirt over her head.

'Hi.' Smiling, she gave me a hug, and there was very little that was soft about her.

Holding her at arm's length, I took a good look at her, just like I always did.

'Uh oh,' she playfully said. 'Inspection time.' She held out her arms and turned around, as if about to be searched.

'Smarty,' I said.

In truth, I would have preferred it had she weighed a little more, but she was keenly pretty and healthy, with auburn hair that was short but softly styled. After all this time, I still could not look at her without envisioning a precocious, obnoxious ten-year-old who had no one, really, but me.

'You pass,' I said.

'Sorry I'm so late.'

'Tell me again what it was you were doing?' I asked, for she had called earlier in the day to say she could not get here until dinner.

'An assistant attorney general decided to drop in with an entourage. As usual, they wanted HRT to put on a show.'

We headed to the kitchen.

'I trotted out Toto and Tin Man,' she added.

They were robots.

'Used fiber optics, virtual reality. The usual things, except it's pretty cool. We parachuted them out of a Huey, and I maneuvered them to burn through a metal door with lasers.'

'No stunts with the helicopters, I hope,' I said.

'The guys did that. I did my shit from the ground.' She wasn't happy about it.

The problem was, Lucy wanted to do stunts with helicopters. There were fifty agents on the HRT. She was the only woman and had a tendency to overreact when they wouldn't let her do dangerous things that, in my opinion, she had no business doing anyway. Of course, I wasn't the most objective judge.

'It suits me fine if you stick with robots,' I said, and we were in the kitchen now. 'Something smells good. What did you fix your tired, old aunt to eat?'

'Fresh spinach sautéed in a little garlic and olive oil, and filets that I'm going to throw on the grill. This is my one day a week to eat beef, so tough luck if it's not yours. I even sprung for a bottle of really nice wine, something Janet and I discovered.'

'Since when can FBI agents afford nice wine?'

'Hey,' she said, 'I don't do too bad. Besides, I'm too damn busy to spend money.'

Certainly, she didn't spend it on clothes. Whenever I saw her, she was either in khaki fatigues or sweats. Now and then she wore jeans and a funky jacket or blazer, and made fun of my offers of hand-me-downs. She would not wear my lawyerly suits and blouses with high collars, and frankly, my figure was fuller than her firm, athletic one. Probably nothing in my closet would fit.

The moon was huge and low in a cloudy, dark sky. We put on

jackets and sat out on the deck drinking wine while Lucy cooked. She had started baked potatoes first, and they were taking a while, so we talked. Over recent years, our relationship had become less mother-daughter as we evolved into colleagues and friends. The transition was not an easy one, for often she taught me and even worked on some of my cases. I felt oddly lost, no longer certain of my role and power in her life.

'Wesley wants me to track this AOL thing,' she was saying. 'Sussex definitely wants CASKU's help.'

'Do you know Percy Ring?' I asked as I thought of what he had said in my office, infuriated again.

'He was in one of my classes and was obnoxious, wouldn't shut up.' She reached for the bottle of wine. 'What a peacock.'

She began filling our glasses. Raising the hood of the grill, she poked potatoes with a fork.

'I believe we're ready,' she said, pleased.

Moments later, she was emerging from the house, carrying the filets. They sizzled as she placed them on the grill. 'Somehow he figured out you're my aunt.' She was talking about Ring again. 'Not that it's a secret, and he asked me about it after class once. You know, if you tutored me, helped me out with my cases, like I couldn't possibly do what I'm doing on my own, that sort of thing. I just think he picks on me because I'm a new agent and a woman.'

'That may be the biggest miscalculation he's ever made in his life,' I said.

'And he wanted to know if I was married.' Her eyes were shadowed as porch lights shone on one side of her face.

'I worry about what his interest really is,' I commented.

She glanced at me as she cooked. 'The usual.' She shrugged it off, for she was surrounded by men and paid no attention to their comments or their stares.

'Lucy, he made a reference to you in my office today,' I said. 'A veiled reference.'

'To what?'

'Your status. Your roommate.'

No matter how often or delicately we talked about this, she always got frustrated and impatient.

'Whether it's true or not,' she said, and the sizzling of the grill seemed to match her tone, 'there would still be rumors because I'm an agent. It's ridiculous. I know women married with kids, and the guys think all of them are gay, too, just because they're cops, agents, troopers, secret service. Some people even think it about you. For the same reason. Because of your position, your power.'

'This is not about accusations,' I reminded her, gently. 'This is about whether someone could hurt you. Ring is very smooth. He comes across as credible. I expect he resents that you're FBI, HRT and he's not.'

'I think he's already demonstrated that.' Her voice was hard.

'I just hope the jerk doesn't keep asking you out.'

'Oh, he already is. At least half a dozen times.' She sat down. 'He's even asked Janet out, if you can believe that.' She laughed. 'Talk about not getting it.'

'The problem is I think he does get it,' I said, ominously. 'It's like he's building a case against you, gathering evidence.'

'Well, gather away.' She abruptly ended our discussion. 'So tell me what else went on today.'

I told her what I had learned at the labs, and we talked about fibers embedded in bone and Koss's analysis of them as we carried steaks and wine inside. We sat at the kitchen table with a candle lit, digesting information few people would serve with food.

'A cheap motel curtain could have a backing like that,' Lucy said.

'That or something like a drop cloth, because of the paint-like substance,' I replied. 'The spinach is wonderful. Where did you get it?'

'Ukrops. I'd give anything to have a store like that in my neighborhood. So this person wrapped the victim in a drop cloth and then dismembered her through it?' she asked as she cut her meat.

'That's certainly the way it's looking.'

'What does Wesley say?' She met my eyes.

'I haven't had a chance to talk to him yet.' This wasn't quite true. I had not even called.

For a moment, Lucy was silent. She got up and brought a bottle of Evian to the table. 'So how long do you plan to run from him?'

I pretended not to hear her, in hopes she would not start in.

'You know that's what you're doing. You're scared.'

'This is not something we should discuss,' I said. 'Especially when we're having such a pleasant evening.'

She reached for her wine.

'It's very good, by the way,' I said. 'I like pinot noir because it's light. Not heavy like a merlot. I'm not in the mood for anything heavy right now. So you made a good choice.'

She stabbed another bite of steak, getting my point.

'Tell me how things are going with Janet,' I went on. 'Mostly doing white-collar crime in D.C.? Or is she getting to spend more time at ERF these days?'

Lucy stared out the window at the moon as she slowly swirled wine in her glass. 'I should get started on your computer.'

While I cleaned up, she disappeared into my office. I did not disturb her for a very long time, if for no other reason than I knew she was put out with me. She wanted complete openness, and I had never been good at that, not with anyone. I felt bad, as if I had let down everyone I loved. For a while, I sat at the kitchen desk, talking to Marino on the phone, and I called to catch up with my mother. I put on a pot of decaffeinated coffee and carried two mugs down the hall.

Lucy was busy at my keyboard, glasses on, a slight frown furrowing her young, smooth brow as she concentrated. I set her coffee down and looked over her head at what she was typing. It made no sense to me. It never did.

'How's it going?' I asked.

I could see my face reflected in the monitor as she struck the enter key again, executing another UNIX command.

'Good and not good,' she replied with an impatient sigh. 'The problem with applications like AOL is you can't track files unless you get into the original programming language. That's where I am now. And it's like following bread crumbs through a universe with more layers than an onion.'

I pulled up a chair and sat next to her. 'Lucy,' I said, 'how did someone send these photographs to me? Can you tell me, step by step?'

She stopped what she was doing, slipping off her glasses and setting them on the desk. She rubbed her face in her hands and massaged her temples as if she had a headache.

'You got any Tylenol?' she asked.

'No acetaminophen with alcohol.' I opened a drawer and got out a bottle of Motrin instead.

'For starters,' she said, taking two, 'this wouldn't have been easy if your screen name wasn't the same as your real one: KSCARPETTA.'

'I made it easy *deliberately*, for my colleagues to send me mail,' I explained one more time.

'You made it easy for anyone to send you mail.' She looked accusingly at me. 'Have you gotten crank mail before?'

'I think this goes beyond crank mail.'

'Please answer my question.'

'A few things. Nothing to worry about.' I paused, then went on, 'Generally after a lot of publicity because of some big case, a sensational trial, whatever.'

'You should change your user name.'

'No,' I said. 'Deadoc might want to send me something else. I can't change it now.'

'Oh great.' She put her glasses back on. 'So now you want him to be a pen pal.'

'Lucy, please,' I quietly said, and I was getting a headache, too. 'We both have a job to do.'

She was quiet for a moment. Then she apologized. 'I guess I'm just as overly protective of you as you've always been of me.'

'I still am.' I patted her knee. 'Okay, so he got my screen name from the AOL directory of subscribers, right?'

She nodded. 'Let's talk about your AOL profile.'

'There's nothing in it but my professional title, my office phone number and address,' I said. 'I never entered personal details, such as marital status, date of birth, hobbies, et cetera. I have more sense than that.'

'Have you checked out his profile?' she asked. 'The one for deadoc?'

'Frankly, it never occurred to me that he would have one,' I said.

Depressed, I thought of saw marks I could not tell apart, and felt I had made yet one more mistake this day.

'Oh, he's got one, all right.' Lucy was typing again. 'He wants you to know who he is. That's why he wrote it.'

She clicked to the Member Directory, and when she opened deadoc's profile, I could not believe what was before my eyes. I scanned key words that could be searched by anyone interested in finding other users to whom they applied.

Attorney, autopsy, chief, Chief Medical Examiner, Cornell, corpse, death, dismemberment, FBI, forensic, Georgetown, Italian, Johns Hopkins, judicial, killer, lawyer, medical, pathologist, physician, Scuba, Virginia, woman.

The list went on, the professional and personal information, the hobbies, all describing me.

'It's like deadoc's saying he's you,' Lucy said.

I was dumbfounded and suddenly felt very cold. 'This is crazy.'

Lucy pushed back her chair and looked at me. 'He's got your profile. In cyberspace, on the World Wide Web, you're both the same person with two different screen names.'

'We are not the same person. I can't believe you said that.' I looked at her, shocked.

'The photographs are yours and you sent them to yourself. It was easy. You simply scanned them into your computer. No big deal. You can get portable color scanners for four, five hundred bucks. Attach the file to the message *ten*, which you send to KSCARPETTA, send to yourself, in other words . . .'

'Lucy,' I cut her off, 'for God's sake, that's enough.'

She was silent, her face without expression.

'This is outrageous. I can't believe what you're saying.' I got up from the chair in disgust.

'If your fingerprints were on the murder weapon,' she replied, 'wouldn't you want me to tell you?'

'My fingerprints aren't on anything.'

'Aunt Kay, I'm just making the point that someone out there is stalking you, impersonating you, on the Internet. Of course you didn't do anything. But what I'm trying to impress upon you is every time someone does a search by subject because they need help from an expert like you, they're going to get deadoc's name, too.'

'How could he have known all this information about me?' I went on. 'It's not in my profile. I don't have anything in there about where I went to law school, medical school, that my heritage is Italian.'

'Maybe from things written about you over the years.'

'I suppose.' I felt as if I were coming down with something. 'Would you like a nightcap? I'm very tired.'

But she was lost again in the dark space of the UNIX environment with its strange symbols and commands like *cat*, *:q!* and *vi*.

'Aunt Kay, what's your password in AOL?' she asked.

'The same one I use for everything else,' I confessed, knowing she would be annoyed again.

'Shit. Don't tell me you're still using *Sinbad*.' She looked up at me.

'My mother's rotten cat has never been mentioned in anything ever written about me,' I defended myself.

I watched as she typed the command *password* and entered *Sinbad*.

'Do you do password aging?' she asked as if everyone should know what that meant.

'I have no idea what you're talking about.'

'Where you change your password at least once a month.'

'No,' I said.

'Who else knows your password?'

'Rose knows it. And of course, now you do,' I said. 'There's no way deadoc could.'

'There's always a way. He could use a UNIX password-encryption program to encrypt every word in a dictionary. Then compare every encrypted word to your password . . .'

'It wasn't that complicated,' I said with conviction. 'I bet whoever did this doesn't know a thing about UNIX.'

Lucy closed what she was doing, and looked curiously at me, swiveling the chair around. 'Why do you say that?'

'Because he could have washed the body first so trace evidence didn't adhere to blood. He shouldn't have given us a photo of her hands. Now we may have her prints.' I was leaning against the door frame, holding my aching head. 'He's not that smart.'

'Maybe he doesn't think her prints will ever matter,' she said, getting up. 'And by the way,' she said as she walked by. 'Almost any computer book's going to tell you it's stupid to choose a password that's the name of your significant other or your cat.'

'Sinbad's not my cat. I wouldn't have a miserable Siamese that always gives me the fisheye and stalks me whenever I walk into my mother's house.'

'Well, you must like him a little bit or you wouldn't have wanted to think of him every time you log on to your computer,' she said from down the hall.

'I don't like him in the least,' I said.

The next morning, the air was crisp and clean like a fall apple, stars were out, traffic mostly truckers in the midst of long hauls. I turned off on 64 East, just beyond the state fairgrounds, and minutes later was prowling rows in short-term parking at the Richmond International Airport. I chose a space in S because I knew it would be easy for me to remember, and was reminded of my password again, of other obvious acts of carelessness caused by overload.

As I was getting my bag out of the trunk, I heard footsteps behind me and instantly wheeled around.

'Don't shoot.' Marino held up his hands. It was cool enough out that I could see his breath.

'I wish you'd whistle or something when you walk up on me in the dark,' I said, slamming shut the trunk.

'Oh. And bad people don't whistle. Only good guys like me do.' He grabbed my suitcase. 'You want me to get that, too?'

He reached for the hard, black Pelican case I was taking with me to Memphis today, where it already had been numerous times before. Inside were human vertebrae and bone, evidence that could not leave me.

'This stays handcuffed to me,' I said, grabbing it and my briefcase. 'I'm really sorry to put you out like this, Marino. Are you sure it's necessary for you to come along?'

We had discussed this several times now, and I did not think he should accompany me. I did not see the point.

'Like I told you, some squirrel's playing games with you,' he said. 'Me, Wesley, Lucy, the entire friggin' Bureau think I should come along. For one thing, you've made this exact same trip in every case, so it's gotten predictable. And it's been in the papers that you use this guy at UT.'

Parking lots were well lit and full of cars, and I could not help but notice people slowly driving past, looking for a place that wasn't miles from the terminal. I wondered what else deadoc knew about me, and wished I had worn more than a trench coat. I was cold and had forgotten my gloves.

'Besides,' Marino added, 'I've never been to Graceland.'

At first, I thought he was joking.

'It's on my list,' he went on.

'What list?'

'The one I've had since I was a kid. Alaska, Las Vegas and the Grand Ole Opry,' he said as if the thought filled him with joy. 'Don't you have some place you would go if you could do anything you want?'

We were at the terminal now, and he held the door.

'Yes,' I said. 'My own bed in my own home.'

I headed for the Delta desk, picked up our tickets and went upstairs. Typical for this hour, nothing was open except security. When I placed my hard case on the X-ray belt, I knew what was going to happen.

'Ma'am, you're going to have to open that,' said the female guard.

I unlocked it and unsnapped the clasps. Inside, nestled in foam rubber, were labeled plastic bags containing the bones. The guard's eyes widened.

'I've been through here before with this,' I patiently explained.

She started to reach for one of the plastic bags.

'Please don't touch anything,' I warned. 'This is evidence in a homicide.'

There were several other travelers behind me, now, and they were listening to every word I said.

'Well, I have to look at it.'

'You can't.' I got out my brass medical examiner's shield and showed it to her. 'You touch anything here, and I'll have to include

you in the chain of evidence when this eventually goes to court. You'll
be subpoenaed.'

That was as much of an explanation as she needed, and she let me
go.

'Dumb as a bag of hammers,' Marino mumbled as we walked.

'She's just doing her job,' I replied.

'Look,' he said. 'We don't fly back until tomorrow morning,
meaning unless you spend the whole damn day looking at bones, we
should have some time.'

'You can go to Graceland by yourself. I've got plenty of work to
do in my room. I'm also sitting in nonsmoking.' I chose a seat at our
gate. 'So if you want to smoke, you'll have to go over there.' I pointed.

He scanned other passengers waiting, like us, to board. Then he
looked at me.

'You know what, Doc?' he said. 'The problem is you hate to have
fun.'

I got the morning paper out of my briefcase, shook it open.

He sat next to me. 'I'll bet you've never even listened to Elvis.'

'How could I not listen to Elvis? He's on the radio, on TV, in elevators.'

'He's the king.'

I eyed Marino over the top of the paper.

'His voice, everything about him. There's never been anyone like
him,' Marino went on as if he had a crush. 'I mean, it's like classical
music and those painters you like so much. I think people like that
only come along every couple hundred years.'

'So now you're comparing him with Mozart and Monet.' I turned
a page, bored with local politics and business.

'Sometimes you're a friggin' snob.' He got up, grumpy. 'And maybe
just once in your life you might think of going some place I want to
go. You ever seen me bowl?' He glared down at me, getting out his
cigarettes. 'You ever said anything nice about my truck? You ever
gone fishing with me? You ever eat at my house? No, I gotta go to
yours because you live in the right part of town.'

'You cook for me, I'll come over,' I said as I read.

He angrily stalked off, and I could feel the eyes of strangers on us.
I supposed they assumed that Marino and I were an item, and had
not gotten along in years. Smiling to myself, I turned a page. Not
only would I go to Graceland with him, I planned to buy him barbecue
tonight.

Since it seemed that one could not fly direct from Richmond to anywhere except Charlotte, we were routed to Cincinnati first, where we changed planes. We arrived in Memphis by noon and checked into the Peabody Hotel. I had gotten us a government rate of seventy-three dollars per night, and Marino looked around, gawking at a grand lobby of stained glass and a fountain of mallard ducks.

'Holy shit,' he said. 'I've never seen a joint that has live ducks. They're everywhere.'

We were walking into the restaurant, which was appropriately named Mallards, and displayed behind glass were duck objets d'art. There were paintings of ducks on walls, and ducks were on the staff's green vests and ties.

'They have a duck palace on the roof,' I said. 'And roll out a red carpet for them twice a day when they come and go to John Philip Sousa.'

'No way.'

I told the hostess that we would like a table for two. 'In nonsmoking,' I added.

The restaurant was crowded with men and women wearing big name tags for some real estate convention they were attending at the hotel. We sat so close to other people that I could read reports they were perusing and hear their affairs. I ordered a fresh fruit plate and coffee, while Marino got his usual grilled hamburger platter.

'Medium rare,' he told the waiter.

'Medium.' I gave Marino a look.

'Yeah, yeah, okay.' He shrugged.

'Enterohemorrhagic E. coli,' I said to him as the waiter walked off. 'Trust me. Not worth it.'

'Don't you ever want to do things bad for you?' he said.

He looked depressed and suddenly old as he sat across from me in this beautiful place where people were well dressed and better paid than a police captain from Richmond. Marino's hair had thinned to an unruly fringe circling the top of his ears like a tarnished silver halo shoved low. He had not lost an ounce since I had known him, his belly rising from his belt and touching the edge of the table. Not a day went by that I did not fear for him. I could not imagine his not working with me forever.

At half past one, we left the hotel in the rental car. He drove because he would never have it any other way, and we got on Madison Avenue and followed it east, away from the Mississippi River. The brick university was so close we could have walked it, the Regional Forensic Center across the street from a tire store and the Life Blood Donor

Center. Marino parked in back, near the public entrance of the medical examiner's office.

The facility was funded by the county and about the size of my central district office in Richmond. There were three forensic pathologists, and also two forensic anthropologists, which was very unusual and enviable, for I would have loved to have someone like Dr David Canter on my staff. Memphis had yet another distinction which was decidedly not a happy one. The chief had been involved in perhaps two of the most infamous cases in the country. He had performed the autopsy of Martin Luther King and had witnessed the one of Elvis.

'If it's all the same to you,' Marino said as we got out of the car, 'I think I'll make phone calls while you do your thing.'

'Fine. I'm sure they can find an office for you to use.'

He squinted up at an autumn blue sky, then looked around as we walked. 'I can't believe I'm here,' he said. 'This is where he was posted.'

'No,' I said, because I knew exactly who he was talking about. 'Elvis Presley was posted at Baptist Memorial Hospital. He never came here, even though he should have.'

'How come?'

'He was treated like a natural death,' I replied.

'Well, he was. He died of a heart attack.'

'It's true his heart was terrible,' I said. 'But that's not what killed him. His death was due to his polydrug abuse.'

'His death was due to Colonel Parker,' Marino muttered as if he wanted to kill the man.

I glanced at him as we entered the office. 'Elvis had ten drugs on board. He should have been signed out an accident. It's sad.'

'And we know it was really him,' he then said.

'Oh for God's sake, Marino!'

'What? You've seen the photos? You know it for a fact?' he went on.

'I've seen them. And yes, I know,' I said as I stopped at the receptionist's desk.

'Then what's in them.' He would not stop.

A young woman named Shirley, who had taken care of me before, waited for Marino and me to quit disagreeing.

'That is none of your business,' I sweetly said to him. 'Shirley, how are you?'

'Back again?' She smiled.

'With no good news, I'm sorry to say,' I replied.

Marino began trimming his fingernails with a pocket-knife, glancing around like Elvis might walk in any minute.

'Dr Canter's expecting you,' she said. 'Come on. I'll take you back.'

While Marino ambled off to make phone calls somewhere down the hall, I was shown into the modest office of a man I had known since his residency days at the University of Tennessee. Canter had been as young as Lucy when I had met him for the first time.

A devotee of forensic anthropologist Dr Bass, who had begun the decay research facility in Knoxville known as The Body Farm, Canter had been mentored by most of the greats. He was considered the world's foremost expert in saw marks, and I wasn't quite sure what it was about this state famous for the Vols and Daniel Boone. Tennessee seemed to corner the market on experts in time of death and human bones.

'Kay.' Canter rose, extending his hand.

'Dave, you're always so good to see me on such short notice.' I took a chair across from his desk.

'Well, I hate what you're going through.'

He had dark hair combed straight back from his brow, so that whenever he looked down it fell in his way. He was constantly shoving it out of his way but did not seem aware of it. His face was youthful and interestingly angular, with closely set eyes and a strong jaw and nose.

'How are Jill and the kids?' I inquired.

'Great. We're expecting again.'

'Congratulations. That makes three?'

'Four.' His smile got bigger.

'I don't know how you do it,' I said sincerely.

'Doing it's the easy part. What goodies have you brought me?'

Setting the hard case on the edge of his desk, I opened it and got out the plastic-enclosed sections of bone. I handed them to him and he took out the left femur first. He studied it under a lamp with his lens, slowly turning it end over end.

'Hmmm,' he said. 'So you didn't notch the end you cut.' He glanced at me.

He wasn't chastising, just reminding, and I felt angry with myself again. Usually, I was so careful. If anything, I was known for being cautious to the point of obsession.

'I made an assumption, and I was wrong,' I said. 'I did not expect to discover that the killer used a saw with characteristics very similar to mine.'

'They usually don't use autopsy saws.' He pushed back his chair and got up. 'I've never had a case, really, just studied that type of saw mark in theory, here in the lab.'

'Then that's what this is.' I had suspected as much.

'I can't say with certainty until I get it under the scope. But both ends look like they've been cut with a Stryker saw.'

He gathered the bags of bones, and I followed him out into the hall as my misgivings got worse. I did not know what we would do if he could not tell the saw marks apart. A mistake like this was enough to ruin a case in court.

'Now, I know you're probably not going to tell much about the vertebral bone,' I said, for it was trabecular, less dense than other bone and therefore not a good surface for tool marks.

'Never hurts to bring it anyway. We might get lucky,' he said as we entered his lab.

There was not an inch of empty space. Thirty-five-gallon drums of degreaser and polyurethane varnish were parked wherever they would fit. Shelves from floor to ceiling were crammed with packaged bones, and in boxes and on carts were every type of saw known to man. Dismemberments were rare, and I knew of only three obvious motivations for taking a victim apart. Transporting the body was easier. Identification was slowed, if not made impossible. Or simply, the killer was malicious.

Canter pulled a stool close to an operating microscope equipped with a camera. He moved aside a tray of fractured ribs and thyroid cartilage that he must have been working on before I arrived.

'This guy was kicked in the throat, among other things,' he absently said as he pulled on surgical gloves.

'Such a nice world we live in,' I commented.

Canter opened the Ziploc bag containing the segment of right femur. Because he could not fit it on the microscope's stage without cutting a section that was thin enough to mount, he had me hold the two-inch length of bone against the table's edge. Then he bent a twenty-five-power fiber optics light close to one of the sawn surfaces.

'Definitely a Stryker saw,' he said as he peered into the lenses. 'You got to have a fast-moving, reciprocating motion to create a polish like this. It almost looks like polished stone. See?'

He moved aside and I looked. The bone was slightly beveled, like water frozen in gentle ripples, and it shone. Unlike other power saws, the Stryker had an oscillating blade that did not move very far. It did not cut skin, only the hard surface it was pressed against, like bone or a cast an orthopedist cut from a mending limb.

'Obviously,' I said, 'the transverse cuts across the mid-shaft are mine. From removing marrow for DNA.'

'But the knife marks aren't.'

'No. Absolutely not.'

'Well, we're probably not going to have much luck with them.'

Knives basically covered their own tracks, unless the victim's bone or cartilage was stabbed or hacked.

'But the good news is, we got a few false starts, a wider kerf and TPI,' he said, adjusting the microscope's focus as I continued holding the bone.

I had known nothing about saws until I began spending so much time with Canter. Bone is an excellent surface for tool marks, and when saw teeth cut into it, a groove or kerf is formed. By microscopically examining the walls and floor of a kerf, one can determine exit chipping on the side where the saw exited bone. Determining the characteristics of the individual teeth, the number of teeth per inch (TPI), the spacing of them and the striae, can reveal the shape of the blade.

Canter angled the optic light to sharpen the striations and defects.

'You can see the curve of the blade.' He pointed to several false starts on the shaft, where someone had pushed the saw blade into the bone, and then tried again in another spot.

'Not mine,' I said. 'Or at least I hope I'm more adept than that.'

'Since this also is the end where most of the knife cuts are, I'm going to agree that it wasn't you. Whoever did this had to cut first with something else, since an oscillating blade won't cut flesh.'

'What about the saw blade?' I asked, for I knew what I used in the morgue.

'Teeth are large, seventeen per inch. So this is going to be a round autopsy blade. Let's turn it over.'

I did, and he directed the light at the other end, where there were no false starts. The surface was polished and beveled like the other one, but not identical to Canter's discerning eye.

'Power autopsy saw with a large, sectioning blade,' he said. 'Multidirectional cut since the radius of the blade's too small to cut through the whole bone in one stroke. So, whoever did this just changed directions, going at it from different angles, with a great deal of skill. We have slight bending of the kerfs. Minimal exit chipping.'

Again denoting great skill with a saw. I'm going to bump up the power some and see if we can accentuate the harmonics.'

He referred to the distance between saw teeth.

'Tooth distance is point-oh-six. Sixteen teeth per inch,' he counted. 'Direction is push-pull, tooth-type chisel. I'm voting this is yours.'

'You caught me,' I said with relief. 'Guilty as charged.'

'I would think so.' He was still looking. 'I wouldn't think you use a round blade for anything.'

The large, round autopsy blades were heavy and continuous rolling, and destroyed more bone. Generally, this was a utility blade used in labs or in doctors' offices to saw off casts.

'The rare occasion I might use a round blade is on animals,' I said.

'Of the two- or four-legged variety?'

'I've taken bullets out of dogs, birds, cats and, on one fine occasion, a python shot in a drug raid,' I replied.

Canter was looking at another bone. 'And I thought I was the one who had all the fun.'

'Do you find it unusual that someone would use a meat saw in four dismemberments, and then suddenly switch to an electric autopsy saw?' I asked.

'If your theory's correct about the cases in Ireland, then you're talking nine cases with a meat saw,' he said. 'How about holding this right here so I can get a picture.'

I held the section of left femur in the tips of my fingers, and he pressed a button on the camera.

'To answer your question,' he said. 'I would find it extremely unusual. You're talking two different profiles. The meat saw is manual, physical, usually ten teeth per inch. It will go through tissue and takes a lot of bone with each stroke, the saw marks rougher-looking, more indicative of someone skilled and powerful. And it's also important to remember that in each of those earlier cases the perpetrator cut through joints, versus the shafts, which is also very rare.'

'It's not the same person.' I again voiced my growing belief.

Canter took the bone from my hand and looked at me. 'That's my vote.'

When I returned to the lobby of the M.E.'s office, Marino was still on the phone down the hall. I waited a little while, then stepped outside because I needed air. I needed sunshine and sights that weren't savage. Some twenty minutes passed before he finally walked out and joined me by the car.

'I didn't know you was here,' he said. 'If someone had told me, I would've got off the phone.'

'It's all right. What a gorgeous day.'

He unlocked the car.

'How'd it go?' he asked, sliding into the driver's seat.

I briefly summarized as we sat in the parking lot, not going anywhere.

'You want to go back to the Peabody?' he asked, tapping the steering wheel with his thumb.

I knew exactly what he wanted to do.

'No,' I said. 'Graceland might be just what the doctor ordered.'

He shoved the car in gear and could not suppress a big grin.

'We want the Fowler Expressway,' I said, for I had studied a map.

'I wish you could get me his autopsy report,' he started on that again. 'I want to see for myself what happened to him. Then I'll know and it won't eat at me anymore.'

'What do you want to know?' I looked at him.

'If it was like they said. Did he die on the toilet? That's always bothered the hell out of me. You know how many cases like that I've seen?' He glanced at me. 'Don't matter if you're some drone or the president of the United States. You end up dead with a ring around your butt. Hope to hell that don't happen to me.'

'Elvis was found on the floor of his bathroom. He was nude, and yes, it is believed that he slid off his black porcelain toilet.'

'Who found him?' Marino was entranced in an uneasy way.

'A girlfriend who was staying in the adjoining room. Or that's the story,' I said.

'You mean he walks in there, feels fine, sits down and boom? No warning signs or nothing?'

'All I know is he'd been playing racquetball in the early morning, and seemed fine,' I said.

'You're kidding.' Marino's curiosity was insatiable. 'Now, I never heard that part. I didn't know he played racquetball.'

We drove through an industrialized area, with trains and trucks, then past campers for sale. Graceland stood in the midst of cheap motels and stores, and it did not seem so grand given its surroundings. The white mansion with its columns was completely out of place, like a joke or a set for a bad movie.

'Holy shit,' Marino said, as he pulled into the parking lot. 'Will you look at that. Holy smoke.'

He went on as if it were Buckingham Palace as he parked beside a bus.

'You know, I wish I could've known him,' he wistfully said.

'Maybe you would have, had he taken better care of himself.' I opened my door as he lit a cigarette.

For the next two hours, we wandered through gilt and mirrors, shag carpeting and stained-glass peacocks as the voice of Elvis followed us through his world. Hundreds of fans had arrived on buses, and their passion for this man was on their faces as they walked around listening to the tour on cassette. Many of them placed flowers, cards and letters on his grave. Some wept as if they had known him well.

We wandered around his purple and pink Cadillacs, Stutz Blackhawk and museum of other cars. There were his planes and shooting range, and the Hall of Gold, with Grammy showcases of gold and platinum records, and trophies and other awards that amazed even me. The hall was at least eighty feet long. I could not take my eyes off splendid costumes of gold and sequins, and photographs of what was truly an extraordinarily and sensuously beautiful human being. Marino was blatantly gawking, an almost pained expression on his face that reminded me of puppy love as we inched our way through rooms.

'You know, they didn't want him to move here when he bought this place,' he announced, and we were outside now, the fall afternoon cool and bright. 'Some of the snobs in this city never did accept him. I think that hurt him, in a way, might be what got him in the end. You know, why he took painkillers.'

'He took more than that,' I made the point again as we walked.

'If you had been the medical examiner, could you have done his autopsy?' He got out cigarettes.

'Absolutely.'

'And you wouldn't have covered his face?' He looked indignant as he fired up his lighter.

'Of course not.'

'Not me.' He shook his head, sucking in smoke. 'No friggin' way I'd even want to be in the room.'

'I wish he had been my case,' I said. 'I wouldn't have signed him out as a natural death. The world should know the truth, so maybe somebody else would think twice about popping Percodan.'

We were in front of one of the gift shops now, and people were gathered around televisions inside, watching Elvis videos. Through outdoor speakers, he was singing 'Kentucky Rain,' his voice powerful and playful, unlike any other I had ever heard in my life. I started walking again and told the truth.

'I am a fan and have a rather extensive collection of his CDs, if you really must know,' I said to Marino.

He couldn't believe it. He was thrilled.

'And I'd appreciate it if you didn't spread that around.'

'All these years I've known you, and you never told me?' he exclaimed. 'You're not kidding me, right? I never would've thought that. Not in a million years. Hey, so maybe now you know I got taste.'

This went on as we waited for a shuttle to return us to the parking lot, and then it continued in the car.

'I remember watching him on TV once when I was a kid in New Jersey,' Marino was saying. 'My old man came in drunk, as usual, started yelling at me to switch the channel. I'll never forget it.'

He slowed and turned into the Peabody Hotel.

'Elvis was singing "Hound Dog," July 1956. I remember it was my birthday. My father comes in, cussing, turns the TV off, and I get up and turn it back on. He smacks the side of my head, turns the TV off again. I turn it back on and walk toward him. First time in my life I ever laid a hand on him. I slam him against the wall, get in his face, tell the son of a bitch he ever touches me or my mother again, I'm going to kill him.'

'And did he?' I asked as the valet opened my door.

'Shit no.'

'Then Elvis should be thanked,' I said.

7

Two days later, on Thursday, November 6, I started out early on the ninety-minute drive from Richmond to the FBI Academy at Quantico, Virginia. Marino and I took separate cars, since we never knew when something might happen to send us off somewhere. For me, it could be a plane crash or derailed train, while he had to deal with city government and layers of brass. I wasn't surprised when my car phone rang as we neared Fredericksburg. The sun was in and out of clouds, and it felt cold enough to snow.

'Scarpetta,' I said, on speakerphone.

Marino's voice erupted inside my car. 'City council's freaking,' he said. 'You got McKuen whose little kid's been hit by a car, now more crap about our case, on TV, in the papers, hear it on the radio.'

More leaks had occurred over the past two days. Police had a suspect in serial murders that included five cases in Dublin. An arrest was imminent.

'You believe this shit?' Marino exclaimed. 'We're talking about, what? Someone in his mid-twenties, and somehow he was in Dublin over the past few years? Bottom line is council's suddenly decided to have some public forum about this situation, probably because they think it's about to be resolved. Got to get that credit, right, make the citizens think maybe they did something for once.' He was careful what he said, but seething. 'So I gotta turn my ass right back around and be at city hall by ten. Plus, the chief wants to see me.'

I watched his taillights up ahead as he approached an exit. I-95 was busy this morning with trucks, and people who commuted every day to D.C. No matter how early I started, whenever I headed north, it seemed traffic was terrible.

'Actually, it's a good thing you're going to be there. Cover my back, too,' I said to him. 'I'll get up with you later, let you know what went on.'

'Yo. When you see Ring, do that to his neck,' he said.

I arrived at the Academy, and the guard in his booth waved me through because by now he knew my car and its license plate. The parking lot was so full, I ended up almost in the woods. Firearms training was already in progress on ranges across the road, and Drug Enforcement Agents were out in camouflage, gripping assault rifles, their faces mean. The grass was heavy with dew and soaked my shoes as I took a shortcut to the main entrance of the tan brick building called Jefferson.

Inside the lobby, luggage was parked near couches and the walls, for there were always National Academy, or N.A., police going somewhere, it seemed. The video display over the front desk reminded everyone to have a nice day and properly display his badge. Mine was still in my purse, and I got it out, looping the long chain around my neck. Inserting a magnetized card into a slot, I unlocked a glass door etched with the Department of Justice seal and followed a long glass-enclosed corridor.

I was deep in thought and scarcely cognizant of new agents in dark blue and khaki, and N.A. students in green. They nodded and smiled as they passed, and I was friendly, too, but I did not focus. I was thinking of the torso, of her infirmities and age, of her pitiful pouch in the freezer, where she would stay for several years or until we knew her name. I thought of Keith Pleasants, of deadoc, of saws and sharp blades.

I smelled Hoppes solvent as I turned into the gun-cleaning room with its rows of black counters and compressors blasting air through the innards of guns. I could never smell these smells or hear these sounds without thinking of Wesley, and of Mark. My heart was squeezed by feelings too strong for me when a familiar voice called out my name.

'Looks like we're heading the same way,' said Investigator Ring.

Impeccably dressed in navy blue, he was waiting for the elevator that would take us sixty feet below ground, where Hoover had built his bomb shelter. I switched my heavy briefcase to my other hand, and tucked the box of slides more snugly under an arm.

'Good morning,' I blandly said.

'Here, let me help with some of that.'

He held out a hand as elevator doors parted, and I noticed his nails were buffed.

'I'm fine,' I said, because I didn't need his help.

We boarded, both of us staring straight ahead as we began the ride down to a windowless level of the building directly beneath the indoor firing range. Ring had sat in on consultations before, and he took copious notes, none of which had ended up in the news thus far. He was too clever for that. Certainly, if information divulged during an FBI consultation was leaked, it would be easy enough to trace. There were only a few of us who could be the source.

'I was rather dismayed by the information the press somehow got access to,' I said as we got out.

'I know what you mean,' Ring said with a sincere face.

He held open the door leading into a labyrinth of hallways that comprised what once had begun as Behavioral Science, then changed to Investigative Support, and now was CASKU. Names changed, but the cases did not. Men and women often came to work in the dark and left after it was dark again, spending days and years studying the minutiae of monsters, their every tooth mark and track in mud, the way they think and smell and hate.

'The more information that gets out the worse it is,' Ring went on as we approached another door, leading into a conference room where I spent at least several days a month. 'It's one thing to give details that might help the public help us . . .'

He talked on, but I wasn't listening. Inside, Wesley was already sitting at the head of a polished table, his reading glasses on. He was going through large photographs stamped on the back with the name of the Sussex County Sheriff's Department. Detective Grigg was several chairs away, a lot of paperwork in front of him as he studied a sketch of some sort. Across from him was Frankel from the Violent Criminal Apprehension Program, or VICAP, and at the other end of the table, my niece. She was tapping on a laptop computer, and glanced up at me but did not say hello.

I took my usual chair to the right of Wesley, opened my briefcase and began arranging files. Ring sat on the other side of me and continued our conversation.

'We got to accept as a fact that this guy is following everything in the news,' he said. 'That's part of the fun for him.'

He had everyone's attention, all eyes on him, the room silent except for his own sound. He was reasonable and quiet, as if his only mission was to convey the truth without drawing undue attention to himself. Ring was a superb con man, and what he said next in front of my colleagues incensed me beyond belief.

'For example, and I have to be honest about this,' he said to me, 'I just don't think it was a good idea to give out the race, age and all about the victim. Now maybe I'm wrong.' He looked around the room. 'But it seems like the less said, the better right now.'

'I had no choice,' I said, and I could not keep the edge out of my voice. 'Since someone had already leaked misinformation.'

'But that's always going to happen, and I don't think it should force us to give out details before we're ready,' he said in his same earnest tone.

'It is not going to help us if the public is focused on a missing prepubescent Asian female.' I stared at him, eye to eye, while everyone else looked on.

'I agree.' Frankel, from VICAP, spoke. 'We'd be getting missing person files from all over the country. An error like that has to be straightened out.'

'An error like that never should have happened to begin with,' Wesley said, peering around the room over the top of his glasses, the way he did when he was in a humorless mood. 'With us this morning is Detective Grigg of Sussex, and Special Agent Farinelli.' He looked at Lucy. 'She's the technical analyst for HRT, manages the Criminal Artificial Intelligence Network all of us know as CAIN, and is here to help us with a computer situation.'

My niece did not look up as she hit more keys, her face intense. Ring had her in his sights, staring as if he wanted to eat her flesh.

'What computer situation?' he asked, as his eyes continued to devour her.

'We'll get to that,' Wesley said, and briskly moved on. 'Let me summarize, then we'll move on to specifics. The victimology in this most recent landfill case is so different from the previous four – or nine, if we include Ireland – as for me to conclude that we are dealing with a different killer. Dr Scarpetta is going to review her medical findings which I think will make it abundantly clear that this M.O. is profoundly atypical.'

He went on, and we spent until midday going over my reports, diagrams and photographs. I was asked many questions, mostly by Grigg, who wanted very much to understand every facet and nuance of the serial dismemberments so he could better discern that the one in his jurisdiction was unlike the rest.

'What's the difference between someone cutting through joints and cutting through the bones?' he asked me.

'Cutting through joints is more difficult,' I said. 'It requires knowledge of anatomy, perhaps some previous experience.'

'Like if someone was a butcher or maybe worked in a meat-packing plant.'

'Yes,' I replied.

'Well, I guess that sure would fit with a meat saw,' he added.

'Yes. Which is very different from an autopsy saw.'

'Exactly how?' It was Ring who spoke.

'A meat saw is a hand saw designed to cut meat, gristle, bone,' I went on, looking around at everyone. 'Usually about fourteen inches long with a very thin blade, ten chisel-type teeth per inch. It's push action, requiring some degree of strength on the part of the user. The autopsy saw, in contrast, won't cut through tissue, which must first be reflected back with something like a knife.'

'Which was what was used in this case,' Wesley said to me.

'There are cuts to bone that fit the class characteristics of a knife. An autopsy saw,' I went on to explain, 'was designed to work only on hard surfaces by using a reciprocating action that is basically push-pull, going in only a little bit at a time. I know everyone here is familiar with it, but I've got photos.'

Opening an envelope, I pulled out eight-by-tens of the saw marks the killer had left on the bone ends I had carried to Memphis. I slid one to each person.

'As you can see,' I went on, 'the saw pattern here is multidirectional with a high polish.'

'Now let me get this straight,' said Grigg. 'This is the exact same saw you use in the morgue.'

'No. Not exactly the same,' I said. 'I generally use a larger sectioning blade than was used here.'

'But this is from a medical sort of saw.' He held up the photograph.

'Correct.'

'Where would your average person get something like that?'

'Doctor's office, hospital, morgue, medical supply company,' I replied. 'Any number of places. The sale of them is not restricted.'

'So he could have ordered it without being in the medical profession.'

'Easily,' I said.

Ring said, 'Or he could have stolen it. He could have decided to do something different this time to throw us off.'

Lucy was looking at him, and I had seen the expression in her eyes before. She thought Ring was a fool.

'If we're dealing with the same killer,' she said, 'then why is he suddenly sending files through the Internet when he's never done that before, either?'

'Good point.' Frankel nodded.

'What files?' Ring said to her.

'We're getting to that.' Wesley restored order. 'We've got an M.O. that's different. We've got a tool that's different.'

'We suspect she has a head injury,' I said, sliding autopsy diagrams and the e-mail photos around the table, 'because of blood in her airway. This may or may not be different from the other cases, since we don't know their causes of death. However, radiologic and anthropologic findings indicate that this victim is profoundly older than the others. We also recovered fibers indicating she was covered in something consistent with a drop cloth when she was dismembered, again, inconsistent with the other cases.'

I explained in more detail about the fibers and paint, all the while vividly aware of Ring watching my niece and taking notes.

'So she was probably cut up in someone's workshop or garage,' Grigg said.

'I don't know,' I answered. 'And as you've seen from the photos sent to me through e-mail, we can only know that she's in a room with putty-colored walls, and a table.'

'Let me again point out that Keith Pleasants has an area behind his house that he uses for a workshop,' Ring reminded us. 'It has a big workbench in it and the walls are unpainted wood.' He looked at me. 'Which could pass for putty-colored.'

'Seems like it would be awfully hard to get rid of all the blood,' Grigg dubiously mused.

'A drop cloth with a rubber backing might explain the absence of blood,' Ring said. 'That's the whole point. So nothing leaks through.'

Everyone looked at me to see what I would say.

'It would have been very unusual not to get things bloody in a case like this,' I replied. 'Especially since she still had a blood pressure when she was decapitated. If nothing else, I would expect blood in wood grain, in cracks of the table.'

'We could try some chemical testing for that.' Ring was a forensic scientist now. 'Like luminol. Any blood at all, it's going to react to it and glow in the dark.'

'The problem with luminol is it's destructive,' I replied. 'And we're going to want to do DNA, to see if we can get a match. So we certainly don't want to ruin what little blood we might find.'

'It's not like we got probable cause to go in Pleasants' workshop and start any kind of testing anyway.' Grigg's stare across the table at Ring was confrontational.

'I think we do.' He stared back at him.

'Not unless they changed the rules on me.' Grigg spoke slowly.

Wesley was watching all this, evaluating everyone and every word the way he always did. He had his opinion, and more than likely it was right. But he remained silent as the arguing went on.

'I thought . . .' Lucy tried to speak.

'A very viable possibility is that this is a copycat,' Ring said.

'Oh, I think it is,' said Grigg. 'I just don't buy your theory about Pleasants.'

'Let me finish.' Lucy's penetrating gaze scanned the faces of the men. 'I thought I would give you a briefing on how the two files were sent via America Online to Dr Scarpetta's e-mail address.'

It always sounded odd when she called me by my professional name.

'I know I'm curious.' Ring had his chin propped on a hand now, studying her.

'First, you would need a scanner,' she went on. 'That's not hard. Something with color capabilities and decent resolution, as low as seventy-two dots per inch. But this looks like higher resolution to me, maybe three hundred dpi. We could be talking about something as simple as a hand-held scanner for three hundred and ninety-nine dollars, to a thirty-five-millimeter slide scanner that can run into the thousands . . .'

'And what kind of computer would you hook this up to?' Ring said.

'I was getting to that.' Lucy was tired of being interrupted by him. 'System requirements: Minimum of eight megs RAM, a color monitor, software like Foto Touch or ScanMan, a modem. Could be a Macintosh, a Performa 6116CD or even something older. The point is, scanning files into your computer and sending them through the Internet is very accessible to your average person, which is why telecommunications crimes are keeping us so busy these days.'

'Like that big child pornography, pedophile case you all just cracked,' Grigg said.

'Yes, photos sent as files through the World Wide Web, where children can talk to strangers again,' she said. 'What's interesting in the situation at hand, is scanning black and white is no big deal. But when you move into color, that's getting sophisticated. Also the edges and borders in the photos sent to Dr Scarpetta are relatively sharp, not much background noise.'

'Sounds to me this is someone who knew what he was doing,' Grigg said.

'Yes,' she agreed. 'But not necessarily a computer analyst or graphic artist. Not at all.'

'These days, if you've got access to the equipment and a few instruction books, anyone can do it,' said Frankel, who also worked in computers.

'All right, the photos were scanned into the system,' I said to Lucy. 'Then what? What is the path that led them to me?'

'First you upload the file, which in this case is a graphic or GIF file,' she replied. 'Generally, to send this successfully, you have to determine the number of data bits, stop bits, the parity setting, whatever the appropriate configuration is. That's where it's not user-friendly. But AOL does all that for you. So in this case, sending the files was simple. You upload and off they go.' She looked at me.

'And this was done over the telephone, basically,' Wesley said.

'Right.'

'What about tracing that?'

'Squad Nineteen's already on it.' Lucy referred to the FBI unit that investigated illegal uses of the Internet.

'I'm not sure what the crime would be in this case,' Wesley pointed out. 'Obscenity, if the photos are fakes, and unfortunately, that isn't illegal.'

'The photographs aren't fake,' I said.

'Hard to prove.' He held my gaze.

'What if they're not fake?' Ring asked.

'Then they're evidence,' Wesley said, adding after a pause, 'A violation of Title Eighteen, Section Eight-seventy-six. Mailing threatening communications.'

'Threats towards who?' Ring asked.

Wesley's eyes were still on me. 'Clearly, towards the recipient.'

'There's been no blatant threat,' I reminded him.

'All we want is enough for a warrant.'

'We got to find the person first,' Ring said, stretching and yawning in his chair like a cat.

'We're watching for him to log on again,' Lucy replied. 'It's being monitored around the clock.' She continued hitting keys on her laptop, checking the constant flow of messages. 'But if you imagine a global telephone system with some forty million users, and no directory, no operators, no directory assistance, that's what you've got with the Internet. There's no list of membership, nor does AOL have one, unless you voluntarily choose to fill out a profile. In this case, all we have is the bogus name deadoc.'

'How did he know where to send Dr Scarpetta's mail?' Grigg looked at me.

I explained, and then asked Lucy, 'This is all done by charge card?'

She nodded. 'That much we've traced. An American Express Card in the name of Ken L. Perley. A retired high-school teacher. Norfolk. Seventy, lives alone.'

'Do we have any idea how someone might have gotten access to his card?' Wesley asked.

'It doesn't appear Perley uses his credit cards much. Last time was in a Norfolk restaurant, a Red Lobster. This was on October second, when he and his son went out to dinner. The bill was twenty-seven dollars and thirty cents, including the tip, which he put on AmEx. Neither he nor the son remembers anything unusual that night. But when it was time to pay the bill, the credit card was left on the table in plain view for quite a long interval because the restaurant was very busy. At some point while the card was out, Perley went to the men's room, and the son stepped outside to smoke.'

'Christ. That was intelligent. Did someone from the wait staff notice anyone coming over to the table?' Wesley said to Lucy.

'Like I said, it was busy. We're running down every charge made that night to get a list of customers. Problem's going to be the people who paid cash.'

'And I suppose it's too soon for the AOL charges to have come up on Perley's American Express,' he said.

'Right. According to AOL, the account was just opened recently. A week after the dinner at the Red Lobster, to be exact. Perley's being very cooperative with us,' Lucy added. 'And AOL is leaving the account open without charge in the event the perpetrator wants to send something else.'

Wesley nodded. 'Though we can't assume it, we should consider that the killer, at least in the Atlantic landfill case, may have been in Norfolk as recently as a month ago.'

'This case is definitely sounding local.' I made that point again.

'Possible any of the bodies could have been refrigerated?' Ring asked.

'Not this one,' Wesley was quick to answer. 'Absolutely not. This guy couldn't stand looking at his victim. He had to cover her up, cut through the cloth, and my guess is, didn't go very far away to dispose of her.'

'Shades of "The Tell-Tale Heart",' Ring said.

Lucy was reading something on her laptop screen, quietly hitting keys, her face tense. 'We just got something from Squad Nineteen,' she said, continuing to scroll down. 'Deadoc logged on fifty-six minutes ago.' She looked up at us. 'He sent e-mail to the president.'

The electronic mail was sent directly to the White House, which was no great feat since the address was public and readily available to any user of the Internet. Once again, the message was oddly in lower-case and used spaces for punctuation, and it read: *apologize if not I will start on france.*

'There are a number of implications,' Wesley was saying to me as gunshots from the range upstairs thudded like a distant, muffled war going on. 'And all of them make me nervous about you.'

He stopped at the water fountain.

'I don't think this has anything to do with me,' I said. 'This has to do with the president of the United States.'

'That's symbolic, if you want to know my guess. Not literal.' We started walking. 'I think this killer is disgruntled, angry, feels a certain person in power or perhaps people in power are responsible for his problems in life.'

'Like the Unabomber,' I said as we took the elevator up.

'Very similar. Perhaps even inspired by him,' he said, glancing at his watch. 'Can I buy you a beer before you leave?'

'Not unless someone else is driving.' I smiled. 'But you can talk me into coffee.'

We walked through the gun-cleaning room, where dozens of FBI and DEA agents were breaking down their weapons, wiping them and blasting parts with air. They glanced at us with curious eyes, and I wondered if they had heard the rumors. My relationship with Wesley had been an item of gossip for quite a long time at the Academy, and it bothered me more than I let on. Most people, it seemed, maintained their belief that his wife had left because of me when, in fact, she had left because of another man.

Upstairs, the line was long in the PX, a mannikin modeling the latest sweatshirt and range pants, and Thanksgiving pumpkins and turkeys in the windows. Beyond, in the Boardroom, the TV was loud, and some people were already into popcorn and beer. We sat as far away from everyone as we could, both of us sipping coffee.

'What's your slant on the France connection?' I asked.

'Obviously, this individual is intelligent and follows the news. Our relations with France were very strained during their nuclear weapons testing. You may recall the violence, vandalism, boycotting of French wine and other products. There was a lot of protesting outside French embassies, the U.S. very much involved.'

'But that was a couple years ago.'

'Doesn't matter. Wounds heal slowly.' He stared out the window at darkness gathering. 'And more to the point, France would not appreciate our exporting a serial killer to them. I can only suppose that is what deadoc is implying. Cops from France and other nations have been worrying for years that our problem would eventually become theirs. As if violence is a disease that can spread.'

'Which it is.'

He nodded, reaching for his coffee again.

'Maybe that would make more sense if we believed the same person killed ten people here and in Ireland,' I said.

'Kay, we can't rule out anything.' He sounded tired as he said that again.

I shook my head. 'He's taking credit for someone else's murders and now threatening us. He probably has no idea how different his M.O. is from what we've seen in the past. Of course, we can't rule out anything, Benton. But I know what my findings tell me, and I believe identifying this recent victim is going to be the key.'

'You always believe that.' He smiled, playing with his coffee stirrer.

'I know who I work for. Right this minute, I work for that poor woman whose torso is in my freezer.'

It was now completely dark out, the Boardroom filling fast with healthy, clean-living men and women in color-coded fatigues. The noise was making it difficult to talk, and I needed to see Lucy before I left.

'You don't like Ring.' Wesley reached around to the back of his chair and collected his suit jacket. 'He's bright and seems sincerely motivated.'

'You definitely profiled the last part wrong,' I said as I got up. 'But you are right about what you said first. I don't like him.'

'I thought that was rather obvious by your demeanor.'

We moved around people who were looking for chairs and setting down pitchers of beer.

'I think he's dangerous.'

'He's vain and wants to make a name for himself,' Wesley said.

'And you don't think that's dangerous?' I looked over at him.

'It describes almost everyone I've ever worked with.'

'Except for me, I hope.'

'You, Dr Scarpetta, are an exception to just about everything I can think of.'

We were walking through a long corridor, heading to the lobby, and I did not want to leave him right now. I felt lonely and wasn't sure why.

'I would love for us to have dinner,' I said, 'but Lucy's got something to show me.'

'What makes you think I don't already have plans?' He held the door for me.

The thought bothered me, even though I knew he was teasing.

'Let's wait until I can get away from here,' he said, and we were walking toward the parking lot now. 'Maybe over the weekend, when we can relax a little more. I'll cook this time. Where are you parked?'

'Over here.' I pointed the key's remote control.

Doors unlocked and the interior light went on. Typically, we did not touch. We never had when someone might see.

'Sometimes I hate this,' I said as I got into my car. 'It's fine to talk about body parts, rape and murder all day long, but not to hug each other, hold hands. God forbid anybody should see that.' I started the engine. 'Tell me how normal that is? It's not like we're still having an affair or committing a crime.' I yanked my seatbelt across my chest. 'Is there some don't-ask-don't-tell FBI rule no one's let me in on?'

'Yes.'

He kissed me on the lips as a group of agents walked by.

'So don't tell anyone,' he said.

Moments later, I parked in front of the Engineering Research Facility, or ERF, a huge, space age-looking building where the FBI conducted its classified technical research and development. If Lucy knew all of what went on in the labs here, she did not tell, and there were few areas of the building where I was allowed, even when escorted by her. She was waiting by the front door as I pointed the remote control at my car, which was not responding.

'It won't work here,' she said.

I looked up at the eerie rooftop of antennae and satellite dishes, sighing as I manually locked doors with the key.

'You'd think I'd remember after all these times,' I muttered.

'Your investigator friend, Ring, tried to walk me over here after the consultation,' she said, scanning her thumb in a biometric lock by the door.

'He's not my friend,' I told her.

The lobby was high-ceilinged and arranged with glass cases displaying clunky, inefficient radio and electronic equipment used by law enforcement before ERF was built.

'He asked me out again,' she said.

Corridors were monochromatic and seemed endless, and I was forever impressed with the silence and sense that no one was here. Scientists and engineers worked behind shut doors in spaces big enough to accommodate automobiles, helicopters and small planes. Hundreds of Bureau personnel were employed at ERF, yet they had virtually no contact with any of us across the street. We did not know their names.

'I'm sure there are a million people who would like to ask you out,' I said as we boarded an elevator, and Lucy scanned her thumb again.

'Usually, not after they've been around me very long,' she said.

'I don't know, I haven't gotten rid of you yet.'

But she was very serious. 'Once I start talking shop, the guys turn off. But he likes a challenge, if you know the type.'

'I know it all too well.'

'He wants something from me, Aunt Kay.'

'Would you like to hazard a guess? And where are you taking me, by the way?'

'I don't know. But I just have this feeling.' She opened a door to the virtual environment lab, adding, 'I have a rather interesting idea.'

Lucy's ideas were always more than interesting. Usually they were frightening. I followed her into a room of virtual system processors and graphic computers stacked on top of each other, and countertops scattered with tools, computer boards, chips and peripherals like DataGloves and helmet-mounted displays. Electrical cords were bundled in thick hanks and tied back from the blank expanse of linoleum flooring where Lucy routinely lost herself in cyberspace.

She picked up a remote control and two video displays blinked on, and I recognized the photographs deadoc had sent to me. They were big and in color on the screens, and I began to get nervous.

'What are you doing?' I asked my niece.

'The basic question has always been, does an immersion into an environment actually improve the operator's performance,' she said, typing computer commands. 'You never got a chance to be immersed in this environment. The crime scene.'

Both of us stared at the bloody stumps and lined-up body parts on the monitors, and a chill crept through me.

'But suppose you could have that chance now?' Lucy went on. 'What if you could be inside deadoc's room?'

I started to interrupt, but she would not let me.

'What else might you see? What else might you do?' she said, and when she got like this, she was almost manic. 'What else might you learn about the victim and him?'

'I don't know if I can use something like this,' I protested.

'Sure you can. Now what I haven't had time to do is add the synthetic sound. Well, except for the typical canned auditory cues. So a squelch is something opening, a click's a switch being turned on or off, a ding usually means you've just bumped into something.'

'Lucy,' I said as she took my left arm, 'what the hell are you talking about?'

She carefully pulled a DataGlove over my left hand, making sure it was snug.

'We use gestures for human communication. And we can use gestures, or positions as we call them, to communicate with the computer, too,' she explained.

The glove was black lycra with fiber-optic sensors mounted on the back of it. These were attached to a cable that led to the high-performance host computer that Lucy had been typing on. Next she picked up a helmet-mounted display that was connected to another cable, and fear fluttered through my breast as she headed my way.

'One VPL Eyephone HRX,' she cheerfully said. 'Same thing they're using at NASA's Ames Research Center, which is where I discovered it.' She was adjusting cables and straps. 'Three hundred and fifty thousand color elements. Superior resolution and wide field of vision.'

She placed the helmet on top of my head, and it felt heavy and covered my eyes.

'What you're looking into are liquid crystal displays, or LCDs, your basic video displays. Glass plates, electrodes and molecules doing all kinds of cool things. How does it feel?'

'Like I'm going to fall down and suffocate.'

I was beginning to panic the way I had when I'd first learned how to scuba dive.

'You're not going to do either.' She was very patient, her hand steadying me. 'Relax. It's normal to be phobic at first. I'll tell you what to do. Now you stand still and take deep breaths. I'm going to put you in.'

She made adjustments, tightening the display around my head, then returned to the host computer. I was blind and off balance, a tiny TV in front of each eye.

'Okay, here we go,' she said. 'Don't know if it will do any good, but can't hurt to try.'

Keys clicked, and I was thrown inside that room. She began instructing me about what to do with my hand to fly forward or faster, or in reverse, and how to release and grab. I moved my index finger, made clicking motions, brought my thumb near my palm and moved my arm across my chest as I broke out in a sweat. I spent a good five minutes on the ceiling and walking into walls. At one point, I was on top of the table where the torso lay on its bloody blue cover, stepping on evidence and the dead.

'I think I might throw up,' I said.

'Just hold still for a minute,' Lucy said. 'Catch your breath.'

I gestured as I started to say something more, and was instantly on the virtual floor, as if I had fallen from the air.

'That's why I told you to hold still,' she said as she watched what I was doing on the monitors. 'Now move your hand in and point with your first two fingers toward where you hear my voice coming from. Better?'

'Better,' I said.

I was standing on the floor in the room, as if the photograph had come to life, three-dimensional and large. I looked around and did not actually see anything I hadn't before when Vander had done the image enhancement. It was what this made me feel, and what I felt changed what I saw.

Walls were the color of putty, with faint discolorations that until now I had attributed to water damage, which might be expected in a basement or garage. But they seemed different now, more uniformly distributed, some so faint I could barely see them. Paper had once covered the putty paint on these walls. It had been removed but not replaced, as had the cornice box or drapery rod. Above a window covered with shut Venetian blinds were small holes where brackets once had been.

'This isn't where it happened,' I said as my heart beat harder.

Lucy was silent.

'She was brought in here after the fact to be photographed. This is not where the killing and dismemberment took place.'

'What are you seeing?' she asked.

I moved my hand and walked closer to the virtual table. I pointed at the virtual walls, to show Lucy what I saw. 'Where did he plug in the autopsy saw?' I said.

I could find but one electrical outlet, and it was at the base of a wall.

'And the drop cloth is from here, too?' I went on. 'It doesn't fit with everything else. No paint, no tools.' I kept looking around. 'And look at the floor. The wood's lighter at the border as if there once was a rug. Who puts rugs in workshops? Who has wallpaper and drapes? Where are the outlets for power tools?'

'What do you feel?' she asked.

'I feel this is a room in someone's house where the furniture has been removed. Except there is some sort of table, which has been covered with something. Maybe a shower curtain. I don't know. The room feels domestic.'

I reached out my hand and tried to touch the edge of the table cover, as if I could lift it and reveal what was underneath, and as I looked around, details became so clear to me, I wondered how I could have missed them before. Wiring was exposed in the ceiling directly above the table, as if a chandelier or other type of light fixture had once hung there.

'What about my color perception right now?' I asked.

'Should be the same.'

'Then there's something else. These walls.' I touched them. 'The color lightens in this direction. There's an opening. Maybe a doorway, with light coming through it.'

'There's no doorway in the photo,' Lucy reminded me. 'You can only see what's there.'

It was odd, but for a moment I thought I could smell her blood, the pungency of old flesh that has been dead for days. I remembered the doughy texture of her skin, and the peculiar eruptions that made me wonder if she had shingles.

'She wasn't random,' I said.

'And the others were.'

'The other cases are nothing like this one. I'm getting double imagery. Can you adjust that?'

'Vertical retinal image disparity.'

Then I felt her hand on my arm.

'Usually goes away after fifteen or twenty minutes,' she said. 'It's time to take a break.'

'I don't feel too good.'

'Image rotation misalignment. Visual fatigue, simulation sickness, cybersick, whatever you want to call it,' she said. 'Causing image blurring, tears, even queasiness.'

I couldn't wait to remove the helmet and I was on the table again, facedown in blood before I could get the LCDs away from my eyes.

My hands were shaking as Lucy helped me take off the glove. I sat down on the floor.

'Are you all right?' she asked, kindly.

'That was awful,' I said.

'Then it was good.' She returned the helmet and glove to a counter. 'You were immersed in the environment. That's what should happen.'

She handed me several tissues, and I wiped my face.

'What about the other photograph? Do you want to do that one, too?' she asked. 'The one with the hands and feet?'

'I've been in that room quite enough,' I said.

8

————

I drove home haunted. I had been going to crime scenes most of my professional life, but had never had one come to me. The sensation of being inside that photograph, of imagining I could smell and feel what was left of that body, had shaken me badly. It was almost midnight by the time I pulled into my garage, and I couldn't unlock my door fast enough. Inside my house, I turned the alarm off, then back on the instant I shut and locked the door. I looked around to make sure nothing was out of place.

Lighting a fire, I fixed a drink and missed cigarettes again. I turned on music to keep me company, then went inside my office to see what might await me there. I had various faxes and phone messages, and another communication in e-mail. This time, all deadoc had for me was to repeat, *you think you re so smart*. I was printing this and wondering if Squad 19 had seen it, too, when the telephone rang, startling me.

'Hi,' Wesley said. 'Just making sure you got in okay.'

'There's more mail,' I said, and I told him what it was.

'Save it and go to bed.'

'It's hard not to think about.'

'He wants you to stay up all night thinking. That's his power. That's his game.'

'Why me?' I was out of sorts and still felt queasy.

'Because you're the challenge, Kay. Even for nice people like me. Go to sleep. We'll talk tomorrow. I love you.'

But I did not get to sleep long. At several minutes past four A.M., my phone rang again. It was Dr Hoyt this time, a family practitioner in Norfolk, where he had served as a state-appointed medical examiner for the last twenty years. He was pushing seventy, but spry and as lucid as new glass. I'd never known him to be alarmed by anything, and I was instantly unnerved by his tone.

'Dr Scarpetta, I'm sorry,' he said, and he was talking very fast. 'I'm on Tangier Island.'

All I could think of, oddly, were crab cakes. 'What in the world are you doing there?'

I arranged pillows behind me, reaching for call sheets and pen.

'I got called late yesterday, been out here half the night. The Coast Guard had to bring me in one of their cutters, and I don't like boats worth a damn, beaten and whipped around worse than eggs. Plus it was cold as hell.'

I had no idea what he was talking about.

'The last time I saw anything like this was Texas, 1949,' he went on, talking fast, 'when I was doing my residency and about to get married . . .'

I had to cut him off. 'Slow down, Fred,' I said. 'Tell me what's happened.'

'A fifty-two-year-old Tangier lady. Probably been dead at least twenty-four hours in her bedroom. She's got severe skin eruptions in crops, just covered with them, including the palms of her hands and the bottoms of her feet. Crazy as it sounds, it looks like smallpox.'

'You're right. That's crazy,' I said as my mouth got dry. 'What about chicken pox? Any way this woman was immunosuppressed?'

'I don't know anything about her, but I've never seen chicken pox look like this. These eruptions follow the smallpox pattern. They're in crops, like I said, all about the same age, and the farther away from the center of the body, the denser they get. So they're confluent, on the face, the extremities.'

I was thinking of the torso, of the small area of eruptions that I had assumed were shingles, my heart filled with dread. I did not know where that victim had died, but I believed it was somewhere in Virginia. Tangier Island was also in Virginia, a tiny barrier island in the Chesapeake Bay where the economy was based on crabbing.

'There are a lot of strange viruses out there these days,' he was saying.

'Yes, there are,' I agreed. 'But Hanta, Ebola, HIV, dengue, et al., do not cause the symptoms you have described. That doesn't mean there isn't something else we don't know about.'

'I know smallpox. I'm old enough to have seen it with my own two eyes. But I'm not an expert in infectious diseases, Kay. And I sure as hell don't know the things that you do. But whatever it might be in this case, the fact is, the woman's dead and some type of poxvirus killed her.'

'Obviously, she lived alone.'

'Yes.'

'And she was last seen alive when?'

'The chief's working on that.'

'What chief?' I said.

'The Tangier police department has one officer. He's the chief. I'm in his trailer now, using the phone.'

'He's not overhearing this.'

'No, no. He's out talking to neighbors. I did my best to get information, without a whole lot of luck. You ever been out here?'

'No, I haven't.'

'Let's just say they don't exactly rotate their crops. There are maybe three family names on the whole island. Most folks grow up here, never leave. It's mighty hard to understand a word they're saying. Now that's a dialect you won't hear in any other corner of the world.'

'Nobody touches her until I have a better idea what we're dealing with,' I said, unbuttoning my pajamas.

'What do you want me to do?' he asked.

'Get the police chief to guard the house. No one goes in or near it until I say. Go home. I'll call you later in the day.'

The labs had not completed microbiology on the torso, and now I could not wait. I dressed in a hurry, fumbling with everything I touched, as if my motor skills had completely left me. I sped downtown on streets that were deserted, and at close to five was parking in my space behind the morgue. As I let myself into the bay, I startled the night security guard and he startled me.

'Lord have mercy, Dr Scarpetta,' said Evans, who had watched over the building for as long as I had been here.

'Sorry,' I said, my heart thudding. 'I didn't mean to frighten you.'

'Just making my rounds. Is everything all right?'

'I sure hope so.' I went past him.

'Is something coming in?'

He followed me up the ramp. I opened the door leading inside, and looked at him.

'Nothing I know of,' I replied.

Now he was completely confused, for he did not understand why

I was here at this hour if no case was coming in. He started shaking his head as he headed back toward the door leading out into the parking lot. From there, he would go next door to the lobby of the Consolidated Labs, where he would sit watching a small, flickering TV until it was time to make his rounds again. Evans would not step foot into the morgue. He did not understand how anyone could, and I knew he was scared of me.

'I won't be down here long,' I told him. 'Then I'll be upstairs.'

'Yes, ma'am,' he said, still shaking his head. 'You know where I'll be.'

Midway along the corridor in the autopsy suite was a room not often entered, and I stopped there first, unlocking the door. Inside were three freezers unlike any normally seen. They were stainless steel and oversized, with temperatures digitally displayed on doors. On each was a list of case numbers, indicating the unidentified people inside.

I opened a door and thick fog rolled out as frigid air bit my face. She was in a pouch, and on a tray, and I put on gown, gloves, face shield, every layer of protection we had. I knew I might already be in trouble, and the thought of Wingo and his vulnerable condition thrilled me with fear as I slid out the pouch and lifted it onto a stainless steel table in the middle of the room. Unzipping black vinyl, I exposed the torso to ambient air, and I went out and unlocked the autopsy suite.

Collecting a scalpel and clean glass slides, I pulled the surgical mask back down over my nose and mouth, and returned to the freezer room, shutting the door. The torso's outer layer of skin was moist as thawing began, and I used warm, wet towels to speed that along before unroofing vesicles, or the eruptions clustered over her hip and at the ragged margins of the amputations.

With the scalpel, I scraped vesicular beds, and made smears on the slides. I zipped up the pouch, marking it with blaze orange biological hazard tags, almost could not lift the body back up to its frigid shelf, my arms trembling under the strain. There was no one to call for help but Evans, so I managed on my own, and placed more warnings on the door.

I headed upstairs to the third floor, and unlocked a small lab that would have looked like most were it not for various instruments used only in the microscopic study of tissue, or histology. On a counter was a tissue processor, which fixed and dehydrated samples such as liver, kidney, spleen, and then infiltrated them with paraffin. From there the blocks went to the embedding center, and on to the micro-tome where they were shaved into thin ribbons. The end product was what kept me bent over my microscope downstairs.

While slides air-dried, I rooted around shelves, moving aside stains of bright orange, blue and pink in coplin jars, pulling out Gram's iodine for bacteria. Oil Red for fat in liver, silver nitrate, Biebrach Scarlet and Acridine Orange, as I thought about Tangier Island, where I'd never had a case before. Nor was there much crime, so I had been told, only drunkenness, which was common with men alone at sea. I thought of blue crab again, and irrationally wished Bev had sold me rock fish or tuna.

Finding the bottle of Nicolaou stain, I dipped in an eye dropper and carefully dripped a tiny amount of the red fluid on each slide, then finished with cover slips. These I secured in a sturdy cardboard folder, and I headed downstairs to my floor. By now, people were beginning to arrive for work, and they gave me odd looks as I came down the hall and boarded the elevator in scrubs, mask and gloves. In my office, Rose was collecting dirty coffee mugs off my desk. She froze at the sight of me.

'Dr Scarpetta?' she said. 'What in the world is going on?'

'I'm not sure, but I hope nothing,' I replied as I sat at my desk and took the cover off my microscope.

She stood in the doorway, watching as I placed a slide on the stage. She knew by my mood, if by nothing else, that something was very wrong.

'What can I do to help,' she said in a grim, quiet way.

The smear on the slide came into focus, magnified four hundred and fifty times, and then I applied a drop of oil. I stared at waves of bright red eosinophilic inclusions within infected epithelial cells, or the cytoplasmic Guarnieri bodies indicative of a pox-type virus. I fitted a Polaroid MicroCam to the microscope, and took instant high-resolution color photographs of what I suspected would have cruelly killed the old woman anyway. Death had given her no humane choice, but had it been me, I would have chosen a gun or a blade.

'Check MCV, see if Phyllis has gotten in,' I said to Rose. 'Tell her the sample I sent on Saturday can't wait.'

Within the hour, Rose had dropped me off at Eleventh and Marshall Streets, at the Medical College of Virginia, or MCV, where I had done my forensic pathology residency when I wasn't much older than the students I now advised and presented gross conferences to throughout the year. Sanger Hall was sixties architecture, with a facade of garish bright blue tiles that could be spotted for miles. I got on an elevator packed with other doctors I knew, and students who feared them.

'Good morning.'

'You, too. Teaching a class?'

I shook my head, surrounded by lab coats. 'Need to borrow your TEM.'

'You hear about the autopsy we had downstairs the other day?' a pulmonary specialist said to me as doors parted. 'Mineral dust pneumoconiosis. Berylliosis, specifically. How often you ever see that around here?'

On the fifth floor, I walked quickly to the Pathology Electron Microscopy Lab, which housed the only transmission electron microscope, or TEM, in the city. Typically, carts and countertops had not an inch of room to spare, crowded with photo and light microscopes, and other esoteric instruments for analyzing cell sizes, and coating specimens with carbon for X-ray microanalysis.

As a rule, TEM was reserved for the living, most often used in renal biopsies and specific tumors, and viruses rarely, and autopsy specimens almost never. In terms of my ongoing needs and patients already dead, it was difficult to get scientists and physicians very excited when hospital beds were filled with people awaiting word that might grant them a reprieve from a tragic end. So I never prodded microbiologist Dr Phyllis Crowder into instant action on the occasions I had needed her in the past. She knew this was different.

From the hall, I recognized her British accent as she talked on the phone.

'I know. I understand that,' she was saying as I knocked on the open door. 'But you're either going to have to reschedule or go on without me. Something else has come up.' She smiled, motioning me in.

I had known her during my residency days, and had always believed that kind words from faculty like her had everything to do with why I had come to mind when the chief's position had opened in Virginia. She was close to my age and had never married, her short hair the same dark gray as her eyes, and she always wore the same gold cross necklace that looked antique. Her parents were American, but she had been born in England, which was where she had trained and worked in her first lab.

'Bloody meetings,' she complained as she got off the phone. 'There's nothing I hate more. People sitting around talking instead of doing.'

She pulled gloves from a box and handed a pair to me. This was followed by a mask.

'There's an extra lab coat on the back of the door,' she added.

I followed her into the small, dark room, where she had been at work before the phone had rung. Slipping on the lab coat, I found a chair as she peered into a green phosphorescent screen inside the huge viewing chamber. The TEM looked more like an instrument for oceanography or astronomy than a normal microscope. The chamber always reminded me of the dive helmet of a dry suit through which one could see eerie, ghostly images in an iridescent sea.

Through a thick metal cylinder called the scope, running from the chamber to the ceiling, a hundred-thousand-volt beam was striking my specimen, which in this case was liver that had been shaved to a thickness of six or seven one-hundredths of a micron. Smears like the ones I had viewed with my light microscope were simply too thick for the electron beam to pass through.

Knowing this at autopsy, I had fixed liver and spleen sections in glutaraldehyde, which penetrated tissue very rapidly. These I had sent to Crowder, who I knew would eventually have them embedded in plastic and cut on the ultramicrotome, then the diamond knife, before being mounted on a tiny copper grid and stained with uranium and lead ions.

What neither of us had expected was what we were looking at now, as we peered into the chamber at the green shadow of a specimen magnified almost one hundred thousand times. Knobs clicked as she adjusted intensity, contrast and magnification. I looked at DNA double-stranded, brick-shaped virus particles, two hundred to two hundred and fifty nanometers in size. I stared without blinking at smallpox.

'What do you think?' I said, hoping she would prove me wrong.

'Without a doubt, it's some type of poxvirus,' she hedged her bets. 'The question is which one. The fact that the eruptions didn't follow any nerve pattern. The fact that chicken pox is uncommon in someone this old. The fact that you may now have another case with these same manifestations causes me great concern. Other tests need to be done, but I'd treat this as a medical crisis.' She looked at me. 'An international emergency. I'd call CDC.'

'That's just what I'm going to do,' I replied, swallowing hard.

'What sense do you make of this being associated with a dismembered body?' she asked, making more adjustments as she peered into the chamber.

'I can make no sense of it,' I said, getting up and feeling weak. 'Serial killers here, in Ireland, raping, chopping people up.' I looked at her.

She sighed. 'You ever wish you'd stayed with hospital pathology?'

'The killers you deal with are just harder to see,' I replied.

The only way to get to Tangier Island was by water or air. Since there wasn't a huge tourist business there, ferries were few and did not run after mid-October. Then one had to drive to Crisfield, Maryland, or in my case, go eighty-five miles to Reedville, where the Coast Guard was to pick me up. I left the office as most people were thinking about lunch. The afternoon was raw, the sky cloudy with a strong cold wind.

I had left instructions for Rose to call the Center for Disease Control and Prevention (CDC) in Atlanta, because every time I had tried, I was put on hold. She was also to reach Marino and Wesley and let them know where I was going and that I would call as soon as I could. I took 64 East to 360, and soon found myself in farmland.

Fields were brown with fallow corn, hawks dipping and soaring in a part of the world where Baptist churches had names like *Faith, Victory* and *Zion*. Trees wore kudzu like chain mail, and across the Rappahannock River, in the Northern Neck, homes were sprawling old manors that the present-generation owners couldn't afford anymore. I passed more fields and crepe myrtles, and then the Northumberland Courthouse that had been built before the Civil War.

In Heathsville were cemeteries with plastic flowers and cared-for plots, and an occasional painted anchor in a yard. I turned off through woods dense with pines, passing cornfields so close to the narrow road, I could have reached out my window to touch brown stalks. At Buzzard's Point Marina, sailboats were moored and the red, white and blue tour boat, *Chesapeake Breeze*, was going nowhere until spring. I had no trouble parking, and there was no one in the ticket booth to ask me for a dime.

Waiting for me at the dock was a white Coast Guard boat. Guardsmen wore bright orange and blue antiexposure coveralls, known as mustang suits, and one of the men was climbing up on the pier. He was more senior than the others, with dark eyes and hair, and a nine-millimeter Beretta on his hip.

'Dr Scarpetta?' He carried his authority easily, but it was there.

'Yes,' I said, and I had several bags, including a heavy hard case containing my microscope and MicroCam.

'Let me help with those.' He held out his hand. 'I'm Ron Martinez, the station chief at Crisfield.'

'Thanks. I really appreciate this,' I said.

'Hey, so do we.'

The gap between the pier and the forty-foot patrol boat yawned and narrowed as the surge pushed the boat against the pier. Grabbing the rail, I boarded. Martinez went down a steep ladder, and I followed him into a hold packed with rescue equipment, fire hoses and huge coils of rope, the air heavy with diesel fumes. He tucked my belongings in a secure spot and tied them down. Then he handed me a mustang suit, life vest and gloves.

'You're going to need to put these on, in case you go in. Not a pretty thought but it can happen. The water's maybe in the fifties.' His eyes lingered on me. 'You might want to stay down here,' he added as the boat knocked against the pier.

'I don't get seasick but I am claustrophobic,' I told him as I sat on a narrow ledge and took off my boots.

'Wherever you want, but it's gonna be rough.'

He climbed back up as I began struggling into the suit, which was an exercise in zippers and Velcro, and filled with polyvinyl chloride to keep me alive a little longer should the boat capsize. I put my boots back on, then the life vest, with its knife and whistle, signal mirror and flares. I climbed back up to the cabin because there was no way I was going to stay down there. The crew shut the engine cover on deck, and Martinez strapped himself into the pilot's chair.

'Wind's blowing out of the northwest at twenty-two knots,' a guardsman said. 'Waves cresting at four feet.'

Martinez began pulling away from the pier. 'That's the problem with the bay,' he said to me. 'The waves are too close together so you never get a good rhythm like you do at sea. I'm sure you're aware that we could get diverted. There's no other patrol boat out, so something goes down out here, there's no one but us.'

We began slowly passing old homes with widow's walks and bowling greens.

'Someone needs rescuing, we got to go,' he went on as a member of the crew checked instruments.

I watched a fishing boat go past, an old man in hip-high boots standing as he steered the outboard motor. He stared at us as if we were poison.

'So you could end up on anything.' Martinez enjoyed making this point.

'It wouldn't be the first time,' I said as I began to detect a very revolting smell.

'But one way or another, we'll get you there, like we did the other doctor. Never did get his name. How long have you worked for him?'

'Dr Hoyt and I go way back,' I said blandly.

Ahead were rusting fisheries with rising smoke, and as we got close I could see moving conveyor belts tilted steeply toward the sky, carrying millions of menhaden in to be processed for fertilizer and oil. Gulls circled and waited greedily from pilings, watching the tiny, stinking fish go by as we passed other factories that were ruins of brick crumbling into the creek. The stench now was unbearable, and I was certainly more stoical than most.

'Cat food,' a guardsman said, making a face.

'Talk about cat breath.'

'No way I'd live around here.'

'Fish oil's real valuable. The Algonquin Indians used cogies to fertilize their corn.'

'What the hell's a cogy?' Martinez asked.

'Another name for those nasty little suckers. Where'd you go to school?'

'Doesn't matter. Least I don't got to smell that for a living. Unless I'm out here with a schleps like you.'

'What the hell's a schlep?'

The banter continued as Martinez pushed the throttle up more, engines rumbling, bow dipping. We sailed by duck blinds and floats marking crab pots as rainbows followed in the spray of our wake. He pushed the speed up to twenty-three knots and we cut into the deep blue water of the bay, where no pleasure boats were out this day, only an ocean liner a dark mountain on the horizon.

'How far is it?' I asked Martinez, hanging on to the back of his chair, and grateful for my suit.

'Eighteen miles total.' He raised his voice, riding waves like a surfer, sliding in sideways and over, his eyes always ahead. 'Ordinarily, it wouldn't take long. But this is worse than usual. A lot worse, really.'

His crew continued checking depth and direction detectors as the GPS pointed the way by satellite. I could see nothing but water now, moguls rising in front, and behind, waves clapping hard like hands as the bay attacked us from all sides.

'What can you tell me about where we're going?' I almost had to shout.

'Population of about seven hundred. Until about twenty years ago they generated their own electricity, got one small airstrip made of dredge material. Damn.' The boat slammed down hard in a trough. 'Almost broached that one. That'll turn you over in a flash.'

His face was intense as he rode the bay like a bronco, his crewmen unfazed but alert as they held on to whatever they could.

'Economy's based on blue crabs, soft-shell crabs, ship 'em all over the country,' Martinez went on. 'In fact, rich folks fly private planes in all the time just to buy crabs.'

'Or that's what they say they're buying,' someone remarked.

'We do have a problem with drunkenness, bootlegging, drugs,' Martinez went on. 'We board their boats when we're checking for life jackets, doing drug interdictions, and they call it being *overhauled.*' He smiled at me.

'Yeah, and we're *the guards,*' a guardsman quipped. 'Look out, here come *the guards.*'

'They use language any way they want,' Martinez said, rolling over another wave. 'You may have a problem understanding them.'

'When does crab season end?' I asked, and I was more concerned about what was being exported than I was about the way Tangiermen talked.

'This time of year they're dredging, dragging the bottom for crabs. They'll do that all winter, working fourteen, fifteen hours a day, sometimes gone a week at a time.'

Starboard, in the distance, a dark hulk protruded from the water like a whale. A crewman caught me looking.

'World War Two Liberty ship that ran aground,' he said. 'Navy uses it for target practice.'

At last, we were slowing as we approached the western shore, where a bulkhead had been built of rocks, shattered boats, rusting refrigerators, cars and other junk, to stop the island from eroding more. Land was almost level with the bay, only feet above sea level at its highest ground. Homes, a church steeple and a blue water tower were proud on the horizon on this tiny, barren island where people endured the worst weather with the least beneath their feet.

We chugged slowly past marshes and tidal flats. Old gap-toothed piers were piled high with crab pots made of chicken wire and strung with colored floats, and battle-scarred wooden boats with round and boxy sterns were moored but not idle. Martinez whelped his horn, and the sound ripped the air as we came through. Tangiermen with bibs turned expressionless, raw faces on us, the way people do when they have private opinions that aren't always friendly. They moved about in their crab shanties and worked on their nets as we docked near fuel pumps.

'Like most everybody else here, the chief's name is Crockett,' Martinez said as his crew tied us down. 'Davy Crockett. Don't laugh.' His eyes searched the pier and a snack bar that didn't look open this time of year. 'Come on.'

I followed him out of the boat, and wind blowing off the water felt as cold as January. We hadn't gone far when a small pickup truck quickly rounded a corner, tires loud on gravel. It stopped, and a tense young man got out. His uniform was blue jeans, a dark winter jacket and a cap that said *Tangier Police*, and his eyes darted back and forth between Martinez and me. He stared at what I was carrying.

'Okay,' Martinez said to me. 'I'll leave you with Davy.' To Crockett, he added, 'This is Dr Scarpetta.'

Crockett nodded. 'Y'all come on.'

'It's just the lady who's going.'

'I'll ride you to there.'

I had heard his dialect before in unspoiled mountain coves where people really are not of this century.

'We'll be waiting for you here,' Martinez promised me, walking off to his boat.

I followed Crockett to his truck. I could tell he cleaned it inside and out maybe once a day, and liked Armor All even more than Marino did.

'I assume you've been inside the house,' I said to him as he cranked the engine.

'I haven't. Was a neighbor that did. And when I was noticed about it, I called for Norfolk.'

He began to back up, a pewter cross swinging from the key chain. I looked out the window at small white frame restaurants with hand-painted signs and plastic seagulls hanging in windows. A truck hauling crab pots was coming the other way and had to pull over to let us pass. People were out on bicycles that had neither hand brakes nor gears, and the favorite mode of travel seemed to be scooters.

'What is the decedent's name?' I began taking notes.

'Lila Pruitt,' he said, unmindful that my door was almost touching someone's chain link fence. 'Widder lady, don't know how aged. Sold receipts for the tourists. Crab cakes and things.'

I wrote this down, not sure what he was saying as he drove me past the Tangier Combined School, and a cemetery. Headstones leaned every way, as if they had been caught in a gale.

'What about when she was last seen alive?' I asked.

'In Daby's, she was.' He nodded. 'Oh, maybe June.'

Now I was hopelessly lost. 'I'm sorry,' I said. 'She was last seen in some place called Daby's way back in June?'

'Yes'em.' He nodded as if this made all the sense in the world.

'What is Daby's and who saw her there?'

'The store. Daby's and Son. I can get you to it.' He shot me a look, and I shook my head. 'I was in it for shopping and saw her. June, I think.'

His strange syllables and cadences sprung, tongued and rolled over each other like the water of his world. There was *thur*, can't was *cain't*, things was *thoings*, do was *doie*.

'What about her neighbors? Have any of them seen her?' I asked.

'Not since days.'

'Then who found her?' I asked.

'No one did.'

I looked at him in despair.

'Just Mrs Bradshaw come in for a receipt, went on in and had the smell.'

'Did this Mrs Bradshaw go upstairs?'

'Said she not.' He shook his head. 'She went on straight for me.'

'The decedent's address?'

'Where we are.' He was slowing down. 'School Street.'

Catty-corner to Swain Memorial Methodist Church, the white clapboard house was two stories, with clothes still on the line and a purple martin house on a rusting pole in back. An old wooden rowboat and crab pots were in a yard scattered with oyster shells, and brown hydrangea lined a fence where there was a curious row of white-painted cubbyholes facing the unpaved street.

'What are those?' I asked Crockett.

'For where she sold receipts. Quarter each. Drop it in a slot.' He pointed. 'Mrs Pruitt didn't do direct much with no one.'

I finally realized that he was talking about recipes, and pulled up my door handle.

'I'll here be waiting,' he said.

The expression on his face begged me not to ask him to go inside that house.

'Just keep people away.' I got out of his truck.

'Don't have to worrisome about that none.'

I glanced around at other small homes and trailers in their sandy-soil yards. Some had family plots, the dead buried wherever there was high ground, headstones worn smooth like chalk and tilted or knocked down. I climbed Lila Pruitt's front steps, noticing more headstones in the shadows of junipers in a corner of her yard.

The screen door was rusting in spots, and the spring protested loudly as I entered an enclosed porch sloping toward the street. There was a glider upholstered in floral plastic, and beside it a small plastic table, where I imagined her rocking and drinking iced tea while she watched tourists buying her recipes for a quarter. I wondered if she had spied to make sure they paid.

The storm door was unlocked, and Hoyt had thought to tape on it a homemade sign that warned, *SICKNESS: DO NOT ENTER!!* I supposed he had figured that Tangiermen might not know what a biological hazard was, but he had made his point. I stepped inside a dim foyer, where a portrait of Jesus praying to His Father hung on the wall, and I smelled the foul odor of decomposing human flesh.

In the living room was evidence that someone had not been well for a while. Pillows and blankets were disarrayed and soiled on the couch, and on the coffee table were tissues, a thermometer, bottles of aspirin, liniment, dirty cups and plates. She had been feverish. She had ached, and had come in here to make herself comfortable and watch TV.

Eventually, she had not been able to make it out of bed, and that was where I found her, in a room upstairs with rosebud wallpaper and a rocker by the window overlooking her street. The full-length mirror was shrouded with a sheet, as if she could not bear to see her reflection anymore. Hoyt, old-world physician that he was, had respectfully pulled bed covers over the body without disturbing anything else. He knew better than to rearrange a scene, especially if his visit was to be followed by mine. I stood in the middle of the room, and took my time. The stench seemed to make the walls close in and turn the air black.

My eyes wandered over the cheap brush and comb on the dresser, the fuzzy pink slippers beneath a chair that was covered with clothes she hadn't had the energy to put away or wash. On the bedside table was a Bible with a black leather cover that was dried out and flaking, and a sample size of Vita aromatherapy facial spray that I imagined she had used in vain to cool her raging fever. Stacked on the floor were dozens of mail-order catalogues, page corners folded back to mark her wishes.

In the bathroom, the mirror over the sink had been covered with a towel, and other towels on the linoleum floor were soiled and bloody.

She had run out of toilet paper, and the box of baking soda on the side of the tub told me she had tried her own remedy in her bath to relieve her misery. Inside the medicine cabinet, I found no prescription drugs, only old dental floss, Jergens, hemorrhoid preparations, first-aid cream. Her dentures were in a plastic box on the sink.

Pruitt had been old and alone, with very little money, and probably had been off this island few times in her life. I expected that she had not attempted to seek help from any of her neighbors because she had no phone, and had feared that if anyone had seen her, they would have fled in horror. Even I wasn't quite prepared for what I saw when I peeled back the covers.

She was covered in pustules, gray and hard like pearls, her toothless mouth caved in, and dyed red hair wild. I pulled the covers down more, unbuttoning her gown, noting the density of eruptions was greater on her extremities and face than on her trunk, just as Hoyt had said. Itching had driven her to claw her arms and legs, where she had bled and gotten secondary infections that were crusty and swollen.

'God help you,' I muttered in pain.

I imagined her itching, aching, burning up with fever, and afraid of her own nightmarish image in the mirror.

'How awful,' I said, and my mother flashed in my mind.

Lancing a pustule, I smeared a slide, then went down to the kitchen and set my microscope on the table. I was already convinced of what I'd find. This was not chicken pox. It wasn't shingles. All indicators pointed to the devastating, disfiguring disease *variola major*, more commonly known as smallpox. Turning on my microscope, I put the slide on the stage, bumped magnification up to four hundred, adjusted the focus as the dense center, the cytoplasmic Guarnieri bodies, came into view. I took more Polaroids of something that could not be true.

Shoving back the chair, I began pacing as a clock ticked loudly from the wall.

'How did you get this? How?' I talked to her out loud.

I went back outside to where Crockett was parked on the street. I didn't get close to his truck.

'We've got a real problem,' I said to him. 'And I'm not a hundred percent sure what I'm going to do about it.'

My immediate difficulty was finding a secure phone, which I finally decided simply was not possible. I couldn't call from any of the local businesses, certainly not from the neighbors' houses or from the chief's trailer. That left my portable cellular phone, which ordinarily I would never have used to make a call like this. But I did not see that I had a choice. At three-fifteen, a woman answered the phone at the U.S. Army Medical Research Institute of Infectious Diseases, or USAMRIID, at Fort Detrick, in Frederick, Maryland.

'I need to speak with Colonel Fujitsubo,' I said.

'I'm sorry, he's in a meeting.'

'It's very important.'

'Ma'am, you'll have to call back tomorrow.'

'At least give me his assistant, his secretary . . .'

'In case you haven't heard, all nonessential federal employees are on furlough . . .'

'Jesus Christ!' I exclaimed in frustration. 'I'm stranded on an island with an infectious dead body. There may be some sort of outbreak here. Don't tell me I have to wait until your goddamn furlough ends!'

'Excuse me?'

I could hear telephones ringing nonstop in the background.

'I'm on a cellular phone. The battery could die any minute. For God's sake, interrupt his meeting! Patch me through to him! Now!'

Fujitsubo was in the Russell Building on Capitol Hill, where my call was connected. I knew he was in some senator's office but did not care as I quickly explained the situation, trying to control my panic.

'That's impossible,' he said. 'You're sure it's not chicken pox, measles . . .'

'No. And regardless of what it is, it should be contained, John. I can't send this into my morgue. You've got to handle it.'

USAMRIID was the major medical research laboratory for the U.S. Biological Defense Research Program, its purpose to protect citizens from the possible threat of biological warfare. More to the point, USAMRIID had the largest Bio Level 4 containment laboratory in the country.

'Can't do it unless it's terrorism,' Fujitsubo said to me. 'Outbreaks go to CDC. Sounds like that's who you need to be talking to.'

'And I'm sure I will be, eventually,' I said. 'And I'm sure most of them have been furloughed too, which is why I couldn't get through earlier. But they're in Atlanta, and you're in Maryland, not far from here, and I need to get this body out of here as fast as I can.'

He was silent.

'No one hopes I'm wrong more than I do,' I went on in a cold sweat.

'But if I'm not and we haven't taken the proper precautions . . .'

'I'm clear, I'm clear,' he quickly said. 'Damn. Right now we're a skeleton crew. Okay, give us a few hours. I'll call CDC. We'll deploy a team. When was the last time you were vaccinated for smallpox?'

'When I was too young to remember it.'

'You're coming in with the body.'

'She's my case.'

But I knew what he meant. They would want to quarantine me.

'Let's just get her off the island, and we'll worry about other things later,' I added.

'Where will you be?'

'Her house is in the center of town near the school.'

'God, that's unfortunate. We got any idea how many people might have been exposed?'

'No idea. Listen. There's a tidal creek nearby. Look for that and the Methodist church. It has a tall steeple. According to the map there's another church, but it doesn't have a steeple. There's an airstrip, but the closer you can get to the house, the better, so we don't have to carry her past where people might see.'

'Right. We sure as hell don't need a panic.' He paused, his voice softening a little. 'Are you all right?'

'I sure hope so.' I felt tears in my eyes, my hands trembling.

'I want you to calm down, try to relax now and stop worrying. We'll get you taken care of,' he said as my phone went dead.

It had always been a theoretical possibility that after all the murder and madness I had seen in my career, it would be a disease that quietly killed me in the end. I never knew what I was exposing myself to when I opened a body and handled its blood and breathed the air. I was careful about cuts and needle sticks, but there was more to worry about than hepatitis and HIV. New viruses were discovered all the time, and I often wondered if they would one day rule, at last winning a war with us that began with time.

For a while, I sat in the kitchen listening to the clock tick-tock while the light changed beyond the window as the day fled. I was in the throes of a full-blown anxiety attack when Crockett's peculiar voice suddenly hailed me from outside.

'Ma'am? Ma'am?'

When I went to the porch and looked out the door, I saw on the top step a small brown paper bag and a drink with a lid and a straw. I carried them in as Crockett climbed back inside his truck. He had gone off long enough to bring me supper, which wasn't smart, but kind. I waved at him as if he were a guardian angel, and felt a little better. I sat on the glider, rocking back and forth, and sipping sweetened iced tea from the Fisherman's Corner. The sandwich was fried flounder on white bread, with fried scallops on the side. I didn't think I'd ever tasted anything so fresh and fine.

I rocked and sipped tea, watching the street through the rusting screen as the sun slid down the church steeple in a shimmering ball of red, and geese were black V's flying overhead. Crockett turned his headlights on as windows lit up in homes, and two girls on bicycles pedaled quickly past, their faces turned toward me as they flew. I was certain they knew. The whole island did. Word had spread about doctors and the Coast Guard arriving because of what was in the Pruitt bed.

Going back inside, I put on fresh gloves, slipped the mask back over my mouth and nose and returned to the kitchen to see what I might find in the garbage. The plastic can was lined with a paper bag and tucked under the sink. I sat on the floor, sifting through it one item at a time to see if I could get any sense at all of how long Pruitt had been sick. Clearly, she had not emptied her trash for a while. Empty cans and frozen food wrappers were dry and crusty, peelings of raw turnips and carrots wizened and hard like Naugahyde.

I wandered through every room in her house, rooting through every wastepaper basket I could find. But it was the one in her living room that was the saddest. In it were several handwritten recipes on strips of paper, for Easy Flounder, Crab Cakes and Lila's Clam Stew. She had made mistakes, scratched through words on each one, which was why, I supposed, she had pitched them. In the bottom of the can was a small cardboard tube for a manufacturer's sample she had gotten in the mail.

Getting a flashlight out of my bag, I went outside and stood on the steps, waiting until Crockett got out of his truck.

'There's going to be a lot of commotion here soon,' I said.

He stared at me as if I might be mad, and in lighted windows I could see the faces of people peering out. I went down the steps, to the fence at the edge of the yard, around to the front of it and began shining the flashlight inside the cubbyholes where Pruitt had sold her recipes. Crockett moved back.

'I'm trying to see if I can get any idea how long she's been sick,' I said to him.

There were plenty of recipes in the slots, and only three quarters in the wooden money box.

'When did the last ferry boat come here with tourists?' I shone the light into another cubbyhole, finding maybe half a dozen recipes for Lila's Easy Soft-Shell Crabs.

'In a week ago. Never nothing since weeks,' he said.

'Do the neighbors buy her recipes?' I asked.

He frowned as if this were an odd thing to ask. 'They already got theirs.'

Now people had come out on their porches, slipping quietly into the dark shadows of their yards to watch this wild woman in surgical gown, hair cover and gloves shining a flashlight in their neighbor's cubbyholes and talking to their chief.

'There's going to be a lot of commotion here soon,' I repeated to him. 'The Army's sending in a medical team any minute, and we're going to need you to make sure people stay calm and remain in their homes. What I want you to do right now is go get the Coast Guard, tell them they're going to need to help you, okay?'

Davy Crockett drove off so fast, his tires spun.

9

They descended loudly from the moonlit night at almost nine P.M. The Army Blackhawk thundered over the Methodist church, whipping trees in its terrible turbulence of flying blades as a powerful light probed for a place to land. I watched it settle like a bird in a yard next door as hundreds of awed Tangiermen spilled out onto the streets.

From the porch, I peered out the screen, watching the medical evacuation team climb out of the helicopter as children hid behind parents, silently staring. The five scientists from USAMRIID and CDC did not look of this planet in their inflated orange plastic suits and hoods, and battery-operated air packs. They walked along the road, carrying a litter shrouded in a plastic bubble.

'Thank God you're here,' I said to them when they got to me.

Their feet made a slipping plastic sound on the porch's wooden floor, and they did not bother to introduce themselves as the only woman on the team handed me a folded orange suit.

'It's probably a little late,' I said.

'It can't hurt.' Her eyes met mine, and she didn't look much older than Lucy. 'Go ahead and put it on.'

It had the consistency of a shower liner, and I sat on the glider and pulled it over my shoes and clothes. The hood was transparent with a bib I tied securely around my chest. I turned on the pack at the back of my waist.

'She's upstairs,' I said over the noise of air rushing in my ears.

I led the way and they carried up the litter. For a moment, they were silent when they saw what was on the bed.

A scientist said, 'Jesus. I've never seen anything like that.'

Everyone started talking fast.

'Wrap her up in the sheets.'

'Pouched and sealed.'

'Everything on the bed, linens, gotta go in the autoclave.'

'Shit. What do we do? Burn the house?'

I went into the bathroom and collected towels off the floor while they lifted her shrouded body. She was slippery and uncooperative as they struggled to get her from the bed inside the portable isolator designed with the living in mind. They sealed plastic flaps, and the sight of a pouched body inside what looked like an oxygen tent was jolting, even to me. They lifted the litter by either end and we made our way back down the stairs and out onto the street.

'What about after we leave?' I asked.

'Three of us will stay,' one of them replied. 'We got another chopper coming in tomorrow.'

We were intercepted by another suited scientist carrying a metal canister not so different from what exterminators used. He decontaminated us and the litter, spraying a chemical while people continued to gather and stare. The Coast Guard was by Crockett's truck, Crockett and Martinez talking to each other. I went to speak to them, and they were clearly put off by my protective clothing, and not so subtly stepped away.

'This house has got to be sealed,' I said to Crockett. 'Until we know with certainty what we're dealing with here, no one goes in or near it.'

He had his hands in the pockets of his jacket and was blinking a lot.

'I need to be notified immediately if anyone else here gets sick,' I said to him.

'This time of year they have sickness,' he said. 'They get the bug. Some take the cold.'

'If they get a fever, backache, break out in a rash,' I said to him, 'call me or my office right away. These people are here to help you.' I pointed to the team.

The expression on his face made it very clear he wanted no one staying here, on his island.

'Please try to understand,' I said. 'This is very, very important.'

He nodded as a young boy materialized behind him, from the darkness, and took his hand. The boy looked, at the most, seven, with tangles of unruly blond hair and wide pale eyes that were fixed on me as if I were the most terrifying apparition he had ever seen.

'Daddy, sky people.' The boy pointed at me.

'Darryl, get on,' Crockett said to his son. 'Get home.'

I followed the thudding of helicopter blades. Circulating air cooled my face, but the rest of me was miserable because the suit didn't breathe. I picked my way through the yard beside the church while blades hammered, and scrubby pines and weeds were ripped by the loud wind.

The Blackhawk was open and lit up inside, and the team was tying down the litter the same way they would have were the patient alive. I climbed aboard, took a crew seat to one side and strapped myself in as one of the scientists pulled shut the door. The helicopter was loud and shuddering as we lifted into the sky. It was impossible to hear without headsets on, and those would not work well over hoods.

This puzzled me at first. Our suits had been decontaminated, but the team did not want to take them off, and then it occurred to me. I had been exposed to Lila Pruitt, and the torso before that. No one wanted to breathe my air unless it was passed through a high efficiency particulate air filter, or HEPA, first. So we mutely looked around, glancing at each other and our patient. I shut my eyes as we sped toward Maryland.

I thought of Wesley, Lucy and Marino. They had no idea what was happening, and would be very upset. I worried about when I would see them next, and what condition I might be in. My legs were slippery, my feet baking, and I did not feel good. I could not help but fear that first fateful sign, a chill, an ache, the bleariness and thirst of fever. I had been immunized for smallpox as a child. So had Lila Pruitt. So had the woman whose torso was still in my freezer. I had seen their scars, those stretched, faded areas about the size of a quarter where they had been scratched with the disease.

It was barely eleven when we landed somewhere I could not see. I had slept just long enough to be disoriented, and the return to reality was loud and abrupt when I opened my eyes. The door slid open again, lights blinking white and blue on a helipad across the road from a big angular building. Many windows were lit up for such a late hour, as if people were awake and awaiting our arrival. Scientists unstrapped the litter and hastily loaded it in the back of a truck, while the female scientist escorted me, a gloved hand on my arm.

I did not see where the litter went, but I was led across the road to a ramp on the north side of the building. From there we did not have far to go along a hallway until I was shown into a shower and blasted with Envirochem. I stripped and was blasted again with hot, soapy water. There were shelves of scrubs and booties, and I dried my hair with a towel. As instructed, I left my clothes in the middle of the floor along with all of my possessions.

A nurse waited in the hall, and she briskly walked me past the surgery room, then walls of autoclaves that reminded me of steel diving bells, the air foul with the stench of scalded laboratory animals. I was to stay in the 200 Ward, where a red line just inside my room warned patients in isolation not to cross. I looked around at the small hospital bed with its moist heating blanket, and ventilator, refrigerator and small television suspended from a corner. I noticed the coiled yellow air lines attached to pipes on the walls, the steel pass box in the door, through which meal trays were delivered, and irradiated with UV light when removed.

I sat on the bed, alone and depressed, and unwilling to contemplate how much trouble I might be in. Minutes passed. An outer door loudly shut, and mine swung open wide.

'Welcome to the Slammer,' Colonel Fujitsubo announced as he walked in.

He wore a Racal hood and heavy blue vinyl suit, which he plugged into one of the coiled air lines.

'John,' I said. 'I'm not ready for this.'

'Kay, be sensible.'

His strong face seemed severe, even frightening behind plastic, and I felt vulnerable and alone.

'I need to let people know where I am,' I said.

He walked over to the bed, tearing open a paper packet, a small vial and medicine dropper in a gloved hand.

'Let's see your shoulder. It's time to revaccinate. And we're going to treat you to a little vaccinia immune globulin, too, for good measure.'

'My lucky day,' I said.

He rubbed my right shoulder with an alcohol pad. I stood very still as he incised my flesh twice with a scarifier and dripped in serum.

'Hopefully, this isn't necessary,' he added.

'No one hopes it more than me.'

'The good news is, you should have a lovely anamnestic response, with a higher level of the antibody than ever before. Vaccination within twenty-four to forty-eight hours of exposure will usually do the trick.'

I did not reply. He knew as well as I did that it might already be too late.

'We'll autopsy her at oh-nine-hundred hours and keep you for a few days beyond that, just to be sure,' he said, dropping wrappers in the trash. 'Are you having any symptoms at all?'

'My head hurts and I'm cranky,' I said.

He smiled, his eyes on mine. Fujitsubo was a brilliant physician who had sailed through the ranks of the Army's Armed Forces Institute of Pathology, or AFIP, before taking over the command of USAMRIID. He was divorced and a few years older than me. He got a folded blanket from the foot of the bed, shook it open and draped it around my shoulders. He pulled up a chair and straddled it, his arms on top of the backrest.

'John, I was exposed almost two weeks ago,' I said.

'By the homicide case.'

'I should have it by now.'

'Whatever *it* is. The last case of smallpox was in October 1977, in Somalia, Kay. Since then it has been eradicated from the face of the earth.'

'I know what I saw on the electron microscope. It could have been transmitted through unnatural exposure.'

'Deliberately, you're saying.'

'I don't know.' I was having a hard time keeping my eyes open. 'But don't you find it odd that the first person possibly infected was also murdered?'

'I find all of this odd.' He got up. 'But beyond offering biologically safe containment for the body and you, there isn't much we can do.'

'Of course there is. There isn't anything you can't do.' I did not want to hear of his jurisdictional conflicts.

'At the moment, this is a public health concern, not a military concern. You know we can't just yank this right out from under CDC. At the worst, what we've got is an outbreak of some sort. And that's what they do best.'

'Tangier Island should be quarantined.'

'We'll talk about that after the autopsy.'

'Which I plan to do,' I added.

'See how you feel,' he said as a nurse appeared at the door.

He conferred briefly with her on his way out, then she was walking in, dressed in another blue suit. Young and annoyingly cheerful, she was explaining that she worked out of Walter Reed Hospital but helped here when they had patients in special containment, which, fortunately, wasn't often.

'Last time was when those two lab workers got exposed to partially thawed field mice blood contaminated with Hantavirus,' she said. 'Those hemorrhagic diseases are nasty. I guess they stayed here about fifteen days. Dr Fujitsubo says you want a phone.' She laid a flimsy robe on the bed. 'I'll have to get that for you later. Here's some Advil and water.' She set them on the bedside table. 'Are you hungry?'

'Cheese and crackers, something like that, would be nice.' My stomach was so raw I was almost sick.

'How are you feeling besides the headache?'

'Fine, thanks.'

'Well, let's hope that doesn't change. Why don't you go on in the bathroom, empty your bladder, clean up and get under the covers. There's the TV.' She pointed, speaking simply as if I were in second grade.

'What about all my things?'

'They'll sterilize them, don't you worry.' She smiled at me.

I could not get warm, and took another shower. Nothing would wash away this wretched day, and I continued to see a sunken mouth gaping at me, eyes half open and blind, an arm hanging stiffly off a foul deathbed. When I emerged from the bathroom, a plate of cheese and crackers had been left for me, and the TV was on. But there was no phone.

'Oh hell,' I muttered as I got under the covers again.

The next morning, my breakfast arrived by pass box, and I set the tray on my lap as I watched the 'Today' show, which I ordinarily never got to do. Martha Stewart was whipping up something with meringue while I picked at a soft-boiled egg that wasn't quite warm. I could not eat, and did not know if my back ached because I was tired or from some other reason I would not contemplate.

'How are we doing?' The nurse appeared, breathing HEPA-filtered air.

'Don't you get hot in that thing?' I pointed my fork.

'I guess I would if I stayed in it for long periods of time.' She was carrying a digital thermometer. 'All right. This will just take a minute.'

She inserted it into my mouth while I stared up at the TV. Now a doctor was being interviewed about this year's flu shot, and I shut my eyes until a beep said my time was up.

'Ninety-seven point nine. Your temperature's actually a little low. Ninety-eight point six is normal.'

She wrapped a BP cuff around my upper arm.

'And your blood pressure.' She vigorously squeezed the bulb, pumping air. 'One hundred and eight over seventy. I believe you're almost dead.'

'Thanks,' I mumbled. 'I need a phone. No one knows where I am.'

'What you need is to get lots of rest.' Now she had out the stethoscope, which she pushed down the front of my scrubs. 'Deep breaths.' It was cold everywhere she moved it, her face serious as she listened. 'Again.' Then she moved it to my back as we continued the routine.

'Could you please have Colonel Fujitsubo stop by.'

'I'll certainly leave him a message. Now you cover up.' She pulled the blanket up to my chin. 'Let me get you some more water. How's your headache?'

'Fine,' I lied. 'You really must ask him to stop by.'

'I'm sure he will when he can. I know he's very busy.'

Her patronizing manner was beginning to really get to me. 'Excuse me,' I said in a demanding tone. 'I have repeatedly requested a phone, and I'm beginning to feel like I'm in prison.'

'You know what they call this place,' she sang. 'And usually, patients don't get . . .'

'I don't care what they usually get.' I stared hard at her as her demeanor changed.

'You just calm right down.' Eyes glinted behind clear plastic, her voice raised.

'Isn't she an awful patient? Doctors always are,' Colonel Fujitsubo said as he strode into the room.

The nurse looked at him, stunned. Then her resentful eyes fixed on me as if she did not believe it could possibly be true.

'One phone coming up,' he went on as he carried in a fresh orange suit, which he laid on the foot of the bed. 'Beth, I guess you've been introduced to Dr Scarpetta, chief medical examiner of Virginia and consulting forensic pathologist for the FBI?' To me, he added, 'Put this on. I'll be back for you in two minutes.'

The nurse frowned as she picked up my tray. She cleared her throat, embarrassed.

'You didn't do a very good job on your eggs,' she said.

She set the tray in the pass box. I was pulling on the suit.

'Typically, once you're in here, they don't let you out.' She shut the drawer.

'This isn't typical.' I tied down the hood and turned on my air. 'The case this morning is mine.'

I could tell she was one of those nurses who resented women doctors, because she preferred to be told what to do by men. Or maybe she had wanted to be a doctor and was told that girls grow up to be nurses and marry doctors. I could only guess. But I remembered when I was in medical school at Johns Hopkins, and one day the head nurse grabbed my arm in the hospital. I'd never forget her hate when she snarled that her son hadn't gotten in because I had taken his slot.

Fujitsubo was walking back into the room, smiling at me as he handed me a telephone and plugged it into a jack.

'You got time for one.' He held up his index finger. 'Then we got to roll.'

I called Marino.

Bio Level 4 containment was in back of a normal lab, but the difference between the two areas was serious. BL-4 meant scientists doing open war with Ebola, Hantavirus and unknown diseases for which there was no cure. Air was single-pass and negative pressure to prevent highly infectious microorganisms from flowing into any other part of the building. It was checked by HEPA filters before it entered our bodies or the atmosphere, and everything was scalded by steam in autoclaves.

Though autopsies were infrequent, when they were performed it was in an air-locked space nicknamed 'the Sub,' behind two massive stainless steel doors with submarine seals. To enter, we had to go in another way, through a maze of change rooms and showers, with only colored lights to indicate which gender was in what. Men were green so I put my light on red and took everything off. I put on fresh sneakers and scrubs.

Steel doors automatically opened and closed as I passed through another air-lock, into the inner change, or hot side room where the heavy gauge blue vinyl suits with built-in feet and pointed hoods hung from hooks on a wall. Sitting on a bench, I pulled one on, zipping it up and securing flaps with what looked like a diagonal Tupperware seal. I worked my feet into rubber boots, then layers of heavy gloves, with outer ones taped to cuffs. I was already beginning to feel hot, doors shutting behind me as other ones of even thicker steel sucked open to let me into the most claustrophobic autopsy room I had ever seen.

I grabbed a yellow line and plugged it into the quick-release coupling at my hip, and rushing air reminded me of a deflating wading pool. Fujitsubo and another doctor were labeling tubes and hosing off the body. In her nakedness, her disease was even more appalling. For the most part, we worked in silence for we had not bothered with communication equipment, and the only way to speak was to crimp our air lines long enough to hear what someone else was saying.

We did this as we cut and weighed, and I recorded the pertinent information on a protocol. She suffered the typical degenerative changes of fatty streaks and fatty plaques of the aorta. Her heart was dilated, her congested lungs consistent with early pneumonia. She had ulcers in her mouth and lesions in her gastrointestinal tract. But it was her brain that told the most tragic story of her death. She had cortical atrophy, widening of the cerebral sulci and loss of the parenchyma, the telltale hints of Alzheimer's.

I could only imagine her confusion when she had gotten sick. She may not have remembered where she was or even who she was, and in her dementia may have believed some nightmarish creature was coming through her mirrors. Lymph nodes were swollen, spleen and liver cloudy and swollen with focal necrosis, all consistent with smallpox.

She looked like a natural death, the cause of which we could not prove yet, and two hours later, we were done. I left the same way I had come in, starting with the hot side room, where I took a five-minute chemical shower in my suit, standing on a rubber mat and scrubbing every inch with a stiff brush as steel nozzles pounded me. Dripping, I reentered the outer room, where I hung the suit to dry, showered again and washed my hair. I put on a sterile orange suit and returned to the Slammer.

The nurse was in my room when I walked in.

'Janet is here writing you a note,' she said.

'Janet?' I was stunned. 'Is Lucy with her?'

'She'll slide it through the pass box. All I know is there's a young woman named Janet. She's alone.'

'Where is she? I must see her.'

'You know that isn't possible just now.' She was taking my blood pressure again.

'Even prisons have a place for visitors,' I almost snapped. 'Isn't there some area where I can talk to her through glass? Or can't she put on a suit and come in here like you do?'

Of course, all this required permission, yet again, from the colonel, who decided that the easiest solution was for me to wear a HEPA filter mask and go into the visitors' booth. This was inside the Clinical Research Ward, where studies were conducted on new vaccines. She led me through a BL-3 recreation room, where volunteers were playing Ping-Pong and pool, or reading magazines and watching TV.

The nurse opened the wooden door to Booth B, where Janet was seated on the other side of glass in an uncontaminated part of the building. We picked up our phones at the same time.

'I can't believe this,' was the first thing she said. 'Are you all right?'

The nurse was still standing behind me in my telephone-booth-sized space, and I turned around and asked her to leave. She didn't budge.

'Excuse me,' I said, and I'd about had it with her. 'This is a private conversation.'

Anger flashed in her eyes as she left and shut the door.

'I don't know how I am,' I said into the phone. 'But I don't feel too bad.'

'How long does it take?' Fear shone in her eyes.

'On average, ten days, at the most fourteen.'

'Well, that's good, then, isn't it?'

'I don't know.' I felt depressed. 'It depends on what we're dealing with. But if I'm still okay in a few days, I expect they will let me leave.'

Janet looked very grown-up and pretty in a dark blue suit, her pistol inconspicuous beneath her jacket. I knew she would not have come alone unless something was very wrong.

'Where's Lucy?' I asked.

'Well, actually, both of us are up here in Maryland, outside Baltimore, with Squad Nineteen.'

'Is she all right?'

'Yes,' Janet said. 'We're working on your files, trying to trace them through AOL and UNIX.'

'And?'

She hesitated. 'I think the quickest way to catch him is going to be online.'

I frowned, perplexed by this. 'I'm not sure I understand . . .'

'Is that thing uncomfortable?' She stared at my mask.

'Yes.'

I was sorrier for the way it looked. It covered half of my face like a hideous muzzle and kept knocking the phone as I talked.

'How can you catch him online unless he's still sending messages to me?'

She opened a file folder on her Formica ledge. 'Do you want to hear them?'

I nodded as my stomach tightened.

'*Microscopic worms, multiplying ferments and miasma,*' she read.

'Excuse me?' I said.

'That's it. E-mail sent this morning. The next one came this afternoon. *They are alive, but no one else will be.* And then about an hour after that, *Humans who seize from others and exploit are macro parasites. They kill their hosts.* All in lowercase with no punctuation except spaces.' She looked through the glass at me.

'Classical medical philosophy,' I said. 'Going back to Hippocrates and other Western practitioners, their theories of what causes disease. The atmosphere. Reproducing poisonous particles generated by the decomposition of organic matter. Microscopic worms, et cetera. And then the historian McNeill wrote about the interaction of micro and macro parasites as a way of understanding the evolution of society.'

'Then deadoc has had medical training,' Janet said. 'And it sounds like he's alluding to whatever this disease is.'

'He couldn't know about it,' I said as I began to entertain a terrible new fear. 'I don't see how he possibly could.'

'There was something in the news,' she said.

I felt a rush of anger. 'Who opened his mouth this time? Don't tell me Ring knows about this, too.'

'The paper simply said your office was investigating an unusual death on Tangier Island, a strange disease that resulted in the body being airlifted out by the military.'

'Damn.'

'Point is, if deadoc has access to Virginia news, he could have known about it before he sent the e-mail messages.'

'I hope that's what happened,' I said.

'Why wouldn't it be?'

'I don't know, I don't know.' I was worn out and my stomach was upset.

'Dr Scarpetta.' She leaned closer to the glass. 'He wants to talk to you. That's why he keeps sending you mail.'

I was feeling chills again.

'Here's the idea.' Janet tucked the printouts back inside the file. 'I could get you in a private chat room with him. If we can keep you online long enough, we can trace him from telephone trunk to telephone trunk, until we get a town, then a location.'

'I don't believe for a moment that this person is going to participate,' I said. 'He's too smart for that.'

'Benton Wesley thinks he might.'

I was silent.

'He thinks deadoc is sufficiently fixated on you that he might get into a chat room. It's more than his wanting to know what you think. He wants you to know what he thinks, or at least this is Wesley's theory. I've got a laptop here, everything you need.'

'No.' I shook my head. 'I don't want to get into this, Janet.'

'You've got nothing else to do for the next few days.'

It irritated me when anyone ever accused me of not having enough to do. 'I don't want to communicate with the monster. It's far too risky. I could say the wrong thing and more people die.'

Janet's eyes were intense on mine. 'They're dying, anyway. Maybe others are, too, even as we speak, that we don't know about yet.'

I thought of Lila Pruitt alone in her house, wandering, demented with disease. I saw her in her mirror, shrieking.

'All you need to do is get him talking, a little bit at a time,' Janet went on. 'You know, act reluctant, as if he's caught you unaware, otherwise he'll get suspicious. Build it up for a few days, while we try to find out where he is. Get on AOL. Go into the chat rooms and find one called M.E., okay? Just hang out in there.'

'Then what?' I wanted to know.

'The hope is he'll come looking for you, thinking this is where you do consultations with other doctors, scientists. He won't be able to resist. That's Wesley's theory and I agree with it.'

'Does he know I'm here?'

The question was ambiguous but she knew who I meant.

'Yes,' she said. 'Marino asked me to call him.'

'What did he say?' I asked into the phone.

'He wanted to know if you were okay.' She was getting evasive. 'He has this old case in Georgia. Something about two people stabbed to death in a liquor store, and organized crime is involved. In a little town near St Simons Island.'

'Oh, so he's on the road.'

'I guess so.'

'Where will you be?'

'With the squad. I'll actually be staying in Baltimore, on the harbor.'

'And Lucy?' I asked again, this time in a way she couldn't evade.

'Do you want to tell me what's really going on, Janet?'

I breathed my filtered air, looking through glass at someone I knew could never lie to me.

'Everything okay?' I pressed harder.

'Dr Scarpetta, I'm here by myself for two reasons,' she finally said. 'First, Lucy and I got into a huge fight about your going online with this guy. So everyone involved thought it would be better if she wasn't the one to talk to you about it.'

'I can understand that,' I said. 'And I agree.'

'My second reason is a far more unpleasant one,' she went on. 'It's about Carrie Grethen.'

I was astonished and enraged at the mere mention of her name. Years ago, when Lucy was developing CAIN, she had worked with Carrie. Then ERF had been broken into, and Carrie had seen to it that my niece was blamed. There were murders, too, sadistic and terrible, that Carrie had been accomplice to with a psychopathic man.

'She's still in prison,' I said.

'I know. But her trial is scheduled for the spring,' Janet said.

'I'm well aware of that.' I didn't understand what she was getting at.

'You're the key witness. Without you, the Common-wealth doesn't have much of a case. At least not when you're talking about a jury trial.'

'Janet, I am most confused,' I said, and my headache was back with fury.

She took a deep breath. 'I'm sure you must be aware that there was a time when Lucy and Carrie were close.' She hesitated. 'Very close.'

'Of course,' I impatiently said. 'Lucy was a teenager and Carrie seduced her. Yes, yes, I know all about it.'

'So does Percy Ring.'

I looked at her, shocked.

'It seems that yesterday, Ring went to see the C.A. who's prosecuting the case, uh, Rob Schurmer. Ring tells him, one buddy to another, that he's got a major problem since the star witness's niece had an affair with the defendant.'

'My God in heaven.' I could not believe this. 'That fucking bastard.'

I was a lawyer. I knew what this meant. Lucy would have to take the stand and be questioned about her affair with another woman. The only way to avoid this was for me to be struck as a witness, allowing Carrie to get away with murder.

'What she did has nothing to do with Carrie's crimes,' I said, so angry with Ring I felt capable of violence.

Janet switched the phone to her other ear, trying to be smooth. But I could see her fear.

'I don't need to tell you how it is out there,' she said. 'Don't ask, don't tell. It's not tolerated, no matter what anybody says. Lucy and I are so careful. People may suspect, but they don't really know, and it's not like we walk around in leather and chains.'

'Not hardly.'

'I think this would ruin her,' she matter-of-factly stated. 'The publicity, and I can't imagine HRT when she shows up after that. All those big guys. Ring's just doing this to do her in, and maybe you, too. And maybe me. This won't exactly help my career, either.'

She didn't need to go on. I understood.

'Does anyone know what Schurmer's response was when Ring told him?'

'He freaked, called Marino and said he didn't know what he was going to do, that when the defense found out, he was cooked. Then Marino called me.'

'Marino has said nothing to me.'

'He didn't want to upset you right now,' she said. 'And he didn't think it was his place.'

'I see,' I said. 'Does Lucy know?'

'I told her.'

'And?'

'She kicked a hole in the bedroom wall,' Janet answered. 'Then she said if she had to, she'd take the stand.'

Janet pressed her palm against the glass, spreading her fingers, waiting for me to do the same. It was as close as we could get to touching, and my eyes teared up.

'I feel as if I've committed a crime,' I said, clearing my throat.

10

———

The nurse carried the computer equipment into my room and word-
lessly handed it to me before walking right back out. For a moment,
I stared at the laptop as if it were something that might hurt me. I
was sitting up in bed, where I continued to perspire profusely while
I was cold at the same time.

I didn't know if the way I felt was due to a microbe or if I were
having some sort of emotional attack because of what Janet had just
told me. Lucy had wanted to be an FBI agent since she was a child,
and she was already one of the best ones they'd ever had. This was
so unfair. She had done nothing but make the mistake of being drawn
in by someone evil when she was only nineteen. I was desperate to
get out of this room and find her. I wanted to go home. I was about
to ring for the nurse when one walked in. She was new.

'Do you suppose I could have a fresh set of scrubs?' I asked her.

'I can get you a gown.'

'Scrubs, please.'

'Well, it's a little out of the ordinary.' She frowned.

'I know.'

I plugged the computer into the telephone jack, and pushed a
button to turn it on.

'If they don't get beyond this budget impasse soon, there won't be
anybody to autoclave scrubs or anything else.' The nurse kept talking
in her blue suit, arranging covers over my legs. 'On the news this

morning, the president said Meals on Wheels is going broke, EPA isn't cleaning up toxic waste dumps, federal courts may close and forget getting a tour of the White House. You ready for lunch?'

'Thank you,' I said as she continued her litany of bad news.

'Not to mention Medicaid, air pollution and tracking the winter flu epidemic or screening water supplies for the Cryptosporidium parasite. You're just lucky you're here now. Next week we might not be open.'

I didn't even want to think about budget feuds, since I devoted most of my time to them, haggling with department heads and firing at legislators during General Assembly. I worried that when the federal crisis slammed down to the state level, my new building would never be finished, my meager current funding further ruthlessly slashed. There were no lobbyists for the dead. My patients had no party and did not vote.

'You got two choices,' she was saying.

'I'm sorry.' I tuned her in again.

'Chicken or ham.'

'Chicken.' I wasn't the least bit hungry. 'And hot tea.'

She unplugged her air line and left me to the quiet. I set the laptop on the tray and logged onto America Online. I went straight to my mailbox. There was plenty, but nothing from deadoc that Squad 19 hadn't already opened. I followed menus to the chat rooms, pulled up a list of the member rooms and checked to see how many people were in the one called M.E.

No one was there, so I went in alone and leaned back against my pillows, staring at the blank screen with its row of icons across the top. Literally, there was no one to chat with, and I thought of how ridiculous this must seem to deadoc, were he somehow watching. Wasn't it obvious if I were alone in a room? Wouldn't it seem that I was waiting? I had no sooner entertained this thought when a sentence was written across my screen, and I began to answer.

QUINCY: Hi. What are we talking about today?
SCARPETTA: The budget impasse. How is it affecting you?
QUINCY: I work out of the D.C. office. A nightmare.
SCARPETTA: Are you a medical examiner?
QUINCY: Right. We've met at meetings. We know some of the same people. Not much of a crowd today, but it could always get better if one is patient.

That's when I knew Quincy was one of the undercover agents from Squad 19. We continued our session until lunch arrived, then resumed it afterwards for the better part of an hour. Quincy and I chatted about our problems, asking questions about solutions, anything we could think of that might seem like normal conversation between medical examiners or people they might confer with. But deadoc did not bite.

I took a nap and woke up a little past four. For a moment, I lay very still, forgetting where I was, then it came back to me with depressing alacrity. I sat up, cramped beneath my tray, the computer still open on top of it. I logged onto AOL again and went back into the chat room. This time I was joined by someone who called himself MEDEX, and we talked about the type of computer database I used in Virginia for capturing case information and doing statistical retrievals.

At exactly five minutes past five, a bell sounded off-key inside my computer, and the Instant Message window suddenly dominated my screen. I stared in disbelief as a communication from deadoc appeared, words that I knew no one else in the chat room could see.

DEADOC: you think you re so smart
SCARPETTA: Who are you?
DEADOC: you know who I am I am what you do
SCARPETTA: What do I do?
DEADOC: death doctor death you are me
SCARPETTA: I am not you.
DEADOC: you think you re so smart

He abruptly got quiet, and when I clicked on the Available button, it showed that he had logged off. My heart was racing as I sent another message to MEDEX, saying I had been tied up with a visitor. I got no response, finding myself alone in the chat room again.

'Damn,' I exclaimed, under my breath.

I tried again as late as ten P.M., but no one appeared except QUINCY again, to tell me we should try another meeting in the morning. All of the other docs, he said, had gone home. The same nurse checked on me, and she was sweet. I felt sorry for her long hours, and her inconvenience of having to wear a blue suit every time she came into my room.

'Where is the new shift?' I asked, as she took my temperature.

'I'm it. We're all just doing the best we can.'

I nodded as she alluded to the furlough yet one more time this day.

'There's hardly a lab worker here,' she went on. 'You could wake up tomorrow, the only person in the building.'

'Now I'm sure to have nightmares,' I said as she wrapped the BP cuff around my arm.

'Well, you're feeling okay, and that's the important thing. Ever since I started coming down here, I started imagining I was getting one thing or another. The slightest ache or pain or sniffle, and it's, oh my God. So what kind of doctor are you?'

I told her.

'I was going to be a pediatrician. Then I got married.'

'We'd be in a lot of trouble were it not for good nurses like you,' I smiled and said.

'Most doctors never bother to notice that. They have these attitudes.'

'Some of them certainly do,' I agreed.

I tried to go to sleep, and was restless throughout the night. Street lights from the parking lot beyond my window seeped through the blinds, and no matter which way I turned, I could not relax. It was hard to breathe and my heart would not slow down. At five A.M., I finally sat up and turned on my light. Within minutes, the nurse was back inside my room.

'You all right?' She looked exhausted.

'Can't sleep.'

'Want something?'

I turned on the computer as I shook my head. I logged onto AOL and went back to the chat room, which was empty. Clicking on the Available button, I checked to see if deadoc was on line, and if so, where he might be. There was no sign of him, and I began scrolling through the various chat rooms available to subscribers and their families.

There was truly something for everyone, places for flirts, singles, gays, lesbians, Native Americans, African Americans, and for evil. People who preferred bondage, sadomasochism, group sex, bestiality, incest, were welcome to find each other and exchange pornographic art. The FBI could do nothing about it. All of it was legal.

Dejected, I sat up, propped against my pillows and, without intending to, dozed off. When I opened my eyes again an hour later, I was in a chat room called ARTLOVE. A message was quietly waiting for me on my screen. Deadoc had found me.

DEADOC: a picture s worth a thousand words

I hastily checked to see if he was still logged on, and found him quietly coiled in cyberspace, waiting for me. I typed my response.

SCARPETTA: What are you trading?

He didn't respond right away. I sat staring at the screen for three or four minutes. Then he was back.

DEADOC: I don t trade with traitors I give freely what do you
            think happens to people like that
SCARPETTA: Why don't you tell me?

Silence, and I watched as he left the room, and a minute later was back. He was breaking the trace. He knew exactly what we were doing.

DEADOC: I think you know
SCARPETTA: I don't.
DEADOC: you will
SCARPETTA: I saw the photos you sent. They weren't very clear.
            What was your point?

But he did not answer and I felt slow and dull-witted. I had him and could not engage him. I could not keep him on. I was feeling frustrated and discouraged when another instant message appeared on my screen, this one from the squad again.

QUINCY: A.K.A., Scarpetta. Still need to go over that case
            with you. The self-immolation.

That's when I realized that Quincy was Lucy. A.K.A. was Aunt Kay Always, her code for me. She was watching over me, as I had watched over her all these years, and she was telling me not to go up in flames. I typed a message back.

SCARPETTA: I agree. Your case is very troublesome. How are you
            handling it?
QUINCY: Just watch me in court. More later.

I smiled as I signed off and leaned back in the pillows. I did not feel quite so alone or crazed.

'Good morning.' The first nurse was back.

'Same to you.' My spirits dipped lower.

'Let's check those vitals. How are we feeling today?'

'We're fine.'

'You've got a choice of eggs or cereal.'

'Fruit,' I said.

'That wasn't a choice. But we can probably scrape up a banana.'

The thermometer went into my mouth, the cuff around my arm. All the while she kept talking.

'It's so cold out it could snow,' she was saying. 'Thirty-three degrees. You believe that? I had frost on my wind-shield. The acorns are big this year. That always means a severe winter. You're still not even up to ninety-eight degrees yet. What's wrong with you?'

'Why wasn't the phone left in here?' I asked.

'I'll ask about it.' She took the cuff off. 'Blood pressure's low, too.'

'Please ask Colonel Fujitsubo to stop by this morning.'

She stood back and scrutinized me. 'You going to complain about me?'

'Good heavens, no,' I said. 'I just need to leave.'

'Well, I hate to tell you, but that's not up to me. Some people stay in here as long as two weeks.'

I would lose my mind, I thought.

The colonel did not appear before lunch, which was a broiled chicken breast, carrots and rice. I hardly ate as my tension mounted, and the TV flashed silently in the background because I had turned off the sound. The nurse came back at two P.M. and announced I had another visitor. So I put on the HEPA filter mask again and followed her back down the hall into the clinic.

This time I was in Booth A, and Wesley was waiting for me on the other side. He smiled when our eyes met, and both of us picked up our phones. I was so relieved and surprised to see him that I stammered at first.

'I hope you've come to rescue me,' I said.

'I don't take on doctors. You taught me that.'

'I thought you were in Georgia.'

'I was. Took a look at the liquor store where the two people were stabbed, scouted around the area, in general. Now I'm here.'

'And?'

'And?' He raised an eyebrow. 'Organized crime.'

'I wasn't thinking about Georgia.'

'Tell me what you are thinking. I seem to be losing the art of mind reading. And you look particularly lovely today, let me add,' he said to my mask.

'I'm going to go crazy if I don't get out of here soon,' I said. 'I've got to get to CDC.'

'Lucy tells me you've been communicating with deadoc.' The playful light vanished from his eyes.

'To no great extent and with not much luck,' I angrily said.

To communicate with this killer was infuriating for it was exactly what he wanted. I had made it my mission in life not to reward people like him.

'Don't give up,' Wesley said.

'He makes allusions to medical matters, such as diseases and germs,' I said. 'Doesn't this concern you in light of what is going on?'

'He no doubt follows the news.' He made the same point Janet had.

'But what if it's more than that?' I asked. 'The woman he dismembered seems to have the same disease that the victim from Tangier does.'

'And you can't verify that yet.'

'You know, I didn't get where I am by making assumptions and leaping to conclusions.' I was getting very out of sorts. 'I will verify this disease as soon as I can, but I think we should be guided by common sense in the meantime.'

'I'm not certain I understand what you're saying.' His eyes never left mine.

'I'm saying that we might be dealing with biological warfare. A Unabomber who uses a disease.'

'I hope to God we're not.'

'But the thought has crossed your mind too. Don't tell me you think that a fatal disease somehow linked with a dismemberment is coincidental.'

I studied his face, and I knew he had a headache. The same vein on his forehead always stood out like a bluish rope.

'And you're sure you're feeling all right,' he said.

'Yes. I'm more worried about you.'

'What about this disease? What about the risk to you?' He was getting irritated with me, the way he always did when he thought I was in danger.

'I've been revaccinated.'

'You've been vaccinated for smallpox,' he said. 'What if that's not what it is?'

'Then we're in a world of trouble. Janet came by.'

'I know,' he said into his phone. 'I'm sorry. The last thing you needed right now . . .'

'No, Benton,' I interrupted him. 'I had to be told. There's never a good time for news like that. What do you think will happen?'

But he did not want to say.

'Then you think it will ruin her, too,' I said in despair.

'I doubt she'll be terminated. What usually happens is you stop getting promoted, get lousy assignments, field offices out in the middle of nowhere. She and Janet will end up three thousand miles apart. One or both will quit.'

'How's that better than being fired?' I said in pained outrage.

'We'll take it as it comes, Kay.' He looked at me. 'I'm dismissing Ring from CASKU.'

'Be careful what you do because of me.'

'It's done,' he said.

Fujitsubo did not stop by my room again until early the next morning, and then he was smiling and opening blinds to let in sunlight so dazzling it hurt my eyes.

'Good morning, and so far, so good,' he said. 'I'm very pleased that you do not seem to be getting sick on us, Kay.'

'Then I can go,' I said, ready to leap out of bed right then.

'Not so fast.' He was reviewing my chart. 'I know how hard this is for you, but I'm not comfortable letting you go quite so soon. Stick it out a little longer, and you can leave the day after tomorrow, if all goes well.'

I felt like crying when he left because I did not see how I could endure one more hour of quarantine. Miserable, I sat up under the covers and looked out at the day. The sky was bright blue with wisps of clouds beneath the pale shadow of a morning moon. Trees beyond my window were bare and rocking in a gentle wind. I thought of my home in Richmond, of plants to be potted and work piling up on my desk. I wanted to take a walk in the cold, to cook broccoli and home-made barley soup. I wanted spaghetti with ricotta or stuffed frittata, and music and wine.

For half the day, I simply felt sorry for myself and did not do a thing except stare at television and doze. Then the nurse for the next shift came in with the phone and said there was a call for me. I waited until it was transferred and snatched up the receiver as if this were the most exciting thing that had ever happened in my life.

'It's me,' Lucy said.

'Thank God.' I was thrilled to hear her voice.

'Grans says hi. Rumor has it that you win the bad patient award.'

'The rumor is accurate. All the work in my office. If only I had it here.'

'You need to rest,' she said. 'To keep your defenses up.'

This made me worry about Wingo again.

'How come you haven't been on the laptop?' She then got to the point.

I was quiet.

'Aunt Kay, he's not going to talk to us. He's only going to talk to you.'

'Then one of you sign on as me,' I replied.

'No way. If he senses that's what's going on, we lose him for good. This guy is scary, he's so clever.'

My silence was my comment, and Lucy rushed to fill it.

'What?' she said with feeling. 'I'm supposed to pretend I'm a forensic pathologist with a law degree who's already worked at least one of this guy's cases? I don't think so.'

'I don't want to connect with him, Lucy,' I said. 'People like him get off on that, they want it, want the attention. The more I play his game, the more it might encourage him. Have you thought about that?'

'Yes. But think about this. Whether he's dismembered one person or twenty, he's going to do something else bad. People like him don't just stop. And we have no idea, not one clue, as to where the hell he is.'

'It's not that I'm scared for myself,' I started to say.

'It's all right if you are.'

'I just don't want to do anything to make it worse,' I repeated.

That, of course, was always the risk when one was creative or aggressive in an investigation. The perpetrator was never completely predictable. Maybe it was simply something I sensed, an intuitive vibration I was picking up deep inside. But I felt that this killer was different and motivated by something beyond our ken. I feared he knew exactly what we were doing and was enjoying himself.

'Now, tell me about you,' I said. 'Janet was here.'

'I don't want to get into it.' Cold fury crept into her tone. 'I have better ways to spend my time.'

'I'm with you, Lucy, whatever you want to do.'

'That much I've always been sure of. And this much everybody else can be sure of. No matter what it takes, Carrie's going to rot in jail and hell after that.'

The nurse had returned to my room to whisk the telephone away again.

'I don't understand this,' I complained as I hung up. 'I have a calling card, if that's what you're worried about.'

She smiled. 'Colonel's orders. He wants you to rest and knows you won't if you can be on the phone all day.'

'I am resting,' I said, but she was gone.

I wondered why he allowed me to keep the laptop and was suspicious Lucy or someone had spoken to him. As I logged onto AOL, I felt conspired against. I had barely entered the M.E. chat room when deadoc appeared, this time not as an invisible instant message, but as a member who could be heard and seen by anybody else who decided to walk in.

DEADOC:	where have you been
SCARPETTA:	Who are you?
DEADOC:	I ve already told you that
SCARPETTA:	You are not me.
DEADOC:	he gave them power over unclean spirits to cast them out and to heal all manner of sickness and all manner of disease pathophysiological manifestations viruses like hiv our darwinian struggle against them they are evil or are we
SCARPETTA:	Explain what you mean.
DEADOC:	there are twelve

But he had no intention of explaining, at least not now. The system alerted me that he had left the room. I waited inside it a while longer to see if he might return, as I wondered what he meant by *twelve*. Pushing a button on my headboard, I summoned the nurse, who was beginning to cause me guilt. I didn't know where she waited outside the room, or if she climbed in and out of her blue suit every time she appeared and left. But none of this could have been pleasant, including my disposition.

'Listen,' I said when she got to me. 'Might there be a Bible around here somewhere.'

She hesitated, as if she'd never heard of such a thing. 'Gee, now that I don't know.'

'Could you check?'

'Are you feeling all right?' She looked suspiciously at me.

'Absolutely.'

'They've got a library. Maybe there's one in there somewhere. I'm sorry. I'm not very religious.' She continued talking as she went out again.

She returned maybe half an hour later with a black leather-bound Bible, Cambridge Red Letter edition, that she claimed to have borrowed from someone's office. I opened it and found a name in front written in calligraphy, and a date that showed the Bible had been given to its owner on a special occasion almost ten years before. As I began to turn its pages, I realized I had not been to Mass in months. I envied people with a faith so strong that they kept their Bibles at work.

'Now you're sure you're feeling okay?' said the nurse as she hovered near the door.

'You've never told me your name,' I said.

'Sally.'

'You've been very helpful and I certainly appreciate it. I know it's no fun working on Thanksgiving.'

This seemed to please her a great deal and gave her enough confidence to say, 'I haven't wanted to poke my nose into anything, but I can't help but hear what people are talking about. That island in Virginia where your case came from. All they do is crabbing there?'

'Pretty much,' I said.

'Blue crab.'

'And soft-shell crab.'

'Anybody bothering to worry about that?'

I knew what she was getting at, and yes, I was worried. I had a personal reason to be worried about Wesley and me.

'They ship those things all over the country, right?' she went on.

I nodded.

'What if whatever that lady had is transmitted through water or food?' Her eyes were bright behind her hood. 'I didn't see her body, but I heard. That's really scary.'

'I know,' I said. 'I hope we can get an answer to that soon.'

'By the way, lunch is turkey. Don't expect much.'

She unplugged her air line and stopped talking. Opening the door, she gave me a little wave and went out. I turned back to the Concordance and had to search for a while under various words before I found the passage deadoc had quoted to me. It was Matthew

10, verse one, and in its entirety it read: *And when he had called unto him his twelve disciples, he gave them power against unclean spirits, to cast them out, and to heal all manner of sickness and all manner of disease.*

The next verse went on to identify the disciples by name, and then Jesus invoked them to go out and find lost sheep, and to preach to them that the kingdom of heaven was at hand. He directed his disciples to heal the sick, cleanse the lepers, raise the dead, cast out devils. As I read, I did not know if this killer who called himself deadoc had a message he believed, if *twelve* referred to the disciples, or if he was simply playing games.

I got up and paced, looking out the window as light waned. Night came early now, and it had become a habit for me to watch people walk out to their cars. Their breath was frosted, and the lot was almost empty because of the furlough. Two women chatted while one held open the door to a Honda, and they shrugged and gestured with intensity, as if trying to resolve life's big problems. I stood looking through blinds until they drove away.

I tried to go to sleep early to escape. But I was fitful again, rearranging myself and the covers every few hours. Images floated past the inside of my eyelids, projected like old movies, unedited and illogically arranged. I saw two women talking by a mailbox. One had a mole on her cheek that became eruptions all over her face as she shielded her eyes with a hand. Then palm trees were writhing in fierce winds as a hurricane roared in from the sea, fronds ripped off and flying. A trunk stripped bare, a bloody table lined with severed hands and feet.

I sat up sweating, and waited for my muscles to stop twitching. It was as if there were an electrical disturbance in my entire system, and I might have a heart attack or a stroke. Taking deep, slow breaths, I blanked out my mind. I did not move. When the vision had passed, I rang for the nurse.

When she saw the look on my face, she did not argue about the phone. She brought it right away and I called Marino after she left.

'You still in jail?' he said over the line.

'I think he killed his guinea pig,' I said.

'Whoa. How 'bout starting over again.'

'Deadoc. The woman he shot and dismembered may have been his guinea pig. Someone he knew and had easy access to.'

'I gotta confess, Doc, I got no idea what the hell you're talking about.' I could tell by his tone he was worried about my state of mind.

'It makes sense that he couldn't look at her. The M.O. makes a lot of sense.'

'Now you really got me confused.'

'If you wanted to find a way to murder people through a virus,' I explained, 'first you would have to figure out a way. The route of transmission, for example. Is it a food, a drink, dust? With smallpox, transmission is airborne, spread by droplets or by fluid from the lesions. The disease can be carried on a person or his clothes.'

'Start with this,' he said. 'Where did this person get the virus to begin with? Not exactly something you order through the mail.'

'I don't know. To my knowledge there are only two places in the world that keep archival smallpox. CDC and a laboratory in Moscow.'

'So maybe this is all a Russian plot,' he said, sardonically.

'Let me give you a scenario,' I said. 'The killer has a grudge, maybe even some delusion that he has a religious calling to bring back one of the worst diseases this planet has ever known. He's got to figure out a way to randomly infect people and be sure that it can work.'

'So he needs a guinea pig,' Marino said.

'Yes. And let's suppose he has a neighbor, a relative, someone elderly and not well. Maybe he even takes care of her. What better way to test the virus than on that person? And if it works, you kill her and stage her death to look like something else. After all, he certainly can't have her die of smallpox. Not if there is a connection between him and her. We might figure out who he is. So he shoots her in the head, dismembers her so we'll think it's the serial killings again.'

'Then how do you get from that to the lady on Tangier?'

'She was exposed,' I simply said.

'How? Was something delivered to her? Did she get something in the mail? Was it carried on the air? Was she pricked in her sleep?'

'I don't know how.'

'You think deadoc lives on Tangier?' Marino then asked.

'No, I don't,' I said. 'I think he picked it because the island is the perfect place to start an epidemic. Small, self-contained. Also easy to quarantine, meaning the killer doesn't intend to annihilate all of society with one blow. He's trying a little bit at a time, cutting us up in small pieces.'

'Yeah. Like he did the old lady, if you're right.'

'He wants something,' I said. 'Tangier is an attention-getter.'

'No offense, Doc, but I hope you're wrong about all of this.'

'I'm heading to Atlanta in the morning. How about checking with

Vander, see if he's had any luck with the thumbprint.'

'So far he hasn't. It's looking like the victim doesn't have any prints on file. Anything comes up, I'll call your pager.'

'Damn,' I muttered, for the nurse had taken that, too.

The rest of the day moved interminably slowly, and it wasn't until after supper that Fujitsubo came to say goodbye. Although the act of releasing me implied I was neither infected nor infectious, he was in a blue suit, which he plugged into an air line.

'I should keep you longer,' he said right off, filling my heart with dread. 'Incubation, on average, is twelve to thirteen days. But it can be as long as twenty-one. What I'm saying to you is that you could still get sick.'

'I understand that,' I said, reaching for my water.

'The revaccination may or may not help depending on what stage you were in when I gave it to you.'

I nodded. 'And I wouldn't be in such a hurry to leave if you would just take this on instead of sending me to CDC.'

'Kay, I can't.' His voice was muffled through plastic. 'You know it has nothing to do with what I feel like doing. But I can no more pull something out from under CDC than you can grab a case that isn't your jurisdiction. I've talked to them. They are most concerned over a possible outbreak and will begin testing the moment you arrive with the samples.'

'I fear terrorism may be involved.' I refused to back down.

'Until there is evidence of it – and I hope there won't be – we can do nothing more for you here.' His regret was sincere. 'Go to Atlanta and see what they have to say. They're operating with a skeleton crew, too. The timing couldn't be worse.'

'Or perhaps more deliberate,' I said. 'If you were a bad person planning to commit serial crimes with a virus, what better time than when the significant federal health agencies are in extremis? And this furlough's been going on for a while and not predicted to end anytime soon.'

He was silent.

'John,' I went on, 'you helped with the autopsy. Have you ever seen a disease like this?'

'Only in textbooks,' he grimly replied.

'How does smallpox suddenly just reappear on its own?'

'If that's what it is.'

'Whatever it is, it's virulent and it kills,' I tried to reason with him. But he could do nothing more, and the rest of the night I wandered from room to room in AOL. Every hour, I checked my e-mail. Deadoc remained silent until six o'clock the next morning when he walked into the M.E. room. My heart jumped as his name appeared on screen. My adrenaline began to pump the way it always did when he talked to me. He was on the line, it was up to me. I could catch him, if only I could trip him.

DEADOC: Sunday I went to church bet you didn't
SCARPETTA: What was the homily about?
DEADOC: sermon
SCARPETTA: You are not Catholic.
DEADOC: beware of men
SCARPETTA: Matthew 10. Tell me what you mean.
DEADOC: to say he s sorry
SCARPETTA: Who is he? And what did he do?
DEADOC: ye shall indeed drink of the cup that I drink of

Before I could answer, he was gone, and I began flipping through the Bible. The verse he quoted this time was from Mark, and again, it was Jesus speaking, which hinted to me, if nothing else, that deadoc wasn't Jewish. Nor was he Catholic, based on his comments about church. I was no theologian, but drinking of the cup seemed to refer to Christ's eventual crucifixion. So deadoc had been crucified and I would be, too?

It was my last few hours here and my nurse, Sally, was more liberal with the phone. I paged Lucy, who called me back almost instantly.

'I'm talking to him,' I said. 'Are you guys there?'

'We're there. He's got to stay on longer,' my niece said. 'There are so many trunk lines, and we got to line up all the phone companies to trap and trace. Your last call was coming in from Dallas.'

'You're kidding,' I said in dismay.

'That's not the origin, just a switch it was routed through. We didn't get any farther because he disconnected. Keep trying. Sounds like this guy's some kind of religious nut.'

11

Later that morning I left in a taxi as the sun was getting high in the clouds. I had nothing but the clothes on my back, all of which had been sterilized in the autoclave or gassed. I was in a hurry, and guarding a large white cardboard box printed with PERISHABLE RUSH! RUSH! and IMPORTANT KEEP UPRIGHT and other big blue warnings.

Like a Chinese puzzle, my package was boxes within boxes containing BioPacks. Inside these were Bio-tubes of Lila Pruitt's liver, spleen and spinal fluid, protected by fiber-board shields, and bubble and corrugated wrap. All of it was packed in dry ice with INFEC-TIOUS SUBSTANCE and DANGER stickers warning anyone who got beyond the first layer. Obviously, I could not let my cargo out of sight. In addition to its well-proven hazard, it could be evidence should it turn out that Pruitt was a homicide. At the Baltimore-Washington International airport, I found a pay phone and called Rose.

'USAMRIID has my medical bag and microscope.' I didn't waste time. 'See what you can do about getting them shipped overnight. I'm at BWI, en route to CDC.'

'I've been trying to page you,' she said.

'Maybe they can return that to me, too.' I tried to remember what else I was missing. 'And the phone,' I added.

'You got a report back that you might find interesting. The animal hairs that turned up with the torso. Rabbit and monkey hairs.'

'Bizarre,' was the only thing I could think to say.

'I hate to tell you this news. The media's been calling about the Carrie Grethen case. Apparently, something's been leaked.'

'Goddamn it!' I exclaimed as I thought about Ring.

'What do you want me to do?' she asked.

'How about calling Benton. I don't know what to say. I'm a little overwhelmed.'

'You sound that way.'

I looked at my watch. 'Rose, I've got to go fight my way on a plane. They didn't want to let me through X-ray, and I know what's going to happen when I try to board with this thing.'

It was exactly what I expected. When I walked into the cabin, a flight attendant took one look and smiled.

'Here.' She held out her hands. 'Let me put this in baggage for you.'

'It's got to stay with me,' I said.

'It won't fit in an overhead rack or under your seat, ma'am.' Her smile got tight, the line behind me getting longer.

'Can we discuss this out of traffic?' I said, moving into the kitchen.

She was right next to me, hovering close. 'Ma'am, this flight is overbooked. We simply don't have room.'

'Here,' I said, showing her the paperwork.

Her eyes scanned the red-bordered Declaration For Dangerous Goods, and froze halfway down a column where it was typed that I was transporting 'Infectious substances affecting humans.' She glanced nervously around the kitchen and moved me closer to the rest rooms.

'Regulations require that only a trained person can handle dangerous goods like these,' I reasonably explained. 'So it has to stay with me.'

'What is it?' she whispered, her eyes round.

'Autopsy specimens.'

'Mother of God.'

She immediately grabbed her seating chart. Soon after, I was escorted to an empty row in first class, near the back.

'Just put it on the seat next to you. It's not going to leak or anything?' she asked.

'I'll guard it with my life,' I promised.

'We should have a lot of vacancies up here unless a bunch of people upgrade. But don't you worry. I'll steer everyone.' She motioned with her arms, as if she were driving.

No one came near me or my box. I drank coffee during a very peaceful flight to Atlanta, feeling naked without my pager or phone, but overjoyed to be on my own. In the Atlanta airport, I took one moving sidewalk and escalator after another, traveling what seemed miles, before I got outside and found a taxi.

We followed 85 North to Druid Hills Road, where soon we were passing pawnshops and auto rentals, then vast jungles of poison oak and kudzu, and strip malls. The Center for Disease Control and Prevention was in the midst of the parking decks and parking lots of Emory University. Across the street from the American Cancer Society, CDC was six floors of tan brick trimmed with gray. I checked in at a desk that had guards and closed circuit TV.

'This is going to Bio Level 4, where I'm meeting Dr Bret Martin in the atrium,' I explained.

'Ma'am, you'll need an escort,' one of the guards said.

'Good,' I said as he reached for the phone. 'I always get lost.'

I followed him to the back of the building, where the facility was new and under intense surveillance. There were cameras everywhere, the glass bulletproof, and corridors were catwalks with grated floors. We passed bacteria and influenza labs, and the red brick and concrete area for rabies and AIDS.

'This is impressive,' I said, for I had not been here in several years.

'Yeah, it is. They got all the security you might want. Cameras, motion detectors at all exits and entrances. All the trash is boiled and burned, and they use these filters for the air so anything that comes in is killed. Except the scientists.' He laughed as he used a card key to open a door. 'So what bad news you carrying in?'

'That's what I'm here to find out,' I said, and we were in the atrium now.

BL-4 was really nothing more than a huge laminar flow hood with thick walls of concrete and steel. It was a building within a building, its windows covered with blinds. Labs were behind thick walls of glass, and the only blue-suited scientists working this furloughed day were those who had cared enough to come in anyway.

'This thing with the government,' the guard was saying as he shook his head. 'What they think? These diseases like Ebola gonna wait until the budget gets straight?' He shook his head some more.

He escorted me past containment rooms that were dark, and labs with no one in them, then empty rabbit cages in a corridor and rooms for large primates. A monkey looked at me through bars and glass, his eyes so human they unnerved me, and I thought of what Rose had said. Deadoc had transferred monkey and rabbit hairs to a victim I knew he had touched. He might work in a place like this.

'They throw waste at you,' the guard said as we walked on. 'Same thing their animal rights activists do. Kinda fits, don't you think?'

My anxiety was getting stronger.

'Where are we going?' I asked.

'Where the good doctor told me to bring you, ma'am,' he said, and we were on another level of catwalk now, heading into another part of the building.

We passed through a door, where Revco ultra low temperature freezers looked like computers the size of large copying machines. They were locked and out of place in this corridor, where a heavy man in a lab coat was waiting for me. He had baby-fine blond hair, and was perspiring.

'I'm Bret Martin,' he said, offering me his hand. 'Thanks.' He nodded at the guard, indicating he was dismissed.

I handed Martin my cardboard box.

'This is where we keep our smallpox stock,' he said, nodding at the freezers as he set my box on top of one of them. 'Locked up at seventy degrees centigrade below zero. What can I say?' He shrugged. 'These freezers are out in the hall because we have no room anyplace else in maximum containment. Rather coincidental you should give this to me. Not that I'm expecting your disease to be the same.'

'All of this is smallpox?' I asked, amazed as I looked around.

'Not all, and not for long, though, since for the first time ever on this planet we've made a conscious decision to eliminate a species.'

'The irony,' I said. 'When the species you're talking about has eliminated millions.'

'So you think we should just take all this source disease and autoclave it.'

His expression said what I was used to hearing. Life was much more complicated than I presented it, and only people like him recognized the subtler shades.

'I'm not saying we should destroy anything,' I replied. 'Not at all. Actually, probably we shouldn't. Because of this.' I looked at the box I had just given him. 'Our autoclaving smallpox certainly won't mean it's gone. I guess it's like any other weapon.'

'You and me both. I'd sure like to know where the Russians are hiding their variola stock virus these days, and if they've sold any of it to the Middle East, North Korea.'

'You'll do PCR on this?' I said.

'Yes.'

'Right away?'

'As fast as we can.'

'Please,' I said. 'This is an emergency.'

'That's why I'm standing here now,' he said. 'The government considers me nonessential. I should be at home.'

'I've got photographs that USAMRIID was kind enough to develop while I was in the Slammer,' I said with a trace of irony.

'I want to see them.'

We took the elevator back up, getting off on the fourth floor. He led me into a conference room where staff met to devise strategies against terrible scourges they couldn't always identify. Usually bacteriologists, epidemiologists, people in charge of quarantines, communications, special pathogens and PCR assembled in the room. But it was quiet, no one was here but us.

'Right now,' Martin said, 'I'm all you've got.'

I got a thick envelope out of my purse, and he began to go through the photographs. For a moment, he stared as if transfixed, at color prints of the torso and those of Lila Pruitt.

'Good God,' he said. 'I think we should look at transpiration routes right away. Everybody who might have had contact. And I mean, fast.'

'We can do that on Tangier,' I said. 'Maybe.'

'Definitely not chicken pox or measles. No way, Jose,' he said. 'Definitely pox-related.'

He went through photographs of the severed hands and feet, his eyes wide.

'Wow.' He stared without blinking, light reflecting on his glasses. 'What the hell is this?'

'He calls himself deadoc,' I said. 'He sent me graphic files through AOL. Anonymously, of course. The FBI's trying to track him.'

'And this victim here, he dismembered?'

I nodded.

'She also has manifestations similar to the victim on Tangier.' He was looking at vesicles on the torso.

'So far, yes.'

'You know, monkeypox has been worrying me for years,' he said. 'We survey the hell out of West Africa, from Zaire to Sierra Leone, where cases have occurred, along with whitepox. But so far, no variola virus has turned up. My fear, though, is that one of these days, some poxvirus in the animal kingdom is going to figure out a way to infect people.'

Again, I thought about my telephone conversation with Rose, about murder and animal hairs.

'All that's got to happen is the microorganism gets in the air, let's say, and finds a susceptible host.'

He went back to Lila Pruitt, to her disfigured, tormented body on her foul bed.

'Now she was obviously exposed to enough virus to cause devastating disease,' he said, and he was so engrossed, he seemed to be talking to himself.

'Dr Martin,' I said. 'Do monkeys get monkeypox or are they just the carrier?'

'They get it and they give it where there is animal contact, such as in the rain forests of Africa. There are nine known virulent poxviruses on this planet and transmission to humans happens only in two. The variola virus, or smallpox, which, thank God, we don't see anymore, and molluscum contagiosum.'

'Trace evidence clinging to the torso has been identified as monkey hair.'

He turned to look at me and frowned. 'What?'

'And rabbit hair, too. I'm just wondering if someone out there is conducting their own laboratory experiments.'

He got up from the table.

'We'll start on this now. Where can you be reached?'

'Back in Richmond.' I handed him my card as we walked out of the conference room. 'Could someone maybe call for a taxi?'

'Sure. One of the guards at the desk. Afraid none of the clerical staff is in.'

Carrying the box, he pushed the elevator button with his elbow. 'It's a nightmare. We got salmonella in Orlando from unpasteurized orange juice, another potential cruise ship outbreak of E. coli O-one-five-seven-H-seven, probably undercooked ground beef again. Botulism in Rhode Island, and some respiratory disease in an old folks' home. And Congress doesn't want to fund us.'

'Tell me about it,' I said.

We stopped at each floor, waiting as other people got on. Martin kept talking.

'Imagine this,' he went on. 'A resort in Iowa where we've got suspected shigella because a lot of rain overflowed in private wells. And try to get the EPA involved.'

'It's called *mission impossible*,' someone sardonically said as the doors opened again.

'If they even exist anymore,' Martin quipped. 'We get fourteen thousand calls a year and have only two operators. Actually, right now we got none. Anybody who comes in, answers the phone. Including me.'

'Please don't let this wait,' I said as we reached the lobby.

'Don't worry.' He was into it. 'I got three guys I'm calling in from home right away.'

For half an hour, I waited in the lobby and used a phone, and at last my taxi was here. I rode in silence, staring out at plazas of polished granite and marble, and sports complexes that reminded me of the Olympics, and buildings of silver and glass. Atlanta was a city where everything aspired higher, and lavish fountains seemed a symbol of generosity and no fear. I was feeling light-headed and chilled and unusually tired for one who had just spent the better part of a week in bed. By the time I reached my Delta gate, my back had begun to ache. I could not get warm or think very clearly, and I knew I had a fever.

I was ill by the time I reached Richmond. When Marino met me at the gate, the expression on his face turned to abject fear.

'Geez, Doc,' he said. 'You look like hell.'

'I feel like hell.'

'You got any bags?'

'No. You got any news?'

'Yeah,' he said. 'One tidbit that will piss you off. Ring arrested Keith Pleasants last night.'

'For what?' I exclaimed as I coughed.

'Attempting to elude. Supposedly, Ring was following him out of the landfill after work and tried to pull him for speeding. Supposedly, Pleasants wouldn't stop. So he's in jail, bond set at five grand, if you can believe that. He ain't going nowhere anytime soon.'

'Harassment.' I blew my nose. 'Ring is picking on him. Picking on Lucy. Picking on me.'

'No kidding. Maybe you should've stayed in Maryland, in bed,' he said as we boarded the escalator. 'No offense, but I ain't gonna catch this, am I?'

Marino was terrified of anything he could not see, whether it was radiation or a virus.

'I don't know what I've got,' I said. 'Maybe the flu.'

'Last time I got that I was out for two weeks.' His pace slowed, so he did not keep up with me. 'Plus, you been around other things.'

'Then don't come close, touch or kiss me,' I said, shortly.

'Hey, don't worry.'

This continued as we walked out into the cold afternoon.

'Look. I'm going to take a taxi home,' I said and I was so mad at him I was next to tears.

'I don't want you doing that.' Marino looked frightened and was jumpy.

I waved in the air, swallowing hard and hiding my face as a Blue Bird cab veered toward me.

'You don't need the flu. Rose doesn't need it. No one needs it,' I said, furiously. 'You know, I'm almost out of cash. This is awful. Look at my suit. You think an autoclave presses anything and leaves a pleasant smell? The hell with my hose. I got no coat, no gloves. Here I am, and it's what?' I yanked open the back door of a cab that was Carolina blue. 'Thirty degrees?'

Marino stared at me as I got in. He handed me a twenty-dollar bill, careful his fingers did not brush mine.

'You need anything at the store?' he called out as I drove off.

My throat and eyes swelled with tears. Digging tissues out of my purse, I blew my nose and quietly wept.

'Don't mean to bug ya, lady,' said my driver, a portly old man. 'But where are we going?'

'Windsor Farms. I'll show you when we get there,' I choked as I said.

'Fights.' He shook his head. 'Dontcha hate 'em? I 'member one time me and the wife got to arguing in one these all-you-can-eat fish camps. She takes the car. Me, I take a hike. Five miles home through a bad part of town.'

He was nodding, eyeing me in the rearview mirror as he assumed that Marino and I were having a lovers' quarrel.

'So, you're married to a cop?' he then said. 'I saw him drive in. Not an unmarked car on the road that can fool this guy.' He thumped his chest.

My head was splitting, my face burning. I settled back in the seat and shut my eyes while he droned on about an earlier life in Philadelphia, and his hopes that this winter would not bring much snow. I settled into a feverish sleep. When I awoke, I did not know where I was.

'Ma'am. Ma'am. We're here,' the driver was saying loudly to wake me up. 'Where to next?'

He had just turned onto Canterbury and was sitting at a stop sign.

'Up here, take a right on Dover,' I replied.

I directed him into my neighborhood, the look on his face increasingly baffled as he drove past Georgian and Tudor estates behind walls in the city's wealthiest neighborhood. When he stopped at my front door, he stared at fieldstone, at the wooded land around my home, and he watched me closely as I climbed out.

'Don't worry,' he said as I handed him a twenty and told him to keep the change. 'I seen it all lady, and never say nothing.' He zipped his lips, winking at me.

I was a rich man's wife having a tempestuous affair with a detective.

'A good credo,' I said, coughing.

The burglar alarm welcomed me with its warning beep, and never in my life had I been more relieved to be home. I wasted no time getting out of my scalded clothes, and straight into a hot shower, where I inhaled steam and tried to clear the rattle from my lungs. When I was wrapping up in a thick terry cloth robe, the telephone rang. It was exactly four P.M.

'Dr Scarpetta?' It was Fielding.

'I just got home,' I said.

'You don't sound good.'

'I'm not.'

'Well, my news isn't going to help,' he said. 'They've got possibly two more cases on Tangier.'

'Oh no,' I said.

'A mother and daughter. Fever of a hundred and five, a rash. CDC's deployed a team with bed isolators, the whole nine yards.'

'How's Wingo?' I asked.

He paused, as if puzzled. 'Fine. Why?'

'He helped with the torso,' I reminded him.

'Oh yeah. Well, he's the same as always.'

Relieved, I sat down and shut my eyes.

'What's going on with the samples you took to Atlanta?' Fielding asked.

'They're doing tests, I hope, with what few people they can muster now.'

'So we still don't know what this is.'

'Jack, everything points to smallpox,' I said to him. 'That's the way it looks so far.'

'I've never seen it. Have you?'

'Not before now. Maybe leprosy is worse. It's bad enough to die of a disease, but to be disfigured in the process is cruel.' I coughed again and was very thirsty. 'I'll see you in the morning, and we'll figure out what we're going to do.'

'It doesn't sound to me like you should be going anywhere.'

'You're absolutely right. And I don't have a choice.'

I hung up and tried Bret Martin at CDC, but his phone was answered by voice mail, and he did not call me back. I also left a message for Fujitsubo, but he did not return my call, either, and I figured he was at home, like most of his colleagues. The budget war raged on.

'Damn,' I swore as I put a kettle of water on the stove and dug in a cupboard for tea. 'Damn, damn, damn.'

It was not quite five when I called Wesley. At Quantico, at least, people were still working.

'Thank God someone is answering the phones somewhere,' I blurted out to his secretary.

'They haven't figured out how nonessential I am yet,' she said.

'Is he in?' I asked.

Wesley got on the phone, and sounded so energetic and cheery that it instantly got on my nerves.

'You have no right to feel this good,' I said.

'You have the flu.'

'I don't know what I've got.'

'That's what it is, right?' He was worried and his mood went bad.

'I don't know. We can only assume.'

'I don't mean to be an alarmist . . .'

'Then don't,' I cut him off.

'Kay,' his voice was firm. 'You've got to face this. What if it's not?'

I said nothing because I could not bear to think such thoughts.

'Please,' he said. 'Don't blow this off. Don't pretend it's nothing like you do with most things in your life.'

'Now you're making me mad,' I snapped. 'I fly into this goddamn airport and Marino doesn't want me in his car so I take a taxi and the driver thinks we're having an affair and my rich husband doesn't know, and all the while I have a fever and hurt like hell and just want to go home.'

'The taxi driver thinks you're having an affair?'

'Just forget it.'

'How do you know you've got the flu? That it's not something else?'

'I don't have a rash. Is that what you want to hear?'

There was a long silence. Then he said, 'What if you get one?'

'Then I'm probably going to die, Benton.' I coughed again. 'You'll probably never touch me again. And I'd never want you to see me again, if it goes its course. It's easier to worry about stalkers, serial killers, people you can blow away with a gun. But the invisible ones are who I've always feared. They take you on a sunny day in a public place. They slide in with your lemonade. I've been vaccinated for hepatitis B. But that's just one killer in a huge population. What about tuberculosis and HIV, and Hanta and Ebola? What about this? God.' I took a deep breath. 'It started with a torso and I did not know.'

'I heard about the two new cases,' he said, and his voice had gotten quiet and gentle. 'I can be there in two hours. Do you want to see me?'

'Right now I don't want to see anyone.'

'Doesn't matter. I'm on my way.'

'Benton,' I said, 'don't.'

But he had his mind made up, and when he pulled into my driveway in his throaty BMW, it was almost midnight. I met him at the door, and we did not touch.

'Let's sit in front of the fire,' he said.

We did, and he was kind enough to make me another cup of decaffeinated tea. I sat on the couch, he was in a side chair, and flames fed by gas enveloped an artificial log. I had turned the lights low.

'I don't doubt your theory,' he said as he lingered over cognac.

'Maybe tomorrow, we'll know more.' I was perspiring as I shivered, staring into the fire.

'Right now I don't give a shit about any of that.' He looked fiercely at me.

'You have to give a shit about that.' I wiped my brow with a sleeve. 'No.'

I was silent as he stared at me.

'What I care about is you,' he said.

Still, I did not respond.

'Kay.' He gripped my arm.

'Don't touch me, Benton.' I shut my eyes. 'Don't. I don't want you sick, too.'

'See, and that's convenient for you. To be sick. And I can't touch you. And you the noble doctor caring more about my well-being than your own.'

I was quiet, determined not to cry.

'Convenient. You want to be sick right now so nobody can get close. Marino won't even give you a ride home. And I can't put my hands on you. And Lucy won't see you and Janet has to talk to you behind glass.'

'What is your point?' I looked at him.

'Functional illness.'

'Oh. I guess you studied that in school. Maybe during your master's in psychology or something.'

'Don't make fun of me.'

'I never have.'

I could feel his hurt as I turned my face to the fire, my eyes closed tight.

'Kay. Don't you die on me.'

I did not speak.

'Don't you dare.' His voice shook. 'Don't you dare!'

'You won't get off the hook that easy,' I said, getting out of my chair. 'Let's go to bed.'

He slept in the room where Lucy usually stayed, and I was up most of the night coughing and trying to get comfortable, which simply was not possible. The next morning at half past six he was up, and coffee was brewing when I walked into the kitchen. Light filtered through trees beyond windows, and I could tell by the tight curl of rhododendron leaves that it was bitterly cold.

'I'm cooking,' Wesley announced. 'What will it be?'

'I don't think I can.' I was weak, and when I coughed, it felt as if my lungs were ripping.

'Obviously, you are worse.' Concern flickered in his eyes. 'You should go to a doctor.'

'I am a doctor, and it's too soon to go to one.'

I took aspirin, decongestants and a thousand milligrams of vitamin C. I ate a bagel and was beginning to feel almost human when Rose called and ruined me.

'Dr Scarpetta? The mother from Tangier died early this morning.'

'Oh God no.' I was sitting at the kitchen table and running my fingers through my hair. 'What about the daughter?'

'Condition's serious. Or at least it was several hours ago.'

'And the body?'

Wesley was behind me, rubbing my sore shoulders and neck.

'No one's moved it yet. No one's sure what to do, and the Baltimore Medical Examiner's Office has been trying to reach you. So has CDC.'

'Who at CDC?' I asked.

'A Dr Martin.'

'I need to call him first, Rose. Meanwhile, you get hold of Baltimore and tell them that under no circumstances are they to have that body sent into their morgue until they've heard from me. What is Dr Martin's number?'

She gave it to me and I dialed it immediately. He answered on the first ring and sounded keyed up.

'We did PCR on the samples you brought in. Three primers and two of them match with smallpox, but one of them didn't.'

'Then is it smallpox or not?'

'We ran its genomic sequence, and it doesn't match up with any poxvirus in any reference lab in the world. Dr Scarpetta, I believe you got a virus that's a mutant.'

'Meaning, the smallpox vaccination isn't going to work,' I said as my heart seemed to drop right out of me.

'All we can do is test in the animal lab. We're talking at least a week before we know and can even begin thinking about a new vaccine. For practical purposes, we're calling this smallpox, but we really don't know what the hell it is. I'll also remind you we've been working on an AIDS vaccine since 1986 and are no closer now than we were back then.'

'Tangier Island needs to be quarantined immediately. We've got to contain this,' I exclaimed, alarmed to the edge of panic.

'Believe me, we know. We're getting a team together right now and will mobilize the Coast Guard.'

I hung up and was frantic when I said to Wesley, 'I've got to go. We've got an outbreak of something no one's ever heard of. It's already killed at least two people. Maybe three. Maybe four.'

He was following me down the hall as I talked.

'It's smallpox but not smallpox. We've got to find out how it's being transmitted. Did Lila Pruitt know the mother who just died? Did they have any contact at all, or did the daughter? Did they even live near each other? What about the water supply? A water tower. Blue. I remember seeing one.'

I was getting dressed. Wesley stood in the doorway, his face almost gray and like stone.

'You're going to go back out there,' he said.

'I need to get downtown first.' I looked at him.

'I'll drive,' he said.

12

———

Wesley dropped me off and said he was going to the Richmond Field Office for a while and would check with me later. My heels were loud as I walked down the corridor, bidding good morning to members of my staff. Rose was on the phone when I walked in, and the glimpse of my desk through her adjoining doorway was devastating. Hundreds of reports and death certificates awaited my initials and signature, and mail and phone messages were cascading out of my in-basket.

'What is this?' I said as she hung up. 'You'd think I've been gone a year.'

'It feels like you have.'

She was rubbing lotion into her hands and I noticed the small canister of Vita aromatherapy facial spray on the edge of my desk, the open mailing tube next to it. There was also one on Rose's desk, next to her bottle of Vaseline Intensive Care. I stared back and forth, from my Vita spray to hers, my subconscious processing what I was seeing before my reason did. Reality seemed to turn inside out, and I grabbed the door frame. Rose was on her feet, her chair flying back on its rollers as she lunged around her desk for me.

'Dr Scarpetta!'

'Where did you get this?' I asked, staring at the spray.

'It's just a sample.' She looked bewildered. 'A bunch of them came in the mail.'

'Have you used it?'

Now she was really worried as she looked at me. 'Well, it just got here. I haven't tried it yet.'

'Don't touch it!' I said, severely. 'Who else got one?'

'Gosh, I really don't know. What is it? What's wrong?' She raised her voice.

Getting gloves from my office, I grabbed the facial spray off her desk and triple-bagged it.

'Everybody in the conference room, now!'

I ran down the hall to the front office, and made the same announcement. Within minutes, my entire staff, including doctors still in scrubs, was assembled. Some people were out of breath, and everyone was staring at me, unnerved and frazzled.

I held up the transparent evidence bag containing the sample size of Vita spray.

'Who has one of these?' I asked, looking around the room.

Four people raised their hands.

'Who has used it?' I then asked. 'I need to know if absolutely anybody has.'

Cleta, a clerk from the front office, looked frightened. 'Why? What's the matter?'

'Have you sprayed this on your face?' I said to her.

'On my plants,' she said.

'Plants get bagged and burned,' I said. 'Where's Wingo?'

'MCV.'

'I don't know this for a fact,' I spoke to everyone, 'and I pray I'm wrong. But we might be dealing with product tampering. Please don't panic, but under no circumstances does anyone touch this spray. Do we know exactly how they were delivered?'

It was Cleta who spoke. 'This morning I came in before anybody up front. There were police reports shoved through the slot, as always. And these had been, too. They were in little mailing tubes. There were eleven of them. I know because I counted to see if there was enough to go around.'

'And the mailman didn't bring them. They had just been shoved through the slot of the front door.'

'I don't know who brought them. But they looked like they'd been mailed.'

'Any tubes you still have, please bring them to me,' I said.

I was told that no one had used one, and all were collected and brought to my office. Putting on cotton gloves and glasses, I studied the mailing tube meant for me. Postage was bulk rate and clearly a manufacturer's sample, and I found it most unusual for something like that to be addressed to a specific individual. I looked inside the tube, and there was a coupon for the spray. As I held it up to the light, I noticed edges imperceptibly uneven, as if the coupon had been clipped with scissors versus a machine.

'Rose?' I called out.

She walked into my office.

'The tube you got,' I said. 'Who was it addressed to?'

'Resident, I think.' Her face was stressed.

'Then the only one with a name on it is mine.'

'I think so. This is awful.'

'Yes, it is.' I picked up the mailing tube. 'Look at this. Letters all the same size, the postmark on the same label as the address. I've never seen that.'

'Like it came off a computer,' she said as her amazement grew.

'I'm going across the street to the DNA lab.' I got up. 'Call USAM-RIID right away and tell Colonel Fujitsubo we need to schedule a conference call between him, us, CDC, Quantico, now.'

'Where do you want to do it?' she asked as I hurried out the door.

'Not here. See what Benton says.'

Outside, I ran down the sidewalk past my parking lot, and crossed Fourteenth Street. I entered the Seaboard Building where DNA and other forensic labs had relocated several years before. At the security desk, I called the section chief, Dr Douglas Wheat, who had been given a male family name, despite her gender.

'I need a closed air system and a hood,' I explained to her.

'Come on back.'

A long sloping hallway always polished bright led to a series of glass-enclosed laboratories. Inside, scientists were prepossessed with pipettes and gels and radioactive probes as they coaxed sequences of genetic code to unravel their identities. Wheat, who battled paperwork almost as much as I did, was sitting at her desk, typing something on her computer. She was an attractive woman in a strong way, forty and friendly.

'What trouble are you getting into this time?' She smiled at me, then eyed my bag. 'I'm afraid to ask.'

'Possible product tampering,' I said. 'I need to spray some on a slide, but it absolutely can't get in the air or on me or anyone.'

'What is it?' She was very somber now, getting up.

'Possibly a virus.'

'As in the one on Tangier?'

'That's my fear.'

'You don't think it might be wiser to get this to CDC, let them . . .'

'Douglas, yes, it would be wiser,' I patiently explained as I coughed again. 'But we haven't got time. I've got to know. We have no idea how many of these might be in the hands of consumers.'

Her DNA lab had a number of closed air system hoods surrounded by glass bioguards, because the evidence tested here was blood. She led me to one in the back of a room, and we put on masks and gloves, and she gave me a lab coat. She turned on a fan that sucked air up into the hood, passing it through HEPA filters.

'Ready?' I asked, taking the facial spray out of the bag. 'We'll make this quick.'

I held a clean slide and the small canister under the hood and sprayed.

'Let's dip this in a ten percent bleach solution,' I said when I was done. 'Then we'll triple bag it, get it and the other ten off to Atlanta.'

'Coming up,' Wheat said, walking off.

The slide took almost no time to dry, and I dripped Nicolaou stain on it and sealed it with a cover slip. I was already looking at it under a microscope when Wheat returned with a container of bleach solution. She dipped the Vita spray in it several times while fears coalesced, rolling into a dark, awful thunderhead as my pulse throbbed in my neck. I peered at the Guarnieri bodies I had come to dread.

When I looked up at Wheat, she could tell by the expression on my face.

'Not good,' she said.

'Not good.' I turned off the microscope and dropped my mask and gloves into biohazardous waste.

The Vita sprays from my office were airlifted to Atlanta, and a preliminary warning was broadcast nationwide to anyone who might have had such a sample delivered to them. The manufacturer had issued an immediate recall, and international airlines were removing the sprays from overseas travel bags given to business and first-class passengers. The potential spread of this disease, should deadoc have somehow tampered with hundreds, thousands of the facial sprays, was staggering. We could, once again, find ourselves facing a worldwide epidemic.

The meeting took place at one P.M. in the FBI's field office off Staples

Mill Road. State and federal flags fought from tall poles out front as a sharp wind tore brown leaves off trees and made the afternoon seem much colder than it was. The brick building was new, and had a secure conference room equipped with audio-visual capabilities, so we could see remote people while we talked to them. A young female agent sat at the head of the table, at a console. Wesley and I pulled out chairs and moved microphones close. Above us on walls were video monitors.

'Who else are we expecting?' Wesley asked as the special agent in charge, or S.A.C., walked in with an armload of paperwork.

'Miles,' said the S.A.C., referring to the Health Commissioner, my immediate boss. 'And the Coast Guard.' He glanced at his paperwork. 'Regional chief out of Crisfield, Maryland. A chopper's bringing him in. Shouldn't take him more than thirty minutes in one of those big birds.'

He had no sooner said this than we could hear blades thudding faintly in the distance. Minutes later, the Jayhawk was thundering overhead and settling in the helipad behind the building. I could not remember a Coast Guard recovery helicopter ever landing in our city or even flying over it low, and the sight of it must have been awesome to people on the road. Chief Martinez was slipping off his coat as he joined us. I noted his dark blue commando sweater and uniform pants, and maps rolled up in tubes, and the situation only got grimmer.

The agent at the console was working controls as Commissioner Miles strode in and took a chair next to mine. He was an older man with abundant gray hair that was more contentious than most of the people he managed. Today, tufts were sticking out in all directions, his brow heavy and stern as he put on thick black glasses.

'You look a little under the weather,' he said to me as he made notes to himself.

'The usual stuff going around,' I said.

'Had I known that, I wouldn't have sat next to you.' He meant it.

'I'm beyond the contagious stage,' I said, but he wasn't listening.

Monitors were coming on around the room, and I recognized the face of Colonel Fujitsubo on one of them. Then Bret Martin blinked on, staring straight at us.

The agent at the console said, 'Camera on. Mikes on. Someone want to count for me.'

'Five-four-three-two-one,' the S.A.C. said into his mike.

'How's that level?'

'Fine here,' Fujitsubo said from Frederick, Maryland.

'Fine,' said Martin from Atlanta.

'We're ready anytime.' The agent at the console glanced around the table.

'Just to make sure all of us are up to speed,' I began. 'We have an outbreak of what appears to be a smallpox-like virus that so far seems to be restricted to the island of Tangier, eighteen miles off the coast of Virginia. Two deaths reported so far, with another person ill. It is also likely that a recent homicide victim was infected with this virus. The mode of transmission is suspected to be the deliberate contamination of samples of Vita aromatherapy facial spray.'

'That hasn't been determined yet.' It was Miles who spoke.

'The samples should be getting here any minute,' Martin said from Atlanta. 'We'll begin testing immediately, and will hopefully have an answer by the end of tomorrow. Meanwhile, they're being taken out of circulation until we know exactly what we're dealing with.'

'You can do PCR to see if it's the same virus,' Miles said to the video screens.

Martin nodded. 'That we can do.'

Miles looked around the room. 'So what are we saying here? We got some loonytune out there, some Tylenol killer who's decided to use a disease? How do we know these little spray bottles aren't the hell all over the place?'

'I think the killer wants to take his time.' Wesley began what he did best. 'He started with one victim. When that paid off, he began on a tiny island. Now that's paying off, so he hits a downtown health department office.' He looked at me. 'He will go to the next stage if we don't stop him or develop a vaccine. Another reason I suspect this is still local, is it appears the facial sprays are hand-delivered, with bogus bulk-rate postage on the tubes to give the appearance that they were mailed.'

'You're definitely calling this product tampering, then,' Colonel Fujitsubo said to him.

'I'm calling this terrorism.'

'The point of it being what?'

'We don't know that yet,' Wesley told him.

'But this is far worse than any Tylenol killer or Unabomber,' I said. 'The destruction they cause is limited to whoever takes the capsules or opens the package. With a virus, it's going to spread far beyond the primary victim.'

'Dr Martin, what can you tell us about this particular virus?' Miles said.

'We have four traditional methods for testing for smallpox.' He stared stiffly at us from his screen. 'Electron microscopy, with which we have observed a direct visualization of variola.'

'Smallpox?' Miles almost shouted. 'You're sure about that?'

'Hold on,' Martin interrupted him. 'Let me finish. We also got a verification of antigenic identity using agar gel. Now, chick embryo chorioallantoic membrane culture, other tissue cultures are going to take two, three days. So we don't have those results now, but we do have PCR. It verified a pox. We just don't know which one. It's very odd, nothing currently known, not monkeypox, whitepox. Not classic variola major or minor, although it seems to be related.'

'Dr Scarpetta,' Fujitsubo spoke. 'Can you tell me what's in this facial spray, as best you know?'

'Distilled water and a fragrance. There were no ingredients listed, but generally that's what sprays like this are,' I said.

He was making notes. 'Sterile?' He looked back at us from the monitor.

'I would hope so, since the directions encourage you to spray it over your face and contact lenses,' I replied.

'Then my question,' Fujitsubo went on via satellite, 'is what kind of shelf life might we expect these contaminated sprays to have? Variola isn't all that stable in moist conditions.'

'A good point,' Martin said, adjusting his ear piece. 'It does very well when dried, and at room temperature can survive months to a year. It is sensitive to sunlight, but inside the atomizers, that wouldn't be a problem. Doesn't like heat, which, unfortunately, makes this an ideal time of year.'

'Then depending on what people do when they have these delivered,' I said, 'there could be a lot of duds out there.'

'Could be,' Martin hoped.

Wesley said, 'Clearly, the offender we're looking for is knowledgeable of infectious diseases.'

'Has to be,' Fujitsubo said. 'The virus had to be cultured, propagated, and if this is, in fact, terrorism, then the perpetrator is very familiar with basic laboratory techniques. He knew how to handle something like this and keep himself protected. We're assuming only one person is involved?'

'My theory, but the answer is, we don't know,' Wesley said.

'He calls himself *deadoc*,' I said.

'As in Doctor Death?' Fujitsubo frowned. 'He's telling us he's a doctor?'

Again, it was hard to say, but the question that was most troublesome was also the hardest to ask.

'Dr Martin,' I said as Martinez silently leaned back in his chair, listening. 'Allegedly, your facility and a laboratory in Russia are the only two sources of the viral isolates. Any thoughts on how someone got hold of this?'

'Exactly,' Wesley said. 'Unpleasant thought that it may be, we need to check your list of employees. Any recent firings, layoffs? Anybody quit during recent months and years?'

'Our source supply of variola virus is as meticulously monitored and inventoried as plutonium,' Martin answered with confidence. 'I personally have already checked into this and can tell you with certainty that nothing has been tampered with. Nothing is missing. And it is not possible to get into one of the locked freezers without authorization and knowledge of alarm codes.'

No one spoke right away.

Then Wesley said, 'I think it would be a good idea for us to have a list of those people who have had such authorization over the past five years. Initially, based on experience, I am profiling this individual as a white male, possibly in his early forties. Most likely he lives alone, but if he doesn't or he dates, he has a part of his residence that is off limits, his lab . . .'

'So we're probably talking about a former lab worker,' the S.A.C. said.

'Or someone like that,' Wesley said. 'Someone educated, trained. This person is introverted, and I base this on a number of things, not the least of which is his tendency to write in the lower case. His refusal to use punctuation indicates his belief that he is not like other people and the same rules do not apply to him. He is not talkative and may be considered aloof or shy by associates. He has time on his hands, and most important, feels he has been mistreated by the system. He feels he is due an apology by the highest office in the land, by our government, and I believe this is key to this perpetrator's motivation.'

'Then this is revenge,' I said. 'Plain and simple.'

'It's never plain or simple. I wish it were,' Wesley said. 'But I do think revenge is key, which is why it is important that all government agencies that deal with infectious diseases get us the records of any employees reprimanded, fired, laid off, furloughed or whatever, in recent months and years.'

Fujitsubo cleared his throat. 'Well, let's talk logistics, then.'

It was the Coast Guard's turn to present a plan. Martinez got up from his chair and fastened large maps to flip charts, as camera angles were adjusted so our remote guests could see.

'Can you get these in?' Martinez asked the agent at the console.

'Got them,' she said. 'How about you?' She looked up at the monitors.

'Fine.'

'I don't know. Maybe if you could zoom in more.'

She moved the camera in closer as Martinez got out a laser pointer. He directed its intense pink dot at the Maryland–Virginia line in the Chesapeake Bay that cut through Smith Island, just north of Tangier.

'We got a number of islands going up this way toward Fishing Bay and the Nanticoke River, in Maryland. There's Smith Island. South Marsh Island. Bloodsworth Island.' The pink dot hopped to each one. 'Then we're on the mainland. And you got Crisfield down here, which is only fifteen nautical miles from Tangier.' He looked at us. 'Crisfield's where a lot of watermen bring in their crabs. And a lot of Tangier folks have relatives in Crisfield. I'm real worried about that.'

'And I'm worried that the Tangiermen are not going to cooperate,' Miles said. 'A quarantine is going to cut off their only source of income.'

'Yes, sir,' Martinez said, looking at his watch. 'And we're cutting it off even as we speak. We got boats, cutters coming in from as far away as Elizabeth City to help us circle the island.'

'So as of now, no one's leaving,' Fujitsubo said as his face continued to reign over us from the video screen.

'That's right.'

'Good.'

'What if people resist?' I asked the obvious question. 'What are you going to do with them? You can't take them into custody and risk exposure.'

Martinez hesitated. He looked up at Fujitsubo on the video screen. 'Commander, would you like to field this one, sir?' he asked.

'We've actually already discussed this at great length,' Fujitsubo said to us. 'I have spoken to the secretary of the Department of Transportation, to Vice Admiral Perry, and of course, the Secretary of Defense. Basically, this thing is speeding its way up to the White House for authorization.'

'Authorization for what?' It was Miles who asked.

'To use deadly force, if all else fails,' Martinez said to all of us.

'Christ,' Wesley muttered.

I listened in disbelief, staring up at doomsday gods.

'We have no choice,' Fujitsubo spoke calmly. 'If people panic and start fleeing the island and do not heed Coast Guard warnings, they *will* – not if – but *will* bring smallpox onto the mainland. And we're talking about a population which either has not been vaccinated in thirty years. Or an immunization done so long ago it's no longer effective. Or a disease that has mutated to the extent that our present vaccine is not protective. There isn't a good scenario, in other words.'

I didn't know if I felt sick to my stomach because I wasn't well or because of what I'd just heard. I thought of that weather-beaten fishing village with its leaning headstones and wild, quiet people who just wanted to be left alone. They weren't the sort to obey anyone, for they answered to a higher power of God and storms.

'There must be another way,' I said.

But there wasn't.

'By reputation, smallpox is a highly contagious infectious disease. This outbreak must be contained,' Fujitsubo exclaimed the obvious. 'We've got to worry about houseflies hovering around patients, and crabs headed for the mainland. How do we know we don't have to worry about the possibility of mosquito transmission, as in Tanapox, for God's sake? We don't even know what all we've got to worry about since we can't fully identify the disease yet.'

Martin looked at me. 'We've already got teams out there, nurses, doctors, bed isolators so we can keep these people out of hospitals and leave them in their homes.'

'What about dead bodies, contamination?' I asked him.

'In terms of United States law, this consitutes a Class One public health emergency.'

'I realize that,' I said, impatiently, for he was getting bureaucratic on me. 'Cut to the chase.'

'Burn all but the patient. Bodies will be cremated. The Pruitt house will be torched.'

Fujitsubo tried to reassure us. 'USAMRIID's got a team heading out. We'll be talking to citizens, trying to make them understand.'

I thought of Davy Crockett and his son, of people and their panic when space-suited scientists took over their island and started burning their homes.

'And we know for a fact that the smallpox vaccine isn't going to work?' Wesley said.

'We don't know that for a fact yet,' Martin answered. 'Tests on laboratory animals will take days to weeks. And even if vaccination is protective in an animal model, this may not translate into protection for humans.'

'Since the DNA of the virus has been altered,' Fujitsubo warned, 'I am not hopeful that vaccinia virus will be effective.'

'I'm not a doctor or anything,' Martinez said, 'but I'm just wondering if you could vaccinate everyone anyway, just in case it might work.'

'Too risky,' Martin said. 'If it's not smallpox, why deliberately expose people to smallpox, thereby possibly causing some people to get the disease? And when we develop the new vaccine, we're not going to want to come back several weeks later and vaccinate people again, this time with a different pox.'

'In other words,' Fujitsubo said, 'we can't use the people of Tangier like laboratory animals. If we keep them on that island and then get a vaccine out to them as soon as possible, we should be able to contain this thing. The good news about smallpox is it's a stupid virus, kills its hosts so fast it will burn itself out if you can keep it restricted to one area.'

'Right. So an entire island gets destroyed while we sit back and watch it burn,' Miles angrily said to me. 'I can't believe this. Goddamn it.' He pounded his fist on the table. 'This can't be happening in Virginia!'

He got out of his chair. 'Gentlemen. I would like to know what we should do if we start getting patients in other parts of this state. The health of Virginia, after all, is what the governor appointed me to take care of.' His face was dark red and he was sweating. 'Are we supposed to just do like the Yankees and start burning down our cities and towns?'

'Should this spread,' Fujitsubo said, 'clearly we'll have to utilize our hospitals, have wards, just as we did during earlier times. CDC and my people are already alerting local medical personnel, and will work with them closely.'

'We realize that hospital personnel are at the greatest risk,' Martin added. 'Sure would be nice if Congress would end this goddamn furlough so I don't have one hand and both legs tied behind my back.'

'Believe me, the president, Congress, knows.'

'Senator Nagle assures me it will end by tomorrow morning.'

'They're always certain, say the same thing every time.'

The swelling and itching of the revaccination site on my arm was a constant reminder that I had been inoculated with a virus probably for nothing. I complained to Wesley all the way out to the parking lot.

'I've been reexposed, and I'm sick with something, meaning I'm probably immunosuppressed, on top of it all.'

'How do you know you don't have it?' he carefully asked.

'I don't know.'

'Then you could be infectious.'

'No, I couldn't be. A rash is the first sign of that, and I check myself daily. At the slightest hint of such a thing, I would go back into isolation. I would not come within one hundred feet of you or anybody else, Benton,' I said, my anger unreasonably spiking at his suggestion that I might risk infecting anyone with even a mundane cold.

He glanced over at me as he unlocked doors, and I knew that he was far more upset than he would let on. 'What do you want me to do, Kay?'

'Take me home so I can get my car,' I said.

Daylight was fading fast as I followed miles of woods thick with pines. Fields were fallow with tufts of cotton still clinging to dead stalks, and the sky was moist and cold like thawing cake. When I had gotten home from the meeting, there had been a message from Rose. At two P.M., Keith Pleasants had called from jail, desperately requesting that I come see him, and Wingo had gone home with the flu.

I had been inside the old Sussex County Courthouse many times over the years, and had grown fond of its antebellum quaintness and inconveniences. Built in 1825 by Thomas Jefferson's master brick mason, it was red with white trim and columns, and had survived the Civil War, although the Yankees had managed to destroy all its records first. I thought of cold winter days spent out on the lawn with detectives as I waited to be called to the witness stand. I remembered the cases by name that I had brought before this court.

Now such proceedings took place in the spacious new building next door, and as I drove past, heading to the back, I felt sad. Such constructions were a monument to rising crime, and I missed simpler times when I had first moved to Virginia and was awed by its old brick and its old war that would not end. I had smoked back then. I supposed I romanticized the past like most people tended to do. But I missed smoking and waiting around in miserable weather outside a courthouse that barely had heat. Change made me feel old.

The sheriff's department was the same red brick and white trim, its parking lot and jail surrounded by a fence topped with razor wire. Imprisoned within, two inmates in orange jumpsuits were wiping down an unmarked car they had just washed and waxed. They eyed me slyly as I parked in front, one of them popping the other with a shammy cloth.

'Yo. What's going,' one of them muttered to me as I walked past.

'Good afternoon.' I looked at both of them.

They turned away, not interested in someone they could not intimidate, and I pulled open the front door. Inside, the department was modest on the verge of depressing, and like virtually all other public facilities in the world, had profoundly outgrown its environment. Inside were Coke and snack machines, walls plastered with wanted posters and a portrait of an officer slain while responding to a call. I stopped at the duty post, where a young woman was shuffling through paperwork and chewing on her pen.

'Excuse me,' I said. 'I'm here to see Keith Pleasants.'

'Are you on his guest list?' Her contact lenses made her squint, and she wore pink braces on her teeth.

'He asked me to come, so I should hope I am.'

She flipped pages in a loose-leaf binder, stopping when she got to the right one.

'Your name.'

I told her as her finger moved down a page.

'Here you are.' She got up from her chair. 'Come with me.'

She came around her desk and unlocked a door with bars in the window. Inside was a cramped processing area for fingerprints and mug shots, a banged-up metal desk manned by a heavyset deputy. Beyond was another heavy door with bars, and through it I could hear the noises of the jail.

'You're gonna have to leave your bag here,' the deputy said to me. He got on his radio. 'Can you get on over here?'

'Ten-four. On my way,' a woman answered back.

I set my pocketbook on the desk and dug my hands in the pockets of my coat. I was going to be searched and I did not like it.

'We got a little room here where they meet with their lawyers,' the deputy said, jabbing his thumb as if he were hitching a ride. 'But some a these critters listen to ever word, and if that's a problem, go upstairs. We got an area up there.'

'I think upstairs might be better,' I said as a female deputy, hefty with short frosted hair, came around the corner with her hand-held metal detector.

'Arms out,' she said to me. 'Got anything metal in your pockets?'

'No,' I said as the detector snarled like a mechanical cat.

She tried it up and down one side and the other. It kept going off.

'Let's get rid of your coat.'

I draped it on the desk as she tried again. The detector continued to make its startling sound as she frowned and kept trying.

'What about jewelry,' she said.

I shook my head as I suddenly remembered I was wearing an underwire bra that I had no intention of announcing. She put down the detector and began to pat me down while the other deputy sat at his desk and watched slack-jawed, as if he were gawking at a dirty movie.

'Okay,' she said, satisfied that I was harmless. 'Follow me.'

To get upstairs, we had to walk through the women's side of the jail. Keys jangled as she unlocked a heavy metal door that loudly banged shut behind us. Inmates were young and hard in institutional denim, their cells scarcely big enough for an animal, with a white toilet, bed and sink. Women played solitaire, and leaned against their cages. They had hung their clothes from bars, and trash barrels were close and crammed with what they hadn't wanted for dinner. The smell of old food made my stomach flop.

'Hey mama.'

'What we got here?'

'A *fine* lady. Umm-umm-umm.'

'Hubba-hubba-hubba!'

Hands came through bars, trying to touch me as I went past, and someone was making kissing sounds while other women emitted harsh, wounded outbursts that were supposed to be laughs.

'Leave her in here. Just fifteen minutes. Ooohhh come to mama!'

'I need cigarettes.'

'Shut up, Wanda. You always needin' something.'

'Y'all quiet on down,' the deputy said in a bored singsong as she unlocked another door.

I followed her upstairs and realized I was trembling. The room she put me in was cluttered and disorganized, as if it might have had a function in an earlier time. Cork boards were propped against a wall, a hand cart parked in a corner, and some sort of pamphlets and bulletins were scattered everywhere. I sat in a folding chair at a wooden table scarred with names and crude messages in ballpoint pen.

'Just make yourself at home and he'll be up,' she said, leaving me alone.

I realized that cough drops and tissues were in my pocketbook and coat, neither of which I had with me now. Sniffing, I shut my eyes until I heard heavy feet. When the male deputy escorted Keith Pleasants in, I almost did not recognize him. He was pale and drawn, thin in baggy denims, his hands cuffed awkwardly in front of him. His eyes filled with tears when he looked at me, and his lips quivered when he tried to smile.

'You sit down and stay down,' the deputy ordered him. 'Don't you let me hear no problem up here. Got it? Or I'm back and the visit's history.'

Pleasants grabbed a chair, almost falling.

'Does he really need to be cuffed?' I said to the deputy. 'He's here for a traffic violation.'

'Ma'am, he's out of the secure area. That's why he's cuffed. Be back in twenty minutes,' he said as he left.

'I've never been through anything like this before. You mind if I smoke?' Pleasants laughed with a nervousness that bordered on hysteria as he sat.

'Help yourself.'

His hands were shaking so badly, I had to light it for him.

'Doesn't look like they got an ashtray. Maybe you're not supposed to smoke up here.' He worried, eyes darting around. 'They got me in this cell with this guy who's a drug dealer? He's got all these tattoos and won't leave me alone? Picking on me, calling me sissy names?' He inhaled a lot of smoke and briefly shut his eyes. 'I wasn't eluding anybody.' He looked at me.

I spotted a Styrofoam coffee cup on the floor and retrieved it for him to use as an ashtray.

'Thanks,' he said.

'Keith, tell me what happened.'

'I was just driving home like I always do, from the landfill, and all of a sudden there's this unmarked car behind me with sirens and lights on. So I pulled over right away. It was that asshole investigator who's been driving me crazy.'

'Ring.' My fury began to pound.

Pleasants nodded. 'Said he'd been following me for more than a mile and I wouldn't heed to his lights. Well I'm telling you, that's just a flat-out lie.' His eyes were bright. 'He's got me so jumpy these days there's no way in hell I wouldn't know if he was behind my car.'

'Did he say anything else to you when he pulled you?' I asked.

'Yes, ma'am, he did. He said my troubles had just begun. His exact words.'

'Why did you want to see me?' I thought I knew, but I wanted to hear what he would say.

'I'm in a world of trouble, Dr Scarpetta.' He teared up again. 'My mama's old and got no one to care for her but me, and there are people thinking I'm a murderer! I never killed anything in my life! Not even birds! People don't want to be around me at work anymore.'

'Is your mother bedridden?' I asked.

'No, ma'am. But she's almost seventy and has emphysema. From doing these things.' He sucked on the cigarette again. 'She doesn't drive anymore.'

'Who's looking after her now?'

He shook his head and wiped his eyes. His legs were crossed, one foot jumping like it was about to take off.

'She has no one to bring her food?' I said.

'Just me.' He choked on the words.

I looked around again, this time for something to write with, and found a purple crayon and a brown paper towel.

'Give me her address and phone number,' I said. 'And I promise someone will check in with her to make sure she's all right.'

He was vastly relieved as he gave me the information and I scribbled it down.

'I called you because I didn't know where else to go,' he started talking again. 'Can't somebody do something to get me out of here?'

'I understand your bond has been set at five thousand dollars.'

'That's just it! Like ten times what it usually is for this, according to the guy in my cell. I don't have any money or any way to get it. Means I got to stay here until court, and that could be weeks. Months.' Tears welled in his eyes again, and he was terrified.

'Keith, do you use the Internet?' I said.

'The what?'

'Computers.'

'At the landfill I do. Remember, I was telling you about our satellite system.'

'Then you do use the Internet.'

He did not seem to know what that was.

'E-mail,' I tried again.

'We use GPS.' He looked confused. 'And you know the truck that dumped the body? I'm pretty sure now it was definitely Cole's, and the Dumpster may have come from a construction site. They pick up at a bunch of construction sites on South Side in Richmond. That would be a good place to get rid of something, on a construction site. Just pull up your car after hours and who's to see?'

'Did you tell Investigator Ring this?' I asked.

Hate passed over his face. 'I don't tell him anything. Not anymore. Everything he's been doing is just to set me up.'

'Why do you think he would want to set you up?'

'He's got to arrest someone for this. He wants to be the hero.' He was suddenly evasive. 'Says everybody else doesn't know what they're doing.' He hesitated. 'Including you.'

'What else has he said?' I felt myself turning to cold, hard stone, the way I did when I had moved from anger to determined rage.

'See, when I was showing him around the house and all, he would talk. He really likes to talk.'

He took his cigarette butt and clumsily set it end-up on the table, so it would go out without burning Styrofoam. I helped him light another one.

'He told me you have this niece,' Pleasants went on. 'And that she's a real fox but has no more business in the FBI than you have being a chief medical examiner. Because. Well.'

'Go on,' I said in a controlled voice.

'Because she's not into men. I guess he thinks you aren't, either.'

'That's interesting.'

'He was laughing about it, said he knew from personal experience that neither of you dated because he'd been around both of you. And that I should just sit back and watch what happens to perverts. Because the same thing was about to happen to me.'

'Wait one minute.' I stopped him. 'Did Ring actually threaten you because you're gay or he thinks you are?'

'My mama doesn't know.' He hung his head. 'But some people do. I've been in bars. In fact, I know Wingo.'

I hoped not intimately.

'I'm worried about Mama.' He teared up again. 'She's upset about what's happening to me, and that's not good for her condition.'

'I tell you what. I'm going to check on her myself, on my way home,' I said, coughing again.

A tear slid down his cheek and he roughly wiped it with the backs of cuffed hands.

'One other thing I'm going to do,' I said as footsteps sounded on the stairs again. 'I'm going to see what I can do about you. I don't believe you killed anyone, Keith. And I'm going to post your bond and make sure you have a lawyer.'

His lips parted in disbelief as the deputies loudly entered the room.

'You really are?' Pleasants asked as he almost staggered to his feet, his eyes wide on mine.

'If you swear you're telling the truth.'

'Oh yes, ma'am!'

'Yeah, yeah,' a deputy said. 'You and all the rest of 'em.'

'It will have to be tomorrow,' I said to Pleasants. 'I'm afraid the magistrate's gone home for the night.'

'Come on. Downstairs.' A deputy grabbed his arm.

Pleasants said one last thing to me. 'Mama likes chocolate milk with Hershey's syrup. Not much else she keeps down anymore.'

Then he was gone, and I was led back downstairs and through the women's section of the jail again. Inmates were sullen this time, as if I no longer were fun. It occurred to me someone had told them who I was, when they turned their backs on me and someone spat.

13

———

Sheriff Rob Roy was a legend in Sussex County and ran uncontested every election year. He had been to my morgue many times, and I thought he was one of the finest law enforcement officers I knew. At half-past six, I found him at the Virginia Diner, where he was sitting at the local table, which literally was where the locals gathered.

This was in a long room of red-checked cloths and white chairs, and he was eating a fried ham sandwich and drinking coffee, black, his portable radio upright on the table and full of chatter.

'Can't do that, no sir. Then what? They just keep selling crack, that's what,' he was saying to a gaunt weathered man in a John Deere cap.

'Let 'em.'

'Let 'em?' Roy reached for his coffee, as wiry and bald as he ever was. 'You can't mean that.'

'I sure as hell can.'

'Might I interrupt?' I said, pulling out a chair.

Roy's mouth fell open, and for an instant he did not believe whom he was looking at. 'Well, I'll be damned.' He stood and shook my hand. 'What in tarnation are you doing out in these parts?'

'Looking for you.'

'If you'll excuse me.' The other man tipped his hat to me and got up to leave.

'Don't you tell me you're out here on business,' the sheriff said.

'What else would it be?'

He was sobered by my mood. 'Something I don't know about?'

'You know,' I said.

'Well, what then? What do you want to eat? I recommend the fried chicken sandwich,' he said as a waitress appeared.

'Hot tea.' I wondered if I would ever eat again.

'You don't look like you're feeling too good.'

'I feel like shit.'

'There's this bug going around.'

'You don't even know the half of it,' I said.

'What can I do?' He leaned closer to me, his attention completely focused.

'I'm posting bond for Keith Pleasants,' I said. 'Now this obviously won't happen before tomorrow, I'm sorry to say. But I think you need to understand, Rob, that this is an innocent man who has been set up. He's being persecuted because Investigator Ring is on a witch hunt and wants to make a name for himself.'

Roy looked baffled. 'Since when are you defending inmates?'

'Since whenever they aren't guilty,' I said. 'And this guy is no more a serial killer than you or I. He didn't try to elude the police and probably wasn't even speeding. Ring's hassling him and lying. Look how high the bond was set for a traffic violation.'

He was silent, listening.

'Pleasants has an old, infirm mother who has no one to take care of her. He's about to lose his job. Now I know Ring's uncle is the secretary of public safety, and he's also a former sheriff,' I said. 'And I know how that goes, Rob. I need you to help me out here. Ring has got to be stopped.'

Roy pushed his plate away as his radio called him. 'You really believe that.'

'Yes, I do.'

'This is fifty-one,' he said into the radio, adjusting his belt and the revolver on it.

'We got anything on that robbery yet?' a voice came back.

'Still waiting for it.'

He signed off and said to me, 'You got no doubt in your mind that this boy didn't commit any crime.'

I nodded again. 'No doubt. The killer who dismembered that lady communicates with me on the Internet. Pleasants doesn't even know what that is. There's a very big picture that I can't get into now. But believe me, what's going on has nothing to do with this kid.'

'You're sure about Ring. I mean, you got to be if I'm going to do this.' His eyes were steady on mine.

'How many times do I have to say it?'

He slammed his napkin down on the table. 'Now, this really makes me mad.' He scooted back his chair. 'I don't like it when an innocent person's locked up in my jail and some cop's out there making the rest of us look bad.'

'Do you know Kitchen, the man who owns the landfill?' I said.

'Oh sure. We're in the same lodge.' He pulled out his wallet.

'Someone needs to talk to him so Keith doesn't lose his job. We have to make this thing right,' I said.

'Believe me, I'm going to.'

He left money on the table and strode angrily out the door. I sat long enough to finish my tea, looking around at displays of striped candy, barbecue sauce and peanuts of every description. My head hurt and my skin was hot when I found a grocery store on 460 and stopped for milk, Hershey's syrup, fresh vegetables and soup.

I charged up and down aisles, and next thing I knew my cart was full of everything from toilet paper to deli meats. Then I got out a map and the address Pleasants had given to me. His mother was not too far off the main route, and when I arrived she was asleep.

'Oh dear,' I said from the porch. 'I didn't mean to get you up.'

'Who is it?' She peered blindly into the night as she unhooked the door.

'Dr Kay Scarpetta. You have no reason . . .'

'What kind of doctor?'

Mrs Pleasants was wizened and stooped, her face wrinkled like crepe paper. Long gray hair floated like gossamer, and I thought of the landfill and the old woman deadoc had killed.

'You can come on in.' She shoved open the door and looked frightened. 'Is Keith all right? Nothing happened to him, did it?'

'I saw him earlier, and he's fine,' I assured her. 'I brought groceries.' I had the bags in my hands.

'That boy.' She shook her head, motioning me into her small, tidy home. 'What would I do? You know, he's all I've got in this world. When he was born I said, "Keith, it's just you."'

She was scared and upset and didn't want me to know.

'Do you know where he is?' I gently said.

We entered her kitchen with its old, squat refrigerator and gas stove, and she did not answer me. She started putting groceries away, fumbling with cans and dropping celery and carrots to the floor.

'Here. Let me help,' I tried.

'He didn't do anything wrong.' She began to cry. 'I know he didn't. And that policeman won't leave him be, always coming over, banging on the door.'

She stood in the middle of her kitchen, wiping her face with her hands.

'Keith says you like chocolate milk, and I'm going to make you one. It's just what the doctor ordered.'

I fetched a glass and a spoon from the drain board.

'He'll be home tomorrow,' I said. 'And I don't imagine you'll be hearing from Investigator Ring anymore.'

She stared at me as if I were a miracle.

'I just wanted to make sure you have everything you need until your son gets here,' I said, handing her the glass of chocolate milk mixed medium dark.

'I'm just trying to figure out who you are,' she finally said. 'This is mighty good. Nothing in life any better.' She sipped and smiled and took her time.

I briefly explained how I knew Keith and what I did professionally, but she did not understand. She assumed I was sweet on him and issued medical licenses for a living. On my way home, I played CDs loudly to keep me awake as I drove through thick darkness, where for long stretches there was not a single light except stars. I reached for the phone.

Wingo's mother answered and told me he was sick in bed. But she got him on the line.

'Wingo, I'm worried about you,' I said with feeling.

'I feel terrible.' He sounded like it. 'I guess you can't do anything for the flu.'

'You're immunosuppressed. When I talked to Dr Riley last, your CD4 cell count was not good.' I wanted him to face reality. 'Describe your symptoms to me.'

'My head's killing me, my neck and back are killing me. Last time my temperature was taken it was a hundred and four. I'm so thirsty all the time.'

Everything he said was setting off alarms in my head, for the symptoms also described the early stages of smallpox. But if his exposure was the torso, I was surprised he hadn't gotten sick before now, especially in light of his compromised condition.

'You haven't touched one of those sprays we got at the office,' I said.

'What sprays?'

'The Vita facial sprays.'

He was clueless, and then I remembered that he was out of the office much of today. I explained what had happened.

'Oh my God,' he said suddenly, as fear shot through both of us. 'One came in the mail. Mom had it on the kitchen counter.'

'When?' I said in alarm.

'I don't know. A few days ago. When was that? I don't know. We'd never seen anything so fancy. Imagine, something sweet to cool your face.'

That made twelve canisters deadoc had delivered to my staff, and *twelve* had been his message to me. It was the number of full-time people in my central office, if I included myself. How could he know such trivia as the size of my staff, and even some of their names and where they lived, if he were far away and anonymous?

I dreaded my next question because I already thought I knew. 'Wingo, did you touch it in any way?'

'I tried it. Just to see.' His voice was shaking badly and he was choking from coughing fits. 'When it was sitting there. I picked it up one time, just to see. It smelled like roses.'

'Who else in your house has tried it?'

'I don't know.'

'I want you to make certain no one touches that canister. Do you understand?'

'Yes.' He was sobbing.

'I'm going to send some people to your house to pick it up and take care of you and your family, okay?'

He was crying too hard to answer.

When I got home, it was minutes past midnight, and I was so out of sorts and sick that I did not know what to do first. I called Marino and Wesley, and Fujitsubo. I told everybody what was happening and that Wingo and his family needed a team at their home immediately. My bad news was returned by theirs. The girl on Tangier who had gotten sick had died, and now a fisherman had the disease. Depressed and feeling like hell, I checked my e-mail, and deadoc was there in his small, mean way. I was glad. His message had been sent while Keith Pleasants was in jail.

mirror mirror on the wall where have you been

'You bastard,' I screamed at him.

The day was too much. All of it was too much, and I was achy and woozy and completely fed up. So I should not have gone into that chat room, where I waited for him as if this were the O.K. Corral. I should have left it for another time. But I made my presence known and paced in my mind as I waited for the monster to appear. He did.

DEADOC:	toil and trouble
SCARPETTA:	What do you want?
DEADOC:	we are angry tonight
SCARPETTA:	Yes, we are.
DEADOC:	why should you care about ignorant fishermen and their ignorant families and those inept people who work for you
SCARPETTA:	Stop it. Tell me what you want to make this stop.
DEADOC:	it s too late the damage is done it was done long before this
SCARPETTA:	What was done to you?

But he did not answer. Oddly, he did not leave the room, but he did not respond to any further questions from me. I thought of Squad 19 and prayed they were listening and following from trunk to trunk, tracing him to his lair. Half an hour passed. I finally logged off as my telephone rang.

'You're a genius!' Lucy was so excited she was hurting my ears. 'How the hell have you managed to keep him on that long?'

'What do you mean?' I asked, amazed.

'Eleven minutes so far. You win the prize.'

'I was only on with him maybe two minutes.' I tried to cool my forehead with the back of my hand. 'I don't know what you're talking about.'

But she didn't care. 'We nailed the son of a bitch!' She was ecstatic. 'A campground in Maryland, agents from Salisbury already en route. Janet and I gotta plane to catch.'

Before I got up the next morning, the World Health Organization put out another international alert about Vita aromatic facial spray. WHO reassured people that this virus would be eliminated, that we were working on the vaccine around the clock and would have it soon. But the panic began anyway.

The virus, dubbed by the press Mutantpox, was on the cover of *Newsweek* and *Time,* and the Senate was forming a subcommittee as the White House contemplated emergency measures. Vita was distributed in New York, but the manufacturer was actually French. The obvious concern was that deadoc was making good on his threat. Although there were yet no reports of the disease in France, economic and diplomatic relations were strained as a large plant was forced to shut down, and accusations about where the tampering was done were volleyed back and forth between countries.

Watermen were trying to flee Tangier in their fishing vessels, and the Coast Guard had called in more backups from stations as far south as Florida. I did not know all the details, but based on what I had heard, there was a standoff between law enforcement and Tangiermen in the Tangier Sound, boats anchored and going nowhere as winter winds howled.

Meanwhile, CDC had deployed an isolation team of doctors and nurses to Wingo's house, and word was out. Headlines screamed and people were evacuating a city that would be difficult, if not impossible, to quarantine. I was as distressed and sick as I'd ever been in my life, drinking hot tea in a bathrobe early Friday morning.

My fever had peaked at a hundred and two, and Robitussin DM didn't do a thing except make me vomit. Muscles in my neck and back hurt as if I had been playing football against people with clubs. But I could not go to bed. There was far too much to do. I called a bondsman and received the bad news that the only way to get Keith Pleasants out of jail was for me to drive downtown and pay in person. So I went out to my car, only to have to turn around ten minutes later because I'd left my checkbook on the table.

'God, help me please,' I muttered as I sped up.

Rubber squealed as I drove too fast through my neighborhood, and then moments later, back out, flying around corners in Windsor Farms. I wondered what had happened in Maryland during the night as I worried about Lucy, for whom every event was an adventure. She wanted to use guns and go on foot pursuit, fly helicopters and planes. I feared such a spirit would be crushed in its prime, because I knew too much about life and how it ended. I wondered if deadoc had been caught, but believed if he had, I would have been told.

I had never needed a bondsman in my life, and this one, Vince Peeler, worked out of a shoe repair shop on Broad Street, along a strip of abandoned stores with nothing in their windows but graffiti and dust. He was a short, slight man with waxed black hair and a leather apron. Seated at an industrial-sized Singer sewing machine, he was stitching a new sole on a shoe. As I shut the door he gave me the piercing look of one accustomed to recognizing trouble.

'You Dr Scarpetta?' he asked as he sewed.

'Yes.'

I got out my checkbook and a pen, not feeling the least bit friendly as I wondered how many violent people this man had helped back out on the streets.

'That will be five hundred and thirty dollars,' he said. 'If you want to use a credit card, add three percent.'

He got up and came to his scarred counter piled with shoes and tins of Kiwi paste. I could feel his eyes crawling over me.

'Funny, I thought you'd be a lot older,' he considered. 'You know, you read about people in the news and sometimes get flat-out wrong impressions.'

'He'll be freed today.' It was an order as I tore out the check and handed it to him.

'Oh, sure.' His eyes darted and he looked at his watch.

'When?'

'When?' he echoed rhetorically.

'Yes,' I said. 'When will he be freed?'

He snapped his fingers. 'Like that.'

'Good,' I said as I blew my nose. 'I'm going to be watching for him to be freed like that.' I snapped my fingers, too. 'And if he isn't? Guess what? I'm also a lawyer and in a really, really shitty mood. And I'll come after you. Okay?'

He smiled at me and swallowed.

'What kind of lawyer?' he asked.

'The kind you don't want to know,' I said as I went out the door.

I got to the office maybe fifteen minutes later, and my pager vibrated and the phone rang as I sat behind my desk. Before I could do anything, Rose suddenly appeared and looked unusually stressed.

'Everybody's looking for you,' she said.

'They always are.' I frowned at the number on my pager's display. 'Now who the hell is that?'

'Marino's on his way here,' she went on. 'They're sending a helicopter. To the helipad at MCV. USAMRIID's in the air right now, heading here. They've let the Baltimore Medical Examiner's office know a special team's going to have to handle this, that the body will have to be autopsied in Frederick.'

I gave her my eyes as my blood seemed to freeze. 'Body?'

'Apparently there's some campground where the FBI traced a call.'

'I know about that.' I had no patience. 'In Maryland.'

'They think they've found the killer's camper. I'm not clear on all

the details. But it has what might be a lab of some type. And there's
a body inside.'

I couldn't believe what I was hearing. 'Whose body?'

'They think, his. A possible suicide. Shot.' She peered at me over
the top of her glasses, and shook her head. 'You should be home in
bed with a cup of my chicken soup.'

Marino picked me up in front of my office as wind gusted through
downtown and whipped state flags on tops of buildings. I knew
instantly that he was angry when he pulled out before I'd barely shut
the door. Then he had nothing to say.

'Thanks,' I said, unwrapping a cough drop.

'You're still sick.' He turned onto Franklin Street.

'I certainly am. Thank you for asking.'

'I don't know why I'm doing this,' he said, and he was not in
uniform. 'Last thing I want to do is get near some goddamn lab where
someone's been making viruses.'

'You'll have special protection,' I replied.

'I should probably have it now, being around you.'

'I have the flu and am no longer infectious. Trust me. I know these
things. And don't be mad at me, because I have no intention of putting
up with it.'

'You'd better hope the flu's what you got.'

'If I had something worse, I would be getting worse and my fever
would be higher. I would have a rash.'

'Yeah, but if you're already sick, don't that mean you're more likely
to catch something else? Like, I don't know why you want to be
making this trip. 'Cause I sure the fuck don't. And I don't appreciate
being dragged into it.'

'Then drop me off and be on your way,' I said. 'Don't even think
about whining to me right now. Not when the entire world's going
to hell.'

'How's Wingo?' he asked in a more conciliatory tone.

'I'm frankly scared to death for him,' I replied.

We drove through MCV, turning into a helipad behind a fence
where patients and organs arrived when they were medflighted to
the hospital. USAMRIID had not arrived yet, but in moments we
could hear the powerful Blackhawk, and people in cars and walking
along sidewalks stopped and stared. Several drivers pulled off the
road to watch the magnificent machine darken the sky as it hammered
in, blasting grass and debris as it landed.

The door slid open and Marino and I climbed inside, where crew seats were already occupied by scientists from USAMRIID. We were surrounded by rescue gear, and another portable isolator that was collapsed like an accordion. I was handed a helmet with a microphone, and I put this on and fastened my five-point harness. Then I helped Marino with his as he perched primly on a fold-down seat not built for people his size.

'God knows I hope reporters don't get wind of this,' someone said as the heavy door shut.

I plugged the cord of my microphone into a port in the ceiling. 'They will. Probably already have.'

Deadoc liked attention. I could not believe he would leave this world silently, or without his presidential apology. No, there was something else in store for us, and I did not want to imagine what that might be. The trip to Janes Island State Park was less than an hour, but complicated by the fact that the campground was densely wooded with pines. There was nowhere to land.

Our pilots set us down at the Coast Guard station in Crisfield, in a marina called Somer's Cove, where sailboats and yachts battened down for winter bobbed on the dark blue ruffled water of the Little Annemessex River. We went inside the tidy brick station long enough to put on exposure suits and life vests while Chief Martinez briefed us.

'We got a lot of problems going at the same time,' he was saying as he paced the carpet inside the communication room, where all of us were gathered. 'For one thing, Tangier folk have kin here, and we've had to station armed guards at roads leading out of town because now CDC is concerned about Crisfield people going anywhere.'

'No one's gotten sick here,' Marino said, as he struggled to get cuffs over his boots.

'No, but I'm worried that at the very start of this thing, some people snuck through the cracks, got out of Tangier and came here. Point being, don't expect much friendliness in these parts.'

'Who's at the campground?' someone else asked.

'Right now, the FBI agents that found the body.'

'What about other campers?' Marino said.

'Here's what I've been told,' Martinez said. 'When the agents went in, they found maybe half a dozen campers and only one with a phone hookup. That was campsite sixteen, and they banged on the door. Nothing, so they look in a window and see the body on the floor.'

'The agents didn't go inside?' I said.

'No. Realizing it might be the perp's, they worried it could be contaminated and didn't. But I'm afraid one of the rangers did.'

'Why?' I asked.

'You know what they say. Curiosity killed the cat. Apparently one of the agents had gone to the airstrip where you landed to pick up two other agents. Whatever. At some point, no one was looking and the ranger went inside, came right back out like a ball of fire. Said there was some kind of monster in there straight out of Stephen King. Don't ask me.' He shrugged and rolled his eyes.

I looked at the USAMRIID team.

'We'll take the ranger back with us,' said a young man whose Army pins identified him as a captain. 'By the way, my name is Clark. This is my crew,' he said to me. 'They'll take good care of him, put him in quarantine, keep an eye on him.'

'Campsite sixteen,' Marino said. 'We know anything about who rented that?'

'We don't have those details yet,' Martinez said. 'Everybody suited up?' He scanned us and it was time to go.

The Coast Guard took us in two Boston Whalers because where we were going was too shallow for a cutter or patrol boat. Martinez was piloting mine, standing up and calm as if racing forty miles an hour on choppy waters was a very normal thing to do. I honestly thought I might sail overboard at any moment as I held hard to the rail, sitting on the side. It was like riding a mechanical bull, air rushing so fast into my nose and mouth, I could barely breathe.

Marino was across the boat from me and looked like he might get sick. I tried to mouth a reassurance to him, but he stared blankly at me as he held on with all his strength. We eventually slowed in a cove called Flat Cat, thick with cat-tails and spartina grass, where there were NO WAKE signs as the park got near. I could see nothing but pines. Then as we got closer, there were paths and bathrooms, a small ranger station, and only one camper peeking through. Martinez glided us into the pier, and another Guardsman tied us to a piling as the engine quit.

'I'm gonna puke,' Marino said in my ear as we clumsily climbed out.

'No you're not.' I gripped his arm.

'I ain't going inside that trailer.'

I turned around and looked at his wan face.

'You're right. You're not,' I said. 'That's my job, but first we need to locate the ranger.'

Marino stalked off before the second boat had docked, and I looked through the woods toward the camper that was deadoc's. Rather old and missing whatever had towed it, it was parked as far from the rangers' station as was possible, tucked in the shadow of loblolly pines. When all of us were ashore, the USAMRIID team passed out the familiar orange suits, air packs and extra four-hour batteries.

'Here's what we're doing.' It was the USAMRIID team leader named Clark who spoke. 'We suit up and get the body out.'

'I would like to go in first,' I said. 'Alone.'

'Right.' He nodded. 'Then we see if there's anything hazardous in there, which hopefully there's not. We get the body out, and the camper's hauled out of here.'

'It's evidence,' I said, looking at him. 'We can't just haul it out of here.'

I knew what he was thinking by the look on his face. The killer may be dead, the case closed. The camper was a biological hazard and should be burned.

'No,' I said to him. 'We don't close this so quickly. We can't.'

He hesitated, blowing out in frustration as he stared off at the camper.

'I'll go in,' I said. 'Then I'll tell you what we need to do.'

'Fair enough.' He raised his voice again. 'Guys? Let's go. No one inside but the M.E. until you hear otherwise.'

They followed us through the forest, the portable isolator in our wake, an eerie caisson not meant for this world. Pine needles were crisp beneath my feet, like shredded wheat, and the air was sharp and clean as the camper got closer. It was a Dutchman travel trailer, maybe eighteen feet long, with a fold-out orange-striped awning.

'That's old. Eight years, I bet,' said Marino, who knew about such things.

'What would it take to tow it?' I asked as we put on our suits.

'A pickup,' he said. 'Maybe a van. This doesn't need nothing with a lot of horsepower. What are we supposed to do? Put these over everything else we already got on?'

'Yes,' I said, zipping up. 'What I'd like to know is what happened to the vehicle that hauled this thing here.'

'Good question,' he said, huffing as he struggled. 'And where's the license plate?'

I had just turned on my air when a young man emerged from trees in a green uniform and smoky hat. He seemed rather dazed as he looked at all of us in our orange hoods and suits, and I sensed his fear. He did not get close to us as he introduced himself as the night shift park ranger.

Marino spoke to him first. 'You ever see the person staying in there?'

'No,' the ranger said.

'What about guys on the other shifts?'

'No one remembers seeing anyone, just lights on at night sometimes. Hard to say. As you can see it's parked pretty far from the station. You could go out to the showers or whatever and not necessarily be noticed.'

'No other campers here?' I asked over the rush of air inside my hood.

'Not now. There were maybe three other people when I found the body, but I encouraged them to leave because there might be some kind of disease.'

'Did you question them first?' Marino asked, and I could see he was irritated by this young ranger who had just chased off all of our witnesses.

'Nobody knew a thing, except one person did think he ran into him.' He nodded at the camper. 'Evening before last. In the bathroom. Big grubby guy with dark hair and a beard.'

'Taking a shower?' I asked.

'No, ma'am.' He hesitated. 'Taking a leak.'

'Doesn't the camper have a bathroom?'

'I really don't know.' He hesitated again. 'To tell you the truth, I didn't stay in there. Minute I saw that. Well, whatever it was. I was gone like a second.'

'And you don't know what towed this thing?' Marino then asked.

The ranger was looking very uncomfortable now. 'This time of year it's usually quiet out here, and dark. I had no reason to notice what vehicle it was hooked up to, and in fact don't recall there even being one.'

'But you got a plate number.' Marino's stare was unfriendly through his hood.

'Sure do.' Relieved, the ranger pulled a folded piece of paper from his pocket. 'Got his registration right here.' He opened it. 'Ken A. Perley, Norfolk, Virginia.'

He handed the paper to Marino, who sarcastically said, 'Oh good. The name the asshole stole off a credit card. So I'm sure the plate number you got is accurate, too. How did he pay?'

'Cashier's check.'

'He gave this to someone in person?' Marino asked.

'No. He made the reservation by mail. No one ever saw anything except the paperwork in your hand. Like I said, we never saw him.'

'What about the envelope this thing came in?' Marino said. 'Did you save it so maybe we got a postmark?'

The ranger shook his head. He nervously glanced at suited scientists, who were listening to his every word. He stared at the trailer and wet his lips.

'You mind my asking what's in there. And what's going to happen to me 'cause I went in?' His voice cracked and he looked like he might cry.

'It could be contaminated with a virus,' I said to him. 'But we don't know that for sure. Everybody here is going to take care of you.'

'They said they were going to lock me up in some room, like solitary confinement.' Fear erupted, his eyes wild, voice loud. 'I want to know exactly what's in there that I might have got!'

'You'll be in exactly the same thing I was last week,' I assured him. 'A nice room with nice nurses. For a few days of observation. That's all.'

'Think of it as a vacation. It really ain't that big of a deal. Just because people are in these suits, don't go getting hinky,' Marino said as if he were one to talk.

He went on as if he were the great expert in infectious diseases, and I left the two of them and approached the camper alone. For a moment, I stood within feet of it and looked around. To my left were acres of trees, then the river where our boats were moored. Right of me, through more trees, I could hear the sounds of a highway. The camper was parked on a soft floor of pine needles, and what I noticed first was the scraped area on the white-painted tongue.

Getting close, I squatted and rubbed gloved fingers over deep gouges and scrapes in aluminum in an area where the Vehicle Identification Number, or VIN, should have been. Near the roof, I noticed a patch of vinyl had been scorched, and decided someone had taken a propane torch to the second VIN. I walked around to the other side.

The door was unlocked and not quite shut because it had been pried open by some sort of tool, and my nerves began to sing. My head cleared and I became completely focused, the way I got when evidence was screaming a different story than witnesses claimed. Mounting metal steps, I walked inside and stood very still as I looked around at a scene that might mean nothing to most, but to me confirmed a nightmare. This was deadoc's factory.

First, the heat was up as high as it would go, and I turned it off, startled when a pathetic white creature suddenly hopped across my feet. I jumped and gasped as it stupidly ran into a wall, and then sat, quivering and panting. The pitiful laboratory rabbit had been shaved in patches and scarified with infection, his eruptions horrible and dark. I noticed his wire cage, and that it seemed to have been knocked off a table, the door wide open.

'Come here.' Squatting, I held out my hand as he watched me with pink-rimmed eyes, long ears twitching.

Carefully, I inched my way closer because I could not leave him out. He was a living source of propagating disease.

'Come on, you poor little thing,' I said to the ranger's monster. 'I promise I won't hurt you.'

Then I gently had him in my hands, his heart beating staccato as he violently trembled. I returned him to his cage, then went to the rear of the camper. The doorway I stepped through was small, the body inside practically filling the bedroom. The man was facedown on gold shag carpet that was stained dark from blood. His hair was curly and dark, and when I turned him over, rigor mortis had come and already passed. He reminded me of a lumberjack in a filthy pea coat and trousers. His hands were huge with dirty nails, his beard and mustache unkempt.

I undressed him from the waist up to check the pattern of livor-mortis, or blood settling by gravity after death. Face and chest were reddish purple, with areas of blanching where his body had been against the floor. I saw no indication that he had been moved after death. He had been shot once in the chest at close range, possibly with the Remington double-barreled shotgun by his side, next to his left hand.

The spread of pellets was tight, forming a large hole with scalloped edges in the center of his chest. White plastic filler from the shotgun clung to clothing and skin, which again did not indicate a contact wound. Measuring the gun and his arms, I did not see how he could have reached the trigger. I saw nothing to indicate that he had rigged up anything to help him. Checking pockets, I found no wallet, no identification, only a Buck knife. The blade was scratched and bent.

I spent no more time with him but came outside, and the team from USAMRIID was restless, like people waiting to go somewhere and afraid they're going to miss their flight. They stared as I came down the steps, and Marino hung back. He was almost lost in trees, orange arms folded across his chest, the ranger standing beside him.

'This is a completely contaminated crime scene,' I announced. 'We have a dead white male with no identification. I need someone to help me get the body out. It needs to be contained.' I looked at the captain.

'It goes back with us,' he said.

I nodded. 'Your guys can do the autopsy and maybe get someone from the Baltimore Medical Examiner's office to witness. The camper's another problem. It's got to go somewhere it can be worked up safely. Evidence needs to be collected and decontaminated. This, frankly, is out of my range. Unless you have a containment facility that can accommodate something this big, maybe we'd better get this to Utah.'

'To Dugway?' he said, dubiously.

'Yes,' I said. 'Maybe Colonel Fujitsubo can help with that.'

Dugway Proving Ground was the Army's major range and test facility for chemical and biological defense. Unlike USAMRIID, which was in the heart of urban America, Dugway had the vast land of the Great Salt Lake desert for testing lasers, smart bombs, smoke obscurance or illumination. More to the point, it had the only test chamber in the United States capable of processing a vehicle as large as a battle tank.

The captain thought for a moment, his eyes going from me to the camper as he made up his mind and formalized a plan.

'Frank, get on the phone and let's get this mobilized ASAP,' he said to one of the scientists. 'The colonel will have to work with the Air Force on transport, get something here fast because I don't want this thing sitting out here all night. And we're going to need a flatbed truck, a pickup truck.'

'Should be able to get that around here, with all the seafood they ship,' Marino said. 'I'll get on it.'

'Good,' the captain went on. 'Somebody get me three body bags and the isolator.' Then he said to me, 'I'll bet you need a hand.'

'I certainly do,' I said, and both of us began walking toward the camper.

I pulled open the bent aluminum door, and he followed me inside, and we did not linger as we passed through to the back. I could tell by Clark's eyes that he had never seen anything like this, but with his hood and air pack, at least he did not have to deal with the stench of decomposing human flesh. He knelt at one end and I at the other, the body heavy and the space impossibly cramped.

'Is it hot in here or is it just me?' he said loudly as we struggled with rubbery limbs.

'Someone turned the heat up as high as it would go.' I was already out of breath. 'To hasten viral contamination, decomposition. A popular way to screw up a crime scene. All right. Let's zip him in. This is going to be tight, but I think we can do it.'

We started working him into a second pouch, our hands and suits slippery with blood. It took us almost thirty minutes to get the body inside the isolator, and my muscles were trembling as we carried it out. My heart was pounding and I was dripping sweat. Outside, we were thoroughly doused with a chemical rinse, as was the isolator which was transported by truck back to Crisfield. Then the team started work on the camper.

All of it, except for the wheels, was to be wrapped in heavy blue tinted vinyl that had a HEPA filter layer. I took off my suit with great relief, and retreated into the warm, well-lit rangers' station, where I scrubbed my hands and face. My nerves were jangled and I would have given anything to crawl into bed, down shots of NyQuil and sleep.

'If this ain't a mess,' Marino said as he came in with a lot of cold air.

'Please shut the door,' I said, shivering.

'What's eating you?' He sat on the other side of the room.

'Life.'

'I can't believe you're out here when you're sick. I think you've lost your friggin' mind.'

'Thank you for the words of comfort.' I said.

'Well, this ain't exactly a holiday for me, either. Stuck out here with people to interview, and I got no wheels.' He looked frayed.

'What are you going to do?'

'I'll find something. Rumor has it Lucy and Janet are in the area and have a ride.'

'Where?' I started to get up.

'Don't get excited. They're out trying to find people to interview, like I gotta do. God, I gotta smoke. It's been almost all day.'

'Not in here.' I pointed to a sign.

'People are dying of smallpox and you're bitching about cigarettes.'

I got out Motrin and popped three without water.

'So what will all these space cadets do now?' he asked.

'Some of them will stay in the area, tracking down any other people who may have been exposed either on Tangier or in the campground.

They'll work in shifts with other team members. I guess you'll be in contact with them, too, in case you come across anyone who might have been exposed.'

'What? I'm supposed to walk around in an orange suit all week?' He yawned and cracked his neck. 'Man, aren't they a bitch? Hot as hell except up in the hood.' He was secretly proud that he had worn one.

'No, you won't be wearing a plastic suit,' I said.

'And what happens if I find out someone I'm interviewing was exposed?'

'Just don't kiss him.'

'I don't think this is funny.' He stared at me.

'It's anything but that.'

'What about the dead guy? They going to cremate him when we don't know who he is?'

'He'll be autopsied in the morning,' I said. 'I imagine they'll store his body for as long as they can.'

'The whole thing's just weird.' Marino rubbed his face in his hands. 'And you saw a computer in there.'

'Yes, a laptop. But no printer or scanner. I'm suspicious this is someone's getaway. The printer, the scanner, at home.'

'What about a phone?'

I thought for a minute. 'Don't remember seeing one.'

'Well, the phone line runs from the camper to the utility box. We'll see what we can find out about that, like whose account it is. I'll also tell Wesley what's going on.'

'If the phone line was used only for AOL,' Lucy said as she walked in and shut the door, 'there won't be any telephone account. The only account will be AOL, which will still come back to Perley, the guy whose credit card number got pinched.'

She looked alert but a little tousled in jeans and a leather jacket. Sitting next to me, she examined the whites of my eyes, and felt the glands in my neck.

'Stick out your tongue,' she seriously said.

'Stop it!' I pushed her away, coughing and laughing at the same time.

'How are you feeling?'

'Better. Where's Janet?' I said.

'Talking. Out somewhere. What kind of computer's in there?'

'I didn't take time to study it,' I replied. 'I didn't notice any of the particulars.'

'Was it on?'

'Don't know. I didn't check.'

'I need to get in it.'

'What do you want to do?' I asked, looking at her.

'I think I need to go with you.'

'Will they let you do that?' Marino asked.

'Who the hell is *they*?'

'The drones you work for,' he replied.

'They put me on the case. They expect me to break it.'

Her eyes never stopped moving to windows and the door. Lucy had been infected and would succumb from her exposure to law enforcement. Beneath her jacket she wore a Sig Sauer nine-millimeter pistol in a leather holster with extra magazines. She probably had brass knuckles in her pocket. She tensed as the door opened and another ranger hurried in, his hair still wet from the shower, eyes nervous and excited.

'Can I help you?' he asked us, taking off his coat.

'Yeah,' Marino said, getting up from his chair. 'What kind of car you got?'

14

———

The flatbed truck was waiting when we arrived, the vinyl-shrouded camper on top of it gleaming an eerie translucent blue beneath the stars and moon and still hooked to a pickup truck. We were parking nearby on a dirt road at the edge of a field when a huge plane passed alarmingly low overhead, its roar louder than a commercial jet.

'What the hell?' Marino exclaimed, opening the door of the ranger's Jeep.

'I think that's our ride to Utah,' Lucy said from the back, where she and I were sitting.

The ranger was staring up through his windshield, incredulous, as if the rapture had come. 'Holy shit. Oh my God. We're being invaded!'

A HMMWV came down first, wrapped in corrugated cardboard, a heavy wooden platform underneath. It sounded like an explosion when it landed on the hard-packed dead grass of the field and was dragged by parachutes caught in the wind. Then green nylon wilted over the multiwheeled vehicle, and more rucksacks blossomed in the heavens as more cargo drifted down and tumbled to the ground. Paratroopers followed, oscillating two or three times before landing nimbly on their feet and running out of their harnesses. They gathered up billowing nylon as the sound of their C-17 receded beyond the moon.

The Air Force's Combat Control team out of Charleston, South Carolina, had arrived at precisely thirteen minutes past midnight. We sat in the Jeep and watched, fascinated as airmen began double-checking the compactness of the field, for what was about to land on it weighed enough to demolish a normal landing strip or tarmac. Measurements were made, surveys taken, and the team set out sixteen ACR remote control landing lights, while a woman in camouflage unwrapped the HMMWV, started its loud diesel engine and drove it off its platform, out of the way.

'I got to find some joint to stay around here,' Marino said as he stared out at the spectacle. 'How the hell can they land some big military plane on such a little field?'

'Some of it I can tell you,' said Lucy, who was never at a loss for technical explanation. 'Apparently, the C-17's designed to land with cargo on unusually small, unapproved runways like this. Or a dry lake bed. In Korea, they've even used interstates.'

'Here we go,' Marino said with his usual sarcasm.

'Only other thing that could squeeze into a tight place like this is a C-130,' she went on. 'The C-17 can back up, isn't that cool?'

'No way a cargo plane can do all that,' Marino said.

'Well, this baby can,' she said as if she wanted to adopt it.

He began looking around. 'I'm so hungry I could eat a tire, and I'd give up my paycheck for a beer. I'm gonna roll down this window here and smoke.'

I sensed the ranger did not want anyone smoking in his well-cared-for Jeep, but he was too intimidated to say so.

'Marino, let's go outside,' I said. 'Fresh air would do us good.'

We climbed out and he lit a Marlboro, sucking on it as if it were mother's milk. Members of the USAMRIID team who were in charge of the flatbed truck and its creepy cargo were still in their protective suits and staying away from everyone. They were gathered on the rutted dirt road, watching airmen work on what looked like acres of flat land that in warmer months might be a playing field.

A dark unmarked Plymouth rolled up at almost two A.M., and Lucy trotted to it. I watched her talk to Janet through the open driver's window. Then the car drove away.

'I'm back,' Lucy spoke quietly, touching my arm.

'Everything okay?' I asked, and I knew the life they lived together had to be hard.

'Under control, so far,' she said.

'Double-O-Seven, it was nice of you to come out and help us today,' Marino said to Lucy, smoking as if it were his last hour to enjoy it.

'You know, it's a federal violation to be disrespectful to federal agents,' she said. 'Especially minorities of Italian extraction.'

'I hope to hell you're a minority. Don't want others out there like you.' He flicked an ash as we heard a plane far off.

'Janet's staying here,' Lucy said to him. 'Meaning, the two of you will be working this together. No smoking in the car, and you hit on her, your life is over.'

'Shhhh,' I said to both of them.

The jet's return was loud from the north, and we stood silently, staring up at the sky as lights suddenly blazed on. They formed a fiery dotted line, marking green for approach, white for the safe zone, and finally warning red at the end of the landing strip. I thought how weird it would seem for anyone who had the misfortune of driving by as this plane was coming in. I could see its dark shadow and winking lights on wings as it dropped lower and its noise became awesome. The landing gear unfolded and emerald green light spilled out from the wheel well as the C-17 headed straight for us.

I had the paralyzing sensation that I was witnessing a crash, that this monstrous flat-gray machine with vertical wing tips and stubby shape was going to plow into the earth. It sounded like a hurricane as it roared right over our heads, and we put our fingers in our ears as its huge wheels touched down, grass and dirt flying, great chunks chewed out of ruts made by big wheels and 130 tons of aluminum and steel. Wing flaps were up, engines in thrust reverse as the jet screamed to a stop at the end of a field not big enough for football.

Then pilots threw it in reverse and began loudly backing it up along the grass, in our direction, so there would be enough of a landing strip for it to take off again. When its tail reached the edge of the dirt road, the C-17 stopped, jet exhaust directed up away from us. The back opened like the mouth of a shark as a metal ramp went down, the cargo bay completely open and lighted and gleaming of polished metal.

For a while we watched as the loadmaster and crew worked. They had put on chemical warfare gear, dark hoods and goggles and black gloves that looked rather scary, especially at night. They quickly backed the pickup and camper off the flatbed truck, unhooked them, and the HMMWV towed the camper inside the C-17.

'Come on,' Lucy said, tugging my arm. 'We don't want to miss our ride.'

We walked out onto the field, and I could not believe the power surging and the noise as we followed the automated ramp, picking our way around rollers and rings built into the flat, metal floor, miles

of wires and insulation exposed overhead. The plane looked big
enough to carry several helicopters, Red Cross buses, tanks, and there
were at least fifty jump seats. But the crew was small tonight, only
the loadmaster and paratroopers, and a first lieutenant named Laurel,
who I assumed had been assigned to us.

She was an attractive young woman with short dark hair, and she
shook each of our hands and smiled like a gracious hostess.

'Good news is you're not sitting down here,' she said. 'We'll be up
with the pilots. More good news, I've got coffee.'

'That would be heaven,' I said, metal clanking as the crew secured
the camper and HMMWV to the floor with chains and netting.

The steps leading up from the cargo bay were painted with the
name of the plane, which in this case, appropriately, was *Heavy Metal*.
The cockpit was huge, with an electronic flight control system, and
head-up displays like fighter pilots used. Steering was done with
sticks instead of yokes, and the instrumentation was completely intimidating.

I climbed up on a swivel seat, behind two pilots in green jumpsuits, who were too busy to pay us any mind.

'You got headsets so you can talk, but please don't when the pilots
are,' Laurel told us. 'You don't have to wear them, but it's pretty loud
in here.'

I was clamping on my five-point harness and noting the oxygen
mask hanging by each chair.

'I'm going to be down here and will check on you from time to
time,' the lieutenant went on. 'It's about three hours to Utah, and the
landing shouldn't be too abrupt. They got a runway long enough for
the space shuttle, or that's what they say. You know how the Army
brags.'

She went back downstairs as pilots talked in jargon and codes that
meant nothing to me. We began to take off a mere thirty amazing
minutes after the plane had landed.

'We're going on the runway now,' a pilot said. 'Load?' I assumed
he meant the loadmaster below. 'Is everything secure?'

'Yes, sir,' the voice sounded in my headset.

'Have we got that checklist completed?'

'Yes.'

'Okay. We're rolling.'

The plane surged forward, bumping over the field with gathering
power that was unlike any takeoff I had ever known. It roared more
than a hundred miles an hour, pulling up into the air at an angle so

sharp it flattened me against the back of my chair. Suddenly, stars spangled the sky, the lights of Maryland a winking network.

'We're going about two hundred knots,' a pilot said. 'Command Post aircraft 30601. Flaps up. Execute.'

I glanced over at Lucy, who was behind the co-pilot and trying to see what he was doing as she listened to every word, probably committing it to memory. Laurel returned with cups of coffee, but nothing would have kept me up. I drifted to sleep at thirty-five thousand feet as the jet flew west at six hundred miles an hour. I came to as a tower was talking.

We were over Salt Lake City and descending, and Lucy would never come to earth again as she listened to cockpit talk. She caught me looking but was not to be distracted, and I had never really known anyone like her, not in my entire life. She had a voracious curiosity about anything that could be put together, taken apart, programmed and, in general, made to do something she wanted. People were about the only thing she couldn't figure out.

Clover Control turned us over to Dugway Range Control, and then we were receiving instructions about landing. Despite what we had been told about the length of the runway, it felt like we were going to be torn out of our seats as the jet crescendoed over a tarmac blinking with miles of lights, air roaring against raised slats. The stop was so abrupt, I didn't see how it was physically possible, and I wondered if the pilots might have been practicing.

'Tally ho,' one of them said cheerfully.

15

Dugway was the size of Rhode Island with two thousand people living on the base. But we could see nothing when we got in at half past five A.M. Laurel turned us over to a soldier, who put us in a truck and drove to a place where we could rest and freshen up. There wasn't time for sleep. The plane would be taking off later in the day, and we needed to be on it.

Lucy and I were checked into the Antelope Inn, across from the Community Club. We had a room with twin beds on the first floor, furnished with light oak and wall-to-wall carpet, everything blue. It offered a view of barracks across the green, where lights were already beginning to come on with the dawn.

'You know, there really doesn't seem any point in taking a shower since we'll have to put on the same dirty things,' Lucy said, stretching out on top of her bed.

'You're absolutely right,' I agreed, taking off my shoes. 'You mind if I turn this lamp off?'

'I wish you would.'

The room was dark and I suddenly felt silly. 'This is like a slumber party.'

'Yeah, the one from hell.'

'Remember when you used to come stay with me when you were little?' I said. 'Sometimes we stayed up half the night. You never wanted to go to sleep, always wanting me to read one more story. You wore me out.'

'I remember it the other way around. I wanted to sleep and you wouldn't leave me alone.'

'Untrue.'

'Because you doted on me.'

'Did not. I could scarcely tolerate being in the same room,' I said. 'But I felt sorry for you and wanted to be kind.'

A pillow sailed through the dark and hit me on the head. I threw it back. Then Lucy pounced from her bed to mine, and when she got there didn't quite know what to do, because she was no longer ten and I wasn't Janet. She got up and went back to her bed, loudly fluffing pillows behind her.

'You sound like you're a lot better,' she said.

'Better, but not a lot. I'll live.'

'Aunt Kay, what are you going to do about Benton? You don't even seem to think about him anymore.'

'Oh yes I do,' I answered. 'But things have been a little out of control of late, to say the least.'

'That's always the excuse people give. I should know. I heard it all my life from my mother.'

'But not from me,' I said.

'That's my point. What do you want to do about him? You could get married.'

The mere thought unnerved me again. 'I don't think I can do that, Lucy.'

'Why not?'

'Maybe I'm too set in my ways, on a track I can't get off. Too much is demanded of me.'

'You need to have a life, too.'

'I feel like I do,' I said. 'But it may not be what everybody else thinks it should be.'

'You've always given me advice,' she said. 'Maybe now it's my turn. And I don't think you should get married.'

'Why?' I was more curious than surprised.

'I don't think you ever really buried Mark. And until you do, you shouldn't get married. All of you won't be there, you know?'

I felt sad and was glad she could not see me in the dark. For the first time in our lives, I talked to her as a trusted friend.

'I haven't gotten over him and probably never will,' I said. 'I guess he was my first love.'

'I know all about that,' my niece went on. 'I worry that if something happens, there will never be anybody else for me, either. And

I don't want to go the rest of my life not having what I've got now. Not having someone you can talk to about anything, someone who cares and is kind.' She hesitated, and what she said next was honed to an edge. 'Someone who doesn't get jealous and use you.'

'Lucy,' I said, 'Ring won't wear a badge again in this lifetime, but only you can strip Carrie of her power over you.'

'She has no power over me.' Lucy's temper flared.

'Of course she does. And I can understand it. I'm furious with her, too.'

Lucy got quiet for a moment, and then she spoke in a smaller voice. 'Aunt Kay, what will happen to me?'

'I don't know, Lucy,' I said. 'I don't have the answers. But I promise I will be with you every step of the way.'

The twisted path that had led her to Carrie eventually bent us back around to Lucy's mother, who, of course, was my sister. I wandered the ridges and rills of my growing-up years, and was honest with Lucy about my marriage to her ex-uncle Tony. I spoke of how it felt to be my age and know I probably would not have children. By now, the sky was lighting up, and it was time to start the day. The base commander's driver was waiting in the lobby at nine, a young private who barely needed to shave.

'We got one other person who came in right after you did,' the private said, putting on Ray-Bans. 'From Washington, the FBI.'

He seemed to be very impressed with this and clearly had no idea what Lucy was, nor did the expression change on her face when I asked, 'What does he do with the FBI?'

'Some scientist or something. Pretty hot stuff,' he said, eyeing Lucy, who was striking-looking even when she'd been up all night.

The scientist was Nick Gallwey, head of the Bureau's Disaster Squad, and a forensic expert of considerable reputation. I had known him for years, and when he walked into the lobby, we gave each other a hug, and Lucy shook his hand.

'A pleasure, Special Agent Farinelli. And believe me, I've heard a lot about you,' he said to her. 'So Kay and I are going to do the dirty work while you play with the computer.'

'Yes, sir,' she sweetly said.

'Is there anywhere to have breakfast around here?' Gallwey asked the private, who was tangled in confusion and suddenly shy.

He drove us in the base commander's Suburban beneath an endless sky. Unsettled western mountain ranges surrounded us in the distance, high desert flora like sage, scrub pine and firs, dwarfed by lack of rain. The nearest traffic was forty miles away in this Home of the Mustangs, as the base was called, with its ammunition bunkers, weapons from World War II and air space restricted and vast. There were traces of salt from receding ancient waters, and we spotted an antelope and an eagle.

Stark Road, aptly named, led us toward the test facilities, which were some ten miles from the living area on base. The Ditto diner was on the way, and we stopped long enough for coffee and egg sandwiches. Then it was on to the test facilities, which were clustered in large, modern buildings behind a fence topped with razor wire.

Warning signs were everywhere, promising that trespassers were unwelcome and deadly force used. Codes on buildings indicated what was inside them, and I recognized symbols for mustard gas and nerve agents, and those for Ebola, Anthrax and Hantavirus. Walls were concrete, the private told us, and two feet thick, refrigerators inside explosion-proof. The routine was not so different from what I had experienced before. Guards led us through the toxic containment facilities, and Lucy and I went into the women's changing room while Gallwey went into the men's.

We stripped and put on house clothes that were Army green, and over these went suits, which were camouflage with goggled hoods, and heavy black rubber gloves and boots. Like the blue suits at CDC and USAMRIID, these were attached to air lines inside the chamber, which in this case was stainless steel from ceiling to floor. It was a completely closed system with double carbon filters, where contaminated vehicles like tanks could be bombarded with chemical agents and vapors. We were assured we could work here as long as we needed without placing anyone at risk.

It might even be possible that some evidence could be decontaminated and saved. But it was hard to say. None of us had ever worked a case like this before. We started by propping open the camper's door and arranging lights directed inside. It was peculiar moving around, the steel floor warping loudly like saw blades as we walked. Above us, an Army scientist sat in the control room behind glass, monitoring everything we did.

Again, I went in first because I wanted to thoroughly survey the crime scene. Gallwey began photographing tool marks on the door and dusting for fingerprints, while I climbed inside and looked around as if I had never been there before. The small living area that normally would have contained a couch and table had been gutted and turned into a laboratory with sophisticated equipment that was neither new nor cheap.

The rabbit was still alive, and I fed him and set his cage on top of a counter neatly built of plywood and painted black. Beneath it was a refrigerator, and in it I found Vero and human embryonic lung fibroblast cells. They were tissue cultures routinely used for feeding poxviruses, just as fertilizers are used for certain plants. To maintain these cultures, the mad farmer of this mobile lab had a good supply of Eagle minimal essential medium, supplemented with ten percent fetal calf serum. This and the rabbit told me that deadoc was doing more than maintaining his virus, he was still in the process of propagating it when disaster had struck.

He had kept the virus in a liquid nitrogen freezer that did not need to be plugged in, but refilled every few months. It looked like a ten-gallon stainless steel thermos, and when I unscrewed the lid, I pulled out seven cryotubes so old that instead of plastic, they were made of glass. Codes that should have identified the disease were unlike anything I'd ever seen, but there was a date of 1978, and the location of Birmingham, England, tiny abbreviations written in black ink, neatly, and in lowercase. I returned the tubes of living, frozen horror to their frigid place, and rooted around more, finding twenty sample sizes of Vita facial spray, and tuberculin syringes that the killer, no doubt, had used to inoculate the canisters with the disease.

Of course, there were pipettes and rubber bulbs, petri dishes, and the flasks with screw caps where the virus was actually growing. The medium inside them was pink. Had it begun to turn pale yellow, the pH balance would indicate waste products, acidity, meaning the virus-laden cells had not been bathed in their nutrient-rich tissue culture medium in a while.

I remembered enough from medical school and my training as a pathologist to know that when propagating a virus, the cells must be fed. This is done with the pink culture medium, which must be aspirated off every few days with a pipette, when the nutrients have been replaced by waste. For the medium still to be pink meant this had been done recently, at least within the last four days. Deadoc was meticulous. He had cultivated death with love and care. Yet there were two flasks broken on the floor, perhaps due to an infected rabbit hopping about, somehow accidentally out of its cage. I did not sense suicide here, but an unforeseen catastrophe that had caused deadoc to run.

Slowly, I moved around some more, through the kitchen, where a single bowl and fork had been washed and neatly left to dry on a dish towel by the sink. Cupboards were orderly, too, with rows of simple spices, boxes of cereal and rice and cans of vegetable soup. In the refrigerator was skim milk, apple juice, onions and carrots, but no meat. I closed the door as my mystification grew. Who was he? What did he do in this camper day after day besides make his viral bombs? Did he watch TV? Did he read?

I began to look for clothes, pulling open drawers with no luck. If this man had spent a lot of time here, why had he nothing to wear except what he had on? Why no photographs or personal mementoes? What about books, catalogues for ordering cell lines, tissue cultures, reference material for infectious diseases? Most obvious of all, what had happened to the vehicle that had towed this? Who had driven off in it and when?

I stayed in the bedroom longer, the carpet black from blood that had been tracked through other rooms when we had removed the body. I could not smell or hear anything but air circulating in my suit as I paused to change my four-hour battery. This room, like the rest of the camper, was generic, and I pulled back the flower-printed spread, discovering the pillow and sheets on one side were wrinkled from having been slept on. I found one short gray hair, and collected it with forceps as I remembered that the dead man's hair was longer and black.

A print of a seaside on the wall was cheap, and I took it down to see if I could tell where it had been framed. I tried the love seat beneath a window on the other side of the bed. It was covered in bright green vinyl, and on top was a cactus plant that had to be the only thing alive in the camper except for what was in the cage, the incubator and the freezer. I stirred the soil with my finger and it was not too dry, then I placed it on the carpet and opened up the love seat.

Based on cobwebs and dust, no one had been inside in many years, and I sifted through a rubber cat toy, a faded blue hat and a chewed-on corncob pipe. I did not sense that any of this belonged to the person who lived here now, or had even been noticed by him. I wondered if the camper had been used or in the family, and got down on my hands and knees and crawled around until I found the shot shell and the wad. These, too, I sealed inside an evidence bag.

Lucy was just sitting down at the laptop computer when I returned to the laboratory area.

'Screen saver password,' she said into her voice-activated microphone.

'I was hoping you'd get something difficult,' I said.

She was already rebooting and going into DOS. Knowing her, she would have that password removed in minutes, as I'd seen her do before.

'Kay,' Gallwey's voice sounded inside my hood. 'Got something good out here.'

I went down the steps, careful to keep my air line from tangling. He was in front of the camper, squatting by the area of the tongue where the VIN had been obliterated. Having polished the metal mirror-smooth with fine grit sandpaper, he was now applying a solution of copper chloride and hydrochloric acid to dissolve scarred metal and restore the deeply stamped number underneath that the killer thought he had filed away.

'People don't realize how difficult it is to get rid of one of these things,' his voice filled my ears.

'Unless they're professional car thieves.' I said.

'Well, whoever did this didn't do a very good job.' He was taking photographs. 'I think we got it.'

'Let's hope the camper's registered,' I said.

'Who knows? Maybe we'll get lucky.'

'What about prints?'

The door and aluminum around it were smudged with black dusting powder.

'Some, but God knows whose,' he said getting up and straightening his back. 'In a minute, I'll tear up the inside.'

Meanwhile, Lucy was tearing up the computer, and like me, not coming up with anything that might tell us who deadoc was. But she did find files he had saved of our conversations in the chat rooms, and it was chilling to see them on screen, and wonder how often he had reread them. There were detailed lab notes documenting the propagation of the virus cells, and this was interesting. It appeared work had begun as recently as early in the fall, less than two months before the torso had turned up.

By late afternoon, we had done all we could do with no startling revelations. We took chemical showers as the camper was blasted with formalin gas. I stayed in my army-green house clothes because I did not want my suit after what it had been through.

'Kind of hell on your wardrobe,' Lucy commented as we left the changing room. 'Maybe you should try pearls with that. Dress it up a little.'

'Sometimes you sound like Marino,' I said.

*   *   *

Days crept into the weekend, and next I knew that was gone too with no developments that were anything but maddening. I had missed my mother's birthday. Not once had it crossed my mind.

'What? You got Alzheimer's now?' she unkindly told me over the phone. 'You don't come down here. Now you don't even bother to call. It's not like I'm getting younger.'

She began to cry, and I felt like it.

'Christmas,' I said what I did every year. 'I'll work something out. I'll bring Lucy. I promise. It's not that far away.'

I drove downtown, uninspired and weary to the bone. Lucy had been right. The killer's only use of the phone line at the campground was to dial into AOL, and in the end, all that came back to was Perley's stolen credit card. Deadoc did not call anymore. I had gotten obsessive about checking and sometimes found myself waiting in that chat room when I could not even be sure the FBI was watching anymore.

The frozen virus source I found in the camper's nitrogen freezer remained unknown. Attempts at mapping its DNA continued, and scientists at CDC knew how the virus was different, but not what it was, and thus far, vaccinated primates remained susceptible to it. Four other people, including two watermen who turned up in Crisfield, had come down with only mild cases of the disease. No one else seemed to be getting sick as the quarantine of the fishing village continued and its economy foundered. As for Richmond, only Wingo was ill, his willowy body and gentle face ravaged by pustules. He would not let me see him, no matter how often I tried.

I was devastated, and found it hard to worry about other cases because this one would not end. We knew the dead man in the trailer could not be deadoc. Fingerprints had come back to a drifter with a long arrest record of crimes mostly involving theft and drugs, and two counts of assault and attempted rape. He was out on parole when he had used his pocketknife to pry open the camper door, and no one doubted that his shotgun death was a homicide.

I walked into my office at eight-fifteen. When Rose heard me, she came through her doorway.

'I hope you got some rest,' she said, more worried about me than I'd ever seen.

'I did. Thanks.' I smiled, and her concern made me feel guilty and shamed, as if I were bad somehow. 'Any new developments?'

'Not about Tangier.' I could see the anxiety in her eyes. 'Try to get your mind off it, Dr Scarpetta. We've got five cases this morning.

Look at the top of your desk. If you can find it. And I'm at least two weeks behind on correspondence and micros because of your not being here to dictate.'

'Rose, I know, I know,' I said, not unkindly. 'First things first. Try Phyllis again. And if they still say she's out sick, get a number where she can be reached. I've been trying her home number for days and no one answers.'

'If I get her, you want me to put her through?'

'Absolutely,' I said.

That happened fifteen minutes later when I was about to go into staff meeting. Rose got Phyllis Crowder on the line.

'Where on earth are you? And how are you?' I asked.

'This wretched flu,' she said. 'Don't get it.'

'I did and am still getting rid of it,' I said. 'I've tried your house in Richmond.'

'Oh, I'm at my mother's, in Newport News. You know, I work a four-day week and have been spending the other three days out here for years.'

I did not know that. But we had never socialized.

'Phyllis,' I said, 'I hate to bother you when you're not well, but I need your help with something. In 1978 there was a laboratory accident at the lab in Birmingham, England, where you once worked. I've pulled what I can on it, and know only that a medical photographer was working directly over a smallpox lab . . .'

'Yes, yes,' she interrupted me. 'I know all about it. Supposedly, the photographer was exposed through a ventilator duct, and she died. The virologist committed suicide. The case is cited all the time by people who argue in favor of destroying all frozen source virus.'

'Were you working in that lab when this happened?'

'No, thank goodness. That was some years after I left. I was already in the States by then.'

I was disappointed, and she went into a coughing spell and could hardly talk.

'Sorry.' She coughed. 'This is when you hate living alone.'

'You don't have anyone looking in on you?'

'No.'

'What about food?'

'I manage.'

'Why don't I bring you something,' I said.

'I wouldn't hear of it.'

'I'll help you if you'll help me,' I added. 'Do you have any files on Birmingham? Concerning the work going on when you were there? Anything you could look up?'

'Buried somewhere in this house, I'm sure,' she said.

'Unbury them and I'll bring stew.'

I was out the door in five minutes, running to my car. Heading home, I got several quarts of my homemade stew out of the freezer, then I filled the tank with gas before going east on 64. I told Marino on the car phone what I was doing.

'You've really lost it this time,' he exclaimed. 'Drive over a hundred miles to take someone food? You coulda called Domino's.'

'That's not the point. And believe me, I have one.' I put sunglasses on. 'There may be something here. She may know something that could help.'

'Yo, let me know,' he said. 'You got your pager on, right?'

'Right.'

Traffic was light this time of day, and I kept the cruise control on sixty-nine so I did not get a ticket. In less than an hour, I was bypassing Williamsburg, and about twenty minutes later, following directions Crowder had given me for her address in Newport News. The neighborhood was called Brandon Heights, where the economic class was mixed, and houses got bigger as they got nearer the James River. Hers was a modest two-story frame recently painted eggshell white, the yard and landscaping well maintained.

I parked behind a van and collected the stew, my pocketbook and briefcase slung over a shoulder. When Phyllis Crowder came to the door, she looked like hell, her face pale, and eyes burning with fever. She was dressed in a flannel robe and leather slippers that looked like they might once have belonged to a man.

'I can't believe how nice you are,' she said as she opened the door. 'Either that or crazy.'

'Depends on who you ask.'

I stepped inside, pausing to look at framed photographs along the dark paneled entrance hall. Most of them were of people hiking and fishing and had been taken in long years past. My eyes were fixed on one, an older man wearing a pale blue hat and holding a cat as he grinned around a corncob pipe.

'My father,' Crowder said. 'This was where my parents lived, and my mother's parents were here before that. That's them there.' She pointed. 'When my father's business started doing poorly in England, they came here and moved in with her family.'

'And what about you?' I said.

'I stayed on, was in school.'

I looked at her and did not think she was as old as she wanted me to believe.

'You're always trying to make me assume you're a dinosaur compared to me,' I said. 'But somehow I don't think so.'

'Maybe you just wear the years better than I do.' Her feverish dark eyes met mine.

'Is any of your family still living?' I asked, perusing more photographs.

'My grandparents have been gone about ten years, my father about five. After that, I came out here every weekend to take care of Mother. She hung on as long as she could.'

'That must have been hard with your busy career,' I said, as I looked at an early photograph of her laughing on a boat, holding up a rainbow trout.

'Would you like to come in and sit down?' she asked. 'Let me put this in the kitchen.'

'No, no, show me the way and save your strength,' I insisted.

She led me through a dining room that did not appear to have been used in years, the chandelier gone, exposed wires hanging out over a dusty table, and draperies replaced by blinds. By the time we walked into the large, old-fashioned kitchen, the hair was rising along my scalp and neck, and it was all I could do to remain calm as I set the stew on the counter.

'Tea?' she asked.

She was hardly coughing now, and though she might be ill, this wasn't why she initially had stayed away from her job.

'Not a thing,' I said.

She smiled at me but her eyes were penetrating, and as we sat at the breakfast table, I was frantically trying to figure out what to do. What I suspected couldn't be right, or should I have figured it out sooner? I had been friendly with her for more than fifteen years. We had worked on numerous cases together, shared information, commiserated as women. In the old days, we drank coffee together and smoked. I had found her charming, brilliant, and certainly never sensed anything sinister. Yet I realized this was the very sort of thing people said about the serial killer next door, the child molester, the rapist.

'So, let's talk about Birmingham,' I said to her.

'Let's.' She wasn't smiling now.

'The frozen source of this disease has been found,' I said. 'The vials have labels on them dated 1978, Birmingham. I'm wondering if the lab there might have been doing any research in mutant strains of smallpox, anything that you might know . . . ?'

'I wasn't there in 1978,' she interrupted me.

'Well, I think you were, Phyllis.'

'It doesn't matter.' She got up to put on a pot of tea.

I did not say anything, waiting until she sat back down.

'I'm sick, and by now, you ought to be,' she said, and I knew she was not referring to the flu.

'I'm surprised you didn't create your own vaccine before you started all this,' I said. 'Seems like that was a little reckless for someone so precise.'

'I wouldn't have needed it if that bastard hadn't broken in and ruined everything,' she snapped. 'That filthy, disgusting pig.' Enraged, she shook.

'While you were on AOL, talking to me,' I said. 'That's when you stayed on the line and never logged off, because he started prying open your door. And you shot him and fled in your van. I guess you just went out to Janes Island for your long weekends, so you could passage your lovely disease to new flasks, feed the little darlings.'

I was beginning to feel the rage as I spoke. She did not seem to care, but was enjoying it.

'After all these years in medicine, are people nothing more than slides and petri dishes? What happened to their faces, Phyllis? I have seen the people you did this to.' I leaned closer to her. 'An old woman who died alone in her soiled bed, no one to even hear her cries for water. And now Wingo, who will not let me look at him, a decent, kind young man, dying. You know him! He's been to your lab! What has he ever done to you!'

She was unmoved, her anger flashing, too.

'You left Lila Pruitt's Vita spray in one of the cubbyholes where she sold recipes for a quarter. Tell me if I don't get it right.' My words bit. 'She thought her mail had been delivered to the wrong box, then dropped off by a neighbor. What a nice little something to get for free, and she sprayed it on her face. She had it on her nightstand, spraying it again and again when she was in pain.'

My colleague was silent, her eyes gleaming.

'You probably delivered all of your little bombs to Tangier at once,' I said. 'Then dropped by the ones for me. And my staff. What was your plan after that? The world?'

'Maybe,' was all she had to say.

'Why?'

'People did it to me first. Tit for tat.'

'What did anybody do to you that's even close?' It was an effort to keep my voice controlled.

'I was at Birmingham when it happened. The accident. It was implied that I was partly to blame, and I was forced to leave. It was completely unfair, a total setback to me when I was young, on my own. Scared. My parents had left for the United States, to live here in this house. They liked the outdoors. Camping, fishing. All of them did.'

For a long moment, she stared off as if there, back in those days.

'I didn't matter much, but I had worked hard. I got another job in London, was three grades below what I had been.' Her eyes focused on me. 'It wasn't fair. It was the virologist who caused the accident. But because I was there that day, and he conveniently killed himself, it was easy to pin it all on me. Plus, I was just a kid, really.'

'So you stole the source virus on your way out,' I said.

She smiled coldly.

'And you stored it all these years?'

'Not hard when every place you work has nitrogen freezers and you're always happy to monitor the inventory,' she said with pride. 'I saved it.'

'Why?'

'Why?' Her voice rose. 'I was the one working on it when the accident happened. It was mine. So I made sure I took some of it and my other experiments with me on my way out the door. Why should I let them keep it? They weren't smart enough to do what I did.'

'But this isn't smallpox. Not exactly,' I said.

'Well, that's even worse, now isn't it?' Her lips were trembling with emotion as she recalled those days. 'I spliced the DNA of monkeypox into the smallpox genome.'

She was getting more overwrought, her hands trembling as she wiped her nose with a napkin.

'And then at the beginning of the new academic year, I get passed over as a department chairman,' she went on, eyes flaming with furious tears.

'Phyllis, that's not fair . . .'

'Shut up!' she screamed. 'All I've given to that bloody school? I'm the senior one who has potty-trained everyone, including you. And they give it to a man because I'm not a doctor. I'm *just* a Ph.D.,' she spat.

'They gave it to a Harvard-trained pathologist who is completely justified in getting the position,' I flatly stated. 'And it doesn't matter. There's no excuse for what you've done. You saved a virus all these years? To do this?'

The teakettle was whistling shrilly. I got up and turned the burner off.

'It's not the only exotic disease I've had in my research archives. I've been collecting,' she said. 'I actually thought I might do an important project someday. Study the world's most feared virus and learn something more about the human immune system that might save us from other scourges like AIDS. I thought I might win a Nobel Prize.' She had gotten oddly quiet, as if pleased with herself. 'But no, I wouldn't say that in Birmingham my intention was to one day create an epidemic.'

'Well, you didn't,' I replied.

Her eyes narrowed like evil as she looked at me.

'No one's gotten sick except for those people suspected of using the facial spray,' I said. 'I've been exposed several times to patients, and I'm okay. The virus you created is a dead end, affecting only the primary person but not replicating. There's no secondary infection. No epidemic. What you created was a panic, disease and death for a handful of innocent victims. And crippled the fishing industry for an island full of people who probably have never even heard of a Nobel Prize.'

I leaned back in my chair, studying her, but she did not seem to care.

'Why did you send me photographs and messages?' I demanded. 'Photographs taken in your dining room, on that table. Who was your guinea pig? Your old and infirm mother? Did you spray her with the virus to see if it worked? And when it did, you shot her in the head. You dismembered her with an autopsy saw so no one ever connected that death with your eventual product tampering?'

'You think you're so smart,' she, deadoc, said.

'You murdered your own mother and wrapped her in a drop cloth because you could not bear to look at her as you sawed her apart.'

She averted her eyes as my pager vibrated. I pulled it out and read Marino's number. I got out my phone, my eyes never leaving her.

'Yes,' I said when he answered.

'We got a hit on the camper,' he said. 'Traced it back to a manufacturer, then to an address in Newport News. Thought you'd want to know. Agents should be there right about now.'

'Wish the Bureau had gotten that hit a little sooner,' I said. 'I'll see the agents at the door.'

'What did you say?'

I got off the phone.

'I communicated with you because I knew you would pay attention.' Crowder kept talking at a higher pitch. 'And to make you try and for once finally lose. The famous doctor. The famous chief.'

'You were a colleague and friend,' I said.

'And I resent you!' Her face was flushed, bosom heaving as she raged. 'I always have! The way the system's always treated you better, all the attention you get. The great Dr Scarpetta. The legend. But ha! Look who won. In the end I outsmarted you, didn't I?'

I would not answer her.

'Ran you around, didn't I?' She stared, reaching for a bottle of aspirin and shaking out two. 'Brought you close to death's door and had you waiting in cyberspace. Waiting for me!' she said triumphantly.

Something metal loudly rapped on her front door. I pushed back my chair.

'What are they going to do? Shoot me? Or maybe you should. I bet you've got a gun in one of those bags.' She was getting hysterical. 'I've got one in the other room and I'm going to get it right now.'

She got up as the knocking continued, and a voice demanded, 'Open up, FBI.'

I grabbed her arm. 'No one's going to shoot you, Phyllis.'

'Let go of me!'

I steered her toward the door.

'Let go of me!'

'Your punishment will be to die the way they did.' I pulled her along.

'NO!' she screamed as the door crashed open, slamming against the wall and jarring framed photographs loose from their hooks.

Two FBI agents stepped inside with pistols drawn, and one of them was Janet. They cuffed Dr Phyllis Crowder after she collapsed to the floor. An ambulance transported her to Sentara Norfolk General Hospital, where twenty-one days later she died, shackled in bed, covered with fulminating pustules. She was forty-four.

EPILOGUE

———

I could not make the decision right away but put it off until New Year's Eve when people are supposed to make changes, resolutions, promises they know they'll never keep. Snow was clicking against my slate roof as Wesley and I sat on the floor in front of the fire, sipping champagne.

'Benton,' I said, 'I need to go somewhere.'

He looked confused, as if I meant right now, and said, 'There's not much open, Kay.'

'No. A trip, in February, maybe. To London.'

He paused, knowing what I was thinking. He set his glass on the hearth and took my hand.

'I've been hoping you would,' he said. 'No matter how hard it is, you really should. So you can have closure, peace of mind.'

'I'm not sure it's possible for me to have peace of mind.'

I pulled my hand away and pushed back my hair. This was hard for him, too. It had to be.

'You must miss him,' I said. 'You never talk about it, but he was like a brother. I remember all the times we did things together, the three of us. Cooking, watching movies, sitting around talking about cases and the latest lousy thing government had done to us. Like furloughs, taxes, budget cuts.'

He smiled a little, staring into flames. 'And I would think about what a lucky bastard he was to have you. Wonder what it was like.

Well, now I know, and I was right. He was lucky as hell. He's probably the only person I've ever really talked to, besides you. Kind of strange, in a way. Mark was one of the most self-centered people I've ever met, one of these beautiful creatures, narcissistic as hell. But he was good. He was smart. I don't think you ever stop missing someone like him.'

Wesley was wearing a white wool sweater and cream-colored khakis, and in firelight he was almost radiant.

'You go out tonight and you'll disappear,' I said.

He gave me a puzzled frown.

'Dressed like that in the snow. You fall in a ditch, no one will see you until spring. You should wear something dark on a night like this. You know, contrast.'

'Kay. How about I put on some coffee.'

'It's like people who want a four-wheel-drive vehicle for winter. So they buy something white. Tell me how that makes sense when you're sliding on a white road beneath a white sky with white stuff swirling everywhere.'

'What are you talking about?' His eyes were on me.

'I don't know.'

I lifted the bottle of champagne out of its bucket. Water dripped as I refilled our glasses, and I was ahead of him, about two to one. The CD player was stacked with hits from the seventies, and Three Dog Night was vibrating speakers in the walls. It was one of those rare times I might get drunk. I could not stop thinking about it and seeing it in my mind. I did not know until I was in that room with the wires hanging out of the ceiling and saw where gory severed hands and feet had been lined in a row. It was not until then that the truth seared my mind. I could not forgive myself.

'Benton,' I quietly said, 'I should have known it was her. I should have known before I got to her house and walked in there and saw the photographs and that room. I mean, a part of me must have known, and I didn't listen.'

He did not answer, and I took this as a further indictment.

'I should have known it was her,' I muttered again. 'People might not have died.'

'*Should* is always easy to say after the fact.' His tone was gentle but unwavering. 'People who live next door to the Gacys, the Bundys, the Dahmers of the world are always the last to figure it out, Kay.'

'And they don't know what I do, Benton.' I sipped champagne. 'She killed Wingo.'

'You did the best you could,' he reminded me.

'I miss him,' I said with a sad sigh. 'I haven't been to Wingo's grave.'

'Why don't we switch to coffee?' Wesley said again.

'Can't I just drift now and then?' I didn't want to be present.

He started rubbing the back of my neck, and I shut my eyes.

'Why do I always have to make sense?' I muttered. 'Precise about this, exact about that. *Consistent with*, and *characteristic of*. Words cold and sharp like the steel blades I use. And what good will they do me in court? When it's Lucy in the balance? Her career, her life? All because of that bastard, Ring. Me, the expert witness. The loving aunt.' A tear slid down my cheek. 'Oh God, Benton. I'm so tired.'

He moved over and put his arms around me, pulling me into his lap so I could lean back my head.

'I'll go with you,' he quietly said into my hair.

We took a black cab to London's Victoria Station on February 18, the anniversary of a bombing that had ripped through a trash can and collapsed an underground entrance, a tavern and a coffee bar. Rubble had flown, shattered glass from the roof raining down in shrapnel and missiles with terrible force. The IRA had not targeted Mark. His death had nothing to do with his being FBI. He simply had been in the wrong place at the wrong time like so many people who are victims.

The station was crowded with commuters who almost ran me over as we made our way to the central area where Railtrack ticket agents were busy in their booths, and displays on a wall showed times and trains. Kiosks were selling sweets and flowers, and one could get a passport picture taken or have money changed. Trash cans were tucked inside McDonald's and places like that, but I did not see a single one out in the open.

'No good place to hide a bomb now.' Wesley was observing the same thing.

'Live and learn,' I said as I began to tremble inside.

I silently stared around me as pigeons flapped overhead and trotted after crumbs. The entrance for the Grosvenor Hotel was next to the Victoria Tavern, and it was here that it had happened. No one was completely certain what Mark had been doing at the time, but it was speculated that he had been sitting at one of the small, high tables in front of the tavern when the bomb exploded.

We knew he had been waiting for the train from Brighton to arrive because he was meeting someone. To this day I did not know who, because the individual's identity could not be revealed for security reasons. That's what I had been told. I had never understood many things, such as the coincidence of timing, and whether this clandestine person Mark was meeting may have been killed, too. I scanned the roof of steel girders and glass, the old clock on the granite wall, and archways. The bombing had left no permanent scars, except on people.

'Brighton is a rather odd place to be in February,' I commented to Wesley in an unsteady voice. 'Why would someone be coming from a seaside resort that time of year?'

'I don't know why,' he said, looking around. 'This was all about terrorism. As you know, that was what Mark was working on. So no one's saying much.'

'Right. That was what he was working on, and that was how he died,' I said. 'And no one seems to think there was a link. That maybe it wasn't random.'

He did not respond, and I looked at him, my soul heavy and sinking down into the darkness of a fathomless sea. People, and pigeons, and constant announcements on the PA blended into a dizzying din, and for an instant, all went black. Wesley caught me as I swayed.

'Are you all right?'

'I want to know who he was seeing.' I said.

'Come on, Kay,' he said, gently. 'Let's go someplace where you can sit down.'

'I want to know if the bombing was deliberate because a certain train was arriving at a certain time,' I persisted. 'I want to know if this is all fiction.'

'Fiction?' he asked.

Tears were in my eyes. 'How do I know this isn't some cover-up, some ruse, because he's alive and in hiding? A protected witness with a new identity.'

'He's not.' Wesley's face was sad, and he held my hand. 'Let's go.'

But I wouldn't move. 'I must know the truth. If it really happened. Who was he meeting and where is that person now?'

'Don't do this.'

People were weaving around us, not paying any attention. Feet crashed like an angry surf, and steel clanged as construction workers laid new rail.

'I don't believe he was meeting anyone.' My voice shook and I wiped my eyes. 'I believe this is some great big Bureau lie.'

He sighed, staring off. 'It's not a lie, Kay.'

'Then who! I have to know!' I cried.

Now people were looking our way, and Wesley moved me out of traffic, toward platform 8, where the 11:46 train was leaving for Denmark Hill and Peckham Rye. He led me up a blue and white tile ramp into a room of benches and lockers, where travelers could store belongings and claim left baggage. I was sobbing, and could not help myself. I was confused and furious as we went into a deserted corner and he kindly sat me on a bench.

'Tell me,' I said. 'Benton, please. I've got to know. Don't make me go the rest of my life not knowing the truth,' I choked between tears.

He took both my hands. 'You can put this to rest right now. Mark is dead. I swear. Do you really think I could have this relationship with you if I knew he were alive somewhere?' he passionately said. 'Jesus. How can you even imagine I could do something like that!'

'What happened to the person he was meeting?' I kept pushing.

He hesitated. 'Dead, I'm afraid. They were together when the bomb went off.'

'Then why all the secrecy about who he was?' I exclaimed. 'This isn't making sense!'

He hesitated again, this time longer, and for an instant, his eyes were filled with pity for me and it looked like he might cry. 'Kay, it wasn't a he. Mark was with a woman.'

'Another agent.' I did not understand.

'No.'

'What are you saying?'

The realization was slow because I did not want it, and when he was silent, I knew.

'I didn't want you to find out,' he said. 'I didn't think you needed to know that he was with another woman when he died. They were coming out of the Grosvenor Hotel when the bomb went off. It had nothing to do with him. He was just there.'

'Who was she?' I felt relieved and nauseated at the same time.

'Her name was Julie McFee. She was a thirty-one-year-old solicitor from London. They met through a case he was working. Or maybe through another agent. I'm really not sure.'

I looked into his eyes. 'How long had you known about them?'

'For a while. Mark was going to tell you, and it wasn't my place to.' He touched my cheek, wiping away tears. 'I'm sorry. You have no idea how this makes me feel. As if you haven't suffered enough.'

'In a way it makes it easier,' I said.

A teenager with body piercing and a mohawk slammed a locker door. We waited until he sauntered off with his girl in black leather.

'Typical of my relationship with him, in truth.' I felt drained and could scarcely think as I got up. 'He couldn't commit, take a risk. Never would have, not for anyone. He missed out on so much, and that's what makes me saddest.'

Outside it was damp with a numbing wind blowing, and the line of cabs around the station did not end. We walked hand in hand and bought bottles of Hooper's Hooch, because one could drink alcoholic lemonade on the streets of England. Police on dappled horses clopped past Buckingham Palace, and in St James's Park a band of guards in bearskin caps were marching while people pointed cameras. Trees swayed and drums faded as we walked back to the Athenaeum Hotel on Piccadilly.

'Thank you.' I slipped my arm around him. 'I love you, Benton,' I said.

POINT OF ORIGIN

Every man's work shall be made manifest: for the day shall declare it, because it shall be revealed by fire; and the fire shall try every man's work of what sort it is.

I Corinthians 3:13

Day 523.6
One Pheasant Place
Kirby Woman's Ward
Wards Island, NY

Hey DOC

Tick Tock

Sawed bone and fire.

Still home alone with FIB the liar? Watch the clock BIG
DOC!

Spurt dark light and fright TRAINSTRAINSTRAINS.
GKSFWFY wants photos.

Visit with we. On floor three. YOU trade with we.

TICK TOC DOC! (Will Lucy talk?)

LUCY-BOO on TV. Fly through window. Come with we
Under covers. Come til dawn. Laugh and sing. Same ole
song. LUCY LUCY LUCY and we!

Wait and see.

Carrie

1

Benton Wesley was taking off his running shoes in my kitchen when I ran to him, my heart tripping over fear and hate and remembered horror. Carrie Grethen's letter had been mixed in a stack of mail and other paperwork, all of it put off until a moment ago when I had decided to drink cinnamon tea in the privacy of my Richmond, Virginia home. It was Sunday afternoon, thirty-two minutes past five, June eighth.

'I'm assuming she sent this to your office,' Benton said.

He did not seem disturbed as he bent over, peeling off white Nike socks.

'Rose doesn't read mail marked personal and confidential.' I added a detail he already knew as my pulse ran hard.

'Maybe she should. You seem to have a lot of fans out there.' His wry words cut like paper.

I watched him set pale bare feet on the floor, his elbows on his knees and head low. Sweat trickled over shoulders and arms well defined for a man his age, and my eyes drifted down knees and calves, to tapered ankles still imprinted with the weave of his socks. He ran his fingers through wet silver hair and leaned back in the chair.

'Christ,' he muttered, wiping his face and neck with a towel. 'I'm too old for this crap.'

He took a deep breath and blew out slowly with mounting anger.

The stainless steel Breitling Aerospace watch I had given to him for Christmas was on the table. He picked it up and snapped it on.

'Goddamn it. These people are worse than cancer. Let me see it,' he said.

The letter was penned by hand in bizarre red block printing, and drawn at the top was a crude crest of a bird with long tail feathers. Scrawled under it was the enigmatic Latin word *ergo*, or *therefore*, which in this context meant nothing to me. I unfolded the simple sheet of white typing paper by its corners and set it in front of him on the antique French oak breakfast table. He did not touch a document that might be evidence as he carefully scanned Carrie Grethen's weird words and began running them through the violent database in his mind.

'The postmark's New York, and of course there's been publicity in New York about her trial,' I said as I continued to rationalize and deny. 'A sensational article just two weeks ago. So anyone could have gotten Carrie Grethen's name from that. Not to mention, my office address is public information. This letter's probably not from her at all. Probably some other cuckoo.'

'It probably is from her.' He continued reading.

'She could mail something like this from a forensic psychiatric hospital and nobody would check it?' I countered as fear coiled around my heart.

'Saint Elizabeth's, Bellevue, Mid-Hudson, Kirby.' He did not glance up. 'The Carrie Grethens, the John Hinckley Juniors, the Mark David Chapmans are patients, not inmates. They enjoy our same civil rights as they sit around in penitentiaries and forensic psychiatric centers and create pedophile bulletin boards on computers and sell serial killer tips through the mail. And write taunting letters to chief medical examiners.'

His voice had more bite, his words more clipped. Benton's eyes burned with hate as he finally lifted them to me.

'Carrie Grethen is mocking you, *big chief*. The FBI. Me,' he went on.

'*FIB*,' I muttered, and on another occasion, I might have found this funny.

Wesley stood and draped the towel over a shoulder.

'Let's say it's her,' I started in again.

'It is.' He had no doubt.

'Okay. Then there's more to this than mockery, Benton.'

'Of course. She's making sure we don't forget that she and Lucy were lovers, something the general public doesn't know *yet*,' he said. 'The obvious point is Carrie Grethen hasn't finished ruining people's lives.'

I could not stand to hear her name, and it enraged me that she was now, this moment, inside my West End home. She might as well be sitting at my breakfast table with us, curdling the air with her foul, evil presence. I envisioned her condescending smile and blazing eyes and wondered what she looked like now after five years of steel bars and socializing with the criminally insane. Carrie was not crazy. She had never been that. She was a character disorder, a psychopath, a violent entity with no conscience.

I looked out at wind rocking Japanese maples in my yard and the incomplete stone wall that scarcely kept me from my neighbors. The telephone rang abruptly and I was reluctant to answer it.

'Dr Scarpetta,' I said into the receiver as I watched Benton's eyes sweep back down that red-penned page.

'Yo,' Pete Marino's familiar voice came over the line. 'It's me.'

He was a captain with the Richmond Police Department, and I knew him well enough to recognize his tone. I braced myself for more bad news.

'What's up?' I said to him.

'A horse farm went up in flames last night in Warrenton. You may have heard about it on the news,' he said. 'Stables, close to twenty high-dollar horses, and the house. The whole nine yards. Everything burned to the ground.'

So far, this wasn't making any sense. 'Marino, why are you calling me about a fire? In the first place, Northern Virginia is not your turf.'

'It is now,' he said.

My kitchen seemed to get small and airless as I waited for the rest.

'ATF's just called out NRT,' he went on.

'Meaning us,' I said.

'Bingo. Your ass and mine. First thing in the morning.'

The Bureau of Alcohol, Tobacco and Firearms' National Response Team, or NRT, was deployed when churches or businesses burned, and in bombings or any other disaster in which ATF had jurisdiction. Marino and I were not ATF, but it was not unusual for it and other law enforcement agencies to recruit us when the need arose. In recent years I had worked the World Trade Center and Oklahoma City bombings and the crash of TWA Flight 800. I had helped with the identifications of the Branch Davidians at Waco and reviewed the disfigurement and death caused by the Unabomber. I knew from stressful experience that ATF included me in a call-out only when people were dead, and if Marino was recruited, too, then the suspicion was murder.

'How many?' I reached for my clipboard of call sheets.

'It's not how many, Doc. It's *who*. The owner of the farm is media big shot Kenneth Sparkes, the one and only. And right now it's looking like he didn't make it.'

'Oh God,' I muttered as my world suddenly got too dark to see. 'We're sure?'

'Well, he's missing.'

'You mind explaining to me why I'm just now being told about this?'

I felt anger rising, and it was all I could do not to hurl it at him, for all unnatural deaths in Virginia were my responsibility. I shouldn't have needed Marino to inform me about this one, and I was furious with my Northern Virginia office for not calling me at home.

'Don't go getting pissed at your docs up in Fairfax,' said Marino, who seemed to read my mind. 'Fauquier County asked ATF to take over here, so that's the way it's going.'

I still didn't like it, but it was time to get on with the business at hand.

'I'm assuming no body has been recovered yet,' I said, and I was writing fast.

'Hell no. That's going to be your fun job.'

I paused, resting the pen on the call sheet. 'Marino, this is a single-dwelling fire. Even if arson is suspected, and it's a high-profile case, I'm not seeing why ATF is interested.'

'Whiskey, machine guns, not to mention buying and selling fancy horses, so now we're talking about a business,' Marino answered.

'Great,' I muttered.

'Oh yeah. We're talking a goddamn nightmare. The fire marshal's gonna call you before the day's out. Better get packed because the whirlybird's picking us up before dawn. Timing's bad, just like it always is. I guess you can kiss your vacation goodbye.'

Benton and I were supposed to drive to Hilton Head tonight to spend a week at the ocean. We had not had time alone so far this year and were burned out and barely getting along. I did not want to face him when I hung up the phone.

'I'm sorry,' I said to him. 'I'm sure you've already figured out there's a major disaster.'

I hesitated, watching him, and he would not give me his eyes as he continued to decipher Carrie's letter.

'I've got to go. First thing in the morning. Maybe I can join you in the middle of the week,' I went on.

He was not listening because he did not want to hear any of it.

'Please understand,' I said to him.

He did not seem to hear me, and I knew he was terribly disappointed.

'You've been working those torso cases,' he said as he read. 'The dismemberments from Ireland and here. "Sawed-up bone." And she fantasizes about Lucy, and masturbates. Reaching orgasm multiple times a night under the covers. Allegedly.'

His eyes ran down the letter as he seemed to talk to himself.

'She's saying they still have a relationship, Carrie and Lucy,' he continued. 'The *we* stuff is her attempt to make a case for disassociation. She's not present when she commits her crimes. Some other party doing them. Multiple personalities. A predictable and pedestrian insanity plea. I would have thought she'd be a little more original.'

'She is perfectly competent to stand trial,' I answered with a wave of fresh anger.

'You and I know that.' He drank from a plastic bottle of Evian. 'Where did *Lucy Boo* come from?'

A drop of water dribbled down his chin and he wiped it with the back of his hand.

I stumbled at first. 'A pet name I had for her until she was in kindergarten. Then she didn't want to be called that anymore. Sometimes I still slip.' I paused again as I imagined her back then. 'So I guess she told Carrie the nickname.'

'Well, we know that at one time, Lucy confided in Carrie quite a lot,' Wesley stated the obvious. 'Lucy's first lover. And we all know you never forget your first, no matter how lousy it was.'

'Most people don't choose a psychopath for their first,' I said, and I still could not believe that Lucy, my niece, had.

'Psychopaths are us, Kay,' he said as if I had never heard the lecture. 'The attractive, intelligent person sitting next to you on a plane, standing behind you in line, meeting you backstage, hooking up with you on the Internet. Brothers, sisters, classmates, sons, daughters, lovers. Look like you and me. Lucy didn't have a chance. She was no match for Carrie Grethen.'

The grass in my backyard had too much clover, but spring had been unnaturally cool and perfect for my roses. They bent and shivered in gusting air and pale petals fell to the ground. Wesley, the retired chief of the FBI's profiling unit, went on.

'Carrie wants photos of Gault. Scene photos, autopsy photos. You bring them to her, and in exchange she'll tell you investigative details, forensic jewels you've supposedly missed. Ones that might help the prosecution when the case goes to court next month. Her taunt. That you might have missed something. That it might in some way be connected with Lucy.'

His reading glasses were folded by his place mat, and he thought to slip them on.

'Carrie wants you to come see her. At Kirby.'

His face was tight as he peered at me.

'It's her.'

He pointed at the letter.

'She's surfacing. I knew she would.' He spoke from a spirit that was tired.

'What's the dark light?' I asked, getting up because I could not sit a moment longer.

'Blood.' He seemed sure. 'When you stabbed Gault in the thigh, severing his femoral artery, and he bled to death. Or would have had the train not finished the job. Temple Gault.'

He took his glasses off again, because he was secretly agitated.

'As long as Carrie Grethen is around, so is he. The evil twins,' he added.

In fact, they were not twins, but had bleached their hair and shaved it close to their skulls. They were prepubescently thin and androgenously dressed alike when I last saw them in New York. They had committed murder together until we had captured her in the Bowery and I had killed him in the subway tunnel. I had not intended to touch him or see him or exchange one word with him, for it was not my mission in this life to apprehend criminals and commit judicial homicide. But Gault had willed it so. He had made it happen because to die by my hand was to bond me to him forever. I could not get away from Temple Gault, though he had been dead five years. In my mind were gory pieces of him scattered along gleaming steel rails and rats moiling out of dense shadows to attack his blood.

In bad dreams his eyes were ice blue with irises scattered like molecules, and I heard the thunder of trains with lights that were blinding full moons. For several years after I had killed him, I avoided autopsying the victims of train deaths. I was in charge of the Virginia medical examiner system and could assign cases to my deputy chiefs, and that was what I had done. Even now, I could not look at dissecting knives with the same clinical regard for their cold sharp steel, because he had set me up to plunge one into him, and I had. In crowds I saw dissipated men and women who were him, and at night I slept closer to my guns.

'Benton, why don't you shower and then we'll talk more about our plans for the week,' I said, dismissing recollections I could not bear. 'A few days alone to read and walk the beach would be just what you need. You know how much you love the bike trails. Maybe it would be good for you to have some space.'

'Lucy needs to know.' He got up, too. 'Even if Carrie's confined at the moment, she's going to cause more trouble that involves Lucy. That's what Carrie's promising in her letter to you.'

He walked out of the kitchen.

'How much more trouble can anybody cause?' I called after him as tears rose in my throat.

'Dragging your niece into the trial,' he stopped to say. 'Publicly. Splashed across *The New York Times*. Out on the AP, *Hard Copy*, *Entertainment Tonight*. Around the world. *FBI agent was lesbian lover of deranged serial killer . . .*'

'Lucy's left the FBI with all its prejudices and lies and preoccupations with how the mighty Bureau looks to the world.' Tears flooded my eyes. 'There's nothing left. Nothing further they can do to crush her soul.'

'Kay, this is about far more than the FBI,' he said, and he sounded spent.

'Benton, don't start . . .' I could not finish.

He leaned against the doorway leading into my great room, where a fire burned, for the temperature had not gotten above sixty degrees this day. His eyes were pained. He did not like me to talk this way, and he did not want to peer into that darker side of his soul. He did not want to conjure up the malignant acts Carrie might carry out, and of course, he worried about me, too. I would be summoned to testify in the sentencing phase of Carrie Grethen's trial. I was Lucy's aunt. I supposed my credibility as a witness would be impeached, my testimony and reputation ruined.

'Let's go out tonight,' Wesley said in a kinder tone. 'Where would you like to go? La Petite? Or beer and barbecue at Benny's?'

'I'll thaw some soup.' I wiped my eyes as my voice faltered. 'I'm not very hungry, are you?'

'Come here,' he said to me sweetly.

I melted into him and he held me to his chest. He was salty when we kissed, and I was always surprised by the supple firmness of his body. I rested my head, and the stubble on his chin roughed my hair and was white like the beach I knew I would not see this week. There would be no long walks on wet sand or long talks over dinners at La Polla's and Charlie's.

'I think I should go see what she wants,' I finally said into his warm, damp neck.

'Not in a million years.'

'New York did Gault's autopsy. I don't have those photographs.'

'Carrie knows damn well what medical examiner did Gault's autopsy.'

'Then why is she asking me, if she knows?' I muttered.

My eyes were closed as I leaned against him. He paused and kissed the top of my head again and stroked my hair.

'You know why,' he said. 'Manipulation, jerking you around. What people like her do best. She wants you to get the photos for her. So she can see Gault mangled like chopped meat, so she can fantasize and get off on that. She's up to something and the worst thing you could do is respond to her in any way.'

'And this GKSWF – something or other? Like out of a personal?'

'I don't know.'

'And the One Pheasant Place?'

'No idea.'

We stayed a long time in the doorway of this house I continued to think of singularly and unequivocally as my own. Benton parked his life with me when he was not consulting in big aberrant cases in this country and others. I knew it bothered him when I consistently said *I* this and *my* that, although he knew we were not married and nothing we owned separately belonged to both of us. I had passed the midline of my life and would not legally share my earnings with anyone, including my lover and my family. Maybe I sounded selfish, and maybe I was.

'What am I going to do while you're gone tomorrow?' Wesley got back to that subject.

'Drive to Hilton Head and get groceries,' I replied. 'Make sure there's plenty of Black Bush and Scotch. More than usual. And sunblock SPF 35 and 50, and South Carolina pecans, tomatoes, and Vidalia onions.'

Tears filled my eyes again, and I cleared my throat.

'As soon as I can, I'll get on a plane and meet you, but I don't know where this case in Warrenton is going to go. And we've already been over this. We've done it before. Half the time you can't go, the rest of the time it's me.'

'I guess our lives suck,' he said into my ear.

'Somehow we ask for it,' I replied, and most of all I felt an uncontrollable urge to sleep.

'Maybe.'

He bent down to my lips and slid his hands to favorite places.

'Before soup, we could go to bed.'

'Something very bad is going to happen during this trial,' I said, and I wanted my body to respond to him but didn't think it could.

'All of us in New York again. The Bureau, you, Lucy, at her trial. Yes, I'm sure for the past five years she has thought of nothing else and will cause all the trouble she can.'

I pulled away as Carrie's sharp, drawn face suddenly jumped out of a dark place in my mind. I remembered her when she was strikingly pretty and smoking with Lucy on a picnic table at night near the firing ranges of the FBI Academy at Quantico. I could still hear them teasing in low playful voices and saw their erotic kisses on the mouth, deep and long, and hands tangled in hair. I remembered the strange sensation running through my blood as I silently hurried away, without them knowing what I had seen. Carrie had begun the ruination of my only niece's life, and now the grotesque coda had come.

'Benton,' I said. 'I've got to pack my gear.'

'Your gear is fine. Trust me.'

He hungrily had undone layers of my clothing, desperate for skin. He always wanted me more when I was not in sync with him.

'I can't reassure you now,' I whispered. 'I can't tell you everything is going to be all right, because it won't be. Attorneys and the media will go after Lucy and me. They will dash us against the rocks, and Carrie may go free. There!'

I held his face in my hands.

'Truth and justice. The American way,' I concluded.

'Stop it.'

He went still and his eyes were intense on mine.

'Don't start again,' he said. 'You didn't used to be this cynical.'

'I'm not cynical, and I'm not the one who started anything,' I answered him as my anger rose higher. 'I'm not the one who started with an eleven-year-old boy and cut off patches of his flesh and left him naked by a Dumpster with a bullet in his head. And then killed a sheriff and a prison guard. And Jayne – Gault's own twin sister. Remember that, Benton? Remember? Remember Central Park on Christmas Eve. Bare footprints in snow and her frozen blood dripping from the fountain!'

'Of course I remember. I was there. I know all the same details you do.'

'No, you don't.'

I was furious now and moved away from him and gathered together my clothes.

'You don't put your hands inside their ruined bodies and touch and measure their wounds,' I said. 'You don't hear them speak after they're dead. You don't see the faces of loved ones waiting inside my poor, plain lobby to hear heartless, unspeakable news. You don't see what I do. Oh no, you don't, Benton Wesley. You see clean case files and glossy photos and cold crime scenes. You spend more time with the killers than with those they ripped from life. And maybe you sleep better than I do, too. Maybe you still dream because you aren't afraid to.'

He walked out of my house without a word, because I had gone too far. I had been unfair and mean, and not even truthful. Wesley knew only tortured sleep. He thrashed and muttered and coldly drenched the sheets. He rarely dreamed, or at least he had learned not to remember. I set salt and pepper shakers on corners of Carrie Grethen's letter to keep it from folding along its creases. Her mocking, unnerving words were evidence now and should not be touched or disturbed.

Ninhydrin or a Luma Lite might reveal her fingerprints on the cheap white paper, or exemplars of her writing might be matched with what she had scrawled to me. Then we would prove she had penned this twisted message at the brink of her murder trial in Superior Court of New York City. The jury would see that she had not changed after five years of psychiatric treatment paid for with their taxes. She felt no remorse. She reveled in what she had done.

I had no doubt Benton would be somewhere in my neighborhood because I had not heard his BMW leave. I hurried along new paved streets, passing big brick and stucco homes, until I caught him beneath trees staring out at a rocky stretch of the James River. The water was frigid and the color of glass, and cirrus clouds were indistinct chalky streaks in a fading sky.

'I'll head out to South Carolina as soon as I get back to the house. I'll get the condo ready and get your Scotch,' he said, not turning around. 'And Black Bush.'

'You don't need to leave tonight,' I said, and I was afraid to move closer to him as slanted light brightened his hair and the wind stirred it. 'I've got to get up early tomorrow. You can head out when I do.'

He was silent, staring up at a bald eagle that had followed me since I had left my house. Benton had put on a red windbreaker, but he looked chilled in his damp running shorts, and his arms were crossed tightly at his chest. His throat moved as he swallowed, his pain radiating from a hidden place that only I was allowed to see. At moments like this I did not know why he put up with me.

'Don't expect me to be a machine, Benton,' I said quietly for the millionth time since I had loved him.

Still he did not speak, and water barely had the energy to roll toward downtown, making a dull pouring sound as it unwittingly headed closer to the violence of dams.

'I take as much as I can,' I explained. 'I take more than most people could. Don't expect too much from me, Benton.'

The eagle soared in circles over the tops of tall trees, and Benton seemed more resigned when he spoke at last.

'And I take more than most people can,' he said. 'In part, because you do.'

'Yes, it works both ways.'

I stepped closer to him from behind and slipped my arms around the slick red nylon covering his waist.

'You know damn well it does,' he said.

I hugged him tight and dug my chin into his back.

'One of your neighbors is watching,' he said. 'I can see him through sliding glass. Did you know you have a peeper in this ritzy white-bread place?'

He placed his hands over mine, then lifted one finger at a time with nothing special in mind.

'Of course, if I lived here, I would peep at you too,' he added with a smile in his tone.

'You do live here.'

'Naw. I just sleep here.'

'Let's talk about the morning. As usual, they'll pick me up at the Eye Institute around five,' I told him. 'So I guess if I get up by four . . .' I sighed, wondering if life would always be like this. 'You should stay the night.'

'I'm not getting up at four,' he said.

2

The next morning came unkindly on a field that was flat and barely blue with first light. I had gotten up at four, and Wesley had gotten up, too, deciding he would rather leave when I did. We had kissed briefly and barely looked at each other as we had headed to our cars, for brevity at goodbyes was always easier than lingering. But as I had followed West Cary Street to the Huguenot Bridge, a heaviness seemed to spread through every inch of me and I was suddenly unnerved and sad.

I knew from weary experience that it was unlikely I would be seeing Wesley this week, and there would be no rest or reading or late mornings to sleep. Fire scenes were never easy, and if nothing else, a case involving an important personage in a wealthy bedroom community of D.C. would tie me up in politics and paperwork. The more attention a death caused, the more public pressure I was promised.

There were no lights on at the Eye Institute, which was not a place of medical research nor called such in honor of some benefactor or important personage named *Eye*. Several times a year I came here to have glasses adjusted or my vision checked, and it always seemed strange to park near fields where I was often lifted into the air, headed toward chaos. I opened my car door as the familiar distant sound moved over dark waves of trees, and I imagined burned bones and teeth scattered through black watery debris. I imagined Sparkes's sharp suits and strong face, and shock chilled me like fog.

The tadpole silhouette flew beneath an imperfect moon as I gathered water repellent duffle bags, and the scratched silver Halliburton aluminum flight case that stored my various medical examiner instruments and needs, including photography equipment. Two cars and a pickup truck began slowing on Huguenot Road, the city's twilight travelers unable to resist a helicopter low and about to land. The curious turned into the parking lot and got out to stare at blades slicing air in a slow sweep for power lines, puddles and muck, or sand and dirt that might boil up.

'Must be the governor coming in,' said an old man who had arrived in a rusting heap of a Plymouth.

'Could be someone delivering an organ,' said the driver of the pickup truck as he briefly turned his gaze on me.

Their words scattered like dry leaves as the black Bell LongRanger thundered in at a measured pitch and perfectly flared and gently descended. My niece Lucy, its pilot, hovered in a storm of fresh-mown grass flooded white by landing lights, and settled sweetly. I gathered my belongings and headed into beating wind. Plexiglas was tinted dark enough that I could not see through it as I pulled open the back door, but I recognized the big arm that reached down to grab my baggage. I climbed up as more traffic slowed to watch the aliens, and threads of gold bled through the tops of trees.

'I was wondering where you were.' I raised my voice above rotors chopping as I latched my door.

'Airport,' Pete Marino answered as I sat next to him. 'It's closer.'

'No, it's not,' I said.

'At least they got coffee and a john there,' he said, and I knew he did not mean them in that order. 'I guess Benton headed out on vacation without you,' he added for the effect.

Lucy was rolling the throttle to full power, and the blades were going faster.

'I can tell you right now I got one of those feelings,' he let me know in his grumpy tone as the helicopter got light and began to lift. 'We're headed for big trouble.'

Marino's specialty was investigating death, although he was completely unnerved by possibilities of his own. He did not like being airborne, especially in something that did not have flight attendants or wings. The *Richmond Times Dispatch* was a mess in his lap, and he refused to look down at fast retreating earth and the distant city skyline slowly rising from the horizon like someone tall standing up.

The front page of the paper prominently displayed a story about the fire, including a distant AP aerial photograph of ruins smoldering in the dark. I read closely but learned nothing new, for mostly the coverage was a rehash of Kenneth Sparkes's alleged death, and his power and wealthy lifestyle in Warrenton. I had not known of his horses before or that one named Wind had sailed in last one year at the Kentucky Derby and was worth a million dollars. But I was not surprised. Sparkes had always been enterprising, his ego as enormous as his pride. I set the newspaper on the opposite seat and noted that Marino's seat belt was unbuckled and collecting dust from the floor.

'What happens if we hit severe turbulence when you're not belted in?' I talked loudly above the turbine engine.

'So I spill my coffee.' He adjusted the pistol on his hip, his khaki suit a sausage skin about to split. 'In case you ain't figured it out after all those bodies you've cut up, if this bird goes down, Doc, a seat belt ain't gonna save you. Not airbags either, if we had them.'

In truth, he hated anything around his girth and had come to wear his pants so low I marveled that his hips could keep them up. Paper crackled as he dug two Hardee's biscuits out of a bag stained gray with grease. Cigarettes bunched in his shirt pocket, and his face had its typical hypertensive flush. When I had moved to Virginia from my native city of Miami, he was a homicide detective as obnoxious as he was gifted. I remembered our early encounters in the morgue when he had referred to me as *Mrs Scarpetta* as he bullied my staff and helped himself to any evidence he pleased. He had taken bullets before I could label them, to infuriate me. He had smoked cigarettes with bloody gloves and made jokes about bodies that had once been living human beings.

I looked out my window at clouds skating across the sky and thought of time going by. Marino was almost fifty-five, and I could not believe it. We had defended and irritated each other almost daily for more than eleven years.

'Want one?' He held up a cold biscuit wrapped in waxy paper.

'I don't even want to look at it,' I said ungraciously.

Pete Marino knew how much his rotten health habits worried me and was simply trying to get my attention. He carefully stirred more sugar in the plastic cup of coffee he was floating up and down with the turbulence, using his meaty arm for suspension.

'What about coffee?' he asked me. 'I'm pouring.'

'No thanks. How about an update?' I got to the point as my tension mounted. 'Do we know anything more than we did last night?'

'The fire's still smoldering in places. Mostly in the stables,' he said. 'A lot more horses than we thought. Must be twenty cooked out there, including thoroughbreds, quarter horses, and two foals with race-horse pedigrees. And of course you know about the one that ran the Derby. Talk about the insurance money alone. A so-called witness said you could hear them screaming like humans.'

'What witness?' It was the first I'd heard of it.

'Oh, all kinds of drones have been calling in, saying they saw this and know that. Same old shit that always happens when a case gets a lot of attention. And it don't take an *eyewitness* to know the horses would have been screaming and trying to kick down their stalls.' His tone turned to flint. 'We're gonna get the son of a bitch who did this. Let's see how he likes it when it's his ass burning.'

'We don't know that there is a son of a bitch, at least not for a fact,' I reminded him. 'No one has said it's arson yet, although I certainly am assuming you and I haven't been invited along for the ride.'

He turned his attention out a window.

'I hate it when it's animals.' He spilled coffee on his knee. 'Shit.' He glared at me as if I were somehow to blame. 'Animals and kids. The thought makes me sick.'

He did not seem to care about the famous man who may have died in the fire, but I knew Marino well enough to understand that he targeted his feelings where he could tolerate them. He did not hate human beings half as much as he led others to believe, and as I en-visioned what he had just described, I saw thoroughbreds and foals with terror in their eyes.

I could not bear to imagine screams, or battering hooves splin-tering wood. Flames had flowed like rivers of lava over the Warrenton farm with its mansion, stables, reserve aged whiskey, and collection of guns. Fire had spared nothing but hollow walls of stone.

I looked past Marino into the cockpit, where Lucy talked into the radio, making comments to her ATF copilot as they nodded at a Chinook helicopter below horizon and a plane so distant it was a sliver of glass. The sun lit up our journey by degrees, and it was diffi-cult to concentrate as I watched my niece and felt wounded again.

She had quit the FBI because it had made certain she would. She had left the artificial intelligence computer system she had created and robots she had programmed and the helicopters she had learned to fly for her beloved Bureau. Lucy had walked off from her heart and was no longer within my reach. I did not want to talk to her about Carrie.

I silently leaned back in my seat and began reviewing paperwork on the Warrenton case. Long ago I had learned how to focus my attention to a very sharp point, no matter what I thought and in spite of my mood. I felt Marino staring again as he touched the pack of cigarettes in his shirt pocket, making sure he was not without his vice. The chopping and flapping of blades was loud as he slid open his window and tapped his pack of cigarettes to shake one loose.

'Don't,' I said, turning a page. 'Don't even think about it.'

'I don't see a No Smoking sign,' he said, stuffing a Marlboro into his mouth.

'You never do, no matter how many of them are posted.' I reviewed more of my notes, puzzling again over one particular statement the fire marshal had made to me over the phone yesterday.

'Arson for profit?' I commented, glancing up. 'Implicating the owner, Kenneth Sparkes, who may have accidentally been overcome by the fire he started? Based on what?'

'Is his the name of an arsonist or what?' Marino said. 'Gotta be guilty.' He inhaled deeply and with lust. 'And if that's the case, he got what he deserves. You know, you can take them off the street but can't take the street out of them.'

'Sparkes was not raised on the street,' I said. 'And by the way, he was a Rhodes scholar.'

'*Road* scholar and *street* sound like the same damn thing to me,' Marino went on. 'I remember when all the son of a bitch did was criticize the police through his newspaper chain. Everybody knew he was doing cocaine and women. But we couldn't prove it because nobody would come forward to help us out.'

'That's right, no one could prove it,' I said. 'And you can't assume someone is an arsonist because of his name or his editorial policy.'

'Well, it just so happens you're talking to the expert in weird-ass names and how they fit the squirrels who have them.' Marino poured more coffee as he smoked. '*Gore* the coroner. *Slaughter* the serial killer. *Childs* the pedophile. *Mr Bury* buried his victims in cemeteries. Then we got *Judges Gallow* and *Frye*. Plus Freddie *Gamble*. He was running numbers out of his restaurant when he got whacked. *Dr Faggart* murdered five homosexual males. Stabbed their eyes out. You remember *Crisp*?' He looked at me. 'Struck by lightning. Blew his clothes all over the church parking lot and magnetized his belt buckle.'

I could not listen to all this so early in the morning and reached behind me to grab a headset so I could drown Marino out and monitor what was being said in the cockpit.

'I wouldn't want to get struck by lightning at no church and have everybody read something into it,' Marino went on.

He got more coffee, as if he did not have prostate and urinary troubles.

'I've been keeping a list all these years. Never told no one. Not even you, Doc. You don't write down shit like this, you forget.' He sipped. 'I think there's a market for it. Maybe one of those little books you see up by the cash register.'

I put the headset on and watched rural farms and dormant fields slowly turn into houses with big barns and long drives that were paved. Cows and calves were black-spotted clusters in fenced-in grass, and a combine churned up dust as it slowly drove past fields scattered with hay.

I looked down as the landscape slowly transformed into the wealth of Warrenton, where crime was low and mansions on hundreds of acres of land had guest houses, tennis courts and pools, and very fine stables. We flew lower over private airstrips and lakes with ducks and geese. Marino was gawking.

Our pilots were silent for a while as they waited to be in range of the NRT on the ground. Then I caught Lucy's voice as she changed frequencies and began transmitting.

'Echo One, helicopter niner-one-niner Delta Alpha. Teun, you read me?'

'That's affirmative, niner Delta Alpha,' T. N. McGovern, the team leader, came back.

'We're ten miles south, inbound-landing with passengers,' Lucy said. 'ETA about eight hundred hours.'

'Roger. It feels like winter up here and not getting any warmer.'

Lucy switched over to the Manassas Automated Weather Observation Service, or AWOS, and I listened to a long mechanical rendition of wind, visibility, sky condition, temperature, dew point, and altimeter setting according to Sierra time, which was the most recent update of the day. I wasn't thrilled to learn that the temperature had dropped five degrees Celsius since I had left home, and I imagined Benton on his way to warm sunshine and the water.

'We got rain over there,' Lucy's copilot said into his mike.

'It's at least twenty miles west and the winds are west,' Lucy replied. 'So much for June.'

'Looks like we got another Chinook coming this way, below horizon.'

'Let's remind 'em we're out here,' Lucy said, switching to a different frequency again. 'Chinook over Warrenton, helicopter niner-one-niner Delta Alpha, you up this push? We're at your three o'clock, two miles northbound, one thousand feet.'

'We see you, Delta Alpha,' answered the twin rotor Army helicopter named for an Indian tribe. 'Have a good'n.'

My niece double-clicked the transmit switch. Her calm, low voice seemed unfamiliar to me as it radiated through space and bounced off the antennae of strangers. I continued to eavesdrop and, as soon as I could, butted in.

'What's this about wind and cold?' I asked, staring at the back of Lucy's head.

'Twenty, gusting to twenty-five out of the west,' she sounded in my headset. 'And gonna get worse. You guys doing all right back there?'

'We're fine,' I said as I thought of Carrie's deranged letter again.

Lucy flew in blue ATF fatigues, a pair of Cébé sunglasses blacking out her eyes. She had grown her hair, and it gracefully curled to her shoulders and reminded me of red jarrah wood, polished and exotic, and nothing like my own short silver-blond strands. I imagined her light touch on the collective and cyclic as she worked anti-torque pedals to keep the helicopter in trim.

She had taken to flying like everything else she had ever tried. She had gotten her private and commercial ratings in the minimum required hours and next got her certificated flight instructor rating simply because it gave her joy to pass on her gifts to others.

I needed no announcement that we were reaching the end of our flight as we skimmed over woods littered with felled trees scattered haphazardly like Lincoln Logs. Dirt trails and lanes wound narrowly, and on the other side of gentle hills, gray clouds got vertical as they turned into vague columns of tired smoke left by an inferno that had killed. Kenneth Sparkes's farm was a shocking black pit, a scorched earth of smoldering carnage.

The fire had left its trail as it had slaughtered, and from the air I followed the devastation of splendid stone dwellings and stables and barn to wide charred swaths that had denuded the grounds. Fire trucks had rolled over sections of the white fence surrounding the property and had churned up acres of manicured grass. Miles in the distance were more pasture land and a narrow paved public road, then a Virginia Power substation, and farther off, more homes.

We invaded Sparkes's privileged Virginia farm at not quite eight a.m., landing far enough away from ruins that our rotor wash did not disturb them. Marino climbed out and went on without me as I waited for our pilots to brake the main rotor and turn off all switches.

'Thanks for the lift,' I said to Special Agent Jim Mowery, who had helped Lucy fly this day.

'She did the driving.'

He popped open the baggage door.

'I'll tie her down if you guys want to go on,' he added to my niece.

'Seems like you're getting the hang of that thing,' I lightly teased Lucy as we walked away.

'I limp along the best I can,' she said. 'Here, let me get one of those bags.'

She relieved me of my aluminum case, which did not seem to weigh much in her firm hand. We walked together, dressed alike, although I did not wear gun or portable radio. Our steel-reinforced boots were so battered they were peeling and almost gray. Black mud sucked at our soles as we drew closer to the gray inflatable tent that would be our command post for the next few days. Parked next to it was the big white Pierce supertruck with Department of the Treasury seals and emergency lights, and ATF and EXPLOSIVES INVESTIGATION announced in vivid blue.

Lucy was a step ahead of me, her face shadowed by a dark blue cap. She had been transferred to Philadelphia, and would be moving from D.C. soon, and the thought made me feel old and used up. She was grown. She was as accomplished as I had been at her age, and I did not want her moving farther away. But I had not told her.

'This one's pretty bad.' She initiated the conversation. 'At least the basement is ground level, but there's only one door. So most of the water's in a pool down there. We got a truck on the way with pumps.'

'How deep?'

I thought of thousands of gallons of water from fire hoses and imagined a cold black soup thick with dangerous debris.

'Depends on where you're stepping. If I were you, I wouldn't have taken this call,' she said in a way that made me feel unwanted.

'Yes, you would have,' I said, hurt.

Lucy had made little effort to hide her feelings about working cases with me. She wasn't rude, but often acted as if she barely knew me when she was with her colleagues. I remembered earlier years when I would visit her at UVA and she did not want students to see us together. I knew she was not ashamed of me but perceived me as an overwhelming shadow that I had worked very hard not to cast over her life.

'Have you finished packing?' I asked her with an ease that was not true.

'Please don't remind me,' she said.

'But you still want to go.'

'Of course. It's a great opportunity.'

'Yes, it is, and I am so pleased for you,' I said. 'How's Janet? I know this must be hard . . .'

'It's not like we'll be in different hemispheres,' Lucy answered back.

I knew better, and so did she. Janet was an FBI agent. The two of them had been lovers since their early training days at Quantico. Now they worked for different federal law enforcement agencies and soon would live in separate cities. It was quite possible their careers would never permit their relationship again.

'Do you suppose we can carve out a minute to talk today?' I spoke again as we picked our way around puddles.

'Sure. When we finish up here, we'll have a beer, if we can find an open bar out here in the sticks,' she replied as the wind blew harder.

'I don't care how late it is,' I added.

'Here goes,' Lucy muttered with a sigh as we approached the tent. 'Hey gang,' she called out. 'Where's the party?'

'You're looking at it.'

'Doc, you making house calls these days?'

'Naw, she's babysitting Lucy.'

In addition to Marino and me, NRT on this call-out were nine men, two women, including team leader McGovern. All of us were dressed alike in the familiar dark blue fatigues, which were worn and patched and supple like our boots. Agents were restless and boisterous around the back of the open tailgate of the supertruck with its shiny aluminum interior divided into shelves and jump seats, and its outside compartments packed with reels of yellow crime-scene tape, and dustpans, picks, floodlights, whisk brooms, wrecking bars, and chop saws.

Our mobile headquarters was also equipped with computers, a photocopier and fax machine, and the hydraulic spreader, ram, hammer, and cutter used to deconstruct a scene or save a human life. In fact, I could not think of much the truck did not have except, perhaps, a chef, and more importantly, a toilet.

Some agents had begun decontaminating boots, rakes, and shovels in plastic tubs filled with soapy water. It was a never-ending effort, and in brisk weather, hands and feet never dried or thawed. Even exhaust pipes were swabbed for petroleum residues, and all power tools were run by electricity or hydraulic fluid instead of gasoline, preparing for that day in court when all would be questioned and judged.

McGovern was sitting on a table inside the tent, her boots unzipped, and a clipboard on her knee.

'All right,' she addressed her team. 'We've been through most of this already at the fire station, where you guys missed good coffee and donuts,' she added for the benefit of those of us who had just gotten here. 'But listen up again. What we know so far is the fire is believed to have started day before yesterday, on the evening of the seventh at twenty hundred hours.'

McGovern was about my age and based in the Philadelphia field office. I looked at her and saw Lucy's new mentor, and I felt a stiffening in my bones.

'At least that's the time the fire alarm went off in the house,' McGovern went on. 'When the fire department got here, the house was fully involved. Stables were burning. Trucks really couldn't get close enough to do anything but surround and drown. Or at least make an attempt at it. We're estimating about thirty thousand gallons of water in the basement. That's about six hours total to pump all of it out, assuming we're talking about four pumps going and don't have millions of clogs. And by the way, the power's off, and our local friendly fire department is going to set up lights inside.'

'What was the response time?' Marino asked her.

'Seventeen minutes,' she replied. 'They had to grab people off duty. Everything around here is volunteer.'

Someone groaned.

'Now don't be too hard on them. They used every tanker around to get enough water in, so that wasn't the problem,' McGovern chided her troops. 'This thing went up like paper, and it was too windy for foam, even though I don't think it would have helped.' She got up and moved to the supertruck. 'The deal is, this was a *fast, hot fire*. That much we know for a fact.'

She opened a red-paneled door and began handing out rakes and shovels.

'We got not a clue as to point of origin or cause,' she continued, 'but it's believed that the owner, Kenneth Sparkes, the newspaper tycoon, was inside the house and did not get out. Which is why we got the doc here.'

McGovern looked straight at me with piercing eyes that did not miss much.

'What makes us think he was home at the time?' I asked.

'For one thing, he seems to be MIA. And a Mercedes burned up in the back. We haven't run the tags yet but assume it's probably his,' a fire investigator answered. 'And the farrier who shoes his horses was just here two days before the fire, on Thursday, the fifth, and Sparkes was home then and the farrier didn't say that he indicated he was headed out somewhere.'

'Who took care of his horses when he was out of town?' I asked.

'We don't know,' McGovern said.

'I'd like the farrier's name and number,' I said.

'No problem. Kurt?' she said to one of her investigators.

'Sure. I got it.' He flipped pages in a spiral notebook, his young hands big and rough from years of work.

McGovern grabbed bright blue helmets out of another compartment and began tossing them around as she reminded individuals of their assignments.

'Lucy, Robby, Frank, Jennifer, you're in the hole with me. Bill, you're general assignment, and Mick's going to help him, since this is Bill's first NRT.'

'Lucky you.'

'Ohhh, a virgin.'

'Give me a break, man,' said the agent named Bill. 'It's my wife's fortieth birthday. She'll never speak to me again.'

'Rusty's in charge of the truck,' McGovern resumed. 'Marino and the doc are here as needed.'

'Had Sparkes been receiving any threats?' Marino asked, because it was his job to think murder.

'You know about as much as we do at this point,' the fire investigator named Robby said.

'What's this about this alleged witness?' I asked.

'We got that through a telephone call,' he explained. 'A male, he wouldn't leave his name, and it was an out-of-the-area call, so we got no idea. Got no idea if it's legit.'

'But he said he heard the horses as they were dying,' I persisted.

'Yeah. Screaming like humans.'

'Did he explain how he might have been close enough to have heard that?' I was getting upset again.

'Said he saw the fire from the distance and drove in for a closer look. Says he watched for maybe fifteen minutes and then got the hell out of Dodge when he heard the fire trucks.'

'Now I didn't know that and it bothers me,' Marino said ominously.

'What he's saying is consistent with the response time. And we know how much these squirrels like to hang around and watch their fires burn. Got any idea about race?'

'I didn't talk to him more than thirty seconds,' Robby answered. 'But he had no discernible accent. Was soft-spoken and very calm.'

There was silence for a pause as everyone processed their disappointment in not knowing who this witness was, or if he had been genuine. McGovern went on with her roster of who was doing what this day.

'Johnny Kostylo, our beloved ASAC in Philly, will be working the media and local bigwigs, like the mayor of Warrenton, who's already been calling because he doesn't want his town to look bad.'

She glanced up from her clipboard, scanning our faces.

'One of our auditors is on his way,' she went on. 'And Pepper will be showing up shortly to help us out.'

Several agents whistled their appreciation of Pepper the arson dog.

'And thankfully, Pepper doesn't hit on alcohol.' McGovern put her own helmet on. 'Because there's about a thousand gallons of bourbon out here.'

'We know anything more about that?' Marino asked. 'We know if Sparkes might have been making or selling the stuff? I mean, that's a hell of a lot of hooch for one guy.'

'Apparently Sparkes was a collector of the finer things in life,' McGovern spoke of Sparkes as if he were certainly dead. 'Bourbon, cigars, automatic firearms, expensive horses. We don't know how legal he was, which is one of the reasons why youze guys are here instead of the Feebs.'

'Hate to tell you, but the Feebs are already sniffing around. Wanting to know what they can do to help.'

'Aren't they sweet.'

'Maybe they can show us what to do.'

'Where are they?' McGovern asked.

'In a white Suburban about a mile down the road. Three of 'em hanging out in their FBI flak jackets. They're already talking to the media.'

'Shit. Wherever there are cameras.'

There were groans and derisive laughter directed at the *Feebs*, which was what ATF rudely called the FBI. It was no secret that the two federal agencies were not fond of each other, and that the FBI routinely appropriated credit when it was not always due.

'Speaking of pains in the ass,' another agent spoke up, 'the Budget

Motel doesn't take AmEx, boss. We're going through the heels of our boots, and we're supposed to use our own credit cards?'

'Plus, room service quits at seven.'

'It stinks anyway.'

'Any chance we can move?'

'I'll take care of it,' McGovern promised.

'That's why we love you so much.'

A bright red fire engine rumbled up the unpaved road, churning dust and small rocks, as help arrived to begin draining water from the scene. Two firefighters in turn-out gear and high rubber boots climbed down and briefly conferred with McGovern before uncoiling one-and-three-quarter-inch hoses attached to filters. These they draped over their shoulders and dragged inside the mansion's stone shell and dropped them into the water in four different locations. They returned to the truck and set heavy portable Prosser pumps on the ground and plugged extension cords into the generator. Soon the noise of engines got very loud, and hoses swelled as dirty water gushed through them and over grass.

I gathered heavy canvas fire gloves and a turn-out coat and adjusted the size of my helmet. Then I began cleaning my faithful Red Wing boots, sloshing them through tubs of sudsy cold tap water that seeped through old leather tongues and soaked the laces. I had not thought to wear silk underwear beneath my BDUs because it was June. That had been a mistake. Winds were now strong and from the north, and every drop of moisture seemed to lower my body temperature another degree. I hated being cold. I hated not trusting my hands, because they were either stiff or heavily gloved. McGovern headed toward me as I blew on my fingertips and fastened my heavy turn-out coat up to my chin.

'It's going to be a long day,' she said with a shiver. 'What happened to summer?'

'Teun, I'm missing my vacation for you. You are destroying my personal life.' I gave her a hard time.

'At least you have either.' McGovern started cleaning her boots, too.

Teun was really an odd hybrid of the initials T. N., which stood for something Southern-awful such as Tina Nola, or so I had been told. For as long as I had been on the NRT, she had been Teun, and so that was what I called her. She was capable and divorced. She was firm and fit, her bone structure and gray eyes compelling. McGovern could be fierce. I had seen her anger flash over like a room in flames, but she could also be generous and kind. Her special gift was arson, and it was legend that she could intuit the cause of a fire simply by hearing a description of the scene.

I worked on two pairs of latex gloves as McGovern scanned the horizon, her eyes staying a long time on the blackened pit with its shell of standing granite. I followed her gaze to scorched stables, and in my mind heard screams and panicked hooves battering stalls. For an instant my throat constricted. I had seen the raw, clawed hands of people buried alive, and the defense injuries of victims who struggled with their killers. I knew about life fighting not to die, and I could not bear the vivid footage playing in my mind.

'Goddamn reporters.' McGovern stared up at a small helicopter flying low overhead.

It was a white Schweizer with no identification or mounted cameras I could see. McGovern stepped forward and boldly pointed out every member of the media within five miles.

'That van there,' she let me know. 'Radio, some local-yokel FM dial with a celebrity talent named Jezebel who tells moving stories about life and her crippled son and his three-legged dog named Sport. And another radio over there. And that Ford Escort over that way is some fucking son-of-a-bitch newspaper. Probably some tabloid out of D.C. Then we got the *Post*.' She pointed at a Honda. 'So look out for her. She's the brunette with legs. Can you imagine wearing a skirt out here? Probably thinks the guys will talk to her. But they know better, unlike the Feebs.'

She backed up and grabbed a handful of latex gloves from inside the supertruck. I dug my hands deeper into the pockets of my BDUs. I had gotten used to McGovern's diatribes about the *biased, mendacious media*, and I barely listened.

'And this is just the start,' she went on. 'These media maggots will be crawling all over the place because I already know about this one here. It doesn't take a Boy Scout to guess how this place burned and all those poor horses got killed.'

'You seem more cheerful than usual,' I said dryly.

'I'm not cheerful in the least.'

She propped her foot on the shiny tailgate of the supertruck as an old station wagon pulled up. Pepper the arson dog was a handsome black Labrador retriever. He wore an ATF badge on his collar and was no doubt comfortably curled in the warm front seat, going nowhere until we were ready for him.

'What can I do to help?' I said to her. 'Besides staying out of the way until you need me.'

She was staring off. 'If I were you, I'd hang out with Pepper or in the truck. Both are heated.'

McGovern had worked with me before and knew if I was needed to dive into a river or sift through fire or bombing debris, I was not above the task. She knew I could hold a shovel and did not sit around. I resented her comments and felt she was somehow picking on me. I turned to address her again and found her standing very still, like a bird dog pointing. She had an incredulous expression on her face as she remained fixed to some spot on the horizon.

'Holy Jesus,' she muttered.

I followed her stare to a lone black foal, maybe a hundred yards due east of us, just beyond the smoky ruins of the stables. The magnificent animal looked carved from ebony from where we stood, and I could make out twitching muscles and tail as he seemed to return our attention.

'The stables,' McGovern said, in awe. 'How the hell did he get away?'

She got on her portable radio.

'Teun to Jennifer,' she said.

'Go ahead.'

'Take a look maybe beyond the stables. See what I do?'

'Ten-four. Got the four-legged subject in sight.'

'Make sure the locals know. We need to find out if subject is a survivor from here or a runaway from somewhere else.'

'You got it.'

McGovern strode off, a shovel over her shoulder. I watched her move into the stinking pit and pick a spot near what appeared to have once been the wide front door, cold water up to her knees. Far off, the aloof black horse wavered as if made of fire. I slogged ahead in soggy boots, my fingers getting increasingly uncooperative. It was only a matter of time before I would need a toilet, which typically would be a tree, a mound, an acre somewhere in what was sworn to be a blind with no men within a mile.

I did not enter the remaining stone shell at first but walked slowly around it from the outside perimeter. The caving-in of remaining structures was an obvious and extreme danger at scenes of mass destruction, and although the two-story walls looked sturdy enough, it would have suited me better had they been pulled down by a crane and trucked away. I continued my scan in the bright, cool wind, my heart sinking as I wondered where to begin. My shoulders ached from my aluminum case, and just the thought of dragging a rake through water-logged debris sent pain into my back. I was certain McGovern was watching to see how long I would last.

Through gaping wounds of windows and doors I could see the sooty pit coiling with thousands of flat steel whiskey-barrel hoops that drifted in black water. I imagined reserve bourbon exploding from burning white oak kegs and pouring through the door in a river of fire downhill to the stables that had housed Kenneth Sparkes's precious horses. While investigators began the task of determining where the fire had started and hopefully its cause, I stepped through puddles and climbed atop anything that looked sturdy enough to bear my weight.

Nails were everywhere, and with a Buckman tool that had been a gift from Lucy, I pulled one of them out of my left boot. I stopped inside the perfect stone rectangle of a doorway in the front of the former mansion. For minutes I stood and looked. Unlike many investigators, I did not take photographs with every inch I moved closer into a crime scene. I had learned to bide my time and let my eyes go first. As I quietly scanned around me, I was struck by many things.

The front of the house, unsurprisingly, would have afforded the most spectacular view. From upper stories no longer there, one should have seen trees and gentle hills, and the various activities of the horses that the owner bought, traded, bred, and sold. It was believed that Kenneth Sparkes had been home the night of the fire, on June seventh, and I remembered that the weather had been clear and a little warmer, with a light wind and full moon.

I surveyed the empty shell of what must have been a mansion, looking at soggy couch parts, metal, glass, the melted guts of televisions and appliances. There were hundreds of partially burned books, and paintings, mattresses, and furniture. All had fallen from upper stories and settled into soupy layers in the basement. As I imagined Sparkes in the evening when the fire alarm went off, I imagined him in the living room with its view, or in the kitchen, perhaps cooking. Yet the more I explored where he might have been, the less I understood why he had not escaped, unless he were incapacitated by alcohol or drugs, or had tried to put out the fire until carbon monoxide had overcome him.

Lucy and comrades were on the other side of the pit, prying open an electrical box that heat and water had caused to rust instantly.

'Good luck,' McGovern's voice carried as she waded closer to them. 'That's not going to be what started this one.'

She kept talking as she slung a blackened frame of an ironing board to one side. The iron and what was left of its cord followed. She kicked more barrel hoops out of the way as if she were mad at whoever had caused this mess.

'You notice the windows?' she went on to them. 'The broken glass is on the inside. Makes you think someone broke in?'

'Not necessarily.' It was Lucy who answered as she squatted to look. 'You get thermal impact to the inside of the glass and it heats up and expands more and faster than the exterior, causing uneven stress and heat cracks, which are distinctively different from mechanical breakage.'

She handed a jagged piece of broken glass to McGovern, her supervisor.

'Smoke goes out of the house,' Lucy went on, 'and the atmosphere comes in. Equalization of pressure. It doesn't mean someone broke in.'

'You get a B-plus,' McGovern said to her.

'No way. I get an A.'

Several of the agents laughed.

'But I have to agree with Lucy,' one of them said. 'So far I'm not seeing any sign that someone broke in.'

Their team leader continued turning our disaster site into a classroom for her soon-to-be Certificated Fire Investigators, or CFIs.

'Remember we talked about smoke coming through brick?' she continued, pointing up to areas of stone along the roofline that looked as if they had been scrubbed with steel brushes. 'Or is that erosion from blasts of water?'

'No, the mortar's partially eaten away. That's from smoke.'

'That's right. From smoke pushing through the joints.' McGovern was matter-of-fact. 'Fire establishes its own vent paths. And low around the walls here, here and here' – she pointed – 'the stone is burned clean of all incomplete combustion or soot. We've got melted glass and melted copper pipes.'

'It started low, on the first floor,' Lucy said. 'The main living area.'

'Looks like that to me.'

'And flames went up as high as ten feet to engage the second floor and roof.'

'Which would take a pretty decent fuel load.'

'Accelerants. But forget finding a pour pattern in this shit.'

'Don't forget anything,' McGovern told her team. 'And we don't know if an accelerant was necessary because we don't know what kind of fuel load was on that floor.'

They were splashing and working as they talked, and all around was the constant sound of dripping water and rumbling of the pumps. I got interested in box springs caught in my rake and squatted to pull out rocks and charred wood with my hands. One always had to consider that a fire victim might have died in bed, and I peered up at what once had been the upper floors. I continued excavating, producing nothing remotely human, only the sodden, sour trash of all that had been ruined in Kenneth Sparkes's fine estate. Some of his former possessions still smoldered on tops of piles that were not submerged, but most of what I raked was cold and permeated with the nauseating smell of scorched bourbon.

Our sifting went on throughout the morning, and as I moved from one square of muck to the next, I did what I knew how to do best. I groped and probed with my hands, and when I felt a shape that worried me, I took off my heavy fire gloves and felt some more with fingers barely sheathed by latex. McGovern's troops were scattered and lost in their own hunches, and at almost noon she waded back to me.

'You holding up?' she asked.

'Still standing.'

'Not bad for an armchair detective.' She smiled.

'I'll take that as a compliment.'

'You see how even everything is?' She pointed a sooty gloved finger. 'High-temperature fire, constant from one corner of the house to the other. Flames so hot and high they burned up the upper two floors and pretty near everything in them. We're not talking some electrical arc here, not some curling iron left on or grease that caught fire. Something big and smart's behind this.'

I had noticed over the years that people who battled fire spoke of it as if it were alive and possessed a will and personality of its own. McGovern began working by my side, and what she couldn't sling out of the way, she piled into a wheelbarrow. I polished what turned out to be a stone that could have passed for a finger bone, and she pointed the wooden butt of her rake up at an empty overcast sky.

'The top level's gonna be the last one to fall,' she told me. 'In other words, debris from the roof and second floor should be on top down here. So I'm assuming that's what we're rooting around in right now.' She stabbed the rake at a twisted steel I-beam that once had supported the roof. 'Yes sir,' she went on, 'that's why there's all this insulation and slate everywhere.'

This went on and on, with no one taking breaks that were longer than fifteen minutes. The local fire station kept us supplied in coffee, sodas, and sandwiches, and had set up quartz lights so we could see as we worked in our wet hole. At each end a Prosser pump sucked water through its hose and disgorged it outside granite walls, and after thousands of gallons were gone, our conditions did not seem much better. It was hours before the level dipped perceptibly.

At half past two I could stand it no longer and went outside again. I scanned for the most inconspicuous spot, which was beneath the sweeping boughs of a large fir tree near the smoking stables. My hands and feet were numb, but beneath heavy protective clothing I was sweating as I squatted and kept a nervous watch for anyone who might wander this way. Then I steeled myself to walk past every charred stall. The stench of death pushed itself up into my nostrils and seemed to cling to spaces inside my skull.

Horses were pitifully piled on top of each other, their legs pugilistically drawn, and skin split from the swelling and shrinking of cooking flesh. Mares, stallions, and geldings were burned down to bone with smoke still drifting from carcasses charred like wood. I hoped they had succumbed to carbon monoxide poisoning before flames had touched them.

I counted nineteen bodies, including two yearlings and a foal. The miasma of burned horse hair and death was choking and enveloped me like a heavy cloak as I headed across grass back to the mansion's shell. On the horizon, the sole survivor was watching me again, standing very still, alone and mournful.

McGovern was still sloshing and shoveling and pitching trash out of her way, and I could tell she was getting tired, and I was perversely pleased by that. It was getting late in the day. The sky had gotten darker, and the wind had a sharper edge.

'The foal is still there,' I said to her.

'Wish he could talk.' She straightened up and massaged the small of her back.

'He's running loose for a reason,' I said. 'It doesn't make sense to think he got out on his own. I hope someone plans to take care of him?'

'We're working on it.'

'Couldn't one of the neighbors help?' I would not stop, because the horse was really getting to me.

She gave me a long look and pointed straight up.

'Master bedroom and bath were right up there,' she announced as she lifted a broken square of white marble out of the filthy water. 'Brass fixtures, a marble floor, the jets from a Jacuzzi. The frame of a skylight, which, by the way, was open at the time of the fire. If you reach down six inches to your left, you'll run right into what's left of the tub.'

The water level continued to lower as pumps sucked and formed small rivers over grass. Nearby, agents were pulling out antique oak flooring that was deeply charred on top with very little unburned wood left. This went on, and added to mounting evidence that the origin of the fire was the second floor in the area of the master suite, where we recovered brass pulls from cabinets and mahogany furniture, and hundreds of coat hangers. We dug through burnt cedar and remnants of men's shoes and clothing from the master closet.

By five o'clock, the water had dropped another foot, revealing a ruined landscape that looked like a burned landfill, with scorched hulls of appliances and the carcasses of couches. McGovern and I were still excavating in the area of the master bath, fishing out prescription bottles of pills, and shampoos and body lotions, when I finally discovered the first shattered edge of death. I carefully wiped soot from a jagged slab of glass.

'I think we've got something,' I said, and my voice seemed swallowed by dripping water and the sucking of pumps.

McGovern shone her flashlight on what I was doing and went still.

'Oh Jesus,' she said, shocked.

Milky dead eyes gleamed at us through watery broken glass.

'A window, maybe a glass shower door fell on top of the body, preserving at least some of it from being burned to the bone,' I said.

I moved more broken glass aside, and McGovern was momentarily stunned as she stared at a grotesque body that I instantly knew was not Kenneth Sparkes. The upper part of the face was pressed flat beneath thick cracked glass, and the eyes were a dull bluish-gray because their original color had been cooked out of them. They peered up at us from the burned bone of the brow. Strands of long blond hair had gotten free and eerily flowed as dirty water seeped, and there was no nose or mouth, only chalky, calcined bone and teeth that had been burned until there was nothing organic left in them.

The neck was partially intact, the torso covered with more broken glass, and melted into cooked flesh was a dark fabric that had been a blouse or shirt. I could still make out the weave. Buttocks and pelvis were also spared beneath glass. The victim had been wearing jeans. The legs were burned down to bone, but leather boots had protected the feet. There were no lower arms or hands, and I could not find any trace of those bones.

'Who the hell is this?' McGovern said, amazed. 'Did he live with someone?'

'I don't know,' I said, scooping more water out of the way.

'Can you tell if it's a female?' McGovern said as she leaned closer to look, her flashlight still pointed.

'I wouldn't want to swear to it in court until I can examine her more closely. But yes, I'm thinking female,' I answered.

I looked up at empty sky, imagining the bathroom the woman possibly had died in, and then got cameras out of my kit as cold water lapped around my feet. Pepper the arson dog and his handler had just filled a doorway, and Lucy and other agents were wading our way as word of our find hummed down the line. I thought of Sparkes, and nothing here made sense, except that a woman had been inside his home the night of the fire. I feared his remains might be somewhere in here, too.

Agents came nearer, and one of them brought me a body bag. I unfolded it and took more photographs. Flesh had cooked to glass and would have to be separated. This I would do in the morgue, and I instructed that any debris around the body would need to be sent in as well.

'I'm going to need some help,' I said to everyone. 'Let's get a backboard and some sheets in here, and someone needs to call whatever local funeral home is responsible for body removals. We're going to need a van. Be careful, the glass is sharp. As she is, *in situ*. Face up, just like she is now, so we don't put too much stress on the body and tear the skin. That's good. Now open the bag more. As wide as we can get it.'

'It ain't gonna fit.'

'Maybe we could break off more of the glass around the edges here,' McGovern suggested. 'Somebody got a hammer?'

'No, no. Let's just cover her as is.' I issued more commands, for I was in charge now. 'Drape this over and around the edges to protect your hands. Everybody got their gloves on?'

'Yeah.'

'Those of you who aren't helping here, there may be another body. So let's keep looking.'

I was tense and irritable as I waited for two agents to return with a backboard and blue plasticized sheets to cover it.

'Okay,' I said. 'We're going to lift. On the count of three.'

Water sloshed and splashed as four of us struggled for leverage and balance. It was awful groping for sure footing as we gripped slippery wet glass that was sharp enough to cut through leather.

'Here we go,' I said. 'One, two, three, lift.'

We centered the body on the backboard. I covered it as best I could with the sheets and fastened it snugly with straps. Our steps were small and hesitant as we felt our way through water that no longer came over our boots. The Prosser pumps and generator were a constant humming throb that we scarcely noticed as we ferried our morbid cargo closer to the empty space that once had been a door. I smelled cooked flesh and death, and the acrid rotting odor of fabric, food, furniture, and all that had burned in Kenneth Sparkes's home. I was breathless and numb with stress and cold as I emerged into the pale light of the fast-retreating day.

We lowered the body to the ground, and I kept watch over it as the rest of the team continued their excavation. I opened the sheets and took a close long look at this pitifully disfigured human being, and got a flashlight and lens out of my aluminum case. Glass had melted around the head at the bridge of the nose, and bits of pinkish material and ash were snared in her hair. I used light and magnification to study areas of flesh that had been spared, and wondered if it was my imagination when I discovered hemorrhage in charred tissue in the left temporal area, about an inch from the eye.

Lucy suddenly was by my side, and Wiser Funeral Home was pulling up in a shiny dark blue van.

'Find something?' Lucy asked.

'Don't know with certainty, but this looks like hemorrhage, versus the drying you find with skin splitting.'

'Skin splitting from fire, you mean.'

'Yes. Flesh cooks and expands, splitting the skin.'

'Same thing that happens when you cook chicken in the oven.'

'You got it,' I said.

Damage to skin, muscle, and bone is easily mistaken for injuries caused by violence if one is not familiar with the artifacts of fire. Lucy squatted closer to me. She looked on.

'Anything else turning up in there?' I asked her. 'No other bodies, I hope.'

'Not so far,' she said. 'It will be dark soon, and all we can do is keep the scene secured until we can start again in the morning.'

I looked up as a man in a pinstripe suit climbed out of the funeral home van and worked on latex gloves. He loudly pulled a stretcher out from the back and metal clacked as he unfolded the legs.

'You gonna get started tonight, Doc?' he asked me, and I knew I'd seen him somewhere before.

'Let's get her to Richmond and I'll start in the morning,' I said.

'Last time I saw you was the Moser shooting. That young girl they was fighting over's still causing trouble round here.'

'Oh yes.' I vaguely remembered, for there were so many shootings and so many people who caused trouble. 'Thank you for your help,' I said to him.

We lifted the body by gripping the edges of the heavy vinyl pouch. We lowered the remains onto the stretcher and slid it into the back of the van. He slammed shut tailgate doors.

'I hope it's not Kenneth Sparkes in there,' he said.

'No identification yet,' I told him.

He sighed and slid into the driver's seat.

'Well, let me tell you something,' he said, cranking the engine. 'I don't care what anybody says. He was a good man.'

I watched him drive away and could sense Lucy's eyes on me. She touched my arm.

'You're exhausted,' she said. 'Why don't you spend the night and I'll fly you back in the morning. If we find anything else, we'll let you know right away. No point in your hanging around.'

I had very difficult work ahead and the sensible thing to do was to head back to Richmond now. But in truth, I did not feel like walking inside my empty home. Benton would be at Hilton Head by now, and Lucy was staying in Warrenton. It was too late to call upon any of my friends, and I was too spent for polite conversation. It was one of those times when I could think of nothing that might soothe me.

'Teun's moved us to a better place and I got an extra bed in my room, Aunt Kay,' Lucy added with a smile as she pulled a car key out of her pocket.

'So now I'm Aunt Kay again.'

'As long as nobody's around.'

'I've got to get something to eat,' I said.

3

We bought drive-thru Whoppers and fries at a Burger King on Broadview, and it was dark out and very cool. Approaching headlights hurt my eyes, and no amount of Motrin would relieve the hot pain in my temples or the dread in my heart. Lucy had brought her own CDs and was playing one of them loudly as we glided through Warrenton in a rented black Ford LTD.

'What's this you're listening to?' I asked as a way of registering a complaint.

'Jim Brickman,' she said sweetly.

'Not hardly,' I said over flutes and drums. 'Sounds Native American to me. And maybe we could turn it down a bit?'

Instead, she turned it up.

'David Arkenstone. *Spirit Wind*. Got to open your mind, Aunt Kay. This one right now is called "Destiny".'

Lucy drove like the wind, and my mind began to float.

'You're getting kooky on me,' I said as I imagined wolves and campfires in the night.

'His music's all about connectivity and finding your way and positive force,' she went on as the music got lively and added guitars. 'Don't you think that fits?'

I couldn't help but laugh at her complicated explanation. Lucy had to know how everything worked and the reason why. The music, in truth, was soothing, and I felt a brightening and calm in frightening places in my mind.

'What do you think happened, Aunt Kay?' Lucy suddenly broke the spell. 'I mean, in your heart of hearts.'

'Right now it's impossible to say,' I answered her the way I would anybody else. 'And we shouldn't assume anything, including gender or who might have been staying in the house.'

'Teun is already thinking arson, and so am I,' she matter-of-factly stated. 'What's weird is Pepper didn't alert on anything in any areas where we thought he might.'

'Like the master bathroom on the first floor,' I said.

'Nothing there. Poor Pepper worked like a dog and didn't get fed.'

The Labrador retriever had been food-reward trained since his youth to detect hydrocarbon petroleum distillates, such as kerosene, gasoline, lighter fluid, paint thinner, solvents, lamp oil. All were possible, if not common, choices for the arsonist who wanted to start a major fire with the drop of a match. When accelerants are poured at a scene, they pool and flow as their vapors burn. The liquid soaks into fabric or bedding or carpet. It seeps under furniture and between the cracks in flooring. It is not water-soluble or easy to wash away, so if Pepper had found nothing to excite his nose, chances were good that nothing was there.

'What we got to do is find out exactly what was in the house so we can begin to calculate the fuel load,' Lucy went on as the music turned to violins, and strings and drums got sadder. 'Then we can begin to get a better idea about what and how much would have been needed to get something like that going.'

'There was melted aluminum and glass, and tremendous burning of the body in the upper legs and lower arms, any areas that weren't spared by the glass door,' I said. 'That suggests to me the victim was down, possibly in the bathtub, when the fire reached her.'

'It would be bizarre to think a fire like this started in a marble bathroom,' my niece said.

'What about electrical? Any possibility of that?' I asked, and our motel's red and yellow lighted sign floated above the highway, maybe a mile ahead.

'Look, the place had been electrically upgraded. When fire reached the wires and insulation was degraded by heat, the ground wires came in contact with each other. The circuit failed, the wires arced and the circuit breakers tripped,' she said. 'That's exactly what I would expect to happen whether the fire was set or not. It's hard to say. There's a lot left to look at, and of course the labs will do their thing. But whatever got that fire going, got it going fast. You can tell from some of the flooring. There's a sharp demarcation between really deep charring and the unburned wood, and that means hot and fast.'

I remembered wood near the body looking just as she had described. It was alligatored, or blistered black on top, versus slowly burned all the way through.

'First floor again?' I asked as my private suspicions about this case grew darker.

'Probably. Plus, we know things happened fast anyway based on when the alarm went off and what the firefighters found seventeen minutes later.' She was quiet for a moment, then went on, 'The bathroom, the possible hemorrhage in tissue near her left eye. What? Maybe she was taking a bath or shower? She's overcome by carbon monoxide and falls and hits her head?'

'It appears she was fully dressed when she died,' I reminded her. 'Including boots. If the smoke alarm goes off while you're in the bath or shower, I doubt you'd take time to put on all that.'

Lucy turned the volume up even louder and adjusted the bass. Bells jingled with drums and I thought oddly of incense and myrrh. I wanted to lie in the sun with Benton and sleep. I wanted the ocean to roll over my feet as I walked in the morning exploring the beach, and I remembered Kenneth Sparkes as I had seen him last. I envisioned what was left of him turning up next.

'This is called "The Wolf Hunt,"' Lucy said as she turned into a white brick Shell Food Mart. 'And maybe that's what we're on, huh? After the big bad wolf.'

'No,' I said as she parked. 'I think we're looking for a dragon.'

She threw a Nike windbreaker over her gun and BDUs.

'You didn't see me do this,' she said as she opened her door. 'Teun would kick my ass to the moon.'

'You've been around Marino too long,' I said, for he rarely minded rules and was known to carry beer home in the trunk of his unmarked police car.

Lucy went inside, and I doubted that she fooled anyone in her filthy boots and faded blue pants with so many pockets, and the tenacious smell of fire. A keyboard and cowbell began a different rhythm on the CD as I waited in the car and longed for sleep. Lucy returned with a six-pack of Heineken, and we drove on as I drifted with flute and percussion until sudden images shocked me straight up in my seat. I envisioned bared chalky teeth and dead eyes the grayish-blue of boiled eggs. Hair strayed and floated like dirty cornsilk in black water, and crazed, melted glass was an intricate sparkling web around what was left of the body.

'Are you all right?' Lucy sounded worried as she looked over at me.

'I think I fell asleep,' I said. 'I'm fine.'

Johnson's Motel was just ahead of us on the other side of the highway. It was stone with a red and white tin awning, and a red and yellow lit-up sign out front promised it was open twenty-four hours a day and had air conditioning. The NO part of the vacancy sign was dark, which boded well for those in need of a place to stay. We got out, and a welcome mat announced HELLO outside the lobby. Lucy rang a bell. A big black cat came to the door, and then a big woman seemed to materialize from nowhere to let us in.

'We should have a reservation for a room for two,' Lucy said.

'Check-out's eleven in the morning,' the woman stated as she went around to her side of the counter. 'I can give you fifteen down there at the end.'

'We're ATF,' Lucy said.

'Honey, I already figured out that one. The other lady was just in here. You're all paid up.'

A sign posted above the door said no checks but encouraged MasterCard and Visa, and I thought of McGovern and her resourceful ways.

'You need two keys?' the clerk asked us as she opened a drawer.

'Yes, ma'am.'

'Here's you go, honey, and there's two nice beds in there. If I'm not around when you check out, just leave the keys on the counter.'

'Glad you got security,' Lucy said drolly.

'Sure do. Double locks on every door.'

'How late does room service stay open?' Lucy played with her again.

'Until that Coke machine out front quits,' the woman said with a wink.

She was at least sixty with dyed red hair and jowls, and a squat body that pushed against every inch of her brown polyester slacks and yellow sweater. It was obvious that she was fond of black and white cows. There were carvings and ceramic ones on shelves and tables and fastened to the wall. A small fish tank was populated with an odd assortment of tadpoles and minnows, and I couldn't help asking her about them.

'Home grown?' I said.

She gave me a sheepish smile. 'I catch 'em in the pond out back. One of them turned into a frog not long ago and it drowned. I didn't know frogs can't live under water.'

'I'm gonna use the pay phone,' Lucy said, opening the screen door. 'And by the way, what happened to Marino?'

'I think some of them went out to eat somewhere,' I said.

She left with our Burger King bag, and I suspected she was calling Janet and that our Whoppers would be cold by the time we got to them. As I leaned against the counter, I noticed the clerk's messy desk on the other side, and the local paper with its front page headline: MEDIA MOGUL'S FARM DESTROYED BY FIRE. I recognized a subpoena among her clutter and posted notices of reward money for information about murders, accompanied by composite sketches of rapists, thieves, and killers. All the same, Fauquier was the typical quiet county where people got lulled into feeling safe.

'I hope you aren't working here all by yourself at night,' I said to the clerk, because it was my irrepressible habit to give security tips whether or not anyone wanted them.

'I've got Pickle,' she affectionately referred to her fat black cat.

'That's an interesting name.'

'You leave an open pickle jar around, and she'll get into it. Dips her paw right in, ever since she was a kitten.'

Pickle was sitting in a doorway leading into a room that I suspected was the clerk's private quarters. The cat's eyes were gold coins fixed on me as her fluffy tail twitched. She looked bored when the bell rang and her owner unlocked the door for a man in a tank top who was holding a burned-out lightbulb.

'Looks like it done it again, Helen.' He handed her the evidence.

She went into a cabinet and brought out a box of lightbulbs as I gave Lucy plenty of time to get off the pay phone so I could use it. I glanced at my watch, certain Benton should have made it to Hilton Head by now.

'Here you go, Big Jim.' She exchanged a new lightbulb for bad. 'That's sixty watts?' She squinted at it. 'Uh huh. You here a little longer?' She sounded as if she hoped he would be.

'Hell if I know.'

'Oh dear,' said Helen. 'So things still aren't too good.'

'When have they ever been?' He shook his head as he went out into the night.

'Fighting with his wife again,' Helen the clerk commented to me as she shook her head, too. 'Course, he's been here before, which is partly why they fight so much. Never knew there'd be so many people cheating on each other. Half the business here is from folks just three miles down the road.'

'And they can't fool you,' I said.

'Oh no-sir-ree-bob. But it's none of my business as long as they don't wreck the room.'

'You're not too far from the farm that burned,' I then said.

She got more animated. 'I was working that night. You could see the flames shooting up like a volcano going off.' She gestured broadly with her arms. 'Everyone staying here was out front watching and listening to the sirens. All those poor horses. I can't get over it.'

'Are you acquainted with Kenneth Sparkes?' I wondered out loud.

'Can't say I've ever seen him in person.'

'What about a woman who might have been staying in his house?' I asked. 'You ever heard anything about that?'

'Only what people say.' Helen was looking at the door as if someone might appear any second.

'For example,' I prodded.

'Well, I guess Mr Sparkes is quite the gentleman, you know,' Helen said. 'Not that his ways are popular around here, but he's quite a figure. Likes them young and pretty.'

She thought for a moment and gave me her eyes as moths flickered outside the window.

'There are those who got upset when they'd see him around with the newest one,' she said. 'You know, no matter what anybody says, this is still the Old South.'

'Anybody in particular who got upset?' I asked.

'Well, the Jackson boys. They're always in one sort of trouble or another,' she said, and she was still watching the door. 'They just don't like colored people. So for him to be sporting something pretty, young, and white, he tended to do that a lot . . . Well, there's been talk. I'll just put it like that.'

I was imagining Ku Klux Klansmen with burning crosses, and white supremacists with cold eyes and guns. I had seen hate before. I had dipped my hands in its carnage for most of my life. My chest was tight as I bid Helen the clerk good night. I was trying not to leap to assumptions about prejudice and arson and an intended victim, which may have been only Sparkes and not a woman whose body was now on its way to Richmond. Of course, it may simply have been the former governor's vast property that the perpetrators had been interested in, and they did not know anyone was home.

The man in the tank top was on the pay phone when I went out. He was absently holding his new lightbulb and talking in an intense, low voice. As I walked past, his anger flared.

'Dammit, Louise! That's what I mean. You never shut up,' he snarled into the phone as I decided to call Benton later.

I unlocked the red door to room fifteen, and Lucy pretended that she hadn't been waiting for me as she sat in a wing chair, bent over a spiral notebook, making notes and calculations. But she had not touched her fast-food dinner, and I knew she was starved. I took Whoppers and French fries out of the bag and set paper napkins and food on a nearby table.

'Everything's cold,' I said simply.

'You get used to it.' Her voice was distant and distracted.

'Would you like to shower first?' I asked politely.

'Go ahead,' she replied, buried in math, a scowl furrowing her brow.

Our room was impressively clean for the price and decorated in shades of brown, with a Zenith TV almost as old as my niece. There were Chinese lamps and long-tasseled lanterns, porcelain figurines, static oil paintings and flower-printed spreads. Carpeting was a thick shag Indian design, and wallpaper was woodland scenes. Furniture was Formica or so thickly shellacked that I could not see the grain of the wood.

I inspected the bath and found it a solid pink and white tile that probably went back to the fifties, with Styrofoam cups and tiny wrapped bars of Lisa Luxury soap on the sink. But it was a single plastic red rose in a window that touched me most. Someone had done the best with the least to make strangers feel special, and I doubted that most patrons noticed or cared. Maybe forty years ago such resourcefulness and attention to detail would have mattered when people were more civilized than they seemed to be now.

I lowered the toilet lid and sat to remove my dirty wet boots. Then I fought with buttons and hooks until my clothes retreated to a wilted heap on the floor. I showered until I was warm and cleansed of the smell of fire and death. Lucy was working on her laptop when I emerged in an old Medical College of Virginia T-shirt and popped open a beer.

'What's up?' I asked as I sat on the couch.

'Just screwing around. I don't know enough to do much more than that,' she replied. 'But that was a big fucking fire, Aunt Kay. And it doesn't appear to have been set with gasoline.'

I had nothing to say.

'And someone died in it? In the master bathroom? Maybe? How did that happen? At eight o'clock at night?'

I did not know.

'I mean, she's in there brushing her teeth and the fire horn goes off?'

Lucy stared hard at me.

'And what?' she asked. 'She just stays there and dies?'

She paused to stretch sore shoulders.

'You tell me, Chief. You're the expert.'

'I can offer no explanation, Lucy,' I said.

'And there we have it, ladies and gentlemen. World famous expert Dr Kay Scarpetta doesn't know.' She was getting irritable. 'Nineteen horses,' she went on. 'So who took care of them? Sparkes doesn't have a stable hand? And why did one of the horses get away? The little black stallion?'

'How do you know it's a boy?' I said as someone knocked on our door. 'Who is it?' I asked through wood.

'Yo. It's me,' Marino announced gruffly.

I let him in and could tell by the expression on his face that he had news.

'Kenneth Sparkes is alive and well,' he announced.

'Where is he?' I was very confused again.

'Apparently, he's been out of the country and flew back when he heard the news. He's staying in Beaverdam and don't seem to have a clue about anything, including who the victim is,' Marino told us.

'Why Beaverdam?' I asked, calculating how long the trip would take to that remote part of Hanover County.

'His trainer lives there.'

'His?'

'Horse trainer. Not his trainer, like in weight lifting or nothing.'

'I see.'

'I'm heading out in the morning, around nine A.M.,' he said to me. 'You can go on to Richmond or go with me.'

'I have a body to identify, so I need to talk to him whether he claims to know anything or not. I guess I'm going with you,' I said as Lucy met my eyes. 'Are you planning on our fearless pilot dropping us off, or have you managed to get a car?'

'I'm skipping the whirlybird,' Marino retorted. 'And do I need to remind you that the last time you had a chat with Sparkes, you pissed him off?'

'I don't remember,' I said, and I really did not, for I had irritated Sparkes on more than one occasion when we disagreed about case details he thought should be released to the media.

'I can guarantee he does, Doc. You gonna share the beer or what?'

'I can't believe you don't have your own stash,' Lucy said as she resumed working on her laptop, keys clicking.

He went to the refrigerator and helped himself to one.

'You want my opinion at the end of the day?' he said. 'It's the same as it was.'

'Which is?' Lucy asked without looking up.

'Sparkes is behind this.'

He set the bottle opener on the coffee table and stopped at the door, resting his hand on the knob.

'For one thing, it's just too friggin' convenient that he was suddenly out of the country when it happened,' he talked on as he yawned. 'So he gets someone to do his dirty work. Money.' He slid a cigarette out of the pack in his shirt pocket and shoved it between his lips. 'That's all the bastard's ever cared about, anyway. Money and his dick.'

'Marino, for God's sake,' I complained.

I wanted to shut him up, and I wanted him to leave. But he ignored my cue.

'The worst news of all is now we probably got a homicide on our hands, on top of everything else,' he said as he opened the door. 'Meaning yours truly here is stuck on this case like a fly on a pest strip. And that goes for the two of you. Shit.'

He got out his lighter, the cigarette moving with his lips.

'The last thing I feel like doing right now. You know how many people that asshole's probably got in his pocket?' Marino would not stop. 'Judges, sheriffs, fire marshals . . .'

'Marino,' I interrupted him because he was making everything worse. 'You're jumping to conclusions. In fact, you're jumping to Mars.'

He pointed his unlit cigarette at me. 'Just wait,' he said on his way out. 'Everywhere you turn on this one, you're going to run into a briar patch.'

'I'm used to it,' I said.

'You just think you are.'

He shut the door too hard.

'Hey, don't wreck the joint,' Lucy called out after him.

'Are you going to work on that laptop all night?' I asked her.

'Not all night.'

'It's getting late, and there's something you and I need to discuss,' I said, and Carrie Grethen was back in my mind.

'What if I told you I don't feel like it?' Lucy wasn't kidding.

'It wouldn't matter,' I replied. 'We have to talk.'

'You know, Aunt Kay, if you're going to start in on Teun and Philly . . .'

'What?' I said, baffled. 'What does Teun have to do with anything?'

'I can tell you don't like her.'

'That's utterly ridiculous.'

'I can see through you,' she went on.

'I have nothing against Teun, and she is not relevant to this conversation.'

My niece got silent. She began taking off her boots.

'Lucy, I got a letter from Carrie.'

I waited to see a response and was rewarded with none.

'It's a bizarre note. Threatening, harassing, from Kirby Forensic Psychiatric Center in New York.'

I paused again as Lucy dropped a boot to the shag carpeting.

'She's basically making sure we know that she intends to cause a lot of trouble during her trial,' I explained. 'Not that this should come as any great surprise. But, well, I . . .' I stumbled as she tugged off wet socks and massaged her pale feet. 'We just need to be prepared, that's all.'

Lucy unbuckled her belt and unzipped her pants as if she had not heard a word I'd said. She pulled her filthy shirt over her head and threw it on the floor, stripping down to sports bra and cotton panties. She stalked toward the bathroom, her body beautiful and fluid, and I sat staring after her, stunned, until I heard water run.

It was as if I had never really noticed her full lips and breasts and her arms and legs curved and strong like a hunter's bow. Or maybe I simply had refused to see her as someone apart from me and sexual, because I chose not to understand her or the way she lived. I felt shamed and confused, when for an electric instant, I envisioned her as Carrie's supple, hungry lover. It did not seem so foreign that a woman would want to touch my niece.

Lucy took her time in the shower, and I knew this was deliberate because of the discussion we were about to have. She was thinking. I suspected she was furious. I anticipated she would vent her rage on me. But when she emerged a little later, she was wearing a Philadelphia fire marshal T-shirt that did nothing but darken my mood. She was cool and smelled like lemons.

'Not that it's any of my business,' I said, staring at the logo on her chest.

'Teun gave it to me,' she answered.

'Ah.'

'And you're right, Aunt Kay, it's none of your business.'

'I just wonder why you don't learn . . .' I started in as my own temper flared.

'Learn?'

She feigned a clueless expression that was meant to irritate, eliminate, and make one feel vapid.

'About sleeping with people you work with.'

My emotions hurled down their own treacherous track. I was being unfair, jumping to conclusions with little evidence. But I was scared for Lucy in every way imaginable.

'Someone gives me a T-shirt and suddenly I'm sleeping with this person? Hmmm. Quite a deduction, Dr Scarpetta,' Lucy said with gathering fury. 'And by the way, you're one to talk about sleeping with people you work with. Look who you practically live with, hello?'

I was certain Lucy would have stormed out into the night if she had been dressed. Instead, she stood with her back to me, staring at a curtained window. She wiped outraged tears from her face as I tried to salvage what was left of a moment that I had never intended to turn out like this.

'We're both tired,' I said softly. 'It's been an awful day, and now Carrie has gotten just what she wanted. She has turned us on each other.'

My niece did not move or utter a sound as she wiped her face again, her back solidly to me like a wall.

'I am not at all implying that you are sleeping with Teun,' I went on. 'I'm only warning you of the heartbreak and chaos . . . Well, I can see how it could happen.'

She turned around and stared at me with a challenge in her eyes.

'What do you mean, *you can see how it could happen*?' she demanded to know. 'She's gay? I don't remember her telling me that.'

'Maybe things aren't so good with Janet right now,' I went on. 'And people are people.'

She sat on the foot of my bed, and it was clear she intended to hold me to this conversation.

'Meaning?' she asked.

'Just that. I wasn't born in a cave. Teun's gender makes no difference to me. I do not know a thing about her proclivities. But if you are attracted to each other? Why wouldn't anyone be attracted to either of you? Both of you are striking and compelling and brilliant and heroic. I'm just reminding you that she's your supervisor, Lucy.'

My blood pounded as my voice got more intense.

'And then what?' I asked. 'Will you move from one federal agency to another until you've screwed yourself out of a career? That's my point, like it or not. And that's the last time I will ever bring it up.'

My niece just stared at me as her eyes filled again. She did not wipe them this time, and tears rolled down her face and splashed the shirt Teun McGovern had given to her.

'I'm sorry, Lucy,' I said gently. 'I know your life isn't easy.'

We were silent as she looked away and wept. She took a deep, long breath that trembled in her chest.

'Have you ever loved a woman?' she asked me.

'I love you.'

'You know what I mean.'

'Not in love with one,' I said. 'Not to my knowledge.'

'That's rather evasive.'

'I didn't mean it to be.'

'Could you?'

'Could I what?'

'Love a woman,' she persisted.

'I don't know. I'm beginning to think I don't know anything.' I was as honest as I knew how to be. 'Probably that part of my brain is shut.'

'It has nothing to do with your brain.'

I wasn't sure what to say.

'I've slept with two men,' she said. 'So I know the difference, for your information.'

'Lucy, you don't need to plead your case to me.'

'My personal life should not be a *case*.'

'But it's about to become one,' I went back to that subject. 'What do you think will be Carrie's next move?'

Lucy opened another beer and glanced to see that I still had plenty.

'Send letters to the media?' I speculated for her. 'Lie under oath? Take the stand and go into gory detail about everything the two of you ever said and did and dreamed?'

'How the hell can I know?' Lucy retorted. 'She's had five years to do nothing but think and scheme while the rest of us have been rather busy.'

'What else might she know that could come out?' I had to ask.

Lucy got up and began to pace.

'You trusted her once,' I went on. 'You confided in her, and all the while she was an accomplice to Gault. You were their pipeline, Lucy. Right into the heart of all of us.'

'I'm really too tired to talk about this,' she said.

But she was going to talk about it. I was determined about that. I got up and turned off the overhead light, because I had always found it easier to talk in an atmosphere soft and full of shadows. Then I plumped pillows on her bed and mine and turned down the spreads. At first she did not take me up on my invitation, and she paced some more like a wild thing as I silently watched. Then she reluctantly sat on her bed and settled back.

'Let's talk about something besides your reputation for a moment,' I began in a calm voice. 'Let's talk about what this New York trial is all about.'

'I know what it's all about.'

I was going to give her an opening argument anyway and raised my hand to make her listen.

'Temple Gault killed at least five people in Virginia,' I began, 'and we know Carrie was involved in at least one of these since we have her on videotape pumping a bullet into the man's head. You remember that.'

She was silent.

'You were in the room when we watched that horrific footage right there in gory color on TV,' I went on.

'I know all this.'

Anger was crawling into Lucy's voice again.

'We've been over it a million times,' she said.

'You watched her kill,' I went on. 'This woman who was your lover when you were all of nineteen and naive and doing an internship at ERF, programming CAIN.'

I saw her draw up more into herself as my monologue became more painful. ERF was the FBI's Engineering Research Facility, which housed its Criminal Artificial Intelligence Network computer system known as CAIN. Lucy had conceived CAIN and been the driving force behind its creation. Now she was locked out of it and could not bear to hear its name.

'You watched your lover kill, after she had set you up in her cold-blooded premeditated way. You were no match for her,' I said.

'Why are you doing this?' Lucy's voice was muffled, her face resting on her arm.

'A reality check.'

'I don't need one.'

'I think you do. And by the way, we won't even go into the personal details both Carrie and Gault learned about me. And this brings us to New York, where Gault murdered his own sister and at least one police officer, and now forensic evidence shows that he didn't do it alone. Carrie's fingerprints were later recovered on some of Jayne Gault's personal effects. When she was captured in the Bowery, Jayne's blood was found on Carrie's pants. For all we know, Carrie pulled that trigger, too.'

'She probably did,' Lucy said. 'And I already know about that.'

'But not about Eddie Heath. Remember the candy bar and can of soup he bought at the 7-Eleven? The bag found with his dying, mutilated body? Carrie's thumbprint has since been recovered.'

'No way!' Lucy was shocked.

'There's more.'

'Why haven't you told me this before? She was doing this all along, with him. And probably helped him break out of prison back then, too.'

'We have no doubt. They were Bonnie and Clyde long before you met her, Lucy. She was killing when you were seventeen and had never been kissed.'

'You don't know that I'd never been kissed,' my niece said inanely.

No one spoke for a moment.

Then Lucy said, and her voice quavered, 'So you think she spent two years plotting a way to meet me and become . . . And do the things she did to . . .'

'To seduce you,' I cut in. 'I don't know if she planned it that far in advance. Frankly, I don't care.' My outrage mounted. 'We've moved heaven and earth to extradite her to Virginia for those crimes, and we can't. New York won't let her go.'

My beer bottle was limp and forgotten in my hands as I shut my eyes, and flashes of the dead played through my mind. I saw Eddie Heath propped up against a Dumpster as rain diluted the blood from his wounds, and the sheriff and prison guard killed by Gault and probably Carrie. I had touched their bodies and translated their pain into diagrams and autopsy protocols and dental charts. I could not help it. I wanted Carrie to die for what she had done to them, to my niece and me.

'She's a monster,' I said as my voice shook with grief and fury. 'I will do anything I can to make sure she is punished.'

'Why are you preaching all this to me?' Lucy said in a louder, upset voice. 'Do you somehow think I don't want the same thing?'

'I'm sure you do.'

'Just let me throw the switch or stick the needle in her arm.'

'Don't let your former relationship distract you from justice, Lucy.'

'Jesus Christ.'

'It's already an overwhelming struggle for you. And if you lose perspective, Carrie will have her way.'

'Jesus Christ,' Lucy said again. 'I don't want to hear any more.'

'You wonder what she wants?' I would not stop. 'I can tell you exactly. To manipulate. The thing she does best. And then what? She'll be found not guilty by reason of insanity and the judge will send her back to Kirby. Then she'll suddenly and dramatically improve, and the Kirby doctors will decide she's not insane. Double jeopardy. She can't be tried twice for the same crime. She ends up back on the street.'

'If she walks,' Lucy said coldly, 'I will find her and blow her brains out.'

'What kind of answer is that?'

I watched her silhouette sitting straight up against pillows on her bed. She was very stiff and I could hear her breathing as hatred pounded inside her.

'The world really won't care who or what you slept or sleep with unless you do,' I said to her more quietly. 'In fact, I think the jury will understand how it could have happened back then. When you were so young. And she was older and brilliant and striking to look at. When she was charismatic and attentive, and your supervisor.'

'Like Teun,' Lucy said, and I could not tell if she was mocking me.

'Teun is not a psychopath,' I said.

4

The next morning, I fell asleep in the rented LTD, and woke up to cornfields and silos, and stands of trees as old as the Civil War. Marino was driving, and we passed vast acres of vacant land strung with barbed wire and telephone lines, and front yards dotted with mail-boxes painted like flower gardens and Uncle Sam. There were ponds and creeks and sod farms, and cattle fields high with weeds. Mostly I noticed small houses with leaning fences, and clotheslines sagging with scrubbed garments billowing in the breeze.

I covered a yawn with my hand and averted my face, for I had always considered it a sign of weakness to look tired or bored. Within minutes, we turned right on 715, or Beaverdam Road, and we began to see cows. Barns were bleached gray and it seemed people never thought to haul away their broken-down trucks. The owner of Hootowl Farm lived in a large white brick house surrounded by endless vistas of pasture and fence. According to the sign out front, the house had been built in 1730. Now it had a swimming pool and a satellite dish that looked serious enough to intercept signals from other galaxies.

Betty Foster was out to greet us before we had gotten out of the car. She was somewhere in her fifties with sharp regal features and skin deeply creased by the sun. Her long white hair was tucked in a bun. But she walked with the athletic spring of someone half her age, and her hand was hard and strong when she shook mine and looked at me with pained hazel eyes.

'I'm Betty,' she said. 'And you must be Dr Scarpetta. And you must be Captain Marino.'

She shook his hand too, her movements quick and confident. Betty Foster wore jeans and a sleeveless denim shirt, her brown boots scarred and crusted with mud around the heels. Beneath her hospitality other emotions smoldered, and she seemed slightly dazed by us, as if she did not know where to begin.

'Kenneth is in the riding ring,' she told us. 'He's been waiting for you, and I'll go on and tell you now that he's terribly upset. He loved those horses, everyone of them, and of course, he's devastated that someone died inside his house.'

'What exactly is your relationship to him?' Marino asked as we started walking up the dusty road toward the stables.

'I've bred and trained his horses for years,' she said. 'Ever since he left office and moved back to Warrenton. He had the finest Morgans in the Commonwealth. And quarter horses and thoroughbreds.'

'He would bring his horses to you?' I asked.

'Sometimes he did that. Sometimes it was yearlings he would buy from me and just leave them here to be trained for two years. Then he'd add them to his stable. Or he'd breed racehorses and sell them when they were old enough to be trained for the track. And I also went up there to his farm, sometimes two or three times a week. Basically, I supervised.'

'And he has no stable hand?' I asked.

'The last one quit several months ago. Since then Kenny has been doing most of the work himself. It's not like he can hire just anyone. He has to be careful.'

'I'd like to know more about the stable hand,' Marino said, taking notes.

'A lovely old guy with a very bad heart,' she said.

'It may be that one horse survived the fire,' I told her.

She didn't comment at first, and we drew nearer to a big red barn and a *Beware of Dog* sign on a fence post.

'It's a foal, I guess. Black,' I went on.

'A filly or a colt?' she asked.

'I don't know. I couldn't tell the gender.'

'What about a star-strip-snip?' she asked, referring to the white stripe on the horse's forehead.

'I wasn't that close,' I told her.

'Well, Kenny had a foal named Windsong,' Foster said. 'The mother, Wind, ran the Derby and came in last, but just being in it was enough.

Plus the father had won a few big stake races. So Windsong was probably the most valuable horse in Kenny's stables.'

'Well, Windsong may have gotten out somehow,' I said again. 'And
was spared.'

'I hope he's not still out there running around.'

'If he is, I doubt he will be for long. The police know about him.'

Marino was not particularly interested in the surviving horse, and
as we entered the indoor ring, we were greeted by the sound of hooves
and the clucking of bantam roosters and guinea hens that wandered
about freely. Marino coughed and squinted because red dust was
thick in the air, kicked up by the cantering of a chestnut Morgan mare.
Horses in their stalls neighed and whinnied as horse and rider went
by, and although I recognized Kenneth Sparkes in his English saddle,
I had never seen him in dirty denim and boots. He was an excellent
equestrian, and when he met my eyes as he went by, he showed no
sign of recognition or relief. I knew right then he did not want us
here.

'Is there someplace we can talk to him?' I asked Foster.

'There are chairs outside.' She pointed. 'Or you can use my office.'

Sparkes picked up speed and thundered toward us, and the guinea
hens lifted up their feathery skirts to hurry out of the way.

'Did you know anything about a lady maybe staying with him in
Warrenton?' I asked as we headed back outside again. 'Did you ever
see anyone when you went to work with his horses?'

'No,' Foster said.

We picked plastic chairs and sat with our backs to the arena, overlooking woods.

'But Lord knows, Kenny's had girlfriends before, and I don't always
know about them,' Foster said, turning around in her chair to look
back inside the ring. 'Unless you're right about Windsong, the horse
Kenny's on now is the only one he has left. Black Opal. We call him
Pal for short.'

Marino and I did not respond as we turned around to see Sparkes
dismount and hand the reins to one of Foster's stable hands.

'Good job, Pal,' Sparkes said, patting the horse's handsome neck
and head.

'Any special reason this horse wasn't with the others on his farm?'
I asked Foster.

'Not quite old enough. He's a barely three-year-old gelding who
still needs training. That's why he's still here, lucky for him.'

For a flicker, her face was contorted by grief, and she quickly looked away. She cleared her throat and got up from her chair. She walked away as Sparkes came out of the arena adjusting his belt and the fit of his jeans. I got up and Marino and I respectfully shook his hand. He was sweating through a faded red Izod shirt, and he wiped his face with a yellow bandanna he untied from his neck.

'Please sit down,' he said graciously, as if he were granting us an audience with him.

We took our chairs again, and he pulled his out and turned it around to face us, the skin tight around eyes that were resolute but bloodshot.

'Let me begin by telling you what I firmly believe right now as I sit in this chair,' he said. 'The fire was not an accident.'

'That's what we're here to investigate, sir,' Marino said, more politely than usual.

'I believe the motivation was racist in nature.' Sparkes's jaw muscles began to flex and fury filled his voice. 'And they – whoever *they* are – intentionally murdered my horses, destroying everything I love.'

'If the motive was racism,' Marino said, 'then why wouldn't they have checked to make sure you were home?'

'Some things are worse than death. Perhaps they want me alive to suffer. You put two and two together.'

'We're trying to,' Marino said.

'Don't even consider pinning this on me.'

He pointed a finger at both of us.

'I know exactly how people like you think,' he went on. 'Huh. I torched my own farm and horses for money. Now you listen to me good.'

He leaned closer to us.

'I'm telling you now that I didn't do it. Would never, could never do it, will never do it. I had nothing to do with what happened. I'm the victim here and probably lucky to be alive.'

'Let's talk about the other victim,' I spoke quietly. 'A white female with long blond hair, as it looks now. Is there anyone else who might have been in your house that night?'

'No one should have been in my house!' he exclaimed.

'We are speculating that this person may have died in the master suite,' I went on. 'Possibly the bathroom.'

'Whoever she was, she must have broken in,' he said. 'Or maybe she was the one who set the fire, and couldn't get out.'

'There's no evidence that anyone broke in, sir,' Marino responded.

'And if your burglar alarm was set, it never went off that night. Only the smoke alarm.'

'I don't understand.' Sparkes seemed to be telling the truth. 'Of course, I set the alarm before I left town.'

'And you were headed where?' Marino probed.

'London. I got there and was immediately notified. I never even left Heathrow and instantly caught the next flight back,' he said. 'I got off in D.C. and drove straight here.'

He stared blankly at the ground.

'Drove in what?' Marino asked.

'My Cherokee. I'd left it at Dulles in long-term parking.'

'You've got the receipt?'

'Yes.'

'What about the Mercedes at your house?' Marino went on.

Sparkes frowned. 'What Mercedes? I don't own a Mercedes. I have always bought American cars.'

I remembered that this had been one of his policies that he had been quite vocal about.

'There's a Mercedes behind the house. It burned up, too, so we can't tell much about it yet,' Marino said. 'But it doesn't look like a recent model to me. A sedan, sort of boxy like they were earlier on.'

Sparkes just shook his head.

'Then we might wonder if it was the victim's car,' Marino deduced. 'Maybe someone who had come to see you unexpectedly? Who else had a key to your house, and your burglar alarm code?'

'Good Lord,' Sparkes said as he groped for an answer. 'Josh did. My stable hand, honest as the day is long. He quit for health reasons and I never bothered changing the locks.'

'You need to tell us where to find him,' Marino said.

'He would never . . .' Sparkes started to say, but he stopped and an incredulous expression came over his face. 'My God,' he muttered with an awful sigh. 'Oh my God.'

He looked at me.

'You said she was blond,' he asked.

'Yes,' I said.

'Can you tell me anything else about the way she looked?' His voice was getting panicky.

'Appears to be slender, possibly white. Wearing jeans, some sort of shirt, and boots. Lace-up boots, versus Western.'

'How tall?' he had to know.

'I can't tell. Not until I've examined her.'

'What about jewelry?'

'Her hands were gone.'

He sighed again, and when he spoke his voice trembled. 'Was her hair very long, like down to the middle of her back, and a very pale gold?'

'That's the way it appears at this time,' I replied.

'There was a young woman,' he began, clearing his throat several times. 'My God . . . I have a place at Wrightsville Beach and met her there. She was a student at the university, or at least on and off she was. It didn't last long, maybe six months. And she did stay with me on the farm, several times. The last time I saw her was there, and I ended the relationship because it couldn't go on.'

'Did she own an old Mercedes?' Marino asked.

Sparkes shook his head. He covered his face with his hands as he struggled for composure.

'A Volkswagen thing. Light blue,' he managed to say. 'She didn't have any money. I gave her some in the end, before she left. A thousand dollars cash. I told her to go back to school and finish. Her name is Claire Rawley, and I suppose she could have taken one of my extra keys without my knowing while she was staying on the farm. Maybe she saw the alarm code when I punched it in.'

'And you've had no contact with Claire Rawley for more than a year?' I said.

'Not one word,' he replied. 'That seems so far in my past. It was a foolish fling, really. I saw her surfing and started talking to her on the beach, in Wrightsville. I have to say, she was the most splendid-looking woman I have ever seen. For a while, I was out of my mind, then I came to my senses. There were many, many complications and problems. Claire needed a caretaker, and I couldn't be that.'

'I need to know everything about her that you can tell me,' I said to him with feeling. 'Anything about where she was from, her family. Anything that might help me identify the body or rule Claire Rawley out. Of course, I will contact the university, as well.'

'I've got to tell you the sad truth, Dr Scarpetta,' my former boss said to me. 'I never knew anything about her, really. Our relationship was mainly sexual, with me helping her out with money and her problems as best I could. I did care about her.' He paused. 'But it was never serious, at least not on my side. I mean, marriage was never in the offing.'

He did not need to explain further. Sparkes had power. He exuded it and had always enjoyed almost any woman he wanted. But I felt no judgment now.

'I'm sorry,' he said, getting up. 'I can only tell you that she was rather much a failed artist. A want-to-be actor who spent most of her time surfing or wandering the beach. And after I'd been around her for a while, I began to see that something wasn't right about her. The way she seemed so lacking in motivation, and would act so erratic and glazed sometimes.'

'Did she abuse alcohol?' I asked.

'Not chronically. It has too many calories.'

'Drugs?'

'That's what I began to suspect, and it was something I could have no association with. I don't know.'

'I need for you to spell her name for me,' I said.

'Before you go walking off,' Marino jumped in, and I recognized the bad-cop edge to his tone, 'you sure this couldn't be some sort of a murder-suicide? Only she kills everything you own and goes up in flames along with it? You sure there's no reason she might have done that, Mr Sparkes?'

'At this point, I can't be sure of anything,' Sparkes answered him as he paused near the barn's open door.

Marino got up, too.

'Well, this ain't adding up, no disrespect intended,' Marino said. 'And I do need to see any receipts you have for your London trip. And for Dulles airport. And I know ATF's hot to know about your basement full of bourbon and automatic weapons.'

'I collect World War II weapons, and all of them are registered and legal,' he said with restraint. 'I bought the bourbon from a Kentucky distillery that went out of business five years ago. They shouldn't have sold it to me and I shouldn't have bought it. But so be it.'

'I think ATF's got bigger fish to fry than your barrels of bourbon,' Marino said. 'So if you got any of those receipts with you now, I'd appreciate your handing them over to me.'

'Will you strip search me next, Captain?' Sparkes fixed hard eyes on him.

Marino stared back as guinea hens kicked past again like break-dancers.

'You can deal with my lawyer,' Sparkes said. 'And then I'll be happy to cooperate.'

'Marino,' it was my turn to speak, 'if you'd give me just a minute alone with Mr Sparkes.'

Marino was taken aback and very annoyed. Without a word, he stalked off into the barn, several hens trotting after him. Sparkes and I stood, facing each other. He was a strikingly handsome man, tall and lean, with thick gray hair. His eyes were amber, his features aristocratic, with a straight Jeffersonian nose and skin dark and as smooth as a man half his age. The way he tightly gripped his riding crop seemed to fit his mood. Kenneth Sparkes was capable of violence but had never given in to it, as best I knew.

'All right. What's on your mind?' he asked me suspiciously.

'I just wanted to make sure you understand that our differences of the past . . .'

He shook his head and would not let me finish.

'The past is past,' he said curtly.

'No, Kenneth, it isn't. And it's important for you to know that I don't harbor bad feelings about you,' I replied. 'That what's going on now is not related.'

When he had been more actively involved with the publishing of his newspapers, he had basically accused me of racism when I had released statistics about black on black homicides. I had shown citizens how many deaths were drug-related or involved prostitution or were just plain hate of one black for another.

His own reporters had taken several of my quotes out of context and had distorted the rest, and by the end of the day, Sparkes had summoned me to his posh downtown office. I would never forget being shown into his mahogany space of fresh flowers and colonial furniture and lighting. He had ordered me, as if he could, to demonstrate more sensitivity to African-Americans and publicly retract my bigoted professional assessments. As I looked at him now, with sweat on his face and manure on his boots, it did not seem I was talking to the same arrogant man. His hands were trembling, his strong demeanor about to break.

'Will you let me know what you find out?' he asked as tears filled his eyes, his head held high.

'I'll tell you what I can,' I promised evasively.

'I just want to know if it's her, and that she didn't suffer,' he said.

'Most people in fires don't. The carbon monoxide renders them unconscious long before the flames get close. Usually, death is quiet and painless.'

'Oh, thank God.'

He looked up at the sky.

'Oh, thank you, God,' he muttered.

5

I got home that night in time for a dinner I did not feel like cooking. Benton had left me three messages, and I had not returned any one of them. I felt strange. I felt an odd sensation of doom, and yet I felt a lightness around my heart that spurred me into working in my garden until dark, pulling weeds and clipping roses for the kitchen. The ones I chose were pink and yellow, tightly furled like flags before glory. At dusk, I went out to walk and wished I had a dog. For a while I fantasized about that, wondering just what sort of dog I would have, were it possible and practical.

I decided on a retired greyhound rescued from the track and from certain extermination. Of course, my life was too unkind for a pet. I pondered this as one of my neighbors came out of his grand stone home to walk his small white dog.

'Good evening, Dr Scarpetta,' the neighbor said grimly. 'How long are you in town for?'

'I never know,' I said, still imagining my greyhound.

'Heard about the fire.'

He was a retired surgeon, and he shook his head.

'Poor Kenneth.'

'I suppose you know him,' I said.

'Oh yes.'

'It is too bad. What kind of dog do you have?'

'He's a salad bar dog. Little bit of everything,' my neighbor said.

He walked on, taking out a pipe and lighting up, because his wife, no doubt, would not let him smoke in the house. I walked past the homes of my neighbors, all different but the same because they were brick or stucco and not very old. It seemed fitting that the sluggish stretch of the river in the back of the neighborhood made its way over rocks the same way it had two hundred years before. Richmond was not known for change.

When I reached the spot where I had found Wesley when he had been somewhat mad at me, I stood near that same tree, and soon it was too dark to spot an eagle or the river's rocks. For a time, I stood staring at my neighbors' lights in the night, suddenly not having the energy to move as I contemplated that Kenneth Sparkes was either a victim or a killer. Then heavy footsteps sounded on the street behind me. Startled, I whipped around, gripping the canister of red pepper spray attached to my keys.

Marino's voice was quickly followed by his formidable shape.

'Doc, you shouldn't be out here this late,' he said.

I was too drained to resent his having an opinion on how I was spending my evening.

'How did you know I was here?' I asked.

'One of your neighbors.'

I did not care.

'My car's right over there,' he went on. 'I'll drive you home.'

'Marino, can I never have a moment's peace?' I said with no rancor, for I knew he meant no harm to me.

'Not tonight,' he said. 'I got some really bad news and think you might want to sit down.'

I immediately thought of Lucy and felt the strength go out of my knees. I swayed and put my hand on his shoulder as my mind seemed to shatter into a million pieces. I had always known the day might come when someone would deliver her death notice to me, and I could not speak or think. I was miles beyond the moment, sucked down deeper and deeper into a dark and terrible vortex. Marino grabbed my arm to steady me.

'Jesus,' he exclaimed. 'Let me get you to the car and we'll sit down.'

'No,' I barely said, because I had to know. 'How's Lucy?'

He paused for a moment and seemed confused.

'Well, she don't know yet, unless she's heard it on the news,' he replied.

'Know what?' I asked as my blood seemed to move again.

'Carrie Grethen's escaped from Kirby,' he told me. 'Some time late this afternoon. They didn't figure it out until it was time to take the female inmates down for dinner.'

We began walking quickly to his car as fear made him angry.

'And here you are walking around in the dark with nothing but a keychain,' he went on. 'Shit. Goddamn son of a bitch. Don't you do that anymore, you hear me? We got no idea where that bitch is, but one thing I know for a fact, as long as she's out, you ain't safe.'

'No one in the world is safe,' I muttered as I climbed into his car and thought of Benton alone at the beach.

Carrie Grethen hated him almost as much as she hated me, or at least this was my belief. Benton had profiled her and was the quarterback in the game that had eventually resulted in her capture and Temple Gault's death. Benton had used the Bureau's every resource to lock Carrie away, and until now, it had worked.

'Is there any way she might know where Benton is?' I said as Marino drove me to my house. 'He's alone on an island resort. He probably takes walks on the beach without his gun, unmindful that there might be someone looking for him . . .'

'Like someone else I know,' Marino cut me off.

'Point well taken.'

'I'm sure Benton already knows, but I'll call him,' Marino said. 'And I got no reason to think that Carrie would know about your place in Hilton Head. You didn't have it back then when Lucy was telling her all your secrets.'

'That's not fair,' I said as he pulled into my driveway and came to an abrupt stop. 'Lucy never meant it that way. She never meant to be disloyal, to hurt me.'

I lifted the handle of my door.

'At this point, it don't matter what she meant.'

He blew smoke out his window.

'How did Carrie get out?' I asked. 'Kirby's on an island and not easily accessible.'

'No one knows. About three hours ago, she was supposed to go down to dinner with all the other lovely ladies, and that's when the guards realized she was gone. Boom, no sign of her, and about a mile away there's an old footbridge that goes over the East River into Harlem.'

He tossed the cigarette butt on my driveway.

'All anyone can figure is maybe she got off the island that way. Cops are everywhere, and they got choppers out to make sure she's not still hiding somewhere on the island. But I don't think so. I think she's planned this for a while, and timed it exactly. We'll hear from her, all right. You can bet on that.'

I was deeply unsettled when I went inside my house and checked every door and set the alarm. I then did something that was rare and unnerving for me. I got my Glock nine-millimeter pistol from a drawer in my office, and secured every closet in every room, on each floor. I stepped into each doorway, the pistol firm in both hands as my heart hammered. By now Carrie Grethen had become a monster with supernatural powers. I had begun to imagine that she could evade any security system, and would glide out of the shadows when I was feeling safe and unaware.

There seemed to be no presence in my two-story stone house but me, and I carried a glass of red burgundy into my bedroom and got into my robe. I called Wesley again and felt a chill when he did not pick up the phone. I tried once more at almost midnight, and still he did not answer.

'Dear God,' I said, alone in my room.

Lamplight was soft and cast shadows from antique dressers and tables that had been stripped down to old gray oak, because I liked flaws and the stress marks of time. Pale rose draperies stirred as air flowed out from vents, and every movement unglued me more, no matter the explanation. With each passing moment, my brain was further overruled by fear as I tried to repress images from the past I shared with Carrie Grethen. I hoped Benton would call. I told myself he was okay and that what I needed was sleep. So I tried to read Seamus Heaney's poetry and dozed off somewhere in the middle of *The Spoonbait*. The phone rang at twenty minutes past two A.M., and my book slid to the floor.

'Scarpetta,' I blurted into the receiver as my heart pounded the way it always did when I was startled awake.

'Kay, it's me,' Benton said. 'Sorry to call you this late, but I was afraid you were trying to reach me. Somehow the answering machine got turned off, and, well, I went out to eat and then walked the beach for more than two hours. To think. I guess you know the news.'

'Yes.' I was suddenly very alert.

'Are you all right?' he said, because he knew me well.

'I searched every inch of my house tonight before going to bed. I had my gun out and checked every closet and behind every shower curtain.'

'I thought you probably would.'

'It's like knowing a bomb is on the way in the mail.'

'No, it's not like that, Kay. Because we don't know one is coming or when or in what form. I wish we did. But that's part of her game. To make us guess.'

'Benton, you know how she feels about you. I don't like you there alone.'

'Do you want me to come home?'

I thought about this and had no good answer.

'I'll get in my car right this minute,' he added. 'If that's what you want.'

Then I told him about the body in the ruins of Kenneth Sparkes's mansion, and I went on and on about that, and about my meeting with the tycoon on Hootowl Farm. I talked and explained while he listened patiently.

'The point is,' I concluded, 'that this is turning out to be terribly complicated, if not bizarre, and there is so much to do. It makes no sense for your vacation to be ruined, too. And Marino's right. There's no reason to suspect that Carrie knows about our place in Hilton Head. You're probably safer there than here, Benton.'

'I wish she'd come here.' His voice turned hard. 'I'd welcome her with my Sig Sauer and we could finally put an end to this.'

I knew he truly wanted to kill her, and this was, in a way, the worst damage she could have done. It was not like Benton to wish for violence, to allow a shadow of the evil he pursued to fall over his conscience and heart, and as I listened, I felt my own culpability, too.

'Do you see how destructive this is?' I said, upset. 'We sit around talking about shooting her, strapping her into the electric chair or giving her a lethal injection. She has succeeded in taking possession of us, Benton. Because I admit that I want her dead about as much as I've ever wanted anything.'

'I think I should come on home,' he said again.

We hung up soon after, and insomnia proved the only enemy of the night. It robbed me of the few hours left before dawn and ripped my brain into fragmented dreams of anxiety and horror. I dreamed I was late for an important appointment and got stuck in the snow and was unable to dial the phone. In my twilight state I could not find answers in autopsies anymore and felt my life was over, and suddenly I drove up on a terrible car accident with bleeding bodies inside, and I could not make a move to help. I flipped this way and that, rearranging pillows and covers until the sky turned smoky blue and the stars went out. I got up and made coffee.

I drove to work with the radio on, listening to repeated news breaks about the fire in Warrenton and a body that was found. Speculation was wild and dramatic about the victim being the famed media mogul, and I could not help but wonder if this amused Sparkes just a little. I was curious why he had not issued a statement to the press, letting the world know he was quite alive, and again, doubts about him darkened my mind.

Dr Jack Fielding's red Mustang was parked behind our new building on Jackson Street, between the restored row houses of Jackson Ward, and the Medical College of Virginia campus of Virginia Commonwealth University. My new building, which was also home to the forensic labs, was the anchor of thirty-four acres of rapidly developing data institutes known as Biotech Park.

We had just moved from our old address to this new one but two months before, and I was still adjusting to modern glass and brick, and lintels on top of windows to reflect the neighborhoods once there. Our new space was bright, with tan epoxy flooring and walls that were easily hosed down. There was much still to be unpacked and sorted and rearranged, and as thrilled as I was to finally have a modern morgue, I felt more overwhelmed than I had ever been. The low sun was in my eyes as I parked in the chief's slot inside the covered bay on Jackson Street, and I unlocked a back door to let myself in.

The corridor was spotless and smelled of industrial deodorizer, and there were still boxes of electrical wiring and switch plates and cans of paint parked against walls. Fielding had unlocked the stainless steel cooler, which was bigger than most living rooms, and he had opened the doors to the autopsy room. I tucked my keys into my pocketbook and headed to the lockers, where I slipped out of my suit jacket and hung it up. I buttoned a lab coat up to my neck, and exchanged pumps for the rather gruesome black Reeboks I called my autopsy shoes. They were spattered and stained and certainly a biological hazard. But they supported my less-than-youthful legs and feet, and never left the morgue.

The new autopsy room was much bigger than the one before as it was better designed to utilize space. No longer were large steel tables built into the floor, so they could be parked out of the way when not in use. The five new tables were transportable and could be wheeled out of the refrigerator and wall-mounted dissecting sinks accommodated both right- and left-handed doctors. Our new tables had roller trays so we no longer had to use our backs to lift or move bodies, and there were non-clogging aspirators, and eye wash stations, and a special dual exhaust duct connected to the building's ventilation system.

All in all, the Commonwealth had granted me most of what I needed to ease the Virginia Medical Examiner System into the third millennium, but in truth, there was no such thing as change, at least not for the better. Each year we explored more damage done by bullets and blades, and more people filed frivolous lawsuits against us, and the courts miscarried justice as a matter of course because lawyers lied and jurors did not seem interested in evidence or facts anymore.

Frigid air rushed as I opened the cooler's massive door, and I walked past body bags and bloody plastic shrouds and stiff protruding feet. Brown-paper-bagged hands meant a violent death, and small pouches reminded me of a sudden infant death and the toddler who had drowned in the family pool. My fire case was swathed, broken glass and all, just as I had left it. I rolled the gurney out into a blaze of fluorescent light. Then I changed shoes again and walked to the other end of the first floor, where our offices and conference room were sequestered from the dead.

It was almost eight-thirty, and residents and clerical staff were getting coffee and traveling the hall. We exchanged our usual detached good mornings as I headed toward Fielding's open door. I knocked once and walked in as he talked on the phone and hastily scribbled information on a call sheet.

'Start again?' he said in his strong blunt voice as he cradled the receiver between his shoulder and chin and absently ran his fingers through his unruly dark hair. 'What's the address? What's the officer's name?'

He did not glance up at me as he wrote.

'You got a local phone number?'

He quickly read it back to make sure he'd gotten it right.

'Any idea what kind of death this is? Okay, okay. What cross street and will I see you in your cruiser? All right, you're good to go.'

Fielding hung up and looked harried for so early in the morning.

'What have we got?' I asked him as the business of the day began to mount.

'Looks like a mechanical asphyxiation. A black female with a history of alcohol and drug abuse. She's hanging off the bed, head against the wall, neck bent at an angle inconsistent with life. She's nude, so I think I'd better take a look to make sure this isn't something else.'

'*Someone* definitely should take a look,' I agreed.

He got my meaning.

'We can send Levine if you want.'

'Good idea, because I'm going to start the fire death and would like your help,' I said. 'At least in the early stages.'

'You got it.'

Fielding pushed back his chair and unfolded his powerful body. He was dressed in khakis, a white shirt with sleeves rolled up, Rockports, and an old woven leather belt around his hard, trim waist. Past forty now, he was no less diligent about his physical condition, which was no less remarkable than it had been when I had first hired him shortly after I had taken office. If only he cared about his cases quite so much. But he had always been respectful and faithful to me, and although he was slow and workmanlike, he was not given to assumptions or mistakes. For my purposes, he was manageable, reliable, and pleasant, and I would not have traded him for another deputy chief.

We entered the conference room together, and I took my seat at the head of the long glossy table. Charts and models of muscles and organs and the anatomical skeleton were the only decor, save for the same dated photographs of previous male chiefs who had watched over us in our previous quarters. This morning, the resident, a fellow, my three deputy and assistant chiefs, the toxicologist, and my administrators were present and accounted for. We had a medical student from MCV who was doing her elective here, and a forensic pathologist from London who was making the rounds in American morgues to learn more about serial murders and gunshot wounds.

'Good morning,' I said. 'Let's go over what we've got, and then we'll talk about our fire fatality and the implications of that.'

Fielding began with the possible mechanical asphyxiation, and then Jones, the administrator for the central district, which was the physical office where we were located, quickly ran through our other cases. We had a white male who fired five bullets into his girlfriend's head before blasting away at his own misguided brain. There were the sudden infant death and the drowning, and a young man who may have been changing out of his shirt and tie when he smashed his red Miata into a tree.

'Wow,' said the medical student, whose name was Sanford. 'How do you figure he was doing that?'

'Tank top half on, shirt and tie crumpled on the passenger's seat,' Jones explained. 'Seems he was leaving work to meet some friends at a bar. We've had these cases before – someone changing clothes, shaving, putting on makeup while they're driving.'

'That's when you want the little box on the death certificate that says manner of death was *stupid*,' Fielding said.

'Quite possibly all of you are aware that Carrie Grethen escaped from Kirby last night,' I went on. 'Though this does not directly impact this office, clearly we should be more than a little concerned.'

I tried to be as matter-of-fact as possible.

'Expect the media to call,' I said.

'They already have,' said Jones as he peered at me over his reading glasses. 'The answering service has received five calls since last night.'

'About Carrie Grethen.' I wanted to be sure.

'Yes, ma'am,' he said. 'And four more calls about the Warrenton case.'

'Let's get to that,' I said. 'There will be no information coming from this office at this point. Not about the escape from Kirby nor the Warrenton death. Fielding and I will be downstairs the better part of the day, and I want no interruptions that aren't absolutely necessary. This case is very sensitive.'

I looked around the table at faces that were somber but alive with interest.

'At present I don't know if we're dealing with an accident, suicide, or homicide, and the remains have not been identified. Tim,' I addressed the toxicologist, 'let's get a STAT alcohol and CO. This lady may have been a drug abuser, so I'll want a drug screen for opiates, amphetamines and methamphetamine, barbiturates, cannabinoids, as fast as you can get it.'

He nodded as he wrote this down. I paused long enough to scan newspaper articles that Jones had clipped for me, then I followed the hallway back to the morgue. In the ladies' locker room I removed my blouse and skirt and went to a cabinet to fetch a transmitter belt and mike that had been custom-designed for me by Lanier. The belt went around my upper waist under a long-sleeved blue surgical gown so the mike key would not come into direct contact with bloody hands. Last, I clipped the cordless mike to my collar, laced up my morgue shoes again, covered them with booties, and tied on a face shield and surgical mask.

Fielding emerged into the autopsy room the same time I did.

'Let's get her into X-ray,' I said.

We rolled the steel table across the corridor into the X-ray room and lifted the body and accompanying fire debris by corners of the sheets. This we transferred onto a table beneath the C-arm of the Mobile Digital Imaging System, which was an X-ray machine and fluoroscope in one computer-controlled unit. I went through the various set-up procedures, locking in various connecting cables and turning on the work station with a key. Lighted segments and a time line lit up on the control panel, and I loaded a film cassette into the holder and pressed a floor pedal to activate the video monitor.

'Aprons,' I said to Fielding.

I handed him a lead-lined one that was Carolina blue. Mine was heavy and felt full of sand as I tied it in back.

'I think we're ready,' I announced as I pressed a button.

By moving the C-arm, we were able to capture the remains in real time from many different angles, only, unlike the examination of hospital patients, what we viewed did not breathe or beat or swallow. Static images of dead organs and bones were black and white on the video screen, and I saw no projectiles or anomalies. As we pivoted the C-arm some more, we discovered several radiopaque shapes that I suspected were metal objects mingled with the debris. We watched our progress on screen, digging and sifting with our gloved hands until I closed my fingers around two hard objects. One was the size and shape of a half dollar, the other smaller than that and square. I began cleaning them in the sink.

'What's left of a small silver metal belt buckle,' I said as I dropped it into a plasticized carton, which I labeled with a Magic Marker.

My other find was easier, and I did not have to do much to it to determine that it was a wristwatch. The band had burned off and the sooty crystal was shattered. But I was fascinated by the face, which upon further rinsing turned out to be a very bright orange etched with a strange abstract design.

'Looks like a man's watch to me,' Fielding observed.

'Women wear watches this big,' I said. 'I do. So I can see.'

'Some kind of sports watch, maybe?'

'Maybe.'

We rotated the C-arm here and there, continuing to excavate as radiation from the X-ray tube passed through the body and all the muck and charred material surrounding it. I spotted what looked like the shape of a ring located somewhere beneath the right buttock, but when I tried to grab it, nothing was there. Since the body had been on its back, much of the posterior regions had been spared, including clothing. I wedged my hands under the buttocks and worked my fingers into the back pockets of the jeans, recovering half a carrot and what appeared to be a plain wedding band that at first looked like steel. Then I realized it was platinum.

'That looks like a man's ring, too,' Fielding said. 'Unless she had really big fingers.'

He took the ring from me to examine it more closely. The stench of burned decaying flesh rose from the table as I discovered more strange signs pointing to what this woman may have done prior to dying. There were dark, coarse animal hairs adhering to wet filthy denim, and though I couldn't be certain, I was fairly sure their origin was equine.

'Nothing engraved in it,' he said, sealing the ring inside an evidence envelope.

'No,' I confirmed with growing curiosity.

'Wonder why she had it in her back pocket instead of wearing it.'

'Good question.'

'Unless she was doing something that might have caused her to take it off,' he continued to think aloud. 'You know, like people taking off their jewelry when they wash their hands.'

'She may have been feeding the horses.'

I collected several hairs with forceps.

'Maybe the black foal that got away?' I supposed.

'Okay,' he said, and he sounded very dubious. 'And what? She's paying attention to the little guy, feeding him carrots, and then doesn't return him to his stall? A little later, everything burns, including the stables and the horses in them? But the foal gets away?'

He glanced at me across the table.

'Suicide?' he continued to speculate. 'And she couldn't bring herself to kill the colt? What's his name, Windsong?'

But there were no answers to any of these questions right now, and we continued to make X-rays of personal effects and pathology, to give us a permanent case record. But mostly we explored, in real time on screen, recovering grommets from jeans and an intrauterine device that suggested she had been sexually active with males.

Our findings included a zipper and a blackened lump the size of a baseball that turned out to be a steel bracelet with small links and a serpent silver ring that held three copper keys. Other than sinus configurations, which are as distinct as fingerprints in every human being, and a single porcelain crown on the right maxillary central incisor, we discovered nothing else obvious that might effect an identification.

At close to noon, we rolled her back across the corridor into the autopsy room and attached her table to a dissecting sink in the farthest corner, out of the main traffic. Other sinks were busy and loud as water drummed stainless steel, and stepladders were scooted as other doctors weighed and sectioned organs and dictated their findings into tiny mikes while various detectives looked on. The chatter was typically blunt with fractured sentences, our communication as random and disjointed as the lives of our cases.

'Excuse me, need to be right about where you are.'

'Darn, I need a battery.'

'What kind?'

'Whatever the hell goes in this camera.'

'Twenty dollars, right front pocket.'

'Probably not robbery.'

'Who's gonna count pills. Got a shitload.'

'Dr Scarpetta, we just got another case. Possible homicide,' a resident said loudly as he hung up a phone that was designated for clean hands.

'We may have to hold it until tomorrow,' I responded as our work load worsened.

'We've got the gun from the murder-suicide,' one of my assistant chiefs called out.

'Unloaded?' I answered back.

'Yeah.'

I walked over to make sure, for I never made assumptions when firearms came in with bodies. The dead man was big and still dressed in Faded Glory jeans, the pockets turned inside out by police. Potential gunshot residue on his hands was protected by brown paper bags, and blood trickled from his nose when a wooden block was placed beneath his head.

'Do you mind if I handle the gun?' I asked the detective, above the whine of a Stryker saw.

'Be my guest. I've already lifted prints.'

I picked up the Smith & Wesson pistol and pulled back the slide to check for a cartridge, but the chamber was clear. I dabbed a towel over the bullet wound in the head, as my morgue supervisor, Chuck Ruffin, honed a knife with long sweeps over a sharpening stone.

'See the black around there and the muzzle imprint?' I said as the detective and a resident leaned close. 'You can see the sight here. It's contact right-handed. The exit's here, and you can see by the dripping he was lying on his right side.'

'That's how we found him,' the detective said as the saw whined on and a bony dust drifted through the air.

'Be sure to note the caliber, make, and model,' I said as I returned to my own sad chore. 'And is the ammunition ball versus hollow point?'

'Ball. Remington nine-mill.'

Fielding had parallel-parked another table nearby and covered it with a sheet that he had piled with the fire debris that we had already sifted through. I began measuring the lengths of her badly burned femurs in hopes I could make an estimate of height. The rest of her legs were gone from just above the knees to the ankles, but her feet had been spared by her boots. In addition, she had burn amputations of her forearms and hands. We collected fragments of fabric and drew diagrams and collected more animal hairs, doing all that we could before beginning the difficult task of removing the glass.

'Let's get the warm water going,' I said to Fielding. 'Maybe we can loosen without tearing skin.'

'It's like a damn roast stuck to the pan.'

'Why are you guys always making food analogies?' came a deep, sure voice I recognized.

Teun McGovern, in full morgue protective garb, was walking toward our table. Her eyes were intense behind her face shield, and for an instant we stared straight at each other. I was not the least bit surprised that ATF would have sent a fire investigator to watch the postmortem examination. But I had never expected McGovern to show up.

'How's it going in Warrenton?' I asked her.

'Working away,' she replied. 'We haven't found Sparkes's body, which is a good thing, since he's not dead.'

'Cute,' Fielding said.

McGovern positioned herself across from me, standing far enough back from the table to suggest to me that she had seen very few autopsies.

'So what exactly are you doing?' she asked as I picked up a hose.

'We're going to run warm water between the skin and the glass in hopes we can peel the two apart without further damage,' I replied.

'And what if that doesn't work?'

'Then we got a big fat mess,' Fielding said.

'Then we use a scalpel,' I explained.

But this was not necessary. After several minutes of a constant warm bath, I began to very slowly and gently separate the thick broken glass from the dead woman's face, the skin pulling and distorting as I peeled, making her all the more horrible to look at. Fielding and I worked in silence for a while, gently laying shards and sections of heat-stressed glass into a plastic tub. This took about an hour, and when we were done, the stench was stronger. What was left of the poor woman seemed more pitiful and small, and the damage to her head was even more striking.

'My God,' McGovern said as she stepped closer. 'That's the weirdest thing I've ever seen.'

The lower part of the face was chalky bone, a barely discernible human skull with open jaws and crumbling teeth. Most of the ears were gone, but from the eyes up, the flesh was cooked and so remarkably preserved that I could see the blond fuzz along the hairline. The forehead was intact, although slightly abraded by the removal of the glass, so that it was no longer smooth. If there had been wrinkles, I could not find them now.

'I can't figure out what the hell this is,' Fielding said as he examined the bits of material mingled with hair. 'It's everywhere, all the way down to her scalp.'

Some of it looked like burned paper, while other small pieces were pristinely preserved and a neon pink. I scraped some of it onto my scalpel and placed it into another carton.

'We'll let the labs take a crack at it,' I said to McGovern.

'Absolutely,' she answered.

The hair was eighteen and three-quarters inches long, and I saved a strand of it for DNA should we ever have a premortem sample for comparison.

'If we trace her back to someone missing,' I said to McGovern, 'and you guys can get hold of her toothbrush, we can look for buccal cells. They line the mucosa of the mouth and can be used for DNA comparison. A hairbrush would be good, too.'

She made a note of this. I moved a surgical lamp closer to the left temporal area, using a lens to painstakingly examine what appeared to be hemorrhage in tissue that had been spared.

'It seems we have some sort of injury here,' I said. 'Definitely not skin splitting or an artifact of fire. Possibly an incision with some sort of shiny debris imbedded inside the wound.'

'Could she have been overcome by CO and fallen and hit her head?' McGovern voiced the same question others had.

'She would have had to have hit it on something very sharp,' I said as I took photographs.

'Let me look,' Fielding said, and I handed him the lens. 'I don't see any torn or ragged edges,' he remarked as he peered.

'No, not a laceration,' I agreed. 'This looks more like something inflicted by a sharp instrument.'

He returned the lens to me, and I used plastic forceps to delicately scrape the shiny debris from the wound. I swiped it onto a square of clean cotton twill. On a nearby desk was a dissecting microscope, and I placed the cloth on the stage and moved the light source so that it would reflect off the debris. I looked through the eyepiece lens as I manipulated the coarse and fine adjustments.

What I saw in the circle of reflected illumination were several silvery segments that had the striated, flattened surfaces of metal shavings, such as the turnings made by a lathe. I fitted a Polaroid MicroCam to the microscope and took high-resolution instant color photographs.

'Take a look,' I said.

Fielding, then McGovern, bent over the microscope.

'Either of you ever seen anything like that?' I asked.

I peeled open the developed photographs to make certain they had turned out all right.

'It reminds me of Christmas tinsel when it gets old and wrinkled,' Fielding said.

'Transferred from whatever cut her,' was all McGovern had to say.

'I would think so,' I agreed.

I removed the square of white cloth from the stage and preserved the shavings between cotton balls, which I sealed inside a metal evidence button.

'One more thing for the labs,' I said to McGovern.

'How long will it take?' McGovern said. 'Because if there's a problem, we can do the work at our labs in Rockville.'

'There won't be a problem.' I looked at Fielding and said, 'I think I can handle it from here.'

'Okay,' he said. 'I'll get started on the next one.'

I opened up the neck to look for trauma to those organs and muscles, beginning with the tongue, which I removed while McGovern looked on with stoicism. It was a grim procedure that separated the weak from the strong.

'Nothing there,' I said, rinsing the tongue and blotting it dry with a towel. 'No bite marks that might be indicative of a seizure. No other injuries.'

I looked inside the glistening smooth walls of the airway and found no soot, meaning she was no longer breathing when heat and flames had reached her. But I also found blood, and this was further ominous news.

'More premortem trauma,' I said.

'Possible something fell on her after she was dead?' McGovern asked.

'It didn't happen that way.'

I noted the injury on a diagram and dictated it into the transmitter.

'Blood in the airway means she inhaled it – or aspirated,' I explained. 'Meaning, obviously, that she was breathing when the trauma occurred.'

'What sort of trauma?' she then asked.

'A penetrating injury. The throat stabbed or cut. I see no other signs of trauma to the base of the skull or lungs or to the neck, no contusions or broken bones. Her hyoid's intact, and there's fusion of the greater horn and body, possibly indicating she's older than twenty and most likely wasn't strangled manually or with a ligature.'

I began to dictate again.

'The skin under the chin and superficial muscle are burned away,' I said into the small mike on my gown. 'Heat-coagulated blood in the distal trachea, primary, secondary, and tertiary bronchi. Hemoaspiration, and blood in the esophagus.'

I made the Y incision to open up the dehydrated, ruined body, and for the most part, the rest of the autopsy proved to be rather routine. Although the organs were cooked, they were within normal limits, and the reproductive organs verified the gender as female. There was blood in her stomach, too; otherwise it was empty and tubular, suggesting she hadn't been eating very much. But I found no disease and no other injuries old or new.

Height I could not positively ascertain, but I could estimate by using Trotter and Gleser regression formula charts to correlate femur length to the victim's stature. I sat at a nearby desk and thumbed through Bass's *Human Osteology* until I found the appropriate table for American white females. Based on a 50.2 millimeter, or approximately twenty-inch, femur, the predicted height would have been five-foot-ten.

Weight was not so exact, for there was no table, chart, or scientific calculation that might tell me that. In truth, we usually got a hint of weight from the size of clothing left, and in this case, the victim had been wearing size eight jeans. So based on the data I had, I intuited that she had been between one hundred and twenty and one hundred and thirty pounds.

'In other words,' I said to McGovern, 'she was tall and very slim. We also know she had long blond hair, was probably sexually active, may have been comfortable around horses, and was already dead inside Sparkes's Warrenton house before the fire got to her. I also know that she received significant premortem injury to her upper neck and was cut right here on her left temple.' I pointed. 'How these were inflicted, I can't tell you.'

I got up from my chair and gathered paperwork while McGovern looked at me, her eyes shadowed by thought. She took off her face shield and mask and untied her gown in back.

'If she had a drug problem, is there any way you might be able to tell that?' she asked me as the phone rang and rang.

'Toxicology will certainly tell us if she had drugs on board,' I said. 'There may also be crystals in her lungs or foreign body granulomas from cutting agents like talc, and fibers from the cotton used to strain out impurities. Unfortunately, the areas where we might be most likely to find needle tracks are missing.'

'What about her brain? Would chronic drug abuse cause any damage that you might be able to see? For example, if she started having severe mental problems, was getting psychotic and so on? It sounds like Sparkes thought she had some sort of mental illness,' McGovern then said. 'For example, what if she were depressive or manic-depressive? Could you tell?'

By now the skull had been opened, the rubbery, fire-shrunken brain sectioned and still on the cutting board.

'In the first place,' I answered, 'nothing is going to be helpful post-mortem because the brain is cooked. But even if that were not the case, looking for a morphological correlate to a particular psychiatric syndrome is, in most cases, still theoretical. A widening of the sulci, for example, and reduced gray matter due to atrophy might be a sign-post if we knew what the weight of the brain originally was when she was healthy. Then maybe I could say, *Okay, her brain weighs a hundred grams less now than it did, so she might have been suffering from some sort of mental disease.* Unless she has a lesion or old head injury that might suggest a problem, the answer to your question is no, I can't tell.'

McGovern was silent, and it was not lost on her that I was clinical and not the least bit friendly. Even though I was aware of my rather brittle demeanor around her, I could not seem to soften it. I looked around for Ruffin. He was at the first dissecting sink, suturing a Y incision in long strokes of needle and twine. I motioned to him and walked over. He was too young to worry about turning thirty anytime soon, and had gotten his training in an O.R. and a funeral home.

'Chuck, if you can finish up here and put her back in the fridge,' I said to him.

'Yes, ma'am.'

He returned to his station to finish his present task while I peeled off gloves and dropped them and my mask into one of many red biological hazard containers scattered around the autopsy room.

'Let's go to my office and have a cup of coffee,' I suggested to McGovern in an attempt to be a little more civil. 'And we can finish this discussion.'

In the locker room, we washed with antibacterial soap and I got dressed. I had questions for McGovern, but in truth, I was curious about her, too.

'Getting back to the possibility of drug-induced mental illness,' McGovern said as we followed the corridor. 'Many of these people self-destruct, right?'

'In one way or another.'

'They die in accidents, commit suicide, and that gets us back to the big question,' she said. 'Is that what happened here? Possible she was whacked out and committed suicide?'

'All I know is, she has injury that was inflicted before death,' I pointed out again.

'But that could be self-inflicted if she were not in her right mind,' McGovern said. 'God knows the kinds of self-mutilation we've seen when people are psychotic.'

This was true. I had worked cases in which people had cut their own throats, or stabbed themselves in the chest, or amputated their limbs, or shot themselves in their sexual organs, or walked into a river to drown. Not to mention leaps from high places and self-immolations. The list of horrendous things people did to themselves was much too long, and whenever I thought I'd seen it all, something new and awful was rolled into our bay.

The phone was ringing as I unlocked my office, and I grabbed it just in time.

'Scarpetta,' I said.

'I've got some results for you,' said Tim Cooper, the toxicologist. 'Ethanol, methanol, isopropanol, and acetone are zero. Carbon monoxide is less than seven percent. I'll keep working on the other screens.'

'Thanks. What would I do without you?' I said.

I looked at McGovern as I hung up, and I told her what Cooper had just said.

'She was dead before the fire,' I explained, 'her cause of death exsanguination and asphyxia due to aspiration of blood due to acute neck injury. As for manner, I'm pending that until further investigation, but I think we should work this as a homicide. In the meantime, we need to get her identified, and I'll do what I can to get started on that.'

'I guess I'm supposed to imagine that this woman torched the place and maybe cut her own throat before the fire got her first?' she said as anger flickered.

I did not answer as I measured coffee for the coffeemaker on a nearby countertop.

'Don't you think that's rather far-fetched?' she went on.

I poured in bottled water and pressed a button.

'Kay, no one's going to want to hear homicide,' she said. 'Because of Kenneth Sparkes and what all of this may imply. I hope you realize what you're up against.'

'And what ATF is up against,' I said, sitting across my hopelessly piled desk from her.

'Look, I don't care who he is,' she replied. 'I do every job like I fully intend to make an arrest. I'm not the one who has to deal with the politics around here.'

But my mind wasn't on the media or Sparkes right now. I was thinking that this case disturbed me at a deeper level and in ways I could not fathom.

'How much longer will your guys be at the scene?' I asked her.

'Another day. Two at the most,' she said. 'Sparkes has supplied us and the insurance company with what was inside his house, and just the antique furniture and old wood flooring and paneling alone were a massive fuel load.'

'What about the master bath?' I asked. 'Saying this was the point of origin.'

She hesitated. 'Obviously, that's the problem.'

'Right. If an accelerant wasn't used, or at least not a petroleum distillate, then how?'

'The guys are beating their brains out,' she said, and she was frustrated. 'And so am I. If I try to predict how much energy would be needed in that room for a flashover condition, the fuel load isn't there. According to Sparkes, there was nothing but a throw rug and towels. Cabinets and fixtures were customized brushed steel. The shower had a glass door, the window had sheer curtains.'

She paused as the coffeemaker gurgled.

'So what are we talking about?' she went on. 'Five, six hundred kilowatts total for a ten-by-fifteen-foot room? Clearly, there are other variables. Such as how much air was flowing through the doorway . . .'

'What about the rest of the house? You just said there was a big fuel load there, right?'

'We're only concerned with one room, Kay. And that's the room of origin. Without an origin, the rest of the fuel load doesn't matter.'

'I see.'

'I know a flame was impinged on the ceiling in that bathroom, and I know how high that flame had to be and how many kilowatts of energy were needed for flashover. And a throw rug and maybe some towels and curtains couldn't even come close to causing something like that.'

I knew her engineering equations were pristinely mathematical, and I did not doubt anything she was saying. But it did not matter. I was still left with the same problem. I had reason to believe that we were dealing with a homicide and that when the fire started, the victim's body was inside the master bath, with its noncombustible marble floors, large mirrors, and steel. Indeed, she may have been in the tub.

'What about the open skylight?' I asked McGovern. 'Does that fit with your theory?'

'It could. Because once again, the flames had to be high enough to break the glass, and then heat would have vented through the opening like a chimney. Every fire has its own personality, but certain behaviors are always the same because they conform to the laws of physics.'

'I understand.'

'There are four stages,' she went on, as if I knew nothing. 'First is the fire plume, or column of hot gases, flames, and smoke rising from the fire. That would have been the case, let's say, if the throw rug in the bathroom had ignited. The higher above the flame the gases rise, the cooler and denser they become. They mix with combustion by-products, and the hot gases now begin to fall, and the cycle repeats itself creating turbulent smoke that spreads horizontally. What should have happened next was this hot smoky layer would have continued to descend until it found an opening for ventilation – in this case, we'll assume the bathroom doorway. Next, the smoky layer flows out of the opening while fresh air flows in. If there's enough oxygen, the temperature at the ceiling's going to go up to more than six hundred degrees Celsius, and boom, we have flashover, or a fully developed fire.'

'A fully developed fire in the master bath,' I said.

'And then on into other oxygen-enriched rooms where the fuel loads were enough to burn the place to the ground,' she replied. 'So it's not the spread of the fire that bothers me. It's how it got started. Like I said, a throw rug, curtains, weren't enough, unless something else was there.'

'Maybe something was,' I said, getting up to pour coffee. 'How do you take yours?' I asked.

'Cream and sugar.'

Her eyes followed me.

'None of that artificial stuff, please.'

I drank mine black, and set mugs on the desk as McGovern's gaze wandered around my new office. Certainly, it was brighter and more modern than what I had occupied in the old building on Fourteenth and Franklin, but I really had no more room to evolve. Worst of all, I had been honored with a CEO corner space with windows, and anybody who understood physicians knew that what we needed were walls for bookcases, and not bulletproof glass overlooking a parking lot and the Petersburg Turnpike. My hundreds of medical, legal, and forensic science reviews, journals and formidable volumes were crammed together and, in some cases, double-shelved. It was not uncommon for Rose, my secretary, to hear me swearing when I could not find a reference book I needed right that minute.

'Teun,' I said, sipping my coffee, 'I'd like to take this opportunity to thank you for taking care of Lucy.'

'Lucy takes care of herself,' she said.

'That has not always been true.'

I smiled in an effort to be more gracious, to hide the hurt and jealousy that were a splinter in my heart.

'But you're right,' I said. 'I think she does a pretty admirable job of it now. I'm sure Philadelphia will be good for her.'

McGovern was reading every signal I was sending, and I could tell she was aware of more than I wanted her to be.

'Kay, hers will not be an easy road,' she then stated. 'No matter what I do.'

She swirled the coffee in her mug, as if about to taste the first sip of fine wine.

'I'm her supervisor, not her mother,' McGovern said.

This irked me considerably, and it showed when I abruptly picked up the phone and instructed Rose to hold all calls. I got up and shut my door.

'I would hope she's not transferring to your field office because she needs a mother,' I replied coolly as I returned to my desk, which served as a barrier between us. 'Above all else, Lucy is a consummate professional.'

McGovern held up her hand to stop me.

'Whoa,' she protested. 'Of course she is. I'm just not promising anything. She's a big girl, but she's also got a lot of big obstacles. Her FBI background will be held against her by some, who will assume right off the bat that she has an attitude and has never really worked cases.'

'That stereotype shouldn't last long,' I said, and I was finding it very difficult to objectively discuss my niece with her.

'Oh, about as long as it takes for them to see her land a helicopter or program a robot to remove a bomb from a scene,' she quipped. 'Or zip through Q-dot calculations in her head while the rest of us can't even figure them out on a calculator.'

Q-dot was slang for the mathematical equations, or scientific evaluations, used to estimate the physics and chemistry of a fire as it related to what the investigator observed at the scene or was told by witnesses. I wasn't sure Lucy would make many friends by being able to work such esoteric formulas in her head.

'Teun,' I said, softening my tone. 'Lucy's different, and that isn't always good. In fact, in many ways it is just as much a handicap to be a genius as it is to be retarded.'

'Absolutely. I am more aware of this than you might imagine.'

'As long as you understand,' I said as if I were reluctantly handing her the baton in the relay race of Lucy's difficult development.

'And as long as you understand that she has and will continue to be treated like everybody else. Which includes the other agents' reactions to her baggage, which includes rumors about why she left the FBI and about her alleged personal life,' she stated frankly.

I looked at her long and hard, wondering just how much she really knew about Lucy. Unless McGovern had been briefed by someone at the Bureau, there was no reason I could think of why she should know about my niece's affair with Carrie Grethen and the implications of what that might mean when the case went to court, assuming Carrie was caught. Just the reminder cast a shadow over what had already been a dark day, and my uncomfortable silence invited McGovern to fill it.

'I have a son,' she said quietly, staring into her coffee. 'I know what it's like to have children grow up and suddenly vanish. Go their own way, too busy to visit or get on the phone.'

'Lucy grew up a long time ago,' I said quickly, for I did not want her to commiserate with me. 'She also never lived with me, not permanently, I mean. In a way, she's always been gone.'

But McGovern just smiled as she got out of her chair.

'I've got troops to check on,' she said. 'I guess I'd better be on my way.'

6

_____

At four o'clock that afternoon, my staff was still busy in the autopsy room, and I walked in looking for Chuck. He and two of my residents were working on the burned woman's body, defleshing her as best they could with plastic spatulas, because anything harder might scratch the bones.

Chuck was sweating beneath his surgical cap and mask as he scraped tissue from the skull, his brown eyes rather glazed behind his face shield. He was tall and wiry with short, sandy blond hair that tended to stick out in every direction no matter how much gel he used. He was attractive in an adolescent way and, after a year on the job, still terrified of me.

'Chuck?' I said again, inspecting one of the more ghoulish tasks in forensic medicine.

'Yes, ma'am.'

He stopped scraping and looked up furtively at me. The stench was getting worse by the minute as unrefrigerated flesh continued to decompose, and I was not looking forward to what I needed to do next.

'Let me just check this one more time,' I said to Ruffin, who was so tall he tended to stoop, his neck jutting out like a turtle when he looked at whoever he was talking to. 'Our old battered pots and pans didn't make it in the move.'

'I think somehow they got tossed out,' he said.

'And probably should have,' I told him. 'Which means you and I have an errand to run.'

'Now?'

'Now.'

He wasted no time heading into the men's locker room to get out of his dirty, stinking scrubs and shower just long enough to get the shampoo out of his hair. He was still perspiring, his face pink from scrubbing, when we met in the corridor and I handed him a set of keys. The dark red office Tahoe was parked inside the bay, and I climbed up into the passenger's seat, letting Ruffin drive.

'We're going to Cole's Restaurant Supply,' I told him as the big engine came to life. 'About two blocks west of Parham, on Broad. Just get us on 64 and take the West Broad exit. I'll show you from there.'

He pushed a remote control on the visor and the bay door rolled up heavily, letting in sunlight that I had not noticed all day. Rush hour traffic had just begun and would be awful in another half hour. Ruffin drove like an old woman, dark glasses on and hunched forward as he kept his speed about five miles an hour less than the limit.

'You can go a little faster,' I told him calmly. 'It closes at five, so we sort of need to hurry along.'

He stepped on the gas, lurching us forward, and fumbled in the ashtray for toll tokens.

'You mind if I ask you something, Dr Scarpetta?' he said.

'Please. Go right ahead.'

'It's kind of bizarre.'

He glanced in the rearview mirror again.

'That's all right.'

'You know, I've seen a lot of things, at the hospital and the funeral home and all,' he began nervously. 'And nothing got to me, you know?'

He slowed at the toll plaza and tossed a token into the basket. The red striped arm went up and we rolled on as people in a hurry darted past us. Ruffin rolled his window back up.

'It's normal for what you're seeing now to get to you,' I finished his thought for him, or thought I did.

But this was not what he wanted to tell me.

'You see, most of the time I get to the morgue before you in the morning,' he said instead, his eyes riveted forward as he drove. 'So I'm the one who answers the phones and gets things ready for you, right? You know, because I'm there alone.'

I nodded, having not a clue as to what he was about to say.

'Well, starting about two months ago, when we were still in the old building, the phone started ringing at around six-thirty in the morning, just after I got in. And when I would pick it up, nobody was there.'

'How often has this happened?' I asked.

'Maybe three times a week. Sometimes every day. And it's still happening.'

He was getting my attention now.

'It's happening since we moved.' I wanted to make sure.

'Of course, we have the same number,' he reminded me. 'But yes, ma'am. In fact it happened again this morning, and I've started getting a little spooked. I'm just wondering if we should try to get the calls traced to see what's going on.'

'Tell me exactly what happens when you pick up the phone,' I said as we drove exactly at the speed limit along the interstate.

'I say "Morgue,"' he said. 'And whoever it is doesn't say a word. There's silence, almost like the line is dead. So I say "Hello?" a few times and finally hang up. I can tell there's someone there. It's just something I sense.'

'Why haven't you told me this before?'

'I wanted to make sure it wasn't just me overreacting. Or maybe being too imaginative, because I got to tell you it's kind of creepy in there first thing in the morning when the sun's not up yet and no one else is around.'

'And you say this started about two months ago?'

'More or less,' he answered. 'I didn't really count the first few, you know.'

I was irritated that he had waited until now to pass this along to me, but there was no point in belaboring that.

'I'll pass this along to Captain Marino,' I said. 'In the meantime, Chuck, you need to tell me if this happens again, okay?'

He nodded, his knuckles white on the steering wheel.

'Just beyond the next light, we're looking for a big beige building. It will be on our left, in the nine thousand block, just past JoPa's.'

Cole's was fifteen minutes from closing, and there were but two other cars in the lot when we parked. Ruffin and I got out, and air conditioning was frigid as we entered a wide open space with aisles of metal shelves all the way up to the ceiling. Crowded on them was everything from restaurant-sized ladles and spoons, to food warmers for cafeteria lines, to giant coffeemakers and mixers. But it was potware that I was interested in, and after a quick scan I found the section I needed, halfway to the back, near electric skillets and measuring cups.

I began lifting great aluminum pans and pots when a sales clerk suddenly appeared. He was balding and big-bellied, and sporting a tattoo of a naked woman playing cards on his right forearm.

'Can I help you?' he said to Ruffin.

'I need the biggest cooking pot you've got,' I answered.

'That'd be forty quarts.'

He reached up to a shelf too high for me and handed the monstrous pot to Ruffin.

'I'll need a lid,' I said.

'Will have to be ordered.'

'What about something deep and rectangular,' I then said as I envisioned long bones.

'Got a twenty-quart pan.'

He reached up to another shelf, and metal clanged as he lifted out a pan that had probably been intended for vats of whipped potatoes, vegetables or cobbler.

'And I don't suppose you have a lid for that either,' I said.

'Yeah.'

Different-sized lids clattered as he pulled one out.

'It's got the notch right here for the ladle. I guess you'll be wanting a ladle, too.'

'No, thank you,' I said. 'Just something long to stir with, either wooden or plastic. And heat-resistant gloves. Two pairs. What else?'

I looked at Ruffin as I thought.

'Maybe we should get a twenty-quart pot, too, for smaller jobs?' I mused.

'That'd be a good idea,' he agreed. 'That big pot's going to be mighty heavy when it's filled with water. And there's no point in using it if something smaller will work, but I think you're going to need the bigger pot this time, or it all won't fit. You know?'

The salesman was getting more confused as he listened to our evasive conversation.

'You tell me what you're planning to cook, and maybe I can give you some advice,' he offered, again to Ruffin.

'Different things,' I replied. 'Mostly I'll be boiling things.'

'Oh, I see,' he said, even though he didn't. 'Well, will there be anything else?'

'That's it,' I answered him with a smile.

At the counter, he rang up one hundred and seventy-seven dollars of restaurant cookware while I got out my billfold and hunted for my MasterCard.

'Do you by chance give discounts to state government?' I asked as he took my card from me.

'No,' he said, rubbing his double chin as he frowned at my card. 'I think I've heard your name on the news before.'

He stared suspiciously at me.

'I know.'

He snapped his fingers.

'You're the lady who ran for the senate a few years back. Or maybe it was for lieutenant governor?' he said, pleased.

'Not me,' I answered. 'I try to stay out of politics.'

'You and me both,' he said loudly as Ruffin and I carried our purchases out the door. 'They're all crooks, every single one of 'em!'

When we returned to the morgue, I gave Ruffin instructions to remove the remains of the burn victim from the refrigerator and wheel them and the new pots into the decomposition room. I shuffled through telephone messages, most of them from reporters, and realized I was nervously pulling at my hair when Rose appeared in the doorway that joined my office to hers.

'You look like you've had a bad day,' she said.

'No worse than usual.'

'How about a cup of cinnamon tea?'

'I don't think so,' I said. 'But thanks.'

Rose placed a stack of death certificates on my desk, adding to the never-ending pile of documents for me to initial or sign. She was dressed this day in a smart navy blue pants suit and bright purple blouse, her shoes, typically, black leather lace-ups for walking.

Rose was well past retirement age, although it didn't show in her face, which was regal and subtly made up. But her hair had gotten finer and had turned completely white, while arthritis nibbled at her fingers, lower back, and hips, making it increasingly uncomfortable for her to sit at her desk and take care of me as she had from my first day at this job.

'It's almost six,' she said, looking kindly at me.

I glanced up at the clock as I began to scan paperwork and sign my name.

'I have a dinner at the church,' she diplomatically let me know.

'That's nice,' I said, frowning as I read. 'Damn it, how many times do I have to tell Dr Carmichael that you don't sign out a death as *cardiac arrest.* Jesus, everybody dies of cardiac arrest. You die, your heart quits, right? And he's done the *respiratory arrest* number too, no matter how many times I've amended his certificates.'

I sighed in annoyance.

'He's been the M.E. in Halifax County for how many years?' I continued my tirade. 'Twenty-five at least?'

'Dr Scarpetta, don't forget he's an obstetrician. And an ancient one at that,' Rose reminded me. 'A nice man who's not capable of learning anything new. He still types his reports on an old manual Royal, flying capitals and all. And the reason I mentioned the church dinner is, I'm supposed to be there in ten minutes.'

She paused, regarding me over her reading glasses.

'But I can stay if you want me to,' she added.

'I've got some things to do,' I told her. 'And the last thing I would think of is to interfere with a church dinner. Yours or anyone's. I'm always in enough trouble with God as is.'

'Then I'll say good night,' Rose said. 'My dictations are in your basket. I'll see you in the morning.'

After her footsteps vanished down the corridor, I was enveloped by silence broken only by the sounds of paper I was moving around on my desk. I thought of Benton several times and warded off my desire to call him, because I was not ready to relax, or maybe I simply did not want to feel human quite yet. It is, after all, hard to feel like a normal person with normal emotions when one is about to boil human remains in what is essentially a large soup pot. A few minutes after seven, I followed the corridor to the decomposition room, which was two doors down and across from the cooler.

I unlocked the door and entered what was nothing more than a small autopsy room with a freezer and special ventilation. The remains were covered by a sheet on a transportable table, a new forty-quart pot filled with water on an electric burner beneath a chemical hood. I put on a mask and gloves and turned the burner on a low heat that would not further damage the bones. I poured in two scoops of laundry detergent and a cup of bleach to hasten the loosening of fibrous membranes, cartilage, and grease.

I opened the sheets, exposing bones stripped of most of their tissue, the extremities pitifully truncated like burned sticks. I gently placed femurs and tibias into the pot, then the pelvis and parts of the skull. Vertebrae and ribs followed as water got hotter and a sharp-smelling steam began to rise. I needed to see her bare, clean bones because they might have something to tell me, and there simply was no other way to do it.

For a while I sat in that room, the hood loudly sucking up air as I drifted in my chair. I was tired. I was emotionally drained and feeling all alone. Water heated up, and what was left of a woman I believed had been murdered began to process in the pot, in what seemed one more indignity and callous slight to who she was.

'Oh God,' I sighed, as if God might somehow hear me. 'Bless her, wherever she is.'

It was hard to imagine being reduced to bones cooking in a pot, and the more I thought about it the more depressed I got. Somewhere someone had loved this woman, and she had accomplished something in this life before her body and identity had been so cruelly stripped away. I had spent my existence trying to ward off hate, but by now it was too late. It was true that I hated sadistic evil people whose purpose in life was to torment life and take it, as if it were theirs to appropriate. It was true that executions deeply disturbed me, but only because they resurrected heartless crimes and the victims society barely remembered.

Steam rose in a hot, moist vapor, tainting the air with a nauseating stench that would lessen the longer the bones were processed. I envisioned someone thin and tall and blond, someone wearing jeans and lace-up boots, with a platinum ring tucked in her back pocket. Her hands were gone, and I probably would never know the size of her fingers or if the ring had fit, but it wasn't likely. Fielding probably was right, and I knew I had one more thing to ask Sparkes.

I thought of her wounds and tried to reconstruct how she might have gotten them, and why her fully clothed body had been in the master bathroom. That location, if we were correct about it, was unexpected and odd. Her jeans had not been undone, for when I had recovered the zipper it had been zipped shut, and certainly her buttocks had been covered. Based on the synthetic fabric that had melted into her flesh, I also had no reason to suspect that her breasts had been exposed, not that any of these findings ruled out a sexual assault. But they certainly argued against one.

I was checking the bones through a veil of steam when the telephone rang, startling me. At first I thought it might be some funeral home with a body to deliver, but then I realized that the flashing light was one of the lines for the autopsy room. I could not help but remember what Ruffin had said about spooky early morning calls, and I halfway expected to hear no one on the other end.

'Yes,' I said abruptly.

'Geez, who pissed in your cornflakes?' Marino answered back.

'Oh,' I said, relieved. 'Sorry, I thought it was someone playing pranks.'

'What do you mean, *pranks*?'

'Later,' I said. 'What's going on?'

'I'm sitting in your parking lot and was hoping you might let me in.'

'I'll be right there.'

In fact, I was very pleased to have company. I hurried to the enclosed bay, and I pushed a button on a wall. The huge door began to crank up, and Marino ducked under it, the dark night smudged with sodium vapor lights. I realized the sky had gotten overcast with clouds that portended rain.

'Why are you here so late?' Marino asked in his usual grumpy way as he sucked on a cigarette.

'My office is smoke-free,' I reminded him.

'Like anybody in this joint's gotta worry about secondary smoke.'

'A few of us are still breathing,' I said.

He flicked the cigarette to the concrete floor and irritably crushed it with his foot, as if we had never been through this routine, not even once in our lives. In fact, this had gotten to be a standard act with us that in its own dysfunctional way somehow reaffirmed our bond to each other. I was quite certain that Marino's feelings would be injured if I didn't nag him about something.

'You can follow me into the decomp room,' I said to him as I shut the bay door. 'I'm in the middle of something.'

'I wish I'd known before,' he complained. 'I would've just dealt with you over the phone.'

'Don't worry. It's not too bad. I'm just cleaning up some bones.'

'Maybe that ain't bad to you,' he said, 'but I've never gotten used to smelling people cook.'

We walked inside the decomposition room and I handed him a surgical mask. I checked the processing to see how it was going and turned the heat down fifty degrees to make sure the water did not boil over and knock bones against each other and the sides of the pot. Marino bent the mask to fit over his nose and mouth and tied sloppy bows in the back. He spotted a box of disposable gloves, snatched a pair and worked them on. It was ironical that he was obsessive in his concerns about outside agents invading his health, when in fact the gravest danger was simply the way he lived. He was sweating in khakis and a white shirt and tie and at some point during the day had been assaulted by ketchup.

'Got a couple interesting things for you, Doc,' he said, leaning against a brightly polished sink. 'We ran the tags on the burned-up Mercedes behind Kenneth Sparkes's house, and it comes back to an '81 Benz 240D, blue. The odometer's probably rolled over at least twice. Registration's a little scary, comes back to a Dr Newton Joyce in Wilmington, North Carolina. He's in the book but I couldn't get him, just his answering machine.'

'Wilmington is where Claire Rawley went to school, and close to where Sparkes had his beach house,' I reminded him.

'Right. So far the signs are still pointing that way.'

He stared blankly at the steaming pot on the burner.

'She drives someone else's car to Warrenton and somehow gets inside Sparkes's house when he's not home, and gets murdered and burns up in a fire,' he said, rubbing his temples. 'I tell you, this one stinks about as bad as what you're cooking there, Doc. We're missing a really big piece, because nothing's making sense.'

'Are there any Rawleys in the Wilmington area?' I asked. 'Any possibility she has relatives there?'

'They got two listings, and neither of them have ever heard of a Rawley named Claire,' he said.

'What about the university?'

'Haven't gotten to that yet,' he answered as I went over to check the pot again. 'Thought you were going to do that.'

'In the morning.'

'So. You gonna hang out here all night cooking this shit?'

'As a matter of fact,' I said, turning off the burner, 'I'm going to let it sit so I can go home. What time is it anyway? Oh God, almost nine o'clock. And I've got court in the morning.'

'Let's blow this joint,' he said.

I locked the door to the decomposition room, and I opened the bay door again. Through it I saw mountainous dark clouds blowing across the moon like boats in full sail, and the wind was wild and making eerie rushing sounds around the corners of my building. Marino walked me to my car and seemed in no hurry as he got out his cigarettes and lit one.

'I don't want to put any hinky ideas in your head,' he said, 'but there's something I think you ought to know.'

I unlocked my car door and slid behind the wheel.

'I'm afraid to ask,' I said, and I meant it.

'I got a call about four-thirty this afternoon from Rex Willis at the paper. The editorial columnist,' he said.

'I know who he is.'

I fastened my seat belt.

'Apparently he got a letter today from an anonymous source, kind of in the format of a press release. It's pretty bad.'

'About what?' I said as an alarm shot through my blood.

'Well, it's supposedly from Carrie Grethen, and she's saying that she escaped from Kirby because she was framed by the feds and knew they'd execute her for something she didn't do unless she got away. She claims that at the time of the murders you were having an affair with the chief profiler in the case, Benton Wesley, and all the so-called evidence against her was doctored, made up, a conspiracy between the two of you to make the Bureau look good.'

'And this was mailed from where?' I asked as outrage heated me up.

'Manhattan.'

'And it was addressed specifically to Rex Willis?'

'Yup.'

'And of course, he's not going to do anything with it.'

Marino hesitated.

'Come on, Doc,' he said. 'When's the last time a reporter didn't do something with something?'

'Oh for God's sake!' I blurted out as I started the engine. 'Has the media gone totally mad? They get a letter from a psycho and print it in the paper?'

'I've got a copy if you want to see it.'

He dug a folded sheet of paper out of his back pocket and handed it to me.

'It's a fax,' he explained. 'The original's already at the lab. Documents is going to see what they can do with it.'

I unfolded the copy with shaking hands, and did not recognize the neat printing in black ink. It was nothing like the bizarre red printing that was on the letter I had received from Carrie, and in this epistle, the words were very articulate and clear. For a moment I read, skimming over the ridiculous claims that she had been framed, my eyes stopping cold on the last long paragraph.

As for Special Agent Lucy Farinelli, she has enjoyed a successful career only because the ever influential chief medical examiner, Dr Scarpetta, her aunt, has covered up her niece's mistakes and transgressions for years. When Lucy and I were both at Quantico, it was she who came on to me, not the other way around as it would most certainly be alleged in court. While it is true that we were lovers for a while, this was all manipulation on her part to get me to cover for her when she screwed up CAIN time and time again. Then she went on to take credit for work she'd never done. I'm telling you this is the God's truth. I swear it. And I'm asking you to please print this letter for all to see. I don't want to stay in hiding the rest of my life, convicted by society for terrible deeds I did not do. My only hope for freedom and justice is for people to see the truth and do something about it.

Have Mercy, Carrie Grethen

Marino quietly smoked until I was finished reading, then he said, 'This person knows too much. I got no doubt the bitch wrote it.'

'She writes me a letter that seems the work of someone deranged and then follows it with this, something that seems completely rational?' I said, and I was so upset I felt sick. 'How does that make sense, Marino?'

He shrugged as the first drops of rain began to fall.

'I'll tell you what I think,' he said. 'She was sending you a signal. She wants you to know she's jerking everybody around. It wouldn't be fun for her if she couldn't piss you off and ruin your day.'

'Does Benton know about this?'

'Not yet.'

'And you really think the paper's going to print it,' I asked again, hoping his answer would be different this time.

'You know how it goes.'

He dropped the cigarette butt and it glowed to the ground and scattered in sparks.

'The story will be that this notorious psychopathic killer has contacted them while half of law enforcement is out there looking for the bitch,' he said. 'And the other bad news is that there's nothing to say she hasn't sent the same letter other places, too.'

'Poor Lucy,' I muttered.

'Yeah, well, poor everybody,' Marino said.

7

_____

Rain was slanted and flying down like nails as I made my way home, scarcely able to see. I had turned the radio off because I did not want to hear any more news this day, and I was certain this would be one night when I was too keyed up to sleep. Twice I slowed to thirty miles an hour as my heavy Mercedes sedan splashed through water like a cigarette boat. On West Cary Street, dips and potholes were filled like tubs, and emergency lights streaking red and blue through the downpour reminded me to take my time.

It was almost ten o'clock when I finally pulled into my driveway and a note of fear was plucked in my heart when motion sensor lights did not come on near the garage door. The darkness was complete, with only the rumble of my car engine and drumming of rain to orient my senses as to what world I was in. For a moment, I deliberated about opening the garage door or speeding away.

'This is ridiculous,' I said to myself as I pressed a button on the visor.

But the door did not respond.

'Damn!'

I shifted the car into reverse and backed up without being able to see the driveway or brick border or even the shrubbery, for that matter. The tree I swiped was small and did no harm, but I felt sure I had churned up part of the lawn as I maneuvered to the front of my house, where timers inside had at least turned lamps on and the light

in the foyer. As for motion sensor lights on either side of the front
steps, they were out, too. I reasonably told myself that the weather
had caused a power outage earlier in the evening, causing a circuit
breaker to be thrown.

Rain swept into my car as I opened the door. I grabbed my pocketbook and briefcase and bolted up the front steps. I was soaked to
the skin by the time I unlocked the front door, and the silence that
greeted me thrilled me with fear. Lights dancing across the keypad
by the door meant the burglar alarm had gone off, or perhaps an
electrical surge had screwed that up, too. But it did not matter. By
now I was terrified and afraid to move. So I stood in the foyer, water
dripping on the hardwood floor as my brain raced to the nearest
gun.

I could not remember if I had returned the Glock to a drawer of
the kitchen desk. That certainly would be closer than my office or
bedroom, which were on the other side of the house. Stone walls and
windows were buffeted by the wind and lashed by rain, and I strained
to hear any other sounds, such as the creaking of an upstairs floor
or feet on carpet. In a burst of panic, I suddenly dropped my briefcase and pocketbook from my hands and ran through the dining room
and into the kitchen, my wet feet almost going out from under me.
I yanked open the bottom right drawer in the desk and almost cried
out in relief when I grabbed my Glock.

For a while I searched my house again, flipping on lights in every
room. Satisfied that I had no unwanted guests, I checked the fuse box
in the garage and flipped on the breakers that had tripped. Order
was restored, the alarm reset, and I poured a tumbler of Black Bush
Irish whiskey on the rocks and waited for my nerves to tuck themselves back inside their sheaths. Then I called Johnson's Motel in
Warrenton, but Lucy was not there. So I tried her apartment in D.C.
and Janet answered the phone.

'Hi, it's Kay,' I said. 'I hope I didn't wake anyone.'

'Oh, hello, Dr Scarpetta,' said Janet, who could not call me by my
first name no matter how many times I had told her to. 'No, I'm just
sitting here having a beer and waiting for Lucy.'

'I see,' I said, very disappointed. 'She's on her way home from
Warrenton?'

'Not for long. You ought to see this place. Boxes everywhere. It's
a wreck.'

'How are you holding up through all this, Janet?'

'I don't know yet,' she said, and I detected a quiver in her voice.

'It will be an adjustment. God knows, we've been through adjustments before.'

'And I'm sure you'll get through this one with flying colors.'

I sipped my whiskey and had no faith in what I'd just said, but at the moment I was grateful to hear a warm human voice.

'When I was married – ancient years ago – Tony and I were on two totally different planes,' I said. 'But we managed to find time for each other, quality time. In some ways, it was better like that.'

'And you also got divorced,' she politely pointed out.

'Not at first.'

'Lucy won't be here for at least another hour, Dr Scarpetta. Is there a message I can give her?'

I hesitated, not sure what to do.

'Is everything all right?' Janet then asked.

'Actually, no,' I said. 'I guess you haven't heard. I guess she hasn't heard either, for that matter.'

I gave her a quick summary of Carrie's letter to the press, and after I had finished, Janet was as silent as a cathedral.

'I'm telling you because you'd better be prepared,' I added. 'You could wake up tomorrow and see this in the paper. You might hear it on the late news tonight.'

'It's best you told me,' Janet said so quietly I could barely hear her. 'And I'll let Lucy know when she gets in.'

'Tell her to call me, if she's not too tired.'

'I'll tell her.'

'Good night, Janet.'

'No, it isn't. It isn't a good night at all,' she said. 'That bitch has been ruining our lives for years. One way or another. And I've fucking had enough of it! And I'm sorry to use that word.'

'I've said it before.'

'I was there, for God's sake!' She began to cry. 'Carrie was all over her, the manipulative psycho bitch. Lucy never stood a chance. My God, she was just a kid, this genius kid who probably should have stayed in college where she belonged instead of doing an internship with the Fucking Bureau of Investigation. Look, I'm still FBI, okay? But I see the shit. And they haven't done right by her, which just makes her all the more vulnerable to what Carrie is doing.'

My whiskey was half gone, and there wasn't enough of it in the world to make me feel better right now.

'She doesn't need to get upset, either,' Janet went on in a gush of frankness about her lover that I had never before heard. 'I don't know if she's told you. In fact, I don't think she ever intended to, but Lucy's been seeing a psychiatrist for two years, Dr Scarpetta.'

'Good. I'm glad to hear it,' I said, disguising my hurt. 'No, she hasn't told me, but I wouldn't necessarily expect her to,' I added with the perfect voice of objectivity as the ache in my heart got more intense.

'She's been suicidal,' Janet said. 'More than once.'

'I'm glad she's seeing someone,' was all I could think to say as tears welled.

I was devastated. Why had Lucy not reached out to me?

'Most of the great achievers have their very dark passages,' I said. 'I'm just glad she's doing something about it. Is she taking anything?'

'Wellbutrin. Prozac weirded her out. One minute a zombie and bar-hopping the next.'

'Oh.' I could barely speak.

'She doesn't need any more stress or upheavals or rejections,' Janet went on. 'You don't know what it's like. Something knocks her off balance, and she's down for weeks, up and down, up and down, morbid and miserable one minute and Mighty Mouse the next.'

She placed her hand over the receiver and blew her nose. I wanted to know the name of Lucy's psychiatrist but was afraid to ask. I wondered if my niece were bipolar and undiagnosed.

'Dr Scarpetta, I don't want her . . .' She struggled, choking. 'I don't want her to die.'

'She won't,' I said. 'I can promise you that.'

We hung up and I sat for a while on my bed, still dressed and afraid to sleep because of the chaos inside my head. For a while I wept in fury and in pain. Lucy could hurt me more than anyone, and she knew it. She could bruise me to the bone and crush my heart, and what Janet had told me was, by far, the most devastating blow. I could not help but think of Teun McGovern's inquisitive mind when we had talked in my office, and she had seemed to know so much about Lucy's difficulties. Had Lucy told her and not me?

I waited for Lucy to call, and she didn't. Since I had not called Benton, at midnight, he finally called me.

'Kay?'

'Have you heard?' I said with feeling. 'What Carrie has done?'

'I know about her letter.'

'Damn it, Benton. Damn it all.'

'I'm in New York,' he surprised me by saying. 'The Bureau's called me in.'

'Well, okay. And they should have. You know her.'

'Unfortunately.'

'I'm glad you're there,' I decided out loud. 'Somehow it seems safer. Isn't that an ironical thing to say? Since when is New York safer?'

'You're very upset.'

'Do you know anything more about where she is?' I swirled melting ice in my glass.

'We know she mailed her latest letter from a 10036 zip code, which is Times Square. The postdate is June tenth, yesterday, Tuesday.'

'The day she escaped.'

'Yes.'

'And we still don't know how she did that.'

'We still don't know,' he said. 'It's as if she beamed herself across the river.'

'No, it's not like that,' I said, weary and out of sorts. 'Someone saw something and someone probably helped her. She's always been skilled at getting people to do what she wants.'

'The profiling unit's had too many calls to count,' he said. 'Apparently she did a blitz mailing, all the major newspapers, including the *Post* and *The New York Times*.'

'And?'

'And this is too juicy for them to drop in a basket, Kay. The hunt for her is as big as the one for the Unabomber or Cunanan, and now she's writing to the media. The story's going to run. Hell, they'll print her grocery list and broadcast her belches. To them she's gold. She's magazine covers and movies in the making.'

'I don't want to hear anymore,' I said.

'I miss you.'

'You wouldn't if you were around me right now, Benton.'

We said good night and I fluffed the pillow behind my back and contemplated another whiskey but thought better of it. I tried to imagine what Carrie would do, and the twisted path always led back to Lucy. Somehow, that would be Carrie's tour de force because she was consumed by envy. Lucy was more gifted, more honorable, more everything, and Carrie would not rest until she had appropriated that fierce beauty and sucked up every drop of Lucy's life. It was becoming clear to me that Carrie did not even need to be present to do it. All of us were moving closer to her black hole, and the power of her pull was shockingly strong.

My sleep was tortured, and I dreamed of plane crashes and sheets soaked with blood. I was in a car and then a train, and someone was chasing me. When I awakened at half past six, the sun was announcing itself in a royal blue sky, and puddles gleamed in the grass. I carried my Glock into the bathroom, locked the door and took a quick shower. When I shut the water off, I listened closely to make sure my burglar alarm wasn't going, and then I checked the keypad in my bedroom to make sure the system was still armed. All the while, I was aware of how paranoid and downright irrational my behavior was. But I could not help it. I was scared.

Suddenly Carrie was everywhere. She was the thin woman in sunglasses and baseball cap walking along my street, or the driver pulling up close behind me at the toll plaza, or the homeless woman in a shapeless coat who stared at me as I crossed Broad Street. She was anyone white with punk hair and body piercing, or anyone androgynous or oddly dressed, and all the while I kept telling myself I had not seen Carrie in more than five years. I had no idea what she looked like now and quite possibly would not recognize her until it was too late.

The bay door was open when I parked behind my office, and Bliley's Funeral Home was loading a body into the back of a shiny black hearse, as the rhythm continued of bringing and taking away.

'Pretty weather,' I said to the attendant in his neat dark suit.

'Fine, how are you?' came the reply of someone who no longer listened.

Another well-dressed man climbed out to help, and stretcher legs clacked and the tailgate slammed shut. I waited for them to drive off, and I rolled down the big door after them.

My first stop was Fielding's office. It was not quite quarter after eight.

'How are we doing?' I asked as I knocked on his door.

'Come in,' he said.

He was scanning books on his shelves, his lab coat straining around his powerful shoulders. Life was difficult for my deputy chief, who rarely could find clothes that fit, since he basically had no waist or hips. I remembered our first company picnic at my house, when he had lounged in the sun with nothing but cut-offs on. I had been amazed and slightly embarrassed that I could scarcely take my eyes off him, not because I had any thoughts of bed, but rather his raw physical beauty had briefly held me hostage. I could not comprehend how anyone could find time to look like that.

'I guess you've seen the paper,' he said.

'The letter,' I said as my mood sunk.

'Yes.'

He slid out an outdated PDR and set it on the floor.

'Front page with a photo of you and an old mug shot of her. I'm sorry you have to put up with shit like this,' he said, hunting for other books. 'The phones up front are going crazy.'

'What have we got this morning?' I changed the subject.

'Last night's car wreck from Midlothian Turnpike, passenger and driver killed. They're views, and DeMaio's already started on them. Other than that, nothing else.'

'That's enough,' I said. 'I've got court.'

'Thought you were on vacation.'

'So did I.'

'Seriously. Didn't get it continued. What? You were gonna have to come back from Hilton Head?'

'Judge Bowls.'

'Huh,' Fielding said with disgust. 'He's done this to you how many times now? I think he waits to find out your void dates so he can decide on a court date that will totally screw you. Then what? You bust your butt to get back here and half the time he continues the case.'

'I'm on the pager,' I said.

'And you can guess what I'll be doing.'

He pointed at the paperwork cascading from piles on his desk.

'I'm so behind I need a rearview mirror,' he quipped.

'There's no point in nagging you,' I said.

The John Marshall Courts Building was but a ten-minute walk from our new location, and I thought the exercise would do me good. The morning was bright, the air cool and clean as I followed the sidewalk along Leigh Street and turned south on Ninth, passing police head-quarters, my pocketbook over my shoulder and an accordion file tucked under an arm.

This morning's case was the mundane result of one drug dealer killing another, and I was surprised to see at least a dozen reporters on the third floor, outside the courtroom door. At first I thought Rose had made a mistake on my schedule, for it never occurred to me that the media might have been there for me.

But the minute I was spotted, they hurried my way with tele-vision cameras shouldered, microphones pointed, and flashguns going off. At first I was startled, then I was angry.

'Dr Scarpetta, what is your response to Carrie Grethen's letter?' asked a reporter from Channel 6.

'No comment,' I said as I frantically cast about for the commonwealth's attorney who had summoned me here to testify in his case.

'What about the conspiracy allegation?'

'Between you and your FBI lover?'

'That would be Benton Wesley?'

'What is your niece's reaction?'

I shoved past a cameraman, my nerves hopping like faulty wiring as my heart flew. I shut myself inside the small windowless witness room and sat in a wooden chair. I felt trapped and foolish, and wondered how I could have been so thick as not to consider that something like this might happen after what Carrie had done. I opened the accordion file and began going through various reports and diagrams, envisioning gunshot entrances and exits and which had been fatal. I stayed in my airless space for almost half an hour until the Commonwealth's attorney found me. We spoke for several minutes before I took the stand.

What ensued brought to fruition what had happened in the hallway moments before, and I found myself disassociating from the core of myself to survive what was nothing more than a ruthless attack.

'Dr Scarpetta,' said defense attorney Will Lampkin, who had been trying to get the best of me for years, 'how many times have you testified in this court?'

'I object,' said the C.A.

'Overruled,' said Judge Bowls, my fan.

'I've never counted,' I replied.

'But surely you can give us an estimate. More than a dozen? More than a hundred? A million?'

'More than a hundred,' I said as I felt his lust for blood.

'And you have always told the truth to the juries and the judges?'

Lampkin paced slowly, a pious expression on his florid face, hands clamped behind his back.

'I have always told the truth,' I answered.

'And you don't consider it somewhat dishonest, Dr Scarpetta, to sleep with the FBI?'

'I object!' The C.A. was on his feet.

'Objection sustained,' said the judge as he stared down at Lampkin, egging him on, really. 'What is your point, Mr Lampkin?'

'My point, Your Honor, is conflict of interest. It is widely known that Dr Scarpetta has an intimate relationship with at least one law enforcement individual she has worked cases with, and she has also influenced law enforcement – both the FBI and ATF – when it comes to her niece's career.'

'I object!'

'Overruled. Please get to the point, Mr Lampkin,' said the judge as he reached for his water and goaded some more.

'Thank you, Your Honor,' Lampkin said with excruciating deference. 'What I'm trying to illustrate is an old pattern here.'

The four whites and eight blacks sat politely in the jury box, staring back and forth from Lampkin to me as if they were watching a tennis match. Some of them were scowling. One was picking at a fingernail while another seemed asleep.

'Dr Scarpetta, isn't it true that you tend to manipulate situations to suit you?'

'I object! He's badgering the witness!'

'Overruled,' the judge said. 'Dr Scarpetta, please answer the question.'

'No, I absolutely do not tend to do that,' I said with feeling as I looked at the jurors.

Lampkin plucked a sheet of paper off the table where his felonious nineteen-year-old client sat.

'According to this morning's newspaper,' Lampkin hurried ahead, 'you've been manipulating law enforcement for years . . .'

'Your Honor! I object! This is outrageous!'

'Overruled,' the judge coolly stated.

'It says right here in black and white that you have conspired with the FBI to send an innocent woman to the electric chair!'

Lampkin approached the jurors and waved the photocopied article in their faces.

'Your Honor, for God's sake!' exclaimed the C.A., sweating through his suit jacket.

'Mr Lampkin, please get on with your cross-examination,' Judge Bowls said to the overweight, thick-necked Lampkin.

What I said about distance and trajectories, and what vital organs had been struck by ten-millimeter bullets, was a blur. I could scarcely remember a word of it after I hurried down the courthouse steps and walked swiftly without looking at anyone. Two tenacious reporters followed me for half a block, and finally turned back when they realized it was easier to talk to a stone. The unfairness of what had happened in the witness stand went beyond words. Carrie had needed to fire but one small round and already I was wounded. I knew this would not end.

When I unlocked the back door to my building, for an instant the glare of sunlight made it hard for me to see as I stepped inside the cool shaded bay. I opened the door leading inside and was relieved to see Fielding in the corridor, heading toward me. He was wearing fresh scrubs, and I supposed another case had come in.

'Everything under control?' I asked, tucking my sunglasses inside my pocketbook.

'A suicide from Powhatan. Fifteen-year-old girl shot herself in the head. It seems daddy wouldn't let her see her dirtbag boyfriend anymore. You look terrible, Kay.'

'It's called a shark attack.'

'Uh oh. Damn fucking lawyers. Who was it this time?'

He was ready to beat somebody up.

'Lampkin.'

'Oh, good ole *Lamprey the eel!*' Fielding squeezed my shoulder. 'It's gonna be all right. Trust me. It really will be. You just gotta block out the bullshit and go on.'

'I know.' I smiled at him. 'I'll be in the decomp room if you need me.'

The solitary task of patiently working on bones was a welcome relief, for I did not want anyone on my staff to detect my dejection and fear. I switched on lights and shut the door behind me. I tied a gown over my clothes and pulled on two layers of latex gloves, and turned on the electric burner and took the lid off the pot. The bones had continued processing after I had left last night, and I probed them with a wooden spoon. I spread a plasticized sheet over a table. The skull had been sawn open during autopsy, and I carefully lifted the dripping calvarium, and the bones of the face with its calcined teeth, from tepid, greasy water. I set them on the sheet to drain.

I preferred wooden tongue depressors versus plastic spatulas to scrape tissue from bone. Metal instruments were out of the question because they would cause damage that might obviate our finding true marks of violence. I worked very carefully, loosening and defleshing while the rest of the skeletal remains quietly cooked in their steamy pot. For two hours I cleaned and rinsed until my wrists and fingers ached. I missed lunch, and in fact never thought of it. At almost two P.M. I found a nick in the bone beneath the temporal region where I had found hemorrhage, and I stopped and stared in disbelief.

I pulled surgical lamps closer, blasting the table with light. The cut to bone was straight and linear, no more than an inch in length and so shallow it easily could have been missed. The only time I had ever seen an injury similar to this was in the nineteenth-century skulls of people who had been scalped. In those instances, the nicks or cuts were not generally associated with temporal bone, but that meant nothing, really.

Scalping was not an exact surgical procedure and anything was possible. Although I had found no evidence that the Warrenton victim was missing areas of scalp and hair, I could not swear to it. Certainly, when we had found her, the head was not intact, and while a scalping trophy might involve most of the cranium, it might also mean the excision of a single lock of hair.

I used a towel to pick up the phone because my hands were unfit to touch anything clean. I paged Marino. For ten minutes I waited for him to call back while I continued to carefully scrape. But I found no other marks. This did not mean, of course, that additional injury had not been lost, for at least a third of the twenty-two bones of the skull were burned away. My mind raced through what I should do. I yanked off my gloves and threw them in the trash, and I was flipping through an address book I had gotten out of my purse when Marino called.

'Where the hell are you?' I asked as stress gushed toxins through my body.

'At Liberty Valance eating.'

'Thank you for getting back to me so quickly,' I said irritably.

'Gee, Doc. It must've been lost in space somewhere, because I just got it. What the shit's going on?'

I could hear the background noise of people drinking and enjoying food that was guaranteed to be heavy and rich but worth it.

'Are you on a pay phone?' I asked.

'Yeah, and I'm off duty, just so you know.'

He took a swallow of something that I figured was beer.

'I've got to get to Washington tomorrow. Something significant has come up.'

'Uh oh. I hate it when you say that.'

'I found something else.'

'You gonna tell me or do I have to stay up all night pacing?'

He had been drinking, and I did not want to talk to him about this now.

'Listen, can you go with me, assuming Dr Vessey can see us?'

'The bones man at the Smithsonian?'

'I'll call him at home as soon as we get off the phone.'

'I'm off tomorrow, so I guess I can squeeze you in.'

I did not say anything as I stared at the simmering pot and turned the heat down just a little.

'Point is, count me in,' Marino said, swallowing again.

'Meet me at my house,' I said. 'At nine.'

'I'll be there with bells on.'

Next I tried Dr Vessey's Bethesda home and he answered on the first ring.

'Thank God,' I said. 'Alex? It's Kay Scarpetta.'

'Oh! Well, how are you?'

He was always a bit befuddled and missing in action in the minds of the hoi polloi who did not spend their lives putting people back together again. Dr Vessey was one of the finest forensic anthropologists in the world, and he had helped me many times before.

'I'll be much better if you tell me you're in town tomorrow,' I said.

'I'll be working on the railroad as always.'

'I've got a cut mark on a skull. I need your help. Are you familiar with the Warrenton fire?'

'Can't be conscious and not know about that.'

'Okay. Then you understand.'

'I won't be there until about ten and there's no place to park,' he said. 'I got in a pig's tooth the other day with aluminum foil stuck in it,' he absently went on about whatever he'd been doing of late. 'I guess from a pig roast, dug up in someone's backyard. The Mississippi coroner thought it was a homicide, some guy shot in the mouth.'

He coughed and loudly cleared his throat. I heard him drink something.

'Still getting bear paws now and then,' he went on, 'more coroners thinking they're human hands.'

'I know, Alex,' I said. 'Nothing has changed.'

8

———

Marino pulled into my driveway early, at quarter of nine, because he wanted coffee and something to eat. He was officially not working, so he was dressed in blue jeans, a Richmond Police T-shirt, and cowboy boots that had lived a full life. He had slicked back what little hair had weathered his years, and he looked like an old beer-bellied bachelor about to take his woman to Billy Bob's.

'Are we going to a rodeo?' I asked as I let him in.

'You know, you always have a way of pissing me off.'

He gave me a sour look that didn't faze me in the least. He didn't mean it.

'Well, I think you look pretty cool, as Lucy would say. I've got coffee and granola.'

'How many times do I got to tell you that I don't eat friggin' bird-seed,' he grumbled as he followed me through my house.

'And I don't cook steak-egg biscuits.'

'Well, maybe if you did, you wouldn't spend so many evenings alone.'

'I hadn't thought about that.'

'Did the Smithsonian tell you where we was going to park up there? Because there's no parking in D.C.'

'Nowhere in the entire district? The President should do something about that.'

We were inside my kitchen, and the sun was gold on windows

facing it, while the southern exposure caught the river glinting through trees. I had slept better last night, although I had no idea why, unless my brain had been so overloaded it simply had died. I remembered no dreams, and was grateful.

'I got a couple of VIP parking passes from the last time Clinton was in town,' Marino said, helping himself to coffee. 'Issued by the mayor's office.'

He poured coffee for me, too, and slid the mug my way, like a mug of beer on the bar.

'I figured with your Benz and those, maybe the cops would think we have diplomatic immunity or something,' he went on.

'I'm supposing you've seen the boots they put on cars up there.'

I sliced a poppyseed bagel, then opened the refrigerator door to take an inventory.

'I've got Swiss, Vermont cheddar, prosciutto.'

I opened another plastic drawer.

'And Parmesan reggiano – that wouldn't be very good. No cream cheese. Sorry. But I think I've got honey, if you'd rather have that.'

'What about a Vidalia onion?' he asked, looking over my shoulder.

'That I have.'

'Swiss, prosciutto, and a slice of onion is just what the doctor ordered,' Marino said happily. 'Now that's what I call a breakfast.'

'No butter,' I told him. 'I have to draw the line somewhere so I don't feel responsible for your sudden death.'

'Deli mustard would be good,' he said.

I spread spicy yellow mustard, then added prosciutto and onion with the cheese on top, and by the time the toaster oven had heated up, I was consumed by cravings. I fixed the same concoction for myself and poured my granola back into its tin. We sat at my kitchen table and drank Columbian coffee and ate while sunlight painted the flowers in my yard in vibrant hues, and the sky turned a brilliant blue. We were on I-95 North by nine-thirty, and fought little traffic until Quantico.

As I drove past the exit for the FBI Academy and Marine Corps base, I was tugged by days that no longer were, by memories of my relationship with Benton when it was new, and my anxious pride over Lucy's accomplishments in a law enforcement agency that remained as much a politically correct all-boys club as it had been during the reign of Hoover. Only now, the Bureau's prejudices and power-mongering were more covert as it marched forward like an army in the night, capturing jurisdictions and credits wherever it could as it pushed closer to becoming the official federal police force of America.

Such realizations had been devastating to me and were largely left unspoken, because I did not want to hurt the individual agent in the field who worked hard and had given his heart to what he believed was a noble calling. I could feel Marino looking at me as he tapped an ash out his window.

'You know, Doc,' he said. 'Maybe you should resign.'

He referred to my long-held position as the consulting forensic pathologist for the Bureau.

'I know they're using other medical examiners these days,' he went on. 'Bringing them in on cases instead of calling you. Let's face it, you haven't been to the Academy in over a year, and that's not an accident. They don't want to deal with you because of what they did to Lucy.'

'I can't resign,' I said, 'because I don't work for them, Marino. I work for cops who need help with their cases and turn to the Bureau. There's no way I'll be the one who quits. And things go in cycles. Directors and attorneys general come and go, and maybe someday things will be better again. Besides, you are still a consultant for them, and they don't seem to call you, either.'

'Yo. Well, I guess I feel the same way you do.'

He pitched his cigarette butt and it sailed behind us on the wind of my speeding car.

'It sucks, don't it? Going up there and working with good people and drinking beer in the Boardroom. It all gets to me, if you want to know. People hating cops and cops hating 'em back. When I was getting started, old folks, kids, parents – they was happy to see me. I was proud to put on the uniform and shined my shoes every day. Now, after twenty years, I get bricks throwed at me in the projects and citizens don't even answer if I say good morning. I work my ass off for twenty-six years, and they promote me to captain and put me in charge of the training bureau.'

'That's probably the place where you can do the most good,' I reminded him.

'Yeah, but that's not why I got stuck there.'

He stared out his side window, watching green highway signs fly by.

'They're putting me out to pasture, hoping I'll hurry up and retire or die. And I gotta tell you, Doc, I think about it a lot. Taking the boat out, fishing, taking the RV on the road and maybe going out west to see the Grand Canyon, Yosemite, Lake Tahoe, all those places I've always heard about. But then when it gets right down to it, I wouldn't know what to do with myself. So I just think I'll croak in the saddle.'

'Not anytime soon,' I said. 'And should you retire, Marino, you can do like Benton.'

'With all due respect, I ain't the consultant type,' he said. 'The Institute of Justice and IBM ain't gonna hire a slob like me. Doesn't matter what I know.'

I didn't disagree or offer another word, because, with rare exception, what he had said was true. Benton was handsome and polished and commanded respect when he walked into a room, and that was really the only difference between him and Pete Marino. Both were honest and compassionate and experts in their fields.

'All right, we need to pick up 395 and head over to Constitution,' I thought out loud as I watched signs and ignored urgent drivers riding my bumper and darting around me because going the speed limit wasn't fast enough. 'What we don't want to do is go too far and end up on Maine Avenue. I've done that before.'

I flicked on my right turn signal.

'On a Friday night when I was coming up to see Lucy.'

'A good way to get carjacked,' Marino said.

'Almost did.'

'No shit?' He looked over at me. 'What'd you do?'

'They started circling my car, so I floored it.'

'Run anybody over?'

'Almost.'

'Would you have kept on going, Doc? I mean, if you had run one of them over?'

'With at least a dozen of his buddies left, you bet your boots.'

'Well, I'll tell you one thing,' he said, looking down at his feet. 'They ain't worth much.'

Fifteen minutes later we were on Constitution, passing the Department of the Interior while the Washington Monument watched over the Mall, where tents had been set up to celebrate African American art, and venders sold Eastern Shore crabs and T-shirts from the backs of small trucks. The grass between kiosks was depressingly layered with yesterday's trash, and every other minute another ambulance screamed past. We had driven in circles several times, the Smithsonian coiled in the distance like a dark red dragon. There was not a parking place to be found and, typically, streets were one way or abruptly stopped in the middle of a block, while others were barricaded, and harried commuters did not yield even if it meant your running into the back of a parked bus.

'I tell you what I think we should do,' I said, turning on Virginia Avenue. 'We'll valet park at the Watergate and take a cab.'

'Who the hell would want to live in a city like this?' Marino griped.

'Unfortunately, a lot of people.'

'Talk about a place that's screwed up,' he went on. 'Welcome to America.'

The uniformed valet at the Watergate was very gracious and did not seem to think it odd when I gave him my car and asked him to hail a cab. My precious cargo was in the backseat, packed in a sturdy cardboard box filled with Styrofoam peanuts. Marino and I were let out at Twelfth and Constitution at not quite noon, and climbed the crowded steps of the National Museum of Natural History. Security had been intensified since the Oklahoma bombing, and the guard let us know that Dr Vessey would have to come down and escort us upstairs.

While we waited, we perused an exhibit called *Jewels of the Sea*, browsing Atlantic thorny oysters and Pacific lions' paws while the skull of a duckbill dinosaur watched us from a wall. There were eels and fish and crabs in jars, and tree snails and a mosasaur marine lizard found in a Kansas chalk bed. Marino was beginning to get bored when the bright brass elevator doors opened and Dr Alex Vessey stepped out. He had changed little since I had seen him last, still slight of build, with white hair and prepossessed eyes that, like those of so many geniuses, were perpetually focused somewhere else. His face was tan and perhaps more lined, and he still wore the same thick black-framed glasses.

'You're looking robust,' I said to him as we shook hands.

'I just got back from vacation. Charleston. I trust you've been there?' he said as the three of us boarded the elevator.

'Yes,' I replied. 'I know the chief there very well. You remember Captain Marino?'

'Of course.'

We rose three levels above the eight-ton African bush elephant in the rotunda, the voices of children floating up like wisps of smoke. The museum was, in truth, little more than a huge granite warehouse. Some thirty thousand human skeletons were stored in green wooden drawers stacked from floor to ceiling. It was a rare collection used to study people of the past, specifically Native Americans who of late had been determined to get their ancestors' bones back. Laws had been passed, and Vessey had been through hell on the Hill, his life's work halfway out the door and headed back to the not-so-wild west.

'We've got a repatriation staff that collects data to supply to this group and that,' he was saying as we accompanied him along a crowded, dim corridor. 'Respective tribes have to be informed as to what we've got, and it's really up to them to determine what's done. In another couple years, our American Indian material may be back in the earth again, only to be dug up again by archaeologists in the next century, my guess is.'

He talked on as he walked.

'Every group is so angry these days they don't realize how much they're hurting themselves. If we don't learn from the dead, who do we learn from?'

'Alex, you're singing to the choir,' I said.

'Yeah, well, if it was my great-grandfather in one of these drawers,' Marino retorted, 'I'm not so sure I'd feel too good about that.'

'But the point is we don't know *who* is in these drawers, and neither do any of the people who are upset,' said Vessey. 'What we do know is that these specimens have helped us know a lot more about the diseases of the American Indian population, which is clearly a benefit to those now feeling threatened. Oh well, don't get me started.'

Where Vessey worked was a series of small laboratory rooms that were a jumble of black counter space and sinks, and thousands of books and boxes of slides, and professional journals. Displayed here and there were the usual shrunken heads and shattered skulls and various animal bones mistaken as human. On a corkboard were large, painful photographs of the aftermath of Waco, where Vessey had spent weeks recovering and identifying the decomposing burned remains of Branch Davidians.

'Let's see what you've got for me,' Vessey said.

I set my package on a counter and he slit the tape with a pocket knife. Styrofoam rattled as I dug out the cranium, then the very fragile lower portion of the skull that included the bones of the face. I set these on a clean blue cloth and he turned on lamps and fetched a lens.

'Right here,' I directed him to the fine cut on bone. 'It corresponds with hemorrhage in the temporal area. But around it, the flesh was too burned for me to tell anything about what sort of injury we were dealing with. I didn't have a clue until I found this on the bone.'

'A very straight incision,' he said as he slowly turned the skull to look at it from different angles. 'And we're certain this wasn't perhaps accidentally done during autopsy, when, for example, the scalp was reflected back to remove the skull cap?'

'We're certain,' I said. 'And as you can see by putting the two together' – I fit the cranium back in place – 'the cut is about an inch and a half below where the skull was opened during autopsy. And it's an angle that would make no sense if one were reflecting back the scalp. See?'

My index finger was suddenly huge as I looked through the lens and pointed.

'This incision is vertical versus horizontal,' I made my case.

'You're right,' he said, and his face was vibrant with interest. 'As an artifact of autopsy, that would make no sense at all, unless your morgue assistant was drunk.'

'Could it be maybe some kind of defense injury?' Marino suggested. 'You know, if someone was coming at her with a knife. They struggle and her face gets cut?'

'Certainly that's possible,' Vessey said as he continued to process every millimeter of bone. 'But I find it curious that this incision is so fine and exact. And it appears to be the same depth from one end to the other, which would be unusual if one is swinging a knife at someone. Generally, the cut to bone would be deeper where the blade struck first, and then more shallow as the blade traveled down.'

He demonstrated, an imaginary knife cutting straight down through air.

'We also have to remember that a lot depends on the assailant's position in relation to the victim when she was cut,' I commented. 'Was the victim standing or lying down? Was the assailant in front or behind or to one side of her or on top of her?'

'Very true,' said Vessey.

He went to a dark oak cabinet with glass doors and lifted an old brown skull from a shelf. He carried it over to us and handed it to me, pointing to an obvious coarse cut in the left parietal and occipital area, or on the left side, high above the ear.

'You asked about scalpings,' he said to me. 'An eight- or nine-year-old, scalped, then burned. Can't tell the gender, but I know the poor kid had a foot infection. So he or she couldn't run. Cuts and nicks like this are fairly typical in scalpings.'

I held the skull and for a moment imagined what Vessey had just said. I envisioned a cowering crippled child, and blood running to the earth as his screaming people were massacred and the camp went up in flames.

'Shit,' Marino muttered angrily. 'How do you do something like that to a kid?'

'How do you do something like that at all?' I said. Then to Vessey, I added, 'The cut on this' – I pointed at the skull I had brought in – 'would be unusual for a scalping.'

Vessey took a deep breath and slowly blew out.

'You know, Kay,' he said, 'it's never exact. It's whatever happened at the time. There were many ways that Indians scalped the enemy. Usually, the skin was incised in a circle over the skull down to the galea and periosteum so it could be easily removed from the cranial vault. Some scalpings were simple, others involved ears, eyes, the face, the neck. In some instances multiple scalps were taken from the same victim, or maybe just the scalplock, or small area of the crown of the head, was removed. Finally, and this is what you usually see in old westerns, the victim was violently grabbed by his hair, the skin sliced away with a knife or saber.'

'Trophies,' Marino said.

'That and the ultimate macho symbol of skill and bravery,' said Vessey. 'Of course, there were cultural, religious, and even medicinal motives, as well. In your case,' he added to me, 'we know she wasn't successfully scalped because she still had her hair, and I can tell you the injury to bone strikes me as having been inflicted carefully with a very sharp instrument. A very sharp knife. Maybe a razor blade or box cutter, or even something like a scalpel. It was inflicted while the victim was alive and it was not the cause of death.'

'No, her neck injury is what killed her,' I agreed.

'I can find no other cuts, except possibly here.'

He moved the lens closer to an area of the left zygomatic arch, or bone of the cheek. 'Something very faint,' he muttered. 'Too faint to be sure. See it?'

I leaned close to him to look.

'Maybe,' I said. 'Almost like the thread of a spider web.'

'Exactly. It's that faint. And it may be nothing, but interestingly enough, it's positioned at very much the same angle as the other cut. Vertical versus horizonal or slanted.'

'This is getting sick,' Marino said ominously. 'I mean, let's cut to the chase, no pun intended. What are we saying here? That some squirrel cut this lady's throat and mutilated her face? And then torched the house?'

'I guess that's one possibility,' Vessey said.

'Well, mutilating a face gets personal,' Marino went on. 'Unless you're dealing with a loony tune, you don't find killers mutilating the faces of victims they don't have some sort of connection with.'

'As a rule, this is true,' I agreed. 'In my experience where it hasn't been true is when the assailant is very disorganized and turns out to be psychotic.'

'Whoever burned Sparkes's farm was anything but disorganized, you ask me,' Marino said.

'So you're contemplating that this might be a homicide of a more domestic nature,' Vessey said, now slowly scanning the cranium with the lens.

'We have to contemplate everything,' I said. 'But if nothing else, when I try to imagine Sparkes killing all his horses, I just can't see it.'

'Maybe he had to kill them to get away with murder,' Marino said. 'So people would say what you just did.'

'Alex,' I said, 'whoever did this to her made very sure we would never find a cut mark. And were it not for a glass door falling on top of her, there probably would have been virtually nothing of her left that would have given us any clue as to what happened. If we had recovered no tissue, for example, we wouldn't have known she was dead before the fire because we wouldn't be able to get a CO level. So what happens? She gets signed out as an accidental death, unless we prove arson, which so far we've been unable to do.'

'There's no doubt in my mind that this is a classic case of arson-concealed homicide,' Vessey said.

'Then why the hell hang around to cut on somebody?' Marino said. 'Why not kill her and torch the joint and run like hell? And usually when these whackos mutilate, they get off on people seeing their handiwork. Hell, they display the bodies in a park, on a hillside next to a road, on a jogging trail, in the middle of the living room, right there for all to see.'

'Maybe this person doesn't want us to see,' I said. 'It's very important that we not know he left a signature this time. And I think we need to run as exhaustive a computer search as we can, to see if anything even remotely similar to this has turned up anywhere else.'

'You do that, and you bring in a lot of other people,' Marino said. 'Programmers, analysts, guys who run the computers at the FBI and big police departments like Houston, L.A., and New York. I guarantee you, someone's going to spill the beans and next thing this shit's all over the news.'

'Not necessarily,' I said. 'It depends on who you ask.'

*   *   *

We caught a cab on Constitution and told the driver to head toward the White House and cut over to the six hundred block of Fifteenth Street. I intended to treat Marino to the Old Ebbitt Grill, and at half past five, we did not have to wait in line but got a green velvet booth. I had always found a special pleasure in the restaurant's stained glass, mirrors, and brass gas lamps wavering with flames. Turtles, boars, and antelopes were mounted over the bar, and the bartenders never seemed to slow down no matter the time of day.

A distinguished-looking husband and wife behind us were talking about Kennedy Center tickets and their son's entering Harvard in the fall, while two young men debated whether lunch could go on the expense account. I parked my cardboard box next to me on the seat. Vessey had resealed it with yards of tape.

'I guess we should have asked for a table for three,' Marino said, looking at the box. 'You sure it doesn't stink? What if someone caught a whiff of it in here?'

'It doesn't stink,' I said, opening my menu. 'And I think it would be wise to change the subject so we can eat. The burger here is so good that even I break down now and then and order it.'

'I'm looking at the fish,' he said with great affectation. 'You ever had them here?'

'Go to hell, Marino.'

'All right, you talked me into it, Doc. Burger it is. I wish it were the end of the day so I could have a beer. It's torture to come to a joint like this and not have Jack Black or a tall one in a frosted mug. I bet they make mint juleps. I haven't had one of those since I was dating that girl from Kentucky. Sabrina. Remember her?'

'Maybe if you describe her,' I said absently as I looked around and tried to relax.

'I used to bring her into the FOP. You was in there once with Benton, and I came over and introduced her. She had sort of reddish blond hair, blue eyes, and pretty skin. She used to roller skate competitively?'

I had no earthly idea whom he was talking about.

'Well' – he was still studying the menu – 'it didn't last very long. I don't think she would have given me the time of day if it wasn't for my truck. When she was sitting high in that king cab you would've thought she was waving at everybody from a float in the Rose Bowl parade.'

I started laughing, and the blank expression on his face only made matters worse. I was laughing so hard my eyes were streaming and the waiter paused and decided to come back later. Marino looked annoyed.

'What's wrong with you?' he said.

'I guess I'm just tired,' I said, gasping. 'And if you want a beer, you go right ahead. It's your day off and I'm driving.'

This improved his mood dramatically, and not much later he was draining his first pint of Samuel Adams while his burger with Swiss and my chicken Caesar salad were served. For a while we ate and drifted in and out of a conversation while people around us talked loudly and nonstop.

'I said, do you want to go away for your birthday?' one businessman was telling another. 'You're used to going wherever you want.'

'My wife's the same way,' the other businessman replied as he chewed. 'Acts like I never take her anywhere. Hell, we go out to dinner almost every week.'

'I saw on *Oprah* that one out of ten people owe more money than they can pay,' an older woman confided to a companion whose straw hat was hanging from the hat rack by their booth. 'Isn't that wild?'

'Doesn't surprise me in the least. It's like everything else these days.'

'They do have valet parking here,' one of the businessmen said. 'But I usually walk.'

'What about at night?'

'Shooo. Are you kidding? In D.C.? Not unless you got a death wish.'

I excused myself and went downstairs to the ladies' room, which was large and built of pale gray marble. No one else was there, and I helped myself to the handicap stall so I could enjoy plenty of space and wash my hands and face in private. I tried to call Lucy from my portable phone, but the signal seemed to bounce off walls and come right back. So I used a pay phone and was thrilled to find her at home.

'Are you packing?' I asked.

'Can you hear an echo yet?' she said.

'Ummm. Maybe.'

'Well, I can. You ought to see this place.'

'Speaking of that, are you up for visitors?'

'Where are you?' Her tone turned suspicious.

'The Old Ebbitt Grill. At a pay phone downstairs by the restrooms, to be exact. Marino and I were at the Smithsonian this morning, seeing

Vessey. I'd like to stop by. Not only to see you, but I have a professional matter to discuss.'

'Sure,' she said. 'We're not going anywhere.'

'Can I bring anything?'

'Yeah. Food.'

There was no point in retrieving my car, because Lucy lived in the northwest part of the city, just off Dupont Circle, where parking would be as bad as it was everywhere else. Marino whistled for a cab outside the grill, and one slammed on its brakes and we got in. The afternoon was calm and flags were wilted over roofs and lawns, and somewhere a car alarm would not stop. We had to drive through George Washington University, past the Ritz and Blackie's Steakhouse to reach Lucy and Janet's neighborhood.

The area was bohemian and mostly gay, with dark bars like The Fireplace and Mr P's that were always crowded with well-built, body-pierced men. I knew, because I had been here many times in the past to visit my niece, and I noted that the lesbian bookstore had moved and there seemed to be a new health food store not too far from Burger King.

'You can let us out here,' I said to the driver.

He slammed on the brakes again and swerved near the curb.

'Shit,' Marino said as the blue cab raced away. 'You think there's any Americans in this town?'

'If it wasn't for non-Americans in towns like this, you and I wouldn't be here,' I reminded him.

'Being Italian's different.'

'Really? Different from what?' I asked at the two thousand block of P Street, where we entered the D.C. Cafe.

'From them,' he said. 'For one thing, when our people got off the boat on Ellis Island, they learned to speak English. And they didn't drive taxi cabs without knowing where the hell they was going. Hey, this place looks pretty good.'

The café was open twenty-four hours a day, and the air was heavy with sautéing onions and beef. On the walls were posters of gyros, green teas, and Lebanese beer, and a framed newspaper article boasted that the Rolling Stones had once eaten here. A woman was slowly sweeping as if it were her mission in life. She paid us no mind.

'You relax,' I said to Marino. 'This shouldn't take but a minute.'

He found a table to smoke at while I went up to the counter and studied the yellow lit-up menu over the grill.

'Yes,' said the cook as he pressed sizzling beef and slapped and cut and tossed browning chopped onions.

'One Greek salad,' I said. 'And a chicken gyro in pita and, let me see.' I perused. 'I guess a Kefte Kabob Sandwesh. I guess that's how you say it.'

'To go?'

'Yes.'

'I call you,' he said as the woman swept.

I sat down with Marino. There was a TV, and he was watching *Star Trek* through a swarm of loud static.

'It's not going to be the same when she's in Philly,' he said.

'It won't be.'

I stared numbly at the fuzzy form of Captain Kirk as he pointed his phaser at a Klingon or something.

'I don't know,' he said, resting his chin in his hand as he blew out smoke. 'Somehow it just don't seem right, Doc. She had everything all figured out and had worked hard to get it that way. I don't care what she says about her transferring, I don't think she wants to go. She just doesn't believe she's got a choice.'

'I'm not sure she does if she wants to stay on the track she's chosen.'

'Hell, I believe you always got a choice. You see an ashtray anywhere?'

I spotted one on the counter and carried it over.

'I guess now I'm an accomplice,' I said.

'You just nag me because it gives you something to do.'

'Actually, I'd like you to hang around for a while, if that's all right with you,' I said. 'It seems I spend half my time trying to keep you alive.'

'That's kind of an irony considering how you spend the rest of your time, Doc.'

'Your order!' the cook called out.

'How 'bout getting me a couple of those baklava things. The one with pistachios.'

'No,' I said.

9

Lucy and Janet lived in a ten-story apartment building called The Westpark that was in the two thousand block of P Street, a few minutes' walk away. It was tan brick with a dry cleaner downstairs and the Embassy Mobile station next door. Bicycles were parked on small balconies, and young tenants were sitting out enjoying the balmy night, drinking and smoking, while someone practiced scales on a flute. A shirtless man reached out to shut his window. I buzzed apartment 503.

'Who goes there?' Lucy's voice came over the intercom.

'It's us,' I said.

'Who's *us*?'

'The *us* with your dinner. It's getting cold,' I said.

The lock clicked free to let us into the lobby, and we took the elevator up.

'She could probably have a penthouse in Richmond for what she pays to live here,' Marino commented.

'About fifteen hundred a month for a two-bedroom.'

'Holy shit. How's Janet going to make it alone? The Bureau can't be paying her more than forty grand.'

'Her family has money,' I said. 'Other than that, I don't know.'

'I tell you, I wouldn't want to be starting out these days.'

He shook his head as elevator doors parted.

'Now back in Jersey when I was just revving up my engines, fifteen hundred could've kept me in clover for a year. Crime wasn't like it is, and people were nicer, even in my bad-ass neighborhood. And here we are, you and yours truly, working on some poor lady who was all cut up and burned in a fire, and after we finish with her, it will be somebody else. It's like what's-his-name rolling that big rock up the hill, and every time he gets close, down it rolls again. I swear, I wonder why we bother, Doc.'

'Because it would be worse if we didn't,' I said, stopping before the familiar pale orange door and ringing the bell.

I could hear the deadbolt flip open, and then Janet was letting us in. She was sweating in FBI running shorts and a Grateful Dead T-shirt that looked left over from college.

'Come in,' she said with a smile as Annie Lennox played loudly in the background. 'Something smells good.'

The apartment was two bedrooms and two baths forced into a very tight space that overlooked P Street. Every piece of furniture was stacked with books and layered with clothing, and dozens of boxes were on the floor. Lucy was in the kitchen, rattling around in cupboards and drawers as she gathered silverware and plates, and paper towels for napkins. She cleared a space on the coffee table and took the bags of food from me.

'You just saved our lives,' she said to me. 'I was getting hypoglycemic. And by the way, Pete, nice to see you, too.'

'Damn, it's hot in here,' he said.

'It's not so bad,' Lucy said, and she was sweating, too.

She and Janet filled their plates. They sat on the floor and ate while I propped up on an armrest of the couch and Marino carried in a plastic chair from the balcony. Lucy was in Nike running shorts and a tank top, and dirty from head to heel. Both young women looked exhausted, and I could not imagine what they were feeling. Surely this was an awful time for them. Every emptying of a drawer and taping shut a box had to be another blow to the heart, a death, an end to who you were at that time in your life.

'The two of you have lived here, what? Three years?' I asked.

'Close to it,' said Janet as she speared a forkful of Greek salad.

'And you'll stay in this same apartment,' I said to Janet.

'For the time being. There's really no reason to move, and when Lucy pops in and out, she'll have some room.'

'I hate to bring up an unpleasant subject,' Marino said. 'But is there any reason Carrie might know where you guys live?'

There was silence for a moment as both women ate. I reached over to the CD player to turn down the volume.

'*Reason*?' Lucy finally spoke. 'Why would there be a reason for her to know anything about my life these days?'

'Hopefully there's no reason at all,' Marino said. 'But we got to think about it whether you two birds like it or not. This is the sort of neighborhood she would hang in and fit right in, so I'm asking myself, if I was Carrie and back out on the street, would I want to find where Lucy is?'

No one said a word.

'And I think we all know what the answer is,' he went on. 'Now finding where the doc lives is no big problem. It's been in the newspapers enough, and if you find her, you find Benton. But you?'

He pointed at Lucy.

'You're the challenge, because Carrie'd been locked up for several years by the time you moved here. And now you're moving to Philly, and Janet's left here alone. And to be honest, I don't like that worth a damn, either.'

'Neither of you is listed in the phone book, right?' I asked.

'No way,' Janet said, and she was listlessly picking at her salad.

'What if someone called this building and asked for either of you?'

'They're not supposed to give out info like that,' Janet said.

'*Not supposed to*,' Marino said sardonically. 'Yeah, I'm sure this joint's got state-of-the-art security. Must be all kinds of *high profile* people living here, huh?'

'We can't sit around worrying about this all of the time,' Lucy said, and she was getting angry. 'Can't we talk about something else?'

'Let's talk about the Warrenton fire,' I said.

'Let's do.'

'I'll be packing in the other room,' Janet said appropriately, since she was FBI and not involved in this case.

I watched her disappear into a bedroom, and then I said, 'There were some unusual and disturbing findings during the autopsy. The victim was murdered. She was dead before the fire started, which certainly points at arson. Have we made any further headway on how the fire might have been set?'

'Only through algebra,' Lucy said. 'The only hope here is fire modeling, since there's no physical evidence that points at arson, only circumstantial evidence. I've spent a lot of time fooling around with Fire Simulator on my computer, and the predictions keep coming back to the same thing.'

'What the hell is Fire Simulator?' Marino wanted to know.

'One of the routines in FPEtool, the software we use for fire modeling,' Lucy explained patiently. 'For example, we'll assume that flashover is reached at six hundred degrees Celsius – or one thousand, one hundred and twelve degrees Fahrenheit. So we plug in the data we know, such as the vent opening, area of surface, energy available from the fuel, fire virtual point of origin, room lining materials, wall materials, and so on and so on. And at the end of the day, we should get good predictions as to the suspect, or the fire in question. And guess what? No matter how many algorithms, procedures, or computer programs you try with this one, the answer's always the same. There's no logical explanation for how a fire this fast and hot could have started in the master bathroom.'

'And we're absolutely sure it did,' I said.

'Oh yeah,' Lucy said. 'As you probably know, that bathroom was a relatively modern addition built out from the master bedroom. And if you look at the marble walls, the cathedral ceiling we recovered, you can piece together this really narrow, sharply defined V pattern, with the apex pointing somewhere in the middle of the floor, most likely where the rug was, meaning the fire developed really fast and hot in that one spot.'

'Let's talk about this famous rug,' Marino said. 'You light it, and what kind of fire do we get?'

'A lazy flame,' Lucy answered. 'Maybe two feet tall.'

'Well, that didn't do it,' I said.

'And what's also really telling,' she went on, 'is the destruction to the roof directly above. Now we're talking flames at least eight feet high above the fire's origin, with the temperature reaching about eighteen hundred degrees for the glass in the skylight to melt. About eighty-eight percent of all arsons are up from the floor, in other words the radiant heat flux . . .'

'What the hell's radiant flux?' Marino wanted to know.

'Radiant heat is in the form of an electromagnetic wave, and is emitted from a flame almost equally in all directions, three hundred and sixty degrees. Following me so far?'

'Okay,' I said.

'A flame also emits heat in the form of hot gases, which weigh less than air, so up they go,' Lucy, the physicist, went on. 'A *convective* transfer of heat, in other words. And in the early stages of the fire, most of the heat transfer is convective. It moves up from its point of origin. In this case, the floor. But after the fire was going for a while and hot gas-smoke layers formed, the dominant form of heat transfer became *radiant*. It was at this stage that I think the shower door fatigued and fell on top of the body.'

'And what about the body?' I asked. 'Where would that have been during all this?'

Lucy grabbed a legal pad off the top of a box and clicked open a pen. She drew the outline of a room with a tub and shower and, in the middle of the floor, a tall narrow fire that was impinging upon the ceiling.

'If the fire was energetic enough to project flames to the ceiling, then we're talking about a high radiant flux. The body was going to be severely damaged unless there was a barrier between it and the fire. Something that absorbed radiant heat and energy – the tub and shower door – which would have protected areas of the body. I also think the body was at least some small distance from the point of origin. We could be talking feet, maybe a yard or two.'

'I don't see any other way it could have happened,' I agreed. 'Clearly something protected much of it.'

'Right.'

'How the hell do you set off a torch like that without some sort of accelerant?' Marino asked.

'All we can hope is that something turns up in the labs,' my niece said. 'You know, since the fuel load can't account for the observed fire pattern, then something was added or modified, indicating arson.'

'And you guys are working on a financial audit,' Marino said to her.

'Naturally almost all of Sparkes's records burned up in the fire. But his financial people and accountant have been pretty helpful, to give the guy credit. So far there's no indication that money was a problem.'

I was relieved to hear it. Everything I knew about this case so far argued against Kenneth Sparkes being anything but a victim. But this was not an opinion that was shared by most, I felt sure.

'Lucy,' I said as she finished her gyro pita, 'I think we're all in agreement that the MO of this crime is distinctive.'

'Definitely.'

'Let's just suppose,' I went on, 'for the sake of argument, that some-thing similar has happened before, somewhere else. That Warrenton is simply part of a pattern of fires used to disguise homicides that are being committed by the same individual.'

'It's certainly possible,' Lucy said. 'Anything is.'

'Can we do a search?' I then asked. 'Is there any database that might connect similar MOs in fires?'

She got up and threw food containers in a large trash bag in the kitchen.

'You want to, we can,' she said. 'With the Arson Incident System, or AXIS.'

I was well acquainted with it and the new supersonic ATF wide area computer network called ESA, which was an acronym for Enterprise System Architecture, the result of ATF being mandated by Congress to create a national arson and explosive repository. Two hundred and twenty sites were hooked up to ESA, and any agent, no matter where he was, could access the central database, could pipe himself into AXIS with his laptop as long as he had a modem or a secure cellular line. This included my niece.

She led us back to her tiny bedroom, which was now depressingly bare save for cobwebs in corners and dust balls on the scuffed hardwood floor. The box springs were empty, the mattress still made with wrinkled peach sheets and upended against a wall, and rolled up in a corner was the colorful silk rug that I had given her for her last birthday. Empty dresser drawers were stacked on the floor. Her office was a Panasonic laptop on top of a cardboard box. The portable computer was in a shark-gray steel and magnesium case that met military specifications for being ruggedized, meaning it was vapor-proof and dust-proof and everything-proof and supposedly could be dropped and run over by a Humvee.

Lucy sat before it on the floor, Indian style, as if she were about to worship the great god of technology. She hit the enter key to turn the screen saver off, and ESA lit up rows of pixels at a time in electric blue, flashing a map of the United States on the next vivid screen. At a prompt, she typed in her user name and password, answered other secure prompts to work her way into the system, invisibly cruising through secret gateways on the Web, passing through one level at a time. When she had logged on to the case repository, she motioned for me to sit next to her.

'I can get you a chair if you want,' she said.

'No, this is fine.'

The floor was hard and unkind to my lower lumbar spine. But I was a good sport. A prompt asked her to enter a word or words or phrases that she wished the system to search for throughout the database.

'Don't worry about the format,' Lucy said. 'The text search engines can handle complete stream of consciousness. We can try everything from the size of the fire hose used to the materials the house was made of – all that fire safety info and stuff that's in your set forms fire departments fill out. Or you can go with your own key queries.'

'Let's try *death, homicide, suspected arson,*' I said.

'*Female,*' Marino added. 'And *wealth.*'

'*Cut, incision, hemorrhage, fast, hot,*' I continued thinking.

'What about *unidentified,*' Lucy said as she typed.

'Good,' I said. 'And *bathroom*, I suppose.'

'Hell, put *horses* in there,' Marino said.

'Let's go ahead and give it a shot,' Lucy proposed. 'We can always try more words as we think of them.'

She executed a search and then stretched her legs out and rolled her neck. I could hear Janet in the kitchen washing dishes, and in less than a minute, the computer came back with 11,873 records searched and 453 keywords found.

'That's since 1988,' Lucy let us know. 'And it also includes any cases from overseas in which ATF was called in to assist.'

'Can we print out the four hundred and fifty-three records?' I asked.

'You know, the printer's packed, Aunt Kay.' Lucy looked up apologetically at me.

'Then how about downloading the records to my computer,' I said.

She looked uncertain.

'I guess that's all right,' she said, 'as long as you make sure . . . Oh, never mind.'

'Don't worry, I'm used to confidential information. I'll make sure no one else gets hold of them.'

I knew it was stupid when I said it. Lucy stared longingly into the computer screen.

'This whole thing's UNIX-based SQL.' She seemed to be talking to no one. 'Makes me crazy.'

'Well, if they had a brain in their head, they'd have you here doing their computer shit,' Marino said.

'I haven't made an issue of it,' Lucy replied. 'I'm trying to pay my dues. I'll ship those files to you, Aunt Kay.'

She walked out of the room. We followed her into the kitchen, where Janet was rolling glasses in newspaper and carefully packing them into a Stor-All box.

'Before I head out,' I said to my niece, 'could we maybe go for a walk around the block or something? And just catch up?'

She gave me a look that was something less than trustful.

'What?' she said.

'I may not see you again for a while,' I said.

'We can sit out on the porch.'

'That would be fine.'

We chose white plastic chairs in the open air above the street, and I shut the sliders behind us and watched crowds come alive at night. Taxis were not stopping, and the fireplace in the window of The Flame danced behind glass while men drank in the dark with each other.

'I just want to know how you are,' I said to her. 'I don't feel like you talk to me much.'

'Ditto.'

She stared out with a wry smile, her profile striking and strong.

'I'm all right, Lucy. As all right as I ever am, I guess. Too much work. What else has changed?'

'You always worry about me.'

'I have since you were born.'

'Why?'

'Because somebody should.'

'Did I tell you Mother's getting a facelift?'

Just the thought of my only sibling made my heart turn hard.

'She had half her teeth crowned last year, now this,' Lucy went on. 'Her current boyfriend, Bo, has hung in there for almost a year and a half. *How 'bout that*? How many times can you screw before you need something else nipped and tucked?'

'Lucy.'

'Oh, don't be self-righteous, Aunt Kay. You feel the same way about her that I do. How did I end up with such a piece of shit for a mother?'

'This isn't helping you in the least,' I said quietly. 'Don't hate her, Lucy.'

'She hasn't said one fucking word about my moving to Philadelphia. She never asks about Janet, or you, for that matter. I'm getting a beer. Do you want one?'

'Help yourself.'

I waited for her in the growing dark, watching the shapes of people flow by, some loud and holding on to each other, while others moved alone with purpose. I wanted to ask Lucy about what Janet had told me, but I was afraid to bring it up. Lucy should tell me on her own, I reminded myself, as my physician's voice ordered that I should take control. Lucy popped open a bottle of Miller Lite as she returned to the balcony.

'So let's talk about Carrie just long enough for you to put your mind at ease,' Lucy matter-of-factly stated, taking a swallow. 'I have a Browning High-Power, and my Sig from ATF, and a shotgun – twelve gauge, seven rounds. You name it, I can get it. But you know? I think my bare hands would be enough if she dared to come around. I've had enough, you know?'

She lifted the bottle again. 'Eventually you just make a decision and move on.'

'What sort of decision?' I asked.

She shrugged.

'You decide you can't give someone any more power than you already have. You can't spend your days in fear of them or hating them,' she explained her mindset. 'So you give it up, in a sense. You go about your business, knowing that if the monster ever steps into your path, she'd better be ready for life or death.'

'I think that's a pretty good attitude,' I said. 'Maybe the only attitude. I'm just not sure you really feel that way, but I hope so.'

She stared up at an irregular moon, and I thought she was blinking back tears, but I couldn't be sure.

'The truth is, Aunt Kay, I could do all their computer stuff with one arm. You know?'

'You could probably do all the Pentagon's computer stuff with one arm,' I said gently as my heart hurt more.

'I just don't want to push it.'

I did not know how to answer her.

'I pissed off enough people because I can fly a helicopter and . . . Well, you know.'

'I know all the things you can do, and that the list will probably only grow longer, Lucy. It's very lonely being you.'

'Have you ever felt like that?' she whispered.

'Only all my life,' I whispered back. 'And now you know why I've always loved you the way I do. Maybe I get it.'

She looked over at me. She reached out and sweetly touched my wrist.

'You'd better go,' she said. 'I don't want you driving when you're tired.'

10

It was almost midnight when I slowed at the guard booth in my neighborhood, and the security officer on duty stepped out to stop me. This was highly unusual, and I feared he would tell me that my burglar alarm had been going half the night or yet one more oddball had tried to drive through to see if I was at home. Marino had been dozing for the past hour and a half, and he came to as I rolled down my window.

'Good evening,' I said to the guard. 'How are you doing, Tom?'

'I'm fine, Dr Scarpetta,' he said, leaning close to my car. 'But you've had a few unusual events within the past hour or so, and I figured something wasn't right when I kept trying to reach you and you weren't home.'

'What sort of events?' I asked as I began to imagine any number of threatening things.

'Two pizza delivery guys showed up at almost the same time. Then three taxis came to take you to the airport, one right after the other. And someone tried to deliver a construction Dumpster to your yard. When I couldn't get hold of you, I turned every one of them around. They all said you had called them.'

'Well, I certainly did not,' I said with feeling as my bewilderment grew. 'All this since when?'

'Well, I guess the truck with the Dumpster was here maybe around five this afternoon. Everything else since then.'

Tom was an old man who probably wouldn't have had a clue as to how to defend the neighborhood should true danger ever come around the bend. But he was courteous and considered himself a true officer of the law and in his mind was probably armed and experienced in combat. He was especially protective of me.

'Did you get the names of any of these guys who showed up?' Marino asked loudly from the passenger seat.

'Domino's and Pizza Hut.'

Tom's animated face was shadowed beneath the brim of his baseball cap.

'And the cabs were Colonial, Metro, and Yellow Cab. The construction company was Frick. Now I took the liberty to make a few calls. Every one of 'em had orders in your name, Dr Scarpetta, including the times you called. I got it written down.'

Tom could not hide how pleased he was when he slipped a square of notepaper from a back pocket and handed it to me. His role had been more than the usual this night, and he was almost intoxicated by it. I turned on the interior light and Marino and I scanned the list. The taxi and pizza orders had been placed between ten-ten and eleven, while the Dumpster order had been placed earlier in the afternoon with instructions for a late afternoon delivery.

'I know at least Domino's said it was a woman who called. I talked to the dispatcher myself. A young kid. According to him, you called and said to just bring a large thick crust pizza supreme to the gate and you'd get it from there. I got his name written down, too,' Tom reported with great pride. 'So none of this came from you, Dr Scarpetta?' He wanted to make sure.

'No sir,' I answered. 'And if anything else shows up tonight, I want you to call me right away.'

'Yo, call me, too,' said Marino, and he jotted his home number on a business card. 'I don't give a shit what time it is.'

I handed Marino's card out my window and Tom looked at it carefully, even though Marino had passed through these gates more times than I could guess.

'You got it, Captain,' Tom said with a deep nod. 'Yes sir, anybody else shows up, I'm on the horn, and I can hold 'em till you get here, if you want me to.'

'Don't do that,' Marino said. 'Some kid with a pizza's not going to know a damn thing. And if it's real trouble, I don't want you tangling with whoever it is.'

I knew right then that he was thinking about Carrie.

'I'm pretty spry. But you got it, Captain.'

'You did a great job, Tom,' I complimented him. 'I can't thank you enough.'

'That's what I'm here for.'

He pointed his remote control and raised the arm to let us through.

'I'm listening,' I said to Marino.

'Some asshole harassing you,' he said, his face grim in the intermittent bath of street lamps. 'Trying to upset you, scare you, piss you off. And doing a pretty damn good job, I might add.'

'You don't think Carrie . . .' I went ahead and started to say.

'I don't know,' Marino cut me off. 'But it wouldn't surprise me. Your neighborhood's been in the news enough times.'

'I guess what would be good to know is if the orders were placed locally,' I said.

'Christ,' he said as I turned into my driveway and parked behind his car. 'I sure as hell hope not. Unless it's someone else who's jerking you around.'

'Take a number and stand in line.'

I cut the engine.

'I can sleep on your couch if you want me to,' Marino said as he opened his door.

'Of course not,' I said. 'I'll be fine. As long as no construction Dumpsters show up. That would be the last straw with my neighbors.'

'I don't know why you live here, anyway.'

'Yes, you do.'

He got out a cigarette and clearly did not want to go anywhere.

'Right. The guard booth. Shit, talk about a placebo.'

'If you don't feel okay to drive, I'd be pleased to have you stay on my couch,' I said.

'Who, me?'

He fired his lighter and puffed smoke out the open car door.

'It ain't me I'm worried about, Doc.'

I got out of my car and stood on the driveway, waiting for him. His shape was big and tired in the dark, and I suddenly was overwhelmed by sad affection for him. Marino was alone and probably felt like hell. He couldn't have memories worth much, between violence on the job and bad relationships the rest of the time. I supposed I was the only constant in his life, and although I was usually polite, I wasn't always warm. It simply wasn't possible.

'Come on,' I said. 'I'll fix you a toddy and you can crash here.

You're right. Maybe I don't want to be alone and have five more pizza deliveries and cabs show up.'

'That's what I'm thinking,' he said with feigned cool professionalism.

I unlocked my front door and turned off the alarm, and very shortly Marino was on the wrap-around couch in my great room, with a Booker's bourbon on the rocks. I made his nest with sweet-smelling sheets and a baby-soft cotton blanket, and for a while we sat in the dark talking.

'You ever think we might lose in the end?' he muttered sleepily.

'Lose?' I asked.

'You know, *good guys always win*. How realistic is that? Not so for other people, like that lady that burned up in Sparkes's house. Good guys don't always win. Uh uh, Doc. No fucking way.'

He halfway sat up like a sick man, and took a swallow of bourbon and struggled for breath.

'Carrie thinks she's gonna win, too, in case that thought's never entered your mind,' he added. 'She's had five fucking years at Kirby to think that.'

Whenever Marino was tired or half drunk, he said *fuck* a lot. In truth, it was a grand word that expressed what one felt by the very act of saying it. But I had explained to him many times before that not everyone could deal with its vulgarity, and for that matter, some perhaps took it all too literally. I personally never thought of *fuck* as sexual intercourse, but rather of wishing to make a point.

'I can't entertain the thought that people like her will win,' I said quietly as I sipped red burgundy. 'I will never think that.'

'Pie in the sky.'

'No, Marino. Faith.'

'Yo.' He swallowed more bourbon. 'Fucking faith. You know how many guys I've known to drop dead of heart attacks or get killed on the job? How many of them do you think had faith? Probably every goddamn one of them. Nobody thinks they're gonna die, Doc. You and me don't think it, no matter how much we know. My health sucks, okay? You think I don't know I'm taking a bite of a poison cookie every day? Can I help it? Naw. I'm just an old slob who has to have his steak biscuits and whiskey and beer. I've given up giving a shit about what the doctors say. So soon enough, I'm gonna stoop over in the saddle and be outta here, you know?'

His voice was getting husky and he was beginning to get maudlin.

'So a bunch of cops will come to my funeral, and you'll tell the next detective to come along how it wasn't all that bad to work with me,' he went on.

'Marino, go to sleep,' I said. 'And you know that's not how I feel at all. I can't even think of something happening to you, you big idiot.'

'You really mean that?' He brightened a bit.

'You know damn well I do,' I said, and I was exhausted, too.

He finished his bourbon and softly rattled the ice in the glass, but I didn't respond, because he'd had enough.

'Know what, Doc?' he said thickly. 'I like you a lot, even if you are a pain in the fucking ass.'

'Thank you,' I said. 'I'll see you in the morning.'

'It is morning.'

He rattled ice some more.

'Go to sleep,' I said.

I did not turn off my bedside lamp until two A.M., and thank God it was Fielding's turn to spend Saturday in the morgue. It was almost nine when I got motivated to put my feet on the floor, and birds were raucous in my garden, and the sun was bouncing light off the world like a manic child with a ball. My kitchen was so bright it was almost white, and stainless steel appliances were like mirrors. I made coffee and did what I could to clear my head as I thought of the files downloaded into my computer. I thought of opening sliders and windows to enjoy spring air, and then Carrie's face was before me again.

I went into the great room to check on Marino. He slept the way he lived, struggling against his physical existence as if it were the enemy, the blanket kicked practically to the middle of the floor, pillows beaten into shape, and sheets twisted around his legs.

'Good morning,' I said.

'Not yet,' he mumbled.

He turned over and punched the pillow to submission under his head. He wore blue boxer shorts and an undershirt that stopped six inches short of covering his swollen belly, and I always marveled that men were not shy about fat the way women were. In my own way I very much cared about staying in shape, and when my clothes starting feeling tight around the waist, both my general disposition and libido turned much less agreeable.

'You can sleep a few more minutes,' I said to him.

I gathered up the blanket and spread it across him. He resumed snoring like a wounded wild boar, and I moved to the kitchen table and called Benton at his New York hotel.

'I hope I didn't wake you,' I said.

'Actually, I was almost out the door. How are you?'

He was warm but distracted.

'I'd be better if you were here and she were back behind bars.'

'The problem is, I know her patterns and she knows I know them. So I may as well not know them, if you see what I mean,' he said in that controlled tone that meant he was angry. 'Last night, several of us disguised ourselves as homeless people and went down into the tunnels in the Bowery. A lovely way to spend the evening, I might add. We revisited the spot where Gault was killed.'

Benton was always very careful to say *where Gault was killed* instead of *where you killed Gault*.

'I am convinced she's gone back there and will again,' he went on. 'And not because she misses him, but that any reminder of the violent crimes they committed together excites her. The thought of his blood excites her. For her it's a sexual high, a power rush that she's addicted to, and you and I both know what that means, Kay. She'll need a fix soon, if she hasn't already gotten one that we just haven't found out about yet. I'm sorry to be a doomsayer, but I have a gut feeling that whatever she does is going to be far worse than what she did before.'

'It's hard to imagine anything could be worse than that,' I said, though I really did not mean it.

Whenever I had thought that human beings could get no worse, they did. Or perhaps it was simply that primitive evil seemed more shocking in a civilization of highly evolved humans who traveled to Mars and communicated through cyberspace.

'And so far no sign of her,' I said. 'Not even a hint.'

'We've gotten hundreds of leads going nowhere. NYPD's set up a special task force, as you know, and there's a command center with guys taking calls twenty-four hours a day.'

'How much longer will you stay up there?'

'Don't know.'

'Well, I'm sure if she's still in the area, she knows damn well where you are. The New York Athletic Club, where you always stay. Just two buildings from where she and Gault had a room back then.' I was upset again. 'I guess that's the Bureau's idea of sticking you in a shark cage and waiting for her to come and get it.'

'A good analogy,' he said. 'Let's hope it works.'

'And what if it does?' I said as fear cut through my blood and made me angrier. 'I wish you'd come home and let the FBI do its job.

I can't get over it, you retire and they don't give you the time of day until they want to use you for bait . . . !'

'Kay . . .'

'How can you let them use you . . .'

'It's not like that. This is my choice, a job I have to finish. She was my case from the start, and as far as I'm concerned, she still is. I can't just relax at the beach knowing she's loose and going to kill again. How can I just look the other way when you, Lucy, Marino – when all of us are very possibly in danger?'

'Benton, don't turn into a Captain Ahab, okay? Don't let this become your obsession. Please.'

He laughed.

'Take me seriously, goddamn it.'

'I promise I'll stay away from white whales.'

'You're already chasing the hell out of one.'

'I love you, Kay.'

As I followed the hallway to my office, I wondered why I bothered saying the same old words to him. I knew his behavior almost as well as I knew my own, and the idea that he wouldn't be doing exactly what he was right now was about as unthinkable as my letting another forensic pathologist take over the Warrenton case because it was my right to take it easy at this stage in my life.

I turned on the light in my spacious paneled office, and opened the blinds to let the morning in. My work space adjoined my bedroom, and not even my housekeeper knew that all of the windows in my private quarters, like those in my downtown office, were bulletproof glass. It wasn't just the Carries of the world who worried me. Unfortunately, there were the countless convicted killers who blamed me for their convictions, and most of them did not stay locked up forever. I had gotten my share of letters from violent offenders who promised to come see me when they got out. They liked the way I looked or talked or dressed. They would do something about it.

The depressing truth, though, was that one did not have to be a detective or profiler or chief medical examiner to be a potential target of predators. Most victims were vulnerable. They were in their cars or carrying groceries into their homes or walking through a parking lot, simply, as the saying goes, in the wrong place at the wrong time. I logged onto America Online and found Lucy's ATF repository research files in my mailbox. I executed a print command and returned to the kitchen for more coffee.

Marino walked in as I was contemplating something to eat. He was dressed, his shirttail hanging out, his face dirty with stubble.

'I'm outta here,' he said, yawning.

'Would you like coffee?'

'Nope. Something on the road. Probably stop at Liberty Valance,' he said as if we'd never had our discussion about his eating habits.

'Thanks for staying over,' I said.

'No problem.'

He waved at me as he walked out, and I set the alarm after him. I returned to my study, and the growing stack of paper was rather disheartening. After five hundred pages, I had to refill the paper tray, and the printer ran another thirty minutes. The information included the expected names, dates, and locations, and narratives from investigators. In addition, there were scene drawings and laboratory results, and in some instances, photographs that had been scanned in. I knew it would take me the rest of the day, at the very least, to get through the stack. I was already feeling that this had probably been a Pollyanna idea that would prove a waste of time.

I had gone through no more than a dozen cases when I was startled by my doorbell. I was not expecting anyone, and I almost never had unannounced visitors in my private, gated neighborhood. I suspected it might be one of the local children selling raffle tickets or magazine subscriptions or candy, but when I looked into the video screen of my camera system, I was stunned to see Kenneth Sparkes standing outside my door.

'Kenneth?' I said into the Aiphone, and I could not keep the surprise out of my voice.

'Dr Scarpetta, I apologize,' he said into the camera. 'But I really need to speak to you.'

'I'll be right there.'

I hurried across the house, and opened the front door. Sparkes looked weary in wrinkled khaki slacks and a green polo shirt spotted with sweat. He wore a portable phone and a pager on his belt, and carried a zip-up alligator portfolio.

'Please come in,' I said.

'I know most of your neighbors,' he said. 'In case you're wondering how I got past the guard booth.'

'I've got coffee made.'

I caught the scent of his cologne as we entered the kitchen.

'Again, I hope you'll forgive me for just showing up like this,' he said, and his concern seemed genuine. 'I just don't know who else to talk to, Dr Scarpetta, and I was afraid if I asked you first, you would say no.'

'I probably would have.'

I got two mugs out of a cabinet.

'How do you take it?'

'The way it comes out of the pot,' he said.

'Would you like some toast or anything?'

'Oh no. But thank you.'

We sat at the table before the window, and I opened the door leading outside because my house suddenly seemed warm and stuffy. Misgivings raced through my mind as I was reminded that Sparkes was a suspect in a homicide, and that I was deeply involved in the case, and here I was alone with him in my house on a Saturday morning. He set the portfolio on the table and unzipped it.

'I suppose you know everything about what goes on in an investigation,' he said.

'I never know everything about anything, really.'

I sipped my coffee.

'I'm not naive, Kenneth,' I said. 'For example, if you didn't have clout, you wouldn't have gotten inside my neighborhood, and you wouldn't be sitting here now.'

He withdrew a manila envelope from the portfolio and slid it across the table to me.

'Photographs,' he said quietly. 'Of Claire.'

I hesitated.

'I spent the last few nights in my beach house,' he went on to explain.

'In Wrightsville Beach?' I said.

'Yes. And I remembered these were in a filing cabinet drawer. I hadn't looked at them or even thought of them since we broke up. They were from some photo shoot. I don't recall the details, but she gave me copies when we first started seeing each other. I guess I told you she did some photographic modeling.'

I slid what must have been about twenty eight-by-ten color prints from the envelope, and the one on top was startling. It was true what the governor had said to me at Hootowl Farm. Claire Rawley was physically magnificent. Her hair was to the middle of her back, perfectly straight, and seemed spun of gold as she stood on the beach in running shorts and a skimpy tank top that barely covered her breasts. On her right wrist she wore what appeared to be a large diving watch with a black plastic band and an orange face. Claire

Rawley looked like a Nordic goddess, her features striking and sharp, her tan body athletic and sensual. Behind her on the sand was a yellow surfboard, and in the distance a sparkling ocean.

Other photographs had been taken in other dramatic settings. In some she was sitting on the porch of a decaying Gothic southern mansion, or on a stone bench in an overgrown cemetery or garden, or playing the part of hard-working mate surrounded by weathered fishermen on one of Wilmington's trawlers. Some of the poses were rather slick and contrived, but it made no difference. In all, Claire Rawley was a masterpiece of human flesh, a work of art whose eyes revealed fathomless sadness.

'I didn't know if these might be of any use to you,' Sparkes said after a long silence. 'After all, I don't know what you saw, I mean what was . . . Well.'

He tapped the table nervously with his index finger.

'In cases such as these,' I told him calmly, 'a visual identification simply isn't possible. But you never know when something like this might help. At the very least, there's nothing in these photos that might tell me the body *isn't* Claire Rawley.'

I scanned the photographs again, to see if I noted any jewelry.

'She's wearing an interesting watch,' I said, shuffling through the photographs again.

He smiled and stared. Then he sighed.

'I gave that to her. One of these trendy sports watches that's very popular with surfers. It had an off-the-wall name. *Animal*? Does that sound right?'

'My niece may have had one of those once,' I recalled. 'Relatively inexpensive? Eighty, ninety dollars?'

'I don't remember what I paid. But I bought it at the surf shop where she liked to hang out. Sweetwater Surf Shop on South Lumina, where Vito's, Reddog's, and Buddy's Crab are. She lived near there with several other women. An old not-so-nice condo on Stone Street.'

I was writing this down.

'But it was on the water. And that's where she wanted to be.'

'And what about jewelry? Do you remember her wearing anything unusual?'

He had to think.

'Maybe a bracelet?'

'I don't recall.'

'Her keychain?'

He shook his head.

'What about a ring?' I then asked.

'She wore funky ones now and then. You know, silver ones that didn't cost much.'

'What about a platinum band?'

He hesitated, knocked off balance.

'You said platinum?' he asked.

'Yes. And a fairly large size, too.'

I stared at his hands.

'In fact, it might fit you.'

He leaned back in his chair and looked up at the ceiling.

'My God,' he said. 'She must have taken it. I have a simple platinum band I used to wear when Claire and I were together. She used to joke that it meant I was married to myself.'

'So she took it from your bedroom?'

'From a leather box. She must have.'

'Are you aware of anything else missing from the house?' I then asked.

'One gun from my collection is unaccounted for. ATF recovered all the rest. Of course, they're ruined.'

He was getting more depressed.

'What kind of gun?'

'A Calico.'

'I hope that's not out on the street somewhere,' I said with feeling.

A Calico was an especially nasty submachine gun that looked rather much like an Uzi with a large cylinder attached to the top of it. It was nine-millimeter and capable of firing as many as a hundred rounds.

'You need to report all this to the police, to ATF,' I told him.

'Some of it I already have.'

'Not some. All of it, Kenneth.'

'I understand,' he said. 'And I will. But I want to know if it's her, Dr Scarpetta. Please understand that I don't care about much else at the moment. I will confess to you that I have called her condo. Neither of her roommates have seen her for over a week. Last she spent the night in her place was the Friday night before the fire, the day before it, in other words. The young lady I talked to said Claire seemed distracted and depressed when they ran into each other in the kitchen. She made no mention of going out of town.'

'I see that you are quite an investigator,' I said.

'Wouldn't you be if you were me?' he asked.

'Yes.'

Our eyes met and I read his pain. Tiny beads of sweat followed the line of his hair, and he talked as if his mouth were dry.

'Let's get back to the photos,' I said. 'Exactly why were these photos taken? Modeling for whom? Do you know?'

'Something local, as I vaguely recall it,' he said, staring past me out the window. 'I think she told me it might have been a Chamber of Commerce thing, something to help advertise the beach.'

'And she gave you all these for what reason?'

I continued slowly going through the pictures.

'Just because she liked you? Perhaps she wanted to impress you?'

He laughed ruefully.

'I wish those were the only reasons,' he replied. 'She knows I have influence, that I know people in the film industry and so on. And I'd like you to hang on to these photos, please.'

'So she was hoping you might help her career,' I said, looking up at him.

'Of course.'

'And did you?'

'Dr Scarpetta, it's a simple fact of life that I have to be careful of who and what I promote,' he stated candidly. 'And it would not have looked especially appropriate if I were handing around photos of my beautiful, young white lover in hopes that I might help her career. I tend to keep my relationships as private as possible.'

Indignation shone in his eyes as he fingered his coffee mug.

'It isn't me who broadcasts my personal life. Never has been. And I might add that you shouldn't believe everything you read.'

'I never do,' I said. 'I of all people know better than that, Kenneth. To be honest, I'm not as interested in your personal life as I am in knowing why you have chosen to give these photos to me instead of to Fauquier County investigators or ATF.'

He looked steadily at me, and then replied, 'For identification reasons I've already stated. But I also trust you, and that's the more important element in the equation. No matter our differences, I know you would not railroad anyone or falsely accuse.'

'I see.'

I was feeling more uncomfortable by the moment and frankly wished he would decide to leave so I didn't have to do it for him.

'You see, it would be far more convenient to blame everything on me. And there are plenty of people out there who have been after me for years, people who would love to see me ruined or locked up or dead.'

'None of the investigators I'm working with feel that way,' I said.

'It's not you or Marino or ATF I'm worried about,' he quickly replied. 'It's factions who have political power. White supremacists, militia types who are secretly in bed with people whose names you know. Trust me.'

He stared off, his jaw muscles knotting.

'The deck's stacked against me,' he went on. 'If someone doesn't get to the bottom of what happened here, my days are numbered. I know it. And anyone who can slaughter innocent, helpless horses can do anything.'

His mouth trembled and his eyes brightened with tears.

'Burning them alive!' he exclaimed. 'What kind of monster could do something like that!'

'A very terrible monster,' I said. 'And it seems there are many terrible monsters in the world these days. Can you tell me about the foal? The one I saw when I was at the scene? I assumed one of your horses somehow got away?'

'Windsong,' he verified what I expected as he wiped his eyes on his napkin. 'The beautiful little fella. He's actually a yearling, and he was born right on my farm, both parents were very valuable race-horses. They died in the fire.' He got choked up again. 'How Windsong got out I have no clue. It's just bizarre.'

'Unless Claire – if it is Claire – perhaps had him out and never got a chance to put him back in his stall?' I suggested. 'Perhaps she had met Windsong during one of her visits to your farm?'

Sparkes took a deep breath, rubbing his eyes. 'No, I don't think Windsong had been born yet. In fact, I remember Wind, his mother, was pregnant during Claire's visits.'

'Then Claire might have assumed that Windsong was Wind's year-ling.'

'She might have figured that out.'

'Where is Windsong now?' I asked.

'Thankfully he was captured and is at Hootowl Farm, where he is safe and will be well taken care of.'

The subject of his horses was devastating to him, and I did not believe he was performing. Despite his skills as a public figure whose talent was to change polls and people, Sparkes could not be this good an actor. His self-control was about to collapse, and he was strug-gling mightily and about to succumb. He pushed back his chair and got up from my table.

'One other thing I should tell you,' he said as I walked him to the front door. 'If Claire were alive, I believe she would have tried to contact me, somehow. If nothing else, through a letter. Providing she knew about the fire, and I don't know how she couldn't have known about it. She was very sensitive and kind, no matter her difficulties.'

'When was the last time you saw her?' I opened the front door.

Sparkes looked into my eyes, and once again I found the intensity of his personality as compelling as it was disturbing. I could not abide the thought that he still somewhat intimidated me.

'I suppose a year ago or so.'

His silver Jeep Cherokee was in the drive, and I waited until he was inside it before I shut the door. I could not help but wonder what my neighbors might have thought had they recognized him in my driveway. On another occasion, I might have laughed, but I found nothing the least bit amusing about his visit. Why he had come in person instead of having the photographs delivered to me was my first important question.

But he had not been inappropriate in his curiosity about the case. He had not used his power and influence to try to manipulate me. He had not attempted to influence my opinions or even my feelings about him, at least not that I could tell.

11

I heated up my coffee and returned to my study. For a while, I sat in my ergonomically correct chair and went through Claire Rawley's photographs again and again. If her murder was premeditated, then why did it just so happen to occur while she was somewhere she was not supposed to be?

Even if Sparkes's enemies were to blame, wasn't it a bit too coincidental for them to strike when she just happened to have showed up, uninvited, at his house? Would even the coldest racist burn horses alive, just to punish their owner?

There were no answers, and I began going through the ATF cases again, scanning page after page as hours sped by and my vision went in and out of focus. There were church burnings, residential and business fires, and a series of bowling alleys with the point of origin always the same lane. Apartments and distilleries and chemical companies and refineries had blazed into annihilation, and in all instances, the causes were suspicious even if arson could not be proven.

As for homicides, they were more unusual and usually perpetrated by the relatively unskilled robber or spouse who did not understand that when an entire family disappears and bone fragments turn up in a pit where trash is burned in the back, the police most likely will be called. Also, people already dead don't breathe CO or have bullets in them that show up on X-ray. By ten o'clock that evening, I had, however, come across two deaths that held my attention. One had happened this past March, the other six months before that. The more recent case had occurred in Baltimore, the victim a twenty-five-year-old male named Austin Hart who was a fourth-year medical student at Johns Hopkins when he died in a house fire not far off campus. He had been the only one home at the time because it was spring break.

According to the brief police narrative, the fire started on a Sunday evening and was fully involved by the time the fire department got there. Hart was so badly burned, he could be identified only by striking similarities of tooth root and trabecular alveolar bone points in antemortem and postmortem radiographs. The origin of fire was a bathroom on the first floor, and no electrical arcing, no accelerants were detected.

ATF had been involved in the case upon invitation by the Baltimore fire department. I found it interesting that Teun McGovern had been called in from Philadelphia to lend her expertise, and that after weeks of painstaking sifting through debris and interviewing witnesses and conducting examinations at ATF's Rockville labs, the evidence suggested the fire was incendiary, and the death, therefore, a homicide. But neither could be proven, and fire modeling could not begin to account for how such a fast-burning fire could have started in a tiny tile bathroom that had nothing in it but a porcelain sink and toilet, a window shade, and a tub enclosed in a plastic curtain.

The fire before that, in October, happened in Venice Beach, California, again at night, in an ocean front house within ten blocks of the legendary Muscle Beach gym. Marlene Farber was a twenty-three-year-old actress whose career consisted mainly of small parts on soap operas and sitcoms, with most of her income generated from television commercials. The details of the fire that burned her cedar shake house to the ground were just as sketchy and inexplicable as those of Austin Hart's.

When I read that the fire was believed to have started in the master bathroom of her spacious dwelling, adrenaline kicked in. The victim was so badly burned, she was reduced to white, calcinated fragments, and a comparison of antemortem and postmortem X-rays of her remains was made to a routine chest film taken two years before. She was identified, basically, by a rib. No accelerants were detected, nor was there any explanation of what in the bathroom could have ignited a blaze that had shot up eight feet to set fire to the second floor. A toilet, tub, sink, and countertop with cosmetics, of course, were not enough. Nor, according to the National Weather Service satellite, had lightning struck within a hundred miles of her address during the past forty-eight hours.

I was mulling over this with a glass of pinot noir when Marino called me at almost one A.M.

'You awake?' he asked.

'Does it matter?'

I had to smile, for he always asked that when he called at impolite hours.

'Sparkes owned four Mac tens with silencers that he supposedly bought for around sixteen hundred dollars apiece. He had a claymore mine he bought for eleven hundred, and an MP40 sub. And get this, ninety empty grenades.'

'I'm listening,' I said.

'Says he was into World War II shit and just collected it as he went along, like his kegs of bourbon, which came from a distillery in Kentucky that went kaput five years ago. The bourbon he gets nothing more than a slap on the hand, because in light of everything else, who gives a shit about that. As for the guns, all are registered and he's paid the taxes. So he's clean on those scores, but this cockeyed investigator in Warrenton has a notion that Sparkes's secret thing is selling arms to anti-Castro groups in South Florida.'

'Based on what?' I wanted to know.

'Shit, you got me, but the investigators in Warrenton are running after it like a dog chasing the postman. The theory is that the girl who burned up knew something, and Sparkes had no choice but to get rid of her, even if it meant torching everything he owned, including his horses.'

'If he were dealing arms,' I said impatiently, 'then he would have had a lot more than a couple old submachine guns and a bunch of empty grenades.'

'They're going after him, Doc. Because of who he is, it may take a while.'

'What about his missing Calico?'

'How the hell do you know about that?'

'A Calico is unaccounted for, am I correct?'

'That's what he says, but how do you . . .'

'He came to see me today.'

There was a long pause.

'What are you talking about?' he asked, and he was very confused. 'Came to see you where?'

'My house. Uninvited. He had photographs of Claire Rawley.'

Marino was silent so long this time I wondered if we had been disconnected.

'No offense,' he finally said. 'You sure you're not getting sucked in because of who . . .'

'No,' I cut him off.

'Well, could you tell anything from what you looked at?' He backed down.

'Only that his alleged former girlfriend was extraordinarily beautiful. The hair is consistent with the victim's, and the height and weight estimates. She wore a watch that sounds similar to the one I found and hasn't been seen by her roommates since the day before the fire. A start, but certainly not enough to go on.'

'And the only thing Wilmington P.D.'s been able to get from the university is that there is a Claire Rawley. She's been a student off and on but not since last fall.'

'Which would have been close to the time Sparkes broke up with her.'

'If what he said was true,' Marino pointed out.

'What about her parents?'

'The university's not telling us anything else about her. Typical. We got to get a court order. And you know how that goes. I'm thinking you could try to talk to the dean or someone, soften them up a little. People would rather deal with doctors than cops.'

'What about the owner of the Mercedes? I guess he still hasn't turned up?'

'Wilmington P.D.'s got his house under surveillance,' Marino answered. 'They've looked through windows, sniffed through the mail slot to see if anyone's decomposing in there. But so far, nothing. It's like he disappeared in thin air, and we don't have probable cause to bust in his door.'

'He's how old?'

'Forty-two. Brown hair and eyes, five-foot-eleven and weighs one-sixty.'

'Well, someone must know where he is or at least when he was seen last. You don't just walk away from a practice and not have anyone notice.'

'So far it's looking like he has. People have been driving up to his house for appointments. They haven't been called or nothing. He's a no-show. Neighbors haven't seen him or his car in at least a week. Nobody noticed him driving off, either with somebody or alone. Now apparently some old lady who lives next door spoke to him the morning of June fifth – the Thursday before the fire. They was both picking up their newspapers at the same time, and waved and said good morning. According to her, he was in a hurry and not as friendly as usual. At the moment, that's all we got.'

'I wonder if Claire Rawley might have been his patient.'

'I just hope he's still alive,' Marino said.

'Yes,' I said with feeling. 'Me, too.'

A medical examiner is not an enforcement officer of the law, but an objective presenter of evidence, an intellectual detective whose witnesses are dead. But there were times when I did not care as much about statutes or definitions.

Justice was bigger than codes, especially when I believed that no one was listening to the facts. It was little more than intuition when I decided Sunday morning at breakfast to visit Hughey Dorr, the farrier who had shoed Sparkes's horses two days before the fire.

The bells of Grace Baptist and First Presbyterian churches tolled as I rinsed my coffee cup in the sink. I dug through my notes for the telephone number one of the ATF fire investigators had given to me. The farrier, which was a modern name for an old-world blacksmith, was not home when I called, but his wife was, and I introduced myself.

'He's in Crozier,' she said. 'Will be there all day at Red Feather Point. It's just off Lee Road, on the north side of the river. You can't miss it.'

I knew I could miss it easily. She was talking about an area of Virginia that was virtually nothing but horse farms, and quite frankly, most of them looked alike to me. I asked her to give me a few landmarks.

'Well, it's right across the river from the state penitentiary. Where the inmates work on the dairy farms, and all,' she added. 'So you probably know where that is.'

Unfortunately, I did. I had been there in the past when inmates hanged themselves in their cells or killed each other. I got a phone number and called the farm to make certain it was all right for me to come. As was the nature of privileged horse people, they did not seem the least bit interested in my business but told me I would find the farrier inside the barn, which was green. I went back to my bedroom to put on a tennis shirt, jeans, and lace-up boots, and called Marino.

'You can go with me, or I'm happy to do this on my own,' I told him.

A baseball game was playing loudly on his TV, and the phone clunked as he set it down somewhere. I could hear him breathing.

'Crap,' he said.

'I know,' I agreed. 'I'm tired, too.'

'Give me half an hour.'

'I'll pick you up to save you a little time,' I offered.

'Yeah, that will work.'

He lived south of the James in a neighborhood with wooded lots just off the strip-mall-strewn corridor called Midlothian Turnpike, where one could buy handguns or motorcycles or Bullet burgers, or indulge in a brushless carwash with or without wax. Marino's small aluminum-sided white house was on Ruthers Road, around the corner from Bon Air Cleaners and Ukrop's. He had a large American flag in his front yard and a chainlink fence around the back, and a carport for his camper.

Sunlight winked off strands of unlit Christmas lights that followed every line and angle of Marino's habitat. The multi-colored bulbs were tucked in shrubs and entwined in trees. There were thousands of them.

'I still don't think you should leave those lights up,' I said one more time when he opened the door.

'Yo. Then you take them down and put 'em back again come Thanksgiving,' he said as he always did. 'You got any idea how long that would take, especially when I keep adding to them every year?'

His obsession had reached the point where he had a separate fuse box for his Christmas decorations, which in full blaze included a Santa pulled by eight reindeer, and happy snowmen, candy canes, toys, and Elvis in the middle of the yard crooning carols through speakers. Marino's display had become so dazzling that its radiance could be seen for miles, and his residence had made it into Richmond's official *Tacky Tour*. It still bewildered me that someone so antisocial didn't mind endless lines of cars and limousines, and drunken people making jokes.

'I'm still trying to figure out what's gotten into you,' I said as he got into my car. 'Two years ago you would never do something like this. Then out of the blue, you turn your private residence into a carnival. I'm worried. Not to mention the threat of an electrical fire. I know I've given you my opinion before on this, but I feel strongly . . .'

'And maybe I feel strongly, too.'

He fastened his seat belt and got out a cigarette.

'How would you react if I started decorating my house like that and left lights hanging around all year round?'

'Same way I would if you bought an RV, put in an above-the-ground pool and started eating Bojangles biscuits every day. I'd think you lost your friggin' mind.'

'And you would be right,' I said.

'Look.'

He played with the unlit cigarette.

'Maybe I've reached a point in life where it's do it or lose it,' he said. 'The hell with what people think. I ain't going to live more than once, and shit, who knows how much longer I'm gonna be hanging around, anyway.'

'Marino, you're getting entirely too morbid.'

'It's called reality.'

'And the reality is, if you die, you'll come to me and end up on one of my tables. That ought to give you plenty of incentive to hang around for a long time.'

He got quiet, staring out his window as I followed Route 6 through Goochland County, where woods were thick and I sometimes did not see another car for miles. The morning was clear but on its way to being humid and warm, and I passed unassuming homes with tin roofs and gracious porches, and bird baths in the yards. Green apples bent gnarled branches to the ground, and sunflowers hung their heavy heads as if praying.

'Truth is, Doc,' Marino spoke again. 'It's like a premonition, or something. I keep seeing my time running short. I think about my life, and I've pretty much done it all. If I didn't do nothing else, I still would have done enough, you know? So in my mind I see this wall ahead and there's nothing behind it for me. My road ends. I'm out of here. It's just a matter of how and when. So I'm sort of doing what-ever the hell I want. May as well, right?'

I wasn't sure what to say, and the image of his garish house at Christmas brought tears to my eyes. I was glad I was wearing sunglasses.

'Don't make it a self-fulfilled prophecy, Marino,' I said quietly. 'People think about something too much and get so stressed out they make it happen.'

'Like Sparkes,' he said.

'I really don't see what this has to do with Sparkes.'

'Maybe he thought about something too much and made it happen. Like you're a black man with a lot of people who hate your guts, and you worry so much about the assholes taking what you got, you end up burning it down yourself. Killing your horses and white girlfriend in the process. Ending up with nothing. Hell, insurance money won't replace what he lost. No way. Truth is, Sparkes is screwed any way you slice it. Either he's lost everything he loved in life, or he's gonna die in prison.'

'If we were talking about arson alone, I'd be more inclined to suspect he was the torch,' I said. 'But we're also talking about a young woman who was murdered. And we're talking about all his horses being killed. That's where the picture gets distorted for me.'

'Sounds like O.J. again, you ask me. Rich, powerful black guy. His former white girlfriend gets her throat slashed. Don't the parallels bother you just a little bit? Listen, I gotta smoke. I'll blow it out the window.'

'If Kenneth Sparkes murdered his former girlfriend, then why didn't he do it in some place where nobody might associate it with him?' I pointed out. 'Why destroy everything you own in the process and cause all the signs to point back at you?'

'I don't know, Doc. Maybe things got out of control and went to shit. Maybe he never planned to whack her and torch his joint.'

'There's nothing about this fire that strikes me as impetuous,' I said. 'I think someone knew exactly what he was doing.'

'Either that or he got lucky.'

The narrow road was dappled with sunlight and shade, and birds on telephone lines reminded me of music. When I drew upon the North Pole restaurant, with its polar bear sign, I was reminded of lunches after court in Goochland, of detectives and forensic scientists who since had retired. Those old homicide cases were vague because by now there were so many murders in my mind, and the thought of them and colleagues I missed made me sad for an instant. Red Feather Point was at the end of a long gravel road that led to an impressive farm overlooking the James River. Dust bloomed behind my car as I wound through white fences surrounding smooth green pastures scattered with leftover hay.

The three-story white frame house had the imperfect slanted look of a building not of this century, and silos cloaked in creeper vines were also left over from long ago. Several horses wandered a distant field, and the red dirt riding ring was empty when we parked. Marino and I walked inside a big green barn and followed the noise of steel ringing from the blows of a hammer. Fine horses stretched their splendid necks out of their stalls, and I could not resist stroking the velvet noses of fox hunters, thoroughbreds, and Arabians. I paused to say sweet things to a foal and his mother as both stared at me with huge brown eyes. Marino kept his distance, waving at flies.

'Looking at them is one thing,' he commented. 'But being bit by one once was enough for me.'

The tack and feed rooms were quiet, and rakes and coils of hoses hung from wooden walls. Blankets were draped over the backs of doors, and I encountered no one but a woman in riding clothes and helmet who was carrying an English saddle.

'Good morning,' I said as the distant hammering grew silent. 'I'm looking for the farrier. I'm Dr Scarpetta,' I added. 'I called earlier.'

'He's that way.'

She pointed, without slowing down.

'And while you're at it, Black Lace doesn't seem to be feeling so hot,' she added, and I realized she thought I was a veterinarian.

Marino and I turned a corner to find Dorr on a stool, with a large white mare's right front hoof clamped firmly between his knees. He was bald, with massive shoulders and arms, and wore a leather farrier's apron that looked like baggy chaps. He was sweating profusely and covered with dirt as he yanked nails out of an aluminum shoe.

'Howdy,' he said to us as the horse laid her ears back.

'Good afternoon, Mr Dorr. I'm Dr Scarpetta and this is Captain Pete Marino,' I said. 'Your wife told me I might find you here.'

He glanced up at us.

'Folks just call me Hughey, 'cause that's my name. You a vet?'

'No, no, I'm a medical examiner. Captain Marino and I are involved with the Warrenton case.'

His eyes darkened as he tossed the old shoe to one side. He snatched a curved knife out of a pocket in his apron and began trimming the frog until marbled white hoof showed underneath. An embedded rock kicked out a spark.

'Whoever did that ought to be shot,' he said, grabbing nippers from another pocket and trimming the hoof wall all the way around.

'We're doing everything we can to find out what happened,' Marino let him know.

'My part in it is to identify the woman who died in the fire,' I explained, 'and get a better idea of exactly what happened to her.'

'For starters,' Marino said, 'why that lady was in his house.'

'I heard about that. Strange,' Dorr answered.

Now he was using a rasp as the mare irritably drew her lips back.

'Don't know why anybody should have been in his house,' he said.

'As I understand it, you had just been on his farm several days earlier?' Marino went on, scribbling in a notepad.

'The fire was Saturday night,' Dorr said.

He began cleaning the bottom of the hoof with a wire brush.

'I was there the better part of Thursday. Everything was just business as usual. I shoed eight of his horses and took care of one that had white line disease, where bacteria gets inside the hoof wall. Painted it with formaldehyde – something I guess you know all about,' he said to me.

He lowered the right leg and picked up the left, and the mare jerked a little and swished her tail. Dorr tapped her nose.

'That's to give her something to think about,' he explained to us. 'She's having a bad day. They're nothing more than little children, will test you any way they can. And you think they love you, and all they want is food.'

The mare rolled her eyes and showed her teeth as the farrier yanked out more nails, working with amazing speed that never slowed as he talked.

'Were you ever there when Sparkes had a young woman visiting?' I asked. 'She was tall and very beautiful with long blond hair.'

'Nope. Usually when I showed up, we spent our time with the horses. He'd help out any way he could, was absolutely nuts about them.'

He picked up the hoof knife again.

'All these stories about how much he ran around,' Dorr went on. 'I never saw it. He's always seemed like a kind of lonely guy, which surprised me at first because of who he is.'

'How long have you worked for him?' Marino asked, shifting his position in a way that signaled he was taking charge.

'Going on six years,' Dorr said, grabbing the rasp. 'A couple times a month.'

'When you saw him that Thursday, did he mention anything to you about going out of the country?'

'Oh sure. That's why I came when I did. He was leaving the next day for London, and since his ranch hand had quit, Sparkes had no one else to be there when I came around.'

'It appears that the victim was driving an old blue Mercedes. Did you ever see a car like that on his ranch?'

Dorr pushed himself back on his low wooden stool, scooting the shoeing box with him. He picked up a hind leg.

'I don't remember ever seeing a car like that.'

He tossed aside another horseshoe.

'But nope. Can't say I remember the one you just described. Now *whoa*.'

He steadied the horse by placing his hand on her rump.

'She's got bad feet,' he let us know.

'What's her name?' I asked.

'Molly Brown.'

'You don't sound as if you're from around here,' I said.

'Born and raised in South Florida.'

'So was I. Miami,' I said.

'Now that's so far south it's South America.'

12

———

A beagle had trotted in and was snuffling around the hay-strewn floor, going after hoof shavings. Molly Brown daintily perched her other hind leg on the hoof stand as if about to be treated to a manicure in a salon.

'Hughey,' I said, 'there are circumstances about this fire that raise many, many questions. There's a body, yet no one was supposed to have been inside Sparkes's house. The woman who died is my responsibility, and I want to do absolutely everything I can to find out why she was there and why she didn't get out when the fire started. You may have been the last person to visit the farm before the fire, and I'm asking you to search your memory and see if there's anything – absolutely anything – that might have struck you as unusual that day.'

'Right,' Marino said. 'For example, did it appear that Sparkes might have been having a private, personal conversation on the phone? You get any idea that he might have been expecting company? You ever heard him mention the name Claire Rawley?'

Dorr got up and patted the mare on her rump again, while my instincts kept me far out of the reach of her powerful hind legs. The beagle bayed at me as if suddenly I were a complete stranger.

'Come here, little fella.'

I bent down and held out my hand.

'Dr Scarpetta, I can tell you trust Molly Brown, and she can tell.

As for you' – he nodded at Marino – 'you're scared of 'em, and they can sense that. Just letting you know.'

Dorr walked off, and we followed him. Marino clung to the wall as he walked behind a horse that was at least fourteen hands high. The farrier went around a corner to where his truck was parked. It was a red pickup, customized with a forge in back that burned propane gas. He turned a knob and a blue flame popped up.

'Since her feet aren't so great, I have to draw clips on shoes to make them fit. Kind of like orthotics for humans,' he commented, gripping an aluminum shoe in tongs and holding it in the fire.

'I give it a count of fifty unless the forge's warmed up,' he went on as I smelled heating metal. 'Otherwise I go to thirty. There's no color change in aluminum, so I just warm it a bit to make it malleable.'

He carried the shoe to the anvil and punched holes. He fashioned clips and hammered them flat. To take off sharp edges he used a grinder, which sounded like a loud Stryker saw. Dorr seemed to be using his trade to stall us, to buy himself time to ponder or perhaps work his way around what we wanted to know. I had no doubt that he was fiercely loyal to Kenneth Sparkes.

'At the very least,' I said to him, 'this lady's family has a right to know. I need to notify them about her death, and I can't do that until I am certain who she is. And they're going to ask me what happened to her. I need to know that.'

But he had nothing to say, and we followed him back to Molly Brown. She had defecated and stepped in it, and he irritably swept manure away with a worn-out broom while the beagle wandered around.

'You know, the horse's biggest defense is flight,' Dorr finally spoke again as he secured a front leg between his knees. 'All he wants is to get away, no matter how much you think he loves you.'

He drove nails through the shoe, bending points down as they went through the outside wall of the hoof.

'People aren't all that different, if you corner them,' he added.

'I hope I'm not making you feel cornered,' I said as I kneaded the beagle behind his ears.

Dorr bent the sharp ends of the nails over with a clincher and rasped them smooth, once again taking his time to answer me.

'Whoa,' he said to Molly Brown, and the smell of metal and manure was heavy on the air. 'Point is,' he went on as he tapped the rounding hammer, 'you two walking in here and thinking I'll trust you just like that is no different than your thinking you could shoe this horse.'

'I don't blame you for feeling like that,' I said.

'No way I could shoe that horse,' Marino said. 'No way I'd want to, either.'

'They can pick you up by the teeth and throw you. They paw, cow kick, slap their tail in your eyes. It better'd be plain as day who's in charge, or you're in for a world of trouble.'

Dorr straightened up, rubbing his lower back. He returned to his forge to fire another shoe.

'Look, Hughey,' Marino said as we followed. 'I'm asking you to help because I think you want to. You cared about those horses. You gotta care that someone's dead.'

The farrier dug in a compartment on the side of his truck. He pulled out a new shoe and grabbed it with tongs.

'All I can do is give you my private theory.'

He held the shoe in the forge's flame.

'I'm all ears,' Marino said.

'I think it was a professional hit and that the woman was part of it but for some reason didn't get out.'

'So you're saying she was an arsonist.'

'Maybe one of them. But she got the short end of the stick.'

'What makes you think that?' I asked.

Dorr clamped the warm shoe into a foot vice.

'You know, Mr Sparkes's lifestyle pisses off a lot of people, especially your Nazi types,' he answered.

'I'm still not clear why you think the woman had anything to do with it,' Marino said.

Dorr paused to stretch his back. He rotated his head and his neck cracked.

'Maybe whoever did it didn't know he was leaving town. They needed a girl to get him to open his door – maybe even a girl he had a past with.'

Marino and I let him talk.

'He's not the kind of guy to turn someone he knew away from his door. In fact, in my opinion he's always been too laid back and nice for his own damn good.'

The grinding and hammering punctuated the farrier's anger, and the shoe seemed to hiss a soft warning as Dorr dipped it in a bucket of water. He said nothing to us as he returned to Molly Brown, seating himself on the stool again. He began trying on the new shoe, rasping away an edge and pulling out the hammer. The mare was fidgety, but mostly she seemed bored.

'I may as well tell you another thing that in my mind fits with my theory,' he said as he worked. 'While I was on his farm that Thursday, this same damn helicopter kept flying overhead. It's not like they do crop dusting around there, so Mr Sparkes and I couldn't figure if it was lost or having a problem and looking for a place to land. It buzzed around for maybe fifteen minutes and then took off to the north.'

'What color was it?' I asked as I recalled the one that had circled the fire scene when I was there.

'White. Looked like a white dragonfly.'

'Like a little piston-engine chopper?' Marino asked.

'I don't know much about whirlybirds, but yup, it was small. A two-seater, my guess is, with no number painted on it. Kind of makes you wonder, now, doesn't it? Like maybe somebody doing a little surveillance from the air?'

The beagle's eyes were half shut and his head was on my shoe.

'And you've never seen that helicopter around his farm before?' Marino asked, and I could tell he remembered the white helicopter, too, but didn't want to seem especially interested.

'No sir. Warrenton's not a fan of helicopters. They spook the horses.'

'There's an air park, flying circus, a bunch of private air strips in the area,' Marino added.

Dorr got up again.

'I've put two and two together for you the best I can,' he said.

He grabbed a bandanna out of a back pocket and mopped his face.

'I've told you all I know. Damn. I'm sore all over.'

'One last thing,' Marino said. 'Sparkes is an important, busy man. He must've used helicopters now and then. To get to the airport, for example, since his farm was sort of out in the middle of nowhere.'

'Sure, they've landed on his farm,' Dorr said.

He gave Marino a lingering look that was filled with suspicion.

'Anything like the white one you saw?' Marino then asked.

'I already told you I've never seen it before.'

Dorr stared at us while Molly Brown jerked against her halter and bared long stained teeth.

'And I'll tell you another thing,' Dorr said. 'If you're out to rail-road Mr Sparkes, don't bother poking your nose around me again.'

'We're not out to railroad anyone,' Marino said, and he was getting defiant, too. 'Just looking for the truth. Like they say, it speaks for itself.'

'That would be nice for a change,' Dorr said.

I drove home deeply troubled as I tried to sort through what I knew and what had been said. Marino had few comments, and the closer we got to Richmond, the darker his mood. As we pulled into his driveway, his pager beeped.

'The helicopter ain't fitting with nothing,' he said as I parked behind his truck. 'And maybe it has nothing to do with nothing.'

There was always that possibility.

'Now what the hell is this?'

He held up his pager and read the display.

'Shit. Looks like something's up. Maybe you better come in.'

It was not often that I was inside Marino's house, and it seemed that the last time was during the holidays when I had stopped by with home-baked bread and a container of my special stew. Of course, his outlandish decorations had been up then, and even the inside of his house was strung with lights and crowded with an overburdened tree. I remembered an electric train whirring in circles along its tracks, going around and around a Christmas town dusted with snow. Marino had made eggnog with one hundred proof Virginia Lightning moonshine, and quite frankly, I should not have driven home.

Now his home seemed dim and bare, with its shag-carpeted living room centered by his favorite reclining chair. It was true the mantle over his fireplace was lined with various bowling trophies he had won over the years, and yes, the big-screen television was his nicest piece of furniture. I accompanied him to the kitchen and scanned the greasy stovetop and overflowing garbage can and sink. I turned on hot water and ran it through a sponge, then I began wiping up what I could while he dialed the phone.

'You don't need to do that,' he whispered to me.

'Someone has to.'

'Yo,' he said into the receiver. 'Marino here. What's up?'

He listened for a long, tense time, his brow furrowed and his face turning a deeper red. I started on the dishes, and there were plenty of them.

'So how closely do they check?' Marino asked. 'No, I mean, do they make sure someone's in their seat? Oh, they do? And we know they did it this time? Yeah, right. No one remembers. The whole friggin' world's full of people who don't remember shit. That and they didn't see a thing, right?'

I rinsed glasses carefully and set them on a towel to drain.

'I agree the luggage thing raises a question,' he went on.

I used the last of Marino's dishwashing liquid and had to resort to a dried-out bar of soap I found under the sink.

'While you're at it,' he was saying, 'how 'bout seeing what you can find out about a white helicopter that was flying around Sparkes's farm.' He paused, then said, 'Maybe before, and definitely after because I saw it with my own two eyes when we were at the scene.'

Marino listened some more as I started on the silverware, and to my amazement he said, 'Before I hang up, you want to say hi to your aunt?'

My hands went still as I stared at him.

'Here.'

He handed me the phone.

'Aunt Kay?'

Lucy sounded as surprised as I was.

'What are you doing in Marino's house?' she asked.

'Cleaning.'

'What?'

'Is everything all right?' I asked her.

'Marino will fill you in. I'll check out the white bird. It had to get fuel from somewhere. Maybe filed a flight plan with FSS in Leesburg, but somehow I doubt it. Gotta go.'

I hung up and suddenly felt preempted and angry, and I wasn't completely sure why.

'I think Sparkes is in a lot of trouble, Doc,' Marino said.

'What's happened?' I wanted to know.

'Turns out that the day before the fire, Friday, he showed up at Dulles for a nine-thirty P.M. flight. He checked baggage but never picked it up at the other end, in London. Meaning it's possible he could have checked his bags and given the flight attendant the ticket at the gate, then turned right around and left the airport.'

'They do head counts on international flights,' I argued. 'His absence on the plane would have been noticed.'

'Maybe. But he didn't get where he is without being clever.'

'Marino . . .'

'Hold on. Let me finish giving you the rundown. What Sparkes is saying is that security was waiting for him the minute his plane landed at Heathrow at nine-forty-five the next morning – on Saturday. And we're talking England time, making it four-forty-five A.M. back here. He was told about the fire and turned right around and caught a United flight back to Washington without bothering with his bags.'

'I guess if you were upset enough, you might do that,' I said.

Marino paused, looking hard at me as I set the soap on top of the sink and dried my hands.

'Doc, you got to quit sticking up for him,' he said.

'I'm not. I'm just trying to be more objective than I think some people are being. And certainly security at Heathrow should remember notifying him when he got off that plane?'

'Not so far. And we can't quite figure out how security knew about the fire anyway. Course Sparkes has got an explanation for everything. Says security always makes special provisions when he travels and meets him at the gate. Apparently the fire had already hit the early-morning news in London, and the businessman that Sparkes was supposed to meet with called British Air to alert them to give Sparkes the news the second he was on the ground.'

'And someone's talked to this businessman?'

'Not yet. Remember, this is Sparkes's story. And I hate to tell you this, Doc, but don't think people wouldn't lie for him, either. If he's behind all this, I can guarantee that he planned it right down to the fine print. And let me also add that by the time he'd arrived at Dulles to catch the flight to London, the fire was already going and the woman was dead. Who's to say he didn't kill her and then use some kind of timer to get the fire going after he'd left the farm?'

'There's nothing to say it,' I agreed. 'There's also nothing to prove it. And there doesn't seem to be much chance of our knowing such a thing unless some material turns up in forensic exams that might point to some sort of explosive device used remotely as an igniter.'

'These days half the stuff in your house can be used as a timer. Alarm clocks, VCRs, computers, digital watches.'

'That's true. But something has to initiate low explosives, like blasting caps, sparks, a fuse, fire,' I said. 'Unless you have any other cleaning to do,' I added dryly, 'I'll be heading out.'

'Don't be pissed at me,' Marino said. 'You know, it's not like this whole damn thing is my fault.'

I stopped at his front door and looked at him. Thin gray wisps of hair clung to his sweating pate. He probably had dirty clothes flung all around his bedroom, and no one could clean and tidy up enough for him, not in a million years. I remembered Doris, his wife, and could imagine her docile servitude until the day she suddenly left and fell in love with another man.

It was as if Marino had been transfused with the wrong blood type. No matter how well his meaning or brilliant his work, he was in terrible conflict with his environment. And slowly it was killing him.

'Just do me one favor,' I said with my hand on the door.

He wiped his face on his shirt sleeve and got out his cigarettes.

'Don't encourage Lucy to jump to conclusions,' I said. 'You know as well as I do that the problem is local law enforcement, local politics. Marino, I don't believe we've even come close to what this is all about, so let's not crucify anyone just yet.'

'I'm amazed,' he said. 'After all that son of a bitch did to run you out of office. And now suddenly he's this saint?'

'I didn't say he was a saint. Frankly, I don't know any saints.'

'Sparkes-the-ladies' man,' Marino went on. 'If I didn't know better, I'd wonder if you were getting sweet on him.'

'I won't dignify that with a response.'

I walked out onto the porch, halfway tempted to slam the door in his face.

'Yeah. Same thing everyone says when they're guilty.'

He stepped out after me.

'Don't think I don't know it when you and Wesley aren't getting along . . .'

I turned to face him and pointed my finger like a gun.

'Not one more word,' I warned him. 'You stay out of my business, and don't you dare question my professionalism, Marino. You know better than that, goddamn it.'

I went down the front steps and got inside my car. I backed out slowly and with deliberate skill. I did not look at him as I drove off.

13

Monday morning was carried in on a storm that thrashed the city with violent winds and pelting rains. I drove to work with windshield wipers going fast and air conditioning on to defog the glass. When I opened my window to toss a token into the toll bin, my suit sleeve got drenched, and then of all days for this to happen, two funeral homes had parked inside the bay, and I had to leave my car outside. The fifteen seconds it took me to dash through the parking lot and unlock the back door of my building concluded my punishment. I was soaked. Water dripped from my hair and my shoes squished as I walked through the bay.

I checked the log in the morning office to see what had come in during the night. An infant had died in his parents' bed. An elderly woman appeared to be a suicidal overdose, and, of course, there was a drug-related shooting from one of the housing projects on the fringes of what had become a more civilized and healthy downtown. In the last several years, the city had been ranked as one of the most violent in the United States, with as many as one hundred and sixty homicides in one year for a population of less than a quarter of a million people.

Police were blamed. Even I was if the statistics compiled by my office didn't suit the politicians or if convictions were slow to come in court. The irrationality of it all never ceased to appall me, for it did not seem to occur to those in power that there is such a thing as preventive medicine, and it is, after all, the only way to halt a lethal disease. It truly is better to vaccinate against polio, for example, than to deal with it after the fact. I closed the log and walked out of the office, my shoes carrying me wetly along the empty corridor.

I turned into the locker room because I was already getting chilled. I hurried out of my sticky suit and blouse and struggled into scrubs, which were always more unwilling the more I rushed. I put on my lab coat, and dried my hair with a towel, running my fingers through it to push it out of my way. The face staring back at me in the mirror looked anxious and tired. I had been neither eating nor sleeping well, and was less disciplined with coffee and alcohol. All of it showed around my eyes. A good deal of it was due to my underlying helpless anger and fear brought about by Carrie. We had no idea where she was, but in my mind she was everywhere.

I went into the break room, where Fielding, who avoided caffeine, was making herb tea. His healthy obsessions did not make me feel any better. I had not exercised in over a week.

'Good morning, Dr Scarpetta,' he said cheerfully.

'Let's hope so,' I replied, reaching for the coffeepot. 'Looks like our caseload is fairly light so far. I'm leaving it up to you, and you can run staff conference. I've got a lot to do.'

Fielding was crisp and fresh in a yellow shirt with French cuffs, and vivid tie and creased black slacks. He was cleanly shaven and smelled good. Even his shoes were shined, because unlike me, he never let life's circumstances interfere with how he took care of himself.

'I don't see how you do it,' I said, looking him up and down. 'Jack, don't you ever suffer from normal things, like depression, stress, cravings for chocolate, cigarettes, Scotch?'

'I tend to overcondition when I get whacked out,' he said, sipping his tea and eyeing me through steam. 'That's when I get injured.'

He thought for a moment.

'I guess the worst thing I do, now that you have me thinking about it, is I shut out my wife and kids. Find excuses not to be home. I'm an insensitive bastard and they hate me for a while. So yes, I'm self-destructive, too. But I promise,' he said to me, 'if you would just find time to fast-walk, ride a bike, do a few push-ups, maybe crunches, I swear you'd be amazed.'

He walked off, adding, 'The body's natural morphines, right?'

'Thanks,' I called after him, sorry I asked.

I had barely settled behind my desk when Rose appeared, her hair pinned up, fit for a CEO in her smart, navy blue suit.

'I didn't know you were here,' she said, setting dictated protocols on top of a stack. 'ATF just called. McGovern.'

'Yes?' I asked with interest. 'Do you know about what?'

'She said she was in D.C. over the weekend and needs to see you.'

'When and about what?'

I began signing letters.

'She should be here soon,' Rose said.

I glanced up in surprise.

'She called from her car and told me to let you know that she was almost to Kings Dominion and should be here in twenty or thirty minutes,' Rose went on.

'Then it must be important,' I muttered, opening a cardboard file of slides.

I swung around and removed the plastic cover from my microscope and turned on the illuminator.

'Don't feel you have to drop everything,' said the ever protective Rose. 'It's not as if she made an appointment or even asked if you could fit her in.'

I set a slide on the stage and peered through the eyepiece lens at a tissue section of pancreas, at pink and shrunken cells that looked hyalinized, or scarred.

'His tox came back as zip,' I said to Rose as I put another slide on the stage. 'Except for acetone,' I added. 'The byproduct of inadequate metabolism of glucose. And kidneys show hyperosmolar vacuolization of the proximal convoluted tubular lining cells. Meaning, instead of cuboidal and pink, they're clear, bulging and enlarged.'

'Sonny Quinn again,' Rose said dismally.

'Plus we've got a clinical history of fruity-smelling breath, weight loss, thirst, frequent urination. Nothing that insulin wouldn't have cured. Not that I don't believe in prayer, contrary to what the family has told reporters.'

Sonny Quinn was the eleven-year-old son of Christian Science parents. He had died eight weeks ago, and although there had never been any question as to his cause of death, at least not in my mind, I had finalized nothing until further studies and tests had been completed. In short, the boy had died because he had not received proper medical treatment. His parents had violently protested the autopsy. They had gone on television and accused me of religious persecution and of mutilating their child's body.

Rose had endured my feelings about this many times by now, and she asked, 'Do you want to call them?'

'Want has nothing to do with it. So, yes.'

She shuffled through Sonny Quinn's thick case file and jotted down a phone number for me.

'Good luck,' she said as she passed through the adjoining doorway.

I dialed, with dread in my heart.

'Mrs Quinn?' I said when a woman answered.

'Yes.'

'This is Dr Kay Scarpetta. I have the results from Sonny's . . .'

'Haven't you hurt us enough?'

'I thought you might like to know why your son died . . .'

'I don't need you to tell me anything about my son,' she snapped.

I could hear someone taking the phone from her as my heart hammered.

'This is Mr Quinn,' said the man whose shield was religious freedom and whose son, as a result, was dead.

'Sonny's cause of death was acute pneumonia due to acute diabetic ketoacidosis due to acute onset of diabetes mellitis. I'm sorry for your pain, Mr Quinn.'

'This is all a mistake. An error.'

'There's no mistake, Mr Quinn. No error,' I said, and it was all I could do to keep the anger out of my voice. 'I can only suggest that if your other young children show Sonny's same symptoms that you get them medical treatment immediately. So you don't have to suffer this way again . . .'

'I don't need some medical examiner telling me how to raise my children,' he said coldly. 'Lady, I'll see you in court.'

That you will, I thought, for I knew the Commonwealth would charge him and his wife with felony child abuse and neglect.

'Don't you call us anymore,' said Mr Quinn, and he hung up on me.

I returned the receiver to its cradle with a heavy heart and looked up to see Teun McGovern standing in the hallway, just outside my door. I could tell by the look on her face that she had heard every word.

'Teun, come in,' I said.

'And I thought my job was hard.' Her eyes were on mine as she took a chair and moved it directly across from me. 'I know you have to do this all the time, but I guess I've never really heard it. It's not that I don't talk to families all the time, but thankfully it's not my job to tell them exactly what inhaling smoke did to their loved one's trachea or lungs.'

'It's the hardest part,' I said simply, and the weight inside me would not go away.

'I guess you're the messenger they want to kill.'

'Not always,' I said, and I knew that in the solitude of my raw inner self, I would hear the Quinns' accusing, harsh words replay for the rest of my days.

There were so many voices now, screams and prayers of rage and pain and sometimes blame, because I had dared to touch the wounds, and because I would listen. I did not want to talk about this with McGovern. I did not want her to get any closer to me.

'I've got one more phone call to make,' I said. 'So if you want to get coffee? Or just relax for a minute. I'm sure you'll be interested in what I find out.'

I called the University of North Carolina at Wilmington, and although it was not quite nine, the registrar was in. He was excruciatingly polite but not at all helpful.

'I completely understand why you're calling and promise that we very much want to help,' he was saying. 'But not without a court order. We can't simply decide to release personal information about any of our students. Certainly not over the phone.'

'Mr Shedd, we're talking about a homicide,' I reminded him as impatience tugged at me.

'I understand,' he said again.

This went on and got me nowhere. Finally I gave up and got off the line. I was dejected when I returned my attention to McGovern.

'They're just covering their asses in case the family tries to come after them later.' McGovern told me what I already knew. 'They need us to give them no choice, so I guess that's what we'll do.'

'Right,' I said dully. 'So what brings you here?' I asked.

'I understand the lab results are in, or at least some of them. I called late Friday,' she said.

'News to me.'

I was irked. If the trace evidence examiner had called McGovern before me, I was going to be really hot. I picked up the phone and called Mary Chan, a young examiner who was new with the labs.

'Good morning,' I said. 'I understand you have some reports for me?'

'I was just getting ready to bring them downstairs.'

'These are the ones you've sent to ATF.'

'Yes. The same ones. I can fax them or bring them in person.'

I gave her the number of the fax machine in my office, and I did not let her know my irritation. But I did give her a hint.

'Mary, in the future, it's best if you let me know about my cases *before* you start sending lab results to others,' I said calmly.

'I'm sorry,' and I could tell she very much was. 'The investigator called at five as I was halfway out the door.'

The reports were in my hands two minutes later, and McGovern opened her battered briefcase to retrieve her copies. She watched me as I read. The first was an analysis of the metal-like shaving that I had recovered from the dead woman's cut to the left temporal region. According to the scanning electron microscope and energy dispersive X-ray, or SEM/EDX, the elemental composition of the material in question was magnesium.

As for the melted debris recovered from the victim's hair, those results were just as inexplicable. A FTIR, or Fourier transform infrared spectrophotometer, had caused the fibers to selectively absorb infrared light. The characteristic pattern turned out to be that of the chemical polymer polysiloxane, or silicone.

'A little strange, don't you think?' McGovern asked me.

'Let's start with magnesium,' I said. 'What comes to mind is sea water. There's plenty of magnesium in that. Or mining. Or the person was an industrial chemist or worked in a research lab? What about explosives?'

'If potassium chloride came up, then yes. That could be flash powder,' she answered. 'Or RDX, lead styphnate, lead azide of mercury fulminate if we're talking about blasting caps, for example. Or nitric acid, sulfuric acid, glycerin, ammonium nitrate, sodium nitrate. Nitroglycerin, dynamite, and so on and so on. And I will add that Pepper would have picked up on high explosives like that.'

'And magnesium?' I asked.

'Pyrotechnics, or fireworks,' she said. 'To produce the brilliant white light. Or flares.' She shrugged. 'Although aluminum powder is preferred, because it keeps better, unless the magnesium particles are coated with something like linseed oil.'

'Flares,' I thought out loud. 'You light flares, strategically place them, and leave? That could buy you several minutes, at least.'

'With the appropriate fuel load, it could.'

'But that doesn't explain an unburned turning or shaving of it embedded in her wound, that would appear to have been transferred by the sharp instrument she was cut with.'

'They don't use magnesium to make knives,' McGovern observed.

'No, nothing like that. It's too soft. What about the aerospace industry, because it's so light?'

'Most definitely. But in those instances, there are alloys that would have come up during testing.'

'Right. Let's move on to silicone, which doesn't seem to make any sense. Unless she had silicone breast implants before they were banned, which she clearly didn't.'

'I can tell you that silicone rubber is used in electrical insulation, hydraulic fluids, and for water repellency. None of which makes sense, unless there was something in the bathroom, maybe in the tub. Something pink – I don't know what.'

'Do we know if Sparkes had a bathmat – anything rubbery and pink in that bathroom?' I asked.

'We've only begun going through his house with him,' she said. 'But he claims that the decor of the master bath was mostly black and white. The marble floor and walls were black. The sink, cabinets, and tub, white. The shower door was European and wasn't tempered glass, meaning it didn't disintegrate into a billion little glass balls when the temperature exceeded four hundred degrees Fahrenheit.'

'Explaining why it basically melted over the body,' I said.

'Yeah, almost shrink-wrapped it.'

'Not quite,' I said.

'The door had brass hinges and no frame. What we recovered was consistent with that. So your friendly media tycoon's memory holds true at least on that score.'

'And on others?'

'God only knows, Kay.'

She unbuttoned her suit jacket as if it suddenly occurred to her to relax, while she paradoxically glanced up at the clock.

'We're dealing with a very smart man,' she said. 'That much all of us know.'

'And the helicopter? What do you make of that, Teun? I'm assuming you've gotten word about the little white Schweizer, or Robinson, or whatever it was that the farrier saw two days before the fire? Perhaps the same one you and I saw two days later?'

'This is just a theory,' she said. 'A groping one at that, okay?'

Her look was penetrating.

'Maybe he sets the fire and needs to get to the airport fast,' she went on. 'So the day before, the helicopter does a recon over the farm because the pilot knows he'll have to land and take off after dark. Following so far?'

I nodded.

'Saturday rolls around. Sparkes murders the girl and torches his place. He runs out to the pasture and gets on the helicopter, which transports him somewhere near Dulles, where his Cherokee is stashed. He gets to the airport and does his thing with receipts and maybe baggage. Then he makes himself scarce until it's time to show up at Hootowl Farm.'

'And the reason the helicopter showed up on Monday, when we were working the scene?' I then asked. 'How does that fit?'

'Pyros like to watch the fun,' she stated. 'Hell, for all we know, Sparkes was up there himself watching us work our asses off. Paranoid, if nothing else. Figured we'd think it was a news bird, which we did.'

'This is all speculation at this point,' I said, and I had heard enough.

I began rearranging the infinite flow of paperwork that began where it stopped and stopped where it began. McGovern was studying me again. She got up and shut the doors.

'Okay, I think it's time we had a little talk,' she said. 'I don't think you like me. And maybe if you come clean about it, maybe we can do something about it, one way or another.'

'I'm not sure what I think of you, if you must know.'

I stared at her.

'The most important thing is that all of us do our jobs, lest we lose perspective. Since we are dealing with someone who was murdered,' I added.

'Now you're pissing me off,' she said.

'Not intentionally, I assure you.'

'As if someone murdered makes no difference to me? Is that what you're implying? You think I got where I am in life by not giving a shit about who set a fire and why?'

She shoved up her sleeves, as if ready for a fight.

'Teun,' I said. 'I don't have time for this, because I don't think it's constructive.'

'This is about Lucy. You think I'm replacing you, or God knows what. That's what this is all about, isn't it, Kay?'

Now she was making me angry, too.

'You and I have worked together before, right?' she went on. 'We've never had a big problem before now. So one has to ask, what's different? I think the answer's pretty obvious. The difference is that even as we speak, your niece is moving into her new apartment in Philadelphia, to be in my field office, under my supervision. Mine. Not yours. And you don't like it. And guess what else? If I were in your shoes, maybe I wouldn't like it either.'

'It is neither the time nor the place for this discussion,' I said firmly.

'Fine.'

She got up and draped her jacket over her arm.

'Then we'll go somewhere else,' she decided. 'I intend to resolve this before I drive back north.'

For an instant I was stymied as I reigned from the empire of my wrap-around desk, with its foremen of files, and guards demanding the hard labor of journal articles, and legions of messages and correspondence that would never set me free. I took my glasses off and massaged my face. When McGovern was blurred, it was easier for me.

'I'll take you to lunch,' I said. 'If you're willing to hang around three more hours. In the meantime' – I got up from my chair – 'I have bones in a pot that need heating up. You can come with me, if you have a strong stomach.'

'You won't scare me off with that.' McGovern seemed pleased.

McGovern was not the sort to follow anyone around, and after I had turned on the burner in the decomposition room, she lingered long enough for steam to rise. Then she headed out to ATF's Richmond field office, and reappeared suddenly within an hour. She was breathless and tense when she walked in. I was carefully stirring simmering bones.

'We got another one,' she said quickly.

'Another one?' I asked.

I set the long plastic spoon on a countertop.

'Another fire. Another whacko one. This time in Lehigh County, about an hour from Philadelphia,' she said. 'Are you coming with me?'

My mind raced through all the possibilities of what might happen if I dropped everything and left with her. For one thing, I was unnerved by the thought of the two of us alone for five hours inside a car.

'It's residential,' she went on. 'It started early yesterday morning, and a body has been recovered. A woman. In the master bathroom.'

'Oh no,' I said.

'It's clear the fire was intended to conceal that she had been murdered,' she said, and then went on to explain why it was possible the case was related to the one in Warrenton.

When the body was discovered, Pennsylvania state police had immediately requested assistance from ATF. Then ATF fire investigators at the scene had entered data on their laptops, and ESA got a hit almost instantly. By last night the Lehigh case had begun to take on huge significance, and the FBI offered agents and Benton, and the state police had accepted.

'The house was built on a slab,' McGovern was explaining as we got on I-95 North. 'So no basement to worry about, thank God. Our guys have been there since three o'clock this morning, and what's curious is in this case, the fire didn't do the job well at all. The areas of the master suite, a guest room right above it on the second floor, and the living room downstairs are pretty badly burned, with extensive ceiling damage in the bathroom, and spalling of the concrete floor in the garage.'

Spalling occurs when rapid, intense heat causes moisture trapped in concrete to boil, fragmenting the surface.

'The garage was located where?' I asked as I tried to envision what she was describing.

'On the same side of the house as the master suite. Again, a fast, hot fire. But the burning wasn't complete, a lot of alligatoring, a lot of surface charring. As for the rest of the house, we're talking mostly smoke and water damage. Which isn't consistent with the work of the individual who torched the Sparkes farm. Except for one important thing. So far, it doesn't appear that any type of accelerant was used, and there wasn't a sufficient fuel load in the bathroom to account for the height of the flames.'

'Was the body in the tub?' I asked.

'Yes. Makes my hair stand on end.'

'It should. What kind of shape is she in?' I asked the most important question as McGovern held our speed ten miles over the limit in her government Ford Explorer.

'Not so burned that the medical examiner couldn't tell her throat was cut.'

'Then she's already been autopsied,' I assumed.

'To be honest, I really don't know how much has been done. But she's not going anywhere. That's your turf. Mine's to see what the hell else we can find at the fire scene.'

'So you're not going to use me to shovel out debris?' I asked.

McGovern laughed and turned on the CD player. I was not expecting *Amadeus*.

'You can dig all you want,' she said with a smile that relieved a lot of tension. 'You're not bad at it, by the way, for someone who probably doesn't run unless she's being chased. Or work out anything except intellectual problems.'

'You do enough autopsies and move enough bodies, and you don't need to lift weights,' I distorted the truth, badly.

'Hold out your hands.'

I did, and she glanced over at them, changing lanes at the same time.

'Damn. I guess it didn't occur to me what saws and scalpels and hedge pruners will do for muscle tone,' she commented.

'*Hedge pruners*?'

'You know, what you use to open the chest.'

'Rib shears, please.'

'Well, I've seen hedge pruners in some morgues, and knitting needles used to track bullet wounds.'

'Not in my morgue. At least not in the one I have now. Although I will admit that in the early days one learned to improvise,' I felt compelled to say as Mozart played.

'One of those little trade secrets you don't want to ever come out in court,' McGovern confessed. 'Sort of like stashing the best jar of confiscated moonshine in a secret desk drawer. Or cops keeping souvenirs from scenes, like marijuana pipes and whacko weapons. Or medical examiners hanging on to artificial hips and parts of fractured skulls that in truth should be buried with the bodies.'

'I won't deny that some of my colleagues aren't always appropriate,' I said. 'But keeping body parts without permission is not in the same category as pinching a jar of moonshine, if you ask me.'

'You're awfully straight and narrow, aren't you, Kay?' McGovern stated. 'Unlike the rest of us, you never seem to use poor judgment or do anything wrong. You probably never overeat or get drunk. And to be honest, it makes the rest of us schleps afraid to be around you, afraid you'll look at us and disapprove.'

'Good Lord, what an awful image,' I exclaimed. 'I hope that's not how I'm perceived.'

She said nothing.

'Certainly I don't see myself that way,' I said. 'Quite to the contrary, Teun. Maybe I'm just more reserved because I have to be. Maybe I'm more self-contained because I always have been, and no, it's not my tendency to publicly confess my sins. But I don't look around and judge. And I can promise I'm much harder on myself than I'd ever be on you.'

'That's not been my impression. I think you size me up and down and inside out to make sure I'm suitable to train Lucy and won't be a pernicious influence.'

I could not answer that charge, because it was true.

'I don't even know where she is,' I suddenly realized.

'Well, I can tell you. She's in Philly. Bouncing back and forth between the field office and her new apartment.'

For a while, music was our only conversation, and as the beltway carried us around Baltimore, I could not help but think of a medical student who also had died in a suspicious fire.

'Teun,' I said. 'How many children do you have?'

'One. A son.'

I could tell this was not a happy subject.

'How old is he?' I asked.

'Joe is twenty-six.'

'He lives nearby?'

I stared out the window at reflective signs flowing by, announcing exits to Baltimore streets I used to know very well when I studied medicine at Johns Hopkins.

'I don't know where he lives, to tell you the truth,' she said. 'We were never close. I'm not sure anyone has ever been close to Joe. I'm not sure anyone would want to be.'

I did not pry, but she wanted to talk.

'I knew something was wrong with him when he started sneaking into the liquor cabinet at the tender age of ten, drinking gin, vodka, and putting water in the bottles, thinking he would fool us. By sixteen, he was a raging alcoholic, in and out of treatment, DUIs, drunk and disorderlies, stealing, one thing after another. He left home at nineteen, skipping around here and there and eventually cut off all contact. To be honest, he's probably a street person somewhere.'

'You've had a hard life,' I said.

14

The Atlanta Braves were staying at the Sheraton Hotel on Society Hill when McGovern dropped me off at almost seven P.M. Groupies, old and young, were dressed in baseball jackets and caps, prowling hallways and bars with huge photographs in hand to be signed by their heroes. Security had been called, and a desperate man stopped me as I was coming through the revolving door.

'Have you seen them?' he asked me, his eyes wildly darting around.

'Seen who?' I said.

'The Braves!'

'What do they look like?' I asked.

I waited in line to check in, not interested in anything but a long soak in the tub. We had been held up two hours in traffic just south of Philadelphia, where five cars and a van had smashed into each other, sending broken glass and twisted metal across six lanes. It was too late to drive another hour to the Lehigh County morgue. That would have to wait until morning, and I took the elevator to the fourth floor and slid in my plastic card to open the electronic lock. I opened curtains and looked out at the Delaware River, and masts of the *Moshulu* moored at Penn's Landing. Suddenly, I was in Philadelphia with a turn-out bag, my aluminum case, and my purse.

My message light was blinking, and I listened to Benton's recorded voice saying that he was staying at my same hotel, and should be arriving as soon as he could break free of New York and its traffic. I was to expect him around nine. Lucy had left me her new phone number and didn't know if she'd see me or not. Marino had an update that he would relay when I called, and Fielding said the Quinns had gone on the television news earlier this evening to say they were suing the medical examiner's office and me for violating the separation of church and state and causing irreparable emotional damage.

I sat on the edge of the bed and took off my shoes. My pantyhose had a run, and I wadded them and hurled them into the trash. My clothes had bitten into me because I had worn them too long, and I imagined the stench of cooking human bones lingering in my hair.

'Shit!' I exclaimed under my breath. 'What kind of goddamn life is this?'

I snatched off my suit, blouse, and slip and flung them inside out on the bed. I made sure the deadbolt was secure and began filling the tub with water as hot as I could stand it. The sound of it pouring on top of itself began to soothe me, and I dribbled in foaming bath gel that smelled like sun-ripened raspberries. I was confused about seeing Benton. How had it all come to this? Lovers, colleagues, friends, whatever we were supposed to be had blended into a mixture, like paintings in sand. Our relationship was a design of delicate colors, intricate and dry and easily disturbed. He called as I was drying off.

'I'm sorry it's so late,' he said.

'How are you?' I asked.

'Are you up for the bar?'

'Not if the Braves are there. I don't need a riot.'

'The Braves?' he asked.

'Why don't you come to my room? I have a mini-bar.'

'In two minutes.'

He showed up in his typical uniform of dark suit and white shirt. Both showed the harshness of his day, and he needed to shave. He gathered me in his arms and we held each other without speaking for a very long time.

'You smell like fruit,' he said into my hair.

'We're supposed to be in Hilton Head,' I muttered. 'How did we suddenly end up in Philadelphia?'

'It's a bloody mess,' he said.

Benton gently pulled away from me and took off his jacket. He draped it over my bed and unlocked the mini-bar.

'The usual?' he asked.

'Just some Evian.'

'Well, I need something stronger.'

He unscrewed the top of a Johnnie Walker.

'In fact, I'll make that a double, and the hell with ice,' he let me know.

He handed me the Evian, and I watched him as he pulled out the desk chair and sat. I propped up pillows on the bed and made myself comfortable as we viewed each other from a distance.

'What's wrong?' I asked. 'Besides everything.'

'The usual problem when ATF and the Bureau are suddenly thrown together on a case,' he said, sipping his drink. 'It makes me glad I'm retired.'

'You don't seem very retired,' I said wryly.

'That's the damn truth. As if Carrie isn't enough for me to worry about. Then I'm called in on this homicide, and to be honest, Kay, ATF has its own profilers and I don't think the Bureau should be poking its nose into this at all.'

'Tell me something I don't know, Benton. And I don't see how they're justifying their involvement, for that matter, unless they're saying this lady's death is an act of terrorism.'

'The potential link to the Warrenton homicide,' he told me. 'As you know. And it wasn't hard for the unit chief to call state police investigators to let them know the Bureau would do anything to help. So then the Bureau's invited in, and here I am. There were two agents at the fire scene earlier today, and already everybody's pissed off.'

'You know, Benton, supposedly we're all on the same side,' I said, and this same old subject made me angry again.

'Apparently this one FBI guy who's with the Philly field office hid a nine-millimeter cartridge at the scene to see if Pepper would hit on it.'

Benton slowly swirled Scotch in his glass.

'Of course Pepper didn't because he hadn't even been told to go to work yet,' he went on. 'And the agent thought this was funny, saying something about the dog's nose needing to go back to the shop.'

'What kind of fool would do something like that?' I asked, incensed. 'He's lucky the handler didn't beat the hell out of him.'

'So here we are,' he went on with a sigh. 'Same old shit. In the good ole days, FBI agents had better sense than that. They weren't always flashing their shields in front of the camera and taking over investigations they aren't qualified to handle. I'm embarrassed. I'm more than embarrassed, I'm enraged that these new idiots out there are ruining my reputation along with their own, after I worked twenty-five years . . . Well. I just don't know what I'm going to do, Kay.'

He met my eyes as he drank.

'Just do your good job, Benton,' I said to him quietly. 'Trite as that may sound, it's all any of us can do. We're not doing it for the Bureau, not for ATF or the Pennsylvania state police. It's for the victims and potential victims. Always for them.'

He drained his glass and set it on the desk. The lights of Penn's Landing were festive outside my window, and Camden, New Jersey, glittered on the other side of the river.

'I don't think Carrie's in New York anymore,' he then said as he stared out into the night.

'A comforting thought.'

'And I have no evidence for that beyond there being no sightings or any other indicators that she is in the city. Where is she getting money, for example? Often that's how the trail begins. Robbery, stolen credit cards. Nothing so far to make us think she's out there doing things like that. Of course, that doesn't mean she isn't. But she has a plan, and I feel quite confident that she's following it.'

His profile was sharp in shadows as he continued staring out at the river. Benton was depressed. He sounded worn out and defeated, and I got up and went to him.

'We should go to bed,' I said, massaging his shoulders. 'We're both tired, and everything seems worse when we're tired, right?'

He smiled a little and closed his eyes as I worked on his temples and kissed the back of his neck.

'How much do you charge per hour?' he muttered.

'You can't afford me,' I said.

We did not sleep together because the rooms were small and both of us needed rest. I liked my shower in the morning and he liked his, and that was the difference between being new with each other versus comfortable. There had been a time when we stayed up all night consuming each other, because we worked together and he was married and we could not help our hunger. I missed feeling that alive. Often when we were with each other now, my heart was dull or felt sweet pain, and I saw myself getting old.

The skies were gray and the streets were wet from washing when Benton and I drove through downtown on Walnut Street a little past seven the following morning. Steam rose from grates and manholes, the morning damp and cool. The homeless slept on sidewalks or beneath filthy blankets in parks, and one man looked dead beneath a *No Loitering* sign across from the police department. I drove while Benton went through his briefcase. He took notes on a yellow legal pad and thought about matters beyond my ken. I turned onto Interstate 76 West, where taillights were strung like red glass beads as far ahead as I could see, and the sun behind us was bright.

'Why would someone pick a bathroom as a point of origin?' I asked. 'Why not some other area of the house?'

'Obviously, it means something to him, if we're talking about serial crimes,' he said, flipping a page. 'Symbolic, perhaps. Maybe convenient for some other reason. My guess is that if we're dealing with the same offender, and the bathroom is the point of origin that all of the fires have in common, then it is symbolic. Represents something to him, perhaps his own point of origin for his crimes. If something happened to him in a bathroom when he was a young child, for example. Sexual abuse, child abuse, witnessing something terribly traumatic.'

'Too bad we can't search prison records for that.'

'Problem is, you'd come up with half the prison population. Most of these people come from abuse. Then they do unto others.'

'They do worse unto others,' I said. 'They weren't murdered.'

'They were, in a sense. When you are beaten and raped as a child, your life is murdered even if your body isn't. Not that any of this really explains psychopathy. Nothing I know of does, unless you believe in evil and that people make choices.'

'That's exactly what I believe.'

He looked over at me and said, 'I know.'

'What about Carrie's childhood? How much do we know about why she's made the choices she has?' I asked.

'She would never let us interview her,' he reminded me. 'There isn't much in her psychiatric evaluations, except whatever her manipulation of the moment was. Crazy today, not tomorrow. Disassociating. Depressed and noncompliant. Or a model patient. These squirrels have more civil rights than we do, Kay. And prisons and forensic psychiatric centers are often so protective of their wards that you would think we're the bad guys.'

The morning was getting lighter and the sky was streaked violet and white in perfect horizontal bands. We drove through farmland and intermittent cliffs of pink granite corrugated with drill holes from the dynamite that had blasted in the roads. Mist rising from ponds reminded me of pots of simmering water, and when we passed tall smokestacks with steamy plumes, I thought of fire. In the distance, mountains were a shadow, and water towers dotted the horizon like bright balloons.

It took an hour to reach Lehigh Valley Hospital, a sprawling concrete complex still under construction, with a helicopter hangar and level one trauma center. I parked in a visitor's lot, and Dr Abraham Gerde met us inside the bright, new lobby.

'Kay,' he said warmly, shaking my hand. 'Who would have ever thought you'd be visiting me here some day? And you must be Benton? We have a very good cafeteria here if you'd like coffee or something to eat first?'

Benton and I politely declined. Gerde was a young forensic pathologist with dark hair and startling blue eyes. He had rotated through my office three years earlier, and was still new enough at his profession to rarely have his status as an expert witness stipulated in court. But he was humble and meticulous, and those attributes were far more valuable to me than experience, especially in this instance. Unless Gerde had changed dramatically, it was unlikely he had touched the body after learning I was coming.

'Tell me where we are in this,' I said as we walked down a wide, polished gray hallway.

'I had her weighed, measured and was doing the external exam when the coroner called. As soon as he said ATF was involved and you were on the way, I stopped the presses.'

Lehigh County had an elected coroner who decided which cases would be autopsied and then determined the manner of death. Fortunately for Gerde, the coroner was a former police officer who did not interfere with the forensic pathologists and usually deferred to the decisions they made. But this was not true in other states or other counties in Pennsylvania, where autopsies were sometimes performed on embalming tables in funeral homes, and some coroners were consummate politicians who did not know an entrance from an exit wound, or care.

Our footsteps echoed in the stairwell, and at the bottom, Gerde pushed through double doors and we found ourselves in a warehouse stacked with collapsed cardboard boxes and busy with people in hard hats. We passed through to a different part of the building and followed another hallway to the morgue. It was small, with a pink tile floor and two stationary stainless steel tables. Gerde opened a cabinet and handed us sterile single-use surgical gowns, plastic aprons, and full coverage disposable boots. We pulled these over our clothes and shoes and then donned latex gloves and masks.

The dead woman had been identified as Kellie Shephard, a thirty-two-year-old black female who had worked as a nurse at the very hospital where she was now being stored with the dead. She was inside a black pouch on top of a gurney inside a small walk-in refrigerator that held no other guests this day except bright orange packages of surgical specimens and stillborn infants awaiting cremation. We rolled the dead woman into the autopsy room and unzipped the pouch.

'Have you X-rayed her?' I asked Gerde.

'Yes, and we've gotten her fingerprints. The dentist charted her teeth yesterday, as well, and matched them with premortem records.'

Gerde and I unzipped the pouch and opened it, and we unwrapped bloody sheets, exposing the mutilated body to the harsh glare of surgical lamps. She was rigid and cold, her blind eyes half open in a gory face. Gerde had not washed her yet, and her skin was crusty with blackish-red blood, her hair stiff with it like a Brillo pad. Her wounds were so numerous and violent that they radiated an aura of rage. I could feel the killer's fury and hate, and I began to envision her fierce struggle with him.

The fingers and palms of both hands had been cut to the bone when she had tried to protect herself by grabbing the knife blade. She had deep cuts to the backs of her forearms and wrists, again from trying to shield herself, and slashes to her legs that most likely were from her being down on the floor and trying to kick the swings of the knife away. Stab wounds were clustered in a savage constellation over her breasts, abdomen, and shoulders, and also on her buttocks and back.

Many of the wounds were large and irregular, and caused by the knife twisting as the victim moved or from the blade being withdrawn. The pattern of the individual wound configurations suggested a single-edged knife with a guard that had left squared-off abrasions. A somewhat superficial cut ran from her right jaw up to her cheek, and her throat had been laid open in a direction that began below the right ear and went downward, and then across the midline of the neck.

'Consistent with her throat being cut from behind,' I said as Benton looked on silently and took notes. 'Head pulled back, throat exposed.'

'I'm assuming cutting her throat was his grand finale,' Gerde said.

'If she had received an injury like this in the beginning, she would have bled out too quickly to put up any kind of fight. So yes, it's very possible he cut her throat last, perhaps when she was face down on the floor. What about clothing?'

'I'll get it,' Gerde said. 'You know, I get the strangest cases here. All these awful car crashes that turn out to be from some guy having a heart attack while he's driving. So he ends up airborne and takes out three or four other people. We had an Internet murder not so long ago. And husbands don't just shoot their wives around here, either. They strangle and bludgeon and decapitate them.'

He kept talking as he headed to a distant corner where clothing dried from hangers over a shallow basin. The garments were separated by sheets of plastic, to insure that trace evidence and body fluids from one weren't inadvertently transferred to another. I was covering the second autopsy table with a sterile sheet when Teun McGovern was shown in by a morgue assistant.

'Thought I'd check by before heading out to the scene,' she said.

She was dressed in BDUs and boots, and carrying a manila envelope. McGovern did not bother with gown or gloves as she slowly surveyed the carnage.

'Good Lord,' she said.

I helped Gerde spread out a pair of pajamas on top of the table I had just covered. Tops and bottoms reeked of dirty smoke and were so sooty and saturated with blood that I could not tell their color. The cotton fabric was cut and punctured front and back.

'She came in clothed in these?' I wanted to make sure.

'Yes,' Gerde replied. 'Everything buttoned and snapped. And I have to wonder if possibly some of the blood is his. In a fight like this, I wouldn't be surprised if he cut himself.'

I smiled at him. 'Someone taught you well,' I said.

'Some lady in Richmond,' he answered.

'At a glance this would seem domestic.' It was Benton who spoke. 'She's home in her pajamas, perhaps late at night. A classic case of overkill, such as you often find in homicides where the two people had a relationship. But what's a little unusual' – he stepped closer to the table – 'is her face. Other than this one cut here,' He pointed, 'there doesn't appear to be any injury. Typically, when the assailant has a relationship with the victim, he directs much of his violence at the face, because the face is the person.'

'The cut to her face is shallower than the others,' I noted, gently spreading open the wound with my gloved fingers. 'Deepest at her jaw, and then tapering off as it travels up her cheek.'

I stepped back and looked at the pajamas again.

'It's interesting that none of the buttons or snaps are missing,' I said. 'And no tears, such as you might expect after a struggle like this when the assailant grabs the victim and tries to control her.'

'I think *control* is the important word here,' Benton said.

'Or lack of it,' said McGovern.

'Exactly,' Benton agreed. 'This is a blitz attack. Something set this guy off and he went berserk. I seriously doubt he intended for this to go down anything like it did, which is also evidenced by the fire. It appears he lost control of that, too.'

'In my mind, the guy didn't hang around very long after he killed her,' McGovern said. 'He torched the place on his way out, thinking it would cover up his dirty work. But you're absolutely right. He didn't do a good job. And added to that, when the lady's fire alarm went off at one-fifty-eight A.M., trucks got there in less than five minutes. So the damage was minimal.'

Kellie Shephard had second-degree burns to her back and feet, and that was all.

'What about a burglar alarm?' I asked.

'Wasn't armed,' McGovern replied.

She opened the manila envelope and began spreading scene photographs over a desk. Benton, Gerde, and I took our time studying them. The victim in her bloody pajamas was facedown in the bathroom doorway, one arm under her body, the other straight out in front of her as if she had been reaching for something. Her legs were straight and close together, her feet almost reaching the toilet. Sooty water on the floor made it impossible to find bloody drag marks, had they existed, but close-ups of the door frame and surrounding wall showed obvious cuts to the wood that appeared fresh.

'The fire's point of origin,' McGovern said, 'is right here.'

She pointed to a photograph of the interior of the scorched bathroom.

'This corner near the tub where there's an open window with a curtain,' she said. 'And in that area, as you can see, are burned remnants of wooden furniture and pillows from a couch.'

She tapped the photograph.

'So we've got an open door and an open window, or a flue and a chimney, so to speak. Just like a fireplace,' she went on. 'The fire starts here on the tile floor, and involves the curtains. But the flames didn't quite have the energy this time to fully engage the ceiling.'

'Why do you suppose that is?' I asked.

'Can only be one good reason,' she replied. 'The damn thing wasn't built right. I mean, it's clear as day the killer piled furniture, couch cushions, and whatever into the bathroom to build his fire. But it just never got going the way it needed to. The initial fire was unable to involve the piled fuel load because of the open window and the flame bending toward it. He also didn't stand around and watch, either, or he would have realized he screwed up. This time his fire didn't do much more than lick over the body like a dragon's tongue.'

Benton was so silent and still he looked like a statue as his eyes traveled over photographs. I could tell he had much on his mind, but typically, he was guarded in his words. He had never worked with McGovern before, and he did not know Dr Abraham Gerde.

'We're going to be a long time,' I said to him.

'I'm heading out to the scene,' he replied.

His face was stony, the way it got when he felt evil like a cold draft. I gave him my eyes, and his met mine.

'You can follow me,' McGovern offered him.

'Thanks.'

'One other thing,' McGovern said. 'The back door was unlocked, and there was an empty cat pan in the grass by the steps.'

'So you think she went outside to empty the cat pan?' Gerde asked both of them. 'And this guy was waiting for her?'

'It's just a theory,' said McGovern.

'I don't know,' Wesley said.

'Then the killer knew she had a cat?' I said dubiously. 'And that she eventually was going to let it out that night or clean out the cat pan?'

'We don't know that she didn't empty the litter box earlier that evening and leave it in the yard to air out,' Wesley pointed out as he ripped off his gown. 'She may have turned off her alarm and opened the door late that night or in the early morning hours for some other reason.'

'And the cat?' I asked. 'Has it shown up?'

'Not yet,' McGovern said, and she and Benton left.

'I'm going to start swabbing,' I said to Gerde.

He reached for a camera and started shooting as I adjusted a light. I studied the cut to her face, and collected several fibers from it, and a wavy brown hair, four and a half inches long, that I suspected was her own. But there were other hairs, red and short, and I could tell they had been recently dyed because one-sixteenth of an inch at the root was dark. Of course, cat fur was everywhere, most likely transferred to bloody surfaces of the body when the victim was on the floor.

'A Persian, maybe?' Gerde asked. 'Long, very fine fur?'

'Sounds good to me,' I said.

15

The task of collecting trace evidence was overwhelming and had to be done before anything else. People generally have no idea what a microscopic pigpen they carry with them until someone like me starts scouring clothing and bodies for barely visible debris. I found splinters of wood, likely from the floor and walls, and cat litter, dirt, bits and pieces of insects and plants, and the expected ash and trash from the fire. But the most telling discovery came from the tremendous injury to her neck. Through a lens, I found two shiny, metallic specks. I collected them with the tip of my little finger, and delicately transferred them to a square of clean white cotton cloth.

There was a dissecting microscope on top of an old metal desk, and I set the magnification to twenty and adjusted the illuminator. I could scarcely believe it when I saw the tiny flattened and twisted silvery shavings in the bright circle of light.

'This is very important,' I started talking fast. 'I'm going to pack them in cotton inside an evidence container, and we need to make double sure there's no other debris like this in any of the other wounds. To the naked eye, it flashes like a piece of silver glitter.'

'Transferred from the weapon?'

Gerde was excited, too, and he came over to take a look.

'They were embedded deep inside the wound to her neck. So yes, I'd say that was a transfer, similar to what I found in the Warrenton case,' I answered him.

'And we know what about that?'

'A magnesium turning,' I answered. 'And we don't mention anything about this to anyone. We don't want this leaking to the press. I'll let Benton and McGovern know.'

'You got it,' he said with feeling.

There were twenty-seven wounds, and after a painful scrutinizing of all of them, we found no other bits of the shiny metal, and this struck me as a little puzzling since I had assumed the throat had been cut last. If that were the case, why wasn't the turning transferred to an earlier wound? I believed it would have been, especially in those instances when the knife had penetrated up to the guard and was swiped clean by muscular and elastic tissue as the blade was withdrawn.

'Not impossible but inconsistent,' I said to Gerde as I began measuring the cut to the throat. 'Six and three-quarters inches long,' I said, jotting it down on a body diagram. 'Shallow up around the right ear, then deep, through the strap muscles and trachea, then shallow again higher on the opposite side of the neck. Consistent with the knife drawn across the neck from behind, by a left-handed assailant.'

It was almost two P.M. when we finally began washing the body, and for minutes, water draining through the steel tabletop was bright red. I scrubbed stubborn blood with a big soft sponge, and her wounds seemed even more gaping and mutilating when her taut brown skin was clean. Kellie Shephard had been a beautiful woman, with high cheekbones and a flawless complexion as smooth as polished wood. She was five-foot-eight, with a lean, athletic figure. Her fingernails were unpainted, and she had been wearing no jewelry when she was found.

When we opened her up, her pierced chest cavity was filled with almost a liter of blood that had hemorrhaged from the great vessels leading to and from her heart and from her lungs. After receiving these injuries, she would have bled to death in, at the most, minutes, and I placed the timing of those attacks later in the struggle, when she was weakening and slowing down. The angles of those wounds were slight enough for me to suspect she had been moving very little on the floor when they had been inflicted from above. Then she had managed to roll over, perhaps in her last dying effort to protect herself, and I conjectured that this was when her throat was slashed.

'Someone should have had an awful lot of blood on him,' I commented as I began measuring the cuts to the hands.

'No kidding.'

'He had to clean up somewhere. You don't walk into a motel lobby looking like that.'

'Unless he lives around here.'

'Or got into his vehicle and hoped he didn't get pulled for something.'

'She's got a little brownish fluid in her stomach.'

'So she hadn't eaten recently, probably not since dinner, at any rate,' I said. 'I guess we need to find out if her bed was unmade.'

I was getting an image of a woman asleep when something happened either late Saturday night or in the early hours of Sunday morning. For some reason, she got up and turned off the alarm and unlocked the back door. Gerde and I used surgical staples to close the Y incision at shortly past four. I cleaned up in the morgue's small dressing room, where a mannikin used for staging violent deaths in court was in a state of disarray and undress on the shower floor.

Other than teenagers burning down old farmhouses, arsons in Lehigh were rare. Violence in the tidy middle-class subdivision called Wescosville where Shephard had lived was unheard of, as well. Crime there had never been more serious than smash and grabs, when a thief spied a pocketbook or wallet in plain view inside a house, and broke in and grabbed. Since there was no police department in Lehigh, by the time state troopers responded to the clanging burglar alarm, the thief was long gone.

I got my BDUs and steel-reinforced boots from my turn-out bag and shared the same changing room with the mannikin. Gerde was kind enough to give me a ride to the fire scene, and I was impressed by lush fir trees and roadside flower gardens, and every now and then, a well-kept, unassuming church. We turned on Hanover Drive, where homes were modern brick and wood, two-story and spacious, with basketball hoops, bicycles, and other signs of children.

'Do you have any idea of the price range?' I said, watching more houses flow past.

'Two-to-three-hundred-K range,' he said. 'Got a lot of engineers, nurses, stock brokers, and executives back here. Plus, I-78 is the main artery through Lehigh Valley, and you can shoot straight out on that and be in New York in an hour and a half. So some people commute back and forth to the city.'

'What else is around here?' I asked.

'A lot of industrial parks are just ten or fifteen minutes away. Coca-Cola, Air Products, Nestlé warehouses, Perrier. You pretty much name it. And farmland.'

'But she worked at the hospital.'

'Right. And that's at most a ten-minute drive, as you can tell.'

'Are you aware of ever having seen her before?'

Gerde thought for a minute as thin smoke drifted up from behind trees at the end of the street.

'I'm fairly certain I've seen her in the cafeteria before,' he answered. 'It's hard not to notice someone who looked like that. She may have been at a table with other nurses, I don't really recall. But I don't think we ever spoke.'

Shephard's house was yellow clapboard with white trim, and although the fire may not have been difficult to contain, the damage from water, and from axes chopping great holes to vent the fire out of the roof, was devastating. What was left was a sad, sooty face with a caved-in head, and shattered windows that were depressed, lifeless eyes. Borders of wildflowers were trampled, the neatly mown grass turned to mud, and a late-model Camry parked in the drive was covered with cinders. Fire department and ATF investigators were working inside, while two FBI agents in flak jackets were prowling the perimeter.

I found McGovern in the backyard talking to an intense young woman dressed in cut-off jeans, sandals, and a T-shirt.

'And that was what? Close to six?' McGovern was saying to her.

'That's right. I was getting dinner ready and saw her pull into her driveway, parking exactly where her car is now,' the woman recounted excitedly. 'She went inside, then came out maybe thirty minutes later and began pulling weeds. She liked to work in the yard, cut her own grass and everything.'

McGovern watched me as I walked up.

'This is Mrs Harvey,' she said to me. 'The next-door neighbor.'

'Hello,' I said to Mrs Harvey, whose eyes were bright with excitement that bordered on fear.

'Dr Scarpetta is a medical examiner,' McGovern explained.

'Oh,' said Mrs Harvey.

'Did you see Kellie again that night?' McGovern then asked.

The woman shook her head.

'She went in,' she said, 'I guess, and that was it. I know she worked real hard and usually didn't stay up late.'

'What about a relationship? Was there anybody she saw?'

'Oh, she's been through them,' Mrs Harvey said. 'A doctor here and there, different folks from the hospital. I remember last year she started seeing this man who had been her patient. Nothing lasted very long, it seems to me. She's so beautiful, that's the problem. The men wanted one thing, and she had something different in mind. I know because she used to make remarks about it.'

'But nobody recently?' McGovern asked.

Mrs Harvey had to think.

'Just her girlfriends,' she replied. 'She has a couple people she works with, and sometimes they dropped by or went off somewhere together. But I don't remember any activity that night. I mean, that's not saying I would know. Someone could have come over, and I wouldn't necessarily have heard a thing.'

'Have we found her cat?' I asked.

McGovern did not answer.

'That darn cat,' Mrs Harvey said. 'Pumpkin. Spoiled, spoiled, spoiled.'

She smiled and her eyes filled with tears.

'That was her child,' Harvey said.

'An indoor cat?' I then asked.

'Oh, absolutely. Kellie never let that cat out of the house, treated him like a hothouse tomato.'

'His litter box was found in the backyard,' McGovern told her. 'Did Kellie sometimes empty it and leave it out all night? Or for that matter, did she have a habit of emptying it at night? Going out after dark, the door unlocked and the alarm off.'

Harvey looked confused, and I suspected she had no idea that her neighbor had been murdered.

'Well,' she said, 'I do know that I've seen her empty the litter before, but always in a trash bag that went into the super can. So it wouldn't make sense for her to do that at night. My guess is she might have emptied it and left it outside to air, you know? Or maybe she just didn't have time to hose it off and was going to do it the next morning. But whatever the case, that cat knew how to use the toilet. So it wouldn't be any big deal for him to be without his litter box for a night.'

She stared off at a state police car cruising by.

'No one's said how the fire started,' Harvey went on. 'Do we know?'

'We're working on it,' McGovern said.

'She didn't die . . . well, it was quick, wasn't it?'

She squinted in the setting sun, and she bit her lower lip.

'I just don't want to think she suffered,' she said.

'Most people who die in fires don't suffer,' I answered, evading her question with gentle words. 'Usually carbon monoxide overcomes them and they aren't conscious.'

'Oh, thank God,' she said.

'I'll be inside,' McGovern said to me.

'Mrs Harvey,' I said, 'did you know Kellie very well?'

'We've been neighbors for almost five years. Not that we did a whole lot together, but I certainly knew her.'

'I'm wondering if you might have any recent photographs of her, or know someone who might?'

'I might have something.'

'I have to make sure of the identification,' I then said, although my motive was other than that.

I wanted to see for myself what Shephard had looked like in life.

'And if there's anything else you can tell me about her, I would appreciate it,' I went on. 'For example, does she have family here?'

'Oh no,' Harvey said, staring at her neighbor's ruined house. 'She was from all over. Her father was military, you know, and I think he and her mom live somewhere in North Carolina. Kellie was very worldly from having moved around so much. I used to tell her I wished I could be as strong and smart as her. She didn't take crap off anyone, let me tell you. One time there was a snake on my deck, and I called her, all hysterical. She came on and chased it in the yard and killed it with a shovel. I guess she had to get that way because the men just wouldn't leave her alone. I always told her she could be a movie star, and she would say, *But Sandra, I can't act.* And I would say, *But neither can most of them!*'

'She was pretty streetwise, then,' I said.

'You bet. That's why she had that burglar alarm put in. Feisty and streetwise, that's Kellie. If you want to come in with me, I'll see what I can do about pictures.'

'If you don't mind,' I said. 'That's very nice of you.'

We cut through a hedge and I followed her up steps into her big, bright kitchen. It was apparent that Harvey liked to cook, based on a well-stocked pantry and every conceivable appliance. Cookware hung from hooks in the ceiling, and whatever was simmering on the stove smelled rich with beef and onions, perhaps a stroganoff or stew.

'If you want to sit right over there by the window, I'll go get what I've got from the den,' she said.

I took a seat at the breakfast table and looked out the window at Kellie Shephard's house. I could see people passing behind broken windows, and someone had set up lights because the sun was low and smoldering. I wondered how often her neighbor had watched her come and go.

Certainly, Harvey was curious about the life of a woman exotic enough to be a movie star, and I wondered if someone could have stalked Shephard without her neighbor noticing a strange car or person in the area. But I had to be careful what I asked, because it was not publicly known that Shephard had died a violent death.

'Well, I can't believe it,' Harvey called out to me as she returned to the kitchen. 'I got something better. You know, some television crew was at the hospital last week filming a feature about the trauma center. It showed on the evening news, and Kellie was in it, so I taped it. I can't believe it took me this long to think of it, but my brain's not working all that well, if you know what I mean.'

She was holding a videotape. I accompanied her into the living room, where she inserted the tape into the VCR. I sat in a blue wing chair in a sea of blue carpet while she rewound and then hit the *play* button. The first few frames were of Lehigh Valley hospital from the perspective of a helicopter swooping in with an emergency case. It was then I realized that Kellie was really a medflight paramedic, and not merely a nurse on a ward.

Footage showed Kellie in a jumpsuit dashing down a corridor with other members of the flight crew who had just been paged.

'Excuse me, excuse me,' she said on tape as they darted around people in the way.

She was a spectacular example of the human genome working just right, her teeth dazzling, and the camera in love with every angle of her fine features and bones. It was not hard to imagine patients getting major crushes on her, and then the film showed her in the cafeteria after another impossible mission had been accomplished.

'It's always a race against time,' Shephard was telling the reporter. 'You know even a minute's delay could cost a life. Talk about an adrenaline rush.'

As she continued her rather banal interview, the angle of the camera shifted.

'I can't believe I taped that, but it's not often someone I know is on TV,' Harvey was saying.

It didn't penetrate at first.

'Stop the tape!' I said. 'Rewind. Yes, right there. Freeze it.'

The frame was of someone in the background eating lunch.

'No,' I said under my breath. 'No way.'

Carrie Grethen was wearing jeans and a tie-dye shirt, and eating a sandwich at a table with other busy hospital personnel. I had not recognized her at first because her hair was below her ears and henna red, and last I had seen her, it was short and bleached white. But it was her eyes that finally pulled at me like a black hole. She was staring straight into the camera as she chewed, her eyes as coldly bright and evil as I remembered.

I came out of the chair and went straight to the VCR and popped out the tape.

'I need to take this,' I said, my voice on the verge of panic. 'I promise you'll get it back.'

'Okay. As long as you don't forget. It's my only copy.' Sandra Harvey got up, too. 'Are you all right? You look like you've seen a ghost.'

'I've got to go. Thank you again,' I said.

I ran next door and trotted up steps into the back of the house, where cold water was an inch deep on the floor and dripping slowly from the roof. Agents were moving about, taking photographs and talking amongst themselves.

'Teun!' I called out.

I carefully moved further inside, stepping over missing areas of flooring and doing my best not to trip. I was vaguely aware of an agent dropping the burned carcass of a cat into a plastic bag.

'Teun!' I called out again.

I heard sure feet splashing and stepping over fallen roofing and collapsed walls. Then she was mere inches from me and steadying my arm with her hand.

'Whoa. Careful,' she started to say.

'We've got to find Lucy,' I said.

'What's going on?'

She began to carefully escort me out.

'Where is she?' I demanded.

'There's a two-alarm fire downtown. A grocery store, probably an arson. Kay, what the hell . . . ?'

We were out on the lawn and I was clutching the videotape as if it were my only hope in life.

'Teun, please.' I held her gaze. 'Take me to Philadelphia.'

'Come on,' she said.

16

McGovern made the trip back to Philadelphia in forty-five minutes, because she was speeding. She had radioed her field office and talked on a secure tac channel. Although she was still very careful what she relayed, she had made it clear that she wanted every available agent out on the street looking for Carrie. While this was going on, I reached Marino on my cellular phone and told him to get on a plane now.

'She's here,' I said.

'Oh shit. Do Benton and Lucy know?'

'As soon as I find them.'

'I'm out the door,' he said.

I did not believe, nor did McGovern, that Carrie was still in Lehigh County. She wanted to be where she could do the most damage, and I was convinced she somehow knew that Lucy had moved to Philadelphia. Carrie could have been stalking Lucy, for that matter. One thing I believed but could not make sense of was that the murders in Warrenton and now here were intended to lure those of us who had defeated Carrie in the past.

'But Warrenton happened before she escaped from Kirby,' McGovern reminded me as she turned onto Chestnut Street.

'I know,' I said as fear turned my pulse to static. 'I don't understand any of it except that somehow she's involved. It's not coincidence that she was on that news clip, Teun. She knew that after Kellie Shephard's murder we would review everything we could find. Carrie knew damn well we would see that tape.'

The fire was located on a seedy strip on the western fringes of the University of Pennsylvania. Darkness had fallen, and flashing emergency lights were visible miles away. Police cars had closed off two blocks of the street. There were at least eight fire engines and four ladder trucks, and more than seventy feet in the air, firefighters in buckets blasted the smoking roof with deluge guns. The night rumbled with diesel engines, and the blasting of high pressure water drummed over wood and shattered more glass. Tumescent hoses snaked across the street, and water was up to the hubcaps of parked cars that would be going nowhere anytime soon.

Photographers and news crews prowled sidewalks and were suddenly on alert when McGovern and I got out of her car.

'Is ATF involved in this case?' asked a TV reporter.

'We're just here taking a look,' McGovern answered as we walked without pause.

'Then it's a suspected arson, like the other grocery stores?'

The microphone followed as our boots splashed.

'It's under investigation,' McGovern said. 'And you need to stay back, ma'am.'

The reporter was left at the hood of a fire engine while McGovern and I drew closer to the store. Flames had jumped to the barbershop next door, where firefighters with axes and pike poles chopped square holes in the roof. Agents in ATF flak jackets were interviewing potential witnesses, and investigators in turn-outs and helmets moved in and out of a basement. I overheard something about toggle switches and the meter and stealing service. Black smoke billowed, and there seemed to be only one area in the plenum that stubbornly smoldered and spurted flame.

'She might be inside,' McGovern said in my ear.

I followed her in closer. The plate-glass storefront was wide open, and part of the inventory flowed out on a cold river of water. Cans of tuna fish, blackened bananas, sanitary napkins, bags of potato chips, and bottles of salad dressing flowed by, and a firefighter rescued a can of coffee and shrugged as he tossed it inside his truck. The strong beams of flashlights probed the smoky, black interior of the devastated store, illuminating girders twisted like taffy and exposed wires hanging in tangles from I-beams.

'Is Lucy Farinelli in there?' McGovern called inside.

'Last I saw her she was out back talking to the owner,' a male voice called back.

'Be careful in there,' McGovern said loudly.

'Yeah, well, we're having a real problem getting the power to shut down. Must be an underground feed. Maybe if you could look into that?'

'Will do.'

'So this is what my niece does,' I said as McGovern and I waded back out to the street and more ruined produce and canned goods floated past.

'On her good days. I think her unit number's 718. Let me see if I can raise her.'

McGovern held the portable radio to her lips and searched for Lucy on the air.

'What'cha got?' my niece's voice came back.

'You in the middle of something?'

'Finishing up.'

'Can you meet us in front?'

'On my way.'

My relief was apparent, and McGovern smiled at me as lights strobed and water arched. Firefighters were black with soot and sweating. I watched them moving slowly in their boots, dragging hoses over their shoulders and drinking cups of a green thirst quencher that they mixed in plastic jugs. Bright lights had been set up in a truck, and the glare was harsh and confusing as the scene became surreal. Fire buffs, or *whackers*, as ATF agents called them, had crawled out of the dark and were taking photographs with disposable cameras, while entrepreneurial venders hawked incense and counterfeit watches.

By the time Lucy got to us, the smoke had thinned and was white, indicating a lot of steam. Water was getting to the source.

'Good,' McGovern commented, observing the same thing. 'I think we're almost there.'

'Rats chewing wires,' Lucy said first thing. 'That's the owner's theory.'

She looked at me oddly.

'What brings you out?' she asked.

'It's looking like Carrie is involved in the Lehigh arson-homicide,' McGovern answered for me. 'And it's possible she's still in the area, maybe even here in Philadelphia.'

'What?' Lucy looked stunned. 'How? What about Warrenton?'

'I know,' I replied. 'It seems inexplicable. But there are definite parallels.'

'So maybe this one's a copycat,' my niece then said. 'She read about it and is jerking us around.'

I thought of the metal shaving again, and of the point of origin. There had been nothing in the news about details like that. Nor had it ever been released that Claire Rawley had been killed with a sharp cutting instrument, such as a knife, and I could not get away from one other similarity. Both Rawley and Shephard were beautiful.

'We've got a lot of agents on the street,' McGovern said to Lucy. 'The point is for you to be aware and alert, all right? And Kay.' She looked at me. 'This may not be the best place for you to be.'

I did not answer her, but instead said to Lucy, 'Have you heard from Benton?'

'No.'

'I just don't understand,' I muttered. 'I wonder where he could be.'

'When did you have contact with him last?' Lucy asked.

'At the morgue. He left saying he was going to the scene. And he what? Stayed there maybe an hour?' I said to McGovern.

'If that. You don't think he would have gone back to New York, or maybe Richmond?' she asked me.

'I'm sure he would have told me. I'll keep paging him. Maybe when Marino gets here, he'll know something,' I added as fire hoses blasted and a fine mist settled over us.

It was almost midnight when Marino came to my hotel room, and he knew nothing.

'I don't think you should be here by yourself,' he said right off, and he was keyed up and disheveled.

'You want to tell me where I might be safer? I don't know what's happening. Benton's left no messages. He isn't answering his pager.'

'You two didn't get in a fight or something, did you?'

'For God's sake,' I said in exasperation.

'Look, you asked me, and I'm just trying to help.'

'I know.'

I took a deep breath and tried to settle down.

'What about Lucy?'

He sat on the edge of my bed.

'There was a pretty big fire near the university. She's probably still there,' I answered.

'Arson?'

'I'm not sure they know yet.'

We were quiet for a moment, and my tension grew.

'Look,' I said. 'We can stay here and wait for God knows what. Or we can go out. I can't sleep.'

I began to pace.

'I'm not sitting here all night worrying that Carrie might be lying in wait, damn it.'

Tears filled my eyes.

'Benton's out there somewhere. Maybe at the fire scene with Lucy. I don't know.'

I turned my back to him and stared out at the harbor. My breath trembled in my breast, and my hands were so cold the fingernails had turned blue.

Marino got up, and I knew he was watching me.

'Come on,' he said. 'Let's check it out.'

When we reached the fire scene on Walnut Street, the activity had diminished considerably. Most of the fire trucks had left, and those few firefighters still on the job were exhausted and coiling hoses. Steamy smoke drifted up from the plenum area of the store, but I could see no flames, and from within voices and footsteps sounded as the strong beam of flashlights cut the darkness and were caught in shards of broken glass. I sloshed through water as more groceries and debris floated past, and when I reached the entrance, I heard McGovern's voice. She was saying something about a medical examiner.

'Get him here now,' she barked. 'And watch it over there, okay? No telling where it's all scattered, and I don't want us stepping on anything.'

'Someone got a camera?'

'Okay, I got a watch, stainless steel, men's. Crystal's shattered. And we got one pair of handcuffs?'

'What did you say?'

'You heard me. Handcuffs, Smith & Wesson, the genuine article. Closed and locked like someone had them on. In fact, they're *double* locked.'

'You're shittin' me.'

I made my way inside as large drops of cold water smacked my helmet and dripped down my neck. I recognized Lucy's voice, but I could not make out what she was saying. She sounded almost hysterical, and there was suddenly a lot of splashing and commotion.

'Hold on, hold on!' McGovern commanded. 'Lucy! Someone get her out of here!'

'No!' Lucy screamed.

'Come on, come on,' McGovern was saying. 'I've got your arm. Take it easy, okay?'

'No!' Lucy screamed. 'NO! NO! NO!'

Then there was a loud splash and a surprised outcry.

'My God. Are you all right?' McGovern said.

I was halfway inside when I saw McGovern helping Lucy to her feet. My niece was hysterical, and her hand was bleeding, but she didn't seem to care. I waded to them as my heart constricted and my blood seemed to turn as cold as the water I waded through.

'Let me see,' I said as I gently took Lucy's hand and shone my light on it.

She was shaking all over.

'When's the last time you had a tetanus shot?' I asked.

'Aunt Kay,' she moaned. 'Aunt Kay.'

Lucy locked her arms around my neck, and both of us almost fell. She was crying so hard she could not speak, and her embrace was a vise against my ribs.

'What's happened?' I demanded of McGovern.

'Let's get both of you out of here now,' she said.

'Tell me what's happened!'

I wasn't going anywhere until she told me. She hesitated again.

'We've found some remains. A burn victim. Kay, please.'

She took my arm and I yanked it away.

'We need to go out,' she said.

I pulled away from her as I looked toward the back corner, where investigators were talking amongst themselves and splashing and wading as fingers of light probed.

'More bones over here,' someone was saying. 'Nope, scratch that. Burned wood.'

'Well, this isn't.'

'Shit. Where the fuck's the medical examiner?'

'I'll take care of this,' I said to McGovern as if this were my scene. 'Get Lucy out and wrap a clean towel around her hand. I'll tend to her shortly. Lucy,' I then said to my niece. 'You're going to be fine.'

I unlocked her arms from my neck, and I was beginning to tremble. Somehow I knew.

'Kay, don't go over there,' McGovern raised her voice. 'Don't!'

But by now I knew I must, and I abruptly left them for that corner, splashing and almost tripping as I got weak in the knees. The investigators grew quiet with my approach, and at first I did not know what I was looking at as I followed the beams of their flashlights to something charred that was mingled with soggy paper and insulation, something on top of fallen plaster and chunks of blackened wood.

Then I saw the shape of a belt and its buckle, and the protruding femur that looked like a thick, burned stick. My heart was beating out of my chest as the shape became the burned ruins of a body attached to a blackened head that had no features, only patches of sooty silver hair.

'Let me see the watch,' I said, staring wildly at the investigators.

One of them held it out and I took it from his hand. It was a men's stainless steel Breitling, an Aerospace.

'No,' I muttered as I knelt in the water. 'Please, no.'

I covered my face with my hands. My mind shorted out. My vision failed as I swayed. Then a hand was steadying me. Bile crept up my throat.

'Come on, Doc,' a male voice said gently as hands lifted me to my feet.

'It can't be him,' I cried out. 'Oh, God, please don't let it be. Please, please, please.'

I couldn't seem to keep my balance, and it took two agents to get me out as I did what I could to gather the fragments that were left of me. I spoke to no one when I was returned to the street, and I walked weirdly, woodenly, to McGovern's Explorer, where she was with Lucy in the back, holding a blood-soaked towel around Lucy's left hand.

'I need a first aid kit,' I heard myself say to McGovern.

'It might be better to get her to the hospital,' her voice came back as she stared hard at me, fear and pity shining in her eyes.

'Get it,' I said.

McGovern reached in back, over the seat to grab something. She set an orange Pelican case on the seat and unfastened the latches. Lucy was almost in shock, shaking violently, her face white.

'She needs a blanket,' I said.

I removed the towel and washed her hand with bottled water. A thick flap of skin on her thumb was almost avulsed, and I swabbed it profusely with betadine, the iodine odor piercing my sinuses as all that I had just seen became a bad dream. It was not true.

'She needs stitches,' McGovern said.

It had not happened. A dream.

'We should go to the hospital so she can get stitches.'

But I already had out the steri-strips and benzoin glue, because I knew that stitches would not work with a wound like this. Tears were streaming down my face as I topped off my work with a thick layer of gauze. When I looked up and out the window, I realized Marino was standing by my door. His face was distorted by pain and rage. He looked like he might vomit. I got out of the Explorer.

'Lucy, you need to come on with me,' I said, taking her arm. I had always been able to function better when I was taking care of someone else. 'Come on.'

Emergency lights flashed in our faces, the night and the people in it disconnected and strange. Marino drove away with us as the medical examiner's van pulled up. There would be X-rays, dental charts, maybe even DNA used to confirm the identification. The process most likely would take a while, but it did not matter. I already knew. Benton was dead.

17

As best anyone could reconstruct events at this time, Benton had been lured to his dreadful death. We had no clue as to what had drawn him to the small grocery store on Walnut Street, or if, perhaps, he simply had been abducted somewhere else and then forced up a ladder into the plenum of that small building in its bad part of town. We believed he had been handcuffed at some point, and the continuing search had also turned up wire twisted into a figure eight that most likely had restrained the ankles that had burned away.

His car keys and wallet were recovered, but not his Sig Sauer nine-millimeter pistol or gold signet ring. He had left several changes of clothing in his hotel room, and his briefcase, which had been searched and turned over to me. I stayed the night in Teun McGovern's house. She had posted agents on the property, because Carrie was still out there somewhere, and it was only a matter of time.

She would finish what she had started, and the important question, really, was who would be next and if she would succeed. Marino had moved into Lucy's tiny apartment and was keeping watch from her couch. The three of us had nothing to say to each other because there was nothing to say, really. What was done was done.

McGovern had tried to get through to me. Several times the previous night she had brought tea or food into my room with its blue-curtained window overlooking the old brick and brass lanterns of the row houses in Society Hill. She was wise enough not to force anything, and I was too ruined to do anything but sleep. I continued to wake up feeling sick and then remember why.

I did not remember my dreams. I wept until my eyes were almost swollen shut. Late Thursday morning, I took a long shower and walked into McGovern's kitchen. She was wearing a Prussian blue suit, drinking coffee and reading the paper.

'Good morning,' she said, surprised and pleased that I had ventured out from behind my closed door. 'How are you doing?'

'Tell me what's happening,' I said.

I sat across from her. She set her coffee cup on the table and pushed back her chair.

'Let me get you coffee,' she said.

'Tell me what is going on,' I repeated. 'I want to know, Teun. Have they found out anything yet? At the morgue, I mean?'

She was at a loss for a moment, staring out the window at an old magnolia tree heavy with blossoms that were limp and brown.

'They're still working on him,' she finally spoke. 'But based on indications so far, it appears his throat may have been cut. There were cuts to the bones of his face. Here and here.'

She pointed to her left jaw and space between his eyes.

'There was no soot or burns in his trachea, and no CO. So he was already dead when the fire was set,' she said to me. 'I'm sorry, Kay. I . . . Well, I don't know what to say.'

'How can it be that no one saw him enter the building?' I asked as if I had not comprehended the horror of what she had just said. 'Someone forces him inside at gunpoint, maybe, and no one saw a thing?'

'The store closed at five P.M.,' she answered. 'There's no sign of forcible entry and for some reason the burglar alarm hadn't been set, so it didn't go off. We've had trouble with these places being torched for insurance money. Same Pakistani family always involved one way or another.'

She sipped her coffee.

'Same MO,' she went on. 'Small inventory, the fire starts shortly after business hours, and no one in the neighborhood saw a thing.'

'This has nothing to do with insurance money!' I said with sudden rage.

'Of course, it doesn't,' she answered quietly. 'Or at least not directly. But if you want to hear my theory, I'll tell you.'

'Tell me.'

'Maybe Carrie was the torch . . .'

'Of course!'

'I'm saying she might have conspired with the owner to torch the place for him. He may have even paid her to do it, not having any idea what her real agenda was. Granted, this would have taken some planning.'

'She's had nothing to do for years but plan.'

My chest tightened again and tears formed a lump in my throat and filled my eyes.

'I'm going home,' I told her. 'I've got to do something. I can't stay here.'

'I think you are better off . . .' she started to protest.

'I've got to figure out what she will do next,' I said, as if this were possible. 'I've got to figure out how she's doing what she's doing. There's some master plan, some routine, something more to all this. Did they find any metal shavings?'

'There wasn't much left. He was in the plenum, the point of origin. There was some kind of big fuel load up there, but we don't know what, except there were a lot of Styrofoam peanuts floating around. And those things will really burn. No accelerants detected, so far.'

'Teun, the metal shavings from the Shephard case. Let us take them to Richmond so we can compare them with what we've got. Your investigators can receipt them to Marino.'

She looked at me with eyes that were skeptical, tired, and sad.

'You need to deal with this, Kay,' she said. 'Let us do the rest of it.'

'I am dealing with it, Teun.'

I got up from my chair and looked down at her.

'The only way I can,' I said. 'Please.'

'You really should not be on this case anymore. And I'm placing Lucy on administrative leave for at least a week.'

'You won't pull me off this case,' I told her. 'Not in this life.'

'You're not in a position to be objective.'

'And what would you do if you were me?' I demanded. 'Would you go home and do nothing?'

'But I'm not you.'

'Answer me,' I said.

'No one could stop me from working the case. I would be obsessed. I would do just what you're doing,' she said, getting up, too. 'I'll do what I can to help.'

'Thank you,' I said. 'Thank God for you, Teun.'

She studied me for a while, leaning against the counter, her hands in the pockets of her slacks.

'Kay, don't blame yourself for this,' she said.

'I blame Carrie,' I replied with a sudden flow of bitter tears. 'That's exactly who I blame.'

18

———

Several hours later, Marino was driving Lucy and me back to Richmond. It was the worst car trip I could remember, with the three of us staring out and saying nothing, an oppressive depression heavy on the air. It did not seem true, and whenever truth struck again, it was with the blow of a heavy fist into my chest. Images of Benton were vivid. I did not know if it were grace or a bigger tragedy that we had not spent our last night together in the same bed.

In a way, I wasn't sure I could bear the fresh memories of his touch, his breath, the way he felt in my arms. Then I wanted to hold him and make love again. My mind tumbled down different hills into dark spaces where thoughts got caught on the realities of dealing with his possessions at my house, including his clothing.

His remains would have to be shipped to Richmond, and despite all I knew about death, the two of us had never devoted much attention to our own or the funeral service we might want and where we should be buried. We had not wanted to think about our own, and so we hadn't.

I-95 South was a blur of highway running forever through stopped time. When tears filled my eyes, I turned to my window and hid my face. Lucy was silent in the back seat, her anger, grief, and fear as palpable as a concrete wall.

'I'm going to quit,' she finally said when we passed through

Fredericksburg. 'This is it for me. I'll find something somewhere. Maybe in computers.'

'Bullshit,' Marino answered, his eyes on her in the rearview mirror. 'That's just what the bitch wants you to do. Quit law enforcement. Be a loser and a big fuck-up.'

'I am a loser and a fuck-up.'

'Bull fucking shit,' he said.

'She killed him because of me,' she went on in the same heartless monotone.

'She killed him because she wanted to. And we can sit here and have a pity party, or we can figure out what we're gonna do before she whacks the next one of us.'

But my niece was not to be consoled. Indirectly, she had exposed all of us to Carrie a long time ago.

'Carrie wants you to blame yourself for this,' I said to her.

Lucy did not respond, and I turned around to look at her. She was dressed in dirty BDUs and boots, her hair a mess. She still smelled of fire, because she had not bathed. She had not eaten or slept, as best I knew. Her eyes were flat and hard. They glinted coldly of the decision she had made, and I had seen the look before, when hopelessness and hostility made her self-destructive. A part of her wanted to die, or maybe a part of her already had.

We reached my house at half past five, and the slanted rays of the sun were hot and bright, the sky hazy blue but cloudless. I carried in newspapers from the front steps and was sickened again by this morning's front-page headline about Benton's death. Although identification was tentative, it was believed he had died in a fire under very suspicious circumstances while assisting the FBI in the nationwide hunt for the escaped killer Carrie Grethen. Investigators would not say why Benton had been inside the small grocery store that had burned, or if he might have been lured there.

'What do you want to do with this?' Marino asked.

He had opened the car trunk, where three large brown paper bags contained the personal effects collected from Benton's hotel room. I could not decide.

'Want me to just put them in your office?' he asked. 'Or I can go through them if you want, Doc.'

'No, no, just leave them,' I said.

Stiff paper crackled as he carried the bags into the house and down the hall. His footsteps were burdened and slow, and when he returned to the front of the house, I was still standing by the open door.

'I'll talk to you later,' he said. 'And don't go leaving this door open, you hear me? The alarm stays on and you and Lucy shouldn't go out anywhere.'

'I don't think you have a worry.'

Lucy had dropped her luggage in her bedroom near the kitchen and was staring out the window at Marino driving away. I came behind her and gently put my hands on her shoulders.

'Don't quit,' I said, and I leaned my forehead against the back of her neck.

She did not turn around, and I felt grief shudder through her.

'We're in this together, Lucy,' I went on quietly. 'We're all that's left, really. Just you and me. Benton would want us united in this. He wouldn't want you giving up. Then what will I do, huh? If you give up, you'll be giving up on me, too.'

She began to sob.

'I need you.' I could barely talk. 'More than ever.'

She turned around and clung to me the way she used to when she was a frightened child starved for someone who cared. Her tears wet my neck, and for a while we stood in the middle of a room still packed with computer equipment and school books, and plastered with posters of her adolescent heroes.

'It's my fault, Aunt Kay. It's all my fault. I killed him!' she cried out.

'No,' I said, holding her tight as my own tears flowed.

'How can you ever forgive me? I took him away from you!'

'That's not the way it is. You did nothing, Lucy.'

'I can't live with this.'

'You can and you will. We need to help each other live with this.'

'I loved him, too. Everything he did for me. Getting me started with the Bureau, giving me a chance. Being supportive. About everything.'

'It's going to be all right,' I said.

She pulled away from me and collapsed on the edge of the bed, wiping her face with the tail of her sooty blue shirt. She rested her elbows on her knees and hung her head, staring at her own tears falling like rain on the hardwood floor.

'I'm telling you, and you've got to listen,' she said in a low, hard voice. 'I'm not sure I can go on, Aunt Kay. Everybody has a point. Where it begins and ends.' Her breath shook. 'Where they can't go on. I wish she had killed me instead. Maybe she would have done me a favor.'

I watched her with gathering resolve as she willed herself to die before my eyes.

'If I don't go on, Aunt Kay, you've got to understand and not blame yourself or anything,' she muttered, wiping her face with her sleeve.

I went over to her and lifted her chin. She was hot and smoky, her breath and body odor bad.

'You listen to me,' I said with an intensity that would have frightened her in the past. 'You get this goddamn notion out of your head right now. You are glad you didn't die, and you aren't committing suicide, if that's what you're implying, and I believe it is. You know what suicide is all about, Lucy? It's about anger, about payback. It's the final *fuck-you*. You will do that to Benton? You will do that to Marino? You will do that to me?'

I held her face in my hands until she looked at me.

'You're going to let that no-good piece of trash Carrie do that to you?' I demanded. 'Where's that fierce spirit I know?'

'I don't know,' she whispered with a sigh.

'Yes you do,' I said. 'Don't you dare ruin my life, Lucy. It's been damaged enough. Don't you dare make me spend the rest of my days with the echo of a gunshot sounding on and on in my mind. I didn't think you were a coward.'

'I'm not.'

Her eyes focused on mine.

'Tomorrow we fight back,' I said.

She nodded, swallowing hard.

'Go take a shower,' I said.

I waited until I heard the water in her bathroom running, and then went into the kitchen. We needed to eat, although I doubted either of us felt like it. I thawed chicken breasts and cooked them in stock with whatever fresh vegetables I could find. I was liberal with rosemary, bay leaves, and sherry, but nothing stronger, not even pepper, for we needed to be soothed. Marino called twice while we were eating, to make certain we were all right.

'You can come over,' I said to him. 'I've made soup, although it might be kind of thin by your standards.'

'I'm okay,' he said, and I knew he did not mean it.

'I've got plenty of room, if you'd like to stay the night. I should have thought to ask you earlier.'

'No, Doc. I got things to do.'

'I'm going to the office first thing in the morning,' I said.

'I don't know how you can,' he replied in a judgmental way, as if my thinking about work meant I wasn't showing what I should be showing right now.

'I have a plan. And come hell or high water, I'm going to carry it out,' I said.

'I hate it when you start planning things.'

I hung up and collected empty soup bowls from the kitchen table, and the more I thought about what I was going to do, the more manic I got.

'How hard would it be for you to get a helicopter?' I said to my niece.

'What?' She looked amazed.

'You heard me.'

'Do you mind if I ask what for? You know, I can't just order one like a cab.'

'Call Teun,' I said. 'Tell her I'm taking care of business and need all of the cooperation I can get. Tell her if all goes as I'm hoping, I'm going to need her and a team to meet us in Wilmington, North Carolina. I don't know when yet. Maybe right away. But I need free rein. They're going to have to trust me.'

Lucy got up and went to the sink to fill her glass with more water.

'This is nuts,' she said.

'Can you get a helicopter or not?'

'If I get permission, then yes. Border Patrol has them. That's usually what we use. I can probably get one in from D.C.'

'Good,' I said. 'Get it as fast as you can. In the morning I'm hitting the labs to confirm what I think I already know. Then we may be going to New York.'

'Why?'

She looked interested but skeptical.

'We're going to land at Kirby and I intend to get to the bottom of things,' I answered her.

Marino called again at close to ten, and I reassured him one more time that Lucy and I were as fine as could be expected, and that we felt safe inside my house, with its sophisticated alarm system, lighting, and guns. He sounded bleary and thick, and I could tell he had been drinking, his TV turned up loud.

'I need you to meet me at the lab at eight,' I said.

'I know, I know.'

'It's very important, Marino.'

'It's not like you need to tell me that, Doc.'

'Get some sleep,' I said.

'Ditto.'

But I couldn't. I sat at my desk in my study, going through the suspicious fire deaths from ESA. I studied the Venice Beach death, and
then the one from Baltimore, struggling to see what, if anything, the
cases and victims had in common besides the point of origin and the
fact that although arson was suspected, investigators could find no
evidence of it. I called the Baltimore police department first, and found
someone in the detective division who seemed amenable to talking.

'Johnny Montgomery worked that one,' the detective said, and I
could hear him smoking.

'Do you know anything about it?' I asked.

'Best you talk to him. And he probably will need some way of
knowing you're who you say you are.'

'He can call me at my office in the morning for verification.' I gave
him the number. 'I should be no later than eight. What about e-mail?
Does Investigator Montgomery have an address I could send a note
to?'

'Now that I can give you.'

I heard him open a drawer, and then he gave me what I needed.

'Seems I've heard of you before,' the detective said thoughtfully.
'If you're the ME I'm thinking of. I know it's a lady. A good-looking
one, too, based on what I've seen on TV. Hmmm. You ever get up to
Baltimore?'

'I went to medical school in your fair city.'

'Well, now I know you're smart.'

'Austin Hart, the young man who died in the fire, was also a
student at Johns Hopkins.' I prodded him.

'He was also a homo. I personally think it was a hate crime.'

'What I need is a photograph of him and anything about his life,
his habits, his hobbies.' I took advantage of the detective's momen-
tary lapse.

'Oh yeah.' He smoked. 'One of these pretty boys. I heard he did
modeling to pay his way through med school. Calvin Klein underwear ads, that sort of thing. Probably some jealous lover. You come
to Baltimore next, Doc, and you got to try Camden Yards. You know
about the new stadium, right?'

'Absolutely,' I replied as I excitedly processed what he had just said.

'I can get you tickets if you want.'

'That would be very nice. I'll get in touch with Investigator
Montgomery, and I thank you so much for your help.'

I got off the phone before he could ask me about my favorite baseball team, and I immediately sent Montgomery an e-mail that outlined my needs, although I felt I already had enough. Next I tried the Pacific Division of the Los Angeles Police Department, which covered Venice Beach, and I got lucky. The investigator who had worked Marlene Farber's case was on evening shift and had just come in. His name was Stuckey, and he did not seem to require much verification from me that I was who I claimed to be.

'Wish somebody would solve this one for me,' he said right off. 'Six months and still nothing. Not one tip that's turned out to be worth anything.'

'What can you tell me about Marlene Farber?' I asked.

'Was on *General Hospital* now and then. And *Northern Exposure*. I guess you've seen that?'

'I don't watch much TV. PBS, that's about it.'

'What else, what else? Oh right. *Ellen.* No big parts, but who knows how far she might have gone. Prettiest thing you ever saw. Was dating some producer, and we're pretty sure he had nothing to do with what happened. Only thing that guy really cared about was coke and screwing all the young stars he got parts for. You know, after I got the case, I went through a bunch of tapes of shows she was on. She wasn't bad. It's a shame.'

'Anything unusual about the scene?' I asked.

'Everything was unusual about that scene. Don't have a clue how a fire like that could have started in the master bathroom on the first floor, and ATF couldn't figure it out, either. There wasn't anything to burn in there except toilet paper and towels. No sign of forcible entry, either, and the burglar alarm never went off.'

'Investigator Stuckey, were her remains by chance found in the bathtub?'

'That's another freaky thing, unless she was a suicide. Maybe set the fire and cut her wrists or something. A lot of people cut their wrists in the tub.'

'Any trace evidence to speak of?'

'Ma'am, she was chalk. Looked like she'd been in the crematorium. There was enough left of the torso area for them to ID her through X-rays, but beyond that, we're talking a few teeth, pieces and parts of bones, and some hair.'

'Did she by chance do any modeling?' I then asked.

'That, TV commercials, magazine ads. She made a pretty good living. Drove a black Viper and lived in a damn nice house right on the ocean.'

'I'm wondering if you could e-mail photos and any reports to me.'
'Give me your address, and I'll see what I can do.'
'I need them fast, Investigator Stuckey,' I said.

I hung up and my mind was whirling. Each victim was physically beautiful and involved in photography or television. It was a common denominator that could not be ignored, and I believed that Marlene Farber, Austin Hart, Claire Rawley, and Kellie Shephard had been selected for a reason that was important to the killer. This was where everything unraveled. The pattern fit that of a serial killer, like Bundy, who selected women with long straight hair who resembled his estranged girlfriend. What didn't fit was Carrie Grethen. In the first place, she had been locked up in Kirby when the first three deaths had occurred, and her MO had never been anything like this.

I was baffled. Carrie was not there and yet she was. I dozed for a while in my chair, and at six A.M., I came to with a start. My neck burned from being bent in the wrong position, and my back was achy and stiff. I got up slowly and stretched, and knew what I had to do but wasn't certain I could. Just the thought filled me with terror, and my heart kicked in with violent force. I could feel my pulse pounding like a fist against a door, and I stared at the brown paper bags Marino had placed in front of a bookcase packed with law reviews. They were taped shut and labeled, and I picked them up. I followed the hallway to Benton's room.

Although we typically had shared my bed, the opposite wing of the house had been his. Here he had worked and stored his day-to-day belongings, for as both of us had gotten older, we had learned that space was our most reliable friend. Our retreats made our battles less bloody, and absences during the day made nights more inviting. His door was open wide, as he had left it. The lights were out, the curtains drawn. Shadows got sharper as I stood, frozen for an instant, staring in. It required all of the courage I had ever demonstrated in my life to turn on the overhead light.

His bed with its bold blue duvet and sheets was neatly made, because Benton was always meticulous, no matter his hurry. He had never waited for me to change his linens or attend to his laundry, and part of this was due to an independence and strong sense of self that never really relented, not even with me. He had to do it his way. In that regard, we were so much alike, I marveled we had ever gotten together. I collected his hairbrush from the dresser, because I knew it might be useful for a DNA comparison, should there be no other avenue for identification. I went to the small cherry bedside table to look at the books and thick file folders stacked there.

He had been reading *Cold Mountain*, and had used the torn flap of an envelope to mark his place not quite halfway through. Of course, there were the pages of the latest revision of a crime classification manual he was editing, and the sight of his scratchy penmanship crashed me to earth. I tenderly turned manuscript pages and trailed my fingers over the barely legible words he had penned as tears ambushed me again. Then I set the bags on the bed and ripped them open.

Police had hastily riffled through his closet and drawers, and nothing they had packed inside the bags was neatly folded, but rather bunched and rolled. One by one I smoothed open white cotton shirts and bold ties and two pairs of suspenders. He had packed two light-weight suits, and both of them were crinkled like crêpe paper. There were dress shoes, and running clothes and socks and jockey shorts, but it was his shaving kit that stopped me.

Methodical hands had rummaged through it, and the screw cap to a bottle of Givenchy III was loose and cologne had leaked. The familiar sharp, masculine scent seized me with emotion. I could feel his smooth shaven cheeks. Suddenly, I saw him behind his desk in his former office at the FBI Academy. I remembered his striking features, his crisp dress and the smell of him, back then when I was already falling in love and did not know it. I neatly folded his clothing in a stack and fumbled, ripping and tearing open another bag. I placed the black leather briefcase on the bed and sprung open the locks.

Noticeably missing inside was the Colt Mustang .380 pistol that he sometimes had strapped to his ankle, and I found it significant that he had taken the pistol with him the night of his death. He always carried his nine-millimeter in its shoulder holster, but the Colt was his backup if he felt a situation to be threatening. This singular act indicated to me that Benton had been on a mission at some point after he had left the Lehigh fire scene. I suspected he had gone to meet someone, and I didn't understand why he hadn't let anybody know, unless he had become careless, and this I doubted.

I picked out his brown leather date book and flipped through it in search of any recent appointment that caught my eye. There were a hair cut, dentist's appointment, and trips coming up, but nothing penciled in for the day of his death except the birthday of his daughter, Michelle, the middle of next week. I imagined she and her sisters were with their mother, Connie, who was Benton's former wife. I dreaded the idea that eventually I would need to share their sorrow, no matter how they might feel about me.

He had scribbled comments and questions about the profile of Carrie, the monster who soon after had caused his death. The irony of that was inconceivable, as I envisioned him trying to dissect Carrie's behavior in hopes of anticipating what she might do. I didn't suppose he had ever entertained the notion that even as he had concentrated on her, she quite likely had been thinking about him, too. She had been planning Lehigh County and the videotape, and by now, most likely, was parading as a member of a production crew.

My eyes stumbled over penned phrases such as *offender-victim relationship/fixation*, and *fusion of identity/erotomania* and *victim perceived as someone of higher status*. On the back of the page, he had jotted *patterned life after. How fits Carrie's victimology? Kirby. What access to Claire Rawley? Seemingly none. Inconsistent. Suggestive of a different offender? Accomplice? Gault. Bonnie and Clyde. Her original MO. May be on to something here. Carrie not alone. W/M 28–45? White helicopter?*

Chills lifted my flesh as I realized what Benton had been thinking when he had been standing in the morgue taking notes and watching Gerde and me work. Benton had been contemplating what suddenly seemed so obvious. Carrie was not alone in this. She had somehow allied herself with an evil partner, perhaps while she was incarcerated at Kirby. In fact, I was certain that this allegiance predated her escape, and I wondered if during the five years she was there, she might have met another psychopathic patient who later was released. Perhaps she had corresponded with him as freely and audaciously as she had with the media and me.

It was also significant that Benton's briefcase had been found inside his hotel room, when I knew it had accompanied him earlier at the morgue. Clearly, he had returned to his room some time after leaving the Lehigh fire scene. Where he had gone after that and why remained an enigma. I read more notes about Kellie Shephard's murder. Benton had emphasized *overkill, frenzied* and *disorganized*. He had jotted, *lost control* and *victim response not according to plan. Ruination of ritual.* **Wasn't supposed to happen like this.** *Rage.* **Will kill again soon.**

I snapped shut the briefcase and left it on the bed as my heart ached. I walked out of the bedroom, turned off the light, and shut the door, knowing that the next time I entered it would be to clean out Benton's closet and drawers, and somehow decide to live with his resounding absence. I quietly checked on Lucy, finding her asleep, her pistol on the table by her bed. My restless wanderings took me to the foyer, where I turned off the alarm long enough to snatch the paper off the porch. I went into the kitchen to make coffee. By seven-thirty I was ready to leave for the office, and Lucy had not stirred. I quietly entered her room again, and the sun glowed faintly around the windowshade, touching her face with soft light.

'Lucy?' I softly touched her shoulder.

She jerked awake, sitting half up.

'I'm leaving,' I said.

'I need to get up, too.'

She threw back the covers.

'Want to have a cup of coffee with me?' I asked.

'Sure.'

She lowered her feet to the floor.

'You should eat something,' I said.

She had slept in running shorts and a T-shirt, and she followed me with the silence of a cat.

'How about some cereal?' I said as I got a coffee mug out of a cupboard.

She said nothing but simply watched me as I opened the tin of homemade granola that Benton had eaten most mornings with fresh banana or berries. Just the toasty aroma of it was enough to crush me again, and my throat seemed to close and my stomach furled. I stood helplessly for a long moment, unable to lift out the scoop or reach for a bowl or do the smallest thing.

'Don't, Aunt Kay,' said Lucy, who knew exactly what was happening. 'I'm not hungry anyway.'

My hands trembled as I clamped the top back on the tin.

'I don't know how you're going to stay here,' she said.

She poured her own coffee.

'This is where I live, Lucy.'

I opened the refrigerator and handed her the carton of milk.

'Where's his car?' she asked, whitening her coffee.

'The airport at Hilton Head, I guess. He flew straight to New York from there.'

'What are you going to do about that?'

'I don't know.'

I got increasingly upset.

'Right now, his car is low on my list. I've got all his things in the house,' I told her.

I took a deep breath.

'I can't make decisions about everything at once,' I said.

'You should clear every bit of it out today.'

Lucy leaned against the counter, drinking coffee and watching me with that same flat look in her eyes.

'I mean it,' she went on in a tone that carried no emotion.

'Well, I'm not touching anything of his until his body has come home.'

'I can help you, if you want.'

She sipped her coffee again. I was getting angry with her.

'I will do this my way, Lucy,' I said as pain seemed to radiate to every cell in me. 'For once I'm not going to slam the door on something and run. I've done it most of my life, beginning when my father died. Then Tony left and Mark got killed, and I got better and better at vacating each relationship as if it were an old house. Walking off as if I had never lived there. And guess what? It doesn't work.'

She was staring down at her bare feet.

'Have you talked to Janet?' I asked.

'She knows. Now she's all bent out of shape because I don't want to see her. I don't want to see anybody.'

'The harder you run, the more you stay in one place,' I said. 'If you've learned nothing else from me, Lucy, at least learn that. Don't wait until half your life has passed.'

'I've learned a lot of things from you,' my niece said as windows caught the morning and brightened my kitchen. 'More than you think.'

For a long moment she stared at the empty doorway leading into the great room.

'I keep thinking he's going to walk in,' she muttered.

'I know,' I said. 'I keep thinking it, too.'

'I'll call Teun. As soon as I know something, I'll page you,' she said.

The sun was strong to the east and other people heading to work squinted in the glare of what promised to be a clear, hot day. I was carried in the flow of traffic on Ninth Street past the wrought-iron-enclosed Capitol Square, with its Jeffersonian pristine white buildings and monuments to Stonewall Jackson and George Washington. I thought of Kenneth Sparkes, of his political influence. I remembered my fear and fascination when he would call with demands and complaints. I felt terribly sorry for him now.

All that had happened of late had not cleared his name of suspicion for the simple reason that even those of us who knew we might be dealing with serial murders were not at liberty to release such information to the news. I was certain that Sparkes did not know. I desperately wanted to talk to him, to somehow ease his mind, as if perhaps in doing so I might ease my own. Depression crushed my chest with cold, iron hands, and when I turned off Jackson Street into the bay of my building, the sight of a hearse unloading a black pouched body jolted me in a way it had not before.

I tried not to imagine Benton's remains enveloped so, or the darkness of his cold, steel space at the shutting of the cooler door. It was awful to know all that I did. Death was not an abstraction, and I could envision every procedure, every sound and smell in a place where there was no loving touch, only a clinical objective and a crime to be solved. I was climbing out of my car when Marino rolled up.

'Mind if I stick my car in here?' he asked, even though he knew the bay parking was not for cops.

Marino was forever breaking rules.

'Go ahead,' I replied. 'One of the vans is in the shop. Or at least I think it is. You're not going to be here long.'

'How the hell do you know?'

He locked his car door and flicked an ash. Marino was his rude self again, and I found this incredibly reassuring.

'You going to your office first?' he asked, as we followed a ramp to doors that led inside the morgue.

'No. Straight upstairs.'

'Then I'll tell you what's probably already on your desk,' he said. 'We got a positive I.D. for Claire Rawley. From hair in her brush.'

I wasn't surprised, but the confirmation weighed me down with sadness again.

'Thanks,' I told him. 'At least we know.'

19

The trace avidence laboratories were on the third floor, and my first stop was the scanning electron microscope, or SEM, which exposed a specimen, such as the metal shaving from the Shephard case, to a beam of electrons. The elemental composition making up the specimen emitted electrons, and images were displayed on a video screen.

In short, the SEM recognized almost all of the one hundred and three elements, whether it was carbon, copper, or zinc, and because of the microscope's depth of focus, high resolution, and high magnification, trace evidence such as gunshot residue or the hairs on a marijuana leaf could be viewed in amazing, if not eerie, detail.

The location of the Zeiss SEM was enthroned within a windowless room of teal and beige wall cupboards and shelves, counter space, and sinks. Because the extremely expensive instrument was very sensitive to mechanical vibration, magnetic fields, and electrical and thermal disturbances, the environment was precisely controlled.

The ventilation and air conditioning system were independent of the rest of the building, and photographically safe lighting was supplied by filament lamps that did not cause electrical interference and were directed up at the ceiling to dimly illuminate the room by reflection. Floors and walls were thick steel-beamed reinforced concrete impervious to human bustling or the traffic of the expressway.

Mary Chan was petite and fair-skinned, a first-rate microscopist, this minute on the phone and surrounded by her complex apparatus.

With its instrument panels, power units, electron gun and optical column, X-ray analyzer, and vacuum chamber attached to a cylinder of nitrogen, the SEM looked like a console for the space shuttle. Chan's lab coat was buttoned to her chin, and her friendly gesture told me she would be but a minute.

'Take her temperature again and try the tapioca. If she doesn't keep that down, call me back, okay?' Chan was saying to someone. 'I've got to go now.'

'My daughter,' she said to me as an apology. 'A stomach upset, most likely from too much ice cream last night. She got into the Chunky Monkey when I wasn't looking.'

Her smile was brave but tired, and I suspected she had been up most of the night.

'Man, I love that stuff,' Marino said as he handed her our packaged evidence.

'Another metal shaving,' I explained to her. 'I hate to spring this on you, Mary, but if you could look at it now. It's urgent.'

'Another case or the same one?'

'The fire in Lehigh County, Pennsylvania,' I replied.

'No kidding?' She looked surprised as she slit taped brown paper with a scalpel. 'Lord,' she said, 'that one sounds pretty awful, based on what I heard on the news, anyway. Then the FBI guy, too. Weird, weird, weird.'

She had no reason to know about my relationship with Benton.

'Between those cases and the one in Warrenton, you have to wonder if there isn't some whacko pyro on the loose,' she went on.

'That's what we're trying to find out,' I said.

Chan took the cap off the small metal evidence button and with tweezers removed a layer of snowy cotton, revealing the two tiny bright turnings. She pushed back her roller chair to a counter behind her and proceeded to place a double-sided adhesive square of black carbon tape on a tiny aluminum stub. On this she mounted the shaving that seemed to have the most surface area. It was maybe half the size of a normal eyelash. She turned on a stereo-optical microscope, positioned the sample on the stage, and adjusted the light wand to take a look at a lower magnification before she resorted to the SEM.

'I'm seeing two different surfaces,' she said as she adjusted the focus. 'One real shiny, the other sort of dull gray.'

'That's different from the Warrenton sample,' I said. 'Both surfaces were shiny, right?'

'Correct. My guess would be that one of the surfaces here was exposed to atmospheric oxidation. For whatever reason that might be.'

'Do you mind?' I asked.

She scooted out of the way and I peered through the lenses. At a magnification of four, the metal turning looked like a ribbon of crumpled foil, and I could just barely make out the fine striations left by whatever had been used to shave the metal. Mary took several Polaroid photographs and then rolled her chair back to the SEM console. She pushed a button to vent the chamber, or release the vacuum.

'This will take a few minutes,' she said to us. 'You can wait or go and come back.'

'I'm getting coffee,' said Marino, who had never been a fan of sophisticated technology and most likely wanted to smoke.

Chan opened a valve to fill the chamber with nitrogen to keep contamination, such as moisture, out. Next she pushed a button on the console and placed our sample on an electron optics table.

'Now we got to get it to ten to the minus six millimeters of mercury. That's the vacuum level needed to turn on the beam. Usually takes two or three minutes. But I like to pump it down a little more than that to get a really good vacuum,' she explained, reaching for her coffee. 'I think the news accounts are very confusing,' she then said. 'A lot of innuendo.'

'So what else is new?' I commented wryly.

'Tell me about it. Whenever I read accounts of my court testimony, I always wonder if someone else had been on the stand instead of me. My point is, first they drag Sparkes into it, and to be honest, I was about to think that maybe he had burned his own place and some girl. Probably for money, and to get rid of her because she knew something. Then, lo and behold, there are these two other fires in Pennsylvania, and two more people killed, and there's the suggestion all of it's related? And where's Sparkes been during all this?'

She reached for her coffee.

'Excuse me, Dr Scarpetta. I didn't even ask. Can I get you some?'

'No thank you,' I said.

I watched the green light move across the gauge as the mercury level slowly climbed.

'I also find it odd that this psycho woman escapes from the loony bin in New York – what's her name? Carrie something? And the FBI profiler guy in charge of that investigation suddenly ends up dead.

I think we're ready to go,' she said.

She turned on the electron beam and the video display. The magnification was set for five hundred, and she turned it down and we began to get a picture of the filament's current on the screen. At first it looked like a wave, then it began to flatten. She hit more keys, backing off the magnification again, this time to twenty, and we began to get a picture of the signals coming off the sample.

'I'll change the spot size of the beam to get a little more energy.'

She adjusted buttons and dials as she worked.

'Looks like our shaving of metal, almost like a curled ribbon,' she announced.

The topography was simply an enlarged version of what we had seen under the optical microscope moments earlier, and since the picture wasn't terribly bright, this suggested an element with a lower atomic number. She adjusted the scanning speed of the live picture and took away some of the noise, which looked like a snowstorm on the screen.

'Here you can clearly see the shiny versus the gray,' she said.

'And you think that's due to oxidation,' I said, pulling up a chair.

'Well, you've got two surfaces of the same material. I would venture that the shiny side was recently shaved while the other wasn't.'

'Makes sense to me.'

The crinkled metal looked like shrapnel suspended in space.

'We had a case last year,' Chan spoke again as she pressed the frame store button to make photographs for me. 'A guy bludgeoned with a pipe from a machine shop. And tissue from his scalp had a metal filing from a lathe. It was transferred right into the wound. Okay, let's change the back scatter image and see what kind of X-ray we get off that.'

The video screen went gray and digital seconds began to count. Mary worked other buttons on her control panel, and a bright orange spectrum suddenly appeared on the screen against a background of vivid blue. She moved the cursor and expanded what looked like a psychedelic stalagmite.

'Let's see if there are other metals.'

She made more adjustments.

'Nope,' she said. 'It's very clean. Think we got our same suspect again. We'll call up magnesium and see if there's an overlapping of lines.'

She superimposed the spectrum for magnesium over the one for our sample, and they were the same. She called up a table of elements on the video screen, and the square for magnesium was lit up red.

We had confirmed our element, and although I had expected the answer we got, I was still stunned by it.

'Do you have any explanation as to why pure magnesium might be transferred to a wound?' I asked Chan as Marino returned.

'Well, I told you my pipe story,' she replied.

'What pipe?' Marino said.

'Only thing I can think of is a metal shop,' Chan went on. 'But I would think that machining magnesium would be unusual. I mean, I can't imagine what for.'

'Thanks, Mary. We've got one more stop to go, but I'm going to need you to let me have the shaving from the Warrenton case so I can take it over to firearms.'

She glanced at her watch as the phone rang again, and I could only imagine the caseload awaiting her.

'Right away,' she said to me generously.

The firearms and toolmarks labs were on the same floor and were really the same section of science, since the lands and grooves and firing pin impressions left on cartridge cases and bullets were, in fact, the toolmarks made by guns. The space in the new building was a stadium compared to the old, and this spoke sadly to the continuing deterioration of the society beyond our doors.

It was not unusual for schoolchildren to hide handguns in their lockers, or show them off in the bathrooms, and carry them on the school bus, it seemed, and it was nothing for violent offenders to be eleven and twelve years old. Guns were still the top choice for killing oneself or one's spouse, or even the neighbor with the constantly barking dog. More frightening were the disgruntled and insane who entered public places and started blasting away, explaining why my office and the lobby were protected by bulletproof glass.

Rich Sinclair's work area was carpeted and well lighted, and overlooked the coliseum, which had always reminded me of a metal mushroom about to take flight. He was using weights to test the trigger pull of a Taurus pistol, and Marino and I walked in to the sound of the hammer clicking against the firing pin. I was not in a chatty mood and did my best not to seem rude as I told Sinclair outright what I needed, and that I needed it now.

'This is the metal turning from Warrenton,' I said, opening that evidence button. 'And this is the one recovered from the body in the Lehigh fire.'

I opened that evidence button next.

'Both have striations that are clearly visible on SEM,' I explained.

The point was to see if the striations, or toolmarks, matched, indicating that the same instrument had been used to produce the magnesium shavings that had been recovered this far. The ribbons of metal were very fragile and thin, and Sinclair used a narrow plastic spatula to pick them up. They weren't very cooperative and tended to jump around as if they were trying to escape as he coaxed them from their sea of cotton. He used squares of black cardboard to center the shaving from Warrenton on one, and the shavings from Lehigh on the other. These he placed on stages of the comparison microscope.

'Oh yeah,' Sinclair said without pause. 'We've got some good stuff.'

He manipulated the shavings with the spatula, flattening them some as he bumped the magnification up to forty.

'Maybe a blade of some type,' he said. 'The striations are probably from the finishing process and end up being a defect because no finishing process is going to be perfectly smooth. I mean, the manufacturer's going to be happy, but he's not at our end seeing this. There, here's an even better area, I think.'

He moved aside so we could take a look. Marino bent over the eyepieces first.

'Looks like ski tracks in snow,' was his comment. 'And that's from the blade, right? Or whatever?'

'Yes, imperfections, or toolmarks, made by whatever shaved this metal. Do you see the match, when one shaving is lined up with the other?'

Marino didn't.

'Here, Doc, you look.' Sinclair got out of my way.

What I saw through the microscope was good enough for court, the striations of the Warrenton shaving in one field of light matching the striations of the shaving in the other. Clearly, the same tool had shaved something made of magnesium in both homicide cases. The question was what this tool might be, and because the shavings were so thin, one had to consider a sharp blade of some type. Sinclair made several Polaroid photographs for me and slid them into glyassine envelopes.

'Okay, now what?' Marino asked as he followed me through the center of the firearms lab, past scientists busy processing bloody clothing under biohazard hoods, and others examining a Phillips screwdriver and machete at a big U-shaped counter.

'Now I go shopping,' I said.

I did not slow down as I talked but, in fact, was getting more frantic because I knew I was getting closer to reconstructing what Carrie or her accomplice or someone had done.

'What do you mean, *shopping*?'

Through the wall I could hear the muffled bangs of test fires in the range.

'Why don't you check on Lucy?' I said. 'And I'll get back to both of you later.'

'I don't like it when you do this *later* shit,' Marino said as elevator doors parted. 'That means you're running around on your own and poking your nose in things that maybe you shouldn't. And this ain't the time for you to be out on the street with nobody around. We got not a clue where Carrie is.'

'That's right, we don't,' I said. 'But I'm hoping that's going to change.'

We got out on the first floor, and I headed with purpose to the door leading to the bay, where I unlocked my car. Marino looked so frustrated, I thought he might launch into a tantrum.

'You want to tell me where the hell you're going?' he demanded at the top of his voice.

'A sports store,' I said, cranking the engine. 'The biggest one I can find.'

That turned out to be Jumbo Sports south of the James, very close to the neighborhood where Marino lived, which was the only reason I was aware of the store, since prowling for basketballs, frisbees, free weights, and golf clubs rarely entered my mind.

I took the Powhite Parkway, and two toll booths later was exiting on Midlothian Turnpike, heading toward downtown. The sports store was big and built of red brick, with stick figures of red-painted athletes framed in white on the outside walls. The parking lot was unexpectedly full for this time of day, and I wondered how many well-toned people spent their lunch hours here.

I had no idea where anything was and had to take a few moments to study the signs above miles of rows. Boxing gloves were on sale, and there were exercise machines capable of tortures I did not know. Racks of clothes for every sport were endless and in blazing colors, and I wondered what had happened to civilized white, which was still what I wore on the much-appreciated occasion I found time to play tennis. I deduced that knives would be with camping and hunting gear, a generous area against the back wall. There were bows and arrows, targets, tents, canoes, mess kits, and camouflage, and at this hour, I was the only woman who seemed interested. At first, no one was inclined to wait on me as I hovered patiently over a show-case of knives.

A sunburnt man was looking for a BB gun for his son's tenth birthday, while an older man in a white suit was inquiring about snakebite kits and mosquito repellent. When my patience was no more, I interrupted.

'Excuse me,' I said.

The clerk, who was college age, didn't seem to hear me at first.

'Thing is, you should check with your doctor before using a snakebite kit,' the clerk was saying to the elderly man in white.

'How the hell am I supposed to do that when I'm out in the middle of the woods somewhere and some copperhead's just bit me?'

'I meant check with him before you go out in the woods, sir.'

As I listened to their backward logic I could stand it no longer.

'Snakebite kits are not only useless, but they're harmful,' I said. 'Tourniquets and local incision, sucking out the venom and all that just make matters worse. If you get bitten,' I said to the man in white, 'what you need to do is immobilize that part of your body, and avoid damaging first aid, and get to a hospital.'

The two men were startled.

'So there's no point in taking anything along?' the man in white asked me. 'No point in buying anything, you're saying?'

'Nothing but a good pair of boots and a walking stick you can poke around with,' I replied. 'Stay out of tall grass and don't stick your hands into hollows or holes. Since venom is transported through the body by the lymphatic system, broad compression bandages – like an Ace bandage – are good, and a splint to keep the limb absolutely immobilized.'

'You some kind of doctor?' the clerk asked.

'I've dealt with snake bites before.'

I didn't add that in those instances, the victims had not lived.

'I'm just wondering if you have knife sharpeners here,' I said to the clerk.

'Kitchen sharpeners or ones for camping?'

'Let's start with camping,' I said.

He pointed to a wall where a vast variety of whetstones and other types of sharpeners hung from pegs. Some were metal, others ceramic. All of the brands were proprietary enough not to reveal the compo-sition on the packages. I scanned some more, my eyes stopping on a small package on the bottom row. Beneath clear plastic was a simple rectangular block of grayish-silver metal. It was called a *fire starter* and was made of magnesium. Excitement mounted as I read the instructions. To start a fire, one simply needed to scrape a knife on the surface of the magnesium and build a pile of shavings as small as the size of a quarter. Matches weren't necessary, for the fire starter included a sparking insert for ignition.

I hurried back through the store with half a dozen of the magnesium starters in hand, and in my haste got tangled up in one section, then another. I wound through bowling balls and shoes, and baseball gloves, and ended up in swimming, where I was instantly captivated by a display of neon-colored swimming caps. One of them was hot pink. I thought of the residue found in Claire Rawley's hair. I had believed from the start that she had been wearing something on her head when she was murdered, or at least when the fire reached her.

A shower cap had been considered but briefly, for its thin, plastic material wouldn't have lasted five seconds in the heat. What had never entered my mind was a swimming cap, and as I quickly riffled through racks of them, I discovered that all were made of Lycra or latex or silicone.

The pink one was silicone, which I knew would hold up in extreme temperatures far better than the others. I purchased several of them. I drove back to my office and was lucky I didn't get a ticket because I was passing people, no matter the lane. Images seized my mind, and they were too painful and horrific to entertain. This was one time I hoped my theory was wrong. I was speeding back to the labs because I had to know.

'Oh Benton,' I muttered as if he were near me. 'Please don't let this be so.'

20

It was one-thirty when I parked inside the bay again and got out of my car. I walked quickly to the elevator and keyed myself back up to the third floor. I was looking for Jerri Garmon, who had examined the pink residue in the beginning and reported to me that it was silicone.

Ducking into doorways, I located her inside a room housing the latest instrumentation used in analyzing organic substances, ranging from heroin to paint binders. She was using a syringe to inject a sample into a heated chamber of the gas chromatograph and did not notice me until I spoke.

'Jerri,' I said, and I was out of breath. 'I hate to disturb you but I've got something I think you'll want to look at.'

I held up the pink swimming cap. Her reaction was completely blank.

'Silicone,' I said.

Her eyes lit up.

'Wow! A swimming cap? Boy howdy. Who would have thought that?' she said. 'Just goes to show you, there's too much to keep up with these days.'

'Can we burn it?' I asked.

'This has got to run for a while anyway. Come on. Now you've got me curious, too.'

The actual trace evidence labs, where evidence was processed before it was routed through complicated instruments such as the SEM and mass spectrometer, was spacious but already running out of room. Scores of airtight aluminum paint cans used in the collection of fire debris and flammable residues were in pyramids on shelves, and there were big jars of granular blue Drierite, and petri dishes, beakers, charcoal tubes, and the usual brown paper bags of evidence. The test I had in mind was easy and quick.

The muffle furnace was in a corner and looked rather much like a small beige ceramic crematorium, the size of a hotel mini-bar, to be exact, that could heat up to as much as twenty-five-hundred degrees Fahrenheit. She turned it on, and a gauge very soon began registering its warming up. Jerri placed the cap inside a white porcelain dish not so different from a cereal bowl, and opened a drawer to get out a thick asbestos glove that would protect her up to her elbow. She stood poised with tongs while the temperature crept to a hundred degrees. At two hundred and fifty, she checked on our cap. It wasn't the least bit affected.

'I can tell you right now that at this temperature latex and Lycra would be smoking up a storm and beginning to melt,' Jerri let me know. 'But this stuff's not even getting tacky yet and the color hasn't changed.'

The silicone cap did not begin to smoke until five hundred degrees. At seven hundred and fifty, it was turning gray at the edges. It was getting tacky and beginning to melt. At not quite one thousand degrees, it was flaming and Jerri had to find a thicker glove.

'This is amazing,' Jerri said.

'Guess we can see why silicone's used for insulation,' I marveled, too.

'Better stand back.'

'Don't worry.'

I moved far out of harm's way as she pulled the bowl forward with tongs and carried our flaming experiment in her asbestos-covered hand. The exposure to fresh air fueled the fire more, and by the time she had placed it under a chemical hood and turned on the exhaust, the outer surface of the cap was blazing out of control, forcing Jerri to cover it with a lid.

Eventually, flames were suffocated, and she took off the lid to see what was left. My heart thudded as I noted papery white ash and areas of spared silicone that were still visibly pink. The swimming cap had not turned gooey or become a liquid at all. It simply had disintegrated until either cooling temperatures or an absence of oxygen or perhaps even a dousing with water had thwarted the process. The end result of our experiment was completely consistent with what I had recovered from Claire Rawley's long blond hair.

The image of her body in the bathtub, a pink swimming cap on her head, was ghastly, and its implication was almost more than I could comprehend. When the bathroom had gone to flashover, the shower door had caved in. Sections of glass and the sides of the tub had protected the body as flames shot up from the point of origin, engaging the ceiling. The temperature in the tub had never climbed above one thousand degrees, and a small telltale part of the silicone swimming cap had been preserved for the simple freakish reason that the shower door was old and made of a single thick sheet of solid glass.

As I drove home, rush hour traffic hemmed me in and seemed more aggressive the greater my hurry. Several times I almost reached for the phone, desperate to call Benton and tell him what I had discovered. Then I saw water and debris in the back corner of a burned-out grocery store in Philadelphia. I saw what was left of a stainless steel watch I had given to him for Christmas. I saw what was left of him. I imagined the wire that had confined his ankles, and handcuffs that had been locked with a key. I now knew what had happened and why. Benton had been killed like the others, but this time it was for spite, for revenge, to satisfy Carrie's diabolical lust to make him her trophy.

Tears blinded me as I pulled into my driveway. I ran, primitive sounds welling up in me as I slammed the front door behind me. Lucy emerged from the kitchen. She was dressed in khaki range pants and a black T-shirt, and holding a bottle of salad dressing.

'Aunt Kay!' she exclaimed, hurrying to me. 'What is it, Aunt Kay? Where's Marino? My God, is he all right?'

'It's not Marino,' I said chokily.

She slipped an arm around me and helped me to the couch in my great room.

'Benton,' I said. 'Like the others,' I moaned. 'Like Claire Rawley. A swimcap to keep her hair out of the way. The bathtub. Like surgery.'

'What?' Lucy was dazed.

'They wanted her face!'

I sprang up from the couch.

'Don't you understand?' I yelled at her. 'The nicks to bone at the temple, at the jaw. Like a scalping, only worse! He doesn't build fires to disguise homicide! He burns everything because he doesn't want

us to know what he's done to them! He steals their beauty, everything beautiful about them, by removing their faces.'

Lucy's lips were parted in shock.

Then she stuttered, 'But Carrie? Now she's doing that?'

'Oh no,' I said. 'Not entirely.'

I was pacing and wringing my hands.

'It's like Gault,' I said. 'She likes to watch. Maybe she helps. Maybe
she fucked things up with Kellie Shephard, or maybe Kellie simply
resisted her because Carrie was a woman. Then there was a fight, the
slashing and stabbing until Carrie's partner intervened and finally
cut Kellie's throat, which is where the magnesium shavings were
found. From his knife, not Carrie's. He's the torch, the fire builder,
not Carrie. And he didn't take Kellie's face because it had been cut,
ruined, during the struggle.'

'You don't think they did that to, to . . . ?' Lucy started to say, her
fists clenched in her lap.

'To Benton?' I raised my voice more. 'Do I think they took his face,
too?'

I kicked the paneled wall and leaned against it. Inside I went still
and my mind felt dark and dead.

'Carrie knew he could imagine everything she might do to him,'
I said in a slow, low voice. 'She would have enjoyed every minute of
it as he sat there, shackled. As she taunted him with the knife. Yes. I
think they did that to him, too. In fact, I know it.'

The last thought was almost impossible to complete.

'I just hope he was already dead,' I said.

'He would have been, Aunt Kay.'

Lucy was crying, too, as she came to me and wrapped her arms
around my neck.

'They wouldn't have taken the chance that someone might hear
him scream,' she said.

Within the hour, I passed on news of the latest developments to Teun
McGovern, and she agreed that it was critical for us to find out who
Carrie's partner was, if possible, and how she might have met him.
McGovern was more angered than she would show when I explained
what I suspected and knew. Kirby might be our only hope, and she
concurred that in my professional position, I had a better chance of
making that visit successfully than did she. She was law enforcement.
I was a physician.

Border Patrol had ferried a Bell JetRanger to HeloAir, near

Richmond International Airport, and Lucy wanted to take off this minute and fly through the night. I had told her this was out of the question, if for no other reason than once we got to New York, we had no place to stay, and certainly we couldn't sleep on Ward's Island. I needed a chance first thing in the morning to alert Kirby that we were coming. It would not be a request, but a statement of fact. Marino thought he should accompany us, but I would not hear of it.

'No cops,' I told him when he dropped by my house at almost ten in the evening.

'You're out of your friggin' mind,' he said.

'Would you blame me if I were?'

He stared down at worn-out running shoes that had never been given a chance to perform their primary function in this world.

'Lucy's law enforcement,' he said.

'As far as they're concerned, she's my pilot.'

'Huh.'

'I have to do this my way, Marino.'

'Gee, Doc, I don't know what to say. I don't know how you can deal with any of this.'

His face was deeply flushed, and when he looked up at me, his eyes were bloodshot and filled with pain.

'I want to go because I want to find those motherfuckers,' he said. 'They set him up. You know that, don't you? The Bureau's got a record that some guy called Tuesday afternoon at three-fourteen. Said he had a tip about the Shephard case that he'd only give to Benton Wesley. They gave the usual song and dance, that *sure, everybody says the same thing*. They're special. Got to talk to the man direct. But this informant had the goods. He said, and I quote, *Tell him it's about some weirdo woman I saw at Lehigh County Hospital. She was sitting one table away from Kellie Shephard.*'

'Damn!' I exclaimed as rage thundered in my temples.

'So as best we know, Benton calls the number this asshole left. Turns out to be a pay phone near the grocery that got burned,' he went on. 'My guess is, Benton met up with the guy – Carrie's psycho partner. Has no idea who he's talking to until BOOM!'

I jumped.

'Benton's got a gun, maybe a knife to his throat. They cuff him, double-locking with the key. And why do that? Because he's law enforcement and knows that your average Joe don't know about double-locking. Usually, all cops do is click shut the jaws of the cuff when they're hauling somebody in. The prisoner squirms, the cuffs tighten. And if he manages to get a hairpin or something similar up there to override the ratchets, then he might even spring himself free. But with double-locking, no way. Can't get out without a key or something exactly like a key. It's something Benton would've known about when it was happening to him. A big bad signal that he was dealing with someone who knew what the shit he was doing.'

'I've heard enough,' I said to Marino. 'Go home. Please.'

I had the beginning of a migraine. I could always tell when my entire neck and head began to hurt and my stomach felt queasy. I walked Marino to the door. I knew I had wounded him. He was loaded with pain and had no place to shoot, because he did not know how to show what he felt. I wasn't even sure he knew what he felt.

'He ain't gone, you know,' he said as I opened the door. 'I don't believe it. I didn't see it, and I don't believe it.'

'They will be sending him home soon,' I said as cicadas sawed in the dark, and moths swarmed in the glow of the lamp over my porch. 'Benton is dead,' I said with surprising strength. 'Don't take away from him by not accepting his death.'

'He's gonna show up one of these days.' Marino's voice was at a higher pitch. 'You wait. I know that son of a bitch. He don't go down this easy.'

But Benton had gone down this easy. It was so often like that, Versace walking home from buying coffee and magazines or Lady Diana not wearing her seat belt. I shut the door after Marino drove away. I set the alarm, which by now was a reflex that sometimes got me into trouble when I forgot I had armed my house and opened a slider. Lucy was stretched out on the couch, watching the Arts and Entertainment network in the great room, the lights out. I sat next to her and put my hand on her shoulder.

We did not speak as a documentary about gangsters in the early days of Las Vegas played on. I stroked her hair and her skin felt feverish. I wondered what was going on inside that mind of hers. I worried greatly about it, too. Lucy's thoughts were different. They were distinctly her own and not to be interpreted by any Rosetta stone of psychotherapy or intuition. But this much I had learned about her from the beginning of her life. What she didn't say mattered most, and Lucy wasn't talking about Janet anymore.

'Let's go to bed so we can get an early start, Madame Pilot,' I said.

'I think I'll just sleep in here.'

She pointed the remote control and turned down the volume.

'In your clothes?'

She shrugged.

'If we can get to HeloAir around nine, I'll call Kirby from there.'

'What if they say don't come?' my niece asked.

'I'll tell them I'm on my way. New York City is Republican at the moment. If need be, I'll get my friend Senator Lord involved, and he'll get the health commissioner and mayor on the warpath, and I don't think Kirby will want that. Easier to let us land, don't you think?'

'They don't have any ground-to-air missiles there, do they?'

'Yes, they're called patients,' I said, and it was the first time we had laughed in days.

Why I slept as well as I did, I could not explain, but when my alarm clock went off at six A.M., I turned over in bed. I realized I had not gotten up once since shortly before midnight, and this hinted of a cure, of a renewing that I desperately needed. Depression was a veil I could almost see through, and I was beginning to feel hope. I was doing what Benton would expect me to do, not to avenge his murder, really, for he would not have wanted that.

His wish would have been to prevent harm to Marino, Lucy, or me. He would have wanted me to protect other lives I did not know, other unwitting individuals who worked in hospitals or as models and had been sentenced to a terrible death in the split second it took for a monster to notice them with evil eyes burning with envy.

Lucy went running as the sun was coming up, and although it unnerved me for her to be out alone, I knew she had a pistol in her butt pack, and neither of us could let our lives stop because of Carrie. It seemed she had such an advantage. If we went on as usual, we might die. If we aborted our lives because of fear, we still died, only in a way that was worse, really.

'I'm assuming everything was quiet out there?' I said when Lucy returned to the house and found me in the kitchen.

I set coffee on the kitchen table, where Lucy was seated. Sweat was rolling down her shoulders and face, and I tossed her a dishtowel. She took off her shoes and socks, and I was slammed with an image of Benton sitting there, doing the same thing. He always hung around the kitchen for a while after running. He liked to cool down, to visit with me before he took a shower and buttoned himself up in his neat clothes and deep thoughts.

'A couple people out walking their dogs in Windsor Farms,' she said. 'Not a sign of anybody in your neighborhood. I asked the guy at the guard gate if anything was going on, like any more taxi cabs or pizza deliveries showing up for you. Any weird phone calls or unexpected visitors trying to get in. He said no.'

'Glad to hear it.'

'That's chicken shit. I don't think she's the one who did that.'

'Then who?' I was surprised.

'Hate to tell you, but there are other people out there who are none too fond of you.'

'A large segment of the prison population.'

'And people who aren't in prison, at least not yet. Like the Christian Scientists whose kid you did. You think it might occur to them to harass you? Like sending taxis, a construction Dumpster, or calling the morgue early in the morning and hanging up on poor Chuck? That's all you need, is a morgue assistant who's too spooked to be alone in your building anymore. Or worse, the guy quits. Chicken shit,' she said again. 'Petty, spiteful, chicken shit generated by an ignorant, little mind.'

None of this had ever occurred to me before.

'Is he still getting the hang-ups?' she asked.

She eyed me as she sipped her coffee, and through the window over the sink, the sun was a tangerine on a dusky blue horizon.

'I'll find out,' I said.

I picked up the phone and dialed the number for the morgue. Chuck answered immediately.

'Morgue,' he said nervously.

It was not quite seven, and I suspected he was alone.

'It's Dr Scarpetta,' I said.

'Oh!' He was relieved. 'Good morning.'

'Chuck? What about the hang-ups? You still getting them?'

'Yes, ma'am.'

'Nothing said? Not even the sound of somebody breathing?'

'Sometimes I think I hear traffic in the background, like maybe the person's at a pay phone somewhere.'

'I've got an idea.'

'Okay.'

'Next time it happens, I want you to say, *Good morning, Mr and Mrs Quinn.*'

'What?' Chuck was baffled.

'Just do it,' I said. 'And I have a hunch the calls will stop.'

Lucy was laughing when I hung up.

'Touché,' she said.

21

After breakfast, I wandered about in my bedroom and study, deliberating over what to bring on our trip. My aluminum briefcase would go, because it was habit to take it almost everywhere these days. I also packed an extra pair of slacks and a shirt, and toiletries for overnight, and my Colt .38 went into my pocketbook. Although I was accustomed to carrying a gun, I had never even thought about taking one to New York, where doing so could land one in jail with no questions asked. When Lucy and I were in the car, I told her what I had done.

'It's called situational ethics,' she said. 'I'd rather be arrested than dead.'

'That's the way I look at it,' said I, who once had been a law-abiding citizen.

HeloAir was a helicopter charter service on the western edge of the Richmond airport, where some of the area's Fortune 500 companies had their own terminals for corporate King Airs and Lear Jets and Sikorskys. The Bell JetRanger was in the hangar, and while Lucy went on to take care of that, I found a pilot inside who was kind enough to let me use the phone in his office. I dug around in my wallet for my AT&T calling card and dialed the number for Kirby Forensic Psychiatric Center's administrative offices.

The director was a woman psychiatrist named Lydia Ensor who was very leery when I got her on the line. I tried to explain to her in more detail who I was, but she interrupted.

'I know exactly who you are,' she said with a Midwestern tongue. 'I'm completely aware of the current situation and will be as cooperative as I can. I'm not clear, however, on what your interest is, Dr Scarpetta. You're the chief medical examiner of Virginia? Correct?'

'Correct. And a consulting forensic pathologist for ATF and the FBI.'

'And of course, they've contacted me, too.' She sounded genuinely perplexed. 'So are you looking for information that might pertain to one of your cases? To someone dead?'

'Dr Ensor, I'm trying to link a number of cases right now,' I replied. 'I have reason to suspect that Carrie Grethen may be either indirectly or directly involved in all of them and may have been involved even while she was at Kirby.'

'Impossible.'

'Clearly, you don't know this woman,' I said firmly. 'I, on the other hand, have worked violent deaths caused by her for half of my career, beginning when she and Temple Gault were on a spree in Virginia and finally in New York, where Gault was killed. And now this. Possibly five more murders, maybe more.'

'I know Miss Grethen's history all too well,' Dr Ensor said, and she wasn't hostile, but defensiveness had crept into her tone. 'I can assure you that Kirby handled her as we do all maximum security patients . . .'

'There's almost nothing useful in her psychiatric evaluations,' I cut her off.

'How could you possibly know about her medical records . . . ?'

'Because I am part of the ATF national response team that is investigating these fire-related homicides,' I measured my words. 'And I work with the FBI, as I've already said. All of the cases we're talking about are my jurisdiction because I'm a consultant for law enforcement at a federal level. But my duty is not to arrest anyone or smear an institution such as yours. My job is to bring justice to the dead and give as much peace as possible to those they left behind. To do that, I must answer questions. And most important, I am driven to do anything I can to prevent one more person from dying. Carrie will kill again. She may already have.'

The director was silent for a moment. I looked out the window and could see the dark blue helicopter on its pad being towed out onto the tarmac.

'Dr Scarpetta, what would you like us to do?' Dr Ensor finally spoke, her voice tense and upset.

'Did Carrie have a social worker? Someone in legal aid? Anyone she really talked to?' I asked.

'Obviously, she spent a fair amount of time with a forensic psychologist, but he isn't on our staff. Mainly he's there to evaluate and make recommendations to the court.'

'Then she probably manipulated him,' I said as I watched Lucy climb up on the helicopter's skids and begin her preflight inspection. 'Who else? Anyone she may have gotten close to?'

'Her lawyer, then. Yes, legal aid. If you would like to speak to her, that can be arranged.'

'I'm leaving the airport now,' I said. 'We should be landing in approximately three hours. Do you have a helipad?'

'I don't remember anyone ever landing here. There are several parks nearby. I'll be happy to pick you up.'

'I don't think that will be necessary. My guess is we'll land close by.'

'I'll watch for you, then, and take you to legal aid, or wherever it is you need to go.'

'I would like to see Carrie Grethen's ward and where she spent her time.'

'Whatever you need.'

'You are very kind,' I said.

Lucy was opening access panels to check fluid levels, wiring, and anything else that might be amiss before we took to the air. She was agile and sure of what she was doing, and when she climbed on top of the fuselage to inspect the main rotor, I wondered how many helicopter accidents happened on the ground. It wasn't until I had climbed up into the copilot's seat that I noticed the AR-15 assault rifle in a rack behind her head, and at the same time, I realized the controls on my side had not been taken out. Passengers were not entitled to have access to the collective and cyclic, and the antitorque pedals were supposed to be cranked back far enough that the uninitiated did not accidentally push them with their feet.

'What's this?' I said to Lucy as I buckled my four-point harness.

'We've got a long flight.'

She cracked the throttle several times to make certain there was no binding and it was closed.

'I realize that,' I said.

'Cross country's a good time to try your hand at it.'

She lifted the collective and made big X's with the cyclic.

'Whose hand at what?' I said as my alarm grew.

'Your hand at flying when all you got to do is hold your altitude and speed and keep her level.'

'No way.'

She pressed the starter and the engine began to whirr.

'Yes, *way*.'

The blades began to turn as the windy roar got louder.

'If you're going to fly with me,' my niece, the pilot and certificated flight instructor, said above the noise, 'then I'd like to know you could help out if there was a problem, okay?'

I said nothing more as she rolled the throttle and raised the rpms. She flipped switches and tested caution lights, then turned on the radio and we put our headsets on. Lucy lifted us off the platform as if gravity had quit. She turned us into the wind and moved forward with gathering speed until the helicopter seemed to soar on its own. We climbed above trees, the sun high in the east. When we were clear of the tower and the city, Lucy began lesson one.

I already knew what most of the controls were and what they were for, but I had an extremely limited understanding of how they worked together. I did not know, for example, that when you raise the collective and increase power, the helicopter will yaw to the right, meaning you have to depress your left antitorque pedal to counter the torque of the main rotor and keep the aircraft in trim, and as your altitude climbs, due to the pulling up on the collective, your speed decreases, meaning you have to push the cyclic forward. And so on. It was like playing the drums, as best I knew, only in this instance I had to watch for dim-witted birds, towers, antennae, and other aircraft.

Lucy was very patient, and the time moved fast as we forged ahead at one hundred and ten knots. By the time we were north of Washington, I actually could keep the helicopter relatively steady while adjusting the directional gyro at the same time to keep it consistent with the compass. Our heading was 050 degrees, and although I could juggle not one more thing, such as the Global Positioning System, or GPS, Lucy said I was doing a fine job keeping us on course.

'We got a small plane at three o'clock,' she said through her mike. 'See it?'

'Yes.'

'Then you say, *tally-ho*. And it's above horizon. You can tell that, right?'

'Tally-ho.'

Lucy laughed. 'No. Tally-ho does not mean ten-four. And if something's above horizon, that means it's also above us. That's important, because if both aircraft are at horizon and the one we're looking at also doesn't seem to be moving, then that means it's at our altitude and either heading away from us or straight for us. Kind of smart to pay attention and figure out which one, right?'

Her instruction went on until the New York skyline was in view, then I was to have nothing more to do with the controls. Lucy flew us low past the Statue of Liberty and Ellis Island, where my Italian ancestors had gathered long ago to begin with nothing in a new world of opportunity. The city gathered around us and the buildings in the financial district were huge as we flew at five hundred feet, the shadow of our helicopter moving below us along the water. It was a hot, clear day, and tour helicopters were making their rounds while others carried executives who had everything but time.

Lucy was busy with the radio, and approach control did not seem to want to acknowledge us because air traffic was so congested, and controllers were not very interested in aircraft flying at seven hundred feet. At this altitude in this city, the rules were see and avoid, and that was about it. We followed the East River over the Brooklyn, Manhattan, and Williamsburg bridges, moving at ninety knots over crawling garbage barges, fuel tankers, and circling white tour boats. As we passed by the crumbled buildings and old hospitals of Roosevelt Island, Lucy let La Guardia know what we were doing. By now Ward's Island was straight ahead. It was appropriate that the part of the river at the southwestern tip was called Hell Gate.

What I knew about Ward's Island came from my enduring interest in medical history, and as was true of many of New York's islands in earlier times, it was a place of exile for prisoners, the diseased, and mentally ill. Ward's Island's past was particularly unhappy, as I recalled, for in the mid-eighteen hundreds, it had been a place of no heat or running water, where people with typhus were quarantined and Russian Jewish refugees were warehoused. At the turn of the century, the city's lunatic asylum had been moved to the island. Certainly conditions were better here now, although the population was far more maniacal. Patients had air conditioning, lawyers, and hobbies. They had access to dental and medical care, psychotherapy, support groups, and organized sports.

We entered the Class B airspace above Ward's Island in a deceptively civilized way, flying low over green parks shaded with trees as the ugly tan brick high-rises of the Manhattan Psychiatric and Children's Psychiatric Centers and Kirby loomed straight ahead. The Triborough Bridge Parkway ran through the middle of the island, where incongruous to all was a small circus going on, with bright striped tents, ponies, and performers on unicycles. The crowd was small, and I could see kids eating cotton candy, and I wondered why they weren't in school. A little farther north was a sewage disposal plant and the New York City fire department training academy, where a long ladder truck was practicing turns in a parking lot.

The forensic psychiatric center was twelve stories of steel mesh covered windows, opaque glass, and air conditioning units. Sloppy coils of razor wire bent in over walkways and recreation areas, to prevent an escape that Carrie apparently had found so easy. The river here was about a mile wide, rough and foreboding, the current swift, and I did not think it likely that anyone could swim across it. But there was a footbridge, as I had been told. It was painted the teal of oxidized copper and was maybe a mile south of Kirby. I told Lucy to fly over it, and from the air I saw people crossing it from both directions, moving in and out of the East River Housing of Harlem.

'I don't see how she could have gotten across that in broad daylight,' I transmitted to Lucy. 'Not without being seen by someone. But even if she could and did, what next? The police were going to be all over the place, especially on the other side of the bridge. And how did she get to Lehigh County?'

Lucy was doing slow circles at five hundred feet, the blades flapping loudly. There were remnants of a ferry that at one time must have allowed passage from East River Drive at 106th Street, and the ruins of a pier, which was now a pile of rotting, creosote-treated wood jutting out into unfriendly waters from a small open field on Kirby's western side. The field looked suitable for landing, providing we stayed closer to the river than to the screened-in walkways and benches of the hospital.

As Lucy began a high reconnaissance, I looked down at people on the ground. All were dressed in civilian clothes, some stretching or lying in the grass, others on benches or moving along walkways between rusting barrels of trash. Even from five hundred feet, I recognized the slovenly, ill-fitting dress and odd gaits of those broken beyond repair. They stared up, transfixed, as we scoured the area for problems, such as power lines, guy wires, and soft, uneven ground. A low reconnaissance confirmed our landing was safe, and by now, more people had emerged from buildings or were looking out windows and standing in doorways to see what was going on.

'Maybe we should have tried one of the parks,' I said. 'I hope we don't start a riot.'

Lucy lowered into a five-foot hover, weeds and tall grass thrashing violently. A pheasant and her brood were appropriately startled and darted along the bank and out of view amid rushes, and it was hard to imagine anything innocent and vulnerable living so close to disturbed humanity. I suddenly thought of Carrie's letter to me, of her odd listing of Kirby's address as *One Pheasant Place*. What was she telling me? That she had seen the pheasants, too? If so, why did it matter?

The helicopter settled softly and Lucy rolled the throttle to flight idle. It was a very long two-minute wait to cut the engine. Blades turned as digital seconds did, and patients and hospital personnel stared. Some stood perfectly still, pinning us with glazed eyes, while others were oblivious, tugging on fences or walking with jerky motions and staring at the ground. An old man rolling a cigarette waved, a woman in curlers was muttering, and a young man wearing headphones started into a loose knee rhythm on the sidewalk, for our benefit, it seemed.

Lucy rolled the throttle to idle cut-off and braked the main rotor, shutting us down. When the blades had fully stopped and we were climbing out, a woman emerged from the gathering crowd of the mentally deranged and those who took care of them. She was dressed in a smart herringbone suit, her jacket on despite the heat. Her dark hair was short and smartly styled. I knew before being told that she was Dr Lydia Ensor, and she seemed to pick me out as well, for she shook my hand first, then Lucy's, as she introduced herself.

'I must say, you've created a lot of excitement,' she said with a slight smile.

'And I apologize for that,' I said.

'Not to worry.'

'I'm staying with the helicopter,' Lucy said.

'You sure?' I asked.

'I'm sure,' she replied, looking around at the unnerving crowd.

'Most of these are outpatients at the psychiatric center right over there.' Dr Ensor pointed at another high rise. 'And Odyssey House.'

She nodded at a much smaller brick building beyond Kirby, where there appeared to be a garden, and an eroded asphalt tennis court with a billowing torn net.

'Drugs, drugs, and more drugs,' she added. 'They go in for counseling, and we've caught them rolling a joint on their way out.'

'I'll be right here,' Lucy said. 'Or I can head out to get fuel, and then come back,' she added to me.

'I'd rather you wait,' I said.

Dr Ensor and I began the brief walk to Kirby while eyes glared and poured out black unspeakable pain and hate. A man with a matted beard shouted out to us that he wanted a ride, making gestures towards the heavens, flapping arms like a bird, jumping on one foot. Ravaged faces were in some other realms or vacant or filled with a bitter contempt that could only come from being on the inside looking out at people like us who were not enslaved to drugs or dementia. We were the privileged. We were the living. We were God to those who were helpless to do anything except destroy themselves and others, and at the end of the day, we went home.

The entrance to Kirby Forensic Psychiatric Center was that of a typical state institution, with walls painted the same teal as the footbridge over the river. Dr Ensor led me around a corner to a button on a wall, which she pressed.

'Come to the intercom,' an abrupt voice sounded like the Wizard of Oz.

She moved on, needing no direction, and spoke through the intercom.

'Dr Ensor,' she said.

'Yes, ma'am.' The voice became human. 'Step on up.'

The entrance into the heart of Kirby was typical for a penitentiary, with its airlocked doors that never allowed two of them to be opened at the same time, and its posted warnings of prohibited items, such as firearms, explosives, ammunition, alcohol, or objects made of glass. No matter how adamant politicians, health workers, and the ACLU might be, this was not a hospital. Patients were inmates. They were violent offenders housed in a maximum security facility because they had raped and beaten. They had shot their families, burned up their mothers, disemboweled their neighbors, and dismembered their lovers. They were monsters who had become celebrities, like Robert Chambers of the Yuppie murder fame, or Rakowitz, who had murdered and cooked his girlfriend and allegedly fed parts of her to street people, or Carrie Grethen, who was worse than any of them.

The teal-painted barred door unlocked with an electronic click, and peace officers in blue uniforms were most courteous to Dr Ensor, and also to me, since I clearly was her guest. Nonetheless, we were made to pass through a metal detector, and our pocketbooks were carefully gone through. I was embarrassed when reminded that one could enter with only enough medication for one dose, while I had enough Motrin, Immodium, Tums, and aspirin to take care of an entire ward.

'Ma'am, you must not be feeling good,' one of the guards said good-naturedly.

'It accumulates,' I said, grateful that I had locked my handgun in my briefcase, which was safely stored in the helicopter's baggage compartment.

'Well, I'm gonna have to hold on to it until you come out. It will be waiting right here for you, okay? So make sure you ask.'

'Thank you,' I said, as if he had just granted me a favor.

We were allowed to pass through another door that was posted with the warning, *Keep Hands Off Bars*. Then we were in stark, color-less hallways, turning corners, passing closed doors where hearings were in session.

'You need to understand that legal aid attorneys are employed by the Legal Aid Society, which is a nonprofit, private organization under contract with New York City. Clearly, the personnel they have here are part of their criminal division. They are not on the Kirby staff.'

She wanted to make sure I understood that.

'Although, after a number of years here, they certainly may get chummy with my staff,' she kept talking as we walked, our heels clicking over tile. 'The lawyer in question, who worked with Miss Grethen from the beginning, will most likely arch her back at any questions you might ask.'

She glanced over at me.

'I have no control over it,' she said.

'I understand completely,' I replied. 'And if a public defender or legal aid attorney didn't arch his back when I appeared, I would think the planet had changed.'

Mental Hygiene Legal Aid was lost somewhere in the midst of Kirby, and I could only swear that it was on the first floor. The director opened a wooden door for me, and then was showing me into a small office that was so overflowing with paper that hundreds of case files were stacked on the floor. The lawyer behind the desk was a disaster of frumpy clothing and wild frizzy black hair. She was heavy, with ponderous breasts that could have benefited from a bra.

'Susan, this is Dr Kay Scarpetta, chief medical examiner of Virginia,'

Dr Ensor said. 'Here about Carrie Grethen, as you know. And Dr Scarpetta, this is Susan Blaustein.'

'Right,' said Ms Blaustein, who was neither inclined to get up nor shake my hand as she sifted through a thick legal brief.

'I'll leave the two of you, then. Susan, I trust you will show Dr Scarpetta around, otherwise I will get someone on staff to do it,' Dr Ensor said, and I could tell by the way she looked at me that she knew I was in for the tour from hell.

'No problem.'

The guardian angel of felons had a Brooklyn accent as coarse and tightly packed as a garbage barge.

'Have a seat,' she said to me as the director disappeared.

'When was Carrie remanded here?' I asked.

'Five years ago.'

She would not look up from her paperwork.

'You're aware of her history, of the homicide cases that have yet to go to trial in Virginia?'

'You name it, I'm aware of it.'

'Carrie escaped from here ten days ago, on June tenth,' I went on. 'Has anyone figured out how that might have happened?'

Blaustein flipped a page and picked up a coffee cup.

'She didn't show up for dinner. That's it,' she replied. 'I was as shocked as anyone when she disappeared.'

'I bet you were,' I said.

She turned another page and had yet to give me her eyes. I'd had enough.

'Ms Blaustein,' I said in a hard voice as I leaned against her desk. 'With all due respect to your clients, would you like to hear about mine? Would you like to hear all about men, women, and children who were butchered by Carrie Grethen? A little boy abducted from a 7-Eleven where he'd been sent to buy his mother a can of mushroom soup? He's shot in the head and areas of his flesh are removed to obliterate bitemarks, his pitiful body clad only in undershorts propped against a Dumpster in a freezing rain?'

'I told you, I know about the cases.' She continued to work.

'I suggest you put down that brief and pay attention to me,' I warned. 'I may be a forensic pathologist, but I'm also a lawyer, and your shenanigans get nowhere with me. You just so happen to represent a psychopath who as we speak is on the outside murdering people. Don't let me find out at the end of the day that you had information that might have spared even one life.'

She gave me her eyes, cold and arrogant, because her only power in life was to defend losers and jerk around people like me.

'Let me just refresh your memory,' I went on. 'Since your client has escaped from Kirby, it is believed she has either murdered or served as an accomplice to murder in two cases, happening within a matter of days of each other. Vicious homicides in which an attempt was made to disguise them by fire. These were predated by other fire-homicides which we now believe are linked, yet in these earlier ones, your client was still incarcerated here.'

Susan Blaustein was silent as she stared at me.

'Can you help me with this?'

'All of my conversations with Carrie are privileged. I'm sure you must know that,' she remarked, yet I could tell she was curious about what I was saying.

'Possible she was connecting with someone on the outside?' I went on. 'And if so, how and who?'

'You tell me.'

'Did she ever talk to you about Temple Gault?'

'Privileged.'

'Then she did,' I said. 'Of course, she did. How could she not? Did you know she wrote to me, Ms Blaustein, asking me to come see her and bring her Gault's autopsy photos?'

She said nothing, but her eyes were coming alive.

'He was hit by a train in the Bowery. Scattered along the tracks.'

'Did you do his autopsy?' she asked.

'No.'

'Then why would Carrie ask you for the photos, Dr Scarpetta?'

'Because she knew I could get them. Carrie wanted to see them, blood and gore and all. This was less than a week before she escaped. I'm just wondering if you knew she was sending out letters like that? A clear indication, as far as I'm concerned, that she had premeditated all she was about to do next.'

'No.'

Blaustein pointed her finger at me.

'What she was thinking was how she was being framed to take the heat because the FBI couldn't find its damn way out of a paper bag and needed to hang all this on someone,' she accused.

'I see you read the papers.'

Her face turned angry.

'I talked to Carrie for five years,' she said. 'She wasn't the one sleeping with the Bureau, right?'

'In a way she was.' I thought honestly of Lucy. 'And quite frankly, Ms Blaustein, I'm not here to change your opinion of your client. My purpose is to investigate a number of deaths and do what I can to prevent others.'

Carrie's legal aid attorney began shoving around paperwork again.

'It seems to me that the reason Carrie had been here so long is that every time an evaluation of her mental status came up, you made sure it was clear that she had not regained competency,' I went on. 'Meaning she is also incompetent to stand trial, right? Meaning she is so mentally ill that she's not even aware of the charges against her? And yet she must have been somewhat aware of her situation, or how else could she have trumped up this whole business about the FBI framing her? Or was it you who trumped that up?'

'This meeting has just ended,' Blaustein announced, and had she been a judge, she would have slammed down the gavel.

'Carrie's nothing but a malingerer,' I said. 'She played it up, manipulated. Let me guess. She was very depressed, couldn't remember anything when it was important. Was probably on Ativan, which probably didn't put a dent in her. She clearly had the energy to write letters. And what other privileges might she have enjoyed? Telephone, photocopying?'

'The patients have civil rights,' Blaustein said evenly. 'She was very quiet. Played a lot of chess and spades. She liked to read. There were mitigating and aggravating circumstances at the time of the offenses, and she was not responsible for her actions. She was very remorseful.'

'Carrie always was a great salesperson,' I said. 'Always a master at getting what she wanted, and she wanted to be here long enough to make her next move. And now she's made it.'

I opened my pocketbook and got out a copy of the letter Carrie had written to me. I dropped it in front of Blaustein.

'Pay special attention to the return address at the top of it. *One Pheasant Place, Kirby Women's Ward,*' I said. 'Do you have any idea what she meant by that, or would you like me to hazard a guess?'

'I don't have a clue.' She was reading the letter, a perplexed expression on her face.

'Possibly the *one-place* part is a play off *One Hogan Place,* or the address of the District Attorney that eventually would have prosecuted her.'

'I don't have a clue as to what was going through her mind.'

'Let's talk about *pheasants,*' I then said. 'You have pheasants along the riverbank right outside your door.'

'I haven't noticed.'

'I noticed because we landed in the field there. And that's right, you wouldn't have noticed unless you waded through half an acre of overgrown grass and weeds and went to the water's edge, near the old pier.'

She said nothing, but I could tell she was getting unsettled.

'So my question is, how might Carrie or any of the inmates have known about the pheasants?'

Still, she was silent.

'You know very well why, don't you?' I forced her.

She stared at me.

'A maximum security patient should never have been in that field or even close to it, Ms Blaustein. If you don't wish to talk to me about it, then I'll just let the police take it up with you, since Carrie's escape is rather much a priority for law enforcement these days. Indeed, I'm sure your fine mayor isn't happy about the continuing bad publicity Carrie brings to a city that has become famous for defeating crime.'

'I don't know how Carrie knew,' Ms Blaustein finally said. 'This is the first I've ever heard of fucking pheasants. Maybe someone on the staff said something to her. Maybe one of the delivery people from the store, someone from the outside, such as yourself, in other words.'

'What store?'

'The patient privilege programs allow them to earn credits or money for the store. Snacks, mostly. They get one delivery a week, and they have to use their own money.'

'Where did Carrie get money?'

Blaustein would not say.

'What day did her deliveries come?'

'Depends. Usually early in the week, Monday, Tuesday, late in the afternoon, usually.'

'She escaped late in the afternoon, on a Tuesday,' I said.

'That's correct.' Her eyes got harder.

'And what about the deliveryperson?' I then asked. 'Has anybody bothered to see if he or she might have had anything to do with this?'

'The deliveryperson was a he,' Blaustein said with no emotion. 'No one has been able to locate him. He was a substitute for the usual person, who apparently was out sick.'

'A *substitute*? Right. Carrie was interested in more than potato chips!' My voice rose. 'Let me guess. The delivery people wear uniforms and drive a van. Carrie puts on a uniform and walks right out with her deliveryman. Gets in the van and is out of here.'

'Speculation. We don't know how she got out.'

'Oh, I think you do, Ms Blaustein. And I'm wondering if you didn't help Carrie with money, too, since she was so special to you.'

She got to her feet and pointed her finger at me again.

'If you're accusing me of helping her escape . . .'

'You helped her in one way or another,' I cut her off.

I fought back tears as I thought of Carrie free on the streets, as I thought about Benton.

'You monster,' I said, and my eyes were hot on hers. 'I'd like you to spend just one day with the victims. Just one goddamn day, putting your hands in their blood and touching their wounds. The innocent people the Carries of the world butcher for sport. I think there would be some people who would not be too happy to know about Carrie, her privileges, and unaccounted source of income,' I said. 'Others besides me.'

We were interrupted by a knock on her door, and Dr Ensor walked in.

'I thought I might take you on your tour,' she said to me. 'Susan seems busy. Are you finished up here?' she asked the legal aid attorney.

'Quite.'

'Very good,' she said with a chilly smile.

I knew then that the director was perfectly clear on how much Susan Blaustein had abused power, trust, and common decency. In the end, Blaustein had manipulated the hospital as much as Carrie had.

'Thank you,' I said to the director.

I left, turning my back on Carrie's defender.

May you rot in hell, I thought.

I followed Dr Ensor again, this time to a large stainless steel elevator that opened onto barren beige hallways closed off with heavy red doors that required codes for entry. Everything was monitored by closed circuit TV. Apparently Carrie had enjoyed working in the pet program, which entailed daily visits to the eleventh floor, where animals were kept in cages inside a small room with a view of razor wire.

The menagerie was dimly lit and moist with the musky smells of animals and wood chips, and the skittering of claws. There were parakeets, guinea pigs, and a Russian dwarf hamster. On a table was a box of rich soil thick with tender shoots.

'We grow our own birdseed here,' Dr Ensor explained. 'The patients are encouraged to raise and sell it. Of course, we're not talking mass production here. There's barely enough for our own birds, and as you can see by what's in some of the cages and on the floor, the patients tend to be fond of feeding their pets cheese puffs and potato chips.'

'Carrie was up here every day?' I asked.

'So I've been told, now that I've been looking into everything she did while she was here.' She paused, looking around the cages as small animals with pink noses twitched and scratched.

'Obviously I didn't know everything at the time. For example, co-incidentally, during the six months Carrie supervised the pet program, we had an unusual number of fatalities and inexplicable escapes. A parakeet here, a hamster there. Patients would come in and find their wards dead in their cages, or a cage door open and a bird nowhere to be found.'

She walked back out into the hallway, her lips firmly pressed.

'It's too bad you weren't here on those occasions,' she said wryly. 'Perhaps you could have told me what they were dying from. Or who.'

There was another door down the hall, and this one opened onto a small, dimly lit room where there was one relatively modern computer and printer on a plain wooden table. I also noted a phone jack in the wall. A sense of foreshadowing darkened my thoughts even before Dr Ensor spoke.

'This was perhaps where Carrie spent most of her free time,' she said. 'As you no doubt know, she has an extensive background in computers. She was extremely good about encouraging other patients to learn, and the PC was her idea. She suggested we find donors of used equipment, and we now have one computer and printer on each floor.'

I walked over to the terminal and sat down in front of it. Hitting a key, I turned off the screen saver and looked at icons that told me what programs were available.

'When patients worked in here,' I said, 'were they supervised?'

'No. They were shown in and the door was shut and locked. An hour later, they were shown back to their ward.' She grew thoughtful. 'I'd be the first to admit that I was impressed with how many of the patients have started learning word processing, and in some instances, spread sheets.'

I went into America Online and was prompted for a username and password. The director watched what I was doing.

'They absolutely had no access to the Internet,' she said.

'How do we know that?'

'The computers aren't hooked up to it.'

'But they do have modems,' I said. 'Or at least this one does. It's simply not connecting because there's no telephone line plugged into the telephone jack.'

I pointed to the tiny receptacle in the wall, then turned around to face her.

'Any chance a telephone line might have disappeared from somewhere?' I asked. 'Perhaps from one of the offices? Susan Blaustein's office, for example?'

The director glanced away, her face angry and distressed as she began to see what I was getting at.

'God,' she muttered.

'Of course, she may have gotten that from the outside. Perhaps from whoever delivered her snacks from the store?'

'I don't know.'

'The point is, there's a lot we don't know, Dr Ensor. We don't know, for example, what the hell Carrie was really doing when she was in here. She could have been in and out of chat rooms, putting feelers out in personals, finding pen pals. I'm sure you've kept up with the news enough to know how many crimes are committed on the Internet? Pedophilia, rape, homicide, child pornography.'

'That's why this was closely supervised,' she said. 'Or supposed to have been.'

'Carrie could have planned her escape this way. And you say she started working with the computer how long ago?'

'About a year. After a long run of ideal behavior.'

'*Ideal behavior,*' I repeated.

I thought of the cases in Baltimore, Venice Beach, and more recently in Warrenton. I wondered if it were possible that Carrie might have met up with her accomplice through e-mail, through a Web site or a chat room. Could it be that she committed computer crimes during her incarceration? Might she have been working behind the scenes, advising and encouraging a psychopath who stole human faces? Then she escaped, and from that point on her crimes were in person.

'Is there anyone who's been discharged from Kirby in the past year who was an arsonist, especially someone with a history of homicide?

Anyone Carrie might have come to know? Perhaps someone in one of her classes?' I asked, just to be sure.

Dr Ensor turned off the overhead light and we returned to the hall.

'No one comes to mind,' she said. 'Not of the sort you're talking about. I will add that a peace officer was always present.'

'And male and female patients did not mix during recreational times.'

'No. Never. Men and women are completely segregated.'

Although I did not know for a fact that Carrie had a male accomplice, I suspected it, and I recalled what Benton had written in his notes at the end, about a white male between the ages of twenty-eight and forty-five. Peace officers, who were simply guards not wearing guns, might have insured that order was maintained in the classrooms, but I doubted seriously they would have had any idea that Carrie was making contact on the Internet. We boarded the elevator again, this time getting off on the third floor.

'The women's ward,' Dr Ensor explained. 'We have twenty-six female patients at the moment, out of one hundred and seventy patients overall. That's the visitors' room.'

She pointed through glass at a spacious open area with comfortable chairs and televisions. No one was in there now.

'Did she ever have visitors?' I asked as we kept walking.

'Not from the outside, not once. Inspiring more sympathy for her, I suppose.' She smiled bitterly. 'The women actually stay in there.'

She pointed out another area, this one arranged with single beds.

'She slept over there by the window,' Dr Ensor said.

I retrieved Carrie's letter from my pocketbook and read it again, stopping at the fifth paragraph:

LUCY-BOO on TV. Fly through window. Come with we. Under covers. Come til dawn. Laugh and sing. Same ole song. LUCY LUCY LUCY and we!

Suddenly I thought about the videotape of Kellie Shephard, and of the actress in Venice Beach who played bit parts on television shows. I thought of photo shoots and production crews, becoming more convinced that there was a connection. But what did Lucy have to do with any of this? Why would Carrie see Lucy on TV? Or was it simply that she somehow knew that Lucy could fly, could fly helicopters?

There was a commotion around a corner, and female peace officers were herding the women patients in from recreation. They were sweating and loud, with tormented faces, and one was being escorted in a preventive aggressive device, or a PAD, which was a politically correct term for a restraint that chained wrists and ankles to a thick leather strap about the waist. She was young and white, with eyes that scattered when they fixed on me, her mouth bowed in a simpering smile. With her bleached hair and pale androgynous body, she could have been Carrie, and for a moment, in my imagination, she was. My flesh crawled as those irises seemed to swirl, sucking me in, while patients jostled past us, several making it a point to bump into me.

'You a lawyer?' an obese black woman almost spat as her eyes smoldered on me.

'Yes,' I said, unflinching as I stared back, for I had learned long ago not to be intimidated by people who hate.

'Come on.' The director pulled me along. 'I'd forgotten they were due up at this time. I apologize.'

But I was glad it had happened. In a sense, I had looked Carrie in the eye and had not turned away.

'Tell me exactly what happened the night she disappeared, please,' I said.

Dr Ensor entered a code into another keypad and pushed through another set of bright red doors.

'As best anyone can reconstruct it,' she replied, 'Carrie went out with the other patients for this same recreation hour. Her snacks were delivered, and at dinner she was gone.'

We rode the elevator down. She glanced at her watch.

'Immediately, a search began and the police were contacted. Not one sign of her, and that's what continued to eat at me,' she went on. 'How did she get off the island in broad daylight with no one seeing her? We had cops, we had dogs, we had helicopters . . .'

I stopped her there, in the middle of the first floor hall.

'Helicopters?' I said. 'More than one?'

'Oh yes.'

'You saw them?'

'Hard not to,' she replied. 'They were circling and hovering for hours, the entire hospital was in an uproar.'

'Describe the helicopters,' I said as my heart began to hammer. 'Please.'

'Oh gosh,' she answered. 'Three police at first, then the media flew in like a swarm of hornets.'

'By chance, was one of the helicopters small and white? Like a dragonfly?'

She looked surprised.

'I do remember seeing one like that,' she said. 'I thought it was just some pilot curious about all of the commotion.'

22

————

Lucy and I lifted off from Ward's Island in a hot wind and low baro-
metric pressure that made the Bell JetRanger sluggish. We followed
the East River and continued to fly through the Class B airspace of
La Guardia, where we landed long enough to refuel and buy cheese
crackers and sodas from vending machines, and for me to call the
University of North Carolina at Wilmington. This time I was
connected to the director of student counseling. I took that as a good
sign.

'I understand your need to protect yourself,' I said to her from
behind the shut door of a pay phone booth inside Signatures terminal.
'But please reconsider. Two more people have been murdered since
Claire Rawley was.'

There was a long silence.

Then Dr Chris Booth said, 'Can you come in person?'

'I was planning to,' I told her.

'All right then.'

I called Teun McGovern next to tell her what was going on.

'I think Carrie escaped from Kirby in the same white Schweizer
we saw flying over Kenneth Sparkes's farm when we were working
the scene,' I said.

'Does she fly?' McGovern's confused voice came back.

'No, no. I can't imagine that.'

'Oh.'

'Whoever she's with,' I said. 'That's the pilot. Whoever helped her escape and is doing all this. The first two cases were warm-ups. Baltimore and Venice Beach. We might never have known about them, Teun. I believe Carrie waited to drag us in. She waited until Warrenton.'

'Then you're thinking Sparkes was the intended target,' she stated thoughtfully.

'To get our attention. To make sure we came. Yes,' I said.

'Then Claire Rawley figures in how?'

'That's what I'm going to Wilmington to find out, Teun. I believe she's somehow the key to all of this. She's the connection to him. Whoever he is. And I also believe that Carrie knows I will think this, and that she's expecting me.'

'You think she's there.'

'Oh yes. I'm betting on it. She expected Benton to come to Philadelphia, and he did. She expects Lucy and me to come to Wilmington. She knows how we think, how we work, at least as much about us as we know about her.'

'You're saying that you're her next hits.'

The thought was cold water in my stomach.

'Intended ones.'

'Not a chance we can take, Kay. We'll be there when you land. The university must have a playing field. We'll get that arranged very discreetly. Whenever you land to refuel or whatever, page me and we'll keep up with each other.'

'You can't let her know you're there,' I said. 'That will ruin it.'

'Trust me. She won't,' McGovern said.

We flew out of La Guardia with seventy-five gallons of fuel and an unbearably long flight to look forward to. Three hours in a helicopter was always more than enough for me. The weight of the headsets and the noise and vibration gave me a hot spot on the top of my head and seemed to rattle me loose at the joints. To endure this beyond four hours generally resulted in a serious headache. We were lucky with a generous tail wind, and although our airspeed showed one hundred and ten knots, the GPS showed our ground speed was actually one hundred and twenty.

Lucy made me take the controls again, and I was smoother as I learned not to overcontrol and fight. When thermals and winds shook us like an angry mother, I gave myself up to them. Trying to outmaneuver gusts and updrafts only made matters worse, and this was hard for me. I liked to make things better. I learned to watch for birds, and now and then I spotted a plane at the same time Lucy did.

Hours became monotonous and blurred as we snuggled up to the coastline, over the Delaware River and on to the Eastern Shore. We refueled near Salisbury, Maryland, where I used the bathroom and drank a Coke, then continued into North Carolina, where hog farms slaughtered the topography with long aluminum sheds and waste treatment lagoons the color of blood. We entered the airspace of Wilmington at almost two o'clock. My nerves began to scream as I imagined what might await us.

'Let's go down to six hundred feet,' Lucy said. 'And lower the speed.'

'You want me to do it.' I wanted to make sure.

'Your ship.'

It wasn't pretty, but I managed.

'My guess is, the university's not going to be on the water, and is probably a bunch of brick buildings.'

'Thank you, Sherlock.'

Everywhere I looked I saw water, condominium complexes, and water treatment and other plants. The ocean was to the east, sparkling and ruffled, oblivious to dark, bruised clouds gathering on the horizon. A storm was on its way and did not seem to be in a hurry but threatened to be bad.

'Lord, I don't want to get grounded here,' I said over my mike as, sure enough, a cluster of Georgian brick buildings came into view.

'I don't know about this.' Lucy was looking around. 'If she's here. Where, Aunt Kay?'

'Wherever she thinks we are.' I sounded so sure.

Lucy took over.

'I've got the controls,' she said. 'I don't know if I hope you're right or not.'

'You hope it,' I answered her. 'In fact, you hope it so much it scares me, Lucy.'

'I'm not the one who brought us here.'

Carrie had tried to ruin Lucy. Carrie had murdered Benton.

'I know who brought us here,' I said. 'It was her.'

The university was close below us, and we found the athletic field where McGovern was waiting. Men and women were playing soccer, but there was a clearing near the tennis courts, and this was where Lucy was to land. She circled the area twice, once high, once low, and neither of us spotted any obstructions, except for an odd tree here and there. Several cars were on the sidelines, and as we settled to the grass, I noted that one of them was a dark blue Explorer with a driver inside. Then I realized that the intramural soccer game was coached by Teun McGovern in P.E. gym shorts and shirt. She had a whistle around her neck, and her teams were co-ed and very fit.

I looked around as if Carrie were observing all this, but skies were empty, and nothing offered even the scent of her. The instant we were on the ground and in flight idle, the Explorer drove across the grass and stopped a safe distance from our blades. It was driven by an unfamiliar woman, and I was stunned to see Marino in the passenger's seat.

'I don't believe it,' I said to Lucy.

'How the hell did he get here?' She was amazed, too.

Marino stared at us through the windshield as we waited out our two minutes and shut down. He didn't smile and wasn't the least bit friendly when I climbed into the back of the car while Lucy tied down the main rotor blades. McGovern and her soccer players went on with their staged game, paying no attention to us at all. But I noticed the gym bags beneath benches on the sidelines, and I had no doubt what was inside them. It was as if we were expecting an approaching army, an ambush by enemy troops, and I could not help but wonder if Carrie had made a mockery of us once again.

'I wasn't expecting to see you,' I commented to Marino.

'You think it's possible US Airways could fly somewhere without dumping your ass out in Charlotte first?' he complained. 'Took me as long to get here as it probably did you.'

'I'm Ginny Correll.' Our driver turned around and shook my hand.

She was at least forty, a very attractive blond dressed primly in a pale green suit, and had I not known the truth, I might have assumed she was on the university's faculty. But there was a scanner and a two-way radio inside the car, and I caught a flicker of the pistol in the shoulder holster beneath her jacket. She waited until Lucy was inside the Explorer, and then began turning around in the grass as the soccer game went on.

'Here's what's going on,' Correll began to explain. 'We didn't know whether the suspect or suspects might be waiting for you, following you, whatever, so we prepared for that.'

'I can see that you did,' I said.

'They'll be heading off the field in about two minutes, and the important point is we got guys all over the place. Some dressed as students, others hanging out in town, checking out the hotels and bars, things like that. Where we're heading now is the student counseling center, where the assistant director's going to meet us. She was Claire Rawley's counselor and has all her records.'

'Right,' I said.

'Just so you know, Doc,' Marino said, 'we got a campus police officer who thinks he may have spotted Carrie yesterday in the student union.'

'The Hawk's Nest, to be specific,' Correll said. 'That's the cafeteria.'

'Short dyed red hair, weird eyes. She was buying a sandwich, and he noticed her because she stared holes in him when she walked past his table, and then when we started passing her photo around, he said it might have been her. Can't swear to it, though.'

'It would be like her to stare at a cop,' Lucy said. 'Jerking people around is her favorite sport.'

'I'll also add that it's not unusual for college kids to look like the homeless,' I said.

'We're checking pawn shops around here to see if anybody fitting Carrie's description might have bought a gun, and we're also checking for stolen cars in the area,' Marino said. 'Assuming if she and her sidekick stole cars in New York or Philadelphia, they aren't going to show up here with those plates.'

The campus was an immaculate collection of modified Georgian buildings tucked amid palms, magnolias, crêpe myrtles, and lobolly and long-leaf pines. Gardenias were in bloom and when we got out of the car, their perfume clung to the humid, hot air and went to my head.

I loved the scents of the South, and for a moment, it did not seem possible that anything bad could happen here. It was summer session, and the campus was not heavily populated. Parking lots were half full, with many of the bike racks empty. Some of the cars driving on College Road had surfboards strapped to their roofs.

The counseling center was on the second floor of Westside Hall, and the waiting area for students with health problems was mauve and blue and full of light. Thousand-piece puzzles of rural scenes were in various stages of completion on coffee tables, offering a welcome distraction for those who had appointments. A receptionist was expecting us and showed us down a corridor, past observation and group rooms, and spaces for GRE testing. Dr Chris Booth was energetic with kind, wise eyes, a woman approaching sixty, I guessed, and one who loved the sun. She was weathered in a way that gave her character, her skin deeply tanned and lined, her short hair white, and her body slight but vital.

She was a psychologist with a corner office that overlooked the fine arts building and lush live oak trees. I had always been fascinated by the personality behind offices. Where she worked was soothing and unprovocative but shrewd in its arrangement of chairs that suited very different personalities. There was a papasan chair for the patient who wanted to curl up on deep cushions and be open for help, and a cane-back rocker and a stiff love seat. The color scheme was gentle green, with paintings of sailboats on the walls, and elephant ear in terracotta pots.

'Good afternoon,' Dr Booth said to us with a smile as she invited us in. 'I'm very glad to see you.'

'And I'm very glad to see you,' I replied.

I helped myself to the rocking chair, while Ginny perched on the love seat. Marino looked around with self-conscious eyes and eased his way into the papasan, doing what he could not to be swallowed by it. Dr Booth sat in her office chair, her back to her perfectly clean desk that had nothing on it but a can of Diet Pepsi. Lucy stood by the door.

'I've been hoping that someone would come see me,' Dr Booth began, as if she had called this meeting. 'But I honestly didn't know who to contact or even if I should.'

She gave each of us her bright gray eyes.

'Claire was very special – and I know that's what everyone says about the dead,' she said.

'Not everyone,' Marino cynically retorted.

Dr Booth smiled sadly. 'I'm just saying that I have counseled many students here over the years, and Claire deeply touched my heart and I had high hopes for her. I was devastated by news of her death.'

She paused, staring out of the window.

'I saw her last about two weeks prior to her death, and I've tried to think of anything I could that might hold an answer as to what might have happened.'

'When you say you saw her,' I said, 'do you mean in here? For a session?'

She nodded. 'We met for an hour.'

Lucy was getting increasingly restless.

'Before you get into that,' I said, 'could you give us as much of her background as possible?'

'Absolutely. And by the way, I have dates and times for her appointments, if you need all that. I'd been seeing her on and off for three years.'

'Off and on?' Marino asked as he sat forward in the deep seat and starting sliding back into its deep cushions again.

'Claire was paying her own way through school. She worked as a waitress at the Blockade Runner at Wrightsville Beach. She'd do nothing but work and save, then pay for a term, then drop out again to earn more money. I didn't see her when she wasn't in school, and this is where a lot of her difficulties began, it's my belief.'

'I'm going to let you guys handle this,' Lucy said abruptly. 'I want to make sure someone's staying with the helicopter.'

Lucy went out and shut the door behind her, and I felt a wave of fear. I didn't know that Lucy wouldn't hit the streets alone to look for Carrie. Marino briefly met my eyes, and I could tell he was thinking the same thing. Our agent escort, Ginny, was stiff on the love seat, appropriately unobtrusive, offering nothing but her attention.

'About a year ago,' Dr Booth went on, 'Claire met Kenneth Sparkes, and I know I'm not telling you something you're not already aware of. She was a competitive surfer and he had a beach house in Wrightsville. The long and short of it is they got involved in a brief, extremely intense affair, which he cut off.'

'This was while she was enrolled in school,' I said.

'Yes. Second term. They broke up in the summer, and she didn't return to the university until the following winter. She didn't come in to see me until that February when her English professor noticed that she was constantly falling asleep in class and smelled of alcohol. Concerned, he went to the dean, and she was put on probation, with the stipulation that she had to come back to see me. This was all related to Sparkes, I'm afraid. Claire was adopted, the situation a very unhappy one. She left home when she was sixteen, came to Wrightsville, and did any kind of work she could to survive.'

'Where are her parents now?' Marino asked.

'Her birth parents? We don't know who they are.'

'No. The ones who adopted her.'

'Chicago. They have had no contact with her since she left home. But they do know she's dead. I have spoken to them.'

'Dr Booth,' I said, 'do you have any idea why Claire would have gone to Sparkes's house in Warrenton?'

'She was completely incapable of dealing with rejection. I can only speculate she went there to see him, in hopes she might resolve something. I do know she stopped calling him last spring, because he finally changed to another unlisted phone number. Her only possible contact was to just show up, my guess is.'

'In an old Mercedes that belonged to a psychotherapist named Newton Joyce?' Marino asked, adjusting his position again.

Dr Booth was startled. 'Now I didn't know that,' she said. 'She was driving Newton's car?'

'You know him?'

'Not personally, but certainly I know his reputation. Claire started going to him because she felt she needed a male perspective. This was within the past two months. He certainly wouldn't have been my choice.'

'Why?' Marino asked.

Dr Booth gathered her thoughts, her face tight with anger.

'This is all very messy,' she said finally. 'Which might begin to explain my reluctance to talk about Claire when you first began to call. Newton is a spoiled rich boy who has never had to work but decided to go into psychotherapy. A power trip for him, I suppose.'

'He seems to have vanished in thin air,' Marino said.

'Nothing out of the ordinary about that,' she replied shortly. 'He's in and out as he pleases, sometimes for months or even years at a time. I've been here at the university for thirty-some years now, and I remember him as a boy. Could charm the birds out of the trees and talk people into anything, but he's all about himself. And I was most concerned when Claire began to see him. Let's just say that no one would ever accuse Newton of being ethical. He makes his own rules. But he's never been caught.'

'At what?' I asked. 'Caught at what?'

'Controlling patients in a way that is most inappropriate.'

'Having sexual relations with them?' I asked.

'I've never heard proof of that. It was more of a mind thing, a dominance thing, and it was very apparent that he completely dominated Claire. She was utterly dependent on him just like that.' She snapped her fingers. 'After their very first session. She would come in here and spend the entire time talking about him, obsessing. That's what's so odd about her going to see Sparkes. I truly thought she was over him and besotted with Newton. I honestly think she would have done anything Newton told her to do.'

'Possible he might have suggested she go see Sparkes? For therapeutic reasons, such as closure?' I said.

Dr Booth smiled ironically.

'He may have suggested she go see him, but I doubt it was to help her,' she replied. 'I'm sorry to say that if going there was Newton's idea, then it most likely was manipulative.'

'I sure would like to know how the two of them got hooked up,' Marino said, scooting forward in the papasan chair. 'I'm guessing that someone referred her to him.'

'Oh no,' she replied. 'They met on a photo shoot.'

'What do you mean?' I said as my blood stopped in my veins.

'He's quite enamored with all things Hollywood and has finagled his way into working with production crews for movies and photo shoots. You know Screen Gems studio is right here in town, and Claire's minor was film studies. It was her dream to be an actress. Heaven knows, she was beautiful enough. Based on what she told me, she was doing a modeling job at the beach, for some surfing magazine, I think. And he was part of the production crew, the photographer, in this instance. Apparently he is accomplished in that.'

'You said he was in and out a lot,' Marino said. 'Maybe he had other residences?'

'I don't know anything more about him, really,' she replied.

Within an hour, the Wilmington Police Department had a warrant to search Newton Joyce's property in the historic district, several blocks from the water. His white frame house was one story with a broken-pitch gable roof that covered the porch in front at the end of a quiet street of other tired nineteenth-century homes with porches and piazzas.

Huge magnolias darkly shadowed his yard with only patches of wan sunlight seeping through, and the air was fitful with insects. By now, McGovern had caught up with us, and we waited on the slumping back porch as a detective used a tactical baton to break out a pane of glass from the door. Then he reached his hand inside and freed the lock.

Marino, McGovern, and a Detective Scroggins went first with pistols close to their bodies and pointed to shoot. I was close behind, unarmed and unnerved by the creepiness of this place Joyce called home. We entered a small sitting area that had been modified to accommodate patients. There was a rather ghastly old red velvet Victorian couch, a marble-topped end table centered by a milkglass lamp, and a coffee table scattered with magazines that were many months old. Through a doorway was his office, and it was even stranger.

Yellowed knotty pine walls were almost completely covered with framed photographs of what I assumed were models and actors in various publicity poses. Quite literally, there were hundreds of them, and I assumed Joyce had taken them himself. I could not imagine a patient pouring out his problems in the midst of so many beautiful bodies and faces. On Joyce's desk were a Rolodex, date book, paperwork, and a telephone. While Scroggins began playing messages from the answering machine, I looked around some more.

On bookcases were worn-out cloth and leather volumes of classics that were too dusty to have been opened in many years. There was a cracked brown leather couch, presumably for his patients, and next to it a small table bearing a single water glass. It was almost empty and smeared around the rim with pale peach lipstick. Directly across from the couch was an intricately carved, high-back mahogany armchair that brought to mind a throne. I heard Marino and McGovern checking other rooms while voices drifted out of Joyce's answering machine. All of the messages had been left after the evening of June fifth, or the day before Claire's death. Patients had called about their appointments. A travel agent had left word about two tickets to Paris.

'What'd you say that fire starter thing looks like?' Detective Scroggins asked as he opened another desk drawer.

'A thin bar of silvery metal,' I answered him. 'You'll know it when you see it.'

'Nothing like that in here. But the guy sure is into rubber bands. Must be thousands of them. Looks like he was making these weird little balls.'

He held up a perfectly shaped sphere made completely of rubber bands.

'Now how the hell do you think he did that?' Scroggins was amazed. 'You think he started with just one and then kept winding others all around like golf ball innards?'

I didn't know.

'What kind of mind is that, huh?' Scroggins went on. 'You think he was sitting here doing that while he was talking with his patients?'

'At this point,' I replied, 'not much would surprise me.'

'What a whacko. So far I've found thirteen, fourteen . . . uh, nineteen balls.'

He was pulling them out and setting them on top of the desk, and then Marino called me from the back of the house.

'Doc, think you'd better come here.'

I followed the sounds of him and McGovern through a small

kitchen with old appliances that were layered in the civilizations of former meals. Dishes were piled in cold scummy water in the sink, and the garbage can was overflowing, the stench awful. Newton Joyce was more slovenly than Marino, and I would not have thought that possible, nor did it square with the orderliness of Joyce's rubber band balls or what I believed were his crimes. But despite criminalist texts and Hollywood renditions, people were not a science and they were not consistent. A prime example was what Marino and McGovern had discovered in the garage.

It was connected to the kitchen by a door that had been made inaccessible by a padlock that Marino had handily removed with bolt cutters that McGovern had fetched from her Explorer. On the other side was a work area with no door leading outside, for it had been closed in with cinder block. Walls were painted white, and against one were fifty-gallon drums of aviation gasoline. There was a stainless steel Sub-Zero freezer and its door, ominously, was padlocked. The concrete floor was very clean, and in a corner were five aluminum camera cases and Styrofoam ice chests of varying sizes. Central was a large plyboard table covered with felt and here were arranged the instruments of Joyce's crimes.

Half a dozen knives were lined in a perfect row, with precisely the same spacing between each. All were in their leather cases, and in a small redwood wooden box were sharpening stones.

'I'll be damned,' Marino said, pointing out the knives to me. 'Let me tell you what these are, Doc. The bone-handled ones are R.W. Loveless skinner knives, made by Beretta. For collectors, numbered, and costing around six hundred bucks a pop.'

He stared at them with lust but did not touch.

'The blued steel babies are Chris Reeves, at least four hundred a pop, and the butts of the handles unscrew if you want to store matches in them,' he went on.

I heard a distant door shut, and then Scroggins appeared with Lucy. The detective was as awed by the knives as Marino was, and then the two of them and McGovern resumed opening drawers of tool chests, and prying open two cabinets that held other chilling signs that we had found our killer. In a plastic Speedo bag were eight silicone swim caps, all of them hot pink. Each was zipped inside a plastic pouch with price stickers that said Joyce had paid sixteen dollars apiece for them. As for fire starters, there were four of them in a Wal-Mart bag.

Joyce also had a modular desk in his concrete cave, and we left it to Lucy to access whatever she could. She sat in a folding chair and began working the keyboard while Marino took the bolt cutters to the freezer, which, eerily, was precisely the same model I had at home.

'This is too easy,' Lucy said. 'He's downloaded his e-mail onto a disk. No password or anything. Stuff he sent and received. About eighteen months' worth. We got a username of FMKIRBY. *From Kirby,* I presume. Now I wonder who that pen pal might be,' she added sarcastically.

I moved closer and looked over her shoulder as she scrolled through notes that Carrie had sent to Newton Joyce, whose username horrifically was *skinner,* and those he had sent to her. On May tenth he wrote:

Found her. A connection to die for. How does a major media tycoon sound? Am I good?

And the next day, Carrie had written back:

Yes, GOOD. I want them. Then fly me out of here, bird man. You can show me later. I want to look in their empty eyes and see.

'My God,' I muttered. 'She wanted him to kill in Virginia, and do so in a way that would insure my participation.'

Lucy scrolled some more, and her tapping of the down arrow was impatient and angry.

'So he happens upon Claire Rawley at a photo shoot, and she turns out to be the bait. The perfect lure because of her past relationship to Sparkes,' I went on. 'Joyce and Claire go to his farm, but he's out of town. Sparkes is spared. Joyce murders and mutilates her, and burns the place.' I paused, reading more old mail. 'And now here we are.'

'Here we are because she wants us here,' Lucy said. 'We were supposed to find all this.'

She tapped the key hard.

'Don't you get it?' she asked.

She turned around and looked at me.

'She reeled us in, here, so we would see all this,' she said.

Bolt cutters suddenly snapped loudly through steel, and the freezer door sucked open.

'Jesus fucking Christ,' Marino shouted. 'Fuck!' he cried.

23

On the top wire shelf were two bald mannikin heads, one male, one female, with blank faces smeared black with frozen blood. They had been used as forms for the faces Joyce had stolen, each one laid over the mannikin's face, then frozen hard to give his trophies shape. Joyce had shrouded his mask-like horrors in triple layers of plastic freezer bags that were labeled like evidence, with case numbers, locations, and dates.

The most recent was the one on top, and I robotically picked it up as my heart began to pound so hard that for an instant, the world went black. I began to shake and was aware of nothing else until I came to in McGovern's arms. She was helping me into the chair where Lucy had been seated at the desk.

'Someone bring her some water,' McGovern was saying. 'It's all right, Kay. It's all right.'

I focused on the freezer with its wide-open door and stacks of plastic bags hinting of flesh and blood. Marino was pacing the garage, running his fingers through his thinning strands of hair. His face was the hue of a stroke about to happen, and Lucy was gone.

'Where's Lucy?' I asked with a dry mouth.

'She's gone to get a first aid kit,' McGovern answered in a gentle voice. 'Just be quiet, try to relax, and we're going to get you out of here. You don't need to be seeing all this.'

But I already had. I had seen the empty face, the misshapen mouth and nose that had no bridge. I had seen the orange-tinted flesh sparkling with ice. The date on the freezer bag was June 17, the location Philadelphia, and that had penetrated at the same time I was looking, and then it was too late, or maybe I would have looked anyway, because I had to know.

'They've been here,' I said.

I struggled to get up and got light-headed again.

'They came here long enough to leave that. So we'd find it,' I said.

'Goddamn son of a bitch!' Marino screamed. 'GODDAMN-MOTHER-FUCKING-SON-OF-A-BITCH!'

He roughly wiped his eyes on his fist as he continued to pace like a madman. Lucy was coming down the steps. She was pale, her eyes glassy. My niece seemed dazed.

'McGovern to Correll,' she said into her portable radio.

'Correll,' the voice came back.

'You guys get on over here.'

'Ten-four.'

'I'm calling our forensic guys,' said Detective Scroggins.

He was stunned, too, but not the same way we were. For him, this wasn't personal. He had never heard of Benton Wesley. Scroggins was carefully going through the bags in the freezer, his lips moving as he counted.

'Holy God,' he said in amazement. 'There's twenty-seven of these things.'

'Dates and locations,' I said, mustering my reserved strength to walk over to him.

We looked together.

'London, 1981. Liverpool, 1983. Dublin, 1984, and one-two-three-four-five-six-seven-eight-nine-ten-eleven. Eleven, total, from Ireland, through 1987. It looks like he really started getting into it,' Scroggins said, and he was getting excited, the way people do when they are on the verge of hysteria.

I was looking on with him, and the location of Joyce's kills began in Northern Ireland in Belfast, then continued into the Republic in Galway, followed by nine murders in Dublin in neighborhoods such as Malahide, Santry and Howth. Then Joyce had begun his predation in the United States, mainly out west, in remote areas of Utah, Nevada, Montana, and Washington, and once in Natches, Mississippi, and this explained a lot to me, especially when I remembered what Carrie had said in her letter to me. She had made an odd reference to *sawed bone*.

'The torsos,' I said as the truth ran through me like lightning. 'The unsolved dismemberments in Ireland. And then he was quiet for eight years because he killed out west and the bodies were never found, or else never centrally reported. So we didn't know about them. He never stopped, and then he came to Virginia, where his presence definitely got my attention and drove me to despair.'

It was 1995 when two torsos had turned up, the first near Virginia Beach, the next in Norfolk. The following year there were two more, this time in the western part of the state, one in Lynchburg, the other in Blacksburg, very close to the campus of the Virginia Tech. In 1997, Joyce seemed to have gotten silent, and this was when I suspected Carrie had allied herself with him.

The publicity about the dismemberments had become overwhelming, with only two of the limbless, headless bodies identified by X-rays matching the premortem films of missing people, both of them male college students. They had been my cases, and I had made a tremendous amount of noise about them, and the FBI had been brought in.

I now realized that Joyce's primary purpose was not only to foil identification, but more importantly, to hide his mutilation of the bodies. He did not want us to know he was stealing his victims' beauty, in effect, stealing who they were by taking his knife to their faces and adding them to his frigid collection. Perhaps he feared that additional dismemberments might make the hunt for him too big, so he had switched his modus operandi to fire, and perhaps it was Carrie who had suggested this. I could only assume that somehow the two of them had connected on the Internet.

'I don't get it,' Marino was saying.

He had calmed a little and had brought himself to sift through Joyce's packages.

'How did he get all of these here?' he asked. 'All the way from England and Ireland? From Venice Beach and Salt Lake City?'

'Dry ice,' I said simply, looking at the metal camera cases and Styrofoam ice chests. 'He could have packed them well and put them through baggage without anyone ever knowing.'

Further searching of Joyce's house produced other incriminating evidence, all within plain view, for the warrant had listed magnesium fire starters, knives, and body parts, and that gave police license to rummage through drawers and even tear out walls, if they so chose. While a local medical examiner removed the contents of the freezer to transport it to the morgue, cabinets were gone through and a safe drilled open. Inside were foreign money and thousands of photographs of hundreds of people who had been granted the good fortune not to have turned up dead.

There also were photographs of Joyce, we presumed, sitting in the pilot's seat of his white Schweizer or leaning against it with his arms crossed at his chest. I stared at his image and tried to take it in. He was a short, slight man with brown hair, and might have been handsome had he not been terribly scarred by acne.

His skin was pitted down his neck and into the open shirt he wore, and I could only imagine his shame as an adolescent, and the mockery and derisive laughter of his peers. I had known young men like him as I was growing up, those disfigured by birth or disease and unable to enjoy the entitlement of youthfulness or being the object of love.

So he had robbed others of what he did not have. He had destroyed as he had been destroyed, the point of origin his own miserable lot in life, his own wretched self. I did not feel sorry for him. Nor did I think that he and Carrie were still here in this city, or even anywhere around. She had gotten what she'd wanted, at least for now. The trap I had set had caught only me. She had wanted me to find Benton, and I had.

The final word, I felt sure, would be what she eventually did to me, and at the moment, I was too beaten up to care. I felt dead. I found silence in sitting on an old, worn marble bench in the riotous tangle of Joyce's overgrown backyard. Hostas, begonias, and fig bushes fought with pampas grass for the sun, and I found Lucy at the edge of intermittent shadows cast by live oak trees, where red and yellow hibiscus were loud and wild.

'Lucy, let's go home.'

I sat next to my niece on cold, hard stone I associated with cemeteries.

'I hope he was dead before they did that to him,' she said one more time.

I did not want to think about it.

'I just hope he didn't suffer.'

'She wants us to worry about things like that,' I said as anger peeked through my haze of disbelief. 'She's taken enough from us, don't you think? Let's not give her any more, Lucy.'

She had no answer for me.

'ATF and the police will handle it from here,' I went on, holding her hand. 'Let's go home, and we'll move on from there.'

'How?'

'I'm not sure I know.' I was as truthful as I could be.

We got up together and went around to the front of the house, where McGovern was talking to an agent out by her car. She looked at both of us, and compassion softened her eyes.

'If you'll take us back to the helicopter,' Lucy said with a steadiness she did not feel, 'I'll take it on in to Richmond and Border Patrol can pick it up. If that's all right, I mean.'

'I'm not sure you should be flying right now.' McGovern suddenly was Lucy's supervisor again.

'Trust me, I'm fine,' Lucy replied, and her voice got harder. 'Besides, who else is going to fly it? And you can't leave it here on a soccer field.'

McGovern hesitated, her eyes on Lucy. She unlocked the Explorer.

'Okay,' she said. 'Climb in.'

'I'll file a flight plan,' Lucy said as she sat in front. 'So you can check on where we are, if that will make you feel better.'

'It will,' McGovern said, starting the engine.

McGovern got on the radio and called one of the agents inside the house.

'Put Marino on,' she said.

After a brief wait, Marino's voice came over the air.

'Go ahead,' he said.

'Party's taking off. You going along?'

'I'll stick to the ground,' his answer came back. 'Gonna help out here first.'

'Got it. We appreciate it.'

'Tell them to fly safe,' Marino said.

A campus police officer on bicycle patrol was standing sentry at the helicopter when we got there, and tennis was going strong on the courts next door, balls clopping, while several young men practiced soccer near a goal. The sky was bright blue, trees barely stirring, as if nothing bad had happened here. Lucy went through a thorough preflight check while McGovern and I waited in the car.

'What are you going to do?' I asked her.

'Bombard the news with pictures of them and any other info that might cause someone out there to recognize them,' she answered. 'They've got to eat. They've got to sleep. And he's got to have Avgas. He can't fly forever without it.'

'It doesn't make sense that it hasn't been spotted before, refueling, landing, flying, what all.'

'Looks like he had plenty of his own Avgas right there in his garage. Not to mention there are so many small airfields where he could land and gas up,' she said. 'All over. And he doesn't have to contact the tower in uncontrolled airspace, and Schweizers aren't exactly rare. Not to mention' – she looked at me – 'it *has* been spotted. We saw it ourselves, and so did the farrier and the director of Kirby. We just didn't know what we were looking at.'

'I suppose.'

My mood was getting heavier by the moment. I did not want to go home. I did not want to go anywhere. It was as if the weather had turned gray, and I was cold and alone and could escape none of it. My mind churned with questions and answers, and deductions and screams. Whenever it went still, I saw him. I saw him in smoldering debris. I saw his face beneath heavy plastic.

'. . . Kay?'

I realized McGovern was talking to me.

'I want to know how you're doing. Really.' Her eyes were fastened to me.

I took a deep, shaky breath, and my voice sounded cracked when I said, 'I'm going to make it, Teun. Beyond that, I don't know how I'm doing. I'm not even sure what I'm doing. But I know what I've done. I've ruined everything. Carrie played me like a hand of cards, and Benton's dead. She and Newton Joyce are still out there, ready to do something bad again. Or maybe they already have. Nothing I've done has made a goddamn difference, Teun.'

Tears filled my eyes as I watched a blurry Lucy checking to make sure the fuel cap was tight. Then she began untying the main rotor blades. McGovern handed me a Kleenex. She gently squeezed my arm.

'You were brilliant, Kay. For one thing, had you not found out what you did, we wouldn't have had a thing to list on the warrant. We couldn't have even gotten one, and then where would we be? Yes, we haven't caught them yet, but at least we know *who*. And we will find them.'

'We found what they wanted us to,' I told her.

Lucy had finished her inspection and looked my way.

'I guess I'd better go,' I said to McGovern. 'Thank you.'

I took her hand and squeezed it.

'Take care of Lucy,' I said.

'I think she does a pretty good job of taking care of herself.'

I got out and turned around once to wave goodbye. I opened the copilot's door and climbed up in the seat, then fastened my harness. Lucy slipped her checklist out of a pocket on the door, and went down it, zeroing in on switches and circuit breakers, and making sure the collective was down, the throttle off. My heart would not beat normally, and my breathing was shallow.

We took off and nosed around into the wind. McGovern watched us climb, a hand shielding her eyes. Lucy handed me a sectional chart and said I was to help navigate. She lifted into a hover and contacted Air Traffic Control.

'Wilmington tower, this is helicopter two-one-niner Sierra Bravo.'

'Go ahead, helicopter two-one-niner, Wilmington tower.'

'Requesting clearance from university athletic field, direct to your location for ISO Aero. Over.'

'Contact tower when entering pattern. Cleared from present position, on course, stay with me and report down and secure at ISO.'

'Two Sierra Bravo, wilco.'

Then Lucy transmitted to me, 'We'll be following a three-three-zero heading. So your job after we gas up will be keeping the gyro consistent with the compass and helping out with the map.'

She climbed to five hundred feet and the tower contacted us again.

'Helicopter two Sierra Bravo,' the voice came over the air. 'Traffic is unidentified and at your six o'clock, three hundred feet, closing.'

'Two Sierra Bravo is looking, no joy.'

'Unidentified aircraft two miles southeast of airport, identify yourself,' the tower transmitted to all who could hear.

We were answered by nothing.

'Unidentified aircraft in Wilmington airspace, identify yourself,' the tower repeated.

Silence followed.

Lucy saw the aircraft first, directly behind us and below horizon, meaning its altitude was lower than ours.

'Wilmington tower,' she said over the air. 'Helicopter two Sierra Bravo. Have low-flying aircraft in sight. Will maintain separation.

'Something's not right,' Lucy commented to me, turning around in her seat to look behind us again.

24

———

It was a dark speck at first, flying after us, directly in our path and gaining on us. As it got closer it became white. Then it turned into a Schweizer with sunlight glinting off the bubble. My heart jumped as I was seized by fear.

'Lucy!' I exclaimed.

'I've got it in sight,' she said, instantly angry. 'Fuck. I don't believe this.'

She pulled up on the collective and we began a steep climb. The Schweizer maintained the same altitude, moving faster than we were for as we gained altitude, our speed dropped to seventy knots. Lucy pushed the cyclic forward as the Schweizer gained on us, swerving in closer on our starboard side, where Lucy was sitting. Lucy keyed the mike.

'Tower. Unidentified aircraft making aggressive moves,' she said. 'Will be making evasive maneuvers. Contact local police authorities, suspect in unidentified aircraft known armed and dangerous fugitive. Will avoid built-up areas, will take evasive actions towards water.'

'Roger helicopter. Am contacting local authorities.'

Then the tower switched to over-the-guard frequency.

'Attention any aircraft, this is Wilmington tower on-guard, aircraft traffic area is now closed to incoming traffic. Any ground traffic, halt movement. Repeat, aircraft traffic area is now closed to incoming traffic. Any ground traffic, halt movement. All aircraft this frequency, immediately switch to Wilmington approach control on Victor 135.75 or Uniform 343.9. I say again, all aircraft this frequency immediately switch to Wilmington approach control on Victor 135.75 or Uniform 343.9. Helicopter two Sierra Bravo, remain this frequency.'

'Roger, two Sierra Bravo,' Lucy returned.

I knew why she was heading toward the ocean. If we went down, she didn't want it to be in a populated area where others might get hurt or killed. I also was certain that Carrie had predicted Lucy would do exactly this, because Lucy was good. She would always put others first. She turned to the east, the Schweizer following our every move but maintaining the same distance behind us of maybe a hundred yards, as if confident that it didn't need to be in a hurry. That's when I realized that Carrie had probably been watching us all along.

'It can't go over ninety knots,' Lucy said to me, and our tension was rising like heat.

'She saw us come in straight to the field earlier today,' I said. 'She knows we haven't refueled.'

We flew at an angle over the beach and followed it briefly over bright splashes of color that were swimmers and sunbathers. They stopped what they were doing and stared straight up at two helicopters speeding over them and out to sea. Half a mile over the ocean, Lucy began to slow down.

'We can't keep this up,' she told me, and it seemed a pronouncement of doom. 'We lose our engine, we'll never make it back, and we're low on fuel.'

The gauge read less than twenty gallons. Lucy pushed us into a sharp one-hundred-and-eighty-degree turn. The Schweizer was maybe fifty feet below us and head on. The sun made it impossible to see who was inside, but I knew. I had not a single doubt, and when it was no more than five hundred feet from us and coming up on Lucy's side, I felt several rapid-fire jolts, like quick slaps, and we suddenly swerved. Lucy grabbed her pistol from her shoulder holster.

'They're shooting at us!' she exclaimed to me.

I thought of the submachine gun, the Calico missing from Sparkes's collection.

Lucy fought to open her door. She jettisoned it and it tumbled through the air, sailing down and away. She slowed our speed.

'They're firing!' Lucy got back on the air. 'Returning fire! Keep all traffic away from Wrightsville Beach area!'

'Roger! Do you request further assistance?'

'Dispatch land emergency crews, Wrightsville Beach! Expect casualty situation!'

As the Schweizer flew directly under us, I saw muzzle flashes and the tip of a barrel barely protruding from the copilot's window. I felt more quick jolts.

'I think they hit the skids,' Lucy almost screamed, and she was trying to position her pistol out her open door and fly at the same time, her shooting hand bandaged.

I instantly dug inside my pocketbook, dismayed to realize my .38 was still inside my briefcase, which remained safe inside the baggage compartment. Then Lucy handed me her pistol and reached behind her head for the AR-15 assault rifle. The Schweizer swooped around, to pursue us inland, knowing we were cornered because we would not risk the safety of people on the ground.

'We've got to go back over the water!' Lucy said. 'Can't shoot at them here. Kick your door open. Get it off the hinges and dump it!'

I somehow managed, the door ripping away as rushing air blasted me and the ground suddenly seemed closer. Lucy made another turn, and the Schweizer turned, too, as the needle on the fuel gauge slipped lower. This went on for what seemed forever, the Schweizer chasing us out to sea, and our trying to return to land so we could get down. It could not shoot up without hitting the rotor blades.

Then at an altitude of eleven hundred feet, when we were over water at a hundred knots, the fuselage got hit. Both of us felt the kicks right behind us, as close as the left rear passenger door.

'I'm turning right now,' Lucy said to me. 'Can you keep us straight at this altitude?'

I was terrified. We were going to die.

'I'll try,' I said, taking the controls.

We were heading straight toward the Schweizer. It couldn't have been more than fifty feet from us, and maybe a hundred feet below when Lucy pulled back the bolt, chambering a round.

'Shove the cyclic down! Now!' she yelled as me as she pushed the barrel of the rifle out her open door.

We were going down a thousand feet per minute, and I was certain we would fly right into the Schweizer. I tried to veer out of its path, but Lucy would have none of it.

'Straight at it!' she yelled.

I could not hear the gunfire as we flew directly over the Schweizer, so close I thought we would be devoured by its blades. She fired more, and I saw flashes, and then Lucy had the cyclic and was ramming it into a hard left, cutting it away from the Schweizer as it exploded into a ball of flames that rolled us almost over on our side. Lucy had the controls as I went into a crash position.

Then as suddenly as the violent shock waves had hit, they were gone, and I caught a glimpse of flaming debris showering into the Atlantic Ocean. We were steady and making a wide turn. I stared at my niece in stunned disbelief.

'Fuck you,' she said coldly as fire and broken fuselage rained into sparkling water.

She got on the air, as calm as I had ever seen her.

'Tower,' she said. 'Fugitive aircraft has exploded. Debris two miles off Wrightsville Beach. Negative survivors seen. Circling for signs of life.'

'Roger. Do you need assistance?' came the rattled response.

'A little late. But negative. Am returning to your location for immediate refuel.'

'Uh. Roger.' The omnipotent tower was stuttering. 'Proceed direct. Local authorities will meet you at ISO.'

But Lucy circled twice more, down to fifty feet as fire engines and police cars sped toward the beach with emergency lights flashing. Panicked swimmers were running out of the water, kicking and falling and fighting waves, arms flying, as if a great white shark were in pursuit. Floating debris rocked with the surge. Bright orange life jackets bobbed, but no one was in them.

ONE WEEK LATER
HILTON HEAD ISLAND

The morning was overcast, the sky the same gray as the sea, when the few of us who had loved Benton Wesley assembled on an empty, undeveloped point on the plantation of Sea Pines.

We parked near condominiums and followed a path that led to a dune. From there we made our way through sand spurs and sea oats. The beach was more narrow here, the sand less firm, and driftwood marked the memory of many storms.

Marino was in a pinstripe suit he was sweating through, and a white shirt and dark tie, and I thought it might have been the first time I had ever seen him so properly dressed. Lucy was in black, but I knew I would not see her until later, for she had something very important to do.

McGovern had come and so had Kenneth Sparkes, not because they had known him, but because their presence was their gift to me. Connie, Benton's former wife, and their three grown daughters were a knot near the water, and it was odd looking at them now and feeling nothing but sorrow. We had no resentment, no animosity or fear left in us. Death had spent it all as completely as life had brought it about.

There were others from Benton's precious past, retired agents and the former director of the FBI Academy who long years before had believed in Benton's prison visits and research in profiling. Benton's expertise was an old, tired word now, ruined by TV and the movies, but once it had been novel. Once Benton had been the pioneer, the creator of a better way of understanding humans who were truly psychotic, or remorseless and evil.

There was no leader of a church, for Benton had not gone since I had known him, only a Presbyterian chaplain who had counseled agents in distress. His name was Judson Lloyd, and he was frail with only a faint new moon of white hair. Reverend Lloyd wore a clerical collar and carried a small black leather Bible. There were fewer than twenty of us gathered on the shore.

We had no music or flowers, no eulogies or notes in our heads, for Benton had made it clear in his will what he wanted done. He had left me in charge of his mortal remains, because, as he had drafted himself, *It is what you are so good at, Kay. I know you will guard my wishes well.*

He had desired no ceremony. He had not wanted the military burial he was entitled to, no police cars leading the way, no gun salutes or flag-draped casket. His simple request was to be cremated and scattered over the place he loved best, the civilized Never-Never-Land of Hilton Head, where we had sequestered ourselves together whenever we could, and had forgotten for the brevity of a dream what we battled.

I would always be sorry that he had spent his last days here without me, and I would never recover from the heartless irony that I had been detained by the butchery Carrie had wrought. It had been the beginning of the end that would be Benton's end.

It was easy for me to wish I had never gotten involved in the case. But had I not, someone else would be attending a funeral somewhere in the world, as others had in the past, and the violence would not have stopped. Rain began to fall lightly. It touched my face like cool, sad hands.

'Benton brought us together here this day not to say goodbye,' began Reverend Lloyd. 'He wanted us to gather strength from each other and go on doing what he had done. Upholding good and condemning bad, fighting for the fallen and holding it all inside, suffering the horrors alone because he would not bruise the gentle souls of others. He left the world better than he found it. He left us better than he found us. My friends, go do as he had done.'

He opened his Bible to the New Testament.

'And let us not be weary in well doing: for in due season we shall reap, if we faint not,' he read.

I felt hot and arid inside and could not stop the tears. I dabbed my eyes with tissues and stared down at the sand dusting the toes of my black suede shoes. Reverend Lloyd touched a fingertip to his lips and voiced more verses from Galatians, or was it Timothy?

I was vague about what he said. His words became a continuous stream, like water flowing in a brook, and I could not make out the meaning as I fought and blocked images that without fail won. Mostly I remembered Benton in his red windbreaker, standing out and staring at the river when he was hurt by me. I would have given the world to take back every harsh word. Yet he had understood. I knew he had.

I remembered his clean profile and the imperviousness of his face when he was with people other than me. Perhaps they found him cold, when in fact his was a shell around a kind and tender life. I wondered if we had married if I would feel any different now. I wondered if my independence had been born of a seminal insecurity. I wondered if I had been wrong.

'Knowing this, that the law is not made for a righteous man, but for the lawless and disobedient, for the ungodly and for sinners, for unholy and profane, for murderers of fathers and murderers of mothers, for manslayers,' the reverend was preaching.

I felt the air stir behind me as I stared at a sluggish, depressed sea. Then Sparkes was next to me, our arms barely touching. His gaze was straight ahead, his jaw strong and resolute as he stood so straight in his dark suit. He turned to me and offered eyes of great sympathy. I nodded slightly.

'Our friend wanted peace and goodness.' Reverend Lloyd had turned to another book. 'He wanted the harmony the victims he championed never had. He wanted to be free of outrage and sorrow, unfettered by anger and his dreamless nights of dread.'

I heard the blades in the distance, the thudding that would forever be the noise of my niece. I looked up, and the sun barely shone behind clouds that danced the dance of veils, sliding endlessly, never fully exposing what we longed to see. Blue shown through, fragmented and brilliant like stained glass over the horizon to the west of us, and the dune at our backs was lit up as the troops of bad weather began to mutiny. The sound of the helicopter got louder, and I looked back over palms and pines, spotting it with nose slightly down as it flew lower.

'I will therefore ask that people pray everywhere, lifting up holy hands, without wrath and doubting,' the reverend went on.

Benton's ashes were in the small brass urn I held in my hands.

'Let us pray.'

Lucy began her glide slope over trees, the chop-chop hard air against the ear. Sparkes leaned close to speak to me, and I could not hear, but the closeness of his face was kind.

Reverend Lloyd continued to pray, but all of us were no longer capable of or interested in a petition to the Almighty. Lucy held the JetRanger in a low hover beyond the shore, and spray flew up from her wind on the water.

I could see her eyes fixed on me through the chin bubble, and I gathered my splintered spirit into a core. I walked forward into her storm of turbulent air as the reverend held on to his barely present hair. I waded out into the water.

'God bless you, Benton. Rest your soul. I miss you, Benton,' I said words no one else could hear.

I opened the urn and looked up at my niece who was there to create the energy he had wanted when it was his time to move on. I nodded at Lucy and she gave me a thumbs-up that rent my heart and let loose more tears. Ashes were like silk, and I felt his bits of chalky bone as I dug in and held him in my hand. I flung him into the wind. I gave him back to the higher order he would have made, had it been possible.